D0908493

100

Astounding Little

ALIEN

Stories

100

Astounding Little

ALIEN

Stories

Edited by

Stefan Dziemianowicz,

Robert Weinberg,

and Martin H. Greenberg

BARNES
&NOBLE
BOOKS
NEW YORK

Contents

Introduction   xv

All Cats Are Gray   1
Andre Norton

And So On, and So On   8
James Tiptree, Jr.

A Bad Day for Vermin   11
Keith Laumer

The Beautiful Doll Caper   17
William F. Nolan

Beyond Lies the Wub   21
Philip K. Dick

The Big Trek   29
Fritz Leiber

Blood Lands   34
Alfred Coppel

Brave New Hamburger   43
Philip Sidney Jennings

Capsule   53
Rosalind Greenberg

The Client from Hell   55
Richard Curtis

Collector's Fever   64
Roger Zelazny

The Crawling Chaos   67
Elizabeth Neville Berkeley *and* H. P. Lovecraft

Crazy Annaoj   74
Fritz Leiber

A Cup of Hemlock   80
Lee Killough

The Dark and the Damp   81
John DeChancie

Dear Pen Pal   92
A. E. van Vogt

The Demon of the Flower   99
Clark Ashton Smith

Disguise   109
Donald A. Wollheim

Dog Star   113
Mack Reynolds

Doing Alien   115
Gregory Benford

Down the Digestive Tract and into the Cosmos with Mantra, Tantra, and Specklebang   122
Robert Sheckley

Dry Spell   124
Bill Pronzini

Dueling Clowns   126
Barry Longyear

Emergency Refueling   132
James Blish

Eripmav   137
Damon Knight

Evensong   138
Lester del Rey

Exile   142
Edmond Hamilton

The Exterminator   147
A. Hyatt Verrill

The Eyes Have It   152
Philip K. Dick

Feeding Time   156
James E. Gunn

The Finest Hunter in the World   162
Harry Harrison

The Flame Midget   165
Frank Belknap Long, Jr.

Gift of U'Thang   177
Basil Wells

The Good Neighbors   186
Edgar Pangborn

The Grapes of The Rath   191
jan howard finder

The Great God Awto   193
Clark Ashton Smith

The Great Slow Kings   199
Roger Zelazny

The Green Meadow   206
Translated by Elizabeth Neville Berkeley
and H. P. Lovecraft

The Grof   211
Philip Sidney Jennings

The Happy Traitor   220
Morris Hershman

The Harvest   223
Tom Godwin

How Now Purple Cow   225
Bill Pronzini

The Hurkle Is a Happy Beast   229
Theodore Sturgeon

An Incident on Route 12   237
James H. Schmitz

Interstellar Way-Station   242
Bob Tucker

Into Your Tent I'll Creep 252
Eric Frank Russell

Itself! 261
A. E. van Vogt

Kindergarten 264
James E. Gunn

The King of the Beasts 267
Philip Jose Farmer

Landscape with Sphinxes 268
Karen Anderson

The Last Men 271
Frank Belknap Long, Jr.

Last Warning 279
Mack Reynolds

Later Than You Think 287
Fritz Leiber

The Life Hater 294
Fred Saberhagen

Linkage 303
Barry N. Malzberg

Listen, Love 306
George Zebrowski *and* Jack Dann

Mail Supremacy 310
Hayford Peirce

Man of Destiny 313
John Christopher

The Man Who Came Back   320
Brian M. Stableford

The Martians and the Leadfoot   324
William F. Nolan

A Matter of Taste   326
Esther M. Friesner

The Mission   336
Arthur Tofte

Mister Magister   338
Thomas F. Monteleone

Mr. Iper of Hamilton   343
Carl Jacobi

Open, Sesame!   351
Stephen Grendon

The Opening   356
Bruce Boston

The Other Tiger   362
Arthur C. Clarke

The Pair   365
Joe L. Hensley

Paths   371
Edward Bryant

Punch   375
Frederick Pohl

The Rebel Slug   379
Basil Wells

The Remorseful 385
Cyril M. Kornbluth

Ripples 392
Ray Russell

Roadside Rescue 394
Pat Cadigan

Roog 401
Philip K. Dick

Sequence 407
Carl Jacobi

The Sky's an Oyster; the Stars Are Pearls 413
David Bischoff

Slow 416
Ramsey Campbell

The Spy 425
Theodore L. Thomas

Starting from Scratch 430
Robert Sheckley

Steel 434
Alan Brennert

A Stranger from Atlanta 440
Hugh B. Cave

Strangers to Straba 448
Carl Jacobi

A Tale of the Lonely Larva 458
Del Stone, Jr.

That Strain Again   460
Charles Sheffield

They Live Forever   462
Lloyd Biggle, Jr.

They're Playing Our Song   468
Harry Harrison

Three Fingers in Utopia   469
Philip Sidney Jennings

To Serve Man   478
Damon Knight

Too Many Eggs   486
Kris Neville

Top Secret   489
Donald A. Wollheim

Tu Quoque   491
John DeChancie

The Twerlik   500
Jack Sharkey

Upstart   508
Steven Utley

Varieties of Technological Experience   511
Barry N. Malzberg

Very Much Like a Game   516
Adam Niswander

The Voice from the Curious Cube   519
Nelson Bond

A Walk in the Wet   522
Dennis Etchison

What's He Doing in There?   530
Fritz Leiber

Zoo   536
Edward D. Hoch

Acknowledgments   *539*

Introduction

Science fiction has given readers a variety of entertaining story types, including space travel, time travel, first contact, and alternative history. Probably the most popular story type—if only because it traverses the boundaries of all others—is the alien story.

The alien story's history predates the actual coining of the term *science fiction* in the 1920s. In 1897, H. G. Wells wrote one of the landmark alien invasion tales: *The War of the Worlds.* Several years later, he wrote of an earthly "invasion" of the moon in *The First Men in the Moon,* and the discovery of a race, the Selenites, who were natural to their environment but alien to earth beings. Nearly a century before, in what many scholars consider the first true science-fiction novel—*Frankenstein*—Mary Shelley envisioned a creature of reanimated body parts as alien to imaginations of her day as Wells's extraterrestrials were to those of his.

The vast differences between these works of fiction raise many questions regarding our definition of the subject: Is the alien merely the inhuman? Does it pertain only to what falls outside the boundaries of normal human experience? Does our conception of it change with our species' accelerating acclimation and accommodation to the new and strange? These questions have become increasingly unanswerable as alien stories have proliferated. Tens of thousands of alien stories have been written in the last two centuries, and adventurous science-fiction readers quickly find that as fast as they can absorb one portrait of the alien, a new and unforeseen rendering is ready to take its place.

It is impossible to generalize from the abundance of alien stories an all-encompassing understanding of what we mean by "alien." It is possible, however, to discern their common objective: Ultimately, all stories about aliens are about ourselves.

Science fiction is a literature of projection. It extrapolates future possibilities from current trends. It speculates about the unknown based on what *is* known. When it offers an image of the alien, science fiction presupposes a norm for humanity from which the alien deviates. No matter how far in the future it is set, or how bizarre its life-forms, the alien story is ultimately a mirror in which we see a reflection of who we are, in the here and now.

In the 100 stories collected here, the reader will encounter just some of the many alien life-forms that afford us an opportunity for self-examination. Some, like those in Dennis Etchison's "A Walk in the Wet" and Adam Niswander's "Very Much Like a Game," look deceptively like ourselves. Others, like the beings in Basil Wells's "The Rebel Slug" and Ramsey Campbell's "Slow," have markedly nonhuman physical appearances. Another feature that differs from story to story is social distance between aliens and earthlings. The invaders in Philip K. Dick's "Roog" are hostile to human beings, whereas Frank Belknap Long, Jr.'s "The Last Men" are comparatively benign. Geographic distance also receives varied treatment: The entities in Donald A. Wollheim's "Top Secret" originate from somewhere outside the galaxy, those in William F. Nolan's "The Martians and the Leadfoot" live within our solar system, and those in Del Stone, Jr.'s "A Tale of the Lonely Larva" come possibly from within our minds.

The shortness of these stories confirms their purpose: It only takes the slightest glimpse to recognize our mirror images.

Herewith, 100 close encounters—of the brief kind.

—Stefan Dziemianowicz
New York, 1996

All Cats Are Gray

Andre Norton

Steena of the spaceways—that sounds just like a corny title for one of the Stellar-Vedo spreads. I ought to know, I've tried my hand at writing enough of them. Only this Steena was no glamour babe. She was as colorless as a Lunar plant—even the hair netted down to her skull had a sort of grayish cast and I never saw her but once draped in anything but a shapeless and baggy gray spaceall.

Steena was strictly background stuff and that is where she mostly spent her free hours—in the smelly smoky background corners of any stellar-port dive frequented by free spacers. If you really looked for her you could spot her—just sitting there listening to the talk—listening and remembering. She didn't open her own mouth often. But when she did spacers had learned to listen. And the lucky few who heard her rare spoken words—these will never forget Steena.

She drifted from port to port. Being an expert operator on the big calculators she found jobs wherever she cared to stay for a time. And she came to be something like the master-minded machines she tended—smooth, gray, without much personality of her own.

But it was Steena who told Bub Nelson about the Jovan moon-rites—and her warning saved Bub's life six months later. It was Steena who identified the piece of stone Keene Clark was passing around a table one night, rightly calling it unworked Slitite. That started a rush which made ten fortunes overnight for men who were down to their last jets. And, last of all, she cracked the case of the *Empress of Mars*.

All the boys who had profited by her queer store of knowledge and her photographic memory tried at one time or another to balance the scales. But she wouldn't take so much as a cup of Canal water at their expense, let alone the credits they tried to push on her. Bub Nelson was the only one who got around her refusal. It was he who brought her Bat.

About a year after the Jovan affair he walked into the Free Fall one night and dumped Bat down on her table. Bat looked at Steena and growled. She looked calmly back at him and nodded once. From then on they traveled together—the thin gray woman and the big gray tomcat. Bat learned to know the inside of more stellar bars than even most spacers visit in their lifetimes. He developed a liking for Vernal juice, drank it neat and quick, right out of a glass. And he was always at home on any table where Steena elected to drop him.

This is really the story of Steena, Bat, Cliff Moran and the *Empress of Mars,* a story which is already a legend of the spaceways. And it's a damn good story too. I ought to know, having framed the first version of it myself.

For I was there, right in the Rigel Royal, when it all began on the night that Cliff Moran blew in, looking lower than an antman's belly and twice as nasty. He'd had a spell of luck foul enough to twist a man into a slug-snake and we all knew that there was an attachment out for his ship. Cliff had fought his way up from the back courts of Venaport. Lose his ship and he'd slip back there—to rot. He was at the snarling stage that night when he picked out a table for himself and set out to drink away his troubles.

However, just as the first bottle arrived, so did a visitor. Steena came out of her corner, Bat curled around her shoulders stole-wise, his favorite mode of travel. She crossed over and dropped down without invitation at Cliff's side. That shook him out of his sulks. Because Steena never chose company when she could be alone. If one of the manstones on Ganymede had come stumping in, it wouldn't have made more of us look out of the corners of our eyes.

She stretched out one long-fingered hand and set aside the bottle he had ordered and said only one thing, "It's about time for the *Empress of Mars* to appear again."

Cliff scowled and bit his lip. He was tough, tough as jet lining—you have to be granite inside and out to struggle up from Venaport to a ship command. But we could guess what was running through his mind at that moment. The *Empress of Mars* was just about the biggest prize a spacer could aim for. But in the fifty years she had been following her queer derelict orbit through space many men had tried to bring her in—and none had succeeded.

A pleasure-ship carrying untold wealth, she had been mysteriously abandoned in space by passengers and crew, none of whom had ever been seen or heard of again. At intervals thereafter she had been sighted, even boarded. Those who ventured into her either vanished or returned swiftly without any believable explanation of what they had seen—wanting only to get away from her as quickly as possible. But the man who could bring her in—or even strip her clean in space—that man would win the jackpot.

"All right!" Cliff slammed his fist down on the table. "I'll try even that!"

Steena looked at him, much as she must have looked at Bat the day Bub Nelson brought him to her, and nodded. That was all I saw. The rest of the story came to me in pieces, months later and in another port half the System away.

Cliff took off that night. He was afraid to risk waiting—with a writ out that could pull the ship from under him. And it wasn't until he was in space that he discovered his passengers—Steena and Bat. We'll never know what happened then. I'm betting that Steena made no explanation at all. She wouldn't.

It was the first time she had decided to cash in on her own tip and she was there—that was all. Maybe that point weighed with Cliff, maybe he just didn't care. Anyway the three were together when they sighted the *Empress* riding, her dead-lights gleaming, a ghost ship in night space.

She must have been an eerie sight because her other lights were on too, in addition to the red warnings at her nose. She seemed alive, a Flying Dutchman of space. Cliff worked his ship skillfully alongside and had no trouble in snapping magnetic lines to her lock. Some minutes later the three of them passed into her. There was still air in her cabins and corridors. Air that bore a faint corrupt taint which set Bat to sniffing greedily and could be picked up even by the less sensitive human nostrils.

Cliff headed straight for the control cabin but Steena and Bat went prowling. Closed doors were a challenge to both of them and

Steena opened each as she passed, taking a quick look at what lay within. The fifth door opened on a room which no woman could leave without further investigation.

I don't know who had been housed there when the *Empress* left port on her last lengthy cruise. Anyone really curious can check back on the old photo-reg cards. But there was a lavish display of silks trailing out of two travel kits on the floor, a dressing table crowded with crystal and jeweled containers, along with other lures for the female which drew Steena in. She was standing in front of the dressing table when she glanced into the mirror—glanced into it and froze.

Over her right shoulder she could see the spider-silk cover on the bed. Right in the middle of that sheer, gossamer expanse was a sparkling heap of gems, the dumped contents of some jewel case. Bat had jumped to the foot of the bed and flattened out as cats will, watching those gems, watching them and—something else!

Steena put out her hand blindly and caught up the nearest bottle. As she unstoppered it she watched the mirrored bed. A gemmed bracelet rose from the pile, rose in the air and tinkled its siren song. It was as if an idle hand played . . . Bat spat almost noiselessly. But he did not retreat. Bat had not yet decided his course.

She put down the bottle. Then she did something which perhaps few of the men she had listened to through the years could have done. She moved without hurry or sign of disturbance on a tour about the room. And, although she approached the bed she did not touch the jewels. She could not force herself to that. It took her five minutes to play out her innocence and unconcern. Then it was Bat who decided the issue.

He leaped from the bed and escorted something to the door, remaining a careful distance behind. Then he mewed loudly twice. Steena followed him and opened the door wider.

Bat went straight on down the corridor, as intent as a hound on the warmest of scents. Steena strolled behind him, holding her pace to the unhurried gait of an explorer. What sped before them both was invisible to her but Bat was never baffled by it.

They must have gone into the control cabin almost on the heels of the unseen—if the unseen had heels, which there was good reason to doubt—for Bat crouched just within the doorway and refused to move on. Steena looked down the length of the instrument panels and officers' station-seats to where Cliff Moran worked. On the heavy carpet her boots made no sound and he did not glance up but sat humming through set teeth as he tested the tardy and reluctant responses to buttons which had not been pushed in years.

To human eyes they were alone in the cabin. But Bat still followed a moving something with his gaze. And it was something which he had at last made up his mind to distrust and dislike. For now he took a step or two forward and spat—his loathing made plain by every raised hair along his spine. And in that same moment Steena saw a flicker—a flicker of vague outline against Cliff's hunched shoulders as if the invisible one had crossed the space between them.

But why had it been revealed against Cliff and not against the back of one of the seats or against the panels, the walls of the corridor or the cover of the bed where it had reclined and played with its loot? What could Bat see?

The storehouse memory that had served Steena so well through the years clicked open a half-forgotten door. With one swift motion she tore loose her spaceall and flung the baggy garment across the back of the nearest seat.

Bat was snarling now, emitting the throaty rising cry that was his hunting song. But he was edging back, back toward Steena's feet, shrinking from something he could not fight but which he faced defiantly. If he could draw it after him, past that dangling spaceall . . . He had to—it was their only chance.

"What the . . ." Cliff had come out of his seat and was staring at them.

What he saw must have been weird enough. Steena, bare-armed and shouldered, her usually stiffly-netted hair falling wildly down her back, Steena watching empty space with narrowed eyes and set mouth, calculating a single wild chance. Bat, crouched on his belly, retreating from thin air step by step and wailing like a demon.

"Toss me your blaster." Steena gave the order calmly—as if they still sat at their table in the Rigel Royal.

And as quietly Cliff obeyed. She caught the small weapon out of the air with a steady hand—caught and leveled it.

"Stay just where you are!" she warned. "Back, Bat, bring it back!"

With a last throat-splitting screech of rage and hate, Bat twisted to safety between her boots. She pressed with thumb and forefinger, firing at the spacealls. The material turned to powdery flakes of ash—except for certain bits which still flapped from the scorched seat—as if something had protected them from the force of the blast. Bat sprang straight up in the air with a scream that tore their ears.

"What. . . ?" began Cliff again.

Steena made a warning motion with her left hand. *"Wait!"*

She was still tense, still watching Bat. The cat dashed madly around the cabin twice, running crazily with white-ringed eyes and flecks of foam on his muzzle. Then he stopped abruptly in the doorway, stopped and looked back over his shoulder for a long silent moment. He sniffed delicately.

Steena and Cliff could smell it too now, a thick oily stench which was not the usual odor left by an exploding blaster-shell.

Bat came back, treading daintily across the carpet, almost on the tips of his paws. He raised his head as he passed Steena and then he went confidently beyond to sniff, to sniff and spit twice at the unburned strips of the spaceall. Having thus paid his respects to the late enemy he sat down calmly and set to washing his fur with deliberation. Steena sighed once and dropped into the navigator's seat.

"Maybe now you'll tell me what in the hell's happened?" Cliff exploded as he took the blaster out of her hand.

"Gray," she said dazedly, "it must have been gray—or I couldn't have seen it like that. I'm colorblind, you see. I can see only shades of gray—my whole world is gray. Like Bat's—his world is gray too—all gray. But he's been compensated for he can see above and below our range of color vibrations and—apparently—so can I!"

Her voice quavered and she raised her chin with a new air Cliff had never seen before—a sort of proud acceptance. She pushed back her wandering hair, but she made no move to imprison it under the heavy net again.

"That is why I saw the thing when it crossed between us. Against your spaceall it was another shade of gray—an outline. So I put out mine and waited for it to show against that—it was our only chance, Cliff.

"It was curious at first, I think, and it knew we couldn't see it—

which is why it waited to attack. But when Bat's actions gave it away it moved. So I waited to see that flicker against the spaceall and then I let him have it. It's really very simple . . ."

Cliff laughed a bit shakily. "But what *was* this gray thing? I don't get it."

"I think it was what made the *Empress* a derelict. Something out of space, maybe, or from another world somewhere." She waved her hands. "It's invisible because it's a color beyond our range of sight. It must have stayed in here all these years. And it kills—it must—when its curiosity is satisfied." Swiftly she described the scene in the cabin and the strange behavior of the gem pile which had betrayed the creature to her.

Cliff did not return his blaster to its holder. "Any more of them on board, d'you think?" He didn't look pleased at the prospect.

Steena turned to Bat. He was paying particular attention to the space between two front toes in the process of a complete bath. "I don't think so. But Bat will tell us if there are. He can see them clearly, I believe."

But there weren't any more and two weeks later Cliff, Steena and Bat brought the *Empress* into the Lunar quarantine station. And that is the end of Steena's story because, as we have been told, happy marriages need no chronicles. And Steena had found someone who knew of her gray world and did not find it too hard to share with her—someone besides Bat. It turned out to be a real love match.

The last time I saw her she was wrapped in a flame-red cloak from the looms of Rigel and wore a fortune in Jovan rubies blazing on her wrists. Cliff was flipping a three-figure credit bill to a waiter. And Bat had a row of Vernal juice glasses set up before him. Just a little family party out on the town.

And So On, and So On

James Tiptree, Jr.

In a nook of the ship's lounge the child had managed to activate a viewscreen.

"Rovy! They *asked* you not to play with the screen while we're Jumping. We've told you and told you there isn't anything there. It's just pretty lights, dear. Now come back and we'll all play—"

As the young clanwife coaxed him back to their cocoons something happened. It was a very slight something, just enough to make the drowsy passengers glance up. Immediately a calm voice spoke, accompanied by the blur of multiple translation.

"This is your captain. The momentary discontinuity we just experienced is quite normal in this mode of paraspace. We will encounter one or two more before reaching the Orion complex, which will be in about two units of ship's time."

The tiny episode stimulated talk.

"Declare I feel sorry for the youngers today." The large being in mercantile robes tapped his Galnews scanner, blew out his ear sacs comfortably. "We had all the fun. Why, when I first came out this was all wild frontier. Took courage to go beyond the Coalsack. They had you make your will. I can even remember the first cross-Gal Jump."

"How fast it has all changed!" admired his talking minor. Daringly it augmented: "The youngers are so apathetic. They accept all these marvels as natural, they mock the idea of heroism."

"Heroes!" the merchant snorted. "Not them!" He gazed challengingly around the luxe cabin, eliciting a few polite nods. Suddenly a cocoon swivelled around to face him, revealing an Earth-typer in Pathman grey.

"Heroism," said the Pathman softly, eyeing the merchant from under shadowed brows. "Heroism is essentially a spatial concept.

No more free space, no more heroes." He turned away as if regretting having spoken, like a man trying to sustain some personal pain.

"Ooh, what about Ser Orpheian?" asked a bright young reproducer. "Crossing the Arm alone in a single pod. I think that's heroic!" It giggled flirtatiously.

"Not really," drawled a cultivated Galfad voice. The lutroid who had been using the reference station removed his input leads and smiled distantly at the reproducer. "Such exploits are merely an expiring gasp, a gleaning after the harvest if you will. Was Orpheian launching into the unknown? Not so. He faced merely the problem of whether he himself could do it. Playing at frontiers. No," the lutroid's voice took on a practiced Recorder's clarity. "The primitive phase is finished. The true frontier is within now. Inner space." He adjusted his academic fourragère.

The merchant had returned to his scanner.

"Now here's a nice little offering," he grunted. "Ringsun for sale, Eridani sector. That sector's long overdue for development, somebody'll make a sweet thing. If some of these young malcontents would just blow out their gills and pitch in!—" He thumped his aquaminor on the snout, causing it to mew piteously.

"But that's too much like work," echoed his talker soothingly.

The Pathman had been watching in haggard silence. Now he leaned over to the lutroid.

"Your remark about inner space. I take it you mean psychics? Purely subjective explorations?"

"Not at all," said the lutroid, gratified. "The psychic cults I regard as mere sensationalism. I refer to reality, to that simpler and deeper reality that lies beyond the reach of the trivial methodologies of science, the reality which we can only approach through what is called aesthetic or religious experience, god-immanent if you will—"

"I'd like to see art or religion get you to Orion," remarked a grizzed spacedog in the next cocoon. "If it wasn't for science you wouldn't be end-running the parsecs in an aleph Jumpship."

"Perhaps we end-run too much," the lutroid smiled. "Perhaps our technological capabilities are end-running, as you call it, our—"

"What about the Arm wars?" cried the young reproducer. "Ooh, science is *horrible*. I cry every time I think of the poor Armers." Its large eyes steamed and it hugged itself seductively.

"Well, now, you can't blame science for what some power-hounds do with it," the spacedog chuckled, hitching his cocoon over toward the reproducer's stay.

"That's right," said another voice, and the conversation group drifted away.

The Pathman's haunted eyes were still on the lutroid.

"If you are so certain of this deeper reality, this inner space," he said quietly, "why is your left hand almost without nails?"

The lutroid's left hand clenched and then uncurled slowly to reveal the gnawed nails; he was not undisciplined.

"I recognise the right of your order to unduly personal speech," he said stiffly. Then he sighed and smiled. "Ah, of course; I admit I am not immune to the universal *angst,* the failure of nerve. The haunting fear of stagnation and decline, now that life has reached to the limits of this galaxy. But I regard this as a challenge to transcendence, which we must, we will meet, through our inner resources. We will find our *true* frontier." He nodded. "Life has never failed the ultimate challenge."

"Life has never before met the ultimate challenge," the Pathman rejoined somberly. "In the history of every race, society, planet or system or federation or swarm, whenever they had expanded to their *spatial limits* they commenced to decline. First stasis, then increasing entropy, degradation of structure, disorganisation, death. In every case, the process was only halted by breaking out into new space, or by new peoples breaking in on them from outside. Crude, simple outer space. Inner space? Consider the Vegans—"

"Exactly!" interrupted the lutroid. "That refutes you. The Vegans were approaching the most fruitful concepts of transphysical reality, concepts we must certainly reopen. If only the Myrmidi invasion had not destroyed so much."

"It is not generally known," the Pathman's voice was very low, "when the Myrmidi landed the Vegans were eating their own larvae and using the sacred dream-fabrics for ornaments. Very few could even sing."

"No!"

"By the Path."

The lutroid's nictating membranes filmed his eyes. After a moment he said formally, "You carry despair as your gift."

The Pathman was whispering as if to himself. "Who will come to open our skies? For the first time all life is closed in a finite space. Who can rescue a galaxy? The Clouds are barren and the realms beyond we know cannot be crossed even by matter, let alone life. For the first time we have truly reached the end."

"But the young," said the lutroid in quiet anguish.

"The young sense this. They seek to invent pseudo-frontiers, subjective escapes. Perhaps your inner space can beguile some for a while. But the despair will grow. Life is not mocked. We have come to the end of infinity, the end of hope."

The lutroid stared into the Pathman's hooded eyes, his hand involuntarily raising his academic surplice like a shield.

"You believe that there is nothing, no way?"

"Ahead lies only the irreversible long decline. For the first time *we know there is nothing beyond ourselves.*"

After a moment the lutroid's gaze dropped and the two beings let silence enshroud them. Outside the Galaxy was twisting by unseen, enormous, glittering: a finite prison. No way out.

In the aisle behind them something moved.

The child Rovy was creeping stealthily toward the screens that looked on no-space, his eyes intent and bright.

A Bad Day for Vermin

Keith Laumer

Judge Carter Gates of the Third Circuit Court finished his chicken salad on whole wheat, thoughtfully crumpled the waxed paper bag, and turned to drop it in the waste basket behind his chair—and sat transfixed.

Through his second-floor office window, he saw a forty-foot flower-petal shape of pale turquoise settling gently between the well-tended petunia beds on the courthouse lawn. On the upper, or stem end of the vessel, a translucent pink panel popped up and a slender, graceful form not unlike a large violet caterpillar undulated into view.

Judge Gates whirled to the telephone. Half an hour later, he put it to the officials gathered with him in a tight group on the lawn.

"Boys, this thing is intelligent; any fool can see that. It's putting together what my boy assures me is some kind of talking machine, and any minute now it's going to start communicating. It's been twenty minutes since I notified Washington on this thing. It won't be long before somebody back there decides this is top secret and slaps a freeze on us here that will make the Manhattan Project look like a publicity campaign. Now, I say this is the biggest thing that ever happened to Plum County—but if we don't aim to be put right out of the picture, we'd better move fast."

"What you got in mind, Jedge?"

"I propose we hold an open hearing right here in the courthouse, the minute that thing gets its gear to working. We'll put it on the air—Tom Clembers from the radio station's already stringing wires, I see. Too bad we've got no TV equipment, but Jody Hurd has a movie camera. We'll put Willow Grove on the map bigger'n Cape Canaveral ever was."

"We're with you on that, Carter!"

Ten minutes after the melodious voice of the Fianna's translator had requested escort to the village headman, the visitor was looking over the crowded courtroom with an expression reminiscent of a St. Bernard puppy hoping for a romp. The rustle of feet and throat-clearing subsided and the speaker began:

"People of the Green World, happy the cycle—"

Heads turned at the clump of feet coming down the side aisle; a heavy-torsoed man of middle age, bald, wearing a khaki shirt and trousers and rimless glasses and with a dark leather holster slapping his hip at each step, cleared the end of the front row of seats, planted himself, feet apart, yanked a heavy nickel-plated .44 revolver from the holster, took aim and fired five shots into the body of the Fianna at a range of ten feet.

The violet form whipped convulsively, writhed from the bench to the floor with a sound like a wet fire hose being dropped, uttered a gasping twitter, and lay still. The gunman turned, dropped the pistol, threw up his hands, and called:

"Sheriff Hoskins, I'm puttin' myself in yer pertective custody."

There was a moment of stunned silence; then a rush of spectators for the alien. The sheriff's three-hundred-and-nine-pound bulk bellied through the shouting mob to take up a stand before the khaki-clad man.

"I always knew you was a mean one, Cecil Stump," he said, unlimbering handcuffs, "ever since I seen you makin' up them ground-glass baits for Joe Potter's dog. But I never thought I'd see you turn to cold-blooded murder." He waved at the bystanders. "Clear a path through here; I'm takin' my prisoner over to the jail."

"Jest a dad-blamed minute, Sheriff." Stump's face was pale, his glasses were gone and one khaki shoulder strap dangled—but what was almost a grin twisted one meaty cheek. He hid his hands behind his back, leaned away from the cuffs. "I don't like that word 'prisoner.' I ast you fer pertection. And better look out who you go throwin' that word 'murder' off at, too. I ain't murdered nobody."

The sheriff blinked, turned to roar, "How's the victim, Doc?"

A small gray head rose from bending over the limp form of the Fianna. "Deader'n a mackerel, Sheriff."

"I guess that's it. Let's go, Cecil."

"What's the charge?"

"First-degree murder."

"Who'd I murder?"

"Why, you killed this here . . . this stranger."

"That ain't no stranger. That's a varmint. Murder's got to do with killin' humerns, way I understand it. You goin' to tell me that thing's humern?"

Ten people shouted at once:

"—human as I am!"

"—intelligent being!"

"—tell me you can simply kill—"

"—must be some kind of law—"

The sheriff raised his hands, his jowls drawn down in a scowl. "What about it, Judge Gates? Any law against Cecil Stump killing the . . . uh . . . ?"

The judge thrust out his lower lip. "Well, let's see," he began. "Technically—"

"Good Lord!" someone blurted. "You mean the laws on murder don't define what constitutes—I mean, what—"

"What a humern is?" Stump snorted. "Whatever it says, it sure-bob don't include no purple worms. That's a varmint, pure and simple. Ain't no different killin' it than any other critter."

"Then, by God, we'll get him for malicious damage," a man called. "Or hunting without a license—out of season!"

"—carrying concealed weapons!"

Stump went for his hip pocket, fumbled out a fat, shapeless wallet, extracted a thumbed rectangle of folded paper, offered it.

"I'm a licensed exterminator. Got a permit to carry the gun, too, I ain't broken no law." He grinned openly now. "Jest doin' my job, Sheriff. And at no charge to the county."

A smaller man with bristly red hair flared his nostrils at Stump. "You blood-thirsty idiot!" He raised a fist and shook it. "We'll be a national disgrace—worse than Little Rock! Lynching's too good for you!"

"Hold on there, Weinstein," the sheriff cut in. "Let's not go gettin' no lynch talk started."

"Lynch, is it!" Cecil Stump bellowed, his face suddenly red. "Why, I done a favor for every man here! Now you listen to me! What is that thing over there?" He jerked a blunt thumb toward the judicial bench. "It's some kind of critter from Mars or someplace—you know that as well as me! And what's it here for? It ain't for the good of the likes of you and me, I can tell you that. It's them or us. And this time, by God, we got in the first lick!"

"Why you . . . you . . . hate-monger!"

"Now, hold on right there. I'm as liberal-minded as the next feller. Hell, I like a nigger—and I can't hardly tell a Jew from a white man. But when it comes to takin' in a damned purple worm and callin' it humern—that's where I draw the line."

Sheriff Hoskins pushed between Stump and the surging front rank of the crowd. "Stay back there! I want you to disperse, peaceably, and let the law handle this."

"I reckon I'll push off now, Sheriff," Stump hitched up his belt. "I figgered you might have to calm 'em down right at first, but now they've had a chance to think it over and see I ain't broken no law, ain't none of these law-abiding folks going to do anything illegal—like tryin' to get rough with a licensed exterminator just doin' his job." He stooped, retrieved his gun.

"Here, I'll take that," Sheriff Hoskins said. "You can consider your gun license canceled—and your exterminatin' license, too."

Stump grinned again, handed the revolver over.

"Sure. I'm cooperative, Sheriff. Anything you say. Send it around to my place when you're done with it." He pushed his way through the crowd to the corridor door.

"The rest of you stay put!" A portly man with a head of bushy white hair pushed his way through to the bench. "I'm calling an emergency Town Meeting to order here and now!"

He banged the gavel on the scarred bench top, glanced down at the body of the dead alien, now covered by a flag.

"Gentlemen, we've got to take fast action. If the wire services get hold of this before we've gone on record, Willow Grove'll be a blighted area."

"Look here, Willard," Judge Gates called, rising. "This—this mob isn't competent to take legal action."

"Never mind what's legal, Judge. Sure, this calls for Federal legislation—maybe a Constitutional amendment—but in the meantime, we're going to redefine what constitutes a person within the incorporated limits of Willow Grove!"

"That's the least we can do," a thin-faced woman snapped, glaring at Judge Gates. "Do you think we're going to set here and condone this outrage?"

"Nonsense!" Gates shouted. "I don't like what happened any better than you do—but a person—well, a person's got two arms and two legs and—"

"Shape's got nothing to do with it," the chairman cut in. "Bears walk on two legs! Dave Zawocky lost his in the war. Monkeys have hands."

"Any intelligent creature—" the woman started.

"Nope, that won't do, either; my unfortunate cousin's boy Melvin was born an imbecile, poor lad. Now, folks, there's no time to waste. We'll find it very difficult to formulate a satisfactory definition based on considerations such as these. However, I think we can resolve the question in terms that will form a basis for future legislation on the question. It's going to make some big changes in things. Hunters aren't going to like it—and the meat industry will be affected. But if, as it appears, we're entering into an era of contact with . . . ah . . . creatures from other worlds, we've got to get our house in order."

"You tell 'em, Senator!" someone yelled.

"We better leave this for Congress to figger out!" another voice insisted.

"We got to do something . . ."

The senator held up his hands. "Quiet, everybody. There'll be reporters here in a matter of minutes. Maybe our ordinance won't hold water. But it'll start 'em thinking—and it'll make a lots better copy for Willow Grove than the killing."

"What you got in mind, Senator?"

"Just this:" the Senator said solemnly. "A person is . . . *any harmless creature* . . ."

Feet shuffled. Someone coughed.

"What about a man who commits a violent act, then?" Judge Gates demanded. "What's he, eh?"

"That's obvious, gentlemen," the senator said flatly. "He's vermin."

On the courthouse steps Cecil Stump stood, hands in hip pockets, talking to a reporter from the big-town paper in Mattoon, surrounded by a crowd of late-comers who had missed the excitement inside. He described the accuracy of his five shots, the sound they had made hitting the big blue snake, and the ludicrous spectacle the latter had presented in its death agony. He winked at a foxy man in overalls picking his nose at the edge of the crowd.

"Guess it'll be a while 'fore any more damned reptiles move in here like they owned the place," he concluded.

The courthouse doors banged wide; excited citizens poured forth, veering aside from Cecil Stump. The crowd around him thinned, broke up as its members collared those emerging with the hot news. The reporter picked a target.

"Perhaps you'd care to give me a few details of the action taken by the . . . ah . . . Special Committee, sir?"

Senator Custis pursed his lips. "A session of the Town Council was called," he said. "We've defined what a person is in this town—"

Stump, standing ten feet away, snorted. "Can't touch me with no *ex-post factory* law."

"—and also what can be classified as vermin," Custis went on. Stump closed his mouth with a snap.

"Here, that s'posed to be some kind of slam at me, Custis? By God, come election time . . ."

Above, the door opened again. A tall man in a leather jacket stepped out, stood looking down. The crowd pressed back. Senator Custis and the reporter moved aside. The newcomer came down the steps slowly. He carried Cecil Stump's nickel-plated .44 in his hand.

Standing alone now, Stump watched him.

"Here," he said. His voice carried a sudden note of strain. "Who're you?"

The man reached the foot of the steps, raised the revolver and cocked it with a thumb.

"I'm the new exterminator," he said.

The Beautiful Doll Caper

William F. Nolan

When I got to the office I felt like hell. "Gawdamn," I said. My lip curled around a bottle of hooch and I didn't stop swallowing until the damn thing was empty.

"Hair of the dog, eh, Sam?" cooed a honey-blonde I'd never set eye on before. She perched on my plastodesk like a sleepy siamese, dangling a lush pair of silken gams in my direction. She wore a moongown open to her kneecaps and I liked what she had inside. But definitely. I swore under my breath and went for her like a rocket jockey for a shot of Martian vino. Her lips were red wine and I was bone-dry.

After a while she said, "I'm here for a reason, big man."

"Well?" I snapped, lighting a butt. I put it in the side of my mouth and let it live there.

"You've got a nasty reputation, Mr. O'Slammer. *Real* nasty."

"Been reading my fan mail, doll?" I smiled crookedly.

"Never mind *how* I know. I know."

"So . . ."

"So I want a man killed. I can make it well worth your while." Her tone was ice and fire. And I liked the things the sun did to her hair.

I stubbed the butt to death on the barrel of Suzy, my blaster, and leaned back in my chair. "Daddy's listening."

"Name is Mac. They call him Max. Runs a clip joint on Broadway east of the Ferry building. Short. Bald. Beefy. Red face. Moustache. Cigar. Gold teeth. Glasses. Squinty eyes. Loud clothes. Scar on cheek. Check?"

"Check," I said, and reached for her.

After a while she handed me the key to her apartment and walked out—if you can call that act walking. Lancaster Arms. Room 7-G. But *that* would have to wait. Right now I had a date with a joker named Mac at a clip joint on Broadway east of the Ferry building. I bought a bottle of hooch from a cute little bundle downstairs and caught a helicab.

The joint was called THE SILVER SLIPPER, a seedy firetrap which reminded me how much I needed a shave. But the mouse that opened the door was a knockout. I reached for her.

After a while she said, "I belong to Max."

"Where can I find him?"

"Why should I tell you?" She was playing a close hand but I held all the aces.

I laid the barrel of my blaster along her skull, splitting her skin like a ripe peach. "I'd talk, delicious."

"B-back room. Third door down the hall." Her face was all red and sticky like a circus clown's.

I smiled crookedly and gave her a pat on the fanny. She had guts. And I liked the things the sun did to her hair.

When I reached the door I didn't bother to knock. I blew the lock to hell and gone with Suzy and stepped into the room. A beefy little bastard with a cigar living under his moustache gave me the fish eye behind a pair of horn rims. "They call you Max?" I asked.

"Could be," he said.

I swore under my breath and shot him in the stomach. Three times.

He did a sort of jerky dance—the kind you see in puppet shows—and folded like a wet newspaper. I hoped he was the Joe I came looking for. In my racket you can't be sure of anything. I killed a pint of hooch and thought things over. If Goldilocks wanted Maxieboy rubbed there must be an angle. I didn't like the smell of things.

Ducking out a side exit I flagged down a hellie. "Lancaster Arms," I snapped. "And don't spare the jets!"

I intended getting some fast answers.

One way or another.

Ten minutes later I was in her apartment. She was wearing a transparent softasilk negligee that did things to me. I swore under my breath and reached for her.

After a while I said, "Some answers, doll."

"Such as?" She got out her powder and paints and put on a new face.

"Such as," I drawled, playing the game *my* way, "who was Mac?"

She smiled like a fish-filled kitten. "My husband."

Things were beginning to tally. I didn't have all the answers but I was old enough to add two and two.

"Insurance?" I snapped.

"Maybe."

"Let's be sure," I said, and slapped her around the room four or five times. She whimpered like a sick pup.

"You can turn off the faucets," I growled, "It doesn't go with me." I was getting a little sore. If she wanted to start playing rough—well . . .

She'd had enough and said so.

"Who's in the caper with you?"

"Name is Keener. Hangs around the bookie joint behind a cigar store on Sutter. Tall. Wavy hair. Blue eyes. Fair complexion. Clean-shaven. Pipe. Watch chain. Neat dresser. Smiles a lot. We had it planned."

I'd been taken for a prize chump! Hired to knock off the husband so she and wavy-hair Keener could lam with the insurance loot. Well, I had all the answers now and I was plenty through playing stooge. The roller-coaster ride was over. I grabbed a handful of negligee and jerked.

She was mother-naked underneath and looked good that way.

"No doll pins the sucker label on Sam O'Slammer. Not even one as easy on the optics as you are, Goldilocks," I said, and levelled Suzy at her bellybutton.

"S—Sam, darling—don't—don't shoot!" Her neat breasts heaved like tugs in choppy water. She was screaming in high C when I plopped four charges into her tummy. She coughed and folded like a tired accordion.

Then I did a quick double-take. This was strictly for the birdies! She was the first female I'd ever air-conditioned who *didn't* bleed! I stowed Suzy and hunkered down for a closer look. Four charred holes in that gorgeous alabaster skin and not a trace of blood. Puzzled, I opened her up with my boy scout sticker and got the shock of my young life. She was nothing but a mess of cogs and coils and springs. A mechanical doll! Remembering some earlier events I felt like a damned fool.

"I'm gonna find this bird, Keener," I said aloud. "He's got some tall explaining to do."

"Finding me won't be necessary," a smooth-as-silk voice purred behind me. "Since it seems *I* have found *you.*"

I swung around to face a disintegrater in the hand of a tall, wavy-haired, fair-complexioned, clean-shaven, pipe-smoking, watch-chained, neatly-dressed, smiling man.

"Keener!" I snapped.

"Correct, my impulsive friend."

"What's the pitch?" I asked, pointing to Goldilocks with the toe of one shoe.

"I created her to fulfill my plan for earthly wealth," said Keener. "I arranged her marriage to this fellow Mac, and I also arranged the deal she made with you resulting in his death. I planned on collecting a considerable amount of insurance. I did *not* plan on your destroying my creation, Mr. O'Slammer. How very careless of you!"

As he oiled out the words he did something to his body. His clothes suddenly fell away and I did my third double-take of the day. His *skin* went with 'em—smile and all! The thing that held the disintegrater was seagreen with tentacles and bug eyes.

"Gawdamn!" I breathed, backing toward the couch.

"As you may observe, Earthman, I am not of your planet. The

knowledge you have of my presence here will die with you in one short moment."

I decided it was time to quit playing *What's My Line,* and took a quick dive behind the couch. Suzy was out and working for me by the time Green Gus got over his surprise. I emptied the last charge into him and was mighty relieved to see him fold like any other dead duck. And this one bled—plenty. All green too, inside and out.

The hall was packed like a New York tubeway so I took the fire escape down. Let homicide answer the questions. I smiled crookedly, wondering what Lt. O'Shane would say when he found the bodies.

It was raining outside. I bought a bottle of hooch at a liquor store, turned up my coat collar and headed for the office.

I felt like hell.

Beyond Lies the Wub

Philip K. Dick

They had almost finished with the loading. Outside stood the Optus, his arms folded, his face sunk in gloom. Captain Franco walked leisurely down the gangplank, grinning.

"What's the matter?" he said. "You're getting paid for all this."

The Optus said nothing. He turned away, collecting his robes. The Captain put his boot on the hem of the robe.

"Just a minute. Don't go off. I'm not finished."

"Oh?" The Optus turned with dignity. "I am going back to the village." He looked toward the animals and birds being driven up the gangplank into the spaceship. "I must organize new hunts."

Franco lit a cigarette. "Why not? You people can go out into the veldt and track it all down again. But when we run halfway between Mars and Earth—"

The Optus went off, wordless. Franco joined the first mate at the bottom of the gangplank.

"How's it coming?" he asked. He looked at his watch. "We got a good bargain here."

The mate glanced at him sourly. "How do you explain that?"

"What's the matter with you? We need it more than they do."

"I'll see you later, Captain." The mate threaded his way up the plank, between the long-legged Martian go-birds, into the ship. Franco watched him disappear. He was just starting up after him, up the plank toward the port, when he saw *it*.

"My God!" He stood staring, his hands on his hips. Peterson was walking along the path, his face red, leading *it* by a string.

"I'm sorry, Captain," he said, tugging at the string. Franco walked toward him.

"What is it?"

The wub stood sagging, its great body settling slowly. It was sitting down, its eyes half shut. A few flies buzzed about its flank, and it switched its tail.

It sat. There was silence.

"It's a wub," Peterson said. "I got it from a native for fifty cents. He said it was a very unusual animal. Very respected."

"This?" Franco poked the great sloping side of the wub. "It's a pig! A huge dirty pig!"

"Yes sir, it's a pig. The natives call it a wub."

"A huge pig. It must weigh four hundred pounds." Franco grabbed a tuft of the rough hair. The wub gasped. Its eyes opened, small and moist. Then its great mouth twitched.

A tear rolled down the wub's cheek and splashed on the floor.

"Maybe it's good to eat," Peterson said nervously.

"We'll soon find out," Franco said.

The wub survived the takeoff, sound asleep in the hold of the ship. When they were out in space and everything was running smoothly, Captain Franco bade his men fetch the wub upstairs so that he might perceive what manner of beast it was.

The wub grunted and wheezed, squeezing up the passageway.

"Come on," Jones grated, pulling at the rope. The wub twisted, rubbing its skin off on the smooth chrome walls. It burst into the anteroom, tumbling down in a heap. The men leaped up.

"Good Lord," French said. "What is it?"

"Peterson says it's a wub," Jones said. "It belongs to him." He kicked at the wub. The wub stood up unsteadily, panting.

"What's the matter with it?" French came over. "Is it going to be sick?"

They watched. The wub rolled its eyes mournfully. It gazed around at the men.

"I think it's thirsty," Peterson said. He went to get some water. French shook his head.

"No wonder we had so much trouble taking off. I had to reset all my ballast calculations."

Peterson came back with the water. The wub began to lap gratefully, splashing the men.

Captain Franco appeared at the door.

"Let's have a look at it." He advanced, squinting critically. "You got this for fifty cents?"

"Yes, sir," Peterson said. "It eats almost anything. I fed it on grain and it liked that. And then potatoes, and mash, and scraps from the table, and milk. It seems to enjoy eating. After it eats it lies down and goes to sleep."

"I see," Captain Franco said. "Now, as to its taste. That's the real question. I doubt if there's much point in fattening it up any more. It seems fat enough to me already. Where's the cook? I want him here. I want to find out—"

The wub stopped lapping and looked up at the Captain.

"Really, Captain," the wub said. "I suggest we talk of other matters."

The room was silent.

"What was that?" Franco said. "Just now."

"The wub, sir," Peterson said. "It spoke."

They all looked at the wub.

"What did it say? What did it say?"

"It suggested we talk about other things."

Franco walked toward the wub. He went all around it, examining it from every side. Then he came back over and stood with the men.

"I wonder if there's a native inside it," he said thoughtfully. "Maybe we should open it up and have a look."

"Oh, goodness!" the wub cried. "Is that all you people can think of, killing and cutting?"

Franco clenched his fists. "Come out of there! Whoever you are, come out!"

Nothing stirred. The men stood together, their faces blank, staring at the wub. The wub swished its tail. It belched suddenly.

"I beg your pardon," the wub said.

"I don't think there's anyone in there," Jones said in a low voice. They all looked at each other.

The cook came in.

"You wanted me, Captain?" he said. "What's this thing?"

"This is a wub," Franco said. "It's to be eaten. Will you measure it and figure out—"

"I think we should have a talk," the wub said. "I'd like to discuss this with you, Captain, if I might. I can see that you and I do not agree on some basic issues."

The Captain took a long time to answer. The wub waited good-naturedly, licking the water from its jowls.

"Come into my office," the Captain said at last. He turned and walked out of the room. The wub rose and padded after him. The men watched it go out. They heard it climbing the stairs.

"I wonder what the outcome will be," the cook said. "Well, I'll be in the kitchen. Let me know as soon as you hear."

"Sure," Jones said. "Sure."

The wub eased itself down in the corner with a sigh. "You must forgive me," it said. "I'm afraid I'm addicted to various forms of relaxation. When one is as large as I—"

The Captain nodded impatiently. He sat down at his desk and folded his hands.

"All right," he said. "Let's get started. You're a wub? Is that correct?"

The wub shrugged. "I suppose so. That's what they call us, the natives, I mean. We have our own term."

"And you speak English? You've been in contact with Earthmen before?"

"No."

"Then how do you do it?"

"Speak English? Am I speaking English? I'm not conscious of speaking anything in particular. I examined your mind—"

"My mind?"

"I studied the contents, especially the semantic warehouse, as I refer to it—"

"I see," the Captain said. "Telepathy. Of course."

"We are a very old race," the wub said. "Very old and very ponderous. It is difficult for us to move around. You can appreciate anything so slow and heavy would be at the mercy of more agile forms of life. There was no use in our relying on physical defenses. How could we win? Too heavy to run, too soft to fight, too good-natured to hunt for game—"

"How do you live?"

"Plants. Vegetables. We can eat almost anything. We're very catholic. Tolerant, eclectic, catholic. We live and let live. That's how we've gotten along."

The wub eyed the Captain.

"And that's why I so violently objected to this business about having me boiled. I could see the image in your mind—most of me in the frozen food locker, some of me in the kettle, a bit for your pet cat—"

"So you read minds?" the Captain said. "How interesting. Anything else? I mean, what else can you do along those lines?"

"A few odds and ends," the wub said absently, staring around the room. "A nice apartment you have here, Captain. You keep it quite neat. I respect life-forms that are tidy. Some Martian birds are quite tidy. They throw things out of their nests and sweep them—"

"Indeed." The Captain nodded. "But to get back to the problem—"

"Quite so. You spoke of dining on me. The taste, I am told, is good. A little fatty, but tender. But how can any lasting contact be established between your people and mine if you resort to such barbaric attitudes? Eat me? Rather you should discuss questions with me, philosophy, the arts—"

The Captain stood up. "Philosophy. It might interest you to know that we will be hard put to find something to eat for the next month. An unfortunate spoilage—"

"I know." The wub nodded. "But wouldn't it be more in accord with your principles of democracy if we all drew straws, or something along that line? After all, democracy is to protect the minority from just such infringements. Now, if each of us casts one vote—"

The Captain walked to the door.

"Nuts to you," he said. He opened the door. He opened his mouth.

He stood frozen, his mouth wide, his eyes staring, his fingers still on the knob.

The wub watched him. Presently it padded out of the room, edging past the Captain. It went down the hall, deep in meditation.

The room was quiet.

"So you see," the wub said, "we have a common myth. Your mind contains many familiar myth symbols. Ishtar, Odysseus—"

Peterson sat silently, staring at the floor. He shifted in his chair.

"Go on," he said. "Please go on."

"I find in your Odysseus a figure common to the mythology of most self-conscious races. As I interpret it, Odysseus wanders as an individual aware of himself as such. This is the idea of separation, of separation from family and country. The process of individuation."

"But Odysseus returns to his home." Peterson looked out the port window, at the stars, endless stars, burning intently in the empty universe. "Finally he goes home."

"As must all creatures. The moment of separation is a temporary period, a brief journey of the soul. It begins, it ends. The wanderer returns to land and race. . . ."

The door opened. The wub stopped, turning its great head.

Captain Franco came into the room, the men behind him. They hesitated at the door.

"Are you all right?" French said.

"Do you mean me?" Peterson said, surprised. "Why me?"

Franco lowered his gun. "Come over here," he said to Peterson. "Get up and come here."

There was silence.

"Go ahead," the wub said. "It doesn't matter."

Peterson stood up. "What for?"

"It's an order."

Peterson walked to the door. French caught his arm.

"What's going on?" Peterson wrenched loose. "What's the matter with you?"

Captain Franco moved toward the wub. The wub looked up from where it lay in the corner, pressed against the wall.

"It is interesting," the wub said, "that you are obsessed with the idea of eating me. I wonder why."

"Get up," Franco said.

"If you wish." The wub rose, grunting. "Be patient. It is difficult for me." It stood, gasping, its tongue lolling foolishly.

"Shoot it now," French said.

"For God's sake!" Peterson exclaimed. Jones turned to him quickly, his eyes gray with fear.

"You didn't see him—like a statue, standing there, his mouth open. If we hadn't come down, he'd still be there."

"Who? The Captain?" Peterson stared around. "But he's all right now."

They looked at the wub, standing in the middle of the room, its great chest rising and falling.

"Come on," Franco said. "Out of the way."

The men pulled aside toward the door.

"You are quite afraid, aren't you?" the wub said. "Have I done anything to you? I am against the idea of hurting. All I have done is try to protect myself. Can you expect me to rush eagerly to my death? I am a sensible being like yourselves. I was curious to see your ship, learn about you. I suggested to the native—"

The gun jerked.

"See," Franco said. "I thought so."

The wub settled down, panting. It put its paws out, pulling its tail around it.

"It is very warm," the wub said. "I understand that we are close to the jets. Atomic power. You have done many wonderful things with it—technically. Apparently your scientific hierarchy is not equipped to solve moral, ethical—"

Franco turned to the men, crowding behind him, wide-eyed, silent.

"I'll do it. You can watch."

French nodded. "Try to hit the brain. It's no good for eating. Don't hit the chest. If the rib cage shatters, we'll have to pick bones out."

"Listen," Peterson said, licking his lips. "Has it done anything? What harm has it done? I'm asking you. And anyhow, it's still mine. You have no right to shoot it. It doesn't belong to you."

Franco raised his gun.

"I'm going out," Jones said, his face white and sick. "I don't want to see it."

"Me, too," French said. The men straggled out, murmuring. Peterson lingered at the door.

"It was talking to me about myths," he said. "It wouldn't hurt anyone."

He went outside.

Franco walked toward the wub. The wub looked up slowly. It swallowed.

"A very foolish thing," it said. "I am sorry that you want to do it. There was a parable that your Saviour related—"

It stopped, staring at the gun.

"Can you look me in the eye and do it?" the wub said. "Can you do that?"

The Captain gazed down. "I can look you in the eye," he said. "Back on the farm we had hogs, dirty razorback hogs. I can do it."

Staring down at the wub, into the gleaming, moist eyes, he pressed the trigger.

The taste was excellent.

They sat glumly around the table, some of them hardly eating at all. The only one who seemed to be enjoying himself was Captain Franco.

"More?" he said, looking around. "More? And some wine, perhaps."

"Not me," French said. "I think I'll go back to the chart room."

"Me, too." Jones stood up, pushing his chair back. "I'll see you later."

The Captain watched them go. Some of the others excused themselves.

"What do you suppose the matter is?" the Captain said. He turned to Peterson. Peterson sat staring down at his plate, at the potatoes, the green peas, and at the thick slab of tender, warm meat.

He opened his mouth. No sound came.

The Captain put his hand on Peterson's shoulder.

"It is only organic matter, now," he said. "The life essence is gone." He ate, spooning up the gravy with some bread. "I, myself, love to eat. It is one of the greatest things that a living creature can enjoy. Eating, resting, meditation, discussing things."

Peterson nodded. Two more men got up and went out. The Captain drank some water and sighed.

"Well," he said. "I must say that this was a very enjoyable meal. All the reports I had heard were quite true—the taste of wub. Very fine. But I was prevented from enjoying this in times past."

He dabbed at his lips with his napkin and leaned back in his chair. Peterson stared dejectedly at the table.

The Captain watched him intently. He leaned over.

"Come, come," he said. "Cheer up! Let's discuss things."

He smiled.

"As I was saying before I was interrupted, the role of Odysseus in the myths—"

Peterson jerked up, staring.

"To go on," the Captain said. "Odysseus, as I understand him—"

The Big Trek

Fritz Leiber

I didn't know if I'd got to this crazy place by rocket, space dodger, time twister—or maybe even on foot the way I felt so beat. My memory was gone. When I woke up there was just the desert all around me with the gray sky pressing down like the ceiling of an enormous room. The desert . . . and the big trek. And *that* was enough to make me stop grabbing for my memory and take a quick look at my pants to make sure I was human.

These, well, animals were shuffling along about four abreast in a straggly line that led from one end of nowhere to the other, right past my rocky hole. Wherever they were heading they seemed to have come from everywhere and maybe everywhen. There were big ones and little ones, some like children and some just small. A few went on two feet, but more on six or eight, and there were wrigglers, rollers, oozers, flutterers and hoppers; I couldn't decide whether the low-flying ones were pets or pals. Some had scales, others feathers, bright armor like beetles or fancy hides like zebras, and quite a few wore transparent suits holding air or other gases, or water or other liquids, though some of the suits were tailored for a dozen tentacles and some for no legs at all. And darn if their shuffle—to pick one word for all the kinds of movement—wasn't more like a dance than a lockstep.

They were too different from each other for an army, yet they weren't like refugees either, for refugees wouldn't dance and make music, even if on more feet than two or four and with voices and instruments so strange I couldn't tell which was which. Their higgledy-piggledy variety suggested a stampede from some awful disaster or a flight to some ark of survival, but I couldn't feel panic in them—or solemn purpose either, for that matter. They just shuffled happily along. And if they were a circus parade, as a person might think from their being animals and some of them dressed fancy, then who was bossing the show and where were the guards or the audience, except for me?

I should have been afraid of such a horde of monsters, but I wasn't, so I got up from behind the rock I'd been spying over and I took one last look around for footprints or blastscar or time-twister whorls or some sign of how I'd got there, and then I shrugged my shoulders and walked down toward them.

They didn't stop and they didn't run, they didn't shoot and they didn't come out to capture or escort me; they kept on shuffling along without a break in the rhythm, but a thousand calm eyes were turned on me from the tops of weaving stalks or the depths of bony caverns, and as I got close a dusky roller like an escaped tire with green eyes in the unspinning hub speeded up a little and an opal octopus in a neat suit brimful of water held back, making room for me.

Next thing I knew I was restfully shuffling along myself, wondering how the roller kept from tipping and why the octopus moved his legs by threes, and how so many different ways of moving could be harmonized like instruments in a band. Around me was the murmuring rise and fall of languages I couldn't understand and the rainbow-changing of color patches that might be languages for the eye—the octopus dressed in water looked from time to time like a shaken-up pousse-café.

I tried out on them what I seemed to remember as the lingoes of a dozen planets, but nobody said anything back at me directly—I almost tried Earth-talk on them, but something stopped me. A puffy bird-thing floating along under a gas-bag that was part of its body settled lightly on my shoulder and hummed gently in my ear and dropped some suspicious-looking black marbles and then bobbed off. A thing on two legs from somewhere ahead in the trek waltzed its way to my side and offered me a broken-edged chunk that was milky with light and crusty. The thing looked female, being jauntily built and having a crest of violet feathers, but instead of nose and mouth her face tapered to a rosy little ring and where breasts would be there was a burst of pink petals. I gave my non-Earth lingoes another try. She waited until I was quiet and then she lifted the crusty chunk to her rosy ring, which she opened a little, and then she offered the chunk to me again. I took it and tasted it and it was like brick cheese but flaky and I ate it. I nodded and grinned and she puffed out her petals and traced a circle with her head and turned to go. I almost said, "Thanks, chick," because that seemed the right thing, but again something stopped me.

So the big trek had accepted me, I decided, but as the day wore on (if they had days here, I reminded myself) the feeling of acceptance didn't give me any real security. It didn't satisfy me that I had been given eats instead of being eaten and that I was part of a harmony instead of a discord. I guess I was expecting too much. Or maybe I was finding a strange part of myself and was frightened of it. And after all it isn't reassuring to shuffle along with intelligent animals you can't talk to, even if they act friendly and dance and sing and now and then thrum strange strings. It didn't calm me to feel that I was someplace that was homey and at the same time as lonely as the stars. The monsters around me got to seem stranger and stranger; I quit seeing their little tricks of personality and saw only their outsides. I craned my neck trying to spot the chick with the pink petals but she was gone. After a while I couldn't bear it any longer. Some ruins looking like chopped-off skyscrapers had come in sight earlier and we were just now passing them, not too close, so although the flat sky was getting darker and pressing down lower and although there were distant flashes of lightning and rumbles of thunder (I think that's what they were), I turned at a right angle and walked away fast from the trek.

Nobody stopped me and pretty soon I was hidden in the ruins. They were comforting at first, the little ruins, and I got the feeling my ancestors had built them. But then I came to the bigger ones and they *were* chopped-off skyscrapers and yet some of them were so tall they scratched the dark flat sky and for a moment I thought I heard a distant squeal like chalk on a giant blackboard that set my teeth on edge. And then I got to wondering what had chopped off the skyscrapers and what had happened to the people, and after that I began to see dark things loafing along after me close to the ruined walls. They were about as big as I was, but going on all fours. They began to follow me closer and closer, moving like clumsy wolves, the more notice I took of them. I saw that their faces were covered with hair like their bodies and that their jaws were working. I started to hurry and as soon as I did I began to hear the sounds they were making. The bad thing was that although the sounds were halfway between growls and barks, I could understand them.

"Hello, Joe."

"Whacha know, Joe?"

"That so, Joe?"

"Let's blow, Joe."

"C'mon Joe, let's go, go, go."

And then I realized the big mistake I'd made in coming to these ruins, and I turned around and started to run back the way I had come, and they came loping and lurching after me, trying to drag me down, and the worst thing was that I knew they didn't want to kill me, but just have me get down on all fours and run with them and bark and growl.

The ruins grew smaller, but it was very dark now and at first I was afraid that I had lost my way and next I was afraid that the end of the big trek had passed me by, but then the light brightened under the low sky like the afterglow of a sunset and it showed me the big trek in the distance and I ran toward it and the hairy things stopped skulking behind me.

I didn't hit the same section of the big trek, of course, but one that was enough like it to make me wonder. There was another dusky roller, but with blue eyes and smaller, so that it had to spin faster, and another many-legged creature dressed in water, and a jaunty chick with crimson crest and a burst of orange petals. But the difference didn't bother me.

The trek slowed down, the change in rhythm rippling back to me along the line. I looked ahead and there was a large round hole in the low sky and through it I could see the stars. And through it too the trek itself was swerving, each creature diving upward toward the winking points of light in the blackness.

I kept on shuffling happily forward, though more slowly now, and to either side of the trek I saw heaped on the desert floor spacesuits tailored to fit every shape of creature I could imagine and fly him or her safely through the emptiness above. After a while it got to be my turn and I found a suit and climbed into it and zipped it snug and located the control buttons in the palms of the gloves and looked up. Then I felt more than control buttons in my fingers and I looked to either side of me and I was hand in hand with an octopus wearing an eight-legged spacesuit over his water-filled one and on the other side with a suited-up chick who sported a jet-black crest and pearl-gray petals.

She traced a circle with her head and I did the same, and the octopus traced a smaller circle with a free tentacle, and I knew that one of the reasons I hadn't used Earth-talk was that I was going to keep quiet until I learned or remembered *their* languages, and that another reason was that the hairy four-footers back in the ruins had been men like me and I hated them but these creatures beside me were my kind, and that we had come to take one last look at the Earth that had destroyed itself and at the men who had stayed on Earth and not got away like me—to come back and lose my memory from the shock of being on my degraded ancestral planet.

Then we clasped hands tight, which pushed the buttons in our palms. Our jets blossomed out behind us and we were diving up together out of this world through the smoothly rounded doughnut hole toward the stars. I realized that space wasn't empty and that those points of light in the darkness weren't lonely at all.

Blood Lands

Alfred Coppel

The rendezvous was well away from the charnel, stinking area that had been burned by the starship's landing. Kenyon stood on the edge of a plume-grove that grew down to where the tideless sea lay red and shimmering.

He looked back, cursing the flatness of the island. The spire of the starship commanded a complete view of the territory; there was no place to hide. Kenyon knew that anyone who wished to do so could spy on him easily as he stood waiting for Elyra to come out of the grove.

Not, he told himself defensively, that there was any good reason that he should hide his doings with Elyra. Affairs with native women—while not considered in the best taste—were common enough among starmen. It was simply that the mission here was one of repatriation rather than exploitation, and all members of the expedition had been warned against forming liaisons that could conceivably become embarrassing situations when the natives were moved off Kana.

Kenyon shifted his weight nervously from one foot to another, peering through the picket of quills into the grove. He would have liked to go into the grove to meet the girl, but it was something he had never been able to bring himself to do. One didn't take chances on a planet like Kana—one that had retrogressed from technology into legend-worshipping semi-savagery. And there was that unanswered question about cannibalism . . .

Not Elyra, Kenyon thought quickly; that wouldn't be possible. After all, the mission had been on Kana only a few days. It was only a matter of time until the riddle of the native food-supply was solved.

A soft rustling of the plumes warned him of her approach. Native or not, he reflected, she was a handsome thing. Odd about the red hair—they all had it, men and women alike. And the grey, almost cold, eyes. But there was nothing cold about her body; it was lithe and supple, burned golden by the light of the red sun. Her costume showed most of it, and Kenyon could fully appreciate the rippling play of muscles under the satiny skin as she walked.

She paused at the very edge of the grove, solemn and unsmiling in the slanting light.

"The sunset comes, Kenyon," she said.

Her greeting was always the same. A dwelling on the ending of a day, the fading of light from the sky. Kenyon unconsciously looked toward the east, where the first pale light of a star was breaking through the rusty glow of the sinking sun. Stars were pale on the Edge, he thought vaguely. It filled him with a sense of distance, of vast empty spaces, of the parsecs that separated Kana and its red star from the teeming worlds of the inner systems. Little wonder it had been lost for so long . . .

He shivered slightly and smiled at Elyra. "Shall we walk by the sea?" he asked. "I've brought something for you—a gift."

Ordinarily, the promise of a bauble would have brought a smile to her face, but she remained solemn and, it seemed to Kenyon, unduly aloof. "Tonight you were to walk in the forest."

Kenyon frowned. He had promised her, and she had remembered.

In the far distance, on one of the islands across the red water, a drum began to beat with a deep, thudding insistence. A sense of alienage filled him, and something akin to fear—though he knew nothing that should bring such feelings into a starman's mind. All the teeming billions of a starflung culture backed him with power and machines. There was nothing in the inhabited galaxy a starman should fear; yet Kenyon *was* afraid—he knew it. Afraid of this watery world and its islands. Perhaps he was even afraid of Elyra.

"We have walked by the sea," Elyra said, still standing apart from him, "and now we should walk in the plume-forest. You have come here from the sky to take my people from Kana—"

There was little point in denying this, Kenyon realized, since both Bothwell and Grancor had already announced it to the island chieftain. Manpower was needed in the industrial combines of the inner worlds. It was wasteful to let humans rusticate on a world without commercial value like Kana.

"—I would take you by the hand," Elyra continued in her quaintly-accented and archaic *lingua spacia*, "and show you why my people have no wish to go."

Kenyon's eyes widened at that. No native had yet offered any of the mission's three members a reason for their reluctance to leave Kana. This was the first apparent break in a wall of courteous passive resistance. If he, Kenyon, could be the one to convince the chiefs that they should urge their people to board the starship without coercion and bloodshed, it would be an excellent mark in his record; it could lead to better things than herding troglodytes back into the fold of the galactic State.

"Wait for me, Elyra," he said. "I will be back before the sun is fully down, and I will go with you into the forest."

She smiled, showing sharp white teeth.

Kenyon shuddered slightly and turned back toward the starship. Into the forest he might go, he thought bleakly, but not without weapons—and not without Bothwell and Grancor knowing what he was about to do and where, in the service of the State.

Even in the cargo-holds—the huge pens intended for the natives of Kana—he could hear Grancor and Bothwell arguing.

Bothwell: "You bloody fool—you aren't even able to tell me what happened to the blasted barges! Even a thousand years in this climate wouldn't destroy them—let alone a mere four hundred. So where are they, then?"

And Grancor, in his dry and acid-tinged tones, like those of an academy professor: "Obviously, my dear Bothwell, when the islands formed they were no longer needed. They simply sank them."

Kenyon paused to listen. It was a perpetual argument between the older men, and one he thought both fruitless and exasperating. One he had no wish to join.

It had begun with the planetfall, and the discovery of ten thousand islands in the shallow sea that had once—according to the book—covered the entire planet of Kana.

Five hundred years ago, in the first flush of stellar colonization, Kana had been populated with human beings from the inner galaxy. Since no land of any kind was available, and since there was a ready market for gold salts and nitrates that could be extracted from Kana's sea, a first-stage barge-culture was established. Floating villages, hydroponics, an essential and highly-developed technology. And then came the interregnum—a commercial interregnum that found the products of Kana unneeded. Trade fell off, and eventually the planet and its people were forgotten. A lost colony. It took five hundred years for the manpower of Kana and other worlds like it to become valuable enough to send repatriation missions out to gather it up and bring it into the industrial combines.

Yet the Kana planetfall brought some surprises to Kenyon and Grancor and Bothwell, the mission's nominal head. The barges were gone, the inhabitants strangely changed and uncivilized, and a million islands where none had been before.

"Vulcanism is out," Bothwell was declaring. "Kana and the Kana sun are too old to support that kind of thing."

"You don't know," Grancor said drily; "you are a starman, not a geologist."

"I'm no agronomist, either," bellowed Bothwell, "but I can tell you nothing grows here but those damn feathers!"

"They only *look* like feathers," Grancor said, "you've seen stranger growths—"

Isolation, thought Kenyon, *is sharpening their natural antagonisms. Isolation and failure. A failure that neither of them will face up to.* He knew that, in a matter of days, Bothwell would blow up and order the Kana natives herded into the starship's holds by force. They had the weapons, but somehow Kenyon dreaded taking such a step; there were dangers on Kana that none of the three men from the stars had yet recognized—he was sure of it.

He armed himself and went up the ramp toward the bickering voices; it would be a pleasure to interrupt them.

Bothwell looked up as he entered, a frown on his craggy face. Kenyon decided again, as he had every day for weeks, that he didn't like Bothwell.

"And where do you think you're going?"

"Where indeed?" murmured Grancor. "Booted, armed and armored, our young colleague goes to meet his pretty savage, of course."

Kenyon flushed. "Since we seem to be wasting time here," he

snapped with some bravado, "I'm going into the forest to talk to the chief."

"Is that wise?" Grancor asked Bothwell.

"Let him go," the big man said. "When he's convinced talking won't help, we'll go out with blasters and herd the trogs into the ship."

Kenyon forced down his anger and turned away. At the bulkhead, he stopped, unwilling to go without asking their help, and hating to do it. "Please guard the command channel," he said casually. "I'll report any progress by radio . . ."

Bothwell let out a hoot of coarse laughter. "Progress! Into the forest at night with his pretty trog and he wants to keep us informed!"

Kenyon turned on his heel and almost ran out of the ship, his face burning. Damn them both anyway!

The sun was down and a thick dusk hung over the island. Kenyon's boots sank into the stinking, burned soil as he went, making him stumble. *Like a red, unhealed scar,* he thought. Typical of the improvements made by man on the worlds he exploited.

Elyra was still where he had left her, waiting in the shadow of the tall plumes. The drums sounded louder, their leaden beat drifting across the darkling water of the sea from island to island. The last bloody light was fading from the sky.

Without talk, Kenyon took the girl's extended hand and together they vanished into the forest of waving plumes.

—the night wind and drums in the forest a feeding circle forms to greet a past man from the stars and the anger in the throbbing beat underfoot grows dark and hungry wait the plumes whisper he is coming wait the soil says he is coming to us your father will care for you and feed you and you need not go out among the stars I will protect you—

It seemed to Kenyon that they walked for hours through the darkness. He was conscious of a growing excitement in Elyra, of a feeling of triumph and anticipation. He thought of Grancor's speculations on cannibalism among the Kana people and a sick thrill ran through him.

As they reached a clearing in the forest, the drums stopped; silence fell like a blow. Elyra turned to face him, her eyes wide and dark in the shadows.

He struck a match and lit a cigaret, sucking the smoke deep into his lungs. Elyra flicked her tongue over her lips and Kenyon noticed its sharp tip. He almost succumbed to an impulse to turn back, but the thought of Bothwell and Grancor laughing at him held him where he was.

"Be steadfast, Kenyon," Elyra said, as though she had guessed his thoughts. "Be brave and above all—be wise when you meet the father."

"Father?"

She stamped a bare foot on the resilient ground impatiently. "The father, Kenyon," she said again. "The great one who came to my people after yours had deserted us—"

There it was again, Kenyon thought—that schism between the people of Kana and the rest of the inhabited worlds. *Your* people. *My* people. As though the birth of a legend of gods from space had changed the inhabitants of Kana into something apart from the rest of the human race.

"There are no gods from space, little one," Kenyon said gently. "Only more men."

"The father is not a man," Elyra whispered. Kenyon could almost feel the mystic calm that descended on her as she contemplated the legendary past. "Long ago, when the people of Kana lived on the sea and were dying, the great gods came to us and fed us and made us warm." Her tone grew scornful. *"You* would not understand me; I cannot make you understand. But the father will speak with you, I am sure, and you will know why our people must remain here for always."

"No," Kenyon said. "One way or another, your people will come with us. You are needed elsewhere."

She laughed at him. "When time ends—when the red star dies— we will be here on Kana. *And so will every man who touched the sacred soil . . .*"

She stood on tiptoes and kissed him, and Kenyon felt a stinging pain on his lips.

"Savage!" He stepped back, wiping blood from his mouth where her sharp tongue had pierced his flesh. He struck her across the face, hard, and she fell. It came to him in a sickening flash of completion. Not cannibals—vampires. He felt his stomach heave convulsively. That descendants of civilized men could become so depraved was unbelievable.

Grancor and Bothwell had to be warned. He keyed his pack radio with the message and waited for a response as Elyra watched him from the shadows. There was no response. Damn them! Were they guarding the channel or weren't they? He had no way of knowing.

Elyra laughed. The sound of it was infuriating. He drew his blaster and pointed it at her. "Lead the way back," he commanded with more confidence than he felt.

For answer, she laughed again and vanished into the darkness of the thicket of plumes. Nightmare! Kenyon fired blindly, searing a path through the feathery growth. Again, laughter.

And then a sudden thudding rush of naked feet, and hands laid roughly on him, clawing, beating. He screamed with fright, threshing about in the grip of strong arms. Then there was a stunning pain at the base of his skull and darkness, deep and black as the night of space itself.

When Kenyon awoke, he lay naked in a clearing lit with torches. All about, a sea of faces—the people of Kana. Someone was beating a drum, very softly, with an insistent and hypnotic rhythm. His bare flesh touched the ground, and for the first time, Kenyon was conscious of the peculiar texture of the soil. Smooth, but warm with some kind of latent, inner heat.

The entire tribe of trogs was swaying, self-entranced by the drum beats and the smoky night. Kenyon could hear their murmured chant, made endless by repetition:

"—wake father wake father wake father—"

Kenyon tried to sit up, found that he could not. Unseen, fleshy bands held him firm to the ground. Panic stirred in him, and he suppressed it with all the power of his will and training. He twisted his head about to see if he could find Elyra in the sea of faces, but she was indistinguishable from any other woman. All were naked, all were swaying in their ritual chant. The very air seemed to vibrate with the beat of it.

Kenyon twisted his head aside and froze with horror. Not ten meters from him a stump of a man stood upright—

—no, it was not a stump at all—but a native buried to the armpits in the ground. His eyes were wide open and his mouth worked convulsively. The soil itself was pulsating slowly as the man sank steadily downward.

The man screamed. A liquid mumbling wail that broke into gibberish. A yell erupted from the gathered trogs.

"—father wakes father wakes!"

Kenyon, eyes bulging, lay stiff—waiting for he knew not what. The sinking man raised an arm like an automaton, pointing directly at the captive. As though something had taken control of his vocal cords—something alien that found speech a clumsy thing—the man spoke in a hollow, ragged, sepulchral voice.

"You—man from the stars! Why have you come here?"

Kenyon could not reply.

"To steal my people. To take them from me," the accusing voice thundered. *"When their own kind deserted them—I came across parsecs of space—across the gulf between the galaxies—to live with them and care for them. And now you think to take them away?"* And the buried man laughed. A hollow, booming, awful sound in the firelit forest. The trogs echoed his mirthless laughter.

—it's a trick, Kenyon thought. *Hypnosis. Or I'm going mad. I thought the whole world was speaking through that man's mouth—*

The man swept his arms about in a wild circle. He shouted at the trogs: *"Eat! I feast! Join me, eat!"*

Kenyon struggled against the bonds that held him, panic surging in him. But the trogs did not attack him with their sucking, pointed tongues. They bent over, pressing their mouths against the ground, plunging their tongues into the soil. The buried man screamed once more and vanished, with a wet, sucking noise.

The whole thing leaped into focus in Kenyon's mind, like a picture forming. The soil, the earth—the islands; that was the father. A race of beings from across space, finding refuge in the shallow, warm waters of a world abandoned by the humans of the inner galaxy. Huge, plumed beasts, willing to live in a ghastly symbiosis with the men they found on Kana. Giving them the blood of the land to eat, and taking in return the flesh of men. It was sickening, horrifying. Kenyon could imagine the people leaving the barges for the islands they could see rising in their ocean, and eventually living like parasites on the blood under the tawny skin . . .

* * *

With sick disgust raging in him, Kenyon threshed about, fighting tooth and nail to free himself. He had to get away—out into the cold, clean dark of space—away from this nightmare of alien and human depravity.

And then suddenly, he was free and running through the forest, with the naked horde of trogs running behind him, torches blazing.

The awful plumes tore at his flesh, the hot pulsing soil of the island softened to slow him. He could hear himself screaming in mixed rage and terror as he fled.

He had to get back!

Back to warn the others!

Back to the starship and cold clean metal under his naked feet and sanity again.

Behind him the trogs howled, and the dark forest echoed their cries.

And at last he was running across the burned flesh of the area of the starship's landing. A ragged, craterlike puckered mouth. The ground rippled and heaved in anger. Kenyon stumbled, fell. Picked himself up again and plunged into the open valve with a sobbing, rasping cry.

Grancor and Bothwell sat in the control room, their faces white. They did not move when Kenyon stumbled into the cabin. They did not speak as he babbled his story and yelled at them to lift the ship.

"You've gone mad! Can't you understand what I'm saying? We must get *out!*"

When they did not respond, he took the controls himself and closed the relays. The rockets did not fire.

There was a sinking sensation to the deck. Kenyon felt his sanity totter.

Grancor took him by the arm and led him to a port near the still-open valve.

"Look outside," Grancor said gently.

"You got my message," Kenyon said.

Grancor nodded.

Kenyon stood in the open port, looking out.

The sky was reddening in the east, and in the crimson light the plumes were waving agitatedly. The ground was close. Too close. The red, mutilated mouth had closed on the ship. Kenyon remembered the buried man with a thrill of horror. The ship was sinking. In another few moments it would be completely ingested.

Kenyon was conscious of the nearness of a supernal, mammoth intelligence. It hungered.

Grancor and Kenyon stood in the open port, watching the silent circle of trogs that had formed around the starship. They felt their craft sinking slowly, down and down—into the bloody, living land.

Brave New Hamburger

Philip Sidney Jennings

City 2, Eating House 13 . . . the meat in the mouth of the hamburger grinned greasily up at the pale youthful face of David Church. The red tower of ketchup leaned towards his shaking left hand, his right clawed his belly—years had passed since he had eaten Cog People's food. He unscrewed the top of the ketchup, pumped, and bled three thick gouts on to the meat—the old ritual. He replaced the cap of the ketchup and the bun cap of the meat. It was ready to be eaten. The grease and the ketchup mingled in a conspiring smile. Fear grew big as a baby in David's stomach: the image occurred to David himself, as he mangled the meat and dripped ketchup. Pregnant with fear, he wondered what he would give birth to . . . in the next two, three, ten, thirty minutes—whenever he chose to make "it" happen. He lowered his mouth to the coffee cup and drank without tasting. Circular music was playing throughout the House. David found himself turning around with it, in it; sometimes he thought he recognised tunes from the past but as he strove to hold them in his mind they turned around again and he was listening to another tune which just eluded him, like the one before it. His head began to spin. He glanced nervously around Eating House 13 and suddenly his heart was heavy with despair, the false stare of neon, the smacking pain of plastic . . .

Heads were bobbing over burgers, spinning around as though on the wheel of the meat. And then horror! A wild conductor with long grey hair, a magical wand in his hand, a twisted grin of the uttermost contempt on his pointed face, broke the surface of David's imagination, leapt with the pirouetting grace of a ballerina into the reality of Eating House 13, waved his stick, his arms, his legs, his hair in front of the tables of the chewing children and the children of the children and chanted:

> *"Eat the meat!*
> *The bun is fun!*
> *Have another one!*
> *You've just begun!*
> *Eat the meat!*
> *The bun is fun!"*

The crazy conductor would have gone on like that but David pulled him as fast as he could back down into the dark cave of his imagination, where many other crazy actors sat waiting for a chance to play on the stage. David shuddered at the thought that his fantasy might in some mysterious way have been noticed. But all was peaceful. Heads bobbed, music turned, the flame and yellow walls glared like a permanent sunset. David shifted in his seat and next to his stomach, now receiving the masticated bombs of bun and meat, felt the heavy old gun tucked in his waistband and hidden by a loose jacket.

The three waiters moved backwards and forwards between the kitchen and the tables. David wondered which of these Cog waiters was Anderson, the operator of the Hamburger Machine. He knew it was one of them but Professor Macbeth had only given David the name, nothing more. David had first to discover who Anderson was . . . and then . . . to graduate . . . an M.A. . . . .

Professor Macbeth is a small round man with eyes that shine like small black olives. His rolling movements make him a happy man to see, his habits of rhyming words make him sometimes sound absurd. This confuses some of the students at first, while later they come around to thinking that Professor Macbeth is clever, always trying to say something, to make a point, to teach his ragged assortment of students by whatever means possible. Questioned by his students as to his part in the Cog and Hamburger times in which they live, the Professor often replies:

"I am the power that unites the vacant lots, the empty spaces.

"Between the Schools, the Eating Houses and the Work Places."
David Church is in the Poetry Workshop which Professor Macbeth runs. At first he was ashamed to find himself in such a place but now he is different. He feels he has changed, though many warning voices from the past still plague him . . .

. . . In Eating House 13 a classroom scene from the past arranged itself for David's reality. A square set teacher with a crimson face has caught David doodling on the front of his "Cog and Diet"—part 1 book. The teacher made words:

"Church! Get that poetic behaviour out of your system or I'll have it pumped out like ketchup from the body of a bottle. The last time I supervised that operation was way back in 1983. I don't want to have to go through that again. I'm just too busy!"

The class understood and nodded their heads up and down as though lunch time were approaching. David knew, even then, he was being threatened by powers beyond his control. He stopped scribbling on his book and tried as best he could to draw sharp triangles and perfect circles. He did well enough never to be threatened again . . . in that school, but in his next school for Small Cogs David again found himself in trouble. The food often made him sick. He starved himself for days rather than eat hamburgers and french fries. His mind wandered from the squares and boxes he was required to fill in on the forms, which were part of the daily diet for Small Cogs. As though stumbling through a world of his unsure making David found himself scribbling absurd works on his "The Cogger" book. He wrote:

"A Bureaucrat is like a mouse
He creeps in every little house."

His astute teacher found the lines and this time David was threatened with inoculation. But again David was fortunate. It was time for him to move on to another school for Bigger Cogs.

* * *

David pulled a long blonde hair from his coffee cup. He twirled the hair around his finger nervously. He wondered how it had got there, and while he wondered his mind staged his first affair with a girl in the Bigger Cogs school. She had long blonde hair. Her name was Nena. He saw her wide swollen mouth, her round short body. His lips moved to meet hers. "Stop!" she cried, a look of horror gathering like a storm across her pretty pimply face. "Stop David, you're forgetting the first rule!" David thought for a moment: what was the first rule? Then it trundled into his mind, an ancient cart on creaking wheels. Relationships. Rule No. 1. "Deny the possibility of love in order to avoid unnecessary pains and intimate intricasies." David looked Nena in the eye.

"I do not love you!"

She smiled and they kissed. David learned the rules of love in the Bigger Cogs school, welcoming the diversion and the pleasure. He went right to number twenty-six with Nena, which was as far as the books said it was possible to go. After his good experiences with Nena, David switched his attentions to a small dark girl with freckles on her nose. Her name was Buttons. He walked with her one day into an Adolescent Shelter in the Center Park. Buttons was smiling. She had been glad to hear David—even before they entered the Shelter—recite:

"I do not love you, Buttons."

She considered it a mark of respect. But inside the Shelter she was in for a surprise. David moved from rule number one to rule number twenty-two in the blink of an eyelid. Buttons ran shrieking from the Shelter and called to the nearest Bureaucrat, who just happened to be standing close by. She pointed at David who was just staggering out into the Park:

"He jumped twenty-one rules in less than a few seconds. I'm only thirteen. I hadn't gotten beyond twenty before."

The Bureaucrat looked at Buttons, licked his lips, and turning to David drew a pencil and paper from a holster on his hip. He spoke out of the corner of his mouth to David:

"You're such a poor statistic. We give you Adolescent Shelters and this is what happens. What's your name, boy?"

David was reported to the Dean of Cogs, threatened with inoculation and finally moved on to another school. It was on the outskirts of City 2. A plastic dome in the midst of mounds of broken bricks and shards of crumbling concrete, the mysterious debris of the past. There was little for David to do in this school. The one teacher was thin and wasted. His eyes were blue and far away. He told David:

"Work hard. Draw straight. You may yet return to the city."

David hardly heard the words of the new teacher. He knew the Cog People and the Machines were in City 2. He didn't want to go back there . . . and yet he wasn't sure. He thought of offering himself up for inoculation but when he thought of the teachers who had threatened him with it and when he heard the tone of their voices in his mind he became afraid and abandoned the idea completely. He still had eating problems too. Every other day they were served hamburgers and ketchup and every other day David was sick. He took to taking long walks alone. He stumbled over the rubble of the past. He was a gaunt youth, not knowing where he was walking or what lay beyond the next ancient heap of ruins. Still he walked and walked and stared at the sky and the distant horizon.

One evening he was out walking. It was the purple time of dusk. The sun had all but melted over a broken arch of bricks. The sky was darkening. David stood still as stone. He felt he had never before been this close to the sky and the sun. He spoke aloud to himself:

> *"I do not love you, Sun,*
> *When you are gone,*
> *I am left here alone,*
> *On these ruins I turn my back*
> *To the school . . ."*

"Like a hamburger fool" . . . interrupted a voice behind David. The youth spun around. That was his first meeting with Professor Macbeth. He stared at the bright-eyed man and the Professor stared right back at him.

"You're a terrible poet!" said the Professor at last.

David was confused by this man's tone of voice. He sounded like both a teacher and a friend, a strange combination. David stood poised between hamburgers and school and this stranger and the rubble of bricks.

"Listen, Hamlet," Macbeth smiled, "let's get off this blasted heath, I think I have the school for you."

David heard himself talking in a strange new voice:

"Not another school. I'm not a good Cog."

Professor Macbeth smiled again at these words:

"My young friend, this is not like any other school you have been put through, this is a school with a difference. If you must give my school a name, then let us call it . . . the Poetry Workshop."

That was David's first meeting with Professor Macbeth.

In Eating House 13 there were three waiters. A crooked old man and two shiny pink boys. All three wore the uniform of the House, a giant H was emblazoned on the backs of their jackets. David studied the trio very carefully. The pink-faced boys did most of the work. The old man stared and scowled at them as they ran past him with plates full of hamburgers and french fries as thick as fingers. David watched and listened and finally his attentions were rewarded. A boy paused to speak to the old man:

"Mr. Anderson, I noticed the Machine was two seconds behind in its delivery of the burger."

The old man drew in his pinched cheeks.

"Incorrect! Four seconds, two for the machine . . . and two for you, now . . ."

The boy raced on his way, travelling hard through time to catch up on those seconds. The old man slouched into the back of the Eating House, where the kitchen machinery was singing softly to itself. Fear pinned David before the ruins of his hamburger. It was not yet time to act. But soon . . . the poem of the gun . . . he saw it all so clearly in his mind. Professor Macbeth had trained him well for this moment . . . and still doubts and misgivings for the "life" of the old Cog Anderson flooded his jumping mind.

Professor Macbeth is seated on the floor of his classroom, which is one large building, built by his own hands from the debris of the wasteland which stretches between cities. His students surround him like satellites. The individual history of each student is not unlike that of David. Fate has brought them to the feet of this man. They cannot survive in the Cog world. Professor Macbeth cultivates land behind the classroom and minds inside the classroom. Here for now the students study and work and live until it is time for them to graduate. And sooner or later they must graduate in Assassination. This is an unwritten rule. Each student knows it but is filled with doubts and questions. David Church asks the Professor:

"Professor Macbeth, how can we really be sure that the Cog People are inhuman, not like us at all?"

David is questioning the basic concepts of Macbeth's school. The Professor smiles.

"Your own experiences will have told you something. That is why you are here. Your own minds will have told you that there is a world inside yourselves which is not to be found in the world created by the Cog People. Do you need further proof?"

A pale girl nods her head. She needs further proof.

Macbeth produces a chart and pointing to figures and diagrams, explains:

"It takes just a thousand hamburgers in a Togglers School to metamorphosise a child. After the first thousand it is guaranteed that that child will be at least a small Cog in a big Machine. Think about that! After Togglers School you cannot take the Eating House out of the child. It is true the child may need inoculations, many of you narrowly escaped them, he or she may even need some body changes and replacements but already basically the child has been changed to a Cog Person. Later intercourse with Cogs and the Machines present their own picture. The world head of state at this time has a head made of ploytics. It is well known his head has been changed twice within the last three years. He is a Cog, no longer a person like you or me! His second in command has a wooden heart. His third in command, a woman, has no flesh and blood as we know it. She is totally playtic! Intercourse between Cog Peoples produces rubber mouths, hardboard faces, plastic arms and legs, aluminium thighs, blue steel eyes, gold and diamond teeth, wire hair, screw-in heads . . . the list is endless. We can no more talk of killing one of these 'put-togethers' than we can talk of beheading a bottle to drink its contents. It is an act of poetic mercy to end them as it is an act of poetic survival for you to do it. In Hamburger Times there is no greater poem."

The pale girl, Dyanne, is still plagued with doubts. Graduation through assassination will not be easy for her.

"Professor Macbeth, even granted these Cogs are not human, why must we even bother to destroy them?"

She glances from David, her lover, to Macbeth. She is as nervous as a bird.

"To become a Master of Assassination is to commit yourself to Poetry, to the new way of life here amongst the rubble of the past peoples. That is the first reason. The second is we must do everything in our power to hold up the advancement of the Cogs. We must fight back! There is no other way!"

Professor Macbeth picks up a piece of crumbling brick and snaps it in two between his fingers.

"Cog people are nothing more than this piece of brick. They are already as dead as this. You are not taking life. You are removing a little death from the world. This is hard for you to grasp, Dyanne, I know. The reason it is so hard for you is that your intake of hamburgers in Togglers School was precious close to the thousand mark. But you will grow again. You are saved. Doubts are natural for you."

Dyanne slumps back into silence. David takes up the questioning once more.

"What is it about the hamburger which makes it an ingredient of the Cog People's mechanism?"

Macbeth shakes his head slowly from side to side. His eyes are suddenly small and bright and deep. A horrible mystery writes itself in his warm features.

"Hamburgers are sold as meat and yet they are like no meat we have ever come across in the wasteland. They are not rabbit or cow. I cannot tell you exactly what they are. They are addictive, that is certain. That they contain an active ingredient for Cog People is also certain but what that ingredient is I cannot tell you . . . because I do not know."

The class falls into silence. Macbeth suggests they now turn to the rusty weapons of graduation, a collection of small arms dug up from amongst the bricks . . .

"If you've finished the sauce, it's time for work," the clock on the wall of Eating House 13 spoke. David felt his heart jump inside his body. He thought of returning to Dyanne, to Professor Macbeth, a graduate, able to start his own Poetry Workshop. Students were already clearing land for him. He could not fail them. He could not fail himself. There was no other place in the world left for him.

The Cog People were slowly filing out of the House into City 2, where the machinery was waiting for them. They could not continue without each other. "Symbiosis," Professor Macbeth had called it, "they feed on each other." David pulled his mind back to his immediate task. Within moments the Eating House would be empty. He would be sitting alone, an immediate figure of strangeness to the waiters. They would wonder why he had not gone to work like the Cog People. Perhaps they would even call for a Bureaucrat to examine the stranger. David shuddered. The mutilated hamburger lay broken and crumbling on the plate in front of him. He couldn't finish it. That was suspicious in itself. Gorge rose in his throat. It was time to act. Macbeth had told him of this moment. Action was imperative, without it his legs would turn to stone. He thought about poetic style and technique. He had none. His act would be one of spontaneity, true art in action. No more time for thought. Act! Act now! The last Cogs were rolling out of the door. The two shiny pink boys were standing by the door. David realised he would have to deal with them. So be it, he would graduate with honours! He stood up and joined the line leaving a space between himself and the last Cog. Anderson was not in sight, presumably he was still in the back with the Hamburger Machine. Now the last Cog was out. It was David's turn to leave . . . another three yards and he would be out of the door. The circular music was turning round and round. Another yard and he would be out—opportunity gone. He saw the eyes of the waiters. They could have no feelings. The feelings were all in his mind. It was himself he was overcoming. He had reached the door, was about to step out . . . but it was happening. He turned in the doorway, the gun was in his hand, he raised it, struck twice with the barrel, and before him he saw the waiters fall, breaking like ketchup bottles, one over the other. Then they lay still. David closed the door, shot the bolt. Gun in hand, he went running back into the House. There was no sign of Anderson. He stepped into the kitchen. Gleaming expanses of steel made him screw up his eyes. Inside a frosty cage David saw metal hands moulding meat, patting it flat, cutting it in circles. The cage stretched back as far as his eye could see . . . an infinity of circles of red meat, stacked in columns. He stared more intensely . . . for a moment he thought he saw a man wandering through the columns, but no, now his mind was playing tricks with him, staging things which were not really there. He gripped his pistol more tightly.

"Anderson! John Anderson!"

A machine coughed and set up a steady hum behind him. A hive of pistons had started an indifferent movement. He watched them for a moment. The coldness of the kitchen was touching his mind. He didn't belong here. He wanted out. But where was the old man? Where could he be? There was no visible back way out of the kitchen. He longed to run out, away from all this steel, back to the bricks and the school . . . how could he go back a failure? He turned around and around, shouting out the Cog's name. There was no reply. Everything had gone wrong. The old man was no longer here. He stuck the gun back in his waistband and as he did so a steel plate in a steel wall hissed and out of the dark hole emerged John Anderson, the old man, a Cog, operator of the Hamburger Machine, the "thing" David had come to rid the world of. They stood facing each other—Anderson had a bottle of ketchup in his hand—David was empty handed. His hand would not go to his gun. He stared and stared into the old Cog's eyes. Anderson broke the silence.

"You must be a poet. Nobody else would come here."

David nodded. Did he see weariness in the eyes of the Cog? Was it mental fatigue or was it metal fatigue? The actors in his imagination rose up leaping into the kitchen in a thousand costumes and guises. He was losing himself. His hand moved for the pistol . . . and as it did Anderson's ketchup bottle struck him a full blow on the side of the head. It didn't matter. David was falling to the ground. Nothing mattered. Darkness. On the floor, next to him, the ketchup bottle lay, beheaded, its mouth oozing sauce.

Anderson sucked a claw like finger for a moment. He clicked with chuckles. Ticking and clicking Anderson took David by the ankles and dragged him to the cold storage room, which led to the hamburger processing machine. He spoke aloud to the engine:

"Here he is, a tender young poet, just right."

The Hamburger Machine clicked like the old Cog. Its pistons raced joyfully. The door closed on David Church.

Beneath a crumbling brick archway, as fading sun lit anxious faces, Macbeth told the class of the loss of David Church. He had failed to return within the given period of time. There was silence for many moments, then the pale girl, Dyanne, spoke:

"Professor Macbeth, I am now ready to graduate." The Professor nodded. The girl's words hung over the class, refugees from Cog Schools all over City 2.

In City 2 the Cog People poured into one or other of the million Eating Houses and sat themselves before a hamburger which grinned greasily up at them. Their hands reached for the ketchup. They shook out three gouts of sauce . . . and then the "People," the Hamburger and the Ketchup were, as they would have said in ancient times, as one.

Capsule

Rosalind Greenberg

Byron stares into the bathroom mirror and wonders if his nose will ever be the same again. Only two days into the allergy season and he has reached crisis. "You know I don't like to take medicine," he tells the puffy-faced man in the mirror. "I'm a naturalist. Pure mind. Pure body."

"Right," the puffy-faced man says, "but don't blame *me* when they carry you away and hook you up to the tubes like last time, dummy."

"Yeah," Byron says wearily, "yeah." He sighs and opens the medicine chest, takes out the fresh bottle of capsules and struggles with it. No one ever died from hay fever, he thinks. On the other hand that is a qualified blessing.

He struggles with the difficult top, grunts, opens it convulsively. Tiny time-release beads spew from the vial, scamper over the porcelain and a few split open.

Out of one of them a tiny orange creature, perfectly formed, emerges. Byron can see it well; allergy has left him, if nothing else, clarity of vision. The orange creature is a tenth of an inch high with beautiful hands and piercing, expressive eyes.

"Greetings, earth person," the creature says in a thin but clear voice. "We come in peace—"

Byron shakes his head and shudders. Inside the sink another creature, green this time, emerges from a time-release bead. "I *told* you so," it says furiously in a slightly deeper voice, "you orange-headed fool, you wanted an inanimate object, something inconspicuous; I hope you're satisfied: Look at us. We have no dignity. What will the report say?"

"Shut up," the orange creature says, "I'm a *supervisor,* you green zyxul. I'm following procedure."

"That's easy for you to say," the green creature says and begins to argue floridly in another language. The orange supervisor argues back. Byron feels faint. He props himself against the sink, dreading its contents. How many aliens are in there?

The thought is horrifying. Byron sneezes convulsively.

Beads rattle and the arguing creatures are blown away as if by an explosion.

Byron takes some tissue and wipes his nose mournfully. Guilt struggles with relief. After a while, relief wins.

"After all," he says, "it *was* my first Contac."

The Client from Hell

Richard Curtis

On the day it was reported that a spaceship had touched down in New Guinea, I was scheduled to have lunch with one of my oldest friends in the publishing business, Bob Gorenstein of Random House. The news had come over the radio and because of the remoteness of the location, the only eyewitness account had been phoned in by the Masefields, the family whose plantation had been flattened by the 600 ton mass of the Drunians' "travel disk." I doubt if anyone on our planet within earshot of a radio or television talked about anything else that morning, and in fact by noon the first of an endless crop of alien jokes was already bouncing over the phone lines between Hollywood and New York. And so when Bob called me that morning to set up our lunch, he was ready with his quip.

"I'm surprised to find you in," he said. "I thought you'd already be on a plane to New Guinea to sign these guys."

"I hate representing celebrities," I said. "Even celebrities from outer space."

"What do you have against celebrities?"

"They're impossibly demanding."

"That's certainly true," said Gorenstein. "But I can't believe you'd turn down an opportunity to be the literary agent for the first alien visitors in the history of the world."

"I'm sure they're as big a pain in the ass as any other stars, plus they probably smell bad."

Bob booked lunch at 1 P.M. at An American Place on East 32nd Street, where we continued our banter over drinks. Shortage of time prohibits me from detailing these exchanges, which are irrelevant anyway. Suffice it to say that publishing people are among the wittiest of any profession, and there was much hilarity as we invented scenarios for such things as alien author tours, publishing parties, and talk show interviews.

As Gorenstein donned his reading glasses to review the menu, he flashed a provocative smile. "Buddy Alter is already on his way to Papua."

I shook my head. "Why am I not surprised to hear this?" Buddy Alter stood at the purple end of the spectrum of literary agents, a true parasite who battened on the very worst that human nature had to offer. The moment a news story broke about some lurid murder, sex scandal, or tragedy, Buddy booked a plane to persuade the principals to let him handle their book, movie, and allied merchandise rights. And he didn't particularly care whether he represented perpetrator or victim. Buddy was the literary agent equivalent of an ambulance chaser.

A twinkle in Gorenstein's eyes told me there was something more. An instant later I guessed what it was. "And I suppose Random House has agreed to buy the book from Buddy if he comes back with their exclusive story."

Gorenstein smiled, not very cryptically. "The salmon special sounds very good."

"God almighty, Bob," I said, pounding the table. The china and silver jangled and the hubbub around us died for a moment as heads turned to the source of the disruption. "Have you no shame?" I murmured after the noise level rose again.

Gorenstein chuckled. "We've only bought a right of first refusal," he said, summoning our waiter.

Thus began what might be called The Great Alien Sweepstakes, for as it turned out Buddy Alter was but one of a veritable tsunami of media representatives that swept across the Pacific Ocean that week hoping not merely to witness humanity's first confirmed encounter with members of a non-human race, but to tie up the exclusive rights to their story. The New Guinea government attempted to cordon off the site until it was established that the "alien blokes" were neither hostile nor contagious. But even the best armed military contingent is no match for a determined and resourceful television crew or an aggressive team of newspaper reporters. Certainly the army was no match for the likes of Buddy Alter and his vision of fabulous commissions. It is said he had actually brought his checkbook with him! In what currency? I wondered.

I watched this circus on television and could only shake my head, as I had all during that lunch with Bob Gorenstein while I listened to him justifying his company's decision to get involved in the bidding war.

I suppose my reluctance to jump into this feeding frenzy will puzzle the reader, just as it did my colleagues in the publishing industry. It's a sign of the times that nobody even tried to understand how appalling I found it that people would cast their dignity to the winds to cash in on this event. Realizing that anything I said would sound like sour grapes, I said very little at all, but not a few colleagues thought that my attitude was insufferably smug.

Even my wife suggested I was foolish not to make at least some effort to offer the visitors representation. "Wouldn't they be better off in your hands than in Buddy Alter's? My God, he'll have them endorsing Miller Lite Beer!"

We had just clicked off the evening television news with the latest report on the carnival in New Guinea. Two executives from the Disney Company had offered to transport the spaceship to a site in Texas and create a 10,000 acre theme park around it.

"Not you, too," I moaned.

My wife gazed crossly at me. "Sometimes you wave your dignity around like some crusader's sword. Would it be so terrible for you to make an effort to contact them? Or have you suddenly become allergic to big commissions?"

This last remark stung me. "I thought you understood how I feel."

"Why don't you run it past me once again to make sure."

"The whole thing is . . . well, so undignified."

She peered at me. "The agent for the Butcher of Harlem is suddenly donning the mantle of dignity?"

"I didn't solicit him," I replied feebly.

She scowled. "I see. It's dignified to represent a man who slaughtered and cannibalized fifteen geriatric females because *he* solicited *you*. But it's *infra dignitatem* to solicit a voyager from another star."

"I feel like a prostitute when I chase authors."

"Your nobility is inspiring," she snorted, snapping a newspaper open and terminating the conversation.

I lapsed into a funk. Gazing at the ceiling with its spiderweb tracery of hairline cracks, I brooded on the unfairness of a world that handsomely rewarded prostitutes like Buddy Alter with penthouse apartments, second homes in the Hamptons, and Rolls Royce automobiles, but rewarded virtuous fellows like me with cramped apartments, seven year old Fords, and wives who had not enjoyed a genuine vacation in eight years.

Ultimately I stood stoutly on my moral superiority and opted for the role of spectator. My wife, God bless her, never said another word about the matter. She didn't have to. Her feelings were painfully implicit in her sighs and baleful looks every time the news carried another story of the bidding wars for the Drunians' exclusive story, product endorsement, or participation in one commercial scheme or another.

After two or three months, however, it began to be apparent that no one had succeeded in signing the spacefarers. Newspaper accounts and media industry gossip indicated that the Drunians were being extremely wary. Whether out of confusion or distrust it was not yet clear. Whatever motivated them, they definitely were not biting at offers that would have made even a Michael Jackson envious. Their caution should not have come as such a surprise. Anyone sophisticated enough to develop a means of interstellar propulsion must presumably be shrewd enough to know when he is being hustled. As my Random House friend observed, "Hell, their race is twenty million years old, so we know they weren't born yesterday." He was one of innumerable shell-shocked veterans of the bidding wars returning to corporate headquarters with nothing to show for months in the field but a lot of bills for airfare, hotel accommodations, bar tabs, and diarrhea medicine.

What we now realize is they were simply studying us. They had been attracted to our world by the radio signals broadcast by our Search for Extra-Terrestrial Intelligence program, and for the first few weeks after their landing they established communications with our computers. Quickly reassuring us that their intentions were not hostile, they began requesting digitized information about all earthly things. We were thrilled to oblige, and they consumed data at a prodigious rate. They easily learned several dozen human languages, and began communicating with reporters in their native tongues by means of linguistic conversion devices. Presently they ventured out of the bays of their craft, their elephantine forms gliding with majestic dignity on furry pods, and, to the universal joy of the entire human race, the Intergalactic Epoch was born in that New Guinea field. All this is on film.

What is not on film is the expression on my face when the phone rang about a month later and a low-pitched metallic voice announced, "Mr. Gordon? This is Garto of Drune." The sound was obviously rendered by some sort of speech simulator, but I suspected something else. "Okay, Eddie, stop screwing around. What do you want?"

"Who's that, dear?" My wife called from the kitchen.

"My brother, up to his usual unfunny pranks. He's talking into a cooking pot and expects me to believe it's the guy from outer space. Eddie, we're just sitting down to din. . . ."

"This is Garto, Mr. Gordon. No joke."

"Tell him you'll call him back," my wife shouted. "The chicken will get cold."

"I'll get back to you, okay, *Garto?* Is there a number on the spaceship where I can reach you?"

"Now it's you who are joking," the voice said.

"Listen, chum, if you're Garto, send me a sign."

I had no sooner uttered the words than a shriek came from the kitchen and a horrible clatter of a metal tray crashing to the floor. I dropped the phone and rushed to the kitchen. On the floor was a live chicken flapping and squawking. Standing on the counter was my wife, also flapping and squawking.

Trembling, I picked up the extension in the kitchen. "Okay, Mister, you have my attention."

"I am Garto."

"I'll accept that as a working thesis."

"I wish to tell the story of my people, of our world, of my voyage."

"Could you talk a little louder? There's a woman screaming in here."

He repeated the message. "Now you definitely have my attention," I said. I put my finger over my lips, and my wife, sensing that something extraordinary was happening, fell silent. "And how may I be of help to you?"

"I will need someone to represent me. You are universally admired, and from all we have been able to learn, you are an honest man. We have encountered very few here."

My wife implored me with her eyes to explain what was going on. I cupped my hand over the phone. "It's the guy from outer space. He wants me to be his agent."

"Sure," she said.

"If you need proof, I'll ask him to turn you into a chicken, too."

"No, thank you."

"What do I have to do?" I asked into the phone.

"Cancel your appointments and book a flight to New Guinea. I will contact you tomorrow to arrange details of our meeting."

"I will do so. But you owe me a chicken dinner for two."

As I hung up, the doorman buzzed us. My wife picked up the intercom. Her eyes widened.

"Who is it?" I asked.

"Maxie's Barbecue is on the way up," she said. "With chicken dinner for two."

And that is how I came to be the literary agent and personal manager of Garto and his contingent of Drunians. I will not go into the details of my trip to New Guinea and my personal experiences in getting to know the explorers from that distant world. Nor will I amplify on the way I created a business strategy for them, conducted their negotiations, and exploited their stories in every possible medium. It's fascinating, but not pertinent to this account. And besides, I've chronicled it in my memoir, "Agent to the Starfarers." I cannot, however, resist the temptation to state that my clients made me a rich man, my agent colleagues became practically apoplectic with envy, and my wife treated me with a renewed respect bordering on reverence. I tried not to be insufferably smug with her, and succeeded most of the time.

When did it all go wrong, then? Well, when in the long sad chronicle of human history have things always gone wrong? When people get greedy, that's when. You would think that the countless publishers, movie studios, cable and television networks, media producers, product developers, commercial sponsors, and lawyers would have been content with the fortunes they made on the licenses I negotiated with them. But no, they couldn't let it go at that.

The big trouble began when Garto summoned me to Texas (where Disney had indeed established a theme park around the

Drunian spacecraft). We hadn't talked face to face for six months; our frequent but routine conversations were usually conducted by telephone or televideo. Obviously the matter he had to take up with me was far from routine: I could tell from the agitated timbre of his voice, even though communicated through his translation device. I caught the next plane to Houston.

I felt like a movie star on opening night as a guard ushered me up the spacecraft's ramp before the stares of thousands of fairground visitors. I found Garto in his chamber, the room redolent of his sweet-sour aroma to which I had never quite become accustomed. On the table before him were stacks of documents which I immediately recognized as book and movie contracts, as well as royalty statements issued by publishers, movie companies, and the countless merchandise firms that had licensed the rights to Drunian toys, games, clothes, furniture, tapes and records, and every other exploitable form of Druniana that the resourceful minds of business people can conjure.

"You have reviewed these?" he said without salutation.

"Of course."

"You know then that they are phony."

I sat up sharply and paused to choose my reply carefully. "My accountants routinely audit them and have found no major discrepancies, Garto."

"They represent a fraction of what these works have actually earned. Where is the rest of our money?"

I picked a bunch of the papers up and examined them, finding nothing out of the ordinary.

"Perhaps you have misunderstood or misinterpreted the figures?"

He extended a pod and tapped a publisher's royalty statement. "Half of the money due on sales of this book are not reported."

I uttered a sigh of relief as I immediately saw what was troubling him. "I had told you at the outset that publishers sell books on consignment. They always hold back royalties to authors in case copies are returned."

"There are few returns of my books," Garto declared. I accepted this statement at face value. I had never doubted that Garto had ways of obtaining confidential information that was inaccessible to literary agents and other mere mortals.

"Perhaps your publishers have been overly zealous in withholding some of your money," I said. "Is something else bothering you?"

"They promised me an embossed foil cover. And my author's photo is blurry. But that is of no consequence compared to the missing royalties."

"No, I don't suppose it is. What else?"

He pushed another pile of papers at me. "Where are the rest of my movie profits?" he demanded.

"I told you about that, too, Garto, when you originally asked me to represent you."

"Remind me."

"Movie profits are calculated on a net basis, after deduction of certain defined expenses. The theatre owners take a piece of every ticket sold at the box office, the distributor takes a bite, the movie studio writes off all sorts of deductible items and overhead. . . ."

Garto cut me off with a majestic wave of his pod. "They are all lining their pockets every step of the way."

"That's show biz," I quipped, hoping to lighten the atmosphere a bit, for the air was crackling with danger. "Seriously, Garto, movie studio accountants are among the most creative members of the human race. They have siphoned money from profit participants from the very beginning of the industry."

"That is neither an acceptable explanation nor a satisfactory excuse. I understand capitalism perfectly well and respect the desires of business firms to earn reasonable profits on their investment. The profits being earned by publishers, movie companies, and other licensees are flagrantly unreasonable, however. I want what is coming to me and my crewmates. And, by the way, they reneged on their promise of a full screen credit as technical consultant, and they never reimbursed my per diem expenses on location in Georgia."

"Rectifying that will be easier than making a studio cough up profits," I said. "You're looking at a long and honorable tradition of institutionalized fraud."

"If you cannot accomplish this, I will have to wonder whether, perhaps, even you are benefiting from these diversions of my funds."

"My friend, I am appalled that you should even think such a thing."

"I want what is coming to me," he repeated.

"I will do what I can, Garto."

"You'll do more than that," he said. "And you'll do it within one week from this hour."

The latter was stated in a deadly flat tone that I had never heard in his voice before, but it chilled me to the marrow of my bones. So staggered was I by this ominous warning that it did not occur to me to ask what remedy he contemplated if I failed to carry out my mandate of redressing his grievance. For this oversight it appears that the human race is about to pay dearly.

You will not be surprised to learn that I have spent the six and a half days and nights since that moment exerting the most determined effort in the history of the literary agents' profession to persuade publishers, movie executives, and merchandise manufacturers to refund the profits that Garto considered to be excessive. Most of you reading this narrative have the good fortune never to have encountered the mentality of accountants in the publishing and entertainment field, so you will simply have to take my word for it that my blandishments were greeted with derision to say the least. More common were the cynical jokes, at which I would have laughed had not the matter been as grave and urgent as it was. Indeed, in the good old, pre-Garto days, I had laughed at such jokes, and made up a few myself.

But I could not impress any of Garto's accounts payable that this was not merely a case of some naive author bitching that the system was gypping him. My week of imploring, cajoling, and threatening yielded not a dime of reparations. One movie president summed up the prevailing attitude when he sneered, "Screw him! If he doesn't like the way we do business, he can zap us with his little ray gun."

Which brings us to what I believe to be the last moment of the human race. I calculate that we have about a half hour. The Drunian craft hovers in the stratosphere, its "little ray gun" (or whatever weapon it employs) trained on our planet and its frail populace of fools and knaves. When it became clear, about an hour ago, that Garto had not been bluffing, I was inundated by panicky phone calls from many of Garto's debtors pressing settlements upon me. Their offers were in vain. Garto had stopped taking my phone calls.

As the clock moves inexorably toward doomsday, I am consumed by a single thought: could Buddy Alter have structured Garto's deals any better than I did?

Collector's Fever

Roger Zelazny

What are you doing there, human?"

"It's a long story."

"Good, I like long stories. Sit down and talk. No—not on me!"

"Sorry. Well, it's all because of my uncle, the fabulously wealthy—"

"Stop. What does 'wealthy' mean?"

"Well, like rich."

"And 'rich'?"

"Hm. Lots of money."

"What's money?"

"You want to hear this story or don't you?"

"Yes, but I'd like to understand it too."

"Sorry, Rock, I'm afraid I don't understand it all myself."

"The name is Stone."

"Okay, Stone. My uncle, who is a very important man, was supposed to send me to the Space Academy, but he didn't. He decided a liberal education was a better thing. So he sent me to his old spinster alma mater to major in nonhuman humanities. You with me, so far?"

"No, but understanding is not necessarily an adjunct to appreciation."

"That's what I say. I'll never understand Uncle Sidney, but I appreciate his outrageous tastes, his magpie instinct and his gross meddling in other people's affairs. I appreciate them till I'm sick to the stomach. There's nothing else I can do. He's a carnivorous old family monument, and fond of having his own way. Unfortunately, he also has all the money in the family—so it follows, like a *xxt* after a *zzn,* that he always *does* have his own way."

"This money must be pretty important stuff."

"Important enough to send me across ten thousand light-years to an unnamed world which, incidentally, I've just named Dunghill."

"The low-flying *zatt* is a heavy eater, which accounts for its low flying . . ."

"So I've noted. That *is* moss though, isn't it?"

"Yes."

"Good, then crating will be less of a problem."

"What's 'crating'?"

"It means to put something in a box to take it somewhere else."

"Like moving around?"

"Yes."

"What are you planning on crating?"

"Yourself, Stone."

"I've never been the rolling sort . . ."

"Listen, Stone, my uncle is a rock collector, see? You are the only species of intelligent mineral in the galaxy. You are also the largest specimen I've spotted so far. Do you follow me?"

"Yes, but I don't want to."

"Why not? You'd be lord of his rock collection. Sort of a one-eyed man in a kingdom of the blind, if I may venture an inappropriate metaphor."

"Please don't do that, whatever it is. It sounds awful. Tell me, how did your uncle learn of our world?"

"One of my instructors read about this place in an old space log. *He* was an old space log collector. The log had belonged to a Captain Fairhill, who landed here several centuries ago and held lengthy discourses with your people."

"Good old Foul Weather Fairhill! How is he these days? Give him my regards—"

"He's dead."

"What?"

"Dead. Kaput. Blooey. Gone. Deeble."

"Oh my! When did it happen? I trust it was an esthetic occurrence of major import—"

"I really couldn't say. But I passed the information on to my uncle, who decided to collect you. That's why I'm here—he sent me."

"Really, as much as I appreciate the compliment, I can't accompany you. It's almost deeble time—"

"I know, I read all about deebling in the Fairhill log before I showed it to Uncle Sidney. I tore those page out. I want him to be around when you do it. Then I can inherit his money and console myself in all manner of expensive ways for never having gone to the Space Academy. First I'll become an alcoholic, then I'll take up wenching—or maybe I'd better do it the other way around . . ."

"But I want to deeble here, among the things I've become attached to!"

"This is a crowbar. I'm going to unattach you."

"If you try it, I'll deeble right now."

"You can't. I measured your mass before we struck up this conversation. It will take at least eight months, under Earth conditions, for you to reach deebling proportions."

"Okay, I was bluffing. But have you no compassion? I've rested here for centuries, ever since I was a small pebble, as did my fathers before me. I've added so carefully to my atom collection, building up the finest molecular structure in the neighborhood. And now, to be snatched away right before deebling time, it's—it's quite unrock of you."

"It's not that bad. I promise you'll collect the finest Earth atoms available. You'll go places no other Stone has ever been before."

"Small consolation. I want my friends to see."

"I'm afraid that's out of the question."

"You are a very cruel human. I hope you're around when I deeble."

"I intend to be far away and on the eve of prodigious debaucheries when that occurs."

Under Dunghill's sub-E gravitation Stone was easily rolled to the side of the space sedan, crated, and, with the help of a winch, installed in the compartment beside the atomic pile. The fact that it was a short-jaunt sport model sedan, customized by its owner, who had removed much of the shielding, was the reason Stone felt a sudden flush of volcanic drunkenness, rapidly added select items to his collection and deebled on the spot.

He mushroomed upwards, then swept in great waves across the plains of Dunghill. Several young Stones fell from the dusty heavens wailing their birth pains across the community band.

"Gone fission," commented a distant neighbor, above the static, "and sooner than I expected. Feel that warm afterglow!"

"An excellent deeble," agreed another. "It always pays to be a cautious collector."

The Crawling Chaos

Elizabeth Neville Berkeley and H. P. Lovecraft

Of the pleasures and pains of opium much has been written. The ecstasies and horrors of De Quincey and the *paradis artificiels* of Baudelaire are preserved and interpreted with an art which makes them immortal, and the world knows well the beauty, the terror, and the mystery of those obscure realms into which the inspired dreamer is transported. But much as has been told, no man has yet dared intimate the *nature* of the phantasms thus unfolded to the mind, or hint at the *direction* of the unheard-of roads along whose ornate and exotic course the partaker of the drug is so irresistibly borne. De Quincey was drawn back into Asia, that teeming land of nebulous shadows whose hideous antiquity is so impressive that "the vast age of the race and name overpowers the sense of youth in the individual", but farther than that he dared not go. Those who *have* gone farther seldom returned; and even when they have, they have been either silent or quite mad. I took opium but once—in the year of the plague, when doctors sought to deaden the agonies they could not cure. There was an overdose—my physician was worn out with horror and exertion—and I travelled very far indeed. In the end I returned and lived, but my nights are filled with strange memories, nor have I ever permitted a doctor to give me opium again.

The pain and pounding in my head had been quite unendurable when the drug was administered. Of the future I had no heed; to escape, whether by cure, unconsciousness, or death, was all that concerned me. I was partly delirious, so that it is hard to place the exact moment of transition, but I think the effect must have begun shortly before the pounding ceased to be painful. As I have said, there was an overdose; so my reactions were probably far from normal. The sensation of falling, curiously dissociated from the idea of gravity or direction, was paramount; though there was a subsidiary impression of unseen throngs in incalculable profusion, throngs of infinitely diverse nature, but all more or less related to me. Sometimes it seemed less as though I were falling, than as though the universe or the ages were falling past me. Suddenly my pain ceased, and I began to associate the pounding with an external rather than internal force. The falling has ceased also, giving place to a sensation of uneasy, temporary rest; and when I listened closely, I fancied the pounding was that of the vast, inscrutable sea as its sinister, colossal breakers lacerated some desolate shore after a storm of titanic magnitude. Then I opened my eyes.

For a moment my surroundings seemed confused, like a projected image hopelessly out of focus, but gradually I realised my solitary presence in a strange and beautiful room lighted by many windows. Of the exact nature of the apartment I could form no idea, for my thoughts were still far from settled; but I noticed varicoloured rugs and draperies, elaborately fashioned tables, chairs, ottomans, and divans, and delicate vases and ornaments which conveyed a suggestion of the exotic without being actually alien. These things I noticed, yet they were not long uppermost in my mind. Slowly but inexorably crawling upon my consciousness, and rising above every other impression, came a dizzying fear of the unknown; a fear all the greater because I could not analyse it, and seeming to concern a stealthily approaching menace—not death, but some nameless, unheard-of thing inexpressibly more ghastly and abhorrent.

Presently I realised that the direct symbol and excitant of my fear was the hideous pounding whose incessant reverberations throbbed maddeningly against my exhausted brain. It seemed to come from a point outside and below the edifice in which I stood, and to associate itself with the most terrifying mental images. I felt that some horrible scene or object lurked beyond the silk-hung walls, and shrank from glancing through the arched, latticed windows that opened so bewilderingly on every hand. Perceiving shutters attached to these windows, I closed them all, averting my eyes from the exterior as I did so. Then, employing a flint and steel which I found on one of the small tables, I lit the many candles reposing about the walls in Arabesque sconces. The added sense of security brought by closed shutters and artificial light calmed my nerves to some degree, but I could not shut out the monotonous pounding. Now that I was calmer, the sound became as fascinating as it was fearful, and I felt a contradictory desire to seek out its source despite my still powerful shrinking. Opening a portiere at the side of the room nearest the pounding, I beheld a small and richly draped corridor ending in a carven door and large oriel window. To this window I was irresistibly drawn, though my ill-defined apprehensions seemed almost equally bent on holding me back. As I approached it I could see a chaotic whirl of waters in the distance. Then, as I attained it and glanced out on all sides, the stupendous picture of my surroundings burst upon me with full and devastating force.

I beheld such a sight as I had never beheld before, and which no living person can have seen save in the delirium of fever or the inferno of opium. The building stood on a narrow point of land—or what was *now* a narrow point of land—fully 300 feet above what must lately have been a seething vortex of mad waters. On either side of the house there fell a newly washed-out precipice of red earth, whilst ahead of me the hideous waves were still rolling in frightfully, eating away the land with ghastly monotony and deliberation. Out a mile or more there rose and fell menacing breakers at least fifty feet in height, and on the far horizon ghoulish black clouds of grotesque contour were resting and brooding like unwholesome vultures. The waves were dark and purplish, almost black, and clutched at the yielding red mud of the bank as if with uncouth, greedy hands. I could not but feel that some noxious marine mind had declared a war of extermination upon all the solid ground, perhaps abetted by the angry sky.

Recovering at length from the stupor into which this unnatural spectacle had thrown me, I realised that my actual physical danger was acute. Even whilst I gazed the bank had lost many feet, and it could not be long before the house would fall undermined into the awful pit of lashing waves. Accordingly I hastened to the opposite side of the edifice, and finding a door, emerged at once, locking it after me with a curious key which had hung inside. I now beheld more of the strange region about me, and marked a singular division which seemed to exist in the hostile ocean and firmament. On each side of the jutting promontory different conditions held sway. At my left as I faced inland was a gently heaving sea with great green waves rolling peacefully in under a brightly shining sun. Something about that sun's nature and position made me shudder, but I could not then tell, and cannot tell now, what it was. At my right also was the sea, but it was blue, calm, and only gently undulating, while the sky above it was darker and the washed-out bank more nearly white than reddish.

I now turned my attention to the land, and found occasion for fresh surprise; for the vegetation resembled nothing I had ever seen or read about. It was apparently tropical or at least sub-tropical—a conclusion borne out by the intense heat of the air. Sometimes I thought I could trace strange analogies with the flora of my native land, fancying that the well-known plants and shrubs might assume such forms under a radical change of climate; but the gigantic and omnipresent palm trees were plainly foreign. The house I had just left was very small—hardly more than a cottage—but its material was evidently marble, and its architecture was weird and composite, involving a quaint fusion of Western and Eastern forms. At the corners were Corinthian columns, but the red tile roof was like that of a Chinese pagoda. From the door inland there stretched a path of singularly white sand, about four feet wide, and lined on either side with stately palms and unidentifiable flowering shrubs and plants. It lay toward the side of the promontory where the sea was blue and the bank rather whitish. Down this path I felt impelled to flee, as if pursued by some malignant spirit from the pounding ocean. At first it was slightly uphill, then I reached a gentle crest. Behind me I saw the scene I had left; the entire point with the cottage and the black water, with the green sea on one side and the blue sea on the other, and a curse unnamed and unnamable lowering over all. I never saw it again, and often wonder. . . . After this last look I strode ahead and surveyed the inland panorama before me.

The path, as I have intimated, ran along the right-hand shore as one went inland. Ahead and to the left I now viewed a magnificent valley comprising thousands of acres, and covered with a swaying growth of tropical grass higher than my head. Almost at the limit of vision was a colossal palm tree which seemed to fascinate and beckon me. By this time wonder and escape from the imperilled peninsula had largely dissipated my fear, but as I paused and sank fatigued to the path, idly digging with my hands into the warm, whitish-golden sand, a new and acute sense of danger seized me. Some terror in the swishing tall grass seemed added to that of the diabolically pounding sea, and I started up crying aloud and disjointedly, "Tiger? Tiger? Is it Tiger? Beast? Beast? Is it a Beast that I am afraid of?" My mind wandered back to an ancient and classical story of tigers which I had read; I strove to recall the author, but had difficulty. Then in the midst of my fear I remembered that the tale was by Rudyard Kipling; nor did the grotesqueness of deeming him an ancient author occur to me. I wished for the volume containing this story, and had almost started back toward the doomed cottage to procure it when my better sense and the lure of the palm prevented me.

Whether or not I could have resisted the backward beckoning without the counter-fascination of the vast palm tree, I do not know. This attraction was now dominant, and I left the path and crawled on hands and knees down the valley's slope despite my fear of the grass and of the serpents it might contain. I resolved to fight for life and reason as long as possible against all menaces of sea or land, though I sometimes feared defeat as the maddening swish of the uncanny grasses joined the still audible and irritating pounding of the distant breakers. I would frequently pause and put my hands to my ears for relief, but could never quite shut out the detestable sound. It was, as it seemed to me, only after ages that I finally dragged myself to the beckoning palm tree and lay quiet beneath its protecting shade.

There now ensued a series of incidents which transported me to the opposite extremes of ecstasy and horror; incidents which I tremble to recall and dare not seek to interpret. No sooner had I crawled beneath the overhanging foliage of the palm, than there dropped from its branches a young child of such beauty as I never beheld before. Though ragged and dusty, this being bore the features of a faun or demigod, and seemed almost to diffuse a radiance in the dense shadow of the tree. It smiled and extended its hand, but before I could arise and speak I heard in the upper air the exquisite melody of singing; notes high and low blent with a sublime and ethereal harmoniousness. The sun had by this time sunk below the horizon, and in the twilight I saw that an aureola of lambent light encircled the child's head. Then in a tone of silver it addressed me: "It is the end. They have come down through the gloaming from the stars. Now all is over, and beyond the Arinurian streams we shall dwell blissfully in Teloe." As the child spoke, I beheld a soft radiance through the leaves of the palm tree, and rising greeted a pair whom I knew to be the chief singers among those I had heard. A god and goddess they must have been, for such beauty is not mortal; and they took my hands, saying, "Come, child, you have heard the voices, and all is well. In Teloe beyond the Milky Way and the Arinurian streams are cities all of amber and chalcedony. And upon their domes of many facets glisten the images of strange and beautiful stars. Under the ivory bridges of Teloe flow rivers of liquid gold bearing pleasure-barges bound for blossomy Cytharion of the Seven Suns. And in Teloe and Cytharion abide only youth, beauty, and pleasure, nor are any sounds heard, save of laughter, song, and the lute. Only the gods dwell in Teloe of the golden rivers, but among them shalt thou dwell."

As I listened, enchanted, I suddenly became aware of a change in my surroundings. The palm tree, so lately overshadowing my exhausted form, was now some distance to my left and considerably below me. I was obviously floating in the atmosphere; companioned not only by the strange child and the radiant pair, but by a constantly increasing throng of half-luminous, vine-crowned youths and maidens with wind-blown hair and joyful countenance. We slowly ascended together, as if borne on a fragrant breeze which blew not from the earth but from the golden nebulae, and the child whispered in my ear that I must look always upward to the pathways of light, and never backward to the sphere I had just left. The youths and maidens now chaunted mellifluous choriambics to the accompaniment of lutes, and I felt enveloped in a peace and happiness more profound than any I had in life imagined, when the intrusion of a single sound altered my destiny and shattered my soul. Through the ravishing strains of the singers and the lutanists, as if in mocking, daemoniac concord, throbbed from gulfs below the damnable, the detestable pounding of that hideous ocean. And as those black breakers beat their message into my ears I forgot the words of the child and looked back, down upon the doomed scene from which I thought I had escaped.

Down through the aether I saw the accursed earth turning, ever turning, with angry and tempestuous seas gnawing at wild desolate shores and dashing foam against the tottering towers of deserted cities. And under a ghastly moon there gleamed sights I can never describe, sights I can never forget; deserts of corpse-like clay and jungles of ruin and decadence where once stretched the populous plains and villages of my native land, and maelstroms of frothing ocean where once rose the mighty temples of my forefathers. Around the northern pole steamed a morass of noisome growths and miasmal vapours, hissing before the onslaught of the ever-mounting waves that curled and fretted from the shuddering deep. Then a rending report clave the night, and athwart the desert of deserts appeared a smoking rift. Still the black ocean foamed and gnawed, eating away the desert on either side as the rift in the centre widened and widened.

There was now no land left but the desert, and still the fuming ocean ate and ate. All at once I thought even the pounding sea seemed afraid of something, afraid of dark gods of the inner earth that are greater than the evil god of waters, but even if it was it could not turn back; and the desert had suffered too much from those nightmare waves to help them now. So the ocean ate the last of the land and poured into the smoking gulf, thereby giving up all it had ever conquered. From the new-flooded lands it flowed again, uncovering death and decay; and from its ancient and immemorial bed it trickled loathsomely, uncovering nighted secrets of the years when Time was young and the gods unborn. Above the waves rose weedy, remembered spires. The moon laid pale lilies of light on dead London, and Paris stood up from its damp grave to be sanctified with star-dust. Then rose spires and monoliths that were weedy but not remembered; terrible spires and monoliths of lands that men never knew were lands.

There was not any pounding now, but only the unearthly roaring and hissing of waters tumbling into the rift. The smoke of that rift had changed to steam, and almost hid the world as it grew denser and denser. It seared my face and hands, and when I looked to see how it affected my companions I found they had all disappeared. Then very suddenly it ended, and I knew no more till I awaked upon a bed of convalescence. As the cloud of steam from the Plutonic gulf finally concealed the entire surface from my sight, all the firmament shrieked at a sudden agony of mad reverberations which shook the trembling aether. In one delirious flash and burst it happened; one blinding, deafening holocaust of fire, smoke, and thunder that dissolved the wan moon as it sped outward to the void.

And when the smoke cleared away, and I sought to look upon the earth, I beheld against the background of cold, humorous stars only the dying sun and the pale mournful planets searching for their sister.

Crazy Annaoj

Fritz Leiber

Two things will last to the end of time, at least for the tribes of Western Man, no matter how far his spaceships rove. They are sorcery and romantic love, which come to much the same thing in the end.

For the more that becomes possible to man, the more wildly he yearns for the impossible, and runs after witches and sorcerers to find it.

While the farther he travels, to the star-ribboned rim of the Milky Way and beyond, the more he falls in love with far-off things and yearns for the most distant and unattainable beloved.

Also, witchcraft and sorcery are games it takes two to play; the witch or sorcerer and his or her client.

* * *

The oldest and wealthiest man in the Milky Way and its loveliest girl laughed as they left the gypsy's tent pitched just outside the jewel-pillared spacefield of the most exclusive pleasure planet between the galaxy's two dizzily-whirling, starry arms. The gypsy's black cat, gliding past them back into the tent, only smiled cryptically.

A private, eiderdown-surfaced slidewalk, rolled out like the red carpet of ancient cliché, received the begemmed slippers of the honeymooning couple and carried them toward the most diamond-glittering pillar of them all, the private hyperspace yacht *Eros* of the galactic shipping magnate Piliph Foelitsack and his dazzling young bride Annaoj.

He looked 21 and was 20 times that old. Cosmetic surgery and organ replacements and implanted featherweight power-prosthetics and pacemakers had worked their minor miracles. At any one time there were three physicians in the *Eros* listening in on the functionings of his body.

She looked and was 17, but the wisdom in her eyes was that of Eve, of Helen of Troy, of Cleopatra, of Forzane. It was also the wisdom of Juliet, of Iseult, of Francesca da Rimini. It was a radiant but not a rational wisdom, and it had a frightening ingredient that had been known to make nurses and lady's maids and the wives of planetary presidents and systemic emperors shiver alike.

Together now on the whispering white slidewalk, planning their next pleasures, they looked the pinnacle of cosmic romance fulfilled—he dashing and handsome and young, except that there was something just a shade careful about the way he carried himself; she giddy and slim with a mind that was all sentimental or amorous whim, except for that diamond touch of terrifying fixed white light in her most melting or mischievous glance. Despite or perhaps because of those two exceptions, they seemed more akin to the sparkling stars above them than even to the gorgeous pleasure planet around them.

He had been born in a ghetto on Andvari III and had fought his way up the razor-runged ladder of economic power until he owned fleets of hyperspace freighters, a dozen planets, and the governments of ten times that many.

She had been born in a slum on Aphrodite IV, owning only herself. It had taken her six Terran months to bring herself to the attention of Piliph Foelitsack by way of three beauty contests and one bit part in a stereographic all-senses sex-film, and six more months to become his seventeenth wife instead of one more of his countless casual mistresses.

The beepers of social gossip everywhere had hinted discreetly about the infatuation-potential of fringe senile megabillionaires and the coldly murderous greed of teenage starlets. And Annaoj and Piliph Foelitsack had smiled at this gossip, since they knew they loved each other and why: for their matching merciless determination to get what they wanted and keep it, and for the distance that had been between them and was no longer. Of the two, Annaoj's love was perhaps the greater, accounting for the icy, fanatic glint in her otherwise nymphet's eyes.

They had laughed on leaving the drab tent of the gypsy fortune-teller, who herself owned a small, beat-up spaceship covered with cabalistic signs, because the last thing she had said to the shipping king, fixing his bright youthful eyes with her bleared ones, had been, "Piliph Foelitsack, you have journeyed far, very far, for such a young man, yet you shall make even longer journeys hereafter. Your past travels will be trifles compared to your travels to come."

Both Piliph and Annaoj knew that he had been once to the Andromeda Galaxy and twice to both Magellanic Clouds, though they had not told the silly old gypsy so, being despite their iron wills kindly lovers, still enamored of everything in the cosmos by virtue of their mutual love. They also knew that Piliph had determined to restrict his jauntings henceforth to the Milky Way, to keep reasonably close to the greatest geriatric scientists, and they were both reconciled, at least by day, to the fact that despite all his defenses, death would come for him in ten or twenty years.

Yet, although they did not now tell each other so, the gypsy's words had given a spark of real hope to their silly night-promises under the stars like gems and the galaxies like puffs of powder that: "We will live and love forever." Their loveliest night had been spent a hundred light-years outside the Milky Way—it was to be Piliph's last extragalactic venture—where the *Eros* had emerged briefly from hyperspace and they had lolled and luxuriated for hours under the magnifying crystal skylight of the Master Stateroom, watching only the far-off galaxies, with all of their moiling, toiling home-galaxy out of sight beneath the ship.

But now, as if the cryptic universe had determined to give an instant sardonic rejoinder to the gypsy's prediction, the eiderdown slidewalk had not murmured them halfway to the *Eros* when a look of odd surprise came into Piliph's bright youthful eyes and he clutched at his heart and swayed and would have toppled except that Annaoj caught him in her strong slender arms and held him to her tightly.

Something had happened in the body of Piliph Foelitsack that could not be dealt with by all its pacemakers and its implanted and re-motely controlled hormone dispensers, nor by any of the coded orders frantically tapped out by the three physicians monitoring its organs and systems.

It took thirty seconds for the ambulance of the *Eros* to hurtle out from the yacht on a track paralleling the slidewalk and brake to a bone-jolting silent halt.

During that half minute Annaoj watched the wrinkles come out on her husband's smooth face, like stars at nightfall in the sky of a planet in a star cluster. She wasted one second on the white-hot impulse to have the gypsy immediately strangled, but she knew that the great aristocrats of the cosmos do not take vengeance on its vermin and that in any event she had far more pressing business with which to occupy herself fully tonight. She clasped the pulseless body a trifle more tightly, feeling the bones and prosthetics through the layer of slack flesh.

In two minutes more, in the surgery of the *Eros*, Piliph's body was in a dissipatory neutrino field, which instantly sent all its heat packing off at the speed of light, but in particles billions of times slimmer than the photons of heat, so that the body was supercooled to the temperature of frozen helium without opportunity for a sin-gle disruptive crystal to form.

Then without consulting the spacefield dispatching station or any other authority of the pleasure planet, Annaoj ordered the *Eros* blasted into hyperspace and driven at force speed to the galaxy's foremost geriatrics clinic on Menkar V, though it lay halfway across the vast Milky Way.

During the anxious, grueling trip, she did only one thing quite out of the ordinary. She had her husband's supercooled body sprayed with a transparent insulatory film, which would adequately hold its coolth for a matter of days, and placed in the Master Stateroom. Once a week the body was briefly returned to the dissipatory neutrino field, to bring its temperature down again to within a degree of zero Kelvin.

Otherwise she behaved as she always had, changing costume seven times a day, paying great attention to her coiffure and to her cosmetic and juvenation treatments, being idly charming to the officers and stewards.

But she spent hours in her husband's office, studying his business and working to the edge of exhaustion his three secretaries. And she always took her small meals in the Master Stateroom.

On Menkar V they told her, after weeks of test and study, that her husband was beyond reawakening, at least at the present state of medical skill, and to come back in ten years. More would be known then.

At that, Annaoj nodded frigidly and took up the reins of her husband's business, conducting them entirely from the *Eros* as it skipped about through space and hyperspace. Under her guidance the Foelitsack economic empire prospered still more than it had under its founder. She successfully fought or bought off the claims of Piliph's eleven surviving divorced wives, a hundred of his relatives and a score of his prime managers.

She regularly returned to Menkar V and frequently visited other clinics and sought out famous healers. She became expert at distinguishing the charlatans from the dedicated, the conceited from the profound. Yet at times she also consulted sorcerers and wizards and witchdoctors. Incantations in exotic tongues and lights were spoken and glowed over Philiph's frigid form, extraterrestrial stenches filled the surgery of the *Eros,* and there were focused there the meditations of holy creatures which resembled man less than a spider does—while three or four fuming yet dutiful doctors of the *Eros'* dozen waited for the crucial moment in the ceremony when they would obediently work a five-second reversal of the neutrino field to bring the body briefly to normal temperature to determine whether the magic had worked.

But neither science nor sorcery could revive him.

She bullied many a police force and paid many a detective agency to hunt down the gypsy with the black cat, but the old crone and her runic spaceship had vanished as utterly as the vital spark in Piliph Foelitsack. No one could tell whether Annaoj really believed that the gypsy had had something to do with the striking down of her husband and might be able to bring him alive, or whether the witch had merely become another counter in the sorcery game of which Annaoj had suddenly grown so fond.

In the course of time Annaoj took many lovers. When she tired of one, she would lead him for the first time into the Master Stateroom of the *Eros* and show him the filmed and frosty body of her husband and send him away without as much as a parting touch of her fingertips and then lie down beside the cold, cold form under the cold, cold stars of the skylight.

And she never once let another woman set foot in that room.

Not the humblest, nor ugliest maid. Not the greatest sculptress of the Pleiades. Not the most feared and revered sorceress in the Hyades.

She became known as Crazy Annaoj, though no one thought it to her face or whispered it within a parsec of her.

When she still looked 17, though her age was 70 times that—for the sciences of geriatrics and juvenation had progressed greatly since her husband's collapse—she felt an unfamiliar weariness creeping on her and she ordered the *Eros* to make once more for Menkar V at force speed.

The *Eros* never emerged from hyperspace. Most say she was lost there, scuttled by Annaoj as she felt death coming on her. A few maintain she exited into altogether another universe, where Crazy Annaoj is still keeping up her search for the healer who can revive Piliph, or playing her game with the doctors and witchdoctors and with her lovers.

But in any case the gypsy's prediction was fulfilled, for in the course of Annaoj's voyages, the body of Piliph Foelitsack had been carried twice to Andromeda and also to two galaxies in Virgo, three in Leo and one in Coma Berenices.

A Cup of Hemlock

Lee Killough

T wo days after the Erasco shuttle crashed at the north pole of Chandanna, the local police arrested the man responsible. The trial was likewise speedy, the judgment being that: "Cars Merrivale Bantling, having caused the deaths of fourteen people by industrial espionage, has proven himself contemptuous of life and unfit to remain in society. He is to be confined for a period of thirty days, during which time he shall give up his life, be declared dead, and finally removed when all vital signs have ceased."

"Do you really expect me to kill myself?" Bantling asked his Chandannair lawyer.

"You might donate yourself to the organ banks as many do. Your parts would be of no use to us, but the gesture would express your desire to expiate your offense."

Bantling frowned. "And if I refuse your cup of hemlock? Is it forced down my throat?"

The lawyer was shocked. "Chandanna is a civilized planet. No one will touch you with intent to harm."

Aside from the barred door and windows, the cell was much like a hotel suite. It was comfortable, with a good library and excellent food. The only disturbing note was the altar-like table bearing a chalice of amber liquid. Bantling decided to wait the Chandannan out. He could do worse than live the rest of his life like this.

His appeals were denied and as the thirtieth day approached, Bantling became nervous, but the last day proceeded as the previous ones had. No one sent gas through the vents or poured the poison down his throat. Toward evening he laughed in triumph and hurled the chalice across the room, splashing the poison up the wall.

Then he began to wonder where his dinner was. It was far past the time the meal usually arrived. He tried to turn on the lights. The room remained dark.

Suddenly he was frightened. He rushed to the water taps . . . but though pushed full on, only drops of water came out.

He ran to the door and pounded on it, yelling, "Hey! I want to see my lawyer!"

No one came.

Bantling remembered the judge's words. He would be declared dead and removed when all vital signs were gone. He looked at the empty cup on the floor and the drying stain on the wall. A whimper rose in his throat.

The Dark and the Damp

John DeChancie

He started hearing the voice after he moved back into his mother's house in the village that he had left three decades before. Walton's Mill had been a farm crossroads before the coal mine opened, and now it looked pretty much as it did after it had bloomed into a coal company town in the nineteen twenties: a haphazard grouping of company houses hastily tacked together for the hordes of eastern European immigrants who came to work in the mines. There were newer houses, to be sure, and not a few trailers, but the essential character of the town had not changed in six decades. The company stores were boarded up, as was the Wobbly meeting hall, but the ethnic fraternal clubs were still open. And although the Walton's Mill mine had closed in the fifties, there was coal dust still in the lungs of many an oldtimer.

Stan Tomsic was one of them; he never did collect black lung compensation but he still hacked and coughed from the chronic bronchitis that he swore the coal dust had caused; forget that he had smoked like a stack for forty years before the doctors told him he had to quit. Tobacco was only a weed. That black stuff got into you and turned your lungs the color of the inside of a wood stove. Soot black, coal black. He had not worked in the mines long, but it had been enough, he always claimed. It had nearly killed him. After the mine accident in '54 he moved to the city to work in the steel mills.

He had hated the mines. He hated their damp moldy smell; he loathed the darkness and the dreariness, the oppressive closeness, the feeling that the ceiling was ready to fall in on you, as it sometimes really did. He hated the long ride into the depths, into the suffocating blackness, with the knowledge that you might never leave. He dreaded the endless hours spent there. In the winter, when you went down in the morning it was dark, and when you came up again at quitting time the sun was already down. You never saw light all winter. You spent your life in darkness. And if you died, you died in darkness. They might never find your body, and you would stay there in the dark forever.

Everything was damp in the mine—even the stuff that could kill you, the dangerous gases, had "damp" in the name. Blackdamp, carbon dioxide. Stinkdamp, sulphur gas; you could smell that one. Whitedamp: carbon monoxide. You could keel over in a second. And worst of all, firedamp. Methane. He knew all about that stuff.

He had fled to the mills. There you could only be brained by a falling ingot of pig iron or incinerated when the heat was tapped. Clean, noble deaths. There were windows in the mills. Light. The place reeked of noxious fumes but there was outside air, too. The mines were tombs, deep in the earth where men ought not to go. The mines had given him funny feelings. You could go crazy down there. He almost did. It got so he was talking to himself, sometimes talking to something that lived down there. He didn't know what that thing was, but he felt a presence, and it was a feeling he couldn't shake off.

In 1982 he took early retirement when the steel mill closed. And now, after his mother had died at the age of ninety-one, he was back in Walton's Mill. He had sold his suburban house with its high taxes. Walton's Mill was in a neighboring county with a much lower property rate. He inherited his mother's house free and clear, and the place was in good shape. The lot was big, with a garden plot and fruit trees and woods at the edge.

He first heard the voice in the spring, shortly after he had moved in, when he was turning up earth in the garden. At first he thought someone was calling him from the front of the house, but the voice sounded strange, muffled, hollow. It called his name and he straightened and looked around.

"Yeah?" he called back. He looked into the woods. No one.

He bent and turned over another spadeful of black soil. Then he heard it again.

"What d'you want?" he yelled, turning around and trying to see who the hell it was.

"Stan, you came back."

"Where are you?" Stan answered.

"Below, Stan. Below."

"Where?" Stan didn't know where "below" was supposed to be. The house was on a level lot.

"Underneath, Stan. Where you left me."

Stan let the spade drop. "Hey, look. Come on out and quit playing." He craned his neck, looking at the woods again, then turned to search the bushes at the side of the house.

"I'm where you left me thirty-five years ago, buddy. Still down here."

"Where the hell's that?"

"Where we both worked, kid. Here, where it's dark."

The voice had a dead reverberation to it, and a watery echo.

"Go to hell." Stan picked up the spade and resumed his digging. Some kids playing a joke on him. In the bushes or in the woods.

"Talk to me, Stan."

Something with cold little feet crawled up his spine.

"I'm busy."

"Remember how we all used to bee-ess while we worked? We'd spend hours talking. Remember Matuzak? He could gab your arm off."

"I don't know what you're talking about," Stan said. He was beginning to sweat a little.

"You don't remember Matuzak? He's still here, too. He didn't make it out either."

"I don't remember nobody," Stan muttered.

"Don't you even remember me, your good buddy, Joe Rezik?"

Stan let go of the spade. "No," he said dully.

"No? How could you forget? We used to go drinking together.

Every night at the club. Saturdays we sometimes went into Sturkeyville. Remember that old Studebaker I used to have, the one with the dent in the left door I never got fixed? You always used to ride me about that. I spent the insurance settlement and never got it fixed. You used to laugh about how I was so cheap."

Stan staggered and sank to one knee. "No."

"You remember."

"You're dead."

"No shit. Hey, did that just hit you?"

Stan got up unsteadily. "Somebody playing a trick."

"No trick, Stan. You went away, but now you're back. You don't mind if I talk to you once in a while, do you? Gets lonely down here. It's dark. It's always wet. It stinks down here, Stan. How come you left me?"

He walked slowly back to the house. He almost never drank whiskey straight but he did that night, right out of the bottle, and he got so drunk he didn't make it to bed. He woke up next morning on the couch with the TV still blaring.

He almost forgot all about it that summer. The garden came in, zucchini and beans and cauliflower and then the tomatoes, big beef-steaks, rich, red and delicious. He'd have it all in big salads with olive oil and red wine vinegar, Italian style with strips of salami and cheese thrown in. He ate well that late summer, and he drank a lot of beer—but he took his blood pressure pill every day so it was all right. His cough wasn't so bad. He got a little indigestion now and then, and his chest hurt some, but it was just something he ate, not his heart, the doctor said.

But the voice came back in October, when he was raking leaves.

"Stan."

He stopped raking.

"Stan, it's me. Joe."

He stood, frozen. The voice was the same; deep, echoey, buried somewhere. In the darkness, down there with the *plop . . . plop . . . plop* of dripping water.

"Stan, talk to me, will you? I'm lonely."

He tried to ignore it. He continued raking. It was his mind. Something was wrong. Maybe he was having a stroke, one of those little ones, that didn't affect anything but the mind—what were they called?

"Ah c'mon, Stan. Don't be so stuck-up. Chew the fat with me a little. How you been keepin' yourself?"

He threw down the rake. "Look," he said. "You better leave me alone. I'm warning you."

"Is that any way to talk to an old pal?"

"You can't be Joe Rezik. Joe Rezik's dead. I don't believe in ghosts."

"Then what am I, a piece of kielbasa?"

"I don't know what the hell you are. You're some goddamn thing in my head."

Stan took out his handkerchief and wiped his forehead.

"Jesus Christ, I'm talkin' to the goddamn ground."

"No, Stan, you're talking to me. Me, Joe Rezik."

"I don't believe you. You're dead, and dead people don't speak."

"Why not?"

"Because, goddamn it, they can't! They're dead, is all. Now get the hell away from me."

"I can't go anywhere, Stan. I gotta stay right here. Number Nine Tunnel goes straight under your house."

He picked up the rake and went inside. He didn't take a drink at first. The doctor had given him some mild tranquilizers, just a few, for the nights when he felt a little edgy and his stomach gave him trouble. He took those and waited, but they didn't do any good. They didn't calm him down, not one bit. So he drank a Stoney's beer, then another, then another. No whiskey this time. That stuff was poison.

He felt lonely, so he got dressed and went down to the club, which he had just rejoined after many years. He didn't know very many people; not well, anyway. He hadn't kept up contact with many local people. He had just come out on Sundays once in a while to see his mother, and maybe his sister, too, who lived in nearby Sturkeyville. The club was familiar, though. He'd spent time in here. Drinking. With buddies.

He played the video poker game and lost five dollars. He had a few more beers, watching the TV over the bar. The place was old, and the head stank. He plunked fifty cents into the pool table and shot a few balls. Then he played the pinball machine.

When he went home he was good and tanked up, so he decided to go right to bed, not watch TV like he usually did.

But the voice came up from the basement and he couldn't get to sleep.

"Stan, talk to me."

He rolled over and closed his eyes, but it did no good. He got up and put on slippers. He went down to the basement.

It was a damp basement with a dirt floor. These houses were thrown up so fast they hadn't even bothered to pour a slab; too cheap, the sons of bitches.

"You gotta leave me alone," Stan said.

"How would it be if I ignored an old pal, with you living right above me like you are?"

"You're not Joe Rezik."

"Yeah? Who?"

Stan breathed hard for a while. "I don't know *what* you are, but you live in that goddamn mine."

"But I don't live at all, Stan. I'm dead. Remember? You didn't come back and get me."

"That's not right!"

"What's not right about it, Stan?"

"I couldn't go back! After that firedamp touched off I kept blacking out. I crawled, I kept crawling, blacking out, coming to, blacking out. There was no oxygen down there!"

"You could have helped me. I was just a few steps behind you."

"I would have died! I just made it to the car. I fell in and the car took me up. I was out! I only came to when I reached the surface. I didn't even hear the second explosion!"

"You could have pulled me along with you, Stan. But you saved yourself. Well, I guess I can't blame you. Maybe I would have done the same thing."

"Then leave me alone!"

"But I'm lonely, Stan. I'm lonely. Your house is right over the place where it happened, Stan. Right over it."

"How come you never talked to me before? Like when I was here visiting my mother."

"Didn't want to disturb her, Stan. You know how old women are. Anything upsets them."

"But . . . *I'm* old."

"Yeah, you got old, Stan. I didn't. I'll always be a young man.

Looks like I got the best of the deal, didn't I? Except for being stuck down here."

"You *can't* be down there! You can't be!"

"But I am, Stan. Forever and ever."

"It don't make no sense! Why should you be down there? You didn't do nothin'! You're the one that died. Why should you suffer? I'm the one that—"

There was laughter. "Yeah. Yeah, I know. Tell you what. You can get me out, Stan."

Stan sat on the worn wooden steps. "How?"

"Just dig."

"Dig?"

"Dig me out. Get a shovel and dig. I'm right under you, no kiddin'. You wouldn't believe how close. The tunnel gets about, oh, ten feet from the surface along here. Remember the big pillar we left to hold the roof up? That's why, because the coal seam went almost all the way up."

"I'm not going to dig you out. You're crazy!"

"Okay, Stan, okay. It was just a thought. Take 'er easy, good buddy."

"You're crazy."

He went upstairs and threw up. Nothing but beer came up. His chest hurt, and he started coughing, so he turned the TV on and lay down on the couch.

"Besides, you're not Joe Rezik. I don't believe in ghosts."

He fell asleep in the middle of an old Bette Davis movie.

He spent the next night at his sister's in Sturkeyville. He pleaded a basement leak; he had had to shut the water off, he said. The plumber would be there tomorrow, and could he spend just one night? Of course. All of Alice's children were grown and the house was full of empty beds. It was just Alice and George in the house. They bedded him down in the back room.

He heard the voice again. Far away, coming up through two floors. But he heard it.

"There are mines everywhere, Stan."

It was almost like a whisper in his mind.

"Anywhere you go, Stan. The whole goddamn state. Other states, everywhere. They're all connected. . . ."

He returned home and called a real estate office. The agents came out to see the house—a man and a woman—but they said, don't expect to sell quick. It was a slow market out here. He said he'd sell low and gave them a price. They looked at each other and said, well, you don't have to give it away. He said, that's the price, and they said, okay, fine, you're the owner.

The FOR SALE sign went up that day, but no offers came.

The next night he didn't hear the voice. Something else was happening in the basement. There came the sound of . . .

He didn't know what it was. It was a scraping—or a chipping, or a picking sound. Then something falling with an echoing crash. Chip, chip chip . . . *crash*. Chip, chip, chip . . . *crash*.

He went down to the basement and put his ear to the floor. There was a definite digging sound. Digging, chipping away.

Digging *up*.

The contractors took out the basement window and ran the chute in through there, and the concrete came sliding down, splat, and they got trowels and levels and smoothed it out. And in no time he had a basement with a concrete floor. They told him not to step on it for forty-eight hours, so he waited two days before he went down again. The floor was fine. It had made him a little nervous when they'd had to dig to sink the drainpipe and connect it with the sewer line, but it had gone okay, and now he had a fully drained basement with a nice hard floor. He had ordered it extra thick, eight inches. The contractor had said, what the hell are you building, a bomb shelter?

He ordered a steel fire door from Sears and had them install it at the top of the basement stairs and put a deadbolt lock on it. He had the basement window bricked up.

He still heard it at night. Picking, picking away. He heard the rubble fall.

He went to Florida to visit his brother. Fred was pleased to see him. Clearwater was a nice place, and he had a good time. Fred's kids all lived in the area and they threw a big barbecue for Stan. They brought all the grandchildren. Stan never had kids; his wife, Eileen, had had miscarriage after miscarriage before giving up. Eileen had died ten years ago, and Stan had never remarried. He missed her. And he missed having a woman live with him.

But Florida was fine. He should move here, Fred suggested. Yeah, Stan said. But he had to sell mom's house. Yeah, Fred said. Besides, Stan said, the prices are high down here. How could he afford it? He'd hate to have a mortgage again, and rent was steep.

Stay here for the winter anyway, Fred told him. No, it'd be too much trouble. No trouble at all! Stay, for Christ's sake. We don't see you enough. Don't spend another horrible winter up there in that old rattrap. Call the real estate people and give him our number. By the time spring comes, you'll be out of that house.

Yeah, Stan said. He stayed until March.

But the house didn't sell, and he had to go back.

He took a limo from the airport to the city, then got a bus to Sturkeyville and picked up his car, which he had left in a lot next to Rizzo's Exxon station because the house didn't have a garage and he wanted somebody to watch it, which Lefty Rizzo had done. He drove the four miles to Walton's Mill and pulled into the gravel driveway. The place looked the same: white clapboards, peeling paint, sagging front porch. But not bad for its years.

He carried his suitcases to the front porch, unlocked the door, and opened it.

The house was quiet. He sniffed; there was a dusty smell, a you-haven't-been-here-for-a-while smell. He went upstairs and unpacked, then took a shower.

He stood before the fire door to the basement and listened. No sound. The door was okay, and the deadbolt was still locked.

There was no food in the house and it was late so he went out to the Interstate and ate at the truck stop: chopped steak with onions, mashed potatoes, green beans, with pecan pie and coffee after.

It was dark when he got back. It was an unusually warm night for late March. The whole town was quiet. Too early for crickets. Very quiet. He went inside and turned on the lights, turned the TV on. Then he turned it right off.

He took the key from the rack in the kitchen and went to the basement door. He turned the key and slid the bolt out. Turning the knob, he opened the door and flicked on the basement light.

Wooden steps leading down to new concrete. The house creaked. He took a deep breath and went down the steps.

The floor was just as spanking new as when he left it. He went to the center of the floor, knelt and listened. Nothing.

He exhaled and smiled. He got up and lit the oil furnace in case of a cold snap and turned the water back on. The pipes knocked and rattled happily all over the house. He surveyed the floor once again and chuckled to himself.

Even though people were coming to see the house he decided to go ahead and plant the garden this year. He liked to putter in the backyard, and besides, he liked to eat the stuff he grew.

On April 15th he opened up the tool shed and got out the spade and the hoe and went out to the plot and started to work. It was a nice day, the sun high and warm on his face. He worked steadily, turning over black earth. He could have paid a guy to come in with a rototiller but he liked to do it the old-fashioned way.

He dug and hoed most of the day, working up a fine sweat. He wasn't doing too badly for a guy his age. It was almost all done. He looked at the couple of square yards left and thought, save it for tomorrow, but then he figured, what the hell, go ahead and finish it and tomorrow you can dump fertilizer in the spreader and do that and it'll be all done and ready for planting. Maybe get in the tomatoes early this year.

As he was about to finish he felt queasy and stopped. A dull ache gripped his chest. His left shoulder hurt and the pain radiated down the arm.

He went to the edge of the yard and sat down on two stacked cinderblocks. Nausea came over him and a pain knifed through his chest.

"Oh, Christ."

"Anything the matter, Stan?"

"God!"

"What's the matter, Stan, old buddy? Feeling a little under the weather?"

He felt faint, ready to pass out. He rose and tried to walk to the house. He needed to call the paramedics. He tripped and fell, going to his knees.

"Pretty soon you'll be joining me, Stan, old buddy."

He had to get to the house. The nausea was like a pool of quicksand pulling him down. His chest felt as though someone were sitting on it. He turned and sat on the grass and felt for his pulse. He couldn't find it. He had no pulse.

The sky looked dark. He waited to die, sitting in the grass by the garden. It was the garden that had done it, he thought. The garden, not the voice.

"You're going to like it down here, good buddy. It's a little damp and dark, but we're gonna have a good time."

Something seemed to be working its way up his chest, something big and bloated, a living thing trying to crawl out. He belched. The force of it made him jump.

He tasted the sausages he had eaten for breakfast. They had smelled a little rank but he'd fried them up anyway. The attack had been indigestion. It had been his goddamn stomach.

He burped again and felt much better. The nausea was waning. The pain in his arm was gone, and his chest was free to move again. Just his goddamn stomach. He laughed.

He got up and took a few deep breaths. He was fine. His stomach was a little sour but he was okay.

He laughed again, and, continuing to laugh, crossed the freshly dug garden to fetch the tools.

His right leg sank into the dirt to the knee.

"Hey . . . ?"

Around him the ground was sinking, forming a wide, quickly deepening crater. He fell forward into it, scrabbling with his hands.

"What . . . what the hell is happening?"

"Mine subsidence."

The voice was close now, just under him, down inside the dark hole that opened at the bottom of the crater.

He struggled upwards, clawing damp soil, but the ground gave way beneath him and he sank.

"I know what you are!" came his scream. "You're not Joe Rezik!"

"Okay, you know. There's always a few of you who know. You knew a long time ago. Yet you all came down and helped yourselves to what is mine. You continue to do it. Don't you believe your own legends?"

"*Who* are you, fer crissakes?"

"I am called by various names. Orcus, Pluto, Hades. I prefer my ancient name, Dis."

"Let me go!"

"You came into my realm, you stole my treasures. Now you must pay, thief, as the others did."

The whole garden seemed to turn concave; then the bottom gave way and, with a great roar, tons of earth slid into the hungry darkness. Rock fractured and tumbled, and waterfalls of dirt cascaded from the ragged edge of the hole.

After a while the roaring ceased and the rubble stopped falling and the dust cleared.

The house stood silently by. Time passed. From the bottom of the hole there came the steady sound of dripping water, echoing in the darkness.

Dear Pen Pal

A. E. van Vogt

Planet Aurigae II

Dear Pen Pal:

When I first received your letter from the interstellar correspondence club, my impulse was to ignore it. The mood of one who has spent the last seventy planetary periods—years I suppose you would call them—in an Aurigaen prison, does not make for a pleasant exchange of letters. However, life is very boring, and so I finally settled myself to the task of writing you.

Your description of Earth sounds exciting. I would like to live there for a while, and I have a suggestion in this connection, but I won't mention it till I have developed it further.

You will have noticed the material on which this letter is written. It is a highly sensitive metal, very thin, very flexible, and I have inclosed several sheets of it for your use. Tungsten dipped in any strong acid makes an excellent mark on it. It is important to me that you do write on it, as my fingers are too hot—literally—to hold your paper without damaging it.

I'll say no more just now. It is possible you will not care to correspond with a convicted criminal, and therefore I shall leave the next move up to you. Thank you for your letter. Though you did not know its destination, it brought a moment of cheer into my drab life.

Skander

Aurigae II

Dear Pen Pal:

Your prompt reply to my letter made me happy. I am sorry your doctor thought it excited you too much, and sorry, also, if I have described my predicament in such a way as to make you feel badly. I welcome your many questions, and I shall try to answer them all.

You say the international correspondence club has no record of having sent any letters to Aurigae. That, according to them, the temperature on the second planet of the Aurigae sun is more than 500 degrees Fahrenheit. And that life is not known to exist there. Your club is right about the temperature and the letters. We have what your people would call a hot climate, but then we are not a hydro-carbon form of life, and find 500 degrees very pleasant.

I must apologize for deceiving you about the way your first letter was sent to me. I didn't want to frighten you away by telling you too much at once. After all, I could not be expected to know that you would be enthusiastic to hear from me.

The truth is that I am a scientist, and, along with the other members of my race, I have known for some centuries that there were other inhabited systems in the galaxy. Since I am allowed to experiment in my spare hours, I amused myself in attempts at communication. I developed several simple systems for breaking in on galactic communication operations, but it was not until I developed a subspacewave control that I was able to draw your letter (along with several others, which I did not answer) into a cold chamber.

I use the cold chamber as both sending and receiving center, and since you were kind enough to use the material which I sent you, it was easy for me to locate your second letter among the mass of mail that accumulated at the nearest headquarters of the interstellar correspondence club.

How did I learn your language? After all, it is a simple one, particularly the written language seems easy. I had no difficulty with it. If you are still interested in writing me, I shall be happy to continue the correspondence.

Skander

Aurigae II

Dear Pen Pal:

Your enthusiasm is refreshing. You say that I failed to answer your question about how I expected to visit Earth. I confess I deliberately ignored the question, as my experiment had not yet proceeded far enough. I want you to bear with me a short time longer, and then I will be able to give you the details. You are right in saying that it would be difficult for a being who lives at a temperature of 500 degrees Fahrenheit to mingle freely with the people of Earth. This was never my intention, so please relieve your mind. However, let us drop that subject for the time being.

I appreciate the delicate way in which you approach the subject of my imprisonment. But it is quite unnecessary. I performed forbidden experiments upon my body in a way that was deemed to be dangerous to the public welfare. For instance, among other things, I once lowered my surface temperature to 150 degrees Fahrenheit, and so shortened the radioactive cycle-time of my surroundings. This caused an unexpected break in the normal person to person energy flow in the city where I lived, and so charges were laid against me. I have thirty more years to serve. It would be pleasant to leave my body behind and tour the universe—but as I said I'll discuss that later.

I wouldn't say that we're a superior race. We have certain qualities which apparently your people do not have. We live longer, not because of any discoveries we've made about ourselves, but because our bodies are built of a more enduring element—I don't know your name for it, but the atomic weight is 52.9#.* Our scientific discov-

* A radioactive isotope of chromium. —*Author's Note*.

eries are of the kind that would normally be made by a race with our kind of physical structure. The fact that we can work with temperatures of as high as—I don't know just how to put that—has been very helpful in the development of the subspace energies which are extremely hot, and require delicate adjustments. In the later stages these adjustments can be made by machinery, but in the development the work must be done by "hand"—I put that word in quotes, because we have no hands in the same way that you have.

I am inclosing a photographic plate, properly cooled and chemicalized for your climate. I wonder if you would set it up and take a picture of yourself. All you have to do is arrange it properly on the basis of the laws of light—that is, light travels in straight lines, so stand in front of it—and when you are ready *think* "Ready!" The picture will be automatically taken.

Would you do this for me? If you are interested, I will also send you a picture of myself, though I must warn you. My appearance will probably shock you.

Sincerely,
Skander

Planet Aurigae II

Dear Pen Pal:

Just a brief note in answer to your question. It is not necessary to put the plate into a camera. You describe this as a dark box. The plate will take the picture when you think, "Ready!" I assure you it will be flooded with light.

Skander

Aurigae II

Dear Pen Pal:

You say that while you were waiting for the answer to my last letter you showed the photographic plate to one of the doctors at the hospital—I cannot picture what you mean by doctor or hospital, but let that pass—and he took the problem up with government authorities. Problem? I don't understand. I thought we were having a pleasant correspondence, private and personal.

I shall certainly appreciate your sending that picture of yourself.

Skander

Aurigae II

Dear Pen Pal:

I assure you I am not annoyed at your action. It merely puzzled me, and I am sorry the plate has not been returned to you. Knowing what governments are, I can imagine that it will not be returned to you for some time, so I am taking the liberty of inclosing another plate.

I cannot imagine why you should have been warned against continuing this correspondence. What do they expect me to do?—eat you up at long distance? I'm sorry but I don't like hydrogen in my diet.

In any event, I would like your picture as a memento of our friendship, and I will send mine as soon as I have received yours. You may keep it or throw it away, or give it to your governmental authorities—but at least I will have the knowledge that I've given a fair exchange.

With all best wishes
Skander

Aurigae II

Dear Pen Pal:

Your last letter was so slow in coming that I thought you had decided to break off the correspondence. I was sorry to notice that you failed to inclose the photograph, puzzled by your reference to having a relapse, and cheered by your statement that you would send it along as soon as you felt better—whatever that means. However, the important thing is that you did write, and I respect the philosophy of your club which asks its members not to write of pessimistic matters. We all have our own problems which we regard as overshadowing the problems of others. Here I am in prison, doomed to spend the next 30 years tucked away from the main stream of life. Even the thought is hard on my restless spirit, though I know I have a long life ahead of me after my release.

In spite of your friendly letter, I won't feel that you have completely re-established contact with me until you send the photograph.

Yours in expectation
Skander

Aurigae II

Dear Pen Pal:

The photograph arrived. As you suggest, your appearance startled me. From your description I thought I had mentally reconstructed your body. It just goes to show that words cannot really describe an object which has never been seen.

You'll notice that I've inclosed a photograph of myself, as I promised I would. Chunky, metallic looking chap, am I not, very different, I'll wager, than you expected? The various races with whom we have communicated become wary of us when they discover we are highly radioactive, and that literally we are a radioactive form of life, the only such (that we know of) in the universe. It's been very trying to be so isolated and, as you know, I have occasionally mentioned that I had hopes of escaping not only the deadly imprisonment to which I am being subjected but also the body which cannot escape.

Perhaps you'll be interested in hearing how far this idea has developed. The problem involved is one of exchange of personalities with someone else. Actually, it is not really an exchange in the accepted meaning of the word. It is necessary to get an impress of both individuals, of their mind and of their thoughts as well as their bodies. Since this phase is purely mechanical, it is simply a matter of taking complete photographs and of exchanging them. By complete I mean of course every vibration must be registered. The next step is to make sure the two photographs are exchanged, that is, that each party has somewhere near him a complete photograph of the other. (It is already too late, Pen Pal. I have set in motion the subspace energy interflow between the two plates, so you might as well read on.) As I have said it is not exactly an exchange of personalities. The original personality in each individual is suppressed, literally pushed back out of the consciousness, and the image personality from the "photographic" plate replaces it.

You will take with you a complete memory of your life on Earth, and I will take along memory of my life on Aurigae. Simultaneously, the memory of the receiving body will be blurrily at our disposal. A part of us will always be pushing up, striving to regain consciousness, but always lacking the strength to succeed.

As soon as I grow tired of Earth, I will exchange bodies in the same way with a member of some other race. Thirty years hence, I will be happy to reclaim my body, and you can then have whatever body I last happened to occupy.

This should be a very happy arrangement for us both. You, with your short life expectancy, will have outlived all your contemporaries and will have had an interesting experience. I admit I expect to have the better of the exchange—but now, enough of explanation. By the time you reach this part of the letter it will be me reading it, not you. But if any part of you is still aware, so long for now, Pen Pal. It's been nice having all those letters from you. I shall write you from time to time to let you know how things are going with my tour.

Skander

Aurigae II

Dear Pen Pal:

Thanks a lot for forcing the issue. For a long time I hesitated about letting you play such a trick on yourself. You see, the government scientists analyzed the nature of that first photographic plate you sent me, and so the final decision was really up to me. I decided that anyone as eager as you were to put one over should be allowed to succeed.

Now I know I didn't have to feel sorry for you. Your plan to conquer Earth wouldn't have gotten anywhere, but the fact that you had the idea ends the need for sympathy.

By this time you will have realized for yourself that a man who has been paralyzed since birth, and is subject to heart attacks, cannot expect a long life span. I am happy to tell you that your once

lonely pen pal is enjoying himself, and I am happy to sign myself
with a name to which I expect to become accustomed.

> With best wishes
> Skander

The Demon of the Flower

Clark Ashton Smith

Not as the plants and flowers of Earth, growing peacefully
beneath a simple sun, were the blossoms of the planet
Lophai. Coiling and uncoiling in double dawns; tossing tu-
multuously under vast suns of jade green and balas-ruby orange;
swaying and weltering in rich twilights, in aurora-curtained nights,
they resembled fields of rooted serpents that dance eternally to an
other-world music.

Many were small and furtive, and crept viper-wise on the
ground. Others were tall as pythons, rearing superbly in hieratic
postures to the jeweled light. Some grew with single or dual stems
that burgeoned forth into hydra heads. And some were frilled and
festooned with leaves that suggested the wings of flying lizards, the
pennants of faery lances, the phylacteries of a strange sacerdotal-
ism. Some appeared to bear the scarlet wattles of dragons; others
were tongued as if with black flames or the colored vapors that
issue with weird writhings from out barbaric censers; and others
still were armed with fleshy nets or tendrils, or with huge blossoms
like bucklers perforated in battle. And all were equipped with venomous darts and fangs, all were alive, restless, and sentient.

They were the lords of Lophai, and all other life existed by their
sufferance. The people of the world had been their inferiors from
unrecorded cycles; and even in the most primitive myths there was
no suggestion that any other order of things had ever prevailed.
And the plants themselves, together with the fauna and mankind of
Lophai, gave immemorial obeisance to that supreme and terrible

99

flower known as the Voorqual, in which a tutelary demon, more ancient than the twin suns, was believed to have made its immortal avatar.

The Voorqual was served by a human priesthood, chosen from amid the royalty and aristocracy of Lophai. In the heart of the chief city, Lospar, in an equatorial realm, it had grown from antiquity on the summit of a high pyramid of sable terraces that loomed over the town like the hanging gardens of some greater Babylon, crowded with the lesser but deadly floral forms. At the center of the broad apex, the Voorqual stood alone in a basin level with the surrounding platform of black mineral. The basin was filled with a compost in which the dust of royal mummies formed an essential ingredient.

The demon flower sprang from a bulb so encrusted with the growth of ages that it resembled a stone urn. Above this there rose the gnarled and mighty stalk that had displayed in earler times the bifurcation of a mandrake, but whose halves had now grown together into a scaly, furrowed thing like the tail of some mythic sea-monster. The stalk was variegated with hues of greening bronze, of antique copper, with the livid blues and purples of fleshly corruption. It ended in a crown of stiff, blackish leaves, banded and spotted with poisonous, metallic white, and edged with sharp serrations as of savage weapons. From below the crown issued a long, sinuous arm, scaled like the main stem, and serpentining downward and outward to terminate in the huge upright bowl of a bizarre blossom—as if the arm, in sardonic fashion, should hold out a hellish beggar's cup.

Abhorrent and monstrous was the bowl—which, like the leaves, was legended to renew itself at intervals of a thousand years. It smouldered with sullen ruby at the base; it lightened into zones of dragon's blood, into belts of the rose of infernal sunset, on the full, swelling sides; and it flamed at the rim to a hot yellowish nacarat red, like the ichor of salamanders. To one who dared peer within, the cup was lined with sepulchral violet, blackening toward the bottom, pitted with myriad pores, and streaked with turgescent veins of sulphurous green.

Swaying in a slow, lethal, hypnotic rhythm, with a deep and solemn sibilation, the Voorqual dominated the city of Lospar and the world Lophai. Below, on the tiers of the pyramid, the thronged ophidian plants kept time to this rhythm in their tossing and hissing. And far beyond Lospar, to the poles of the planet and in all its longitudes, the living blossoms obeyed the sovereign tempo of the Voorqual.

Boundless was the power exercised by this being over the people who, for want of a better name, I have called the humankind of Lophai. Myriad and frightful were the legends that had gathered through aeons about the Voorqual. And dire was the sacrifice demanded each year at the summer solstice by the demon: the filling of its proffered cup with the life-blood of a priest or priestess, chosen from amid the assembled hierophants who passed before the Voorqual till the poised cup, inverted and empty, descended like a devil's miter on the head of one of their number.

Lunithi, king of the realms about Lospar, and high-priest of the Voorqual, was the last if not the first of his race to rebel against this singular tyranny. There were dim myths of some primordial ruler who had dared to refuse the required sacrifice; and whose people, in consequence, had been decimated by a mortal war with the serpentine plants which, obeying the angry demon, had uprooted themselves everywhere from the soil and had marched on the cities of Lophai, slaying or vampirizing all who fell in their way. Lunithi, from childhood, had obeyed implicitly and without question the will of the floral overlord; had offered the stated worship, had performed the necessary rites. To withhold them would have been blasphemy. He had not dreamt of rebellion till, at the time of the annual choosing of the victim, and thirty suns before the date of his nuptials with Nala, priestess of the Voorqual, he saw the hesitant, inverted grail come down in deathly crimson on the fair head of his betrothed.

A sorrowful consternation, a dark, sullen dismay which he sought to smother in his heart, was experienced by Lunithi. Nala, dazed and resigned, in a mystic inertia of despair, accepted her doom without question; but a blasphemous doubt formed itself surreptiously in the mind of the king.

Trembling at his own impiety, he asked himself if there was not some way in which he could save Nala, could cheat the demon of its ghastly tribute. To do this, and escape with impunity to himself and his subjects, he knew that he must strike at the very life of the monster, which was believed to be deathless and invulnerable. It seemed impious even to wonder concerning the truth of this belief, which had long assumed the force of a religious tenet and was held unanimously.

Amid such reflections, Lunithi remembered an old myth about the existence of a neutral and independent being known as the Occlith: a demon coeval with the Voorqual, and allied neither to man nor the flower creatures. This being was said to dwell beyond the desert of Aphom, in the otherwise unpeopled mountains of white stone above the habitat of the ophidian blossoms. In latter days no man had seen the Occlith, for the journey through Aphom was not lightly to be undertaken. But this entity was supposed to be immortal; and it kept apart and alone, meditating upon all things but interfering never with their processes. However, it was said to have given, in earlier times, valuable advice to a certain king who had gone forth from Lospar to its lair among the white crags.

In his grief and desperation, Lunithi resolved to seek the Occlith and question it anent the possibility of slaying the Voorqual. If, by any mortal means, the demon could be destroyed, he would remove from Lophai the long-established tyranny whose shadow fell upon all things from the sable pyramid.

It was necessary for him to proceed with utmost caution, to confide in no one, to veil his very thoughts at all times from the occult scrutiny of the Voorqual. In the interim of five days between the choosing of the victim and the consummation of the sacrifice, he must carry out his mad plan.

Unattended, and disguised as a simple hunter of beasts, he left his palace during the short three-hour night of universal slumber, and stole forth toward the desert of Aphom. In the dawn of the balas-ruby sun, he had reached the pathless waste, and was toiling painfully over its knife-sharp ridges of dark stone, like the waves of a mounting ocean petrified in storm.

Soon the rays of the green sun were added to those of the other, and Aphom became a painted inferno through which Lunithi dragged his way, crawling from scarp to glassy scarp or resting at whiles in the colored shadows. There was no water anywhere; but swift mirages gleamed and faded; and the sifting sand appeared to run like rills in the bottom of deep valleys. At setting of the first sun, he came within sight of the pale mountains beyond Aphom, towering like cliffs of frozen foam above the desert's dark sea. They were tinged with transient lights of azure, of jade and orange in the going of the yellow-red orb and the westward slanting of its binary. Then the lights melted into beryl and tourmaline, and the green sun was regnant over all, till it too went down, leaving a twilight whose colors were those of sea-water. In the gloom, Lunithi reached the foot of the pale crags; and there, exhausted, he slept till the second dawn.

Rising, he began his escalade of the white mountains. They rose bleak and terrible before him against the hidden suns, with cliffs that were like the sheer terraces of gods. Like the king who had preceded him in the ancient myth, he found a precarious way that led upward through narrow, broken chasms. At last he came to the vaster fissure, riving the heart of the white range, by which it was alone possible to reach the legendary lair of the Occlith.

The chasm's beetling walls rose higher and higher above him, shutting out the suns but creating with their whiteness a wan and deathly glimmer to illumine his way. The fissure was such as might have been cloven by the sword of a macrocosmic giant. It led downward, steepening ever, like a wound that pierced to the heart of Lophai.

Lunithi, like all of his race, was able to exist for prolonged periods without other nutriment than sunlight and water. He had brought with him a metal flask, filled with the aqueous element of Lophai, from which he drank sparingly as he descended the chasm; for the white mountains were waterless, and he feared to touch the pools and streams of unknown fluids upon which he came at intervals in the dusk. There were sanguine-colored springs that fumed and bubbled before him, to vanish in fathomless rifts; and brooklets of mercurial metal, green, blue, or amber, that wound beside him like liquescent serpents and then slipped away into dark caverns. Acrid vapors rose from clefts in the chasm; and Lunithi felt himself among strange chemistries of nature. In this fantastic world of stone, which the plants of Lophai could never invade, he seemed to have gone beyond the Voorqual's grim, diabolic tyranny.

At last he came to a clear, watery pool, occupying almost the entire width of the chasm. In passing it he was forced to scramble along a narrow, insecure ledge at one side. A fragment of the marble stone, breaking away beneath his footfall, dropped into the pool as he gained the opposite edge; and the hueless liquid foamed and hissed like a thousand vipers. Wondering as to its properties, and fearful of the venomous hissing, which did not subside for some time, Lunithi hurried on; and came after an interval to the fissure's end.

Here he emerged in the huge crater-like pit that was the home of the Occlith. Fluted and columned walls went up to a stupendous height on all sides; and the sun of orange ruby, now at zenith, was pouring down a vertical cataract of gorgeous fires and shadows.

Addorsed against the further wall of the pit in an upright posture, he beheld that being known as the Occlith, which had the likeness of a high cruciform pillar of blue mineral, shining with its own esoteric luster. Going forward he prostrated himself before the pillar; and then, in accents that quavered with a deep awe, he ventured to ask the desired oracle.

For a while the Occlith maintained its aeon-old silence. Peering timidly, the king perceived the twin lights of mystic silver that brightened and faded with a slow, rhythmic pulsation in the arms of the blue cross. Then, from the lofty, shining thing, there issued a voice that was like the tinkling of mineral fragments lightly clashed together, but which somehow shaped itself into articulate words.

'It is possible,' said the Occlith, 'to slay the plant known as the Voorqual, in which an elder demon has its habitation. Though the flower has attained millennial age, it is not necessarily immortal: for all things have their proper term of existence and decay; and nothing has been created without its corresponding agency of death. . . . I do not advise you to slay the plant . . . but I can furnish you with the information which you desire. In the mountain chasm through which you came to seek me, there flows a hueless spring of mineral poison, deadly to all the ophidian plant-life of this world. . . .'

The Occlith went on, and told Lunithi the method by which the poison should be prepared and administered. The chill, toneless, tinkling voice concluded:

'I have answered your question. If there is anything more that you wish to learn, it would be well to ask me now.'

Prostrating himself again, Lunithi gave thanks to the Occlith; and, considering that he had learned all that was requisite, he did not avail himself of the opportunity to question further the strange entity of living stone. And the Occlith, cryptic and aloof in its termless, impenetrable meditation, apparently saw fit to vouchsafe nothing more except in answer to a direct query.

Withdrawing from the marble-walled abyss, Lunithi returned in haste along the chasm; till, reaching the pool of which the Occlith had spoken, he paused to empty his water-flask and fill it with the angry, hissing liquid. Then he resumed his homeward journey.

At the end of two days, after incredible fatigues and torments in the blazing hell of Aphom, he reached Lospar in the time of darkness and slumber, as when he had departed. Since his absence had been unannounced, it was supposed that he had retired to the underground adyta below the pyramid of the Voorqual for purposes of prolonged meditation, as was sometimes his wont.

In alternate hope and trepidation, dreading the miscarriage of his plan and shrinking still from its audacious impiety, Lunithi awaited the night preceding that double dawn of summer solstice when, in a secret room of the black pyramid, the monstrous offering was to be made ready. Nala would be slain by a fellow-priest or priestess, chosen by lot, and her life-blood would drip from the channeled altar into a great cup; and the cup would then be borne with solemn rites to the Voorqual and its contents poured into the evilly supplicative bowl of the sanguinated blossom.

He saw little of Nala during that interim. She was more withdrawn than ever, and seemed to have consecrated herself wholly to the coming doom. To no one—and least of all to his beloved—did Lunithi dare to hint a possible prevention of the sacrifice.

There came the dreaded eve, with a swiftly changing twilight of jeweled hues that turned to a darkness hung with auroral flame. Lunithi stole across the sleeping city and entered the pyramid whose blackness towered massively amid the frail architecture of buildings that were little more than canopies and lattices of stone. With infinite care and caution he made the preparations prescribed by the Occlith. Into the huge sacrificial cup of black metal, in a room lit with stored sunlight, he emptied the seething, sibilant poison he had brought with him from the white mountains. Then, opening adroitly a vein in one of his arms, he added a certain amount of his own life-fluid to the lethal potion, above whose foaming crystal it floated like a magic oil, without mingling; so that the entire cup, to all appearance, was filled with the liquid most acceptable to the Satanic blossom.

Bearing in his hands the black grail, Lunithi ascended a hewn stairway that led to the Voorqual's presence. His heart quailing, his senses swooning in chill gulfs of terror, he emerged on the lofty summit above the shadowy town.

In a luminous azure gloom, against the weird and iridescent streamers of light that foreran the double dawn, he saw the dreamy swaying of the monstrous plant, and heard its somnolent hissing that was answered drowsily by myriad blossoms on the tiers below. A nightmare oppression, black and tangible, seemed to flow from the pyramid and to lie in stagnant shadow on all the lands of Lophai.

Aghast at his own temerity, and deeming that his shrouded thoughts would surely be understood as he drew nearer, or that the Voorqual would be suspicious of an offering brought before the accustomed hour, Lunithi made obeisance to his floral suzerain. The Voorqual vouchsafed no sign that it had deigned to perceive his presence; but the great flower-cup, with its flaring crimsons dulled to garnet and purple in the twilight, was held forward as if in readiness to receive the hideous gift.

Breathless, and fainting with religious fear, in a moment of suspense that seemed eternal, Lunithi poured the blood-mantled poison into the cup. The venom boiled and hissed like a wizard's brew as the thirsty flower drank it up; and Lunithi saw the scaled arm draw back, tilting its demon grail quickly, as if to repudiate the doubtful draught.

It was too late; for the poison had been absorbed by the blossom's porous lining. The tilting motion changed in midair to an agonized writhing of the reptilian arm; and then the Voorqual's huge, scaly stalk and pointed leaf-crown began to toss in a deathly dance, waving darkly against the auroral curtains of morn. Its deep hissing sharpened to an insupportable note, fraught with the pain of a dying devil; and looking down from the platform edge on which he crouched to avoid the swaying growth, Lunithi saw that the lesser plants on the terraces were now tossing in a mad unison with their master. Like noises in an ill dream, he heard the chorus of their tortured sibilations.

He dared not look again at the Voorqual, till he became aware of a strange silence, and saw that the blossoms below had ceased to writhe and were drooping limply on their stems. Then, incredulous, he knew that the Voorqual was dead.

Turning in triumph mingled with horror, he beheld the flaccid stalk that had fallen prone on its bed of unholy compost. He saw the sudden withering of the stiff, sworded leaves, of the gross and hellish cup. Even the stony bulb appeared to collapse and crumble before his eyes. The entire stem, its evil colors fading swiftly, shrank and fell in upon itself like a sere, empty serpent-skin.

At the same time, in some obscure manner, Lunithi was still aware of a presence that brooded above the pyramid. Even in the death of the Voorqual, it seemed to him that he was not alone. Then, as he stood and waited, fearing he knew not what, he felt the passing of a cold and unseen thing in the gloom—a thing that flowed across his body like the thick coils of some enormous python, without sound, in dark, clammy undulations. A moment more and it was gone; and Lunithi no longer felt the brooding presence.

He turned to go; but it seemed that the dying night was full of an unconceived terror that gathered before him as he went down the long, somber stairs. Slowly he descended; and a weird despair was upon him. He had slain the Voorqual, had seen it wither in death. Yet he could not believe the thing he had done; the lifting of the ancient doom was still no more than an idle myth.

The twilight brightened as he passed through the slumbering city. According to custom, no one would be abroad for another hour. Then the priests of the Voorqual would gather for the annual blood-offering.

Midway between the pyramid and his own palace, Lunithi was more than startled to meet the maiden Nala. Pale and ghostly, she glided by him with a swift and swaying movement almost serpentine, which differed oddly from her habitual languor. Lunithi dared not accost her when he saw her shut, unheeding eyes, like those of a somnambulist; and he was awed and troubled by the strange ease, the unnatural surety of her motion, which reminded him of something which he feared to remember. In a turmoil of fantastic doubt and apprehension, he followed her.

Threading the exotic maze of Lospar with the fleet and sinuous glide of a homing serpent, Nala entered the sacred pyramid. Lunithi, less swift than she, had fallen behind; and he knew not where she had gone in the myriad vaults and chambers; but a dark and fearsome intuition drew his steps without delay to the platform of the summit.

He knew not what he should find; but his heart was drugged with an esoteric hopelessness; and he was aware of no surprise when he came forth in the varicolored dawn and beheld the thing which awaited him.

The maiden Nala—or that which he knew to be Nala—was standing in the basin of evil compost, above the withered remains of the Voorqual. She had undergone—was still undergoing—a monstrous and diabolic metamorphosis. Her frail, slight body had assumed a long and dragon-like shape, and the tender skin was marked off in incipient scales that darkened momentarily with a mottling of baleful hues. Her head was no longer recognizable as such, and the human lineaments were flaring into a weird semi-circle of pointed leaf-buds. Her lower limbs had joined together, had rooted themselves in the ground. One of her arms was becoming a part of the reptilian bole; and the other was lengthening into a scaly stem that bore the dark-red bud of a sinister blossom.

More and more the monstrosity took on the similitude of the Voorqual; and Lunithi, crushed by the ancient awe and dark, terrible faith of his ancestors, could feel no longer any doubt of its true identity. Soon there was no trace of Nala in the thing before him, which began to sway with a sinuous, python-like rhythm, and to utter a deep and measured sibilation, to which the plants on the lower tiers responded. He knew then that the Voorqual had returned to claim its sacrifice and preside forever above the city Lospar and the world Lophai.

Disguise

Donald A. Wollheim

We called it Borderland House, because it was a title that tickled our imagination, and because in a way we were all men who made our living by digging and delving along the borderlands of science. Specifically, we were science-fiction fans.

We had met as boys years ago, ten, twelve, some even twenty years before. We had formed clubs, written enthusiastic letters to magazines, feuded, mimeographed fan journals. Then we tried writing stories for the three existing science-fiction magazines, and one of us cracked Gernsback and another sold something to T. O'Conor Sloane, and finally most of us sold a few. As the years went by, we matured, found our places in the world. We married, some of us were still happy with our first wives, others were already divorced three times. We were getting a bit grey, one was balding, others remained surprisingly youthful.

Before we had realized it, we were the editors, the professional writers. We no longer corresponded with fans out of town. Some of us avoided conventions, some of us even pooh-poohed that which had been the making of us all. Basically, we were still fans. And we liked to gather on an evening to chew the fat, to argue the doings of the world, cuss out publishers, tear other writers to pieces, and maybe unravel dianetics or the latest high-jinks of the *stf* world.

One of us had made a lot of money and had bought a house in the suburbs with his former wife. Now his wife had left him, but he still had the house, and we all got together and made it a special hangout. A club for professional science-fictionists. It was a lovely little place, a sort of ranch-house type, with a wonderful picture-window living room, looking down the hill. The location was sufficiently suburban for it to be surrounded by greenery. We could see the road at the base of the hill, along which the bus passes. We had a view of the winding path leading up to our door, and when we sat by the huge wall-length window, we could watch our visitors coming.

It was a summer evening, on a Friday night, and most of us were already gathered there. Friday night is the end of a work week and, married or not, our wives knew we liked to make it our own night. So there were five of us sitting around the living room of Borderland House, cocktail glasses in hand or on the table, some of us smoking, and talking science-fiction.

Fred was sitting idly, chain-smoking and looking bland. Bob was expounding on semantics and arguing with Ted about the matter. I was quietly meditating over an Old-Fashioned and simply listening. I think Sam was reading a book.

My eyes wandered over the scene. The sun was still above the horizon, for this was summer and daylight-saving. A soft light filled the view, the trees were lush and green, and I could see the shingled rooftops of the houses down below us, and very far away the towers of Manhattan. I watched the bus come to a halt at the base of our path, and I saw a man descend, glance up at our house, and start slowly up the path.

"Here comes Evan," I remarked. Eyes swiveled around for a moment to watch our friend make his way up. Evan Carey was not one of the original gang, but he was a good scout. He had sort of joined our clique about seven years ago and had fitted like a glove. We all liked him. He was full of humor and always in good spirits and could roar out an argument like a bull.

Evan Carey was the editor of two science-fiction pulps, both doing nicely. He was one of those who loved fans and delighted to attend fan meetings and make speeches. We watched him toiling slowly up the hill. I thought to myself that he didn't look well.

He seemed, even from that distance, somewhat pale and hesitant. He climbed steadily, slowly, but his face lacked its usual smile. He passed around the bend and reached our door. When he came in, my observations were confirmed.

Evan Carey was looking pretty bad—for him. He seemed to have lost a little weight or, at any rate, he seemed peaked . . . like a man who had not slept for three nights. His face was paler, instead of its usual ruddy color. He failed to give us his usual cheery greeting and bantering opening. He just looked around a bit, tired, and then slumped into a chair.

"You must have been making a day of it, Evan," said Sam. "Yeah, you look like the last rose of summer," put in Ted.

Evan looked at them, looked at us all. He shook his head a bit, wearily. "I dunno. I don't feel so good. I should have gone to bed, I suppose, but I felt that I had to come out here and warn you boys."

I looked at him sharply. "Warn us? What's up?"

He ran a hand nervously over his cheek. "Why, nothing, nothing, but just the same . . ."

He took the drink that Fred handed him, sipped at it, put it down, squirmed a bit. "You know," he started to say, "this science-fiction . . ."

He sort of let his voice peter out, took another sip.

"Letting it get you down, eh?" said Bob.

He shook his head. "No, no, nothing like that," he muttered. "Just that—oh, well—it's just that—you know, it might start something."

"Start what?" I said sharply. "Pull yourself together man! What the hell are you talking about?"

He looked up at me. "Well, you know . . . science-fiction. It deals with all sorts of strange things. I got to thinking today. Suppose there really were intelligent creatures on other planets?"

I shrugged impatiently. "We've been over that a thousand times. What about it?"

"Well," he said hesitantly, "well, suppose they were able to come here, and suppose they knew how skeptical most people would be . . ."

Again he broke off, his face twitched nervously, he took another peck at his cocktail glass. Continued:

"Maybe the only people that would be willing to believe them would be science-fiction fans? Maybe?" More hesitation. "And where would be the first place to look for fans?" A slow breath. "In an office where they publish the stuff. Science-fiction editors. Maybe they'd go to see science-fiction editors first."

He looked around at us, as if glad to get that out. Fred shrugged, lit another cigarette. "I haven't met any, and I'm an editor," he said.

"I'll tell my switchboard girl to keep an eye out for bug-eyed monsters," said Bob.

"Someone been up to visit you?" asked Ted, who was only a writer.

Evan Carey glanced at him hastily. "No, no. Of course not. But I was only thinking about it. Still it was awful odd this afternoon."

"What was odd?" I asked. In heaven's name, what was the matter with him, I thought. I had never seen him act so shaken up, so uncertain.

"Why, the . . . the thing, the idea, I thought I should warn you . . ." Evan took another sip, sort of made a face, sat on the edge of his chair, jumpy.

I was looking out the window for a moment. Another bus was drawing to a stop. I saw someone get off. Another of our friends, I supposed. Evan Carey must have watched my eyes, for he leaned forward, staring sharply.

"Excuse me," he said suddenly and stood up. We all looked up at him. He put down his glass, turned, and went out the room into the kitchen.

"Now, what's eating him?" Fred said. We were puzzled. I was wondering just what had happened to make Evan so jittery.

My eyes went to the window again. The man who had gotten off the bus was now toiling up the hill, swiping at nearby bushes with his hand, and whistling. I thought my eyes would pop out. I just sat and stared.

The others must have noticed my agitation, for there was dead silence as they followed my staring eyes. All five pairs of eyes in our room watched the figure of Evan Carey climb the path to the door of Borderland House. He was ruddy-faced, hale, and bustling with energy. He must have noticed us, for he waved a hand and hollered.

We heard his halloo through the glass. With one accord, all five of us turned and made a dash for the kitchen. But the other Evan Carey was gone.

Do you really think that a visitor from space would visit a science-fiction editor first? And in what disguise?

Dog Star

Mack Reynolds

Whee man's first representatives landed on Sirius Two, hungry to trade for that planet's abundance of pitchblende, they carried with them, as ship's mascot, one of the few dogs left on Earth.

That Gimmick was one of the very last was not due to disease, nor reproductive failure. It was just that man was going through a period of wearying of his ages-long companion. The Venusian *marmoset*, the Martian *trillie*, were much cuter, you know, and much less trouble.

Captain Hanford—leader of the three man, one dog crew—saluted the Sirian delegates snappily, only mildly surprised at the others' appearance. In a small saddle, topping what appeared almost identical to an Earthside airedale, was an octopus-looking creature. It was not until later that the captain and his men realized that dog-like creature was the intelligent of the two, and the octopus a telepathically-controlled set of useful tentacles.

Telepathic communication can be confusing, since it is almost impossible when the group consists of several individuals, to know who is "talking."

When the amenities had been dispensed with, the Sirian leader remarked in friendly fashion, "I would say our domesticated animals were somewhat superior to yours. Eight tentacles would seem more efficient than two five-fingered limbs, such as yours possess."

Captain Hanford blinked.

"In fact," the Sirian continued, somewhat apologetically, "if you don't mind my saying so, your creatures are somewhat repulsive in appearance."

"I suppose we are used to them," Hanford replied, swallowing quickly.

Later, in the space ship, the ship's captain looked at his men indignantly. "Do you realize," he said, "that they think Gimmick is the leader of this expedition and that we're domesticated animals?"

Ensign Jones said happily, "Possibly you're right, Skipper, but they were certainly friendly enough. And they sure came through nicely on the uranium exchange deal. The government will be pleased as . . ."

Hanford insisted, "But do you realize what those Sirians would think if it came out that Gimmick was a pet? That we consider him an inferior life form?"

Lieutenant Grant was the first to comprehend. "It means," he said slowly, "that from now on, every time we come in contact with Sirians, a dog is going to have to be along. It means that every ship that comes for a load of pitchblende, is going to have to have several. We've got to continue pretending that the dog is Earth's dominant life form, and man his servant. Everytime we *talk* to a Sirian, we're going to have to pretend it's the dog *talking*."

"Holy Smokes," Jones said, "there aren't that many dogs left on Earth. We're going to have to start breeding them back as fast as we can."

The Captain looked down to where Gimmick, his red tongue out as he panted so that he looked as though he was grinning, lay on the floor.

"You son-of-a——" the Captain snapped at him.

But Gimmick's tail went left, right, left, right.

Doing Alien

Gregory Benford

I remember how Mitchell was putting the moves on some major league pussy when the news about the aliens came in.

That Mitchell, he stopped in mid-line and cocked his big square head and said kind of whispery, "Double dog damn." Then he went back to the little redhead he had settled onto the stool next to his, way down at the end of the mahogany bar at Nan's.

But I could tell he was distracted. He's the kind of fella always drawn to a touch of weirdness. At Mardi Gras he just loved the confusion, not being able to tell guys from gals, or who was what, the whole thing.

He left with the redhead before ten, which was pretty quick even for Mitchell. When he's headed for the sheets there isn't much can get in Mitchell's way. But he kept glancing over at the Alphas on the TV. Going out, he gave me the old salute and big smile but I could tell he was thinking off somewhere, not keeping his mind and his hands on the redhead. Which wasn't like him.

Mitchell's been my buddy since the earth's crust cooled off. I can read him pretty well. We graduated high school about the time the dinosaurs started up and went into farm equipment sales together when there were still a few nickels to make in that game. I've seen Mitchell bareass in the woods howling around a campfire, watched him pulling in six-foot tuna off the back of McKenzie's old boat, laughed when he was drunk up to his eyeballs with a big brassy broad on each arm and a shitass happy grin. For sure I know him better than any of his goddamn two ex-wives or his three kids. None of them'd recognize him on the street, pretty near.

So when the Alphas showed up right here in Fairhope I could tell right away that Mitchell took it funny. These Alphas come in slick as you please, special escort in limos and all. They go down to the wharf and look at the big new Civic Center and all, but nobody has a dime's worth of idea what they're here for.

Neither does the escort. Two suits on every Alpha, dark glasses and shoulder-slung pistols and earplug radios and the like. You could see it plain, the way their tight mouths twitched. They dunno from sour owl shit what to expect next.

For sure nobody thought they'd go into Nan's. Just clank on in, look around, babble that babble to each other, plunk down on those chrome stools.

Then they order up. Mitchell and me, we was at the other end of the bar. The Alphas, they are ordering up and putting them down pretty quick. Nobody knows their chemistry but they must like something in gimlets and fireballs and twofers, cause they sure squirt them in quick.

Pretty soon there's a crowd around them. The suits stand stiff as boards, but the locals ooze around them, curious. The Alphas don't pay any attention. Maybe they're used to it or maybe they don't even know people are there unless they need something. Way they act, you could believe that.

But Mitchell, he keeps eyeing them. Tries to talk to them. They don't pay him no never mind. Buys one a drink, even, but the Alpha won't touch it.

I could see it got to him. Not the first day maybe or the second. By the third, though, he was acting funny. Studying them. The Alphas would show up at Nan's, suck in plenty of the sauce, then blow out of town in those limos.

News people around, crowds waiting to see them, the whole goddamn shooting match. Made Fairhope hell to get around in.

I was gone three days to Birmingham on a commission job with International Harvester, so I didn't see what started him on it. I come into town all busted out from chasing tail in Birmingham and first thing you know, phone rings and Mitchell wants help.

"I'm in that beat up shack back of Leroy's TV," he said.

"That place's no biggern a coffin and smells worse."

"They spruced it up since Briggs run that poker game in here."

"So who you pokin there now?"

"Fred, if your dick fell off your I.Q. would be zero."

"That happen, what'd I need to think for?"

"Get your dumb ass over here."

So I did. Walk in on Mitchell in a chair, this brunette working on him. First I figured she was from over Bessie's, giving him a manicure with her kit all spread out. Turns out she's a makeup gal from clear over to New Orleans. Works Mardi Gras and like that.

Only she's not making Mitchell up to be a devil or in blackface or anything. This is serious. She's painting shellac all over him. He's already got a crust on him like dried mud in a hog wallow, only it's orange.

"Christ on a crutch," is all I can say.

"Mix me a bourbon and branch." Mitchell's voice came out muffled by all these pink pancake-size wattles on his throat, like some kind of rooster.

So I do. Only he doesn't like it, so he gets up and makes his own. "Got to add a twist sometimes," he says.

Mitchell was always picky about drinks. He used to make coffee for the boys, morning after a big carouse, and it had to be Colombian and ground just so and done up in this tricky filter rig he made himself out of tin sheeting.

That's how he was with this makeup girl, too. She layered on ridges of swarthy gum all down his arms, then shaped it with little whittling tools. She was sweating in that firebox shack. Mitchell was, too, under all the makeup.

I'm wondering what the hell, and Mitchell says, "Go take a squint, see if they're in Nan's yet."

So I'm catching on. Mitchell's always had something working on the side, see, but he takes his time about letting on. Kind of subtle, too. When Mr. Tang moved into Fairhope with his factory, Mitchell was real respectful and polite and called him Poon for a year before that Tang caught on.

As I go out the shack and down the alley I see why he used that place. I angle across Simpson's parking lot and down by those big air conditioners and pop out on Ivy right next to Nan's. That way, none of the suits can see you coming. Slip in the side door and sure as God's got a beard, there's three Alphas. Got a crowd around them but the room is dead quiet. People just looking and wondering and the aliens drinking.

I'd heard that plenty of fastlane operators were trying to get information out of Alphas, seeing as they got all this technology. We didn't even see them coming, that's how good their stuff is.

First thing anybody knew, they were bellying up to Venus, this other planet out there. Covered in clouds, it was. Then the Alphas start to work on her. First thing you know, you can see those volcanoes and valleys.

Anybody who can clear up muggy air like that inside a week, you got to pay attention. Turned out that was just cleaning off the work bench. Next they spun a kind of magnetic rod, rammed it in at the pole, clean down into the core of the whole damn planet. Easy as sticking an ice pick through an apple. Only the ice pick was hollow and they sucked the liquid metal out of there. Up the rod like it was a straw, and out into space. To make those metal city kind of things, huge and all.

That's when people started getting really afraid. And some others got really interested. The way they figured, any little scrappy thing you got from an Alpha might just be a billion-buck trick.

That's the scoop I heard on CNN coming down from Birmingham, anyway. Now here was the whole circus in Fairhope, big as life and twice as ugly. Snoops with those directional microphones. Cameras in the backs of vans, shooting out through dark windows. Guys in three-piece suits kind of casual slouched against the bar and trying to get an Alpha to notice them.

So back I go. Mitchell is getting some inflated bags stuck on him by the makeup girl. Bags all over his back and chest and neck even. He's all the Alpha colors now, from Georgia clay red here to sky blue there.

"Three of 'em sucking it up in there," I said.

"Holy shit, let's go," Mitchell croaks back at me. The girl had fitted him out with this voicebox thing, made him sound like a frog at the bottom of a rain barrel.

The girl pats him all over with that fine, rusty dust the Alphas are always shedding. She straightens the pouches so you can hardly see that his arms are too short for an Alpha.

"Let's make tracks," Mitchell says, and proceeds to do just that. Alpha tracks, fat and seven-toed.

We go across the parking lot, so the escorts can't see. In a minute we're in Nan's. The other Alphas don't take any notice of Mitchell but all the people do. They move out of the way fast and we parade in, me a little behind so it'll seem like I was just a tourist. Mitchell's got the Alpha shuffle down just right, to my eye.

Bold as brass, he sits down. The suits look at each other, dunno what to do. But they buy it, that Mitchell's one of them.

The Alphas still don't notice him. Bartender asks and Mitchell orders, making a kind of slithery noise.

He slurps down two drinks before anything happens. An Alpha makes a gesture with that nose thing of theirs and Mitchell does, too. Then there's some more gesturing and they talk like wet things moving inside a bag.

I sit and listen but I can't make sense out of any of it. Mitchell seems to know what he's doing. He keeps it up for maybe five more minutes. I can see it's wearing on him. He gives me the signal.

I clear some space for him so he can get back up—that crap he was wearing weighs real considerable. He gets up smooth and shuffles some and then we're out the door. Free and clean. We got back to the shack before we let go with the whooping and hollering.

We pull it off four more times in the next three weeks. Each time the Alphas take more notice of Mitchell. Hard to know what they think of him. The girl comes over from New Orleans and does him up, getting better each time. I keep an ear open for word on the street and it's all good.

Or seems so to me, anyway. Everybody thinks Mitchell's the real thing. Course that's people talking, not Alphas. After the fourth time I couldn't hold back anymore. "You got some money angle on this, right?"

"Money?"

"What I want to know is, how you going to get anything out of them?"

"I'm not in for money."

"You figure maybe you can get one of those little tool kits they carry? They don't look hooked on real firm or anything."

Mitchell grinned. "Wouldn't try that, if I was you. Fella in Cincinnati went to lift one, came up an arm short."

"Then what the hell you in for?"

Mitchell gave me this funny look. "Cause it's *them*."

I blinked. "So goddamn what?"

"You don't get it, Fred. Thing about aliens is, they're alien." In his eyes there's this look. Like he was seeing something different, something important, something way bigger than Fairhope.

I couldn't make any more sense out of what he said after that.

That's when I realized. Mitchell just wanted to be close to them, was all.

That pretty well took the wind out of my sails. I'd figured Mitchell was onto something for sure. I went with him one more time, that's all. And a few days later I heard that the same Alpha was coming back to Nan's every day, just sitting and waiting for more Alphas to come in, and hanging out with them when they did.

It went that way for a while and I was feeling pretty sour about it. I went on a carouse with the Perlotti brothers and had me a pretty fair time. Next morning I was lying in bed with a head that barely fit in the room and in walks Mitchell. "Heard you maybe needed some revivin' from last night."

He was grinning and I was glad to see him even if he did waste a slab of my time. We'd do little things like that for each other sometimes, bring a fella a drink or a hundred dollar bill when he was down and could sure use it. So I crawled up out of bed and pulled on some jeans and went into the kitchen.

Mitchell was filling a pot and popping open one of his Colombian coffee packs. I got some cups and we watched the water boil without saying anything. That's when it happened.

Mitchell was fooling with the coffee and I was still pretty bleary-eyed, so I'm not sure just exactly what I saw. Mitchell was stirring the coffee and he turned to me. "Ummm. Smell those enzymes."

He said it perfectly natural and I wouldn't have taken much notice of the funny word. I looked it up later at the library and it's a chemical term, I forget what it means. Mitchell would never have said something like that. And I wouldn't have given it any mind, except that just then his arm stuck a little farther out of the denim work shirt he had on. He has big arms and thick wrists. As the shirt slid up I saw the skin and curly hair and then something else.

At first I thought it was leather. Then it seemed like cloth, real old fabric, wrinkled and coarse. Mitchell turned further and looked at me and that's when I heard the sound of him moving. It was like dry leaves rustling. Old and blowing in a wind. In the next second I caught a whiff of it and the worse smell I ever knew came swarming up into my head and I finally really saw what the thing next to me was.

I don't want to describe that. It sent me banging back against the plywood wall of the kitchen and then out the door. The smell stayed with me somehow even in the open. I was off into the pines way back of my place before I knew it.

I had the shakes for hours. Made myself circle around for three miles. Got to my sister's place. Didn't tell her anything about it but I think she might of guessed. I was pale and woozy.

I got my truck and went off to Pensacola for a week. There was maybe some work there but it didn't pan out and I hadn't gone for that anyway.

I didn't go back into my place for another week. And I was real careful when I did.

It was all picked up, neat as you please. Not a sign. Mitchell was a fine man but he would never have done that.

I stood in the kitchen and tried to work out what had happened, how it had been. Couldn't. There was that one second when I saw straight into whatever was there and being Mitchell, and that was all.

He had tried to blend in with them. And I'd helped him. So in some way maybe this was the reverse. Or a pay back, kind of. Or maybe a signal or something. No way to tell.

Only, you know what I think? I figure there isn't any Mitchell anymore. There's something else.

Now, could be there's still some Mitchell in there, only he can't get out. Or maybe that thing's Alpha for sure. I guess it could be something in between. Only thing I know is, it isn't anything I ever want to know.

Maybe it's something I *can't* know. Thing about aliens is, they're alien.

They say that one Alpha still hangs out at Nan's. I haven't been to check. I don't even walk down that part of town anymore.

Down the Digestive Tract and into the Cosmos with Mantra, Tantra, and Specklebang

Robert Sheckley

But will I really have hallucinations?" Gregory asked.

"Like I said, I guarantee it," Blake answered. "You should be into something by now."

Gregory looked around. The room was dismayingly, tediously familiar: narrow blue bed, walnut dresser, marble table with wrought-iron base, double-headed lamp, turkey-red rug, beige television set. He was sitting in an upholstered armchair. Across from him, on a white plastic couch, was Blake, pale and plump, poking at three speckled irregularly shaped tablets.

"I mean to say," Blake said, "that there's all sorts of acid going around—tabs, strips, blotters, dots, most of it cut with speed and some of it cut with Drano. But lucky you have just ingested old Doc Blake's special tantric mantric instant freakout special superacid cocktail, known to the carriage trade as Specklebang, and containing absolutely simon-pure LSD-25, plus carefully calculated additives of STP, DMT, and THC, plus a smidgen of Yage, a touch of psilocybin, and the merest hint of oloiuqui; *plus* Doc Blake's own special ingredient—extract of foxberry, newest and most potent of the hallucinogenic potentiators."

Gregory was staring at his right hand, slowly clenching and unclenching it.

"The result," Blake went on, "is Doc Blake's total instantaneous many-splendored acid delight, guaranteed to make you hallucinate on the quarter-hour at least, or I return your money and give up my credentials as the best free-lance underground chemist ever to hit the West Village."

"You sound like you're stoned," Gregory said.

"Not at all," Blake protested. "I am merely on speed, just simple, old-fashioned amphetamines such as truck drivers and high school students swallow by the pound and shoot by the gallon. Speed is nothing more than a stimulant. With its assistance I can do my thing faster and better. My thing is to create my own quickie drug empire between Houston and 14th Street, and then bail out quickly, before I burn out my nerves or get crunched by the narcs or the Mafia, and *then* split for Switzerland where I will freak out in a splendid sanitorium surrounded by gaudy women, plump bank accounts, fast cars, and the respect of the local politicos."

Blake paused for a moment and rubbed his upper lip. "Speed *does* bring on a certain sense of grandiloquence, with accompanying verbosity . . . But never fear, my dear newly met friend and esteemed customer, my senses are more or less unimpaired and I am fully capable of acting as your guide for the superjumbotripout upon which you are now embarked."

"How long since I took that tablet?" Gregory asked.

Blake looked at his watch. "Over an hour ago."

"Shouldn't it be acting by now?"

"It should indeed. It undoubtedly is. *Something* should be happening."

Gregory looked around. He saw the grass-lined pit, the pulsing glowworm, the hard-packed mica, the captive cricket. He was on the side of the pit nearest to the drain pipe. Across from him, on the mossy gray stone, was Blake, his cilia matted and his exoderm mottled, poking at three speckled irregularly shaped tablets.

"What's the matter?" Blake asked.

Gregory scratched the tough membrane over his thorax. His cilia waved spasmodically in clear evidence of amazement, dismay, perhaps even fright. He extended a feeler, looked at it long and hard, bent it double and straightened it again.

Blake's antennae pointed straight up in a gesture of concern. "Hey, baby, speak to me! Are you hallucinating?"

Gregory made an indeterminate movement with his tail. "It started just before, when I asked you if I'd really have any hallucinations. I was into it then but I didn't realize it, everything seemed so natural, so ordinary . . . I was sitting on a *chair,* and you were on a *couch,* and we both had soft exoskeletons like—like mammals!"

"The shift into illusion is often imperceptible," Blake said. "One slides into them and out of them. What's happening now?"

Gregory coiled his segmented tail and relaxed his antennae. He looked around. The pit was dismayingly, tediously familiar. "Oh,

I'm back to normal now. Do you think I'm going to have any more hallucinations?"

"Like I told you, I guarantee it," Blake said, neatly folding his glossy red wings and settling comfortably into a corner of the nest.

Dry Spell

Bill Pronzini

*T*he bane of all writers, John Kensington thought glumly, whether they be poor and struggling or whether they be rich and famous, is the protracted dry spell.

He sat staring at the blank sheet of yellow foolscap in his typewriter. His mind was as blank as that paper. Not a single idea, not a single line of writing that even remotely reached coherency in almost three weeks.

Sighing, Kensington pushed back his chair and got on his feet. He went to the small refrigerator in the kitchenette, opened his last can of beer, and took it to the old Morris chair that reposed near his desk.

I've got to come up with something, he thought. *The rent's due in another week, and if I don't get something down on that grocery bill I can forget about eating for a while.*

He sipped his beer, closing his eyes. *Come on, son,* he thought. *Just an idea, just one little idea . . .*

He let his mind wander. It seemed, however, to be wandering in circles. Nothing. Not even . . .

Wait a minute.

Now wait just a single damned minute here.

The germ of something touched a remote corner of his brain. It was a mere fragment, evanescent, but he seized it the way a man dying of thirst would seize a dipper of water.

Grimly, he hung on. The fragment remained. Slowly, inexorably, it began to blossom.

Kensington sat bolt upright in the chair, his eyes wide open now, the beer forgotten. His fingertips tingled with excitement. The coming of the idea was a catharsis, releasing the tension which had been building within him for the past three weeks.

It would be a science fiction/fantasy story, he thought, probably a novella if he worked it properly. He moistened his lips. *Now, let's see . . .*

Suppose there's this race of aliens plotting to take over Earth, because it is a strategic planet in some kind of inter-galactic war they're involved in. Okay, okay, so it's hackneyed. There are ways to get around that, ways to play that aspect down.

These aliens have infiltrated Earth and set up some kind of base of operations, maybe up in the mountains somewhere. They're assembling a kind of penultimate cybernetic machine which, when fully completed, will have the power to erase all rational thought from the minds of humans, turning them into obsequious zombies. Wait now. Suppose these aliens have a portion of this machine already completed. This portion would be capable of reading, simultaneously, the thoughts of every human on Earth, and of categorizing those thoughts for the aliens to study. That way, if any human somehow happened to blunder on the scheme in one way or another—mental blundering as well as physical would have to be considered, what with clairvoyance and the emanation into space of thought waves, and the like—then the extraterrestrials would immediately know about it. And what they would do would be to train the full strength of this completed portion of the machine on that particular human, and with it eradicate all those thoughts endangering their project, thus ensuring its safety.

Kensington was sweating a bit now, his forehead crinkled in deep thought.

Sure, he thought, *it's a touch far out. But if I handle it right, who knows? At least it's a good, workable idea, which is a hell of a lot better than nothing at all. Now, how am I going to save Earth from this fate? It has to be in some way that is totally plausible, not too gimmicky, and . . .*

All at once the answer popped into his mind. *By God!* Kensington thought. *It's perfect! There's not a flaw in it!* He grinned hugely. *Those damned aliens wouldn't stand a snowball's chance in you-know-where if I set it up this way.*

He stood abruptly and started for his typewriter. The progression of the story was already flowing, plotting itself firmly in Kensington's mind.

He sat at the typewriter, excitement coursing through him because he knew, he could feel, that the dry spell was at an end. His fingers poised over the keys.

Quite suddenly, quite inexplicably, his mind went blank.

He pressed his forehead against the cool surface of his typewriter.

Why, he moaned silently, *why, oh, why can't I come up with just one little story idea?*

Dueling Clowns

Barry Longyear

Lord Allenby raised his eyebrows at the newsteller's apprentice, but the apprentice only shrugged. Allenby looked back at the master newsteller. His eyes fixed on the fire, Boosthit sat crosslegged, elbows on his knees, chin on his hands and a black scowl on his face. "Come, come, Boosthit. I've known you too long for this." The newsteller sat unmoving.

The apprentice scratched his head. "It's no use, Lord Allenby. He's been that way for a week."

Allenby shrugged. "I came by this fire and saw my old friend and expected to have grand times getting reacquainted. When I first came to Momus as the ambassador to the Ninth Quadrant, it was Boosthit who took news of my mission and played it in Tarzak."

The apprentice nodded. "He won't even talk to me."

Allenby looked closely at the apprentice. "You're one of the Montagne soldiers, aren't you?"

"Yes. In a year I'll be taking my retirement here on Momus. I'm on leave now looking into newstelling as an occupation for when I get out."

"Your name?"

"Forgive me. Sergeant Major Gaddis; I'm top soldier at orbital fighter base twenty-six."

Allenby nodded. "I'm pleased to meet you, Sergeant Major. Has newstelling been to your liking?"

The apprentice turned toward Boosthit, shook his head and turned back to Allenby. "I have no idea, Lord Allenby. I've been with him for a week, but I haven't heard any news yet."

Allenby looked at Boosthit. "Come, old friend, you haven't hit a dry spell, have you?" Boosthit's scowl deepened. "Why, there's news of galactic significance transpiring this very moment, with the commission from the United Quadrants coming to Momus. Then, there's the military buildup of the Tenth Quadrant forces to counter the Ninth's defense of this planet, and the ambassador from the Tenth Quadrant will be here in a few days to present his credentials; even my own office as statesman of Momus is in doubt. The UQ Commission will rule—"

Boosthit held up his hands. "Still yourself, Allenby; I have news!"

The sergeant major applauded. "Congratulations. That's more than I've heard him say for the entire week."

Boosthit glowered at the apprentice, then aimed his expression at Allenby. "As I said, I have news. I do not choose to recite it."

Allenby smiled and nodded his head. "That bad, is it? I understand—"

"It is the best news I have ever had; it is great news! And, you would *not* understand!"

"Dear friend," Allenby held up his hands in a gesture of peace, "we have been through and seen much together over the past six years. You think I would lack understanding, or not appreciate great news?"

"It is what I think."

"What caused this? A newsteller with great news refusing to recite it? Do you think I wouldn't pay?"

Boosthit stood, walked to the boulders outside the light of the fire, then returned and sat down. He lifted an eyebrow in Allenby's direction. "You really want to hear my news?"

"Of course. I also want you to explain your strange behavior."

Boosthit pursed his lips, then nodded. "Very well. First, I shall tell you why I am reluctant." He turned to the sergeant major. "I recited my news to others such as this one, and I was treated very badly."

Allenby frowned. "You mean, to soldiers?"

"They were apprenticed, as this one is, but they were soldiers, yes."

Allenby turned to Gaddis. "The rules for visiting planetside are being observed, aren't they?"

"Yes, Lord Allenby. We are all familiarized with customs, traditions and occupations. When I am on duty, that training is part of my responsibility."

Allenby rubbed his chin and turned back to the newsteller. "Tell me what happened, Boosthit."

Boosthit gave the apprentice a suspicious glance, then held up his hands. "Very well. It happened at the first fire from Tarzak several days ago. I had rehearsed my news, and was anxious to take it on the road. As I said, it is great news."

"As you said."

Boosthit shrugged. "I approached the fire in the evening, and heard laughter coming from behind the rocks. I thought to myself that this was a lucky stroke, having a good audience my first night. But, when I stepped through the boulders, I saw that they were soldiers."

"You said they were apprenticed; how did you know they were soldiers?"

"They wear their robes badly, and sit funny." Boosthit cocked his head toward his apprentice. Gaddis had his knees together and sat back on his legs.

Gaddis shrugged. "It takes time to get used to going without trousers."

Allenby nodded. "I remember. Go on, Boosthit."

"Well, I turned to go, but they made such a fuss about me staying, that I changed my mind. That meant, of course, sitting through all of their amateur acts, but, I thought, business is business. I stayed. There was a priest's apprentice, and apprentices representing storytellers, tumblers, knife-throwers, and even one representing your own magicians, Allenby.

"After we bargained and ate, the first to rise was the apprentice priest. He did an almost acceptable job of reciting the epic of the circus ship *Baraboo* that brought our ancestors to Momus. Reluctantly, I parted with two movills for the fellow's performance, thinking to collect twenty times that amount after I dazzled those apprentices with my news.

"Then, the knife-thrower did a few turns on a piece of board he carried with him, but the act was of no consequence since he had no one standing in front of the board. Nevertheless, I parted with another two movills. Let it suffice to say that the tumblers and the magician were of similar quality. I could hardly keep my eyes open.

"Then, may his master's throat turn to stone, the apprentice storyteller began. He went on and on about a boy in a strange land named Pittsburgh, and I could find no start nor middle to the tale. I recognized the ending because he stopped talking and another movill left my purse. But, then," a strange fire lit behind the newsteller's eyes as he stared off in a trance, "then, my turn came. I looked among their faces, and began:

"I, Boosthit of the Faransetti newstellers, sit before the fire this evening to tell you of the great duel between Kamera, Master of the Tarzak clowns, and Spaht, new Master of Clowns from Kuumic. It is news of heroics; a defense of the mighty being attacked by a hungry jackal. I, Boosthit, was witness to this event.

"Four days ago, I sat at the table of the Great Kamera, exchanging my news for entertainment, when the curtain to the street opened. Standing in the doorway was Spaht, garbed in yellow trousers with black polka dots, a vest of green and white stripes over a naked torso. On his bare neck, he wore a collar and bow tie. He wore white grease paint with red nose and upturned lips, the entire effect being capped with an orange fright wig and derby. He bowed to Kamera and said, 'Now is the time, Kamera; be on the street in five minutes.'

"Kamera laughed. 'Fool, I cannot be bothered with challenges from every apprentice that passes by my door.'

" 'Apprentice? I am Spaht, Master of the Kuumic clowns!'

"Kamera waved an idle hand in the direction of the door. 'In that case, out damned Spaht! Out, I say!'

"Spaht bowed. 'I see I have entered the wrong house and found only great chimera.'

"Kamera squinted his eyes. 'Leave me. I shall be out as you requested.' Spaht bowed again, then left. In the quiet room, I saw the great clown sigh and reach under his table for his paints. His face was very sad.

" 'Surely, Great Kamera,' I said, 'this upstart does not worry you?'

"Kamera adjusted a looking glass and began putting on his makeup. 'Boosthit, it is ever thus for the greatest clown on Momus. Always there is another young punslinger lurking in the corners, waiting to build a reputation. It is not an easy life.'

"Kamera finished his makeup and put on a pure white suit, with large pompoms down the front. On his hairless head, he placed a white peaked cone. As he put on white slippers, I could see the frown under the painted smile.

" 'Spaht is different from the usual run of challenger, Great Kamera, isn't he?'

"He nodded. 'You saw what he was wearing. That garish costume, and the bow tie—he winds it up and it spins! Spaht has no sense of tradition; no honor. On the street this day, anything can be expected.'

"The two clowns squared off in the center of the dusty street. Warily, they circled each other, then Spaht opened. 'My uncle, a tailor, once made a magician very angry by making him a shirt that didn't fit.'

" 'Put him in a bad choler, did he?'

" 'Aye, and he turned my uncle into a tree.'

"All could see Kamera struggling, but he had no choice but to feed Spaht the straight line. 'Did it bother your uncle?'

" 'He didn't say; he was board.'

" 'Knot he!'

" 'But I avenged my uncle by thrashing the magician and throwing the rude fellow at my uncle's wooden feet.'

" 'That was casting churl before pine.'

"As the dust cleared from the opening exchange, the two each had the other's measure. Kamera circled to get the sun out of his eyes. Spaht had a look of confidence on his face.

" 'Did you know,' said Spaht, 'that my nephew is related to the tiny flying cave creatures?'

" 'Yes, Spaht, I know. I stepped on one once and heard your nephew say, "Oh, my akin bat!" '

"The crowd moaned. Cued by this, Spaht returned. 'Why should the clowns pay homage to you, Kamera? It seems that you are in your anecdotage.'

"Kamera smiled. 'Obeisance make the heart grow fonder.'

"Staggered, Spaht circled and began spinning his bow tie. 'My uncle, the tree . . . ,' he began.

" 'I saw him the other day, Spaht. I said, "That's yew all over." '

" 'We were so poor that at his funeral we could afford no music. All you could hear was the coughing—'

" 'There was catarrh playing, then?'

" 'Well, there was a coffin.' Spaht tried to rally, but Kamera scented blood. 'My . . . nephew lost consciousness and fell into a vat of stain. . . .'

" 'The good dye stunned.' Spaht fell to all fours and began crawling out of town. A cheer erupted from the crowd, and Kamera followed the beaten clown down the street. 'Crawl in a straight line, Spaht, or you will get contusions of meander. . . .' "

Boosthit looked down to deliver the punchline at Allenby, but the Great Statesman of Momus was gone. ". . . he . . ." He turned and found Gaddis missing as well. Rushing between the boulders, he could see two dark shapes running together toward Tarzak.

"Strange," said the newsteller, rubbing his chin, "if Allenby knew what the soldiers did, why did he ask?"

Emergency Refueling

James Blish

That's the last," growled pilot Stan Dorry, exhibiting the almost empty lead box. His red-haired navigator peered in at the gray handful of powdery metal huddled dispiritedly in the bottom.

"Well, put it in. We could coast and save this for landing, but we'd hit Jupiter sometime early next century at our present speed." (The red-haired Whipple had the gift of gab.) "We'll take the chance on getting enough fuel on Pluto to take us in."

Dorry shoveled the metal into the tube and closed the breechblock, and together they walked back to the control room. Their thoughts revolved in the same groove. Refueling on Pluto. It was beset with entirely unknown dangers, and illegal as well.

They had been driving in from an interesting-looking asteroid calculated to be twenty million miles beyond the orbit of Pluto. When it turned out to be twenty-five there was nothing they could do about it, and to cap the climax the forty-mile chunk of rock was just that, containing just enough scattered bits of nickel to attract the detectors. Now they had just enough fuel to land them on Pluto—and the nearest fueling station was on Ganymede.

There was plenty of fuel on Pluto—that was an established fact. The whole planet seemed radioactive. First of the planets to be thrown from the sun, it was also one of the densest, and the rocks were full of pitchblende. Their little prospector ran on proactinium, but most good motors would burn ore for a limited length of time. Yes, Pluto was an ideal coaling station—

If it weren't for the fact that the IPF had put an iron-bound taboo on the planet. It had never been satisfactorily explored, since prolonged exposure to the lethal radiations, even in heavy armor, was fatal. Perfunctory charting had been undertaken from the air, hampered by the fact that photography was impossible because of the blurring effects of the radiation on film, and, while it was unthinkable that life could exist under such conditions, the IPF didn't like to take chances. Too many space tramps had landed and never taken off.

Consequently there were ten ships circling the planet constantly, detectors overlapping, and one hundred and twenty superbly bored IP-men longing for some ship to try and break through.

Dorry charged the batteries for five minutes, muttering at the fuel consumption involved, and sent out a call. The response was immediate.

"Okay, *Pallas*," snapped the speaker briskly. "We heard your engines half an hour ago. What's wrong with your screen?"

"Nothing," returned Dorry. "We haven't enough fuel to spare. That's what we called about—"

"Turn it on," barked the voice suspiciously.

"We haven't the fuel, I tell you—"

"Turn it ON!"

Dorry resignedly clicked the switch, and a young and irritated face appeared, wearing a cap a little large for it.

"Satisfied?"

"All right, you can turn it off now. What's the trouble with your fuel?"

"Not enough," Dorry repeated. "We want permission to land on Pluto."

"You can't have it, as you ought to know."

"We'll be a floating coffin in no time at all if we don't."

"Can't you reach Ganymede?"

Whipple made a wry face as Dorry answered, "Why the hell do you think we were scraping the power for the screen?"

"Eh. There are ten patrol ships here—you might get a little from each—"

"The amount we'd get that way would just about equal the expenditure in stopping at each one. Use your head."

There was a brief silence, then a series of high keening notes as if consultation was being made with the other ships.

"We can give you fifteen minutes and no more, and in a region designated by us."

"Good," said Whipple heartily. "Where?"

"In Quadrant—eh—Quadrant Three, section ten. There's a

rocky plain there that ought to make a fair landing field, and nearby a set of caves where the deposits are better than usual." The captain seemed to be reading from Sir Christopher Barclay's *Space Manual*. "Get your material from near the mouth of the northmost cave, and do not under any conditions go any farther. There've been twenty tramps like you lost in there, and twice that many IPs looking for them, too."

"Right." The radio went off. "Three minutes. Two minutes extra fuel wasted. Oh, well, no need to worry."

They burned all their fuel in landing, but they felt almost carefree about it now. The field was indeed rocky. In general, however, it was no worse than most of the planetoids at which the *Pallas* had stopped, and they found a prime spot not thirty yards from the cave selected.

"Lead suits?"

"We'll have to make these do. If we're lucky the exposure should be only a few minutes, and any burns we get over that time we can treat easily. Besides, there's the cosmic ray insulation."

They struggled into their spacesuits, charging the batteries from the dregs in the radio. The ground beneath their feet looked like any other ground, although the pair realized that it was at a constant temperature above body heat. The mouth of the cave seemed to be faintly lit with a glow from farther down.

"Like the doorway to hell," crackled Dorry's radio. "Let's go, Jack. Got the pick?"

"Sure 'nuff." They crunched across the rocks and paused at the opening. "Wonder what's here that swallowed sixty men?"

"God knows. It couldn't be anything alive, that's a cinch. Cave-ins, maybe." They entered cautiously, both nervous, and both determined not to show it to the other.

"Saaay," whistled Dorry. "This is good. Look—there's no ore like that on Earth."

"No. It gets better as you go along." Whipple stepped ahead and disappeared around the bend. Dorry heard his gasp. "Cripes, come here."

"What is it, Jack . . . well, I'll be. . . ." They stood like barbaric statues hacked crudely from metal and gazed down the long slanting passage, which was glowing, at first faintly, then as it progressed more and more brightly.

"You know, I'll bet if we got down there, where the bend is, we'd have practically the pure stuff. Well, not quite, but damn good, anyhow, if the vein holds true."

Dorry shook his head. "The IP-men'd say naughty, naughty. Besides, if we stayed long in that stuff it'd be no minor burns we'd have."

"Yeh . . . Lord, though, what a range it would give us. Even with what we hack out here, we'll have to be careful if we're to make Ganymede. Down there we could get more than enough."

Dorry considered that. "You're right, I suppose. If we make it quick, the IPs won't know the difference."

As if he were afraid of a change of heart, Whipple bounded ahead. "Take it easy, Jack," remonstrated the pilot.

"I'm all right. Come along. The light is almost bright down here—and will you look at it pour around the bend! It isn't coming from here though. . . ."

The light was streaming from a small opening which apparently led to a larger cave. It did not flicker as this in the passage did, but burst in a steady, blue-white stream upon them.

"That's the place," said Whipple with conviction. "A few seconds is all we'll need—anyhow the cosmic ray insulation in the suits should hold us for some time." He could not know that it had burned out long ago, for he could not see the bright sympathetic brilliance of his watch-face. He strode into the opening, the pilot on his heels.

The light blinded them temporarily. It came from everywhere, the walls, the floor, the ceiling. Apparently they were in the very heart of a vein, a rich layer of some strange radium isotope.

The glare was blue-white, almost solid in its intensity. Gradually they got used to it.

"What's that?"

"I don't know," said Whipple, blinking. "I'm still half-blind. All I can see is a splotch. There—hey—!"

"Jack . . . I think it's . . . alive." They stared in unison at the fungus-like object. Even as they watched it bloated to a size of eight inches, collapsed, emitting a small cloud of spores.

Tiny blue splotches appeared on the walls and floor, swelling. . . .

"Life-cycle a million times accelerated by the radiation," whispered Dorry with a dry throat. "I wouldn't have believed it."

As their eyes became used to the light they saw others of the rubbery things, which moved slowly about as they went through their instantaneous life-time. The cave seemed enormous, stretching downward in a blue effulgency beyond the limit of their watering eyes. Their radios began to crackle a little.

"No time for gaping," the navigator jerked abruptly. "Come on, Stan. There's a big outcropping we can hack off whole, down just a little to the right."

"I can't hear you very well," complained Dorry. "There's a whale of a lot of static here."

"Yeh—that's funny, we should have heard it up above—I say IT WASN'T HERE BEFORE!" he shouted as Dorry shook his head. The crackling uproar grew startlingly to a deafening pitch, seemed about to die away, then sprang up again. They plodded wordlessly down toward the outcropping, and as they went the static became so violent they were forced to turn the radios off. The immediate silence was worse on Whipple's nerves, and he turned the switch again to low power. A voice rang in his ears.

"Stan, Stan," he screeched. "It isn't static, it's a carrier-wave—telepathic—" Dorry moved deafly on toward the glowing, jutting stone. The voice echoed in Whipple's brain.

"Dead metal," it called. "I sense dead metal."

A subtle change became apparent—another voice? Whipple could not tell. "Another vibration," it said. "A speech radiation and a life force very weak. Do you not feel it?" The voices seemed to become louder. Whipple grabbed his companion and gestured frantically at the radio switch.

The other clicked it over to full, then off again with a despairing wave, made so clumsy by the suit that it looked almost threatening. Whipple seized the switch himself and turned it to low power.

"Very close, yes," said the mental voice. "Near the entrance."

"Let's get out of here," Dorry howled futilely, and jumped for the outcropping, pick raised high. There was a burst of light brighter than all the rest, and Whipple's radio speaker tore resoundingly across. He was deafened achingly. Ahead, the pilot stood in the center of a seven-foot, blue-white flame, and his suit turned very slowly red, then yellow. . . . Other flames shot silently through the glaring, low-roofed space below—

Whipple ran madly, crashing with insensate violence against the walls.

Outside he paused at the airlock. Dorry—dead, roasted. But fuel—

No more of the caves. He seized an armful of the nearest rubble and tumbled into the *Pallas*. Behind, the glow in the mouth of the abyss wavered and sank a little.

Eripmav

Damon Knight

On the planet Veegl, in the Fomalhaut system, we found a curious race of cellulose vampires. The Veeglians, like all higher life on their world, are plants; the Veeglian vampire, needless to say, is a sapsucker.

One of the native clerks in our trade mission, a plant-girl named Xixl, had been complaining of lassitude and showing an unhealthy pink color for some weeks. The girl's parent stock suspected vampirism; we were skeptical, but had to admit that the two green-tinged punctures at the base of her axis were evidence of something wrong.

Accordingly, we kept watch over her sleep-box for three nights running. (The Veeglians sleep in boxes of soil, built of heavy slabs of the hardmeat tree, or *woogl;* they look rather like coffins.) On the third night, sure enough, a translator named Ffengl, a hefty, blue-petaled fellow, crept into her room and bent over the sleep-box.

We rushed out at the blackguard, but he turned quick as a wink and fairly flew up the whitemeat stairs. (The flesh of Veegl's only animal life, the "meat-trees," or *oogl,* petrifies rapidly in air and is much used for construction.) We found him in an unsuspected vault at the very top of the old building, trying to hide under the covers of an antique burial bed. It was an eery business. We sizzled him with blasts from our proton guns, and yet to the end, with unVeeglian vitality, he was struggling to reach us with his tendrils.

Afterward he seemed dead enough, but the local wise-heads advised us to take certain precautions.

So we buried him with a steak through his heart.

Evensong

Lester del Rey

By the time he reached the surface of the little planet, even the dregs of his power were drained. Now he rested, drawing reluctant strength slowly from the yellow sun that shone on the greensward around him. His senses were dim with an ultimate fatigue, but the fear he had learned from the Usurpers drove them outward, seeking a further hint of sanctuary.

It was a peaceful world, he realized, and the fear thickened in him at the discovery. In his younger days, he had cherished a multitude of worlds where the game of life's ebb and flow could be played to the hilt. It had been a lusty universe to roam then. But the Usurpers could brook no rivals to their own outreaching lust. The very peace and order here meant that this world had once been theirs.

He tested for them gingerly while the merest whisper of strength poured into him. None were here now. He could have sensed the pressure of their close presence at once, and there was no trace of that. The even grassland swept in rolling meadows and swales to the distant hills. There were marble structures in the distance, sparkling whitely in the late sunlight, but they were empty, their unknown purpose altered to no more than decoration now upon this abandoned planet. His attention swept back, across a stream to the other side of the wide valley.

There he found the garden. Within low walls, its miles of expanse were a tree-crowded and apparently untended preserve. He could sense the stirring of larger animal life among the branches and along the winding paths. The brawling vigor of all proper life was missing, but its abundance might be enough to mask his own vestige of living force from more than careful search.

It was at least a better refuge than this open greensward and he longed toward it, but the danger of betraying motion held him still where he was. He had thought his previous escape to be assured, but he was learning that even he could err. Now he waited while he tested once more for evidence of Usurper trap.

He had mastered patience in the confinement the Usurpers had designed at the center of the galaxy. He had gathered his power furtively while he designed escape around their reluctance to make final disposition. Then he had burst outward in a drive that should have thrust him far beyond the limits of their hold on the universe. And he had found failure before he could span even the distance to the end of this spiral arm of one galactic fastness.

Their webs of detection were everywhere, seemingly. Their great power-robbing lines made a net too fine to pass. Stars and worlds were linked, until only a series of miracles had carried him this far. And now the waste of power for such miracles was no longer within his reach. Since their near failure in entrapping and sequestering him, they had learned too much.

Now he searched delicately, afraid to trip some alarm, but more afraid to miss its existence. From space, this world had offered the only hope in its seeming freedom from their webs. But only microseconds had been available to him for his testing then.

At last he drew his perceptions back. He could find no slightest evidence of their lures and detectors here. He had begun to suspect that even his best efforts might not be enough now, but he could do no more. Slowly at first, and then in a sudden rush, he hurled himself into the maze of the garden.

Nothing struck from the skies. Nothing leaped upwards from the planet core to halt him. There was no interruption in the rustling of the leaves and the chirping bird songs. The animal sounds went on unhindered. Nothing seemed aware of his presence in the garden. Once that would have been unthinkable in itself, but now he drew comfort from it. He must be only a shadow self now, unknown and unknowable in his passing.

Something came down the path where he rested, pattering along on hoofs that touched lightly on the spoilage of fallen leaves. Something else leaped quickly through the light underbrush beside him.

One was a rabbit, nibbling now at the leaves of clover and twitching long ears as its pink nose stretched out for more. The other was a young deer, still bearing the spots of its fawnhood. Either or both might have seemingly been found on any of a thousand worlds. But neither would have been precisely of the type before him.

This was the Meeting World—the planet where he had first found the ancestors of the Usurpers. Of all worlds in the pested galaxy, it had to be *this* world he sought for refuge!

They were savages back in the days of his full glory, confined to this single world, rutting and driving their way to the lawful self-destruction of all such savages. And yet there had been something odd about them, something that then drew his attention and even his vagrant pity.

Out of that pity, he had taught a few of them, and led them upwards. He had even nursed poetic fancies of making them his companions and his equals as the life span of their sun should near its ending. He had answered their cries for help and given them at least some of what they needed to set their steps toward power over even space and energy. And they had rewarded him by overweening pride that denied even a trace of gratitude. He had abandoned them finally to their own savage ends and gone on to other worlds, to play out the purposes of a wider range.

It was his second folly. They were too far along the path toward unlocking the laws behind the universe. Somehow, they even avoided their own destruction from themselves. They took the worlds of their sun and drove outwards, until they could even vie with him for the worlds he had made particularly his own. And now they owned them all, and he had only a tiny spot here on their world—for a time a least.

The horror of the realization that this was the Meeting World abated a little as he remembered now how readily their spawning hordes possessed and abandoned worlds without seeming end. And again the tests he could make showed no evidence of them here. He began to relax again, feeling a sudden hope from what had been temporary despair. Surely they might also believe this was the one planet where he would never seek sanctuary.

Now he set his fears aside and began to force his thoughts toward the only pattern that could offer hope. He needed power, and power was available in any area untouched by the webs of the Usurpers. It had drained into space itself throughout the aeons, a waste of energy that could blast suns or build them in legions. It was power to escape, perhaps even to prepare himself eventually to meet them with at least a chance to force truce, if not victory. Given even a few hours free of their notice, he could draw and hold that power for his needs.

He was just reaching for it when the sky thundered and the sun seemed to darken for a moment!

The fear in him gibbered to the surface and sent him huddling from sight of the sky before he could control it. But for a brief moment there was still a trace of hope in him. It could have been a phenomenon caused by his own need for power; he might have begun drawing too heavily, too eager for strength.

Then the earth shook, and he knew.

The Usurpers were not fooled. They knew he was here—had never lost him. And now they had followed in all their massive lack of subtlety. One of their scout ships had landed, and the scout would come seeking him.

He fought for control of himself, and found it long enough to drive his fear back down within himself. Now, with a care that disturbed not even a blade of grass or leaf on a twig, he began retreating, seeking the denser undergrowth at the center of the garden where all life was thickest. With that to screen him, he might at least draw a faint trickle of power, a strength to build a subtle brute aura around himself and let him hide among the beasts. Some Usurper scouts were young and immature. Such a one might be fooled into leaving. Then, before his report could be acted on by others, there might still be a chance. . . .

He knew the thought was only a wish, not a plan, but he clung to it as he huddled in the thicket at the center of the garden. And then even the fantasy was stripped from him.

The sound of footsteps was firm and sure. Branches broke as the steps came forward, not deviating from a straight line. Inexorably, each firm stride brought the Usurper nearer to his huddling place. Now there was a faint glow in the air, and the animals were scampering away in terror.

He felt the eyes of the Usurper on him, and he forced himself away from that awareness. And, like fear, he found that he had learned prayer from the Usurpers; he prayed now desperately to a nothingness he knew, and there was no answer.

"Come forth! This earth is a holy place and you cannot remain upon it. Our judgment is done and a place is prepared for you. Come forth and let me take you there!" The voice was soft, but it carried a power that stilled even the rustling of the leaves.

He let the gaze of the Usurper reach him now, and the prayer in him was mute and directed outward—and hopeless, as he knew it must be.

"But—" Words were useless, but the bitterness inside him forced the words to come from him. "But why? I am God!"

For a moment, something akin to sadness and pity was in the eyes of the Usurper. Then it passed as the answer came. "I know. But I am Man. Come!"

He bowed at last, silently, and followed slowly as the yellow sun sank behind the walls of the garden.

And the evening and the morning were the eighth day.

Exile

Edmond Hamilton

I wish now that we hadn't got to talking about science fiction that night! If we hadn't, I wouldn't be haunted now by that queer, impossible story which can't ever be proved or disproved.

But the four of us were all professional writers of fantastic stories, and I suppose shop talk was inevitable. Yet, we'd kept off it through the dinner and the drinks afterward. Madison had outlined his hunting trip with gusto, and then Brazell started a discussion of the Dodgers' chances. And then I had to turn the conversation to fantasy.

I didn't mean to do it. But I'd had an extra Scotch, and that always makes me feel analytical. And I got to feeling amused by the perfect way in which we four resembled a quartet of normal, ordinary people.

"Protective coloration, that's what it is," I announced. "How hard we work at the business of acting like ordinary good guys!"

Brazell looked at me, somewhat annoyed by the interruption. "What are you talking about?"

"About us," I answered. "What a wonderful imitation of solid, satisfied citizens we put up! But we're not satisfied, you know— none of us. We're violently dissatisfied with the Earth and all its works, and that's why we spend our lives dreaming up one imaginary world after another."

"I suppose the little matter of getting paid for it has nothing to do with it?" asked Brazell skeptically.

"Sure it has," I admitted. "But we all dreamed up our impossible worlds and peoples long before we ever wrote a line, didn't we? From back in childhood, even? It's because we don't feel at home here."

Madison snorted. "We'd feel a lot less at home on some of the worlds we write about."

Then Carrick, the fourth of our party, broke into the conversation. He'd been sitting over his drink in his usual silent way, brooding, paying no attention to us.

He was a queer chap, in most ways. We didn't know him very well, but we liked him and admired his stories. He'd done some wonderful tales of an imaginary planet—all carefully worked out.

He told Madison, "That happened to me."

"What happened to you?" Madison asked.

"What you were suggesting—*I* once wrote about an imaginary world and then had to live on it," Carrick answered.

Madison laughed. "I hope it was a more livable place than the lurid planets on which I set my own yarns."

But Carrick was unsmiling. He murmured, "I'd have made it a lot different—if I'd known I was ever going to live on it."

Brazell, with a significant glance at Carrick's empty glass, winked at us and then asked blandly, "Let's hear about it, Carrick."

* * *

Carrick kept looking dully down at his empty glass, turning it slowly in his fingers as he talked. He paused every few words.

"It happened just after I'd moved next to the big power station. It sounds like a noisy place, but actually it was very quiet out there on the edge of the city. And I had to have quiet, if I was to produce stories.

"I got right to work on a new series I was starting, the stories of which were all to be laid on the same imaginary world. I began by working out the detailed physical appearance of that world, as well as the universe that was its background. I spent the whole day concentrating on that. And as I finished, something in my mind went *click!*

"That queer, brief mental sensation felt oddly like a sudden *crystallization.* I stood there, wondering if I were going crazy. For I had a sudden strong conviction that it meant that the universe and world I had been dreaming up all day had suddenly crystallized into physical existence somewhere.

"Naturally, I brushed aside the eerie thought and went out and forgot about it. But the next day, the thing happened again. I had spent most of that second day working up the inhabitants of my story world. I'd made them definitely human, but had decided against making them too civilized—for that would exclude the conflict and violence that must form my story.

"So I'd made my imaginary world a world whose people were still only half-civilized. I figured out all their cruelties and superstitions. I mentally built up their colorful, barbaric cities. And just as I was through—that *click!* echoed sharply in my mind.

"It startled me badly, this second time. For now I felt more strongly than before that queer conviction that my day's dreaming had crystallized into solid reality. I knew it was insane to think that, yet it was an incredible certainty in my mind. I couldn't get rid of it.

"I tried to reason the thing out so that I could dismiss that crazy conviction. If my imagining a world and universe had actually created them, where were they? Certainly not in my own cosmos. It couldn't hold two universes—each completely different from the other.

"But maybe that world and universe of my imagining had crystallized to reality in another and empty cosmos? A cosmos lying in a different dimension from my own? One which had contained only free atoms, formless matter that had not taken on shape until my concentrated thought had somehow stirred it into the forms I dreamed?

"I reasoned along like that, in the queer, dreamlike way in which you apply the rules of logic to impossibilities. How did it come that my imaginings had never crystallized into reality before, but had only just begun to do so? Well, there was a plausible explanation for that. It was the big power station nearby. Some unfathomable freak of energy radiated from it was focusing my concentrated imaginings, as superamplified force, upon an empty cosmos where they stirred formless matter into the shapes I dreamed.

"Did I believe that? No, I didn't believe it—but I knew it. There is quite a difference between knowledge and belief, as someone knew who once pointed out that all men know they will die and none of them believe it. It was like that with me. I realized it was not possible that my imaginary world had come into physical being in a different dimensional cosmos, yet at the same time I was strangely convinced that it had.

"A thought occurred to me that amused and interested me. What if I imagined *myself* in that other world? Would I, too, become physically real in it? I tried it. I sat at my desk, imagining myself as one of the millions of persons in that imaginary world, dreaming up a whole soberly realistic background and family and history for myself over there. And my mind said *click!*"

Carrick paused, still looking down at the empty glass that he twirled slowly between his fingers.

Madison prompted him. "And of course you woke up there, and a beautiful girl was leaning over you, and you asked, 'Where am I?' "

"It wasn't like that," Carrick said dully. "It wasn't like that at all. I woke up in that other world, yes. But it wasn't like a real awakening. I was just suddenly in it.

"I was still myself. But I was the myself I had imagined in that other world. That other me had always lived in it—and so had his ancestors before him. I had worked all that out, you see.

"And I was just as real to myself, in that imaginary world I had created, as I had been in my own. That was the worst part of it.

Everything in that half-civilized world was so utterly, commonplacely real."

He paused again. "It was queer, at first. I walked out into the streets of those barbaric cities, and looked into the people's faces, and I felt like shouting aloud, 'I imagined you all! You had no existence until I dreamed of you!'

"But I didn't do that. They wouldn't have believed me. To them, I was just an insignificant single member of their race. How could they guess that they and their traditions of long history, their world and their universe, had all been suddenly brought into being by my imagination?

"After my first excitement ebbed, I didn't like the place. I had made it too barbaric. The savage violences and cruelties that had seemed so attractive as material for a story, were ugly and repulsive at first hand. I wanted nothing but to get back to my own world.

"And I couldn't get back! There just wasn't any way. I had had a vague idea that I could imagine myself back into my own world, as I had imagined myself into this other one. But it didn't work that way. The freak of force that had wrought the miracle didn't work two ways.

"I had a pretty bad time when I realized that I was trapped in that ugly, squalid, barbarian world. I felt like killing myself, at first. But I didn't. A man can adapt himself to anything. I adapted myself the best I could to the world I had created."

"What did you do there? What was your position, I mean?" Brazell asked.

Carrick shrugged. "I didn't know the crafts or skills of that world I'd brought into being. I had only my one skill—that of story-telling."

I began to grin. "You don't mean to say that you started writing fantastic stories?"

He nodded soberly. "I had to. It was all I could do. I wrote stories about my own real world. To those other people my tales were wild imagination—and they liked them."

We chuckled. But Carrick was deadly serious.

Madison humored him to the end. "And how did you finally get back home from that other world you'd created?"

"I never did get back home," Carrick said with a heavy sigh.

"Oh, come now," Madison protested lightly. "It's obvious that you got back some time."

Carrick shook his head somberly as he rose to leave.

"No, I never got back home," he said soberly. "I'm still here."

The Exterminator

A. Hyatt Verrill

He was a magnificent specimen of his kind. Translucent—white, swift in movement, possessing an almost uncanny faculty for discovering his prey, and invariably triumphing over his natural enemies. But his most outstanding feature was his insatiable appetite. He was as merciless and as indiscriminate a killer as a weasel or a ferret; but unlike those wanton destroyers who kill for the mere lust of killing, the Exterminator never wasted his kill. Whatever he fell upon and destroyed was instantly devoured. To have watched him would have been fascinating. A rush, as he hurled himself upon his prey, a brief instant of immobility, of seeming hesitation, a slight tremor of his substance, and all was over; the unfortunate thing that had been moving, unsuspicious of danger, on its accustomed way had vanished completely, and the Exterminator was hurrying off, seeking avidly for another victim. He moved continually in an evenly flowing stream of liquid in absolute darkness. Hence eyes were non-essential, and he was guided entirely by instinct or by nature rather than by faculties such as we know.

He was not alone. Others of his kind were all about and the current was crowded with countless numbers of other organisms: slowly moving roundish things of reddish hue, wiggling tadpole-like creatures, star-shaped bodies; slender, attenuated things like sticks endowed with life; globular creatures; shapeless things constantly altering their form as they moved or rather swam; minute, almost invisible beings; thread-like, serpentine, or eel-like organisms, and countless other forms. Among all these, threading his way in the overcrowding warm current, the Exterminator moved aimlessly, yet ever with one all-consuming purpose—to kill and devour.

By some mysterious, inexplicable means he recognized friends and could unerringly distinguish foes. The reddish multitudes he avoided. He knew they were to remain unmolested and even when, as often happened, he found himself surrounded, hemmed in, almost smothered by hordes of the harmless red things and was jostled by them, he remained unperturbed and made no attempt to injure or devour them. But the others—the writhing, thread-like creatures; the globular, ovoid, angular, radiate and bar-like things; the rapidly wiggling tadpole-like organisms—were different. Among these he wrought rapid and terrible destruction. Yet even here he exhibited a strange discrimination. Some he passed by without offering to harm them, while others he attacked, slaughtered, and devoured with indescribable ferocity. And on every hand others of his kind were doing the same. They were like a horde of ravenous sharks in a sea teeming with mackerel. They seemed obsessed with the one all-consuming desire to destroy, and so successful were they in this that often, for long periods, the ever moving stream in which they dwelt would be totally destitute of their prey.

Still, neither the Exterminator nor his fellows appeared to suffer for lack of sustenance. They were capable of going for long periods without food and they cruised, or rather swam slowly about, apparently as contented as when on a veritable orgy of killing. And even when the current bore no legitimate prey within reach of the Exterminator and his companions, never did they attempt to injure or molest the ever present red forms or the innumerable smaller organisms which they seemed to realize were friends. In fact, had it been possible to have interpreted their sensations, it would have been found that they were far more content, far more satisfied when there were no enemies to kill and devour than when the stream swarmed with their natural prey and there was a ceaseless ferocious urge to kill, kill, kill.

At the latter times the stream in which the Exterminator dwelt became uncomfortably warm, which aroused him and his fellows to renewed activity for a space, but which brought death to many of the savage beings. And always, following these casualties, the hordes of enemies rapidly increased until the Exterminator found it almost impossible to decimate them. At times, too, the stream flowed slowly and weakly and a lethargy came over the Exterminator. Often at such times he floated rather than swam, his strength ebbed, and his lust to kill almost vanished. But always there followed a change. The stream took on a peculiar bitter taste, countless numbers of the Exterminator's foes died and vanished, while the Exterminator himself became endowed with unwonted sudden strength and fell ravenously upon the remaining enemies. At such times, also, the number of his fellows always increased in some mysterious manner, as did the red beings. They seemed to appear from nowhere until the stream was thick with them.

Time did not exist for the Exterminator. He knew nothing of distance, nor of night or day. He was susceptible only to changes of temperature in the stream where he always had dwelt, and to the absence or presence of his natural foes and natural allies. Though he was perhaps aware that the current followed an erratic course, that the stream flowed through seemingly endless tunnels that twisted and turned and branched off in innumerable directions and formed a labyrinth of smaller streams, he knew nothing of their routes, or their sources or limits, but swam, or rather drifted, anywhere and everywhere quite aimlessly. No doubt, somewhere within the hundreds of tunnels, there were others of his kind as large, as powerful, and as insatiable a destroyer as himself. But as he was blind, as he did not possess the sense of hearing or other senses which enabled the higher forms of life to judge of their surroundings, he was quite unaware of such companions near him. And, as it happened, he was the only one of his kind who survived the unwanted event that eventually occurred, and by so doing was worthy of being called the Exterminator.

For an unusually long period the current in the tunnel had been most uncomfortably warm. The stream had teemed with countless numbers of his foes and these, attacking the reddish forms, had decimated them. There had been a woeful decrease in the Exterminator's fellows also, and he and the few survivors had been forced to exert themselves to the utmost to avoid being overwhelmed. Even then the hordes of wiggling, gyrating, darting, weaving enemies seemed to increase faster than they were killed and devoured.

It began to look as if their army would be victorious and the Exterminator and his fellows would be vanquished, utterly destroyed, when suddenly the slowly flowing hot stream took on a strange, pungent, acrid taste. Instantly, almost, the temperature decreased, the current increased, and as if exposed to a gas attack, the swarming hosts of innumerable strange forms dwindled. And almost instantly the Exterminator's fellows appeared as if from nowhere and fell ravenously upon their surviving foes. In an amazingly short time the avenging white creatures had practically exterminated their multitudinous enemies. Great numbers of the reddish organisms filled the stream and the Exterminator dashed hither and thither seeking chance survivors of his enemies. In eddies and the smaller tunnels he came upon a few. Almost instantly he dashed at them, destroyed them, swallowed them. Guided by some inexplicable power or force he swept along a tiny tunnel. Before him he was aware of a group of three tiny thread-like things, his deadliest foes—and hurled himself forward in chase. Overtaking one, he was about to seize it when a terrific cataclysm occurred. The wall of the tunnel was split asunder, a great rent appeared, and with a rush like water through an opened sluice-way the enclosed stream poured upward through the opening.

Helpless in the grip of the current, the Exterminator was borne whirling, gyrating madly into the aperture. But his one obsession, an all-consuming desire to kill, overcame all terror, all other sensations. Even as the fluid hurled him onward he seized the wriggling foe so near him and swallowed it alive. At the same instant the remaining two were carried by the rushing current almost within his reach. With a sudden effort he threw himself upon the nearest, and as the thing vanished in his maw, he was borne from eternal darkness into blinding light.

Instantly the current ceased to flow. The liquid became stagnant and the countless red beings surrounding the Exterminator moved feebly, slowly, and gathered in clusters where they clung together as if for mutual support. Somewhere near at hand, the Exterminator sensed the presence of the last surviving member of the trio he had been chasing when the disaster took place. But in the stagnant, thick liquid, obstructed by the red beings, he could not move freely. He struggled, fought to reach this one remaining foe; but in vain. He felt suffocating, becoming weaker and weaker. And he was alone. Of all his comrades, he was the only one that had been carried through the rent in the tunnel that for so long had been his home.

Suddenly he felt himself lifted. Together with a few of the reddish things and a small portion of his native element, he was drawn up. Then, with the others, he was dropped, and as he fell, new life coursed through him, for he realized that his hereditary enemy—that wiggling thread-like thing—was close beside him, that even yet he might fall upon and destroy it.

The next instant some heavy object fell upon him. He was imprisoned there with his archenemy an infinitesimal distance from him, but hopelessly out of reach. A mad desire to wreak vengeance swept over him. He was losing strength rapidly. Already the red beings about him had become inert, motionless. Only he and that thread-like, tiny thing still showed signs of life. And the fluid was rapidly thickening. Suddenly, for a fraction of a second, he felt free, and with a final spasmodic effort he moved, reached the enemy, and, triumphant at the last, became a motionless inert thing.

"Strange!" muttered a human voice as its owner peered through the microscope at the blood drop on the slide under the objective. "I could have sworn I caught a glimpse of a bacillus there a moment ago. But there's not a trace of it now."

"That new formula we injected had an almost miraculous effect," observed a second voice.

"Yes," agreed the first. "The crisis is past and the patient is out of danger. Not a single bacillus in this specimen. I would not have believed it possible."

But neither physician was aware of the part the Exterminator had played. To them he was merely a white corpuscle lying dead in the rapidly drying blood drop on the glass-slide.

The Eyes Have It

Philip K. Dick

It was quite by accident I discovered this incredible invasion of Earth by lifeforms from another planet. As yet, I haven't done anything about it; I can't think of anything to do. I wrote to the Government, and they sent back a pamphlet on the repair and maintenance of frame houses. Anyhow, the whole thing is known; I'm not the first to discover it. Maybe it's even under control.

I was sitting in my easy-chair, idly turning the pages of a paperbacked book someone had left on the bus, when I came across the reference that first put me on the trail. For a moment I didn't respond. It took some time for the full import to sink in. After I'd comprehended, it seemed odd I hadn't noticed it right away.

The reference was clearly to a nonhuman species of incredible properties, not indigenous to Earth. A species, I hasten to point out, customarily masquerading as ordinary human beings. Their disguise, however, became transparent in the face of the following observations by the author. It was at once obvious the author knew everything. Knew everything—and was taking it in his stride. The line (and I tremble remembering it even now) read:

. . . *his eyes slowly roved about the room.*

Vague chills assailed me. I tried to picture the eyes. Did they roll like dimes? The passage indicated not; they seemed to move through the air, not over the surface. Rather rapidly, apparently. No one in the story was surprised. That's what tipped me off. No sign of amazement at such an outrageous thing. Later the matter was amplified.

. . . *his eyes moved from person to person.*

There it was in a nutshell. The eyes had clearly come apart from the rest of him and were on their own. My heart pounded and my breath choked in my windpipe. I had stumbled on an accidental mention of a totally unfamiliar race. Obviously non-Terrestrial. Yet, to the characters in the book, it was perfectly natural—which suggested they belonged to the same species.

And the author? A slow suspicion burned in my mind. The author was taking it rather *too easily* in his stride. Evidently, he felt this was quite a usual thing. He made absolutely no attempt to conceal this knowledge. The story continued:

. . . presently his eyes fastened on Julia.

Julia, being a lady, had at least the breeding to feel indignant. She is described as blushing and knitting her brows angrily. At this, I sighed with relief. They weren't *all* non-Terrestrials. The narrative continues:

. . . slowly, calmly, his eyes examined every inch of her.

Great Scott! But here the girl turned and stomped off and the matter ended. I lay back in my chair gasping with horror. My wife and family regarded me in wonder.

"What's wrong, dear?" my wife asked.

I couldn't tell her. Knowledge like this was too much for the ordinary run-of-the-mill person. I had to keep it to myself. "Nothing," I gasped. I leaped up, snatched the book, and hurried out of the room.

In the garage, I continued reading. There was more. Trembling, I read the next revealing passage:

. . . he put his arm around Julia. Presently she asked him if he would remove his arm. He immediately did so, with a smile.

It's not said what was done with the arm after the fellow had removed it. Maybe it was left standing upright in the corner. Maybe it was thrown away. I don't care. In any case, the full meaning was there, staring me right in the face.

Here was a race of creatures capable of removing portions of their anatomy at will. Eyes, arms—and maybe more. Without batting an eyelash. My knowledge of biology came in handy, at this point. Obviously they were simple beings, uni-cellular, some sort of primitive single-celled things. Beings no more developed than starfish. Starfish can do the same thing, you know.

I read on. And came to this incredible revelation, tossed off coolly by the author without the faintest tremor:

. . . outside the movie theater we split up. Part of us went inside, part over to the cafe for dinner.

Binary fission, obviously. Splitting in half and forming two entities. Probably each lower half went to the cafe, it being farther, and the upper halves to the movies. I read on, hands shaking. I had really stumbled onto something here. My mind reeled as I made out this passage:

. . . I'm afraid there's no doubt about it. Poor Bibney has lost his head again.

Which was followed by:

. . . and Bob says he has utterly no guts.

Yet Bibney got around as well as the next person. The next person, however, was just as strange. He was soon described as:

. . . totally lacking in brains.

There was no doubt of the thing in the next passage. Julia, whom I had thought to be the one normal person, reveals herself as also being an alien lifeform, similar to the rest:

. . . quite deliberately, Julia had given her heart to the young man.

It didn't relate what the final disposition of the organ was, but I didn't really care. It was evident Julia had gone right on living in her usual manner, like all the others in the book. Without heart, arms, eyes, brains, viscera, dividing up in two when the occasion demanded. Without a qualm.

. . . *thereupon she gave him her hand.*

I sickened. The rascal now had her hand, as well as her heart. I shudder to think what he's done with them, by this time.

. . . *he took her arm.*

Not content to wait, he had to start dismantling her on his own. Flushing crimson, I slammed the book shut and leaped to my feet. But not in time to escape one last reference to those carefree bits of anatomy whose travels had originally thrown me on the track:

. . . *her eyes followed him all the way down the road and across the meadow.*

I rushed from the garage and back inside the warm house, as if the accursed things were following *me.* My wife and children were playing Monopoly in the kitchen. I joined them and played with frantic fervor, brow feverish, teeth chattering.

I had had enough of the thing. I want to hear no more about it. Let them come on. Let them invade Earth. I don't want to get mixed up in it.

I have absolutely no stomach for it.

Feeding Time

James E. Gunn

Angela woke up with the sickening realization that today was feeding time. She slipped out of bed, hurried to the desk, and leafed nervously through her appointment book. She sighed with relief; it was all right—today was her appointment.

Angela took only forty-five minutes for make-up and dressing: it was feeding time. As she descended in the elevator, walked swiftly through the lobby, and got into a taxi, she didn't even notice the eyes that stopped and swiveled after her: feeding time.

Angela was haunted by a zoo.

She was also haunted by men, but this was understandable. She was the kind of blond, blue-eyed angel men pray to—or for—and she had the kind of measurements—36-26-36—that make men want to take up mathematics.

But Angela had no time for men—not today. Angela was haunted by a zoo, and it was feeding time.

Dr. Bachman had a gray-bearded, pink-skinned, blue-eyed kindliness that was his greatest stock in trade. Underneath, there was something else not quite so kindly which had been influential in his choice of professions. Now, for a moment, his professional mask— his *persona,* as the Jungians call it—slipped aside.

"A zoo?" he repeated, his voice clear, deep, and cultured, with just a trace of accent; Viennese without a doubt. He caught himself quickly. "A zoo. Exactly."

"Well, not exactly a zoo," said Angela, pursing her red lips thoughtfully at the ceiling. "At least not an ordinary zoo. It's really only one animal—if you could call him an animal."

"What do you call him?"

"Oh, I never call him," Angela said quickly, giving a delicious little shiver. "He might come."

"Hm-m-m," hm-m-med Dr. Bachman neutrally.

"But you don't mean that," Angela said softly. "You mean if he isn't an animal, what is he? What he is—is a monster."

"What kind of monster?" Dr. Bachman asked calmly.

Angela turned on one elbow and looked over the back of the couch at the psychoanalyst. "You say that as if you met monsters every day. But then I guess you do." She sighed sympathetically. "It's a dangerous business, being a psychiatrist."

"Dangerous?" Dr. Bachman repeated querulously, caught off guard a second time. "What do you mean?"

"Oh, the people you meet—all the strange ones—and their problems—"

"Yes, yes, of course," he said hurriedly. "But about the monster—?"

"Yes, doctor," Angela said in her obedient tone and composed herself again on the couch. She looked at the corner of the ceiling as if she could see him clinging there. "He's not a nightmare monster, though he's frightening enough. He's too real; there are no blurred edges. He has purple fur—short, rather like the fur on some spiders—and four legs, not evenly distributed like a dog's or a cat's but grouped together at the bottom. They're very strong—much stronger than they need to be. He can jump fifteen feet straight up into the air."

She turned again to look at Dr. Bachman. "Are you getting all this?"

Hastily, the psychoanalyst turned his notebook away, but Angela had already caught a glimpse of his doodling.

"Goodie!" she said, clapping her hands in delight. "You're drawing a picture."

"Yes, yes," he said grumpily. "Go on."

"Well, he has only two arms. He has six fingers on each hand, and they're flexible, as if they had no bones in them. They're elastic, too. They can stretch way out—as if to pick fruit that grows on a very tall vine."

"A vegetarian," said Dr. Bachman, making his small joke.

"Oh, no, doctor!" Angela said, her eyes wide. "He eats everything, but meat is what he likes the best. His face is almost human except it's green. He has very sharp teeth." She shuddered. "Very sharp. Am I going too fast?"

"Don't worry about me!" snapped the psychoanalyst. "It is your subconscious we are exploring, and it must go at its own speed."

"Oh, dear," Angela said with resignation. "The subconscious. It's going to be another one of those."

"You don't believe this nightmare has any objective reality?" Dr. Bachman asked sharply.

"That would make me insane, wouldn't it? Well, I guess there's no help for it. That's what I think."

Dr. Bachman tugged thoughtfully at his beard. "I see. Let's go back. How did this illusion begin?"

"I think it began with the claustrophobia."

Dr. Bachman shrugged. "A morbid fear of confined places is not unusual."

"It is when you're out in the open air. The fear had no relationship to my surroundings. All of a sudden, I'd feel like I was in a fairly large room which had a tremendous weight of rock or masonry above it. I was in the midst of a crowd of people. For moments it became so real that my actual surroundings faded out."

"But the feeling came and went."

"Yes. Then came the smell. It was a distinctive odor—musty and strong like the lion house in the winter, only wrong, somehow. But it made me think of the zoo."

"Naturally you were the only one who smelled it."

"That's right. I was self-conscious, at first. I tried to drown out the odor with perfume, but that didn't help. Then I realized that no one else seemed to smell it. Like the claustrophobia, it came and went. But each time it returned it was stronger. Finally I went to a psychiatrist—a Dr. Aber."

"That was before the illusion became visual?"

"That was sort of Dr. Aber's fault—my seeing the monster, I mean."

"It is to be expected," Dr. Bachman said.

"When nothing else worked, Dr. Aber tried hypnosis. 'Reach into your subconscious,' he said. 'Open the door to the past!' Well, I reached out. I opened the door. And that's when it happened."

"What happened?" Dr. Bachman leaned forward.

"I saw the monster."

"Oh." He lcaned back again, disappointed.

"People were close, but the monster was closer. The odor was stifling as he stared through the door—and saw me. I slammed the door shut, but it was too late. The door was there. I knew it could be opened. And he knew it could be opened. Now I was really afraid."

"Afraid?"

"That the monster might get through the door."

The psychoanalyst tugged at his beard. "You have an explanation for this illusion?"

"You won't laugh?"

"Certainly not!"

"I think, through some strange accident of time, I've become linked to a zoo that will exist in the distant future. The monster—wasn't born on Earth. He's an alien—from Jupiter, perhaps, although I don't think so. Through the door I can see part of a sign; I can read this much."

Angela turned and took the notebook from his surprised fingers and printed quickly:

M'RA
(Larmis
Nativ
Vega

"Just like in the zoo," she said, handing the book back. "There's a star named Vega."

"Yes," said the psychoanalyst heavily. "And you are afraid that this . . . alien will get through the door and—"

"That's it. He can open it now, you see. He can't exist here; that would be impossible. But something from the present can exist in the future. And the monster gets hungry—for meat."

"For meat?" Dr. Bachman repeated, frowning.

"Every few weeks," Angela said, shivering, "it's feeding time."

Dr. Bachman tugged at his beard, preparing the swift, feline stroke which would lay bare the traumatic relationship at the root of the neurosis. He said, incisively, "The monster resembles your father, is that not so?"

It was Angela's turn to frown. "That's what Dr. Aber said. I'd never have noticed it on my own. There might be a slight resemblance."

"This Dr. Aber—he did you no good?"

"Oh, I wouldn't want you to think that," Angela protested quickly. "He helped. But the help was—temporary, if you know what I mean."

"And you would like something more permanent."

"That would be nice," Angela admitted. "But I'm afraid it's too much to hope for."

"No. It will take time, but eventually we will work these subconscious repressions into your conscious mind, where they will be cleansed of their neurotic value."

"You think it's all in my head?" Angela said wistfully.

"Certainly," the psychoanalyst said briskly. "Let us go over the progress of the illusion once more: First came the claustrophobia, then the smell, then, through Dr. Aber's bung . . . treatment, I should say, the dreams—"

"Oh, not dreams, doctor," Angela corrected. "When I sleep, I don't dream of monsters. I dream"—she blushed prettily—"of men. The thing in the zoo—I can see him whenever I close my eyes." She shivered. "He's getting impatient."

"Hungry?"

Angela beamed at him. "Yes. It's almost feeding time. He gets fed, of course. By the keeper, I suppose. But that's just grains and fruits and things like that. And he gets hungry for meat."

"And then?"

"He opens the door."

"And I suppose he sticks through his elastic fingers."

Angela gave him a look of pure gratitude. "That's right."

"And you're afraid that one day he will get hungry enough to eat you."

"That's it, I guess. Wouldn't you be—afraid, that is? There's all the legends about dragons and Minotaurs and creatures like that. They always preferred a diet of young virgins; and where there's all that talk—"

"If that were your only concern," Dr. Bachman commented dryly, "it seems to me that you could make yourself ineligible with no great difficulty."

Angela giggled. "Why, doctor! What a suggestion!"

"Hm-m-m," hm-m-med the psychoanalyst. "So! To return. Every few weeks comes feeding time. And you, feeling nervous and afraid, come to me for help."

"You put it so well."

"And now it's feeding time."

"That's right." Angela's nostrils dilated suddenly. "He's getting close to the door. Don't you smell him, doctor?"

Dr. Bachman sniffed once and snorted. "Certainly not. Now tell me about your father."

"Well," Angela began reluctantly, "he believed in reincarnation—"

"No, no," the psychoanalyst said impatiently. "The important things. How you felt about him when you were a little girl. What he said to you. How you hated your mother."

"I'm afraid there won't be time. He's got one of his hands on the door already."

Despite himself, Dr. Bachman glanced back over his shoulder. "The monster?" His beard twitched nervously. "Nonsense. About your father—"

"The door's opened!" Angela cried out. "I'm scared, doctor. It's feeding time!"

"I won't be tricked again," the psychoanalyst said sternly. "If we're to get anywhere with this analysis, I must have complete—"

"Doctor! Watch out! The fingers—Dr. Bachman! Doctor! Doc—!"

Angela sighed. It was a strange sigh, half hopelessness and half relief. She picked up her purse.

"Doctor?" she said tentatively to the empty room.

She stood up, sniffing the air gingerly. The odor was gone. So was Dr. Bachman.

She walked toward the door. "Doctor?" she tried once more.

There was no answer. There never had been an answer, not from seventeen psychiatrists. There was no doubt about it. The monster did like psychiatrists.

It was a truly terrifying situation she was in, certainly through no fault of her own, and a girl had to do the best she could. She could console herself with the thought that the monster would never take her for food.

She was the trapdoor it needed into this world. Eat her, and feeding time was over.

She was perfectly safe.

As long as she didn't run out of psychiatrists.

The Finest Hunter in the World

Harry Harrison

Y ou of course realize, Mr. Lamb, that not one hunter has ever bagged a Venusian swamp-thing?" Godfrey Spingle spoke into the microphone, then shoved it toward the other man.

"Indeed I do. I've read all the records and studied all the reports. That is why I am here on Venus. I have been called the finest hunter in the world and, to be perfectly honest, I would rather enjoy being called the finest hunter in *two* worlds."

"Well, thank you, Mr. Lamb. And may the best wishes of the Intrasystem Broadcasting Company go with you, as well as all the listening millions out there. This is Godfrey Spingle, in Muckcity, on Venus, signing off." He flipped the switch and stowed the mike back in the recorder case.

Behind them the shuttle rocket roared as it blasted up through the damp air and Lamb waited until the sound had died away before he spoke.

"If the interview is finished, I wonder if you would be kind enough to tell me which of these . . ." He pointed toward the ramshackle collection of tottering structures, ". . . is the hotel."

"None of them." Spingle picked up two of Lamb's bags. "It sank into the mud last week, but I have a cot for you in one of the warehouses."

"That's very kind of you," Lamb said, picking up the other two cases and staggering after his long-legged guide. "I hate to put you to any trouble."

"No trouble," Spingle said, unsuccessfully keeping a thin note of complaint out of his voice. "I used to run the hotel too before it went down. And I'm the customs officer and mailman. There's not much of a population in this place—or any damn reason why there should be."

Spingle was sorry for himself and angry at the injustice of the world. Here he was, six foot two, strong and handsome, and rotting away in this filthy hole. While Lamb, five foot four, round and fat, with bifocals was famous—as a hunter! No justice, no justice at all.

Lamb began rooting in his bags as soon as they were dropped onto the mildewed concrete floor. "I want to go out at once, shoot a swamp-thing before dark so I can get the morning rocket back. Would you be so kind as to tell the guide."

"I'm the guide." He had to control his sneer. "Aren't you being a little, well, optimistic about your chances? The swamp-things can swim, fly, walk, and swing from trees. They are wary, intelligent, and deadly. No one has ever shot one of them."

"I shall," Lamb said, taking a gray coverall from his bag and pulling it on. "Hunting is a science that I alone have mastered. I never fail. Hand me that head, please."

Wordlessly, Spingle passed over a large papier-mâché head that had white teeth and red eyes painted on it. Lamb slipped it over his own head, then pulled on gray gloves, followed by gray boots with white claws dangling from them.

"How do I look?" he asked.

"Like a fat swamp rat," Spingle blurted out.

"Fine." He took a gnarled stick from his bag and placed it between the jaws of the mask. "Lead the way, Mr. Spingle, if you please."

Spingle, at a complete loss for words, belted on his pistol and took the path into the swamp.

"I'll give you a one minute start," Lamb said as the last building vanished behind them in the mist, "then follow your footprints. Be careful, I understand these swamps are quite deadly."

"Deadly! That's an understatement. Take my advice, Lamb, and go back."

"Thank you, Mr. Spingle," the muffled voice said from inside the grotesque head, "but I shall proceed."

Spingle led the way; let the fool get eaten by the swamp-things or any other local beasts. Once the idiot was gone his bags could be gone through and there should be something of value . . .

The unmistakable sound of a blaster echoed through the damp air and, after a moment's paralysis, Spingle ran back down the path with his own handgun ready.

It was not needed. Lamb sat on the rotting trunk of a fallen tree, the discarded mask-head beside him, mopping sweat from his face with a large bandanna. Beyond him, half in and half out of the jungle, was the hideous fang-toothed, claw-winged, poison-green corpse of a swamp-thing, frightful even in death.

"How . . . ?" Spingle gasped. "What . . . you . . . how?"

"A simple story," Lamb said, digging a camera from his pocket, "a discovery I made some years back. I found out that I was heavy of foot and bad of eye, an undistinguished tracker and an unaccomplished woodsman. Though I'm a damn fine shot; I pride myself on that. My ambition was to be a hunter, but I could never get close enough to my prey to get in a shot. So, with impeccable logic, I changed roles. After all—these beasts are born hunters and killers, so why should I compete on their terms? Instead I became prey and let the beasts stalk and attack me—to be killed themselves, of course. In the guise of the oryx, skin-draped and horn-headed, I have knelt by the stream and killed the swift leopard. As a very slow zebra I have bagged my share of lions. It is the same here. My research showed that the swamp-things live almost exclusively off of the giant swamp rat, *rattus venerius.* So I became a rat—with this result." He raised the camera and photographed the dead beast.

"Without a gun?"

Lamb pointed to the twisted stick, leaning now against the log, that he had carried in his rodent teeth. "That is a disguised blaster. These creatures would have recognized a gun at once."

Then the idea came to Spingle. The swamp-thing was dead and *he* had the gun—and the secret. Lamb would vanish in the swamp and he would be the finest hunter in the world. Two worlds. He raised his weapon.

"So long, sucker," he said. "Thanks for the tip."

Lamb only smiled and pressed the flash button on his camera. The blaster, concealed inside, blew a neat hole through Spingle before he could press his own trigger. Lamb shook his head.

"People never listen. I'm fit prey for *all* hunters. Now, let me see, that makes my bag one swamp-thing—and thirteen, no, fourteen would-be assassins."

The Flame Midget

Frank Belknap Long, Jr.

Although the sun was warm and shining brightly, I experienced a sense of dismal foreboding when I drew near to Richard Ashley's little South Carolinian retreat. Live oaks and palmettos screened the small laboratory building and the high yellow fence beyond. Huge, brown mushrooms, which looked like the conical dwellings of gnomes and other demons of fable with a lineage rooted deep in earth, studded the grass about me.

As I advanced over the narrow pathway which led to the laboratory door, I told myself with some bitterness that no other bacteriologist of Ashley's standing would have conducted his researches so far from the citadels of organized science. Ashley had once labored in a great white laboratory by the sea, and this little inland retreat seemed peculiarly noisome by contrast.

I don't like profuse and suggestive vegetation. I don't like little buildings nestling in the midst of clustering shadows, with dank earth odors all about them. But Ashley was a strange chap.

There is a sect of Eastern fanatics which insists that human beings are but thinly disguised counterparts of certain animals. Some men exhibit characteristics which link them with the birds of the air, others with tigers, pigs, and hyenas, and still others with the invertebrate phyla. I have often thought that the imaginative gentlemen who adhere to this cult would have classified Ashley as a mole or an earthworm. I am not being facetious when I say that Ashley was a deep one.

He resented and fled from all warm, human, personal contacts. I don't believe there was ever a woman in his life. Even friendship was impossible to him. But occasionally he'd get into an intellectual jam, or run head-on into a stone wall; and then he'd send for me. I was his good man Friday. As a human being I didn't admire Ashley at all. But as a scientist—and I think scientists are the salt of the earth—I respected and revered him.

I was halfway down the path when the laboratory door opened suddenly and Ashley came out. He came out blinking into the warm, bright sunlight, and stood for an instant with his hand on the doorknob, peering intently through thick-lensed spectacles at the hatless and perspiring young man who was approaching him over the lawn.

He resembled a corpse. His features, especially the skin on his cheek bones, had the sickly pallor which usually accompanies a stoppage of circulation. There were black half moons under both his eyes, and the veins on his forehead stood out horribly. His expression was a peculiar one, difficult to describe. Though torment and apprehension looked out of his eyes, he seemed somehow still master of himself and even a little defiant.

"You took your time getting here, didn't you?" he said, petulantly, as though he was addressing a child.

I had come three hundred miles by bus, in response to his urgent telegram, but it was no good being angry with him. He was tormented and in trouble. A wave of compassion swept over me when I saw how his hands were shaking. When he tried to hold the door open for me he sagged against the jamb. For an instant I thought he was going to fall.

As we passed from the palmetto-shadowed lawn into the interior of the laboratory I watched him out of the corner of my eye, striving to repress his hysteria. I continued to shoot sidewise glances at him until we reached the large, sunlighted room where he worked over his slides and cultures.

His composure seemed to return a little when he shut the door of that room. He seized my hand and pressed it gratefully.

"Glad you came, John," he said. "Really glad. It was decent of you."

I looked at him. A trace of color had crept back into his cheeks. He was standing with his back to the window, gazing in a kind of trance at the long row of microscopes which had claimed his attention for five absorbing months, and the pale-blue jars full of polluted water which contained an astonishing assortment of microscopic organisms—diatoms and wheel animalcules and prototropic bacteria, all tremendously important to him in his patient labors.

The laboratory was bathed in limpid shafts of warm and slowly reddening sunlight, and I remember how the optical tubes of the microscopes glittered as I stared at them. Their brilliant sheen seemed to exert an almost hypnotic influence on my companion. But suddenly he tore his gaze away and his lean fingers fastened on my arm in a grip that made me wince.

"It's under the third microscope from the end of the table," he said, with twitching lips. "It put itself on the slide deliberately. I thought, of course, that it was a microörganism at first. But when he stared steadily up at me I found myself thinking its thoughts and obscurely sharing its incredible emotions. You see, it would have been invisible to the naked eye. With devilish cunning it put itself where I would be sure to see it."

He nodded grimly toward the long, zinc-topped table which ran the length of the laboratory. "You may look at it if you wish. The third microscope."

I turned and stared at him intently for an instant. His eyes seemed abnormally bright, but the pupils were not dilated. I am rather proficient at detecting the stigmata of drugs, hysteria, incipient insanity. Without a word I moved to the end of the table, bent over and glued my eye to the instrument of science.

For a moment I stared down at tiny, moving blobs of matter on an immersion liquid which was tinted a beautiful rose-pink. Shapes grotesque and aberrant, grotesque and revolting, weaved in and out and devoured one another on a mucid area no larger than my thumb. Hundreds of shapes with enormous, greedy "mouths" and repulsively writhing bodies darted in and out between slothful tiger animalcules, and flat, segmented horrors which bore a nauseating resemblance to the proglottides of fish tapeworms and other intestinal Cestoda.

Suddenly, as I stared, an organism shaped like an inverted bell swam toward the center of the slide and remained there with curious oscillatory movements of its tapering body. It was utterly unlike the hundreds of other loathsome, squirming little animals about it.

It was quite large, for one thing, and extremely complex in structure, consisting of an outer translucent shell or chrysalis, and a cone-shaped inner shell, also transparent and curiously iridescent in texture. As I peered more intently I perceived that the inner shell enveloped a little form, serving as a sort of matrix for the actual inhabitant of the bell.

The little form was shockingly anthropomorphic in contour. There is something horribly disturbing about the human form when it is simulated by creatures of nonsimian origin. Vaguely man-shaped fishes, reptiles and insects—and there are a few such in nature—invariably repel me. The debased but distinctly manlike face of a skate or ray fills me with detestation. I shiver when I see a frog with its legs extended. Perhaps this fear reaction is caused by man's primitive, instinct dread of being *supplanted*.

Ordinarily the revulsion is fleeting and quickly forgotten. But as I gazed down at the little shape within the bell, the horror which I experienced was pervasive, unsettling. It wasn't just a shivery pre-monition. I had a feeling I was gazing on something alien to normal experience, something that transcended all the grotesque parallel-isms in Nature's book.

The little shape was in all respects a perfectly formed little man, dark-skinned, with pointed ears and pointed chin. Purely by acci-dent it resembled a whimsical creation of man's fancy. Purely by accident it was goblinlike, gnomelike. But it was not whimsical. It was horrible.

A human shape, starkly nude and so small it was invisible to the naked eye tenuously suspended within a bell-shaped receptacle. It rested on its back, with its little arms tightly folded across its chest. Its abdomen, arms and legs were covered with fine, reddish hair. Suddenly, as I studied it, sick with revulsion and horror, it opened its little slitted eyes and stared steadily up at me.

Something seemed to speak to me then. Words rippled across my mind in slow, sluggish waves.

"You are his friend. I will not harm you. Do not fear me."

I spun from the microscope, gasping out in unbelief and horror. Ashley laid his hand on my arm and drew me swiftly away from the table.

"You saw it?" he asked. "It spoke to you?"

I nodded. I stared at him in furious unbelief. I clenched my hands in blind terror. I said: "What is it, Richard?"

I was trembling like a leaf. My face was twitching; I could feel the blood tingling in my cheeks as it drained away.

"It has traveled for hundreds of light years through interstellar space," he said. "Its home is on a tiny planet encircling a sun of inconceivable density in a star cluster more remote than Earth's nearest stellar neighbors, but an immeasurable distance from the rim of the galaxy. It came in a little space vessel which is hidden somewhere in the laboratory. It refuses to tell me where the vessel is concealed. Through some undreamed-of development of the power of telepathy it can transmit a whole sequence of thought images in a flash."

I nodded grimly. "I know," I said. "It spoke to me. At least, words formed in my mind."

Ashley grasped at that admission as though it were a life line which I had flung him suddenly in sheer compassion and at grave risk to myself.

"Then you do believe, John. I'm glad. Skepticism would be dangerous now. It can sense all opposition to me."

He fell silent an instant. He was staring with fixed intentness at the tube of the microscope which contained the little horror.

"I know that it is difficult to accept a reality in startling opposition to the whole trend of modern scientific thought," he said. "Since the age of Kepler the thinking portion of mankind has inordinately glorified bigness, vastness, extension in space and time. Scientifically minded men have thrown their thoughts occasionally outward toward remote constellations and mysteriously receding nebulæ, and dreamed vain dreams in which mere size has figured as a stepping stone to the eternal.

"But why should size be of any particular importance to the mysterious architect of the mysterious universe?"

"One associates size with force, power," I replied, my eyes on his white face.

"But size and power are not coincidental throughout the universe," exclaimed Ashley. "The radiant force fields at the core of many midget suns would shatter the stellar giants into glowing fragments. Van Maanen's star is no larger than our Earth, but its density exceeds that of the solar disk. If this little star came within a few million miles of Pluto's orbit, it would disrupt the Sun and turn it into a nova. A tiny fragment of its inconceivably concentrated substance no larger than a bolide would pull mighty Jupiter from its orbit. A few spoonfuls of radiant matter from its core colliding with the Earth's crust would cause a more cataclysmic upheaval than the eruption of a major volcano.

"In size it is simply negligible in the cosmic scheme. Compared to the Sun it is a gadfly speck, but it would be capable of blasting a heavenly body millions of times larger than itself.

"The little figure which you have seen was spawned on an unimaginably energized planet no larger than a large meteor, encircling a sun heavier than Van Maanen's star, but smaller in circumference than little Venus. A pygmy sun containing within its tiny bulk a concentration of matter so intense that its atoms may actually have become negative in mass.

"The thin, transparent sheaths in which the little figure appears to float are nonconductive energy sheaths. When the figure extends its arms the sheaths divide laterally, and a searing emanation streams out."

Ashley's voice rose in pitch. He appeared to be approaching a crisis in his recital.

"That radiation surpasses high-frequency electric waves in its destructive power.

"You are, of course, familiar with the theories of the noted research biologist Dr. George Crile as to the nature and origin of life. Crile believes all life is electromagnetic in nature and directly activated by the solar disk. He affirms that the Sun shines with unabated radiance in the protoplasm of animals.

"According to Crile every cell of an animal body contains tiny centers of radiation called radiogens, which have a temperature of six thousand degrees centigrade. These minute hot points are invisible even under the most powerful microscopes. Tiny, incandescent suns, hotter than the solar photosphere and more mysterious than the atom, they generate fields of force within us, producing in all the cells of our bodies the phenomenon of life. But these force fields do not flow outward from our bodies in searing emanations. They are so inconceivably tiny and infrequently spaced that their excess heat is dissipated by the water in our tissues.

"The little figure which you have seen is more lethally endowed. The product of a hotter and more concentrated sun, its radiant energies are not damped by what Crile has defined as interradiogen spaces within itself. Its entire body is a mass of radiogens. When the protective sheaths are withdrawn this terrific energy flows outward in channeled waves, searing everything in its path.

"Two days ago, in my presence, it withdrew the sheaths. One channeled wave streamed eastward across the Atlantic Ocean and was dissipated before it reached the shores of Europe. But the one that streamed westward killed twenty-four human beings.

"One death occurred right in this vicinity. A tenant farmer named Jake Saunders was sitting quietly in the living room of his home with his wife and children when the ray pierced him. He threw up his arms, cried out and slumped jerkily to the floor. His flesh turned black. Although the Sun was shining in a cloudless sky, the local papers blindly assumed that a bolt of lightning had blasted the poor devil. In a New York paper which arrived yesterday all of the other deaths are casually ascribed to freak electrical storms throughout the country. One would think that such tragedies were of everyday occurrence."

"But if the wave crossed the continent thousands should have perished," I gasped. "How do you account for the fact that only a few were fatally affected?"

"The unimaginable thinness of the radiant beam," he said. "It is a single lethal filament, nonspreading until it contacts an animal substance. Then it spreads in all directions, blasting and searing the body in its path. Before it leaves the body it becomes a narrow thread of force again. Extend a thin wire from New York to San Francisco, and the number of men and animals directly in its path would be small indeed."

I was too horrified to comment. I glanced at the microscope, in silent dread and revulsion. Somehow I could not doubt one word of Ashley's recital. I had seen the little shape with my own eyes. It had stared up at me and communicated with me. Only its assurances of amity awakened my skepticism, causing my mood to grow darker as I mused on the implications of Ashley's words.

"I have been in constant communication with it for three days," said Ashley. "It was drawn to me because it believes I am superior to most men in intellectual acumen. The quality of my mind exerted a profound influence upon it, attracting it like a lodestone.

"The world from which it comes would be incomprehensible to us. Its inhabitants are motivated by passions and desires which are alien to humanity. The little shape is a sort of emissary sent across space by its myriad brethren to study conditions on the remote terrestrial globe at first hand. Although they possess instruments of observation infinitely more complex and powerful than our telescopes, and have studied Earth from afar, they have never before attempted to communicate with us. When the little baroque returns its brethren will come in vast numbers.

"When they come they will probably exterminate the entire human race. The little shape does not admire us, and when it returns its observations will reflect no credit on mankind. It thinks us needlessly irrational and cruel. Our custom of settling disputes by a process of wholesale extermination it regards as akin to the savagery of animals. It thinks that our mechanical achievements are less remarkable than the social life of the ants and bees. It regards us as unnecessary excrescences on the face of a comparatively pleasant little globe in space which should afford limitless opportunities for colonization.

"As an isolated individual it respects and even admires me. There is nothing paradoxical in this. Mankind as a whole shuns and fears the dangerous animals which individual men frequently cherish as pets. It regards me as a kind of superior pet—possessing certain likable characteristics, but sharing a heritage, and following conduct patterns which are repellent to it."

I glanced at the microscope in apprehension. His candor disturbed, frightened me.

"Isn't it reading your thoughts now?" I asked.

"No. One must be within two or three feet of it. Its telepathic equipment breaks down beyond a certain radius. It cannot overhear us. It does not even know that I intend to destroy it."

I stared at him, startled.

"If it does not return," he said, "they will not raid Earth immediately. They will send another emissary to search for it. Although they can travel with the velocity of light, the star cluster from which they come is so remote that another emissary would not arrive before the twenty-second century. Another two hundred and fifty years would elapse before that emissary could return and make his report. The first raiders would not arrive before 2700.

"In eight hundred years mankind may succeed in developing some means of defense sufficiently powerful to repel and destroy them. Atomic armaments, perhaps."

He ceased speaking abruptly. I noticed that the muscles of his face were twitching spasmodically. He was obviously laboring under an almost unbearable emotional strain. Suddenly his hands went into one of the spacious pockets of his laboratory frock, and emerged with a flat, metallic object no larger than a cigarette case.

"This is used for purposes of demonstration in the metal industries," he said, as he extended it toward me on the palm of his hand. "It is a midget induction furnace. It will melt virtually all known metals in three or four seconds—even molybdenum, which has a melting point of nearly five thousand degrees Fahrenheit."

I stared at the object, fascinated. Superficially it resembled a little crystal radio set. It consisted merely of a small, spoonlike object about a half inch in height, resting in the center of a flat surface of highly burnished copper. Two curving prongs with insulated stems branched from both sides of the little spool and projected a full inch beyond the gleaming baseboard.

"High-frequency waves set up a searing, blasting heat within the metal a few seconds after the furnace is turned on," he said. "I telegraphed to Charleston for the apparatus yesterday, but it did not arrive until an hour ago."

I had a pretty good idea then why he had sent for me. Richard Ashley was about to endanger his life. If the little horror survived the terrific heat generated by the blast furnace, it would certainly turn upon Ashley and destroy him. It would destroy both Ashley and myself. And since its protective sheaths could resist an *internal* incandescence of thousands of degrees centigrade, Ashley would be taking a long, grim chance.

My friend seemed to sense what was passing through my mind. "Perhaps you'd better not stay, John," he said. "I've no right to ask you to risk your neck."

"You want me to stay, don't you?" I asked.

"Yes, but—"

"Then I will. When do we—burn it?"

He looked at me steadily for an instant. I had a shaky feeling he was weighing the chances against us.

"No sense in putting it off," he said.

Unwaveringly, I met and held his gaze. "Right, Richard," I murmured.

"It will be difficult," he said. "Difficult and—dangerous. It will start reading my mind as soon as I approach the microscope, and if it becomes suspicious it will remove itself before the slide begins to melt."

He smiled with an effort. His hand shot out. "I'll try to make my thoughts behave," he said. "Wish me luck."

"I know you'll succeed, Richard," I murmured, as I returned the pressure of his fingers. He had laid the little induction furnace on the edge of the laboratory table. With a grim nod he picked it up and advanced with rapid steps toward the long row of sun-dappled microscopes. His broad back concealed the gleaming instruments from view as he approached the far end of the laboratory.

I watched him with indrawn breath. When he reached the extremity of the table he swung about and stooped a little. I saw his elbow jerk back. There was a faint, sputtering sound. It was followed by a blinding flash of polychromatic light. For an instant he remained bending above the table. Then he straightened and came slowly back to where I was standing. His face was gray.

"There isn't much left of the microscope," he said. "The slide is liquid, molten. Take a look at it."

Curiosity drew me swiftly toward the end of the table. The little induction furnace had indeed flamed destructively. The microscope was a twisted, blackened wreck. The optical tube lay prone in a gleaming mass of metallic ooze on the zinc tabletop.

Ashley had moved to the opposite side of the laboratory and was stripping off his soiled and faded frock.

"I'm going for a walk," he exclaimed. "I've got to get out in the open, away from all this. I'll crack if I don't."

I nodded sympathetically. "I'll go with you," I said.

A few minutes later we were walking side by side along a narrow dirt road under the open sky. Crickets shrilled in dust barrows under our feet and warblers, wrens and chickadees chirped from the low branches of short-leaf palms and tulip trees. On both sides of us gently rolling hills stretched away to glimmering, haze-obscured horizons.

I glanced at my companion in deep concern. He moved like a man entranced, his body swaying a little as he advanced over the sun-baked soil of the deeply rutted and winding roadway. My concern increased when I perceived that he was silently muttering to himself.

With a shudder I tore my gaze from his white face and stared straight before me. For a long time I continued to keep pace with him in silence, my mind occupied with plans for getting him away from the little laboratory and into an environment where the memories of his grim, three-day ordeal would cease to play on his tormented nerves.

Suddenly he lurched against me. I heard him gasp in horror. A chill premonition swept over me as I swung about, staring. His features were contorted with fright and he was trembling all over.

"It's still alive," he choked. "It just spoke to me again. It has taken refuge *inside my body."*

"Richard," I exclaimed, "have you gone mad?"

"No," he choked. "It is really in my body. It says that when it came to Earth it berthed the space ship in my right kidney."

"Impossible!" I gasped. "How could it—"

"The space ship is microscopic, too. It can pass freely through all the organs and tissues of a human body. For three days the tiny vessel has been suspended in the pelvis of my right kidney by radiant microscopic mooring lines."

His voice rose hysterically. "It suspected that I intended to destroy it. It left the slide and listened while we were discussing it. When I blasted the slide it had already returned to the space ship."

His eyes suddenly took on a glaze of terror. "John—it has decided to kill me. It says that it will *take off* from my body, and carry me with it high above the Earth. It is mocking me, taunting me. It says that I will perish in splendor, will shine as a star. When the ship takes off the energy blast will turn my body into a field of radiant force. I will become a—"

Suddenly his speech congealed. He threw out his arms and staggered violently backward. For four or five seconds he continued to move away from me, his tottering steps swiftly increasing the distance between us. He moved with an incredible acceleration, his limbs trembling and jerking and his torso twisting about as though invisible forces were tugging at every atom of his receding body, pulling him in divergent directions and threatening to tear his fleshly tenement asunder.

There was an instant of utter silence while the air about me seemed visibly to quiver; to quiver and shake and buckle into folds like a film of violently agitated water. The gently sloping hills, the clustering pines and tulip trees and the winding road ahead all quivered in ominous instability. Then, suddenly, the whole of this wavering, fearfully silent world exploded in a blast of sound.

For a moment there was only sound. Then Richard Ashley rose from the Earth. In a burst of salmon-colored flame he shot high into the air, his body rotating like a revolving pinwheel.

He rose with tremendous velocity. As he soared toward the clouds long tongues of sanguineous fire shot from his body, ensheathing his limbs in a radiance so dazzling that even the sunlight failed to obscure it. He became a vessel of lucent flame, a day star throbbingly aglow. For an instant he flamed more redly than red Aldebaran high in the pale heavens. Then, like a comet receding from its zenith, the radiant force fields which streamed luminously outward in all directions from his skyward-soaring body dimmed and dwindled and were lost to view in the wide firmament.

Richard Ashley's body was never found. The local police conducted a thorough search for it, and even attempted to wrest a confession from me by cruel and illegal means. I had made up an absurd little story which they did not believe, but were unable to disprove or discredit. Eventually they were compelled to release me.

But though I am once more free to come and go as I please, I have made the tragic discovery that anxiety can take on many and terrible forms. Night and day I am haunted by a memory which I cannot erase from my mind; a fear which has assumed the compulsive character of a phobia. I know that some day it and its kind will return across wide gulfs of space and wage relentless war on all of humankind. In a peculiar, but very real, sense I have become Richard Ashley's heir. When he vanished into the sky he left behind him a legacy of horror which will darken my days until I am one again with the blind flux of the mysterious universe.

Gift of U'Thang

Basil Wells

Lanky young Sidney Weston looked across the ancient space lighter's cabin at U'Thang, his four foot Asterite companion. Then his eyes went to the view screen of the much-repaired control panel for a last view of the dwindling bulk of Estelle Asteroid.

For the first time since leaving Asteroid Central's School of Mines, for two months' vacation, he felt homesick and miserable.

He and his father had just ended a five week jaunt aboard the space lighter's mother ship, the space tanker, *Redden.* He was used to living in weightlessness. Also he was used to being alone at the college while his father was away piloting spacers. No, it was probably the prospect of having no really experienced adult available if an emergency arose. Plus the ugly secret of why he was here.

U'Thang was two years younger than Sid's nineteen years. Since Sid's knowledge of navigation among the treacherous rocky shards of the denser asteroid belt was very sketchy he knew that U'Thang's skill was all that stood between them and disaster.

The young mute, and deaf, Asterite was taking Sid on a leisurely week-long swing out among some asteroids newly opened to settlement. They had formed a good friendship aboard the *Redden,* and while the tanker was being repaired U'Thang had suggested this swing.

Thoughtfully he studied the scaly-skinned youth's thick body, gray-green as were the head and limbs, but shading to slate gray at the extremities. The sunken ear channels, useless, and the double-hooded, unblinking, gold-flecked eyes, green and set wide above flared shallow nostrils. After the first day he had forgotten these details.

He was remembering his father's parting words earlier today.

"This is a serious business for both of us," said his father. "Until the company medics reinstate my space pilot's license this trouble-shooting assignment helps keep you in school, and me, eating."

"But, wouldn't I be more help here, Dad?" he had asked.

"Not at all. No!" His head jerked in emphatic negation. "I suspect that Ed Torner knows I am an undercover man. I sensed it while aboard his ship. He must know they are checking into his banking ten times his salary last year." He paused. Closed his eyes briefly.

"With you alone out there with your Asterite friend perhaps you can learn something of value. I know you hate it. But it's my job."

"All right, Dad," he had agreed. "I'll try."

Now he looked about the crude, utilitarian ugliness of the tiny craft's interior and his eyes dimmed. He hated this lying and sham.

U'Thang touched his arm. He turned to face the control chair on his right where the Asterite was sitting. U'Thang had been printing in swift, squared, block letters on a large blue pad. His friendly grin bared the triple bony ridges that were his equivalent for teeth. He held out the pad.

"We may find metal, many other deposits—even ice," he had written. "Get many credits. Let you finish school with no worries."

Sid used the swift interplay of fingers and body, in the dumb speech of the mutes, to answer. U'Thang had taught him basics.

"You can then buy your own spacer," he signed, clumsily. "You can hire Captain Torner—instead of him hiring you."

U'Thang's fingers spouted words. He shook his head, grinning.

"Oh, no! Ed Torner my half-brother. Older brother. We share."

Neither of them had suspected this relationship. The surly, small man commanding the space tanker bore no physical resemblance to the hairless, scaly-bodied mutant who was his friend. He was learning that there are thousands of Asterite types.

This would make the prying of information from his new friend about the possible illegal use of the tanker, much more difficult and distasteful. He would be trying to trap U'Thang's brother rather than his superior officer.

The pretense of passing for a wealthy business man and his son, taking a pleasure jaunt aboard one of the old space freighters that service the inhabited mining and hothouse asteroids, no longer amused Sid. He had come to like the men that they spied upon.

Yet there had been no other way, it had seemed. His father's eyesight was deteriorating. The medics had Xed out his permit to pilot spacers—even asteroid-hopping freight runs.

U'Thang was looking at him. Probably wondering why he hesitated.

"Small chance of hitting it lucky," his hands spelled out. "Most of these hunks of rock are already staked-out and recorded."

The Asterite opened his toothless mouth in silent laughter and shook his head. Swiftly he wrote on the blue pad.

"Further out only a few chunks of gravel are taken legally. The cost of registering and recording by the cubic acre is too high for most transient miners. They work pockets of ore or other deposits on unrecorded and unoccupied asteroids."

He flashed Sid a pixy grin, and wrote again.

"They move often and hide their diggings. Use lots of fuel. Good customers for our tanker."

Could that be it? Sid chewed at the idea. Transporting ore or gems or whatever from unreported—even illegal—mining operations? Perhaps purchasing them at a fraction of their true worth and black marketing them? That could account for the swollen bank accounts of U'Thang's brother.

Yet the sales of rocket fuel, and the fuel used on the space tanker's carefully monitored voyages, checked out almost exactly with the craft's optimum performance. Any substantial increase in cargo would increase fuel consumption. Nor could any fuel be sold, unreported, without the shortages becoming immediately apparent.

He would have to keep questioning U'Thang, he thought miserably, until he somehow learned the truth.

"Are we going to search for ore or ice?" he asked, his fingers lamely shaping the question.

"Later." U'Thang's nimble fingers took over the controls to send the little ship sharply upward to avoid a cubic mile or so of dumbbell-shaped, erratically turning rock. "Further out we will prospect. Before that I wish to show you a crystalline world like Estelle—a transparent sponge of bubbles, caverns, and tubes."

A particularly ugly cluster of grinding, spinning boulders demanded all of the Asterite's attention for a few moments. U'Thang was forced to swing almost a hundred miles to his left to clear this spatial debris safely.

* * *

Sid Weston had visited dozens of the sealed, pressurized caverns like those within Estelle Asteroid's thirty mile bulk. Light came through the translucent rock layers. Roughly ground lenses of the crystalline matter concentrated sunlight in a variety of controlled intensities—ranging from comfortable warmth to that of a blast furnace. Ice deposits were towed to Estelle and thawed within it, and oxygen and hydrogen and metals were freed from the debris of space.

The Hothouse Asteroids, a cluster of fifty-three tiny worlds, were similar in structure to the half-developed planetoid they had just quitted. They supplied food and oxygen-freeing vegetation to the half-million Asterites and the thousands of transient Earthmen.

Eventually all the similar compartmented asteroids ready for use by human beings would be tamed and filled with vegetation and atmosphere and people. But it might require centuries . . .

Now U'Thang had regained his plotted course. He wrote again.

"My brother and I hope to settle there—unless someone beats us to it. Once we own our own trading ship, and are free of debt, we will file on our share of it."

"Is it large?" asked Sid's fingers.

"Almost as large as Estelle." U'Thang frowned. "We can claim no more than a fourth of the cubic acreage. That is enough."

Sid started impulsively to say something. Then he closed his fist. Developing a dead airless world, bringing life and atmosphere and warmth to its pellucid inner cavities, intrigued his imagination. There would be a possible modest fortune for the early owners and lease-holders of such a development.

But Captain Torner and his half-brother would hardly welcome a company spy, and his son, as partners in such a venture.

"There it is," U'Thang's pad announced. He pointed ahead.

The asteroid was lumpily triangular as seen from one side, but as they drew closer and circled it the opposite hemisphere was rounded. The entire irregular mass, in the eternal sunlight of space, glowed with a milky lambency. Only a few darker pockets of opaque matter scattered unevenly through the asteroid's substance served to mar the soft glow of the tiny world.

At its thickest the planetoid was less than twenty miles—with a possible twelve miles for the minimum dimension. Rifts and gaping irregular orifices dotted the surface, and ragged spurs of glassy substance jutted upward like miniature mountains.

U'Thang guided the space lighter into a funnel-shaped crater with a diameter of a thousand feet, and an equal depth. At a point midway he eased the craft into a wide crevice and made contact.

"Two inner liners for the space suit," he informed Sid. He grinned. "You soft Big Worlders need them. Cold and radiation bother you."

Sid agreed with what U'Thang had written as he donned the repulsive yellow limpness of the insulating liners. He was soft, and he could be harmed by unshielded radiation. Just as the squat Asterite's own ancestors had given birth to strange, and often ghastly, mutations in the early days of asteroid colonization, so his cells could be harmed.

The scores of divergent Asterite strains testified to the danger. Even yet the Asterites were changing—often without improvement. The ratio of monstrous offspring to the more stable types was very high.

After they had donned their suits U'Thang went first into the undersized airlock—about the size and shape of an upended coffin—and a moment later his space-suited shape was visible through the cloudy viewport. He motioned at Sid to follow suit.

A corridor opened before them from the crater's creviced wall, leading into the asteroid's gleaming depths. Lumps of loose debris, some of them large as the space lighter, cluttered the way but did not block passage.

Gravity was near zero; so low in nickel-iron was the asteroid that Sid's magnetic shoes were worthless. Walking was a shuffling sort of glide. A violent spurt of activity could spell disaster he knew.

U'Thang was securing a small cable from above the mooring fenders of the lighter to an iron ring set into the crystalline rock. Now Sid could see that his younger friend had brought along a half-dozen extra air cylinders and a battered brown plastryn bag filled with tools and equipment from the ship.

The Asterite waved his suit's air-swollen arm to attract Sid's attention. He pointed to the transparent belly panel in his suit where the pad was clipped. U'Thang's indrawn hand was printing a message.

"Come," the pad requested.

Sid had known that audio communication, unless by tapping out code, was impossible, and he had wondered how they were to communicate. He had been working out a visual system that might work well, to be built at some later date. But this makeshift system seemed to be adequate.

U'Thang led the way among and around the mass of debris that half-filled the wide corridor. Sid followed closely after the floating air cylinders and the bag attached by a line to the Asterite's belt.

As they proceeded the way that had been broken and uneven underfoot gradually became smooth and glassy. Overhead the rift opened to a height of as much as a hundred feet—and again it came close down to Sid's helmeted head.

They were soon passing through empty chambers with soaring domed ceilings and uneven floors several acres in extent. There were level miniature plains, wrinkled chains of pygmy mountains, and expanses of canyon-mesa–like crevices and outcroppings. There were clustering series of hollow bubbles nine to thirty feet in diameter reminding Sid of the beaded froth of soapy water, but these were of thick glassy rock.

As they proceeded, U'Thang, at intervals, sprayed fresh scarlet splotches, and brightened older markings, along the walls as they shuffled and slithered alongside them. In such a labyrinth of intersecting ways—often five or six new tunnels opened invitingly—markers were essential.

"How do you like our world?" printed U'Thang. "Picture it with chambers sealed. Full of air and green with life."

Sid nodded his head within the helmet vigorously—and stopped. He withdrew his arm from the suit and groped into his transparent belly pod where he found another pad and a stylus.

"Beats Estelle," he printed. "Good as Complex Nine's hothouse worlds. Would like to own a few cubic miles myself."

"All you need is some money and legal markers," wrote U'Thang. "If you and your father settled here we would have good neighbors, Sid."

Poor hard luck guy, Sid was thinking. Born without voice or hearing and with the appearance of a scaly offworld entity exiled from some video horror tape. From the first he had admired the good nature and even temper of the dwarfish mutant, and with every passing day in his company his liking and respect had grown for U'Thang.

"How far back to the tender?" he printed hastily, trying to dismiss what U'Thang had offered. He was a Judas—a cheat.

"Two, maybe three minutes." U'Thang's improbable pixy grin again. "This is end of a long circle. But now I show you where we build first."

They stood in a narrow opening three feet above the uneven knobs and level stretches of a cavern's two acre floor. The roof was thirty feet above and seemed free of cracks or openings.

"Easy sealed," the printed words came. "Only two openings, Sid."

They crossed the chamber and left through a larger gap that returned them to the same corridor they had used on the inward trek. Eighty feet along this brought them to the wide crevice where the space lighter had been docked.

U'Thang's triple-clawed mechanical hand clamped on Sid's arm. He drew him back behind a roughly pyramidal mass of rock, making signs for caution and concealment as he did so.

"Hard luck miners or outlaws," wrote U'Thang.

Sid felt the bottom drop out of his stomach. He had been anticipating the reassuring tug of his magnetic boots on the ship's metal deck for several minutes now. Out here he weighed only ounces.

Now he saw the second, much larger, ship landed close beside the lighter. The newcomer was a badly scarred, much-patched hulk—a cobbled-together crushed section aft heavily daubed with a light-hued spacetite compound that formed bizarre, almost Oriental, marks.

Three air-bloated figures, protective outer envelopes of yellow over their space armor well-scabbed with patches, were carrying supplies and parts from the stubby cargo lighter to their own vessel.

Sudden rage came to Sid. The stripping of the ship could mean certain death to them both if they were left without fuel or air.

He twisted free from U'Thang's restraining grip and leaped outward toward the plunderers. In so doing he had forgotten how feeble was gravity's clutch on his person. Up and outward he rocketed far above their heads. He was in danger of quitting the tiny world forever.

As he passed close above one of the trio his clawed hands clamped the end of the burden being carried by the suited man—a section of metallic tubing ripped from the lighter. He yanked, pulling his body downward even as the outlaw was catapulted skyward in turn. His body hit crystalline rock and his claws clamped projecting spurs.

He caught a glimpse of a second figure, a ruddy face with a mat of dirty gray whiskers and tiny blue sparks of eyes behind a grimy faceplate. Something slammed into his suit's middle—a length of pipe perhaps—and he was choking for air.

Another bulky shape. He was jammed into a wide crack between two boulders. There was a hiss of escaping air as a knife-edged shard of crystalline rock penetrated. But Sid was grateful. He had not been killed outright. The leak could be sealed.

Rockets blasted. The boulders about him juggled together and went rolling. U'Thang was looking ruefully down at him, and then he saw that both ships were gone. The little Asterite was slapping a temporary patch over the frost-rimmed leak and hauling him upright.

A moment later U'Thang pushed Sid, and the extra air bottles and tools, into a hollow natural cockpit of a fifty-foot slab of the translucent asteroid's substance. He twisted a length of trylon line about a few convenient knobs inside and then climbed aboard too.

So abruptly that Sid almost lost permanently his newly regained power to breathe, the crystalline block lifted from the crevice and shot upward out of the crater into empty space. In a moment they were traveling even faster than had the space lighter.

Only then did U'Thang resort again to the writing pad.

"We had only a few hours' supply of air, Sid," he printed. "I had no choice. I must save your life even though it costs me your friendship . . . You see I have the gift of levitation—and of other powers as well."

"Why, that is wonderful!" wrote back Sid. "I wish I were an esper too. If I could read minds and move objects about. Wow!"

The racing shard of rock gracefully dodged a twisted dark object larger than Lookout Mountain back on Earth, and then swerved far to the right of a grinding jumble of basketball-sized rocks.

"So many people hate our kind," wrote U'Thang, "that we keep our strange talents hidden. They are more curse than gift, Sid."

Sid wanted to itch his nose. Instead he printed a few more words. He was able to breathe freely again by now.

"I suppose you are right," he told his friend. "They envy you. You have something they cannot ever possess."

"My brother has a gift too." The little Asterite's grin was twisted. "He can look into minds. He knows why your father bought passage on the tanker. He knows how much you both dislike the job."

Sid was beginning to understand. Everything was coming out into the open now. He felt a lot better. No reason they couldn't help settle the honeycombed asteroid either. They were still good friends.

"You drove the space tanker?" he questioned. "As you drive this?"

U'Thang dodged another slowly tumbling square mile of striated real estate and nodded. His pad sprouted words again.

"I drove the ship, yes. The fuel we saved my brother sells to the asteroid miners. That is why the bank accounts grow, Sid."

"I can't see anything really wrong about that," printed Sid. "Not morally at least. Legally, well . . . But you're not stealing and I'm sure Dad will report you in clean.

"After that I'm sure we'll want to go in with you at developing the asteroid. Dad has plenty of friends. He can borrow money."

The hooded sunken eyes of the Asterite and the blue eyes of the lanky young Earthman met. They winked at one another. Their suits' arms extended and their triple-clawed iron hands clasped. Agreed.

The improvised rough slab of a vessel that U'Thang drove darted yet more swiftly back toward the planetoid, Estelle, and safety.

The Good Neighbors

Edgar Pangborn

The ship was sighted a few times, briefly and without a good fix. It was spherical, the estimated diameter about twenty-seven miles, and was in an orbit approximately 3400 miles from the surface of the Earth. No one observed the escape from it.

The ship itself occasioned some excitement, but back there at the tattered end of the 20th century, what was one visiting spaceship more or less? Others had appeared before, and gone away discouraged—or just not bothering. Three-dimensional TV was coming out of the experimental stage. Soon anyone could have Dora the Doll or the Grandson of Tarzan smack in his own living-room. Besides, it was a hot summer.

The first knowledge of the escape came when the region of Seattle suffered an eclipse of the sun, which was not an eclipse but a near shadow, which was not a shadow but a thing. The darkness drifted out of the northern Pacific. It generated thunder without lightning and without rain. When it had moved eastward and the hot sun reappeared, wind followed, a moderate gale. The coast was battered by sudden high waves, then hushed in a bewilderment of fog.

Before that appearance, radar had gone crazy for an hour.

The atmosphere buzzed with aircraft. They went up in readiness to shoot, but after the first sighting reports only a few miles offshore, that order was vehemently canceled—someone in charge must have had a grain of sense. The thing was not a plane, rocket or missile. It was an animal.

If you shoot an animal that resembles an inflated gas-bag with wings, and the wingspread happens to be something over four miles tip to tip, and the carcass drops on a city—it's not nice for the city.

The Office of Continental Defense deplored the lack of precedent. But actually none was needed. You just don't drop four miles of dead or dying alien flesh on Seattle or any other part of a swarming homeland. You wait till it flies out over the ocean, if it will—the most commodious ocean in reach.

It, or rather she, didn't go back over the Pacific, perhaps because of the prevailing westerlies. After the Seattle incident she climbed to a great altitude above the Rockies, apparently using an updraft with very little wing-motion. There was no means of calculating her weight, or mass, or buoyancy. Dead or injured, drift might have carried her anywhere within one or two hundred miles. Then she seemed to be following the line of the Platte and the Missouri. By the end of the day she was circling interminably over the huge complex of St. Louis, hopelessly crying.

She had a head, drawn back most of the time into the bloated mass of the body but thrusting forward now and then on a short neck not more than three hundred feet in length. When she did that the blunt turtle-like head could be observed, the gaping, toothless, suffering mouth from which the thunder came, and the soft-shining purple eyes that searched the ground but found nothing answering her need. The skin-color was mud-brown with some dull iridescence and many peculiar marks resembling weals or blisters. Along the belly some observers saw half a mile of paired protuberances that looked like teats.

She was unquestionably the equivalent of a vertebrate. Two web-footed legs were drawn up close against the cigar-shaped body. The vast, rather narrow, inflated wings could not have been held or moved in flight without a strong internal skeleton and musculature. Theorists later argued that she must have come from a planet with a high proportion of water surface, a planet possibly larger than Earth though of about the same mass and with a similar atmosphere. She could rise in Earth's air. And before each thunderous lament she was seen to breathe.

It was assumed that immense air sacs within her body were inflated or partly inflated when she left the ship, possibly with some gas lighter than nitrogen. Since it was inconceivable that a vertebrate organism could have survived entry into atmosphere from an orbit 3400 miles up, it was necessary to believe that the ship had briefly descended, unobserved and by unknown means, probably on

Earth's night-side. Later on the ship did descend as far as atmosphere, for a moment . . .

St. Louis was partly evacuated. There is no reliable estimate of the loss of life and property from panic and accident on the jammed roads and rail lines: 1500 dead, 7400 injured is the conservative figure.

After a night and a day she abandoned that area, flying heavily eastward. The droning and swooping gnats of aircraft plainly distressed her. At first she had only tried to avoid them, but now and then during her eastward flight from St. Louis she made short desperate rushes against them, without skill or much sign of intelligence, screaming from a wide-open mouth that could have swallowed a four-engine bomber. Two aircraft were lost over Cincinnati, by collision with each other in trying to get out of her way. Pilots were then ordered to keep a distance of not less than ten miles until such time as she reached the Atlantic—if she did—when she could safely be shot down.

She studied Chicago for a day.

By that time Civil Defense was better prepared. About a million residents had already fled to open country before she came, and the loss of life was proportionately smaller. She moved on. We have no clue to the reason why great cities should have attracted her, though apparently they did. She was hungry perhaps, or seeking help, or merely drawn in animal curiosity by the endless motion of the cities and the strangeness. It has even been suggested that the life forms of her homeland—her masters—resembled humanity. She moved eastward, and religious organizations united to pray that she would come down on one of the lakes where she could safely be destroyed. She didn't.

She approached Pittsburgh, choked and screamed and flew high, and soared in weary circles over Buffalo for a day and a night. Some pilots who had followed the flight from the West Coast claimed that the vast lamentation of her voice was growing fainter and hoarser while she was drifting along the line of the Mohawk Valley. She turned south, following the Hudson at no great height. Sometimes she appeared to be choking, the labored inhalations harsh and prolonged, like a cloud in agony.

When she was over Westchester, headquarters tripled the swarm of interceptors and observation planes. Squadrons from Connecticut and southern New Jersey deployed to form a monstrous funnel, the small end before her, the large end pointing out to open sea. Heavy bombers closed in above, laying a smoke screen at 10,000 feet to discourage her from rising. The ground shook with the drone of jets, and with her crying.

Multitudes had abandoned the metropolitan area. Other multitudes trusted to the subways, to the narrow street canyons and to the strength of concrete and steel. Others climbed to a thousand high places and watched, trusting the laws of chance.

She passed over Manhattan in the evening—between 8:14 and 8:27 P.M., July 16, 1976—at an altitude of about 2000 feet. She swerved away from the aircraft that blanketed Long Island and the Sound, swerved again as the southern group buzzed her instead of giving way. She made no attempt to rise into the sun-crimsoned terror of drifting smoke.

The plan was intelligent. It should have worked, but for one fighter pilot who jumped the gun.

He said later that he himself couldn't understand what happened. It was court-martial testimony, but his reputation had been good. He was Bill Green—William Hammond Green—of New London, Connecticut, flying a one-man jet fighter, well aware of the strictest orders not to attack until the target had moved at least ten miles east of Sandy Hook. He said he certainly had no previous intention to violate orders. It was something that just happened in his mind. A sort of mental sneeze.

His squadron was approaching Rockaway, the flying creature about three miles ahead of him and half a mile down. He was aware of saying out loud to nobody: "Well, she's too big." Then he was darting out of formation, diving on her, giving her one rocket-burst and reeling off to the south at 840 M.P.H.

He never did locate or rejoin his squadron, but he made it somehow back to his home field. He climbed out of the cockpit, they say, and fell flat on his face.

It seems likely that his shot missed the animal's head and tore through some part of her left wing. She spun to the left, rose perhaps a thousand feet, facing the city, sideslipped, recovered herself and fought for altitude. She could not gain it. In the effort she collided with two of the following planes. One of them smashed into her right side behind the wing, the other flipped end over end across her back, like a swatted dragonfly. It dropped clear and made a mess on Bedloe's Island.

She too was falling, in a long slant, silent now but still living. After the impact her body thrashed desolately on the wreckage between Lexington and Seventh Avenues, her right wing churning, then only trailing, in the East River, her left wing a crumpled slowly deflating mass concealing Times Square, Herald Square and the garment district.

At the close of the struggle her neck extended, her turtle beak grasping the top of Radio City. She was still trying to pull herself up, as the buoyant gases hissed and bubbled away through the gushing holes in her side. Radio City collapsed with her.

For a long while after the roar of descending rubble and her own roaring had ceased, there was no human noise except a melancholy thunder of the planes.

The apology came early next morning.

The spaceship was observed to descend to the outer limits of atmosphere, very briefly. A capsule was released, with a parachute timed to open at 40,000 feet and come down quite neatly in Scarsdale. Parachute, capsule and timing device were of good workmanship.

The communication engraved on a plaque of metal (which still defies analysis) was a hasty job, the English slightly odd, with some evidence of an incomplete understanding of the situation. That the visitors were themselves aware of these deficiencies is indicated by the text of the message itself.

Most sadly regret inexcusable escape of livestock. While petting same, one of our children monkied (sp?) with airlock. Will not happen again. Regret also imperfect grasp of language, learned through what you term Television etc. Animal not dangerous, but observe some accidental damage caused, therefore hasten to enclose reimbursement, having taken liberty of studying your highly ingenious methods of exchange. Hope same will be adequate, having estimated deplorable inconvenience to best of ability. Regret exceedingly impossibility of communicating further, as pressure of time and prior obligations forbids. Please accept heartfelt apologies and assurances of continuing esteem.

The reimbursement was in fact properly enclosed with the plaque and may be seen by the public in the rotunda of the restoration of Radio City. Though technically counterfeit, it looks like perfectly good money, except that Mr. Lincoln is missing one of his wrinkles and the words "FIVE DOLLARS" are upside down.

The Grapes of The Rath

jan howard finder

Sir Nippip Koot, Chief of Special Investigations of the Galactic Scotland Yard, sucked slowly on his favorite meerschaum, while eyeing the wight opposite him. This was Su Gnoma Sugnuf, Chief of the Imperial Police on Oniv, the seventh planet of Anthony's Star. Su was humanoid in appearance, having two legs, two arms, two eyes, two noses, etc.

Chief Sugnuf fidgeted irritably in his chair, which valiantly tried to keep up with his movements in order to provide him with a comfortable seat. His jaw muscles tightened in time with his clenching fists as he strove to compose himself.

"Chief Inspector Koot, you must realize that although this hideous and detestable crime has long gone unsolved, it would not normally bring me here to your esteemed office. However, this moldy excretion of a grape worm has lifted off Oniv. Thus, we cannot carry on without the permission and, hopefully, the help of your office."

"Yes," replied Chief Koot, "I do believe that we can enter the case. I'd appreciate your giving me a full briefing. All I know is that the suspect has apparently stolen some grapevines from the Caesar's Imperial vineyards."

"Ah yes, Chief Inspector Koot, seemingly, belike, a petty crime for such exertions by the Imperial Police. However, Oniv is a poor planet. Our one saving grace is that the Ghreat Ghod Vombato has seen fit to bless us with the soil, climate, and vines to produce the most fabulous wine in the Galaxy. Wine is our sole export. Thus, it is a capital crime to attempt to export the vines. It is very probable the vines would not and could not grow elsewhere; however, we dare not tempt the fates.

"That the criminal in question, this rotted lump of vine leaves from diseased cuttings, has stolen vines is bad enough. That this filth from the shoes of discredited grape stompers has taken the vines off planet is infinitely worse. But this, *this* . . ." he sputtered, "has taken vines from The Rath, the vineyard of the Caesar! The Emperor's own vines!

"Therefore, I have been ordered to search for this scum of contaminated grape seeds until I have found him. And found him I have! He is rooted up in the hills of Germany, along the Mosel River on the Galactic Government's own planet Terra. Yet, he is smarter than we thought. No one can touch him there; it is sanctuary. However, with your office's help, we can at least seize the contraband."

Chief Inspector Nippip Koot mulled over the details of the wine caper. The tangled skein of events wove itself into a pattern demonstrating that while on the sanctuary called Terra, the suspect could not be rooted out—but the same could not be said about the vines. *Any* grapes or berries the suspect had in his possession were fair pickings under Galactic Law.

It was only a hop, skip, and two black hole jumps to Terra. Being himself a wine connoisseur who had heard of the fabled wines of Oniv, Chief Inspector Koot went along with Chief Sugnuf and the Imperial Guard assigned to the chase. The Guard was an impressive lot, being a good head taller than Su, who was not short for an Onivian.

The rolling green hills of „Der Schöne Eifel" gave way to the steep-walled Mosel river valley. The police craft quickly and quietly settled to the earth in front of the small flowered home of the suspect.

Su leapt from the craft as it alighted. Moving like the point man on a cavalry charge, he raced to the door. Pounding on it, not really in a manner becoming the Chief of the Imperial Police, he bellowed, "Nup, Tid Nup, come out here—or *else!*"

The door opened and a small, wizened Onivian came out. Tears streaked his cheeks. "Oh sirrah, please do not kill me."

Su, restraining himself with difficulty, choked out, "Nup, you drippings from cancerous berries, if you don't give us every single one of the vines that you stole, I'll forget my position and also the lamentable fact that you are on sanctuary."

"Oh sirrah," whined Nup, "you have come for naught. Though the Mosel valley is famed, far and wide, for its vines, the Berries from The Rath won't grow here. Only one vine survived and on it merely one berry has grown. Please let me keep it—to remind me of the home I can never return to. It is such a beautiful berry, *please?*"

Tears coursed down the cheeks of the broken-hearted Tid Nup. The hard heart of Su was touched. However, Chief Inspector Nippip Koot knew the consequences of being softhearted.

"Nup," he said in a quiet voice, "I'm sure it is indeed magnificent, but we came to seize your berry, not to praise it."

The Great God Awto

Clark Ashton Smith

Class-room lecture given by the Most Honorable Erru Saggus, Professor of Hamurriquanean Archaeology at the World-University of Toshtush, on the 365th day of the year 5998.

Males, females, androgynes and neuters of the class in archaeology, you have learned, from my previous lectures, all that is known or inferred concerning the crudely realistic art and literature of the ancient Hamurriquanes. With some difficulty, owing to the fragmentary nature of the extant remains, I have reconstructed for you their bizarre and hideous buildings, their rude mechanisms.

Also, you are now familiar with the unimaginably clumsy, corrupt and inefficient legal and economic systems that prevailed among them, together with the garblings of crass superstition and scant knowledge that bore the sacred names of the sciences. You have listened, not without amusement, to my account of their ridiculous amatory and social customs, and have heard with horror the unutterable tale of their addiction to all manner of violent crimes.

Today I shall speak regarding a matter that throws into even grosser relief the low-grade barbarism, the downright savagery, of this bloody and besotted people.

Needless to say, my lecture will concern their well nigh universal cult of human sacrifice and self-immolation to the god Awto: a cult which many of my confreres have tried to associate with the worship of the Heendouan deity, Yokkurnudd, or Jukkernot. In this cult, the wild religious fanaticism of the Hamurriquanes, together with the national blood-lust for which they were notorious, found its most congenial and spacious outlet.

If we grant the much-disputed relationship between Awto and Yokkurnudd, it seems plain that the latter god was an extremely mild and refined variation of Awto, worshipped by a gentler and more advanced people. The rites done to Yokkurnudd were localized and occasional while the sacrifices required by Awto took place at all hours on every street and highway.

However, in the face of certain respected authorities, I am inclined to doubt if the two religions had much in common. Certainly nothing apart from the ritual usage of crushing the sacrificial victims under the wheels of ponderous earth-vehicles, such as you have seen in our museums among the exhumed relics of antiquity.

It is my fond hope that I shall eventually find evidence to confirm this doubt, and thus vindicate the Heendouans of the blackest charge that legend and archaeology have brought against them. I shall have made a worthy contribution to science if I can show that they were among the few ancient peoples who were never tainted by the diabolic cult of Awto originating in Hamurriqua.

Because of a religion so barbarous, it has sometimes been argued that the Hamurriquanean culture—if one can term it such—must have flourished at an earlier period in man's development than the Heendouan. However, in dealing with a realm of research that borders upon prehistory, such relative chronology can be left to theorists.

Excepting, of course, in our own superior modern civilization, human progress has been slow and uncertain, with many intercalated Dark Ages, many reversions to partial or total savagery. I believe that the Hamurriquanean epoch, whether prior to that of the Heendouans or contemporary with it, can well be classified as one of these Dark Ages.

To return to my main theme, the cult of Awto. It is doubtless well known to you that in recent years certain irresponsible so-called archaeologists, misled by a desire to create sensation at the cost of truth, have fathered the fantastic thesis that there never was any such god as Awto. They believe, or profess to believe, that the immolatory vehicles of the ancients, and the huge destruction of life and limb caused by their use, were quite without religious significance.

A premise so absurd could be maintained only by madmen or charlatans. I mention it merely that I may refute and dismiss it with all the contempt that it deserves.

Of course, I cannot deny the dubiousness of some of our archaeological deductions. Great difficulties have attended our researches in the continent-embracing deserts of Hamurriqua, where all food-supplies and water must be transported for thousands of miles.

The buildings and writings of the ancients, often made of the most ephemeral materials, lie deep in ever-drifting sands that no human foot has trod for millenniums. Therefore, it is small wonder that guesswork must sometimes fill the gaps of precise knowledge.

I can safely say, however, that few of our deductions are so completely proven, so solidly based, as those relating to the Awto cult. The evidence, though largely circumstantial, is overwhelming.

Like most religions, it would seem that this cult was obscure and shadowy in its origin. Legend and history have both lost the name of the first promulgator. The earliest cars of immolation were slow and clumsy, and the rite of sacrifice was perhaps rarely and furtively practised in the beginning. There is no doubt, too, that the intended victims often escaped. Awto, at first, can hardly have inspired the universal fear and reverence of later epochs.

Certain scraps of Hamurriquanean printing, miraculously preserved in air-tight vaults and deciphered before they could crumble, have given us the names of two early prophets of Awto, Anriford and Dhodzh. These amassed fortunes from the credulity of their benighted followers. It was under the influence of these prophets that the dark and baleful religion spread by leaps and bounds, until no Hamurriquanean street or highway was safe from the thunderously rolling wheels of the sacrificial cars.

It is doubtful whether Awto, like most other savage and primordial deities, was ever represented by graven images. At least, no such images have been recovered in all our delvings. However, the rusty remains of the iron-built temples of Awto, called *grahges,* have been exhumed everywhere in immense numbers.

Strange vessels and metal implements of mysterious hieratic use have been found in the *grahges,* together with traces of oils by which the sacred vehicles were anointed, and the vehicles lie buried in far-spread, colossal scrapheaps. All this, however, throws little light on the deity himself.

It is probable that Awto, sometimes known as Mhotawr, was simply an abstract principle of death and destruction and was believed to manifest himself through the homicidal speed and fury of the fatal machines. His demented devotees flung themselves before these vehicles as before the embodiment of the god.

The power and influence of Awto's priesthood, as well as its numbers, must have been well nigh beyond estimation. The priesthood, it would seem, was divided into at least three orders:

The *mekniks,* or keepers of the *grahges.* The *shophurs,* who drove the sacred vehicles. And an order—whose special name has been lost—that served as guardians of innumerable wayside shrines. It was at these shrines where a mineral liquid called *ghas,* used in the fueling of the vehicles, was dispensed from crude and curious pumping mechanisms.

Several well preserved mummies of *mekniks,* in sacerdotal raiment blackened by the sacred oils, have been recovered from *grahges* in the central Hamurriquanean deserts, where they were apparently buried by sudden sandstorms.

Chemical analysis of the oiled garments has so far failed to confirm a certain legendary belief current among the degenerate bushmen who form the scant remnant of Hamurriqua's teeming myriads. I refer to a belief that the oils used in anointing those ancient cars were often mixed with unctuous matters obtained from the bodies of their victims.

However, a usage so barbarous would have conformed well enough with the principles of the hideous cult. Further research may establish the old legend as a truth.

From the evidence we have unearthed, it is plain that the cult assumed enormous power and wide-spread proportions within a few decades of its inception. The awful apex was reached in little more than a century. In my opinion, it is no coincidence that the whole period of the Awto cult corresponded very closely with Hamurriqua's decline and ultimate downfall.

Some will consider my statements too definite, and will ask for the evidence above mentioned. In answer, I need only point to the condition of those skeletons exhumed by thousands from tombs and vaults dated according to the Hamurriquanean chronology.

Throughout the time-period we have assigned to the Awto cult there is a steady, accelerative increase of bone-fractures, often of the most horribly complicated nature. Toward the end, when the fearful cult was at its height, we find few skeletons that do not show at least one or two minor, if not major, breakages.

The shattered condition of these skeletons, often decapitated or wholly disarticulated, is almost beyond belief.

The rusty remains of the ancient vehicles bear similar witness. Built with an eye to ever greater speed and deadliness, they fall into types that show the ghastly growth and progress of the cult. The later types, found in prodigious numbers, are always more or less dented, broken, crumpled—often they are mere heaps of indescribably tangled wreckage.

Toward the end, it would seem that virtually the whole population must have belonged to the blood-mad priesthood. Going forth daily in the rituals of Awto, they must have turned their cars upon each other, hurtling together with the violence of projectiles. A universal mania for speed went hand in hand with a mania for homicide and suicide.

Picture, if you can, the ever-mounting horror of it all. The nation-wide madness of immolation. The carnivals of bloody holidays. The highways lined from coast to coast with crushed and dismembered sacrifices!

Can you wonder that this ancient people, their numbers decimated, their mentality sapped and bestialized by dire superstition, should have declined so rapidly? Should have fallen almost without a struggle before the hordes of the Orient?

Let history and archaeology draw the curtain. The moral is plain. But luckily, in our present state of high enlightenment, we have little need to fear the rise of any savage error such as that which attended the worship of Awto.

Obituary item broadcast from Toshtush on the 1st day of the year 5999:

We are sorry to record the sudden death of Professor Erru Saggus, who had just delivered the last of his series of lectures on Hamurriquanean Archaeology at the University of Toshtush.

Returning on the same afternoon to his home in the Himalayas, Professor Saggus was the victim of a most unfortunate accident. His stratosphere ship, one of the very newest and speediest models, collided within a few leagues of its destination with a ship driven by one Jar Ghoshtar, a chemistry student from the great College of Ustraleendia.

Both ships were annihilated by the impact, plunging earthward in a single flaming meteoric mass which ignited and destroyed an entire Himalayan village. Several hundred people are said to have burned to death in the resultant conflagration.

Such accidents are all too frequent nowadays, owing to the crowded condition of stratosphere traffic. We must deplore the recklessness of navigators who exceed the 950 mile speed limit. All who saw the recent accident bear witness that Erru Saggus and Jar Ghoshtar were both driving at a speed very much in excess of 1000 miles per hour.

While regretting this present-day mania for mere mileage, we cannot agree with certain ill-advised satirists who have tried to draw a parallel between the fatalities of modern traffic and the ancient rites of immolation to the god Awto.

Superstition is one thing, Science is another. Such archaeologists as Professor Saggus have proven to us that the worshippers of Awto were the victims of a dark and baleful error. It is unthinkable that such superstition will ever again prevail. With pride for our achieve-ments, and full confidence in the future, we can number the Most Honorable Professor Erru Saggus among the martyrs of Science.

The Great Slow Kings

Roger Zelazny

Drax and Dran sat in the great Throne Hall of Glan, discuss-ing life. Monarchs by virtue of superior intellect and phy-sique—and the fact that they were the last two survivors of the race of Glan—theirs was a divided rule over the planet and their one subject, Zindrome, the palace robot.

Drax had been musing for the past four centuries (theirs was a sluggish sort) over the possibility of life on other planets in the galaxy.

Accordingly, "Dran," said he, addressing the other (who was becoming mildly curious as to his thoughts), "Dran, I've been thinking. There may be life on other planets in the galaxy."

Dran considered his reply to this, as the world wheeled several times about its sun.

"True," he finally agreed, "there may."

After several months Drax shot back, "If there is, we ought to find out."

"Why?" asked Dran with equal promptness, which caused the other to suspect that he, too, had been thinking along these lines.

So he measured his next statement out cautiously, first testing each word within the plated retort of his reptilian skull.

"Our kingdom is rather underpopulated at present," he ob-served. "It would be good to have many subjects once more."

Dran regarded him askance, then slowly turned his head. He closed one eye and half-closed the other, taking full stock of his co-ruler, whose appearance, as he suspected, was unchanged since the last time he had looked.

"That, also, is true," he noted. "What do you suggest we do?"

This time Drax turned, reappraising him, eye to eye.

"I think we ought to find out if there is life on other planets in the galaxy."

"Hmm."

Two quick roundings of the seasons went unnoticed, then, "Let me think about it," he said, and turned away.

After what he deemed a polite period of time, Drax coughed.

"Have you thought sufficiently?"

"No."

Drax struggled to focus his eyes on the near-subliminal streak of bluish light which traversed, re-traversed and re-re-traversed the Hall as he waited.

"Zindrome!" he finally called out.

The robot slowed his movements to a statuelike immobility to accommodate his master. A feather duster protruded from his right limb.

"You called, great Lord of Glan?"

"Yes, Zindrome, worthy subject. Those old spaceships which we constructed in happier days, and never got around to using. Are any of them still capable of operation?"

"I'll check, great Lord."

He seemed to change position slightly.

"There are three hundred eighty-two," he announced, "of which four are in functioning condition, great Lord. I've checked all the operating circuits."

"Drax," warned Dran, "you are arrogating unauthorized powers to yourself once more. You should have conferred with me before issuing that order."

"I apologize," stated the other. "I simply wanted to expedite matters, should your decision be that we conduct a survey."

"You have anticipated my decision correctly," nodded Dran, "but your eagerness seems to bespeak a hidden purpose."

"No purpose but the good of the realm," smiled the other.

"That may be, but the last time you spoke of 'the good of the realm,' the civil strife which ensued cost us our other robot."

"I have learned my lesson and profited thereby. I shall be more judicious in the future."

"I hope so. Now, about this expedition—which part of the galaxy do you intend to investigate first?"

A tension-filled pause ensued.

"I had assumed," murmured Drax, "that you would conduct the expedition. Being the more mature monarch, yours should be a more adequate decision as to whether or not a particular species is worthy of our enlightened rule."

"Yes, but your youth tends to make you more active than I. The journey should be more expeditiously conducted by you." He emphasized the word "expeditiously."

"We could both go, in separate ships," offered Drax. "That would be truly expeditious—"

Their heated debating was cut short by a metallic cough-equivalent.

"Masters," suggested Zindrome, "the half-life of radioactive materials being as ephemeral as it is, I regret to report that only one spaceship is now in operational condition."

"That settles it, Dran. *You* go. It will require a steadier *rrand* to manage an underpowered ship."

"And leave you to foment civil strife and usurp unfranchised powers? No, you go!"

"I suppose we could *both* go," sighed Drax.

"Fine! Leave the kingdom leaderless! *That* is the kind of muddle-headed thinking which brought about our present political embarrassment."

"Masters," said Zindrome, "if *someone* doesn't go soon, the ship will be useless."

They both studied their servant, approving the rapid chain of logic forged by his simple statement.

"Very well," they smiled in unison, *"you* go."

Zindrome bowed quite obsequiously and departed from the great Throne Hall of Glan.

"Perhaps we should authorize Zindrome to construct facsimiles of himself," stated Dran, tentatively. "If we had more subjects, we could accomplish more."

"Are you forgetting our most recent agreement?" asked Drax. "A superfluity of robots tended to stimulate factionalism last time—and certain people grew ambitious . . ." He let his voice trail off over the years, for emphasis.

"I am not certain as to whether your last allusion contains a hidden accusation," began the other carefully. "If so, permit me to caution you concerning rashness—and to remind you who it was who engineered the Mono-Robot Protection Pact."

"Do you believe things will be different in the case of a multitude of organic subjects?" inquired the other.

"Definitely," said Dran. "There is a certain irrational element in the rationale of the organic being, making it less amenable to direct orders than a machine would be. Our robots, at least, were faithful when we ordered them to destroy one another. Irresponsible organic subjects either do it without being told, which is boorish, or refuse to do it when you order them, which is insubordination."

"True," smiled Drax, unearthing a gem he had preserved for millennia against this occasion. "Concerning organic life, the only statement which can be made with certainty is that life is uncertain."

"Hmm." Dran narrowed his eyes to slits. "Let me ponder that a moment. Like much of your thinking it seems to smack of a concealed sophistry."

"It contains none, I assure you. It is the fruit of much meditation."

"Hmm."

Dran's pondering was cut short by the arrival of Zindrome, who clutched two brownish blurs beneath his metal arms.

"Back already, Zindrome? What have you there? Slow them down so we can see them."

"They are under sedation at present, great Masters. It is the movements caused by their breathing which produce the unpleasant vibration pattern on your retinas. To subject them to more narcosis could prove deleterious."

"Nevertheless," maintained Dran, "we must appraise our new subjects carefully, which requires that we see them. Slow them down some more."

"You gave that order without—" began Drax, but was distracted by the sudden appearance of the two hairy bipeds.

"Warm-blooded?" he asked.

"Yes, Lord."

"That bespeaks a very brief lifespan."

"True," offered Dran, "but that kind tends to reproduce quite rapidly."

"That observation tends to be correct," nodded Drax. "Tell me, Zindrome, do they represent the sexes necessary for reproduction?"

"Yes, Master. There are two sexes among these anthropoids, so I brought one of each."

"That was very wise. Where did you find them?"

"Several billion light years from here."

"Turn these two loose outside and go fetch us some more."

The creatures vanished. Zindrome appeared not to have moved.

"Have you the fuel necessary for another such journey?"

"Yes, my Lord. More of it has evolved recently."

"Excellent."

The robot departed.

"What sort of governmental setup should we inaugurate this time?" asked Drax.

"Let us review the arguments for the various types."

"A good idea."

In the midst of their discussion, Zindrome returned and stood waiting to be recognized.

"What is it, Zindrome? Did you forget something?"

"No, great Lords. When I returned to the world from which I obtained the samples, I discovered that the race had progressed to the point where it developed fission processes, engaged in an atomic war, and annihilated itself."

"That was extremely inconsiderate—typical, however, I should say, of warm-blooded instability."

Zindrome continued to shift.

"Have you something else to report?"

"Yes, great Masters. The two specimens I released have multiplied and are now spread over the entire planet of Glan."

"We should have been advised!"

"Yes, great Lords, but I was absent and—"

"They themselves should have reported this action!"

"Masters, I am afraid they are unaware of your existence."

"How could that have happened?" asked Dran.

"We are presently buried beneath several thousand layers of alluvial rock. The geological shifts—"

"You have your orders to maintain the palace and clean the grounds," glowered Dran. "Have you been frittering away your time again?"

"No, great Lords! It all occurred during my absence. I shall attend to it immediately."

"First," ordered Drax, "tell us what else our subjects have been up to, that they saw fit to conceal from us."

"Recently," observed the robot, "they have discovered how to forge and temper metals. Upon landing, I observed that they had developed many ingenious instruments of a cutting variety. Unfortunately they were using them to cut one another."

"Do you mean," roared Dran, "that there is strife in the kingdom?"

"Uh, yes, my Lord."

"I will not brook unauthorized violence among my subjects!"

"*Our* subjects," added Drax, with a meaningful glare.

"*Our* subjects," amended Dran. "We must take immediate action."

"Agreed."

"Agreed."

"I shall issue orders forbidding their engagement in activities leading to bloodshed."

"I presume that you mean a joint proclamation," stated Drax.

"Of course. I was not slighting you, I was simply shaken by the civil emergency. We shall draft an official proclamation. Let Zindrome fetch us writing instruments."

"Zindrome, fetch—"

"I have them here, my Lords."

"Now, let me see. How shall we phrase it . . . ?"

"Perhaps I should clean the palace while your Excellencies—"

"No! Wait right here! This will be very brief and to the point."

"Mm. 'We hereby proclaim . . .' "

"Don't forget our titles."

"True. 'We, the imperial monarchs of Glan, herebeneath undersigned, do hereby . . .' "

A feeble pulse of gamma rays passed unnoticed by the two rulers. The faithful Zindrome diagnosed its nature, however, and tried unsuccessfully to obtain his monarchs' attention. Finally, he dismissed the project with a stoical gesture typical of his kind. He waited.

"There!" they agreed, flourishing the document. "Now you can tell us what you have been trying to say, Zindrome. But make it brief, you must deliver this soon."

"It is already too late, great Lords. This race, also, progressed into civilized states, developed nuclear energy, and eradicated itself while you were writing."

"Barbarous!"

"Warm-blooded irresponsibility!"

"May I go clean up now, great Masters?"

"Soon, Zindrome, soon. First, though, I move that we file the proclamation in the Archives for future use, in the event of similar occurrences."

Dran nodded.

"I agree. *We* so order."

The robot accepted the crumbling proclamation and vanished from sight.

"You know," Drax mused, "there must be lots of radioactive material lying about now . . ."

"There probably is."

"It could be used to fuel a ship for another expedition."

"Perhaps."

"This time we could instruct Zindrome to bring back something with a longer lifespan and more deliberate habits—somewhat nearer our own."

"That would have its dangers. But perhaps we could junk the Mono-Robot Protection Pact and order Zindrome to manufacture extras of himself. Under strict supervision."

"That would have its dangers, too."

"At any rate, I should have to ponder your suggestion carefully."

"And I yours."

"It's been a busy day," nodded Dran. "Let's sleep on it."

"A good idea."

Sounds of saurian snoring emerged from the great Throne Hall of Glan.

The Green Meadow

**Translated by Elizabeth Neville Berkeley
and H. P. Lovecraft**

INTRODUCTORY NOTE: The following very singular narrative or record of impressions was discovered under circumstances so extraordinary that they deserve careful description. On the evening of Wednesday, August 27, 1913, at about 8:30 o'clock, the population of the small seaside village of Potowonket, Maine, U.S.A., was aroused by a thunderous report accompanied by a blinding flash; and persons near the shore beheld a mammoth ball of fire dart from the heavens into the sea but a short distance out, sending up a prodigious column of water. The following Sunday a fishing party composed of John Richmond, Peter B. Carr, and Simon Canfield caught in their trawl and dragged ashore a mass of metallic rock, weighing 360 pounds, and looking (as Mr. Canfield said) like a piece of slag. Most of the inhabitants agreed that this heavy body was none other than the fireball which had fallen from the sky four days before; and Dr. Richmond M. Jones, the local scientific authority, allowed that it must be an aerolite or meteoric stone. In chipping off specimens to send to an expert Boston analyst, Dr. Jones discovered imbedded in the semi-metallic mass the strange book containing the ensuing tale, which is still in his possession.

In form the discovery resembles an ordinary notebook, about 5×3 inches in size, and containing thirty leaves. In material, however, it presents marked peculiarities. The covers are apparently of some dark stony substance unknown to geologists, and unbreakable by any mechanical means. No chemical reagent seems to act upon them. The leaves are much the same, save that they are lighter in colour, and so infinitely thin as to be quite flexible. The whole is bound by some process not very clear to those who have observed it; a process involving the adhesion of the leaf substance to the cover substance. These substances cannot now be separated, nor can the leaves be torn by any amount of force. The writing is *Greek of the purest classical quality,* and several students of palaeography declare that the characters are in a cursive hand used about the second century B.C. There is little in the text to determine the date. The mechanical mode of writing cannot be deduced beyond the fact that it must have resembled that of the modern slate and slate-pencil. During the course of analytical efforts made by the late Prof. Chambers of Harvard, several pages, mostly at the conclusion of the narrative, were blurred to the point of utter effacement before being read; a circumstance forming a well-nigh irreparable loss. What remains of the contents was done into modern Greek letters by the palaeographer Rutherford and in this form submitted to the translators.

Prof. Mayfield of the Massachusetts Institute of Technology, who examined samples of the strange stone, declares it a true meteorite; an opinion in which Dr. von Winterfeldt of Heidelberg (interned in 1918 as a dangerous enemy alien) does not concur. Prof. Bradley of Columbia College adopts a less dogmatic ground; pointing out that certain utterly unknown ingredients are present in large quantities, and warning that no classification is as yet possible.

The presence, nature, and message of the strange book form so momentous a problem, that no explanation can even be attempted. The text, as far as preserved, is here rendered as literally as our language permits, in the hope that some reader may eventually hit upon an interpretation and solve one of the greatest scientific mysteries of recent years.

—E.N.B.—L.T., Jun.

(The Story)

It was a narrow place, and I was alone. On one side, beyond a margin of vivid waving green, was the sea; blue, bright, and billowy, and sending up vaporous exhalations which intoxicated me. So profuse, indeed, were these exhalations, that they gave me an odd impression of a coalescence of sea and sky; for the heavens were likewise bright and blue. On the other side was the forest, ancient almost as the sea itself, and stretching infinitely inland. It was very dark, for the trees were grotesquely huge and luxuriant, and incredibly numerous. Their giant trunks were of a horrible green which blended weirdly with the narrow green tract whereon I stood. At some distance away, on either side of me, the strange forest extended down to the water's edge; obliterating the shore line and completely hemming in the narrow tract. Some of the trees, I observed, stood in the water itself; as though impatient of any barrier to their progress.

I saw no living thing, nor sign that any living thing save myself had ever existed. The sea and the sky and the wood encircled me, and reached off into regions beyond my imagination. Nor was there any sound save of the wind-tossed wood and of the sea.

As I stood in this silent place, I suddenly commenced to tremble; for though I knew not how I came there, and could scarce remember what my name and rank had been, I felt that I should go mad if I could understand what lurked about me. I recalled things I had learned, things I had dreamed, things I had imagined and yearned for in some other distant life. I thought of long nights when I had gazed up at the stars of heaven and cursed the gods that my free soul could not traverse the vast abysses which were inaccessible to my body. I conjured up ancient blasphemies, and terrible delvings into the papyri of Democritus; but as memories appeared, I shuddered in deeper fear, for I knew that I was alone— horribly alone. Alone, yet close to sentient impulses of vast, vague kind; which I prayed never to comprehend nor encounter. In the voice of the swaying green branches I fancied I could detect a kind of malignant hatred and daemoniac triumph. Sometimes they struck me as being in horrible colloquy with ghastly and unthinkable things which the scaly green bodies of the trees half hid; hid from sight but not from consciousness. The most oppressive of my sensations was a sinister feeling of alienage. Though I saw about me objects which I could name—trees, grass, sea, and sky; I felt that their relation to me was not the same as that of the trees, grass, sea, and sky I knew in another and dimly remembered life. The nature of the difference I could not tell, yet I shook in stark fright as it impressed itself upon me.

And then, in a spot where I had before discerned nothing but the misty sea, I beheld the Green Meadow; separated from me by a vast expanse of blue rippling water with sun-tipped wavelets, yet strangely near. Often I would peep fearfully over my right shoulder at the trees, but I preferred to look at the Green Meadow, which affected me oddly.

It was while my eyes were fixed upon this singular tract, that I first felt the ground in motion beneath me. Beginning with a kind of throbbing agitation which held a fiendish suggestion of conscious action, the bit of bank on which I stood detached itself from the grassy shore and commenced to float away; borne slowly onward as if by some current of resistless force. I did not move, astonished and startled as I was by the unprecedented phenomenon; but stood rigidly still until a wide lane of water yawned betwixt me and the land of trees. Then I sat down in a sort of daze, and again looked at the sun-tipped water and the Green Meadow.

Behind me the trees and the things they may have been hiding seemed to radiate infinite menace. This I knew without turning to view them, for as I grew more used to the scene I became less and less dependent upon the five senses that once had been my sole reliance. I knew the green scaly forest hated me, yet now I was safe from it, for my bit of bank had drifted far from the shore.

But though one peril was past, another loomed up before me. Pieces of earth were constantly crumbling from the floating isle which held me, so that death could not be far distant in any event. Yet even then I seemed to sense that death would be death to me no more, for I turned again to watch the Green Meadow, imbued with a curious feeling of security in strange contrast to my general horror.

Then it was that I heard, at a distance immeasurable, the sound of falling water. Not that of any trivial cascade such as I had known, but that which might be heard in the far Scythian lands if all the Mediterranean were poured down an unfathomable abyss. It was toward this sound that my shrinking island was drifting, yet I was content.

Far in the rear were happening weird and terrible things; things which I turned to view, yet shivered to behold. For in the sky dark vaporous forms hovered fantastically, brooding over trees and seeming to answer the challenge of the waving green branches. Then a thick mist arose from the sea to join the sky-forms, and the shore was erased from my sight. Though the sun—what sun I knew not—shone brightly on the water around me, the land I had left seemed involved in a daemoniac tempest where clashed the will of the hellish trees and what they hid, with that of the sky and the sea. And when the mist vanished, I saw only the blue sky and the blue sea, for the land and the trees were no more.

It was at this point that my attention was arrested by the *singing* in the Green Meadow. Hitherto, as I have said, I had encountered no sign of human life; but now there arose to my ears a dull chant whose origin and nature were apparently unmistakable. While the words were utterly undistinguishable, the chant awaked in me a peculiar train of associations; and I was reminded of some vaguely disquieting lines I had once translated out of an Egyptian book, which in turn were taken from a papyrus of ancient Meroë. Through my brain ran lines that I fear to repeat; lines telling of very antique things and forms of life in the days when our earth was exceeding young. Of things which thought and moved and were alive, yet which gods and men would not consider alive. It was a strange book.

As I listened, I became gradually conscious of a circumstance which had before puzzled me only subconsciously. At no time had my sight distinguished any definite objects in the Green Meadow, an impression of vivid homogeneous verdure being the sum total of my perception. Now, however, I saw that the current would cause my island to pass the shore at but a little distance; so that I might learn more of the land and of the singing thereon. My curiosity to behold the singers had mounted high, though it was mingled with apprehension.

Bits of sod continued to break away from the tiny tract which carried me, but I heeded not their loss; for I felt that I was not to die with the body (or appearance of a body) which I seemed to possess. That everything about me, even life and death, was illusory; that I had overleaped the bounds of mortality and corporeal entity, becoming a free, detached thing; impressed me as almost certain. Of my location I knew nothing, save that I felt I could not be on the earth-planet once so familiar to me. My sensations, apart from a kind of haunting terror, were those of a traveller just embarked upon an unending voyage of discovery. For a moment I thought of the lands and persons I had left behind; and of strange ways whereby I might some day tell them of my adventurings, even though I might never return.

I had now floated very near the Green Meadow, so that the voices were clear and distinct; but though I knew many languages I could not quite interpret the words of the chanting. Familiar they indeed were, as I had subtly felt when at a greater distance, but beyond a sensation of vague and awesome remembrance I could make nothing of them. A most extraordinary *quality* in the voices— a quality which I cannot describe—at once frightened and fascinated me. My eyes could now discern several things amidst the omnipresent verdure—rocks, covered with bright green moss, shrubs of considerable height, and less definable shapes of great magnitude which seemed to move or vibrate amidst the shrubbery in a peculiar way. The chanting, whose authors I was so anxious to glimpse, seemed loudest at points where these shapes were most numerous and most vigorously in motion.

And then, as my island drifted closer and the sound of the distant waterfall grew louder, I saw clearly the *source* of the chanting, and in one horrible instant remembered everything. Of such things I cannot, dare not tell, for therein was revealed the hideous solution of all which had puzzled me; and that solution would drive you mad, even as it almost drove me. . . . I knew now the change through which I had passed, and through which certain others who once were men had passed! and I knew the endless cycle of the future which none like me may escape. . . . I shall live forever, be conscious forever, though my soul cries out to the gods for the boon of death and oblivion. . . . All is before me: beyond the deafening torrent lies the land of Stethelos, where young men are infinitely old. . . . The Green Meadow . . . I will send a message across the horrible immeasurable abyss. . . .

[At this point the text becomes illegible.]

The Grof

Philip Sidney Jennings

Alone in the city park with the Spring sunlight pointing out a few white hairs in the general dark of his closely cropped head (old invaders gathering in the dark continent) Ossie did not feel free. At least he didn't feel as he thought he should feel. A whole three days ago he had ended a ten year stretch on the inescapable side of bars and a whole three days ago he had thought ahead to this moment in the Park when he would feel and be free! But it didn't feel that marvellous! He speculated that even if he hadn't spent the last ten years of his life in jail he would have spent it in no extravagant or high flung way—a well-lit room, his stamps, his books, his music; his mother in the next room chatting to Telly, her electrical companion; a chocolate biscuit easiness throughout the apartment. Now he had that world again and no real desire to change it. He began walking briskly. Something was missing or he had changed or . . . He began whistling as he walked.

The City, where Ossie had been born forty-three years ago in 2056 had definitely changed. He paused before the statue of a man on a horse, way up high on a stainless steel stand. The gleaming man drew a short sword from its scabbard, raised it on high, then faster than the eye could follow, brought it down in a hissing sweep, then up it went again and was returned to its place in the scabbard. The green eyes of the metal warrior beamed out of a bronzen face and for a moment Ossie forgot about statues and felt afraid. He walked on through the Park and found a lion which twisted its head, opened its jaws and snapped them shut. He found ancient politicians wagging tall spindly fingers and modern ones shoulder-ing short stun guns, heros, whose giant muscles rippled visibly in cavernous iron chests, and most amazing of all: a small space army of Earthmen repelling an invasion of Trokers, whose unlikely limbs, as they were shed in the furore of the electronic battle, were in-stantly replaced so that it seemed warriors sprouted from the ground, as the oldest stories of ancient mythology might have in-sisted it was.

He bought a dinner stick from a Park peddlar, entered The City Zoo and after staring at the heaving sides of a sleeping lion for several silent minutes, wandered down an avenue of trees up to a squat concrete building, studded with a large plaque, which read:

THE GROF HOUSE

The Grof was brought back from Noah 11 in 2090 by Dr.
  Herbert Von Groff.
It is the first creature to be seen from another planet.
Studies have yet to determine its gender and age.
It is characterised by what appears to be an even temper
  and a "bubbling" sound.
The Grof House is purposely kept dark to simulate the
  conditions on Noah 11.

Ossie had heard of the Grof. He became suddenly anxious to see what the creature looked like. He pushed through a door and found himself alone in a long dark room. Dimly he made out a cage at one end of the room. He approached the cage and stared through the bars. His heart jumped. One moment he had been staring through the darkness, the next he was looking into twin tunnels of deep yellow eyes, which were triangular and moist and without pupils which a human eye could move in and out of with little jumps of understanding and insight. The eyes were in a perfectly round head. There were two breathing holes beneath the eyes and a pair of purple lips which sprang out from the face of the creature on a long thin stem like that of a tulip. Somehow that mouth reminded Ossie of the way his mother often kissed him goodnight, stretching her neck, making a kiss with her lips. This marvellous head was in the middle of four concertina-like limbs, attached to the head by four short crinkly necks. The Grof moved around the cage slowly, using all four limbs which had three fingers at their ends. It moved like a child doing cartwheels in slow motion and was covered like a teddy bear with a thin brown fur; the head, however, was dark and naked like a hazel nut.

"Incredible!" Ossie whispered aloud to himself.

The Grof, whose yellow eyes had never moved from Ossie's, now stopped its turning and came to a standstill in front of the staring human. Two of its limbs contracted. The creature sank from five feet to three in height. Ossie realised the Grof was crouched down now, staring at him. The yellow eyes shone like torch beams and suddenly the "bubbling" sound started. Ossie listened carefully to it. It reminded him of water boiling over a ballet of boiled eggs in a pan. He began to smile and drift along with the liquid music.

"Funny looking fellah, ain't he? Hello Groffy. Chow time soon."

Ossie spun around. The frosty haired Grofkeeper was standing just behind him. Ossie felt an unexpected shot of guilt course through his body, as though, like a little boy, he had been caught doing something he shouldn't. He nodded in some confusion. The Keeper went on:

"He used to be a popular fellah some years ago. Groffy used to be the star attraction of the Zoo. Not anymore. All his admirers have gone back to lions and tigers."

The Keeper shook his head from side to side. Ossie nodded again and with a feeling that his privacy had been invaded, went out into the Park with a memory of yellow eyes and bubbling music. He thought he could still see the eyes and hear the music when he reached Avenue 15, for Ossie a new motorised section of The City. Individuals shot up and down the sidewalk on wheelshoes. Ossie grinned to himself. There seemed to be two speeds: "Don't stop me" miles per hour and "Just cruising" miles per hour. A shadow fell across him. He looked up and saw two Pleesmen hovering in the air just above him. The sun glinted on the tiny heli-blades which revolved with a small whine on their enormous flying boots.

"Wheel problem, sir?"

Ossie shook his head:

"No wheels: no problem."

The Pleesmen shook their heads. One said:

"Wrong sir. No wheels in a motorised section . . ."

"I'm looking fcr the Belt to Branksville, The City."

The Pleesmen, not anxious it seemed to issue a ticket, gave Ossie directions and buzzed away like giant blue bees. He reached the Belt without a hitch and was swept through a tunnel which spat him out almost on the doorstep of his mother's ground level apartment.

He heard Telly talking to his mother in her room and quietly went into his study. With a pair of fine tweezers he began moving postage stamps from a large album into little paper approval booklets. He worked with his stamp business for three or four hours, then he put them aside and lay back on his bed. He wondered if he shouldn't go out, fill himself up with Lastliquors and feel and reciprocate the bold caresses of the leggy women of The City. He closed his eyes. That wasn't what he really wanted to do. His breathing took on a steadier rhythm. Oily patterns seemed to run beneath his eye-lids. They were shapeless and moving and multi-colored like gasoline spills. But then suddenly, as though freed of some hidden impediment, they ran in definite directions, making a shape, forming a form. It was the Grof. There for a moment, yellow eyes pouring light, and then it was gone. Ossie opened his eyes, swung off the bed and reached for the Tellyfone. He dialed: "Hey! Everything that's Known is now on the Fone."

"Request info on Grof, extra-terrestrial creature, located in The City Zoo."

The tape on the Grof told him little. The creature weighed a hundred and five pounds and could extend or contract its limbs. It was the only life form found on Noah 11 or anywhere else. There was a scientific explanation for the bubbling sound, which Ossie could not fully understand but which he felt was somehow absurd. He returned to his stamps until his mother, a frail widow, full of love and anxiety, came into the room. She kissed him on the forehead.

"I'm going to bed, Ossie. Get a good night's sleep yourself. Get that pinched look out of your face."

Ossie grinned: "Don't worry about me, Ma."

She shook her head: "Well I do. Always have done. And we're all on the Fone now. No secrets anywhere."

She went out of the room, and Ossie, filled with curiosity, phoned for info on himself. He was listed he found under C for criminal. He had been charged with rape and savagely resisting arrest. He had bitten a finger off a Pleesman and wounded another. He listened to further details and as they piled one on top of the other he slammed the Fone down. His head was swimming. It wasn't that he couldn't see himself somewhere in the jungle of info, it was just that at the end of it all, he was emerging not as the quietly spoken Ossie Mathews but as some ugly distorted monster, not really himself at all. Oh it was true he had loved a girl who had been legally under age. He had loved her to distraction and she had welcomed him as the first real lover in her life . . . until that day when the door had cracked inwards on its hinges and the girl's father and three Pleesmen had burst in on the lover's nest. Ossie had fought them off like women are said to fight—with their nails and teeth. He had never been that way before, so like an animal . . . "Inside" they had told the story differently again. To murderers, cut-throats and armed robbers he instantly became an animal, a "specimen," a "freak," a "perv"—as though even in a jailed society there existed a need for a higher and lower form of person. Ossie shook his head and felt himself go tight inside. He was not the man on the Fone banks or any of those other versions of himself. He had lost in translation. The original was a mild man, long and stringy in build, the opposite of trembling spars and wavery notions so often attributed to this "type." He turned the lights out and let the day slide away.

"How are you?"

He was alone in the Grof House. His voice had sunk to a whisper of intimacy. The bubbling stopped. The eyes were locked into his. He suddenly thought he was listening for something in the silence. Then the Grof started again: "Lop lop lop . . ."

The Grof paused and began again. Ossie listened for an hour and then a little boy dragged his mother into the House and began to squeal and point.

"Tomorrow," said Ossie and steamed out into the Park but not before he had heard a funny moment in time when the Grof's sudden silence seemed to be filled with: "I'll see you tomorrow, Ossie."

He went straight into an informal soccer match in the Park, exhausted himself, admitted he felt great and took a Bumpacar back home. His mother was sitting on the stoop. It was her place when Telly was too boring and the sun was shining. She looked up at Ossie:

"You've got more colour in your cheeks today. Did you meet a pretty girl?"

Ossie said:

"I met the Grof."

His mother began to laugh, then they laughed together, their family laugh, ladling it out like it was good and ready. He touched her and went into his room and closed the door. A giant sob passed in and out of his body. He crumpled to his knees. Coils in his mind, which had been shelved and placed in small out of the way places, now began to stir and unwind. It occurred to him he was a free man. Why should he resist anything? He didn't. The sobs came and shook his body like a passing storm. And then they were gone. He felt himself settling as though for a moment the floor had disappeared and was back again. He thought of his mother sitting outside. The season had changed. When you could sit outside it was summertime. He went into the shower and beneath the rush of the welcoming water he smelt a memory of coffee beans. Percolating in the pot it would go: "lop lop lop . . ." Ossie felt great again.

"Hello Grof," Ossie said.

"Lop lop lop . . ."

In the spaces when the Grof went silent he heard sounds. They were fantastic whispers from labyrinthine palaces beneath the water and they were words scratched and whispered in caves. He saw or he imagined he saw a younger Grof handwheeling down a mountain slope and the narrow astonished face of Herbert Von Groff as he brought a stun gun up to his shoulder and froze the creature like an old fashioned statue that didn't move. The journey from Noah 11 to Earth had been hell, so had the mental and physical examinations, the tests, and finally the Zoo. Ossie nodded. The bubbling music and the silence that followed had made him drowsy. He understood the way it had been for the Grof.

"I'll come back tomorrow as usual."

He went out into the park past the gyrating statues and beneath the flying eyes of the Pleesmen. Neither bothered him that much anymore. His visits to the Grof became part of the routine of his life. Between the morning hours of nine and eleven he would sit talking and listening to the creature. He was generally undisturbed and that was a blessing. The music of the Grof and the golden days of summer quickened his life. His stamp business picked up. He was busy and tanned and in the arms of several pretty girls, who found him "different" but whom he knew would soon find him "ordinary" because it seemed to Ossie it was all planned to happen that way. He felt loyalty to none and his lack of feeling was welcomed with carefully embroidered intimacies sewn on sheets throughout The City. He never missed a day with the Grof, however. He found the creature to be a sentient like himself. Their communication therefore went on as they continued, the both of them, to put out feelers, exploratory probes. Ossie often found the bubbling music too complex for him to be comfortable. He concentrated on the silence and was rewarded with different sounds. He could hear something indistinct, as though written by the sea and left lingering on the breeze above the water. Day after day he listened.

It was true if you held a shell up to the ear you could hear the whispered memories of the sea. Similarly Ossie began to hear the wings of broken things in the silence that followed the music of the Grof. All summer long he listened. August became September and the people on wheels were no longer "Just cruising," they were moving at "I'm in a hurry" miles per hour. The seasonal changes brought with them their own urgency. Ossie remained patient. His life was set in familiar grooves. He didn't want to rush anything now. Not now that he felt something was about to happen.

In the first week of October it finally happened. The new month had burned the Park red and the kinetic statues were immobile, their moveable parts stuffed up with leaves. Ossie had been listening to the Grof for an hour. He had lost himself in the yellow eyes and the bubbling river of the Grof's music. There was a sudden abrupt silence. Then he heard two words: "Free me!" He bit his lip. They were words he hadn't wanted to hear. Radical words which demanded he break the law. The yellow eyes held him. The bubbling had stopped. He knew he had not been mistaken. The Grof wheeled abruptly into the back of its cage and left Ossie with no alternative but to go home with those magic words dancing in his brain cells. He came back the next day as usual and the message he heard was exactly the same: "Free me!" He wanted to tell the Grof a hundred things about survival in an alien world and how there was no longer any place to hide. The Grof would not listen. He began to explain and the creature disappeared into the back of the cage. Ossie went home in distress. He was being torn in two directions by a hundred conflicting pieces of logic which told him to do one thing, then the other. He put his hands to his head and felt pieces of it could break away in his hands like pieces of cake. He saw himself as Hamlet . . . to free or not to free . . . and the picture and the pun brought him the consolation of a sword's point.

In the quiet of his room he watched himself. He watched his hands. They couldn't really belong to him, could they? Those hands which were cleaning files, polishing a hammer, selecting lengths of sturdy wire which might negotiate where a chisel failed. And now those same hands were wrapping those metal tools of freedom in plain brown paper. He lay back on the bed holding the parcel in his hand. It dawned on him that he had decided to free the Grof. He was breaking the law and ending a friendship which had sustained him since his own freedom from jail. What he was about to do didn't make sense, at least not as he had known it before. He grieved for the Grof who would not survive and he grieved for his actions: his hands which would carry the parcel to the Zoo early on the next day.

Ossie felt the reassuring touch of the Grof's three fingers on his shoulder and through them he felt a river of friendship flow. He passed the bag of metal tools through the bars. The Grof took them, cartwheeled into the back of his cage for a moment, hid the package somewhere and came flying out bubbling at nineteen to the dozen. Ossie listened to his friend until the little boys came pulling their tired mothers behind them. Then he pulled his ears out of the bubbling music and his eyes away from the twin triangles of liquid light. He went quickly out of the Grof House with the music still trailing behind him like oxygen bubbles surfacing from deep deep water.

At home Ossie began to stick his stamps in all the wrong places. Africa was in South America and China was on the Moon. He gave himself up to Telly.

The City was excited that the Grof had escaped. Of course Telly didn't exactly say that, nor did the newspapers that Ossie bought in the days that followed his last meeting with the Grof. There were headlines which shouted: "GROF FREE!" "Mysterious disappearance of extra-terrestrial starts monster hunt!" Several papers said the Grof had been freed by another Grof and that made Ossie smile. Grof sightings ran like brush fire through The City. Telly laughed and reported that the elusive creature had been seen on top of the Empire State Building and in New Mexico at the same time. Ossie waited for the knock on the door which would summon him "downtown" for questioning—but it never came. The Grof had freed itself and left no clues for the Pleesmen to follow. The door in its cage had been picked clean, Ossie read, no tools were found. The Grof was free but its chances of survival, even bearing in mind the flexible nature of its diet, were low. Then Winter drew an icy hand from the North and dropped it over The City. Humans could not leave their homes without their Winta Skins. Telly said one night as though to voice the creeping thought of The City: "If the Grof is out there it must be frozen stiff." Then where is its body? Ossie demanded and Telly answered almost immediately: "Its body, however, has not yet been found." The little flame inside Ossie that said that the Grof was still alive, flickered, as though threatening to go out. He missed his visits to the Zoo in the morning. It had left a hole in his day, an emptiness. Winter froze the emptiness inside him and confined him to the solitary business and pleasure of stamps. Then his mother died. He found her one morning seated in front of Telly who was jabbering on about the fashion needs of the spacesetters. Ossie went numb and became efficient. In a mist of time in which dates were carefully arranged and set and met Ossie dealt with the funeral, the rearrangement of the apartment, his stamp business and the sundry affairs of staying alive. He noted how Telly had lost interest in the Grof and often found himself seated before the electrical companion absorbed in that one fact.

Winter deepened and broke its back only in March. Then the heavy winds came. They punched the buildings and moaned in the throats of the alley-ways and made garbage cans lift up their caps like polite robot boys. They groaned with the thunder of their release. Then the rains came spitefully, spitting and snarling on unexpected street corners. Then they steadied their flow to an established beat.

Ossie sat listening to the sound of the rain. His stamp albums lay open before him. He sighed, closed them carefully and went in to the front room without bothering to put on the light. There was no sound of the rain now, only the silence of the room. He walked over to the window, expecting to see it splashed with the broken lances of the rain. It was dry. He pulled it up and looked out. A smile broke on his face like a mountain slide. He stepped back from the window, leaving it open . . . With a little "lop" the Grof cartwheeled gracefully into the room.

The Happy Traitor

Morris Hershman

All earth rolled out the red carpet for a determined but still dazed Curt Marlin. The honors began with a whopping big parade up Lower Broadway to City Hall.

"My only wish now," Curt said, holding the key to the city, "is to live in peace and obscurity."

In the next few days he was given fourteen civic parades and offered ninety jobs. The blond giant who would break a robot in two with his bare hands received 118 proposals of marriage.

"Darling," Curt told his wife, "I wouldn't have any of these women on a bet. I hope that the general public forgets about me in a few weeks."

Maybe he had no right to expect it, he'd done so much. As an Interplanetary Ranger he had almost single-handedly saved Earth from invasion by another planet. The green men had solemnly promised him that they would never interfere in Earth matters, and there was no telling how many humans were alive because of Curt Marlin.

On this occasion he sincerely thanked everyone: "You've been finer to me than words can say." Then he tried to get back to living quietly on his little farm in the town of Shifting Sands. He was asked to endorse cigarettes, cigars, matches, butters, cheeses, soft drinks, insecticides and beauty creams. A big city toy outfit began selling Curt Marlin interplanetary suits, Curt Marlin masks, and a Curt Marlin space gun with Curt's picture on every bullet. It goes without saying that "The Adventures of Curt Marlin" could be viewed on telescreens from pole to pole.

But his name was generally used without permission. A journalist in Saskatoon founded the Curt Marlin Daily Bugle; a fellow in Des Moines originated Curt Marlin Bicycles ("Smooth as a space trip," ran the ads); and Curt's wife, Mary, nearly hit the ceiling when some enterprising manufacturer of ladies undergarments brought out on the market an item called a Curt Marlin Featherfluff Bra.

On Broadway a teleplay opened called Curt Marlin, Interplanetary Ranger, and Vox Telepix was rumored to be showing considerable interest in the first telepix serial rights. His giant image could now be seen on every can of Curt Marlin Soup ("Marlin Soup is a darlin' soup"). A woman journeyed from Lhasa, Tibet, because she wanted to die in Curt Marlin's arms.

"Enough," said Curt, "is enough. If I don't stop this business, it'll drive us all crazy."

"People would do anything for you," said Mary with her quiet smile, "except leave you alone."

Certainly she was under a strain. In order to give them a little privacy their farmhouse had to be guarded by half a dozen County Troopers. Worst of all, their son Jeremy was being tutored, as any group of public school kids would have mobbed him to death the minute they saw him.

"There is only one way out." Mary thumped her plasteen kitchen table so hard she nearly shattered it. "We must move to another planet. We must!"

Curt applied in secret to the Interplanetary Travel Commission, but the story leaked to the telepapers and he was promptly invited to 700 farewell dinners; Curt Marlin had received a solemn verbal promise of non-intervention from the green men and he'd have to find out that all Earth was grateful.

"Even," as somebody said, "if it kills his family."

Curt settled for 50 dinners, and Mary gritted her teeth. At number 46 the blow fell when a sheet of telescrip was handed up to the toastmaster and a broad smile shone on his face.

"I have some splendid news for all of us here on Earth!" he proclaimed. "Thanks to pressures exerted from all corners of our mighty planet," he went on, after a stage pause for effect, "the Interplanetary Travel Commission has announced that it will not permit Curt Marlin to leave Earth in a civilian capacity. Let's have three cheers for the hero!"

While the crowd was lustily singing "For he's a jolly good Earthman," a white-faced Mary told Curt that she was taking Jeremy and leaving him for good and all.

Ten minutes later Curt Marlin made his decision. He rejoined the Interplanetary Rangers. Soon after, Curt left his company and was seen heading alone for the planet Quuntal, inhabited by the green men. Three days later Earth saw in its skies the first rocketship. No blood was spilled during the invasion.

Curt's status under the new regime couldn't have been nicer. Having freed them from their original promise of non-intervention made Curt a hero to the green men; having made them promise non-intervention in the first place marked him as their enemy. The green men shrugged off the paradox and carried on as if Curt didn't exist.

Mary and Jeremy came back to him after a while, and moved out to another small town. Since Curt had betrayed the mother planet, his neighbors leave Curt, Mary and Jeremy pretty much alone, as a kind of punishment.

The three of them are taking it bravely.

The Harvest

Tom Godwin

It was Harvest time.

The Sky People waited where the last tenuous vestiges of atmosphere met the nothing of outer space, invisible to the land creatures below who had no way of perceiving life forms that were almost pure energy. Harthon and Ledri waited a little apart from the others, soaring restlessly on scintillating wings in the light-stream from the sun.

For many days the Release Field had enveloped the world below, clouding and distorting the surface of it to the perception of the Sky People with the violence of its psycho-persuasion bands. Now the field was lifted, its work done. There remained only the last little while of waiting before the fralings came; the intoxicating, maddeningly delicious fralings that filled the body and mind with a singing, ecstatic fire. . . .

"There are so many of us this time," Ledri said. "Do you think there will be enough fralings?"

"Of course," Harthon reassured her. "There are more of *them,* too, and they've learned how to send us as many as we need. There will be more fralings this time than ever before."

"The Harvest—" Ledri's thought was like a nostalgic sigh. "What fun they are! Do you remember the last one, Harthon? And the night we danced down the moonbeams to meet the fralings coming up, before they had ever reached the nets of the Gatherer?"

"I remember. And afterward we followed the sun-stream out, so far out that the world and the moon were like a big and little star behind us. And we sang . . ."

"And you. And then we were hungry again and we let the sun-stream carry us back to the feast where the others were laughing because someone had almost let a fraling escape. Everyone was so happy and the world and the stars were so beautiful. The poor creatures down below—" a touch of sadness came over her—"they don't know and can never know what it's like . . ."

"It has to be that way," Harthon said. "Would you change it if you could?"

"Oh, no! They have to stay there and we have to watch over them. But what if they should do something beyond our control, as the Wise Ones say they may do some day, and then there would be the Last Harvest and never again any fralings for us?"

"I know. But that may not happen for a long time. And this isn't the day for worrying, little shining one—not when the feast begins so soon."

Their wings touched as they turned in their soaring and looked down upon the great curve of the world below. The eastern sea was blue and cloudless; the western continent going into the evening and the huge mass of the eastern continent coming out of the night. The turning of the world was visible as they watched; the western rim of the western continent creeping very slowly into the extinction of the horizon.

"Can the land people tell when we're watching them like this?" Ledri asked.

"No. They know we're up here, but that's all."

"How did they ever—"

A little sun blazed into being on the western continent, brighter than the real sun. Others followed, swiftly; then they began to flare into life on the eastern continent—two fields of vivid flowers that bloomed briefly and were gone. Where they had been were tall, dark clouds that rose higher still, swelling and spreading, hiding the land beneath.

The Summoner gave the call that was like the song of a trumpet and the one who had been appointed Gatherer poised his far-flung nets.

"They're coming—the fralings!" Ledri cried. "Look at them, Harthon. But there are so many—" the worry came back to her— "so many that maybe this is the Last Harvest."

"There aren't *that* many," Harthon said, and he laughed at her concern. "Besides, will we care tonight?"

The quick darkness of her mood vanished and she laughed with him. "Tonight we'll dance down the moonbeams again. And tomorrow we'll follow the sun-stream out, farther than ever before."

The fralings drew swiftly closer, hurrying like bright silver birds.

"They're coming to us," Ledri said. "They know that this is where they must go. But how did the land people ever learn of us?"

"Once, many centuries ago, a fraling escaped the nets long enough to go back for a little while. But fralings and land people can't communicate very well with one another and the land people misunderstood most of what it tried to tell them about us."

The fralings struck the invisible nets and the Gatherer gave the command to draw them closed.

"Let's go—the others are already starting," Harthon said, and they went with flashing wings toward the nearer net.

"Do the land people have a name for us?" Ledri asked.

"They call us 'angels,' and they call the Gatherer 'God.' "

The fralings, finally understanding, were trying frantically to escape and the terror of the small ones was a frightened, pleading wail.

"And what do they call the fralings?"

"They call them their 'souls.' We'll eat the small, young ones first—they're the best and there will be plenty for all."

How Now Purple Cow

Bill Pronzini

W hen Floyd Anselmo saw the purple cow grazing on a hillside of his dairy ranch one cold morning in October, he thought his mind must be hallucinating.

He brought his pick-up truck to a sharp halt at the side of the access road that wound through his property, set the brake, and leaned across the seat to have another look. But it was still there. He stared, willing it to disappear. It didn't.

Anselmo shook his head slowly and got out of the truck. He stood on the graveled roadbed, shading his eyes from the glare of the winter sun. Still there.

By God, Anselmo thought. Next thing you know, it'll be pink elephants. And me not even a drinking man.

He drew the collar of his coat up against the chill, early morning wind, sighed deeply, and walked around the truck. He made his way carefully through the damp grass at the side of the road, climbed easily over the white fence there, and began to ascend the hillside.

Halfway up, he paused for another look. Damned if the cow *wasn't* purple; a rather pleasant, almost lilac, shade of that color. Still, the contrast with the bright chlorophyll green of the grass, and the dull, brown-and-white of the other cows, was rather startling.

Anselmo climbed to within twenty feet of where the purple cow was grazing. Cautiously, he made a wide circle around the animal. It paid no attention to him.

"Listen, here," he said aloud, "you ain't real."

The cow chewed peacefully, ignoring him.

"Cows ain't purple," Anselmo said.

The animal flicked its tail lightly.

He stood looking at it for quite some time. Then he sighed again, rather resignedly this time, turned and started down the hillside.

His wife was finishing the breakfast dishes in the kitchen when he came in a few minutes later. "Back so soon?" she asked.

"Amy," Anselmo said, "there's a purple cow grazing on a hillside down the road."

She wiped her hands on a dishtowel. "I made some fresh coffee," she told him.

Anselmo tugged at his ear. "I said, there's a purple cow grazing on a hillside down the road."

"Yes, dear," his wife said. She began stacking dishes in the cupboard.

Anselmo went outside. He saw Hank Raiford, his foreman, coming up from the milking barn.

"Morning, Mr. Anselmo," Hank said.

"Hank," Anselmo said, frowning, "I saw this purple cow grazing on a hillside down the road."

Hank looked at him.

"I thought it was an hallucination at first. But I went up there and the damned thing was purple, all right. I can't figure it out."

"Well," Hank said, watching him strangely.

"You haven't seen it by any chance, have you?"

"No, sir."

Anselmo nodded. "Want to come out with me and have a look at it?"

"Well," Hank said, "there are a few things I got to take care of right now."

"Maybe later," Anselmo said.

"Sure," Hank told him, moving away quickly. "Maybe later."

Anselmo went back into the house. He crossed directly to the telephone on the hall table and put in a call to Jim Player, the editor of the local weekly newspaper.

"Floyd Anselmo here," he said when Player came on.

"What can I do for you, Floyd?"

"Well," Anselmo said. "I was coming into town a while ago, and I was driving down my access road when I saw this purple cow grazing on a hillside."

There was silence from the other end.

"Jim?" Anselmo asked.

"Purple cow?" Player said finally.

"That's right," Anselmo told him. "Purple cow."

Another silence, shorter this time. Then Player laughed. "You're putting me on, right?"

"No," Anselmo said seriously.

"Look, Floyd, I'm a busy man," Player said. "With all these silly damned UFO sightings hereabout lately, I haven't had time to . . ." He broke off, chuckling. "Say, maybe this purple cow of yours came in one of those flying saucers people claim to have been seeing."

"Jim," Anselmo said slowly, "I don't know anything about flying saucers. All I know is there's a purple cow grazing on one of my hillsides. If you want to come out here, I'll show it to you."

Player was silent for a moment. Then he said, "All right, I'll come out. But if you're ribbing me . . ."

"The hillside I'm talking about is maybe a mile onto my land from the highway," Anselmo told him. "I'll meet you there."

"Forty-five minutes," Player said unhappily, and hung up.

Anselmo went to the door. His wife came into the room just as he reached it. "Where are you going, dear?"

"To meet Jim Player."

"Whatever for?"

"To show him the purple cow I saw."

Her forehead corrugated worriedly. "Floyd . . ."

"I'll be back in an hour or so," Anselmo said, and stepped outside.

He started his pick-up and drove down the access road. When he reached the hillside, he saw that the purple cow had moved further down it, and was grazing now only a few feet from the white fence.

Anselmo braked the truck and got out. He went through the grass to the fence, climbed over it, and stood facing the cow.

The animal continued to graze, seemingly oblivious to his presence.

Anselmo walked haltingly up to it. He put out a wary hand and touched its head. Then he stepped back. "I was beginning to have some doubts," he said, "but damned if you ain't real, and damned if you ain't purple."

The animal shifted its hind legs.

"Where'd you come from anyway?" Anselmo asked. "Jim Player said something about flying saucers or some such. Now I don't hold much truck with them things, but y—"

Anselmo strangled on the last word. His eyes had riveted on his hand, the hand he had touched the animal's head with seconds earlier.

His fingers were turning purple.

He had a fleeting desire to turn and run. It passed quickly. After a moment, the animal raised its head to look at Anselmo for the first time.

In a distinctly questioning tone, it said, "Moo?"

"Moo," Anselmo answered.

There were two purple cows grazing on the hillside when Jim Player arrived from town a few minutes later.

The Hurkle Is a Happy Beast

Theodore Sturgeon

This is Earth, and it once was horrible with wars, and murders, and young love in the spring. It would be today, but for a man of principle, a man of action. So gather around me, and hear about how it began. It began on Lirht.

Lirht is either in a different universal plane or in another island galaxy. Perhaps these terms mean the same thing. The fact remains that Lirht is a planet with three moons (one of which is unknown) and a sun.

Lirht is inhabited by gwik, its dominant race, and by several less highly developed species which, for purposes of this narrative, can be ignored. Except, of course, for the hurkle. The hurkle are highly regarded by the gwik as pets, in spite of the fact that a hurkle is so affectionate that it can have no loyalty.

The prettiest of the hurkle are blue.

Now, on Lirht, in its greatest city, there was trouble, the nature of which does not matter to us, and a gwik named Hvov, whom you may immediately forget, blew up a building which was important for reasons we cannot understand. This event caused great excitement, and gwik left their homes and factories and strubles and streamed toward the center of town, which is how a certain laboratory door was left open.

In times of such huge confusion, the little things go on. During the "Ten Days That Shook the World" the cafes and theaters of Moscow and Petrograd remained open, people fell in love, sued each other, died, shed sweat and tears; and some of these were tears of laughter. So on Lirht, while the decisions on the fate of the miserable Hvov were being formulated, gwik still fardled, funted, and fupped. The great central hewton still beat out its mighty pulse, and in the anams the corsons grew. . . .

Into the above-mentioned laboratory, which had been left open through the circumstances described, wandered a hurkle kitten. It was very happy to find itself there; but then, the hurkle is a happy beast. It prowled about fearlessly—it could become invisible if frightened—and it glowed at the legs of the tables and at the glittering, racked walls. It moved sinuously, humping its back and arching along on the floor. Its front and rear legs were stiff and straight as the legs of a chair; the middle pair had two sets of knees, one bending forward, one back. It was engineered as ingeniously as a scorpion, and it was exceedingly blue.

Occupying almost a quarter of the laboratory was a huge and intricate machine, unhoused, showing the signs of development projects the galaxies over—temporary hookups from one component to another, cables terminating in spring clips, measuring devices standing about on small tables near the main work. The kitten regarded the machine with curiosity and friendly intent, sending a wave of radiations outward which were its glow, or purr. It arched daintily around to the other side, stepping delicately but firmly on a floor switch.

Immediately there was a rushing, humming sound, like small birds chasing large mosquitoes, and parts of the machine began to get warm. The kitten watched curiously, and saw, high up inside the clutter of coils and wires, the most entrancing muzziness it had ever seen. It was like heat-flicker over a fallow field; it was like a smoke-vortex; it was like red neon lights on a wet pavement. To the hurkle kitten's senses, that red-orange flicker was also like the smell of catnip to a cat, or anise to a terrestrial terrier.

It reared up toward the glow, hooked its forelegs over a busbar—fortunately there was no ground potential—and drew itself upward. It climbed from transformer to power-pack, skittered up a variable condenser—the setting of which was changed thereby—disappeared momentarily as it felt the bite of a hot tube, and finally teetered on the edge of the glow.

The glow hovered in midair in a sort of cabinet, which was surrounded by heavy coils embodying tens of thousands of turns of small wire and great loops of bus. One side, the front, of the cabinet was open, and the kitten hung there fascinated, rocking back and forth to the rhythm of some unheard music it made to contrast this sourceless flame. Back and forth, back and forth it rocked and wove, riding a wave of delicious, compelling sensation. And once, just once, it moved its center of gravity too far from its point of support. Too far—far enough. It tumbled into the cabinet, into the flame.

One muggy, mid-June day a teacher, whose name was Stott and whose duties were to teach seven subjects to forty moppets in a very small town, was writing on a blackboard. He was writing the word Madagascar, and the air was so sticky and warm that he could feel his undershirt pasting and unpasting itself on his shoulder-blades with each round "a" he wrote.

Behind him there was a sudden rustle from the moist seventh-graders. His schooled reflexes kept him from turning from the board until he had finished what he was doing, by which time the room was in a young uproar. Stott about-faced, opened his mouth, closed it again. A thing like this would require more than a routine reprimand.

His forty-odd charges were writhing and squirming in an extraordinary fashion, and the sound they made, a sort of whimpering giggle, was unique. He looked at one pupil after another. Here a hand was busily scratching a nape; there a boy was digging guiltily under his shirt; yonder a scrubbed and shining damsel violently worried her scalp.

Knowing the value of individual attack, Stott intoned, "Hubert, what seems to be the trouble?"

The room immediately quieted, though diminished scrabblings continued. "Nothin', Mister Stott," quavered Hubert.

Stott flicked his gaze from side to side. Wherever it rested, the scratching stopped and was replaced by agonized control. In its wake was rubbing and twitching. Stott glared, and idly thumbed a lower left rib. Someone snickered. Before he could identify the source, Stott was suddenly aware of an intense itching. He checked the impulse to go after it, knotted his jaw, and swore to himself that he wouldn't scratch as long as he was out there, front and center. "The class will—" he began tautly, and then stopped.

There was a—a *something* on the sill of the open window. He blinked and looked again. It was a translucent, bluish cloud which was almost nothing at all. It was less than a something should be, but it was indeed more than a nothing. If he stretched his imagination just a little, he might make out the outlines of an arched crea-ture with too many legs; but of course that was ridiculous.

He looked away from it and scowled at his class. He had had two unfortunate experiences with stink bombs, and in the back of his mind was the thought of having seen once, in a trick-store window, a product called "itching powder." Could this be it, this terrible itch? He knew better, however, than to accuse anyone yet; if he were wrong, there was no point in giving the little geniuses any extra-curricular notions.

He tried again. "The cl—" He swallowed. This itch was . . . "The class will—" He noticed that one head, then another and another, were turning toward the window. He realized that if the class got too interested in what he thought he saw on the window sill, he'd have a panic on his hands. He fumbled for his ruler and rapped twice on the desk. His control was not what it should have been at the moment; he struck far too hard, and the reports were like gunshots. The class turned to him as one; and behind them the thing on the window sill appeared with great distinctness.

It was blue—a truly beautiful blue. It had a small spherical head and an almost identical knob at the other end. There were four stiff, straight legs, a long sinuous body, and two central limbs with a boneless look about them. On the side of the head were four pairs of eyes, of graduated sizes. It teetered there for perhaps ten sec-onds, and then, without a sound, leapt through the window and was gone.

Mr. Stott, pale and shaking, closed his eyes. His knees trembled and weakened, and a delicate, dewy mustache of perspiration ap-peared on his upper lip. He clutched at the desk and forced his eyes open; and then, flooding him with relief, pealing into his terror, swinging his control back to him, the bell rang to end the class and the school day.

"Dismissed," he mumbled, and sat down. The class picked up and left, changing itself from a twittering pattern of rows to a rowdy kaleidoscope around the bottle-necking doorway. Mr. Stott slumped down in his chair, noticing that the dreadful itch was gone, had been gone since he had made that thunderclap with the ruler.

Now, Mr. Stott was a man of method. Mr. Stott prided himself on his ability to teach his charges to use their powers of observation and all the machinery of logic at their command. Perhaps, then, he had more of both at his command—after he recovered himself—than could be expected of an ordinary man.

He sat and stared at the open window, not seeing the sun-swept lawns outside. And after going over these events a half-dozen times, he fixed on two important facts:

First, that the animal he had seen, or thought he had seen, had six legs.

Second, that the animal was of such a nature as to make anyone who had not seen it believe he was out of his mind.

These two thoughts had their corollaries:

First, that every animal he had ever seen which had six legs was an insect, and

Second, that if anything were to be done about this fantastic creature, he had better do it by himself. And whatever action he took must be taken immediately. He imagined the windows being kept shut to keep the thing out—in this heat—and he cowered away from the thought. He imagined the effect of such a monstrosity if it bounded into the midst of a classroom full of children in their early teens, and recoiled. No; there could be no delay in this matter.

He went to the window and examined the sill. Nothing. There was nothing to be seen outside, either. He stood thoughtfully for a moment, pulling on his lower lip and thinking hard. Then he went downstairs to borrow five pounds of DDT powder from the janitor for an "experiment." He got a wide, flat wooden box and an electric fan, and set them up on a table he pushed close to the window, and then he sat down to wait, in case, just in case the blue beast returned.

When the hurkle kitten fell into the flame, it braced itself for a fall at least as far as the floor of the cabinet. Its shock was tremendous, then, when it found itself so braced and already resting on a surface. It looked around, panting with fright, its invisibility reflex in full operation.

The cabinet was gone. The flame was gone. The laboratory with its windows, lit by the orange Lirhtian sky, its ranks of shining equipment, its hulking, complex machine—all were gone.

The hurkle kitten sprawled in an open area, a sort of lawn. No colors were right; everything seemed half-lit, filmy, out-of-focus. There were trees, but not low and flat and bushy like honest Lirhtian trees, but with straight naked trunks and leaves like a portle's tooth. The different atmospheric gases had colors; clouds of fading, changing faint colors obscured and revealed everything. The kitten twitched its cafmors and ruddled its kump, right there where it stood; for no amount of early training could overcome a shock like this.

It gathered itself together and tried to move; and then it got its second shock. Instead of arching over inchworm-wise, it floated into the air and came down three times as far as it had ever jumped in its life.

It cowered on the dreamlike grass, darting glances all about, under, and up. It was lonely and terrified and felt very much put-upon. It saw its shadow through the shifting haze, and the sight terrified it even more; for it had no shadow when it was frightened on Lirht. Everything here was all backwards and wrong way up; it got more visible, instead of less, when it was frightened; its legs didn't work right, it couldn't see properly, and there wasn't a single, solitary malapek to be throdded anywhere. It thought some music; happily, that sounded all right inside its round head, though some-how it didn't resonate as well as it had.

It tried, with extreme caution, to move again. This time its trajec-tory was shorter and more controlled. It tried a small, grounded pace, and was quite successful. Then it bobbed for a moment, seesawing on its flexing middle pair of legs, and, with utter aban-don, flung itself skyward. It went up perhaps fifteen feet, turning end over end, and landed with its stiff forefeet in the turf.

It was completely delighted with this sensation. It gathered itself together, gryting with joy, and leapt up again. This time it made more distance than altitude, and bounced two long, happy bounces as it landed.

Its fears were gone in the exploration of this delicious new free-dom of motion. The hurkle, as has been said before, is a happy beast. It curvetted and sailed, soared and somersaulted, and at last brought up against a brick wall with stunning and unpleasant re-sults. It was learning, the hard way, a distinction between weight and mass. The effect was slight but painful. It drew back and stared forlornly at the bricks. Just when it was beginning to feel friendly again. . . .

It looked upward, and saw what appeared to be an opening in the wall some eight feet above the ground. Overcome by a spirit of high adventure, it sprang upward and came to rest on a window-sill—a feat of which it was very proud. It crouched there, preening itself, and looked inside.

It saw a most pleasing vista. More than forty amusingly ugly animals, apparently imprisoned by their lower extremities in individual stalls, bowed and nodded and mumbled. At the far end of the room stood a taller, more slender monster with a naked head—naked compared with those of the trapped ones, which were covered with hair like a mawson's egg. A few moments' study showed the kitten that in reality only one side of the heads was hairy; the tall one turned around and began making tracks in the end wall, and its head proved to be hairy on the other side too.

The hurkle kitten found this vastly entertaining. It began to radiate what was, on Lirht, a purr, or glow. In this fantastic place it was not visible; instead, the trapped animals began to respond with most curious writhings and squirmings and susurant rubbings of their hides with their claws. This pleased the kitten even more, for it loved to be noticed, and it redoubled the glow. The receptive motions of the animals became almost frantic.

Then the tall one turned around again. It made a curious sound or two. Then it picked up a stick from the platform before it and brought it down with a horrible crash.

The sudden noise frightened the hurkle kitten half out of its wits. It went invisible; but its visibility system was reversed here, and it was suddenly outstandingly evident. It turned and leapt outside, and before it reached the ground, a loud metallic shrilling pursued it. There were gabblings and shufflings from the room which added force to the kitten's consuming terror. It scrambled to a low growth of shrubbery and concealed itself.

Very soon, however, its irrepressible good nature returned. It lay relaxed, watching the slight movement of the stems and leaves—some of them may have been flowers—in a slight breeze.

It turned its attention again to the window, wondering what those racks of animals might be up to now. It seemed very quiet up there. . . . Boldly the kitten came from hiding and launched itself at the window again. It was pleased with itself; it was getting quite proficient at precision leaps in this mad place. Preening itself, it balanced on the window sill and looked inside.

Surprisingly, all the smaller animals were gone. The larger one was huddled behind the shelf at the end of the room. The kitten and the animal watched each other for a long moment. The animal leaned down and stuck something into the wall.

Immediately there was a mechanical humming sound and something on a platform near the window began to revolve. The next thing the kitten knew it was enveloped in a cloud of pungent dust.

It choked and became as visible as it was frightened, which was very. For a long moment it was incapable of motion; gradually, however, it became conscious of a poignant, painfully penetrating sensation which thrilled it to the core.

The hurkle felt strange, transported. It turned and leapt high into the air, out from the building.

Mr. Stott stopped scratching. Disheveled indeed, he went to the window and watched the odd sight of the blue beast, quite invisible now, but coated with dust, so that it was like a bubble in a fog. It bounced across the lawn in huge floating leaps, leaving behind it diminishing patches of white powder in the grass. He smacked his hands, one on the other, and smirking withdrew to straighten up. He had saved the earth from battle, murder and bloodshed, forever, but he did not know that.

And the hurkle kitten?

It bounded off through the long shadows, and vanished in a copse of bushes. There it dug itself a shallow pit, working drowsily, more and more slowly. And at last it sank down and lay motionless, thinking strange thoughts, making strange music, and racked by strange sensations. Soon all its movements ceased, and it stretched out stiffly, motionless.

For about two weeks. At the end of that time, the hurkle, no longer a kitten, was possessed of a fine, healthy litter of just under two hundred young. Perhaps it was the DDT, and perhaps it was the new variety of radiation that the hurkle received from the terrestrial sky, but they were all parthenogenetic females, even as you and I.

And the humans? Oh, we *bred* so! And how happy we were!

But the humans had the slidy itch, and the scratchy itch, and the prickly or tingly or titillative paraesthetic formication. And there wasn't a thing they could do about it.

So they left.

Isn't this a lovely place?

An Incident on Route 12

James H. Schmitz

Phil Garfield was thirty miles south of the little town of Red-mon on Route Twelve when he was startled by a series of sharp, clanking noises. They came from under the Packard's hood.

The car immediately began to lose speed. Garfield jammed down the accelerator, had a sense of sick helplessness at the complete lack of response from the motor. The Packard rolled on, getting rid of its momentum, and came to a stop.

Phil Garfield swore shakily. He checked his watch, switched off the headlights and climbed out into the dark road. A delay of even half an hour here might be disastrous. It was past midnight, and he had another hundred and ten miles to cover to reach the small private airfield where Madge waited for him and the thirty thousand dollars in the suitcase on the Packard's front seat.

If he didn't make it before daylight. . . .

He thought of the bank guard. The man had made a clumsy play at being a hero, and that had set off the fool woman who'd run screaming into their line of fire. One dead. Perhaps two. Garfield hadn't stopped to look at an evening paper.

But he knew they were hunting for him.

He glanced up and down the road. No other headlights in sight at the moment, no light from a building showing on the forested hills. He reached back into the car and brought out the suitcase, his gun, a big flashlight and the box of shells which had been standing beside the suitcase. He broke the box open, shoved a handful of shells and the .38 into his coat pocket, then took suitcase and flashlight over to the shoulder of the road and set them down.

There was no point in groping about under the Packard's hood. When it came to mechanics, Phil Garfield was a moron and well aware of it. The car was useless to him now . . . except as bait.

But as bait it might be very useful.

Should he leave it standing where it was? No, Garfield decided. To anybody driving past, it would merely suggest a necking party, or a drunk sleeping off his load before continuing home. He might have to wait an hour or more before someone decided to stop. He didn't have the time. He reached in through the window, hauled the top of the steering wheel towards him and put his weight against the rear window frame.

The Packard began to move slowly backwards at a slant across the road. In a minute or two he had it in position. Not blocking the road entirely, which would arouse immediate suspicion, but angled across it, lights out, empty, both front doors open and inviting a passerby's investigation.

Garfield carried the suitcase and flashlight across the right-hand shoulder of the road and moved up among the trees and under-growth of the slope above the shoulder. Placing the suitcase be-tween the bushes, he brought out the .38, clicked the safety off and stood waiting.

Some ten minutes later, a set of headlights appeared speeding up Route Twelve from the direction of Redmon. Phil Garfield went down on one knee before he came within range of the lights. Now he was completely concealed by the vegetation.

The car slowed as it approached, braking nearly to a stop sixty feet from the stalled Packard. There were several people inside it; Garfield heard voices, then a woman's loud laugh. The driver tapped his horn inquiringly twice, moved the car slowly forward. As the headlights went past him, Garfield got to his feet among the bushes, took a step down towards the road, raising the gun.

Then he caught the distant gleam of a second set of headlights approaching from Redmon. He swore under his breath and dropped back out of sight. The car below him reached the Packard, edged cautiously around it, rolled on with a sudden roar of acceler-ation.

The second car stopped when still a hundred yards away, the

Packard caught in the motionless glare of its lights. Garfield heard the steady purring of a powerful motor.

For almost a minute, nothing else happened. Then the car came gliding smoothly on, stopped again no more than thirty feet to Garfield's left. He could see it now through the screening bushes—a big job, a long, low four-door sedan. The motor continued to purr. After a moment, a door on the far side of the car opened and slammed shut.

A man walked quickly out into the beam of the headlights and started towards the Packard.

Phil Garfield rose from his crouching position, the .38 in his right hand, flashlight in his left. If the driver was alone, the thing was now cinched! But if there was somebody else in the car, somebody capable of fast, decisive action, a slip in the next ten seconds might cost him the sedan, and quite probably his freedom and life. Garfield lined up the .38's sights steadily on the center of the approaching man's head. He let his breath out slowly as the fellow came level with him in the road and squeezed off one shot.

Instantly he went bounding down the slope to the road. The bullet had flung the man sideways to the pavement. Garfield darted past him to the left, crossed the beam of the headlights, and was in darkness again on the far side of the road, snapping on his flashlight as he sprinted up to the car.

The motor hummed quietly on. The flashlight showed the seats empty. Garfield dropped the light, jerked both doors open in turn, gun pointing into the car's interior. Then he stood still for a moment, weak and almost dizzy with relief.

There was no one inside. The sedan was his.

The man he had shot through the head lay face down on the road, his hat flung a dozen feet away from him. Route Twelve still stretched out in dark silence to east and west. There should be time enough to clean up the job before anyone else came along. Garfield brought the suitcase down and put it on the front seat of the sedan, then started back to get his victim off the road and out of sight. He scaled the man's hat into the bushes, bent down, grasped the ankles and started to haul him towards the left side of the road where the ground dropped off sharply beyond the shoulder.

The body made a high, squealing sound and began to writhe violently.

Shocked, Garfield dropped the legs and hurriedly took the gun from his pocket, moving back a step. The squealing noise rose in intensity as the wounded man quickly flopped over twice like a struggling fish, arms and legs sawing about with startling energy. Garfield clicked off the safety, pumped three shots into his victim's back.

The grisly squeals ended abruptly. The body continued to jerk for another second or two, then lay still.

Garfield shoved the gun back into his pocket. The unexpected interruption had unnerved him; his hands shook as he reached down again for the stranger's ankles. Then he jerked his hands back, and straightened up, staring.

From the side of the man's chest, a few inches below the right arm, something like a thick black stick, three feet long, protruded now through the material of the coat.

It shone, gleaming wetly, in the light from the car. Even in that first uncomprehending instant, something in its appearance brought a surge of sick disgust to Garfield's throat. Then the stick bent slowly halfway down its length, forming a sharp angle, and its tip opened into what could have been three blunt, black claws which scrabbled clumsily against the pavement. Very faintly, the squealing began again, and the body's back arched up as if another sticklike arm were pushing desperately against the ground beneath it.

Garfield acted in a blur of horror. He emptied the .38 into the thing at his feet almost without realizing he was doing it. Then, dropping the gun, he seized one of the ankles, ran backwards to the shoulder of the road, dragging the body behind him.

In the darkness at the edge of the shoulder, he let go of it, stepped around to the other side and with two frantically savage kicks sent the body plunging over the shoulder and down the steep slope beyond. He heard it crash through the bushes for some seconds, then stop. He turned, and ran back to the sedan, scooping up his gun as he went past. He scrambled into the driver's seat and slammed the door shut behind him.

His hands shook violently on the steering wheel as he pressed down the accelerator. The motor roared into life and the big car surged forward. He edged it past the Packard, cursing aloud in horrified shock, jammed down the accelerator and went flashing up Route Twelve, darkness racing beside and behind him.

What had it been? Something that wore what seemed to be a man's body like a suit of clothes, moving the body as a man moves, driving a man's car . . . roach-armed, roach-legged itself!

Garfield drew a long, shuddering breath. Then, as he slowed for a curve, there was a spark of reddish light in the rear-view mirror.

He stared at the spark for an instant, braked the car to a stop, rolled down the window and looked back.

Far behind him along Route Twelve, a fire burned. Approximately at the point where the Packard had stalled out, where something had gone rolling off the road into the bushes.

Something, Garfield added mentally, that found fiery automatic destruction when death came to it, so that its secrets would remain unrevealed.

But for him the fire meant the end of a nightmare. He rolled the window up, took out a cigarette, lit it, and pressed the accelerator. . . .

In incredulous fright, he felt the nose of the car tilt upwards, headlights sweeping up from the road into the trees. Then the headlights winked out. Beyond the windshield, dark tree branches floated down towards him, the night sky beyond. He reached frantically for the door handle.

A steel wrench clamped silently about each of his arms, drawing them in against his sides, immobilizing them there. Garfield gasped, looked up at the mirror and saw a pair of faintly gleaming red eyes watching him from the rear of the car. Two of the things . . . the second one stood behind him out of sight, holding him. They'd been in what had seemed to be the trunk compartment. And they had come out.

The eyes in the mirror vanished. A moist, black roach-arm reached over the back of the seat beside Garfield, picked up the cigarette he had dropped, extinguished it with rather horribly human motions, then took up Garfield's gun and drew back out of sight.

He expected a shot, but none came.

One doesn't fire a bullet through the suit one intends to wear. . . .

It wasn't until that thought occurred to him that tough Phil Garfield began to scream. He was still screaming minutes later when, beyond the windshield, the spaceship floated into view among the stars.

Interstellar Way-Station

Bob Tucker

Hey, kid! She's going over!"

"Hah?" I yelled.

"The mail rocket. . . ." Pinko repeated. "She's just gone over!"

I dropped my paintbrush, shoved the bucket over out of the way, and beat it around the corner of the Guest Hotel in a bee line for the mail chute; it was our first mail this week. Those damned tightwads on the Universal Council began trimming the overhead a couple of years ago, and daily mail to the Service was the first to go.

Pinko was at the chute ahead of me, flapping his wings excitedly.

"Ahhhh! Another letter from the little Lulu over on '3,'" I jeered. Pinko bobbled about and confirmed this without words. He went over by himself to read the letter. I would read her letter later; we always swapped our mail.

You see, Pinko and I are in the Universal Service—and that covers a lot of space and sins. Our particular branch and job is Refueling. Refueling the big liners that drop in here about once or twice a week, stay a few hours to give the passengers a quick peek at a gas station in space (and a dip in our pool if they like—real Earth water!), meanwhile taking on a capacity load of fuel for the big push on to Alpha Centauri.

Get out your charts and space maps, and if you don't have one, phone, don't walk, to your nearest tourist agency. They'll have one to you in three clicks of a mail tube sounder. Find yourself . . . the big symbol "Earth" in the near center of the map. Now swinging in a tight semi-circle toward the upper left-hand corner of the map, trace that dotted line that leads to the page margin (a little box on the margin tells you that line will take you to Alpha Centauri). This little dotted line is known as the Lowden Line. Your ship, however, doesn't exactly follow that line. After all, no one has really faithfully followed a map since the first one was made thousands of years ago for foot travelers on Earth!

What isn't shown on that map are two Passages, known as the "Outer Passage" and the "Inner Passage." All ships follow one of the two channels known as "passages"; ships *from* Earth to Centauri on the Inner Passage; and ships from Centauri *to* Earth on the Outer Passage. This is necessary, you understand, to prevent ships heading in opposite directions from bumping head-on into one another, and various other little things that aren't important enough to tell passengers.

Examine that map, particularly the Lowden Line, a little more closely. At spaced intervals along the Lowden Line (and all other lines) you will notice a small black square containing a number: 1, 2, 3, and so on. A quick consulting of the key and index informs you that here, at these squares in space, are located stopovers, where tourists may spend a few hours resting from the nervous strain of their first day in space (as in the case of our depot. We are "E-1-AC," or, depot number one, on the Inner Passage, approximately one day out from Earth on the long grind to Alpha Centauri up yonder.) We have on our little world, among other wonders, a small pool of genuine Earth water, the last, by the way, that tourists will see until they near Earth again.

And undoubtedly, the tourists, are as amused by us as they amuse. I, I'm from Earth myself—Indiana. Only now and then does someone drop in who finds *me* a strange life form, and spends his hours trailing me around, colorgraphing my every move. But poor old Pinko comes in for more than his share of trouble. These gawks from Earth out of bounds for the first time—especially the children—find Pinko the very first Centaurian birdman they've seen outside the theaters.

"Here's looking at you, kid," Pinko called. He flipped the Lulu's letter over to me. "What else in the mail?"

"Aw, the usual old stuff: coupla trade journals, sixteen letters from sixteen passengers, the said letters containing sixteen varied colorgraphs of you—" For Pinko's benefit, I displayed mock astonishment: "Say, here's a beaut! Somebody caught you with your beak open! Mmmmmm . . . what charm." If you've seen a Centaurian with his beak open, you can appreciate the candidness of the picture.

Pinko snatched the pic, stared long at it, and presently the hundred tiny pieces of the paper were floating softly down to the artificial lawn, pulled there slowly by the artificial gravity.

"Centaurians have a word for that!" he snapped. "What else . . . ?"

"Two mash notes from some girls back home. They want to 'correspond with some romantic young guardsmen of the spaceways!' Jupiter, why do we have to put up with that? Some advertisements. . . . Oh, look for yourself." I flung him the bundle after separating from its mass a picture magazine, and rolled over on my belly. The letter from the Lulu—a female of some species, who superintended the Guest Hotel out on E-3-AC (she and Pinko had struck up quite a cordial correspondence)—I let lay where it had fallen.

These picture magazines, designed as they are for Servicemen, display plenty of beauteous females—of every world imaginable, for we have servicemen from every one of those worlds—for the bored gentlemen who peddle gas in space. Cheesecake abounds, and honestly, if you could but glimpse the cheesecake displayed by *some* of the females, on *some* of the planets, you'd undoubtedly go off by yourself and have a nice little sick spell. I felt that way when I saw my first picture of a Trinorite. Never again will I look at a picture of a "girl" of Trinor unless she is fully dressed. You see, it's all in the point of view . . . male Trinors probably find it interesting, but . . . !

Staring up at my very interested gaze was an Earth girl. A very pretty girl, with "wealth" written into every pretty line of her face. Wealth, position, and of course a bit of snobbishness. I knew her. Oh, very intimately. Her name is Judith Maynard . . . aw, wait a minute. The caption explains that the name *was* Maynard.

"Well, I'll be damned!" I was disgusted.

"Hah?" the beak extracted itself from a profound study of a political advertisement. "Why?"

"Take a look," I tossed him the mag. "Remember her? No . . . not that one, nitwit! *This* one."

Pinko switched his gaze from the undraped legs of a Martian to the face of Maynard.

"So she married? You might of guessed it," he stared at me.

"Yeah, I might of guessed it. But I didn't. I rather thought . . ."

About eight years ago the *Centau-Maid* express roared into our outer port with a fused rocket stud. The mighty ship, then the crack liner on the Lowden Line, could have flown to hyperspace and back without half her studs, but regulations required her to set down in the nearest port for repairs. It was our bad luck that she happened to be a few million miles from us, and down she came.

Her ace pilot hit the dimensions of the outer port not a foot over the lines, and Pinko on the cradle engine brought her inside as smoothly as one could want. The cradle brings the ship down through the two locks to the surface of our midget world; and there she is serviced while the passengers take unheard-of liberties with our and the Council's property. If you can afford the luxury of the *Maid,* you must be somebody on *any* world. No tourists here, but first-class fares exclusively. And any Serviceman will gladly tell you that these fares are twice as nosey and twice as obnoxious as any tourist. I guess it's their wealth that makes them that way.

My Judith Maynard was one of the whirliest whirls on this boat, and immediately made up a colorgraphing party. This is where I came in, being one of their own kind (and Pinko long ago realized the safety of staying with the ship's crew); having bare notice of the *Maid's* coming, I had just skipped into my dress whites, hid paint-cans and brushes under a tarp, and beamed according to Council Regulation S1317.

First stop of course on all tours about the station, is the cradle, the huge and complex bed that reaches up to our outer hull, almost snatches a ship from space, and brings it right down into the ground. Under the cradle proper is a maze of girders and beams, the engine and the controls for the bed.

Cameras clicked.

"Oh, I beg pardon ma'am. Don't touch those girders." I stopped her just in time. "Wet paint, you know. We have to freshen up these things every week. The children just love to carve their names on the beams with toy ray guns. Ha ha, our clever children!" (I had a few hours earlier just finished painting out the slogan *"Gladrz wuv Zir"* that a particularly premature-worldly youngster had etched into a girder with fire.)

"Oh, do you find children a nuisance?" she inquired ever so interestedly.

"Not at all, ma'am, on the contrary, they make life pleasant for we Servicemen out here. But they cause us much work with those real flame-throwing ray guns most of them tote nowadays. Only about two months ago we had a report from some liner over on the Riga run that it was afire in space. Seems some youngster had desired to carve his name into a bunk, and . . ."

But she was gone, half way through my explanation. I ran to catch up.

"Now *this* used to be an ammunition dump, several decades ago when the War was going on." (Cameras clicked.) "The Council stored huge amounts of munitions here, and on every Depot like this between here and Centauri. But that was long ago—" I smiled deprecatingly "—and now forgotten."

"But, porter," (I guess the fat woman meant me—!) "why hasn't the hole been filled in? Someone might get hurt!" and she looked hurt at the very thought.

"Nothing to fill it with, ma'am. Dirt just isn't a payload. There are many more precious things, things needed for life and service, that take up all available ships. Dirt is simply too cheap a thing to transport from Earth in a large enough quantity to fill that hole. So, it is left as is."

We moved on to the next item of interest, the powerhouse. "This is the powerhouse." (Cameras clicked.)

"Every single unit of energy no matter what kind it is, or what it is used for, comes from this building. Here is gathered the power from the Sun, plus the stars, plus the storage batteries—yes, ma'am, those black boxes over there are the batteries—that hold this depot in space, and permit us to live inside it. Here, in these machines and . . . uh, black boxes, is everything needed for our maintenance. Tremendous voltages are handled here. You will note the warning posted on the door"—and I directed their attention to the glaring big sign that read:

We handled nothing like six billion volts here, but Pinko and I had found that a bit of exaggeration paid dividends. A tourist who reports back to the medical officer aboard his ship with electric burns means demerits for us. And the darn fools actually invite electrocution.

"Hah? I beg your pardon, madam, I wasn't listening. Oh no, madam, Senior Serviceman Pinko never lets me ride astride his back. Yes'm, he can fly. Well, madam, possibly you do believe it to be a shame that a Centaurian has seniority over an Earthman; but you see, this is necessary. Serviceman Pinko has been on duty at this station nearly forty-six years. He has four more years to serve until he attains his second-class citizen's rating; and at the same time I step up to senior attendant, and a rookie . . . I mean a new man comes from some world to serve *his* twenty-five years as my junior. Now *this,* ladies, is the control tower." (Cameras clicked.)

I shot a hasty glance around to note if Pinko had been in earshot when the overfed baby demanded to know whether Pinko and I played horse and jockey. He wasn't in sight.

"This is the control tower. Into this building comes all the power, direct from the powerhouse, and here it is split up and fed to many hundreds of pieces of machinery all over the depot. Up there on the second floor—you can see the levers through the windows—are the controls themselves that cause every bit of apparatus to function when and how it is supposed to. No, ma'am, we have no control for weather. You see, the weather is always the same here, being as we are on the inside of an immense metal ball.

"From this tower can be controlled, by remote control of course, the landing cradle that brought your ship in from space; the check needed to hold a depot at a given spot in space; the machinery for putting under a finger the millions upon millions of volts we draw from the sun; and the very electric lights about the place. From this tower the water in the pool is purified every twenty-four hours and made ready for any ship at any time. From this tower the very air you are now breathing is cleansed over and over again to keep it free from fumes and bacteria."

And so, amid the ever-clicking of color cameras, we went clock-wise around the grounds; my three-thousand-and-ninety-sixth journey.

At last I delivered this consignment to the gangplank and the purser. They filed in.

"Thirty-eight," I gritted, "and they're all yours, every damned one of them! I hope I never see you or them again!"

"My eye!" that worthy retorted. "You've snitched one. There should be thirty-nine."

"Thirty-eight was all I counted. And I don't want one of them . . . *any* of them! Check again."

He did, from a list in his hand. The assistant purser joined him in head bobbing. Both looked solemn.

"One short. I'm positive of it. Thirty-nine left the ship. Thirty-eight returned. We have both counted. Let me see . . . ah, yes. Miss Maynard. Miss Judith Maynard is missing. Maynard! Oh glory be . . . her old man has half the gold mines in . . ." He never finished, but hurried off into the darkened interior of the ship. His assistant appeared nervous.

Sighing disgustedly, I turned and started off on a counter-clock-wise tour, half-wondering just what gear she had tangled herself in. I didn't get far. Pinko came bounding out of the ship and an excited captain at his heels.

Prudently, I put a few steps between Pinko and myself. Having lived with him for something like twenty-one years, I recognize danger signals when I see them. His eyes turned a beautiful violet and bored right into mine. He swept the landscape for signs of her, and finding none, returned to me. Three more steps were put between us.

Six sailors tumbled out of the ship behind him on the double.

They were assigned to me, and we continued the counter-clock-wise movement; while Pinko, the captain, and both pursers vanished back into the ship for a room-by-room check.

It had me scared before long. We didn't find her at the fuel tanks, the piping, nor the pumps. She wasn't entangled among the levers and switches in the powerhouse, nor had she neatly or otherwise made a sizzle steak of herself in the powerhouse. With a premonition we approached the old dump, but the premonition was false; she hadn't fallen in there and broken her skinny neck. Nowhere under the cradle was she to be found, and the sailors even went clambering and climbing up into the maze of beams and cross-beams in search of her. No luck.

By the time we had finished this, and were again emerging on the central plaza, Pinko and his party had come out of the ship, as emptyhanded as we. Together, Pinko and I made for the pool. It had been a long time since anyone had fallen in *that*—but . . .

Again nothing.

Pinko methodically and idiotically opened and closed his beak; the ship's master frankly sank down upon an artificial divan and wept. It was on the tip of my tongue to suggest that perhaps she had dug a hole and crawled into it, when it occurred to me that one doesn't dig holes in the artificial ground—not large enough to crawl into, that is. The "sod" was but four inches deep, and then solid, electrical-gravity-plated metal began. The hole underneath the "sod" was sealed solid and airtight, in fact a perfect vacuum existed between the bottom of our metal ball and the "ground" we stood on, marred only by that artificial hole in which ammunition was once kept. The men had silently and without orders taken their leave. If the gravity of the situation didn't penetrate their thick skulls, the sight of their captain crying did.

"Now by the four little hells of Centauria III," Pinko broke the silence, "she *has* to be here. And yet she isn't. She has to be here. And yet she isn't. She has to—Say! She's Outside!"

Roberds groaned: "Oh, God!"

"Clumb the runs and sneaked out the mail chute door! I should have known!" It took something like this to reveal the inner aspects of Pinko's character. It was fascinating to watch him, despite the emergency. After all, I'd spent twenty-one years with him and this was the first show he'd ever performed. "I should have known!"

Six of us broke out suits and rifles—the complete arsenal on hand—and followed him up; how long after her we could not guess. Perhaps *too* long. Again Pinko took unfair advantage: he flew up and we had to climb. It was funny to see his long beak sticking out of the suit (with a special auxiliary covering for the beak). He looked like a man from Mars . . . say, that was funny. If I lived, I must remember to repeat it to him. I say, *"If* I lived."

Topside, Pinko awaited us; despite that everyone took a hasty glance around as if foolishly expecting to find Maynard calmly sitting a few feet away, stargazing. Unable to communicate except by gestures, he roughly grouped two men together and pushed them off in the left direction; two others he started the opposite way. I about-faced and began climbing up towards the slightly flattened "roof" of our metal sphere, while he, reasoning that she would do likewise, followed the line of least resistance and walked down underneath.

It was dark and hard to see, but presently I could see her shadow. Oh, yes, I had to find her! We were pretty close but still hardly discernible to each other. In fairness, I must admit I saw the shark first. I found Judy at just the moment she was a whoop and a holler ahead of a dish of mincemeat. She was to be the mincemeat.

This mess she had wandered into was the third shark I had ever seen! Description? Hah! It has a scientific name a light-year long among the learned men who admitted its existence; and was just a jeering, "Bah!" to the other side of the fence who denied such a thing can live in a void! *"Space-shark,"* the Service called it. Almost everywhere in space it is, except in those zones surrounding the planets and their moons. There still remains to be written an accurate description of the thing! Some of the boys who have had glimpses of 'em claim it's a cross between a shark and a ghost—a description that can't be imagined until you've seen one, and then you realize that is its *only* description!

Laying my gun down against the hull, I fired. Now if only some of the others were walking, and "heard" the vibration of the shot!

Had Judy kept her presence of mind, or remembered her fiction heroes, she'd've stiffened—played dead—and the chances are better than one in ten she would have lived to snap another camera. But like a fool girl, she thrashed and kicked about in semi-hysterics in an effort to swim away from the beast; and as I came closer, it began to nose her, a prelude to the kill. If that damn thing had any sense, it wouldn't touch her with a hundred-foot fuel pipe; the air in her body and suit-tanks would give it one hell of a bellyache! Which goes to show you the loathsome devil had no more common sense than she.

I ran and swam ahead clumsily, threw up the rifle for another shot! Kill it? Don't make me laugh! But I did succeed in one thing:

distracting its attention from her to me! The terrible phosphorescent "eyes" dropped her and fastened on me with a charge like high voltage.

Play dead! I ordered myself. Spreading arms and legs in slow movements, my body began revolving slowly like the human "X" it appeared, watching the beast and the girl from eye-corners. The shark rolled, forgot Maynard, and nosed me! Oozy and wet sweat popped out to tickle the skin of my arms and legs. Sweat popped off my exposed body and floated near me!

Movement made itself felt at my boots and against my will I angled my head and watched! Long, shapeless nose eagerly quizzing the artificial leather in the boots, sniffing for the scent of life. Accidentally it touched bare skin and terror-locked muscles loosened—I jumped! The shark quivered in pure joy! Repeating the experiment it poked its shocking nose flat against my leg, and that leg jerked like a wild thing. Its body-fins rippled in anticipation . . .

Abruptly, the monster stopped nosing and backed away. From then on the moments of my life were a blueprint I knew by heart and hearsay! The shark would leave me—for the space of seconds and perhaps a half-mile—and when it returned, it wouldn't be taking its time! They rush at their hapless victim with the speed of the time-honored express rocket! The great shimmering body, exploding with internal fireworks, literally swallows a man at one gulp in a maw that promised hellfire and brimstone! My "X" wasn't doing me much good, but I held it. This baby stopped just about a half-mile away and angled in an attempt to catch me end-on. Why don't you close eyes? Oh, they still belonged to me, the will to close them no longer existed. They'd be closed soon—permanently! Yeah! Pinko and the Lulu certainly should be happy.

Then it came.

There was no mind-picturing necessary; I was helpless in front of a roaring rocket, a rocket that breathed and squirmed and devoured me with hellish eyes seconds before its mouth did! Glowing body was almost transparent as redfire lit up its insides; slapping tail streaked like a minor comet! It was so close and horrible I could look right into the mouth, so close the tongue was plainly seen uncurling, ready to lick me in and roll up my body, even before the jaws closed over me!

And a streaking pain I knew was a bullet zipped across my forehead, drowning the sight out of my eyes with blood. And awareness from my mind. But not entirely out until I had flopped over on my belly and saw figures racing around the ball; and saw Maynard drop fainting to the surface, my rifle falling from her hands.

Remember? I said that was about eight years ago, more or less. "So she married some other guy?" Pinko repeated. "Yeah, you *should* have guessed it."

Me, what could I answer? He had me. Money she had tenderly pressed upon me, and just as tenderly I had pressed it back, according to Regulation S908. Herself she had tenderly pressed upon me for a few hours I held her, and just as tenderly pressed back into the care of the departing liner. (Regulation S37.)

Marriage? Yeah, I could get married when I had finished out my fifty years. She'd wait, sure she would. She loved me. And she'd pull a few wires, meanwhile, to see if I couldn't be transferred somewhere for a shorter service period or to a job allowing wives.

And she'd sent me an autographed colorpic which I had tacked up over my bunk.

Which, I guess, was all I could expect. . . .

Into Your Tent I'll Creep

Eric Frank Russell

Morfad sat in the midship cabin and gloomed at the wall. He was worried and couldn't conceal the fact. The present situation had the frustrating qualities of a gigantic rattrap. One could escape it only with the combined help of all the other rats.

But the others weren't likely to lift a finger either on his or their own behalf. He felt sure of that. How can you persuade people to try escape a jam when you can't convince them that they're in it, right up to the neck?

A rat runs around a trap only because he is grimly aware of its existence. So long as he remains blissfully ignorant of it, he does nothing. On this very world a horde of intelligent aliens had done nothing about it through the whole of their history. Fifty skeptical Altairans weren't likely to step in where three thousand million Terrans had failed.

He was still sitting there when Haraka came in and informed, "We leave at sunset."

Morfad said nothing.

"I'll be sorry to go," added Haraka. He was the ship's captain, a big, burly sample of Altairan life. Rubbing flexible fingers together, he went on, "We've been lucky to discover this planet, exceedingly lucky. We've become blood brothers of a life-form fully up to our own standard of intelligence, space-traversing like ourselves, friendly and cooperative."

Morfad said nothing.

"Their reception of us has been most cordial," Haraka continued enthusiastically. "Our people will be greatly heartened when they hear our report. A great future lies before us, no doubt of that. A Terran-Altairan combine will be invincible. Between us we can explore and exploit the entire galaxy."

Morfad said nothing.

Cooling down, Haraka frowned at him. "What's the matter with you, Misery?"

"I am not overjoyed."

"I can see that much. Your face resembles a very sour *shamsid* on an aged and withered bush. And at a time of triumph, too! Are you ill?"

"No." Turning slowly, Morfad looked him straight in the eyes. "Do you believe in psionic faculties?"

Haraka reacted as if caught on one foot. "Well, I don't know. I am a captain, a trained engineer-navigator, and as such I cannot pretend to be an expert upon extraordinary abilities. You ask me something I am not qualified to answer. How about you? Do you believe in them?"

"I do—*now.*"

"Now? Why now?"

"The belief has been thrust upon me." Morfad hesitated, went on with a touch of desperation. "I have discovered that I am telepathic."

Surveying him with slight incredulity, Haraka said, "You've discovered it? You mean it has come upon you recently?"

"Yes."

"Since when?"

"Since we arrived on Terra."

"I don't understand this at all," confessed Haraka, baffled. "Do you assert that some peculiarity in Terra's conditions has suddenly enabled you to read my thoughts?"

"No, I cannot read your thoughts."

"But you've just said that you have become telepathic."

"So I have. I can hear thoughts as clearly as if the words were being shouted aloud. But not your thoughts nor those of any member of our crew."

Haraka leaned forward, his features intent. "Ah, you have been hearing *Terran* thoughts, eh? And what you've heard has got you bothered? Morfad, I am your captain, your commander. It is your bounden duty to tell me of anything suspicious about these Terrans." He waited a bit, urged impatiently, "Come on, speak up!"

"I know no more about these humanoids than you do," said Morfad. "I have every reason to believe them genuinely friendly but I don't know what they think."

"But by the stars, man, you—"

"We are talking at cross-purposes," Morfad interrupted. "Whether I do or do not overhear Terran thoughts depends upon what one means by Terrans."

"Look," said Haraka, "whose thoughts *do* you hear?"

Steeling himself, Morfad said flatly, "Those of Terran dogs."

"Dogs?" Haraka lay back and stared at him. *"Dogs?* Are you serious?"

"I have never been more so. I can hear dogs and no others. Don't ask me why because I don't know. It is a freak of circumstance."

"And you have listened to their minds ever since we jumped to Earth?"

"Yes."

"What sort of things have you heard?"

254

"I have had pearls of alien wisdom cast before me," declared Morfad, "and the longer I look at them the more they scare hell out of me."

"Get busy frightening me with a few examples," invited Haraka, suppressing a smile.

"Quote: the supreme test of intelligence is the ability to live as one pleases without working," recited Morfad. "Quote: the art of retribution is that of concealing it beyond all suspicion. Quote: the sharpest, most subtle, most effective weapon in the cosmos is flattery."

"Huh?"

"Quote: if a thing can think it likes to think that it is God—treat it as God and it becomes your willing slave."

"Oh, no!" denied Haraka.

"Oh, *yes!*" insisted Morfad. He waved a hand toward the nearest port. "Out there are three thousand million petty gods. They are eagerly panted after, fawned upon, gazed upon with worshiping eyes. Gods are very gracious toward those who love them." He made a spitting sound that lent emphasis to what followed. "The lovers know it—and love comes cheap."

Haraka said, uneasily, "I think you're crazy."

"Quote: to rule successfully the ruled must be unconscious of it." Again the spitting sound. "Is that crazy? I don't think so. It makes sense. It works. It's working out there right now."

"But—"

"Take a look at this." He tossed a small object into Haraka's lap. "Recognize it?"

"Yes, it's what they call a cracker."

"Correct. To make it some Terrans plowed fields in all kinds of weather, rain, wind and sunshine, sowed wheat, reaped it with the aid of machinery other Terrans had sweated to build. They transported the wheat, stored it, milled it, enriched the flour by various processes, baked it, packaged it, shipped it all over the world. When humanoid Terrans want crackers they've got to put in man-hours to get them."

"So—?"

"When a dog wants one he sits up, waves his forepaws and admires his god. That's all. Just that."

"But, darn it, man, dogs are relatively stupid."

"So it seems," said Morfad, dryly.

"They can't really *do* anything effective."

"That depends upon what one regards as effective."

"They haven't got hands."

"And don't need them—having brains."

"Now see here," declaimed Haraka, openly irritated, "we Altairans invented and constructed ships capable of roaming the spaces between the stars. The Terrans have done the same. Terran dogs have not done it and won't do it in the next million years. When one dog has the brains and ability to get to another planet I'll eat my cap."

"You can do that right now," Morfad suggested. "We have two dogs on board."

Haraka let go a grunt of disdain. "The Terrans have given us those as a memento."

"Sure they gave them to us—at whose behest?"

"It was wholly a spontaneous gesture."

"Was it?"

"Are you suggesting that dogs put the idea into their heads?" Haraka demanded.

"I know they did," retorted Morfad, looking grim. "And we've not been given two males or two females. Oh no, sir, not on your life. One male and one female. The givers said we could breed them. Thus in due course our own worlds can become illuminated with the undying love of man's best friend."

"Nuts!" said Haraka.

Morfad gave back, "You're obsessed with the old, out-of-date idea that conquest must be preceded by aggression. Can't you understand that a wholly alien species just naturally uses wholly alien methods? Dogs employ their own tactics, not ours. It isn't within their nature or abilities to take us over with the aid of ships, guns and a great hullabaloo. It *is* within their nature and abilities to creep in upon us, their eyes shining with hero-worship. If we don't watch out, we'll be mastered by a horde of loving creepers."

"I can invent a word for your mental condition," said Haraka. "You're suffering from caniphobia."

"With good reasons."

"Imaginary ones."

"Yesterday I looked into a dogs' beauty shop. Who was doing the bathing, scenting, powdering, primping? Other dogs? Hah! Humanoid females were busy dolling 'em up. Was *that* imaginary?"

"You can call it a Terran eccentricity. It means nothing whatever. Besides, we've quite a few funny habits of our own."

"You're dead right there," Morfad agreed. "And I know one of yours. So does the entire crew."

Haraka narrowed his eyes. "You might as well name it. I am not afraid to see myself as others see me."

"All right. You've asked for it. You think a lot of Kashim. He always has your ear. You will listen to him when you'll listen to nobody else. Everything he says makes sound sense—to you."

"So you're jealous of Kashim, eh?"

"Not in the least," assured Morfad, making a disparaging gesture. "I merely despise him for the same reason that everyone else holds him in contempt. He is a professional toady. He spends most of his time fawning upon you, flattering you, pandering to your ego. He is a natural-born creeper who gives you the Terradog treatment. You like it. You bask in it. It affects you like an irresistible drug. It works—and don't tell me that it doesn't because all of us know that it *does*."

"I am not a fool. I have Kashim sized up. He does not influence me to the extent you believe."

"Three thousand million Terrans have four hundred million dogs sized up and are equally convinced that no dog has a say in anything worth a hoot."

"I don't believe it."

"Of course you don't. I had little hope that you would. Morfad is telling you these things and Morfad is either crazy or a liar. But if Kashim were to tell you while prostrate at the foot of your throne you would swallow his story hook, line and sinker. Kashim has a Terradog mind and uses Terradog logic, see?"

"My disbelief has better basis than that."

"For instance?" Morfad invited.

"Some Terrans are telepathic. Therefore if this myth of subtle mastery by dogs were a fact, they'd know of it. Not a dog would be left alive on this world." Haraka paused, finished pointedly, "They don't know of it."

"Terran telepaths hear the minds of their own kind but not those of dogs. I hear the minds of dogs but not those of any other kind.

As said before, I don't know why this should be. I know only that it *is*."

"It seems nonsensical to me."

"It would. I suppose you can't be blamed for taking that viewpoint. My position is difficult; I'm like the only one with ears in a world that is stone-deaf."

Haraka thought it over, said after a while, "Suppose I were to accept everything you've said at face value—what do you think I should do about it?"

"Refuse to take the dogs," responded Morfad, promptly.

"That's more easily said than done. Good relations with the Terrans are vitally important. How can I reject a warm-hearted gift without offending the givers?"

"All right, don't reject it. Modify it instead. Ask for two male or two female dogs. Make it plausible by quoting an Altairan law against the importation of alien animals that are capable of natural increase."

"I can't do that. It's far too late. We've already accepted the animals and expressed our gratitude for them. Besides, their ability to breed is an essential part of the gift, the basic intention of the givers. They've presented us with a new species, an entire race of dogs."

"You said it!" confirmed Morfad.

"For the same reason we can't very well prevent them from breeding when we get back home," Haraka pointed out. "From now on we and the Terrans are going to do a lot of visiting. Immediately they discover that our dogs have failed to multiply they'll become generous and sentimental and dump another dozen on us. Or maybe a hundred. We'll then be worse off than we were before."

"All right, all right." Morfad shrugged with weary resignation. "If you're going to concoct a major objection to every possible solution we may as well surrender without a fight. Let's abandon ourselves to becoming yet another dog-dominated species. Requote: to rule successfully the ruled must be unconscious of it." He gave Haraka the sour eye. "If I had my way, I'd wait until we were far out in free space and then give those two dogs the hearty heave-ho out the hatch."

Haraka grinned in the manner of one about to nail down a cockeyed tale once and for all. "And if you did that it would be proof positive beyond all argument that you're afflicted with a delusion."

Emitting a deep sigh, Morfad asked, "Why would it?"

"You'd be slinging out two prime members of the master race. Some domination, eh?" Haraka grinned again. "Listen, Morfad, according to your own story you know something never before known or suspected and you're the only one who does know it. That should make you a mighty menace to the entire species of dogs. They wouldn't let you live long enough to thwart them or even to go round advertising the truth. You'd soon be deader than a low-strata fossil." He walked to the door, held it open while he made his parting shot. "You look healthy enough to me."

Morfad shouted at the closing door, "Doesn't follow that because I can hear their thoughts they must necessarily hear mine. I doubt that they can because it's just a freakish—"

The door clicked shut. He scowled at it, walked twenty times up and down the cabin, finally resumed his chair and sat in silence while he beat his brains around in search of a satisfactory solution.

"The sharpest, most subtle, most effective weapon in the cosmos is flattery."

Yes, he was seeking a means of coping with four-footed warriors incredibly skilled in the use of Creation's sharpest weapon. Professional fawners, creepers, worshipers, man-lovers, ego-boosters, trained to near-perfection through countless generations in an art against which there seemed no decisive defense.

How to beat off the coming attack, contain it, counter it?

"Yes, God!"

"Certainly, God!"

"Anything you say, God!"

How to protect oneself against this insidious technique, how to quarantine it or—

By the stars! that was it—*quarantine* them! On Pladamine, the useless world, the planet nobody wanted. They could breed there to their limits and meanwhile dominate the herbs and bugs. And a soothing reply would be ready for any nosey Terran tourist.

"The dogs? Oh, sure, we've still got them, lots of them. They're doing fine. Got a nice world of their very own. Place called Pladamine. If you wish to go see them, it can be arranged."

A wonderful idea. It would solve the problem while creating no hard feelings among the Terrans. It would prove useful in the future and to the end of time. Once planted on Pladamine no dog could ever escape by its own efforts. Any tourists from Terra who brought dogs along could be persuaded to leave them in the canine heaven specially created by Altair. There the dogs would find themselves unable to boss anything higher than other dogs, and, if they didn't like it, they could lump it.

No use putting the scheme to Haraka who was obviously prejudiced. He'd save it for the authorities back home. Even if they found it hard to credit his story, they'd still take the necessary action on the principle that it is better to be sure than sorry. Yes, they'd play safe and give Pladamine to the dogs.

Standing on a cabin seat, he gazed out and down through the port. A great mob of Terrans, far below, waited to witness the coming take-off and cheer them on their way. He noticed beyond the back of the crowd a small, absurdly groomed dog dragging a Terran female at the end of a thin, light chain. Poor girl, he thought. The dog leads, she follows yet believes *she* is taking *it* some place.

Finding his color-camera, he checked its controls, walked along the corridor and into the open air lock. It would be nice to have a picture of the big send-off audience. Reaching the rim of the lock he tripped headlong over something four-legged and stubby-tailed that suddenly intruded itself between his feet. He dived outward, the camera still in his grip, and went down fast through the whistling wind while shrill feminine screams came from among the watching crowd.

Haraka said, "The funeral has delayed us two days. We'll have to make up the time as best we can." He brooded a moment, added, "I am very sorry about Morfad. He had a brilliant mind but it was breaking up toward the end. Oh well, it's a comfort that the expedition has suffered only one fatality."

"It could have been worse, sir," responded Kashim. "It could have been you. Praise the heavens that it was not."

"Yes, it could have been me." Haraka regarded him curiously. "And would it have grieved you, Kashim?"

"Very much indeed, sir. I don't think anyone aboard would feel the loss more deeply. My respect and admiration are such that—"

He ceased as something padded softly into the cabin, laid its head in Haraka's lap, gazed soulfully up at the captain. Kashim frowned with annoyance.

"Good boy!" approved Haraka, scratching the newcomer's ears.

"My respect and admiration," repeated Kashim in louder tones, "are such that—"

"Good boy!" said Haraka again. He gently pulled one ear, then the other, observed with pleasure the vibrating tail.

"As I was saying, sir, my respect—"

"Good boy!" Deaf to all else, Haraka slid a hand down from the ears and massaged under the jaw.

Kashim favored Good Boy with a glare of inutterable hatred. The dog rolled a brown eye sidewise and looked at him without expression. From that moment Kashim's fate was sealed.

Itself!

A. E. van Vogt

Itself, king of the Philippine Deep—that awesome canyon where the sea goes down six miles—woke from his recharge period and looked around suspiciously.

His Alter Ego said, "Well, how is it with Itself today?"

The Alter Ego was a booster, a goader, a stimulant to action, and, in his limited way, a companion.

Itself did not answer. During the sleep period, he had drifted over a ravine, the walls of which dropped steeply another thousand feet. Suspiciously, Itself glared along the canyon rim.

. . . Not a visual observation. No light ever penetrated from above into the eternal night here at the deepest bottom of the ocean. Itself perceived the black world which surrounded him with high frequency sounds which he broadcast continuously in all directions. Like a bat in a pitch dark cave, he analyzed the structure of all things in his watery universe by interpreting the returning echoes. And the accompanying emotion of suspicion was a device which impelled Itself to record changing pressures, temperatures and current flows. Unknown to him, what he observed became part of the immense total of data by which faraway computers estimated the interrelationship of ocean and atmosphere, and thus predicted water and air conditions everywhere with uncanny exactness.

His was almost perfect perception. Clearly and unmistakably, Itself made out the intruder in the far distance of that twisting ravine. A ship! Anchored to rock at the very edge of the canyon.

The Alter Ego goaded, "You're not going to let somebody invade your territory, are you?"

Instantly, Itself was furious. He activated the jet mechanism in the underslung belly of his almost solid metal body. A nuclear reactor immediately heated the plates of the explosion chamber. The seawater which flowed through the chamber burst into hissing clouds of steam, and he jetted forward like a missile.

Arriving at the ship, Itself attacked the nearest of four anchor lines with the nuclear-powered heat beam in his head. When he had severed it, he turned to the second cable, and burned through it. Then he moved for the third cable.

But the startled beings aboard the alien ship had spotted the twenty-foot monster in the black waters below.

"Analyze its echo pattern!" came the command. That was done, with total skill.

"Feed the pattern back through the infinite altering system till the recorders register a response."

The significant response was: Itself forgot what he was doing. He was drifting blankly away, when his Alter Ego goaded, "Wake up! You're not going to let them get away with that, are you?"

The defeat had galvanized Itself to a more intense level of rage. He became multiples more sensitive. Now, he simply turned out the alien echo copies.

The new greater anger triggered a second weapon.

Itself's echo system of perception, normally monitered to be safe for all living things in the sea, suddenly strengthened. It became a supersonic beam. Purposefully, Itself started toward the ship.

Watching his approach, the enemy decided to take no chances. "Pull the remaining anchors in!"

Itself headed straight for the nearest part of the vessel. Instantly, those ultrasonic waves started a rhythmic vibration on the hard wall, weakening it.

The metal groaned under a weight of water that at these depths amounted to thousands of tons per square inch. The outer wall buckled with a metallic scream.

The inner wall trembled, but held.

At that point, the appalled defenders got a counter-vibration started, nullified the rhythm of Itself's projections, and were safe.

But it was a sorely wounded ship that now drifted helplessly in a slow current. The aliens had thus far used no energy that might be detected from the surface. But they had come to Earth to establish a base for invasion. Their instructions were to accumulate enough data about underwater currents to enable them to leave the Deep, and eventually to be able to drift near land, launch atom bombs, and drift away again. For this purpose they were mightily armed, and they refused to die in these black waters without a fight.

"What can we do about that daemon?"

"Blast it!" someone urged.

"That's dangerous." The alien commander hesitated.

"We can't be in greater danger than we already are."

"True," said the commander, "but frankly I don't know why he's armed at all, and I can't believe he has anything more. Set up a response system. If he does attack with anything new, it will automatically fire back. We'll take that much of a chance."

The second setback had driven Itself completely berserk. He aimed his nuclear pellet gun, firing twice. In the next split-second a blast from the invader pierced his brain.

The Alter Ego yelled, "You're not going to let them get away with that, are you?"

But the king of the Philippine Deep was dead, and could no longer be goaded.

In due course, a report was given to weather headquarters: "Computer Center shows no recent data from Itself. It therefore seems as if another of the wartime antisubmarine water-weather robots has worn out. You may recall that these electronic monsters were programmed to suspicion, anger, and the idea that they owned part of the ocean. After the war, we could never get these creatures to surface; they were too suspicious of us."

The ocean of water, like the ocean of air far above, flowed and rolled and moved in a ceaseless, dynamic, driving motion many, many times more powerful, however, than any comparable air current. Yet, in essence, the quadrillions of water movements solely and only balanced each other out.

Through the Philippine Deep there began presently to flow an enormous balancing river. It carried the aliens' invasion vessel in a long, slanting, upward direction. But several weeks passed before the drifting ship actually broke surface, and another day or two before it was seen.

A naval patrol boarded it, found the aliens dead more than a month from concussion, and—after examining the damage—correctly analyzed what had happened.

And so—a new king "woke" to the first "day" of his reign, and heard *his* Alter Ego say, "Well, Itself, what's the program?"

Itself glared with a royal suspicion.

Kindergarten

James E. Gunn

First day—

Teacher told my parent that I am the slowest youngster in my class, but today I made a star in the third quadrant of kindergarten.

Teacher was surprised. Teacher tried to hide it and said the solar phoenix reaction is artistic, but is it practical?

I don't care. I think it's pretty.

Second day—

Today I made planets: four big ones, two middle-sized ones, and three little ones. Teacher laughed and said why did I make so many when all but three were too hot or too cold to support life and the big ones were too massive and poisonous for any use at all.

Teacher doesn't understand. There is more to creation than mere usefulness.

The rings around the sixth planet are beautiful.

Third day—

Today I created life. I begin to understand why my people place creation above all else.

I have heard the philosophers discussing the purpose of existence, but I thought it was merely age. Before today joy was enough: to have fun with the other kids, to speed through endless space, to explode some unstable star into a nova, to flee before the outrage of some adult—this would fill eternity.

Now I know better. Life must have a function.

Teacher was right: only two of the middle-sized planets and one of the little ones were suitable for life. I made life for all three, but only on the third planet from the sun was it really successful.

I have given it only one function: survive!

Fourth day—

The third planet has absorbed all my interest. The soupy seas are churning with life.

Today I introduced a second function: multiply!

The forms developing in the seas are increasingly complex.

The kids are calling me to come and play, but I'm not going.

This is more fun.

Fifth day—

Time after time I stranded sea-creatures on the land and kept them alive long past the time when they should have died. At last I succeeded. Some of them have adapted.

I was right. The sea is definitely an inhibiting factor.

The success of the land-creatures is pleasing.

Sixth day—

Everything I did before today was nothing. Today I created intelligence.

I added a third function: know!

Out of a minor primate has developed a fabulous creature. It has two legs and walks upright and looks around it with curious eyes. It has weak hands and an insignificant brain, but it is conquering all things. Most of all, it is conquering its environment.

It has even begun speculating about me!

Seventh day—
Today there is no school.

After the pangs and labors of creation, it is fun to play again. It is like escaping the gravitational field of a white dwarf and regaining the dissipated coma.

Teacher talked to my parent again today. Teacher said I had developed remarkably in the last few days but my creation was hopelessly warped and inconsistent. Moreover, it was potentially dangerous.

Teacher said it would have to be destroyed.

My parent objected, saying that the solar phoenix reaction in the sun would lead the dangerous life form on the third planet to develop a thermonuclear reaction of its own. With the functions I had given that life form, the problem would take care of itself.

It wasn't my parent's responsibility Teacher said, and Teacher couldn't take the chance.

I didn't hear who won the argument. I drifted away, feeling funny.

I don't care, really. I'm tired of the old thing anyway. I'll make a better one.

But it was the first thing I ever made, and you can't help feeling a kind of sentimental attachment.

If anyone sees a great comet plunging toward the sun, it isn't me.

Eighth day—

The King of the Beasts

Philip Jose Farmer

The biologist was showing the distinguished visitor through the zoo and laboratory.

"Our budget," he said, "is too limited to re-create all known extinct species. So we bring to life only the higher animals, the beautiful ones that were wantonly exterminated. I'm trying, as it were, to make up for brutality and stupidity. You might say that man struck God in the face every time he wiped out a branch of the animal kingdom."

He paused, and they looked across the moats and the force fields. The quagga wheeled and galloped, delight and sun flashing off his flanks. The sea otter poked his humorous whiskers from the water. The gorilla peered from behind bamboo. Passenger pigeons strutted. A rhinoceros trotted like a dainty battleship. With gentle eyes a giraffe looked at them, then resumed eating leaves.

"There's the dodo. Not beautiful but very droll. And very helpless. Come. I'll show you the re-creation itself."

In the great building, they passed between rows of tall and wide tanks. They could see clearly through the windows and the jelly within.

"Those are African elephant embryos," said the biologist. "We plan to grow a large herd and then release them on the new government preserve."

"You positively radiate," said the distinguished visitor. "You really love the animals, don't you?"

"I love all life."

"Tell me," said the visitor, "where do you get the data for re-creation?"

"Mostly, skeletons and skins from the ancient museums. Excavated books and films that we succeeded in restoring and then translating. Ah, see those huge eggs? The chicks of the giant moa are growing within them. These, almost ready to be taken from the tank, are tiger cubs. They'll be dangerous when grown but will be confined to the preserve."

The visitor stopped before the last of the tanks.

"Just one?" he said. "What is it?"

"Poor little thing," said the biologist, now sad. "It will be so alone. But I shall give it all the love I have."

"Is it so dangerous?" said the visitor. "Worse than elephants, tigers and bears?"

"I had to get special permission to grow this one," said the biologist. His voice quavered.

The visitor stepped sharply back from the tank. He said, "Then it must be . . . But you wouldn't dare!"

The biologist nodded.

"Yes. It's a man."

Landscape with Sphinxes

Karen Anderson

The pride was a small one, even as sphinxes go. An arrogant black mane blew back over Arctanax's shoulders and his beard fluttered against his chest. Ahead and a little below soared Murrhona and Selissa, carrying the remnants of the morning's kill. It was time the cubs were weaned.

The valley lifted smooth and broad from the river, then leaped suddenly in sandstone cliffs where the shadows seemed more solid than the thorny, gray-green scrub. A shimmer of heat ran along wind-scoured edges.

In the tawny rocks about the eyrie, the cubs played at stalk-the-unicorn. They were big-eyed, dappled, and only half fledged. Taph, the boy, crept stealthily up a sun-hot slab, peeking around it from time to time to be sure that the moly blossom still nodded on the other side. He reached the top and shifted his feet excitedly. That moly was about to be a dead unicorn. The tip of his tail twitched at the thought.

His sister Fiantha forgot the blossom at once. Pounce! and his tail was caught between her paws; he rolled back down on top of her, all claws out. They scuffled across baked clay to the edge of a thorn-bush and backed apart.

Taph was about to attack again when he saw the grownups dip down from above. He leaped across Fiantha and bounded toward the cave mouth. She came a jump and a half behind. They couldn't kiss Murrhona and Selissa because of the meat in their jaws, so they kissed Father twice instead.

"Easy, there! Easy!" Arctanax coughed, but he was grinning. "Get back into the cave, the two of you. How often do I have to tell you to stay in the cave?" The cubs laughed and bounced inside.

Selissa dropped the meat she had been carrying and settled down to wash her face, but Murrhona called her cubs over to eat. She watched critically as they experimented with their milk-teeth on this unfamiliar substance.

"Hold it down with your paw, Fiantha," she directed. "If you just tug at it, it'll follow you all over the floor. Like Taph—No, Taph, use your side teeth. They're the biggest and sharpest." And so the lesson went. After a while both cubs got tired of the game and nuzzled for milk.

Selissa licked her right paw carefully and polished the bridge of her broad nose. There was still a trace of blood smell; she licked and polished again.

"You can't rush them," she said rather smugly. "I remember *my* first litter. Time and again I thought they'd learned a taste for meat, but even when they could kill for themselves—only conies and such, but their own kill—they still came back to suck."

"Oh, I remember how put out you were when you realized you still had to hold quiet for nursing," Murrhona smiled lazily. She licked down a tuft behind Fiantha's ear and resettled her wings. "But I really hate to see them grow up. They're so cute with their little spots."

Selissa shrugged and polished the bridge of her nose again for good measure. If you wanted to call them *cute,* with their wings all pinfeathers and down shedding everywhere—! Well, yes, she had to admit they were, in a way. She licked her paw once more, meditatively, put her chin down on it and dozed off.

An hour later Fiantha woke up. Everybody was asleep. She stretched her wings, rolled onto her back, and reached her paws as far as she could. The sun outside was dazzling. She rubbed the back of her head against the cool sandstone floor and closed her eyes, intending to go back to sleep, but her left wing itched. When she licked at it, the itch kept moving around, and bits of down came loose on her tongue.

She rolled over on her stomach, spat out the fluff, and licked again. There—*that* did it!

Fully awake now, she noticed the tip of Arctanax's tail and pounced.

"Scram," he muttered without really waking. She pounced again just as the tail-tip flicked out of reach. Once more and she had it, chewing joyously.

"Scram, I said!" he repeated with a cuff in her general direction. She went on chewing, and added a few kicks. Arctanax rolled over and bumped into Selissa, who jumped and gave Fiantha a swat in case she needed it. Fiantha mewed with surprise. Murrhona sprang up, brushing Taph aside; he woke too and made a dash for Selissa's twitching tail.

"Can't a person get *any* rest around here?" grumbled Arctanax. He heaved himself up and walked a few feet away from his by now well-tangled family.

"They're just playful," Murrhona murmured.

"If this is play, I'd hate to see a fight," said Selissa under her breath. She patted Taph away and he tumbled enthusiastically into a chewing match with Fiantha.

"Go to sleep, children," Murrhona suggested, stretching out again. "It's much too hot for games."

Fiantha rolled obediently away from Taph, and found a good place to curl up, but she wasn't the least bit sleepy. She leaned her chin on a stone and looked out over the valley. Down there, in the brown-roasted grass, something moved toward a low stony ridge.

There were several of them, and they didn't walk like waterbuck or unicorn; it was a queer, bobbing gait. They came slowly up the ridge and out of the grass. Now she could see them better. They had heads like sphinxes, but with skimpy little manes, and no wings at all; and—and—

"Father, *look!*" she squeaked in amazement. "What kind of animal is that?"

He got up to see. "I don't know," he replied. "Never saw anything like it in all my born days. But then, we've had a lot of queer creatures wandering in since the glaciers melted."

"Is it game?" asked Taph.

"Might be," Arctanax said. "But I don't know any game that moves around in the middle of the day like that. It isn't natural."

"And the funny way they walk, too," added Fiantha.

"If they're silly enough to walk around like that at mid-day," Arctanax said as he padded back to an extra-cool corner of the cave, "I'm not surprised they go on two legs."

The Last Men

Frank Belknap Long, Jr.

Maljoc had come of age. On a bright, cold evening in the fall of the year, fifty million years after the last perishing remnant of his race had surrendered its sovereignty to the swarming masters, he awoke proud and happy and not ashamed of his heritage. He knew, and the masters knew, that his kind had once held undisputed sway over the planet. Down through dim aeons the tradition—it was more than a legend—had persisted, and not all the humiliations of the intervening millenniums could erase its splendor.

Maljoc awoke and gazed up at the great moon. It shone down resplendently through the health-prism at the summit of the homorium. Its rays, passing through the prism, strengthened his muscles, his internal organs, and the soft parts of his body.

Arising from his bed, he stood proudly erect in the silver light and beat a rhythmic tattoo with his fists on his naked chest. He was of age, and among the clustering homoriums of the females of his race which hung suspended in the maturing nurseries of Agrahan was a woman who would share his pride of race and rejoice with him under the moon.

As the massive metallic portals of the homorium swung inward, a great happiness came upon him. The swarming masters had instructed him wisely as he lay maturing under the modified lunar rays in the nursery homorium.

He knew that he was a man and that the swarming masters were the descendants of the chitin-armored, segmented creatures called insects, which his ancestors had once ruthlessly despised and trampled under foot. At the front of his mind was this primary awareness of origins; at the back a storehouse of geologic data.

He knew when and why his race had succumbed to the swarming masters. In imagination he had frequently returned across the wide wastes of the years, visualizing with scientific accuracy the post-Pleistocene glacial inundations as they streamed equatorward from the poles.

He knew that four of the earth's remaining continents had once lain beneath ice sheets a half mile thick, and that the last pitiful and cold-weakened remnants of his race had succumbed to the superior sense-endowments of the swarming masters in the central core of a great land mass called Africa, now submerged beneath the waters of the southern ocean.

The swarming masters were almost godlike in their endowments. With their complex and prodigious brains, which seemed to Maljoc as all-embracing as the unfathomable forces which governed the constellations, they instructed their servitors in the rudiments of earth history.

In hanging nursery homoriums thousands of men and women were yearly grown and instructed. The process of growth was unbelievably rapid. The growth-span of the human race had once embraced a number of years, but the swarming masters could transform a tiny infant into a gangling youth in six months, and into a bearded adult, strong-limbed and robust, in twelve or fourteen. Gland injections and prism-ray baths were the chief casual agents of this extraordinary metamorphosis, but the growth process was further speeded up by the judicious administration of a carefully selected diet.

The swarming masters were both benevolent and merciless. They despised men, but they wished them to be reasonably happy. With a kind of grim, sardonic toleration they even allowed them to choose their own mates, and it was the novelty and splendor of that great privilege which caused Maljoc's little body to vibrate with intense happiness.

The great metallic portal swung open, and Maljoc emerged into the starlight and looked up at the swinging constellations. Five hundred feet below, the massive domed dwellings of Agrahan glistened resplendently in the silvery radiance, but only the white, glittering immensity of the Milky Way was in harmony with his mood.

A droning assailed his ears as he walked along the narrow metal terrace toward the swinging nurseries of the women of his race. Several of the swarming masters were hovering in the air above him, but he smiled up at them without fear, for his heart was warm with the splendor of his mission.

The homoriums, sky promenades, and air terraces were suspended above the dwellings of Agrahan by great swinging cables attached to gas-inflated, billowing air floats perpetually at anchor. As Maljoc trod the terrace, one of the swarming masters flew swiftly between the cables and swooped down upon him.

Maljoc recoiled in terror. The swarming masters obeyed a strange, inhuman ethic. They reared their servitors with care, but they believed also that the life of a servitor was simply a little puff of useful energy. Sometimes, when in sportive mood, they crushed the little puffs out between their claws.

A chitin-clad extremity gripped Maljoc about his middle and lifted him into the air. Calmly then, and without reversing its direction, the swarming master flew with him toward the clouds.

Up and up they went, till the air grew rarefied. Then the swarming master laid the cool tips of its antennae on Maljoc's forehead and conversed with him in a friendly tone.

"Your nuptial night, my little friend?" it asked.

"Yes," replied Maljoc. "Yes—yes—it is."

He was so relieved that he stammered. The master was pleased. The warmth of its pleasure communicated itself to Maljoc through the vibrations of its antennae.

"It is well," it said. "Even you little ones are born to be happy.

Only a cruel and thoughtless insect would crush a man under its claw in wanton pleasure."

Maljoc knew, then, that he was to be spared. He smiled up into the great luminous compound-eyes of his benefactor.

"It amused me to lift you into the air," conveyed the master. "I could see that you wanted to soar above the earth; that your little wingless body was vibrant with happiness and desire for expansion."

"That is true," said Maljoc.

He was grateful and—awed. He had never before been carried so high. Almost the immense soaring wings of the master brushed the stratosphere.

For a moment the benevolent creature winged its way above the clouds, in rhythmic glee. Then, slowly, its body tilted, and it swept downward in a slow curve toward the sky terrace.

"You must not pick a too-beautiful mate," cautioned the master. "You know what happens sometimes to the too beautiful."

Maljoc knew. He knew that his own ancestors had once pierced the ancestors of the swarming masters with cruel blades of steel and had set them in decorative rows in square boxes because they were too beautiful. His instructors had not neglected to dwell with fervor on the grim expiation which the swarming masters were in the habit of exacting. He knew that certain men and women who were too beautiful were frequently lifted from the little slave world of routine duties in the dwellings of the masters and anaesthetized, embalmed, and preserved under glass in the museum mausoleums of Agrahan.

The master set Maljoc gently down on the edge of the sky terrace and patted him benevolently on the shoulder with the tip of its hindermost leg. Then it soared swiftly upward and vanished from sight.

Maljoc began to chant again. The Galaxy glimmered majestically in the heavens above him, and as he progressed along the sky promenade he feasted his gaze on the glowing misty fringes of stupendous island universes lying far beyond the milky nebulae to which his little race and the swarming masters belonged.

Nearer at hand, as though loosely enmeshed in the supporting cables, the pole star winked and glittered ruddily, while Sirius vied with Betelgeuse in outshining the giant, cloud-obscured Antares, and the wheeling fire chariot of the planet Mars.

Above him great wings droned, and careening shapes usurped his vision. He quickened his stride and drew nearer, and ever nearer, to the object of his desire.

The nursery homorium of the women of his race was a towering vault of copper on the edge of the cable-suspended walk. As he came abreast of it he began to tremble, and the color ebbed from his face. The women of his race were unfathomable, dark enigmas to him—bewildering shapes of loveliness that utterly eluded his comprehension.

He had glimpsed them evanescently in pictures—the swarming masters had shown him animated pictures in colors—but why the pictures enraptured and disturbed him so he did not know.

For a moment he stood gazing fearfully up at the massive metal portal of the homorium. Awe and a kind of panicky terror contended with exultation in his bosom. Then, resolutely, he threw out his chest and began to sing.

The door of the homorium swung slowly open, and a dim blue light engirded him as he stood limned in the aperture. The illumination came from deep within the homorium. Maljoc did not hesitate. Shouting and singing exultantly, he passed quickly through the luminous portal, down a long, dim corridor, and into a vast, rectangular chamber.

The women of his race were standing about in little groups. Having reached maturity, they were discussing such grave and solemn topics as the past history of their kind and their future duties as obedient servants of the swarming masters. Without hesitation, Maljoc moved into the center of the chamber.

The women uttered little gasping cries of delight when they beheld him. Clustering boldly about him, they ran their slim white hands over his glistening tunic and caressed with fervor his beard and hair. They even gazed exultantly into his boyish gray eyes, and when he flushed they tittered.

Maljoc was disturbed and frightened. Ceasing to sing, he backed away precipitously toward the rear of the chamber.

"Do not be afraid," said a tall, flaxen-haired virago at his elbow. "We will not harm you."

Maljoc looked at her. She was attractive in a bold, flamboyant way, but he did not like her. He tried to move away from her, but she linked her arm in his and pulled him back toward the center of the chamber.

He cried out in protest. "I do not like you!" he exclaimed. "You are not the kind of woman—"

The amazon's lips set in hard lines. "You are far too young to know your own mind," she said. "I will be a good wife to you."

As she spoke, she thrust out a powerful right arm and sent three of her rivals sprawling.

Maljoc was panic-stricken. He pleaded and struggled. The woman was pulling him toward the center of the chamber, and two of the other women were contending with her.

The struggle terminated suddenly. Maljoc reeled, lost his balance, and went down with a thud on the hard metallic floor. The metal bruised his skull, stunning him.

For several seconds a wavering twilight engulfed Maljoc's faculties. Needles pierced his temples, and the relentless eyes of the amazon burned into his brain. Then, slowly and painfully, his senses cleared, and his eyelids flickered open in confused bewilderment.

Two compassionate blue eyes were gazing steadily down at him. Dazedly, Maljoc became aware of a lithely slim form, and a clear, lovely face. As he stared up in wonderment, the apparition moved closer and spoke in accents of assurance.

"I will not let them harm you," she said.

Maljoc groaned, and his hand went out in helpless appeal. Slim, firm fingers encircled his palm, and a gentle caress eased the pain in his forehead.

Gently he drew his comforter close and whispered: "Let us escape from these devils."

The woman beside him hesitated. She seemed both frightened and eager. "I am only eight months old," she told him in a furtive whisper. "I am really too young to go forth. They say, too, that it would be dangerous, for I am—" A blush suffused her cheeks.

"She is dangerously beautiful," said a harsh voice behind her. "The instructors here are indifferent to beauty, but when she goes forth she will be seized and impaled. You had better take me."

Maljoc raised himself defiantly on his elbow. "It is my privilege to choose," he said. "And I take this woman. Will you go forth with me, my little one?"

The woman's eyes opened widely. She looked slowly up at the amazon, who was standing in the shadows behind her, and said in a voice which did not tremble: "I will take this man. I will go forth with him."

The amazon's features were convulsed with wrath. But she was powerless to intervene. Maljoc was privileged to choose, and the woman was privileged to accept. With an infuriated shrug she retreated farther into the shadows.

Maljoc arose from the floor and gazed rapturously at his chosen mate. She did not evade his scrutiny. As Maljoc continued to stare at her, the strained look vanished from his face and mighty energies were released within him.

He stepped to her and lifted her with impassioned chantings into the air. Her long hair descended and enmeshed his shoulders, and as he pressed her to his heart her arms tightened clingingly about him.

The other women clustered quickly about the exultant couple. Laughing and nudging one another, they examined the strong biceps of the bridegroom and ran their fingers enviously through the woman's dark hair.

Maljoc ignored them. Holding his precious burden very firmly in his muscular arms, he walked across the chamber, down the long outer corridor, and out through the massive door. Above him in another moment the Cyclopean luminous cables loomed beneath far-glimmering stars. He walked joyfully along the sky promenade, chanting, singing, unquenchably happy in his little hour of triumph and rapture.

The woman in his arms was unbelievably beautiful. She lay limply and calmly in his embrace, her eyes luminous with tenderness. Orion gleamed more brightly now, and the great horned moon was a silver fire weaving fantastically in and out of the nebulae-laced firmament.

As Maljoc sang and chanted, the enormous droning shapes above him seemed mere alien intruders in a world of imperishable loveliness. He thought of himself now as lord of the earth and the sky, and the burden in his arms was more important in his sight than his destiny as a servitor and the benefits which the swarming masters had promised to bestow upon him if he served them diligently and well.

He no longer coveted slave joys and gratifications. He wished to be forever his own master under the stars. It was a daring and impious wish, and as if aware of his insurgent yearnings a great form came sweeping down upon him out of the sky. For an instant it hovered with sonorously vibrating wings in the air above him. But Maljoc was so obsessed with joy that he ignored the chill menace of its presence. He walked on, and the woman in his arms shared his momentary forgetfulness.

The end of their pathetic and insane dream came with a sickening abruptness. A great claw descended and gripped the woman's slim body, tearing her with brutal violence from Maljoc's clasp.

The woman screamed twice shrilly. With a harsh cry, Maljoc leaped back. As he shook with horror, a quivering feeler brushed his forehead and spoke to him in accents of contempt:

"She is too beautiful for you, little one. Return to the homorium and choose another mate."

Fear and awe of the swarming masters were instinctive in all men, but as the words vibrated through Maljoc's brain he experienced a blind agony which transcended instinct. With a scream he leaped into the air and entwined his little hands about the enormous bulbous hairs on the master's abdomen.

The master made no attempt to brush him off. It spread its gigantic lacy wings and soared swiftly into the sky. Maljoc tore and pulled at the hairs in a fury of defiance. The swiftness of the flight choked the breath in his lungs, and his eyes were blinded by swirling motes of dust. But though his vision was obscured, he could still glimpse dimly the figure of the woman as she swung limply in the clasp of the great claw a few yards above him.

Grimly, he pulled himself along the master's abdomen toward the claw. He pulled himself forward by transferring his fingers from hair to hair. The master's flat, broad stinger swung slowly toward him in a menacing arc, but he was sustained in his struggle by a sacrificial courage which transcended fear.

Yet the stinger moved so swiftly that it thwarted his daring purpose. In a fraction of time his brain grew poignantly aware that the stinger would sear his flesh before he could get to his dear one, and the realization was like a knife in his vitals. In despair and rage, he thrust out his puny jaw and sank his teeth deep into the soft flesh beneath him. The flesh quivered.

At the same instant the master swooped and turned over. Maljoc bit again. It screeched with pain and turned over and over, and suddenly, as it careened in pain, a white shape fell from its claw.

Maljoc caught the shape as it fell. With one hand clinging to the hair of the master's palpitating abdomen, and the other supporting the woman of his choice, he gazed downward into the abyss.

A mile below him the unfriendly earth loomed obscurely through riven tiers of cirrus clouds. But Maljoc did not hesitate. With a proud, exultant cry he tightened his hold on the woman and released his fingers from the hair.

The two lovers fell swiftly to the earth. But in that moment of swooning flight that could end only in destruction, Maljoc knew that he was mightier than the masters, and having recaptured for an imperishable instant the lost glory of his race, he went without fear into darkness.

Last Warning

Mack Reynolds

Despite the widely publicized radar posts encircling our nation and the continuously alerted jet squadrons at its borders, the space ship was about to land before it was detected.

It settled gracefully, quietly, onto an empty field in northern New Jersey. And so unexpected was the event, so unbelievable the fact that man was being visited by aliens from space, that it was a full half hour before the first extra was on the streets in New York, and forty minutes before the news buzzed through the Kremlin.

It might have taken considerably longer for man in earth's more isolated areas to hear of the event had not the alien taken a hand at this point. Approximately an hour after the landing, into the mind of every human on earth, irrespective of nation, language, age, or intellect, came the thought telepathically:

We come in peace. Prepare to receive our message.

It was a month before the message came.

During that period, more than ninety-nine per cent of the earth's population became aware of the visitor from space. Radio, television, newsreel, telegraph and newspapers reached the greater number; but word of mouth and even throbbing drums, played their part. In four weeks, savages along the Amazon and shepherds in Sinkiang knew that visitors from the stars had arrived with a message for man.

And all awaited the message: scientist and soldier, politician and revolutionist, millionaire and vagrant, bishop and whirling dervish, banker and pickpocket, society matron and street walker. And each was hoping for one thing, and afraid he'd hear another.

All efforts at communication with the alien ship had failed. The various welcoming delegations from the State of New Jersey, from the United States, and even from the United Nations, were ignored. No sign of life aboard was evident, and there seemed no means of entrance to the spacecraft. It sat there impassively; its tremendous, saucerlike shape seemed almost like a beautiful monument.

At the end of a month, when world-wide interest in the visitor from space was at its height, the message came. And once again it was impressed upon the mind of every human being on earth:

Man, know this: Your world is fated to complete destruction. Ordinarily, we of the Galactic Union would not have contacted man until he had progressed much further and was ready to take his place among us. But this emergency makes necessary that we take immediate steps if your kind is to be saved from complete obliteration.

In order to preserve your race, we are making efforts to prepare another planet, an uninhabited one, to receive your colonists. Unfortunately, our means for transporting you to your new world are limited; only a handful can be taken. You are safe for another five of your earth years. At the end of that period we will return. Have a thousand of your people ready for their escape.

The President of the United States lifted an eyebrow wearily and rapped again for order.

"Gentlemen, please! . . . Let us get back to the fundamental question. Summed up, it amounts to this: only one thousand persons, out of a world population of approximately two billion, are going to be able to escape the earth's destruction. In other words, one out of every two million. It is going to be most difficult to choose."

Herr Ernst Oberfeld tapped his glasses fretfully on the conference table. "Mr. President, it need not be quite as bad as all that. After all, we must choose the earth's best specimens to carry on our race. I believe we will find that the combined populations of Europe and North America total somewhat less than a billion. If we go still further and eliminate all inferior . . ."

Monsieur Pierre Duclos flushed. "Herr Oberfeld should keep in mind that his presence at this meeting at all was opposed vigorously by some of the delegates. Isn't it somewhat too soon after his country's debacle to again broadcast its super-race theories?"

The British representative spoke up. "My dear Duclos, although I agree with you completely in essence, still it must be pointed out that if we were to handle this allocation on a strictly numerical basis, that our Chinese friends would be alloted something like two hundred colonists, while Great Britain would have perhaps twenty."

Maxim Gregoroff grunted, "Hardly enough for the Royal family, eh?"

Lord Harriman was on his feet. "Sir, I might echo what Monsieur Duclos has said to Herr Oberfeld. It was in spite of the protest from a considerable number of delegates to this conference that your nation is represented at all."

Gregoroff's fist thumped on the table and his face went beet red. "It is as expected! You plan to monopolize the escape ship for the imperialistic nations! The atom bomb will probably be used to destroy all other countries!"

The President of the United States held up his hand. This whole thing was getting more chaotic by the minute. As a matter of fact, instructions from Congress were that he explain that the United States expected to have at least one third of the total. This, in view of the fact that the aliens had landed in New Jersey, obviously seeing that the United States was the foremost nation of the world, and, further, in view of the fact that this country was a melting pot of all nations and consequently produced what might be called the "average" member of the human race.

However, that would have to wait. Order had to be brought to this conference if anything was to be accomplished.

"Gentlemen, gentlemen, please!" he called. "These accusations. We are getting nowhere. I have taken the liberty to make arrangements to have the representative of the newly formed Congress of American Sciences address you. Are you agreeable?" He raised his eyebrows inquiringly, and meeting no objection, pressed the button on the table before him.

Professor Manklethorp was ushered in, bobbed his head to the assembled delegates and came to the point immediately. "The problem which you are discussing has many ramifications. I would like to bring to your attention a few which should be examined with care.

"First, the choice of colonists must not be on a national basis, nor on one based upon political or monetary prominence. If it is, we, as a race, are doomed. This new planet, no matter how well prepared for us by the Galactic Union, is going to be a challenge such as man has never faced before. This challenge cannot be met by politicians, no matter how glib, nor by wealthy men, no matter how many dollars they possess, nor by titled ones, no matter how old and honored their names. We must pick trained specialists who will be able to meet the problems that arise in the new world.

"Our congress recommends that all persons, of all nations, who have college degrees, be given thorough tests both for I.Q. and for accumulated knowledge, and that the highest thousand be chosen irrespective of nation or race."

Pandit Hari Kuanai smiled quietly. "May I ask the learned professor a question?"

"Of course. That is why I am here. We want only to have this matter decided on a strictly scientific basis."

"My poverty stricken country has a population of possibly one fifth of the world total, but fewer university men than one of your large cities might boast. Your desire to choose men by their I.Q. has its merits, but I have no doubt that in my country we have men of tremendous intelligence who cannot even read or write, aside from having a university degree. Must my widely illiterate people go unrepresented in the new world?"

A muscle twitched in the professor's face. "Needless to say, the Congress of American Sciences has considered that. However, we must view this matter in a spirit of sacrifice. The best of the world's population must go to the new world. Possibly whole nations will go without representation. It is too bad . . . but, unfortunately, necessary."

Sven Carlesen put up his finger for recognition. "It seems to me there is another serious loophole in the professor's recommendation. He wants the thousand to be made up of university graduates of high I.Q. and considerable accumulated knowledge. I am afraid I foresee the new world being populated with elderly scholars." He smiled. "Like the professor himself, who, I understand, has a phenomenal I.Q."

Monsieur Duclos nodded. "He is right. We must consider the need to send perfect physical specimens." He looked down at his own small and bent body. "Gentlemen," he said wryly, "has it occurred to you that none of us here at this conference are suitable to be represented among the thousand?"

They ignored him.

A pale faced delegate in black, who had thus far said nothing, spoke up softly, "I have been instructed to inform you that our organization demands that all of the colonists be of the true faith."

His words were drowned by the shouting of half a dozen of the conference delegates. Loud above them all could be heard the bellow of Maxim Gregoroff.

"Our Union now includes the population of approximately half the world. Our allotment, consequently, will be five hundred colonists, of the one thousand. We will choose them by our own methods."

Lord Harriman murmured, "Undoubtedly, by starting at the top of the party membership list and taking the first five hundred names beginning with your leader."

The President of the United States ran his hand through his hair and then roughly down the side of his face. A messenger handed him a slip of paper. He read it and intensified his pounding on the table.

"Gentlemen," he shouted. "If Professor Manklethorp is through, we have here a request from the International Physical Culture Society to have their representative heard."

"I know," Sven Carlesen said. "He wants all of the colonists to be able to chin themselves twenty-five times as the first requisite."

At the end of the five year period the space ship came again, settling into the identical field where it had first landed. This time a delegation awaited it, and a multitude that stretched as far as the eye could see.

A telepathic message came from the visitor from space almost immediately.

Choose from your number three representatives to discuss the situation with us.

Within ten minutes, three advanced and entered the ship by way of a port that opened before them as they approached. Among their number was Pierre Duclos. A passage stretched before them, and, seeing no one, they hesitated a moment before following it to its further end. Monsieur Duclos led the way, depending only slightly on his cane to aid his bent body.

A door opened and they were confronted by the figure of a man seated at a desk. It was several moments before they realized that the entity before them was masked so cleverly that they had been led to believe him human.

He said in faultless English, "I note that you have penetrated my disguise. I thought it would be easier for you if I hid my true appearance. Until your people are used to alien life forms, I must use this measure."

Monsieur Duclos bowed. "We appreciate your consideration, but I assure you that our . . ."

The alien waved a gloved hand. "Please, no argument. My appearance would probably nauseate you. But it is of no importance. Pray be seated." He noted the cane, and nodded to the little Frenchman. "You sir, must be highly thought of to rate being chosen one of the thousand in view of your age and health."

Although he was not at ease in the presence of the representative of the Galactic Union, Monsieur Duclos allowed himself a wry smile. "You misunderstand. I am not one of the colonists. My presence here at this meeting is an honor that has been awarded me in return for some small services in aiding in the selection of the favored ones."

"And what were these services?"

"Of no real importance. I suppose you might say that the most important was that I was the first to refuse to be a colonist."

Bently, one of the other earthmen, spoke up, "Had it not been for Pierre Duclos, it is doubtful if the thousand would have been chosen, and even possible that there would be no earth to which to return for your colonists."

Behind the mask the eyes of the alien gleamed. "Enlighten me further, please."

Duclos demurred. "You honor me overmuch, Mr. Bently. Let us approach the problem of the colonists and their transportation."

But John Bently went on. "For more than two years after your ship's departure, complete confusion reigned in regard to selection of the thousand. Happily, all out warfare between nations had been avoided although conditions were rapidly coming to a point where it was momentarily expected.

"Each race, each nation, each religion, even each sex, thought they should have the greater representation. And each of these groups in turn were divided into sub-groups by wealth, age, class, education and others. Almost everyone on earth knew of some reason why he should be one of the colonists. And most of us were willing to take any steps to make our desire come true."

The alien said, "That was to be expected. And then?"

"And then Pierre Duclos formed his Society of Racial Preservation whose first requisite for membership was a refusal to become one of the colonists. The purpose of the organization was to find the thousand most suitable colonists without regard to race, nationality, creed, color, education, class, wealth or any other grouping.

"At first, the growth of membership was slow, but, after a time, man saw that his chance of survival as an individual was practically nil, that his chance of being chosen was at best less than one in two million. When he realized this, his next desire was to make sure that, even though he as an individual was doomed, the race survived. Membership in the society grew rapidly and internationally.

The members, you might say, were fanatical. Why not? They knew that they had less than five years to live. Why not sacrifice those last years of life to such a noble cause?

"As the society grew in strength, nothing could stand before it. Governments that stood in the way were overthrown, social systems abolished, prejudices and institutions that had stood for centuries were wiped out. It became necessary to institute world government, to guarantee to all equal opportunity. Step by step, the society took the measures necessary to ensure the selection of the best specimens earth had to offer.

"And scientific development was pushed to the utmost. We wished to send our colonists off with as much as earth could possibly give them. We eliminated a dozen diseases that have plagued us for centuries; we devised a thousand new tools and techniques."

"In short," said the alien, "because of this stimulus, man has progressed as much in this past few years as he could have expected in the next fifty."

"That is correct," Pierre Duclos said. "It is unfortunate that now we have on our threshold a world really worth living in, that it is fated to be destroyed."

"I see," said the alien; what would have been a smile on a human face flickered on his. "I am glad to report that the danger which confronted the earth has been removed and the need to populate the new planet with colonists in order to preserve your race is now eliminated.

"Gentlemen, the earth is safe. Man may go on with his plans without fear of destruction."

Monsieur Duclos fingered his cane thoughtfully while the other two earthmen jumped to their feet, thumped each other's backs, shouted, and otherwise demonstrated their joy. They finally dashed from the room and from the spacecraft to give the news to the world.

The alien eyed the little Frenchman. "And why have you remained?"

"I do not believe the world was faced with destruction, monsieur. I have come to the conclusion that you have perpetrated a farce upon mankind."

The alien sat himself down at the desk again. "I see you will need an explanation. But you are wrong, you know. Faced with destruc-

286

tion you were. The destruction, however, was not a matter of collision with some other body, or whatever you might have imagined. The destruction would have come from within. Man was on the verge of destroying himself. One more conflict, or, at most, two, would have done it.

"The Galactic Union has long been aware of man who has developed mechanically in a phenomenal manner but has not been able to develop socially to the point where his science is less than a danger. This ship was sent to you in hopes of accomplishing exactly what has been accomplished. We believed your racial instinct would be strong enough to unite you when the race as a whole thought it was threatened with extinction."

The alien got to his feet. "I am afraid we must leave now. Let me say that I hope that man will soon be able to take his place in the Galactic Union."

Monsieur Duclos winced. "The Galactic Union," he said. "The League of Nations and the United Nations were bad enough." He smiled wryly. "And I thought that with the establishment of a world government, we had abolished such conferences forever. I can just see myself as the first delegate from earth. Heaven forbid!"

Later Than You Think

Fritz Leiber

Obviously the Archeologist's study belonged to an era vastly distant from today. Familiar similarities here and there only sharpened the feeling of alienation. The sunlight that filtered through the windows in the ceiling had a wan and greenish cast and was augmented by radiation from some luminous material impregnating the walls and floor. Even the wide desk and the commodious hassocks glowed with a restful light. Across the former were scattered metal-backed wax tablets, styluses, and a pair of large and oddly formed spectacles. The crammed bookcases were not particularly unusual, but the books were bound in metal and the script on their spines would have been utterly unfamiliar to the most erudite of modern linguists. One of the books, lying open on a hassock, showed leaves of a thin, flexible, rustless metal covered with luminous characters. Between the bookcases were phosphorescent oil paintings, mainly of sea bottoms, in somber greens and browns. Their style, neither wholly realistic nor abstract, would have baffled the historian of art.

A blackboard with large colored crayons hinted equally at the schoolroom and the studio.

In the center of the room, midway to the ceiling, hung a fish with iridescent scales of breathtaking beauty. So invisible was its means of support that—also taking into account the strange paintings and the greenish light—one would have sworn that the object was to create an underwater scene.

The Explorer made his entrance in a theatrical swirl of movement. He embraced the Archeologist with a warmth calculated to startle that crusty old fellow. Then he settled himself on a hassock, looked up and asked a question in a speech and idiom so different from any we know that it must be called another means of communication rather than another language. The import was, "Well, what about it?"

If the Archeologist were taken aback, he concealed it. His expression showed only pleasure at being reunited with a long-absent friend.

"What about what?" he queried.

"About your discovery!"

"What discovery?" The Archeologist's incomprehension was playful.

The Explorer threw up his arms. "Why, what else but your discovery, here on Earth, of the remains of an intelligent species? It's the find of the age! Am I going to have to coax you? Out with it!"

"I didn't make the discovery," the other said tranquilly. "I only supervised the excavations and directed the correlation of material. *You* ought to be doing the talking. *You're* the one who's just returned from the stars."

"Forget that." The Explorer brushed the question aside. "As soon as our spaceship got within radio range of Earth, they started to send us a continuous newscast covering the period of our ablic walls of great strength and toughness. Evidently its makers had intended it for the very purpose of carrying a message down through the ages. It proved to contain artifacts; models of buildings, vehicles, and machines, objects of art, pictures, and books—hundreds of books, along with elaborate pictorial dictionaries for interpreting them. So now we even understand their languages."

"Languages?" interrupted the Explorer. "That's queer. Somehow one thinks of an alien species as having just one language."

"Like our own, this species had several, though there were some words and symbols that were alike in all their languages. These words and symbols seem to have come down unchanged from their most distant prehistory."

The Explorer burst out, "I am not interested in all that dry stuff! Give me the wet! What were they like? How did they live? What did they create? What did they want?"

The Archeologist gently waved aside the questions. "All in good time. If I am to tell you everything you want to know, I must tell it my own way. Now that you are back on Earth, you will have to reacquire those orderly and composed habits of thought which you have partly lost in the course of your wild interstellar adventurings."

"Curse you, I think you're just trying to tantalize me."

The Archeologist's expression showed that this was not altogether untrue. He casually fondled an animal that had wriggled up onto his desk, and which looked rather more like an eel than a snake. "Cute little brute, isn't it?" he remarked. When it became apparent that the Explorer wasn't to be provoked into another outburst, he continued, "It became my task to interpret the contents of the cache, to reconstruct its makers' climb from animalism and savagery to civilization, their rather rapid spread across the world's surface, their first fumbling attempts to escape from the Earth."

"They had spaceships?"

"It's barely possible. I rather hope they did, since it would mean the chance of a survival elsewhere, though the negative results of your expedition rather lessen that." He went on, "The cache was laid down when they were first attempting space flight, just after their discovery of atomic power, in the first flush of their youth. It was probably created in a kind of exuberant fancifulness, with no serious belief that it would ever serve the purpose for which it was

sence. One of the items, exasperatingly brief, mentioned your di
covery. It captured my imagination. I couldn't wait to hear tl
details." He paused, then confessed, "You get so eager out there
space—a metal-filmed droplet of life lost in immensity. You red
cover your emotions. . . ." He changed color, then finished ra
idly. "As soon as I could decently get away, I came straight to you
wanted to hear about it from the best authority—yourself."

The Archeologist regarded him quizzically. "I'm pleased that y
should think of me and my work, and I'm very happy to see y
again. But admit it now, isn't there something a bit odd about yo
getting so worked up over this thing? I can understand that aft
your long absence from Earth, any news of Earth would seem esp
cially important. But isn't there an additional reason?"

The Explorer twisted impatiently. "Oh, I suppose there is. Disa
pointment, for one thing. We were hoping to get in touch wi
intelligent life out there. We were specially trained in techniques 1
establishing mental contact with alien intelligent life forms. We
we found some planets with life upon them, all right. But it w
primitive life, not worth bothering about."

Again he hesitated embarrassedly. "Out there you get to thinki
of the preciousness of intelligence. There's so little of it, and it's
lonely. And we so greatly need intercourse with another intellige
species to give depth and balance to our thoughts. I suppose I s
too much store by my hopes of establishing a contact." He pause
"At any rate, when I heard that what we were looking for, you h
found here at home—even though dead and done for—I felt that
least it was something. I was suddenly very eager. It is odd, I kno
to get so worked up about an extinct species—as if my intere
could mean anything to them now—but that's the way it hit me

Several small shadows crossed the windows overhead. Th
might have been birds, except they moved too slowly.

"I think I understand," the Archeologist said softly.

"So get on with it and tell me about your discovery!" the E
plorer exploded.

"I've already told you that it wasn't my discovery," the Archeol
gist reminded him. "A few years after your expedition left, ther
was begun a detailed resurvey of Earth's mineral resources. In th
course of some deep continental borings, one party discovered
cache—either a very large box or a rather small room—with meta

28

intended." He looked at the Explorer strangely. "If I am not mistaken, we have laid down similar caches."

After a moment the Archeologist continued, "My reconstruction of their history, subsequent to the laying down of the cache, has been largely hypothetical. I can only guess at the reasons for their decline and fall. Supplementary material has been very slow in coming in, though we are still making extensive excavations at widely separated points. Here are the last reports." He tossed the Explorer a small metal-leaf pamphlet. It flew with a curiously slow motion.

"That's what struck me so queer right from the start," the Explorer observed, putting the pamphlet aside after a glance. "If these creatures were relatively advanced, why haven't we learned about them before? They must have left so many things—buildings, machines, engineering projects, some of them on a large scale. You'd think we'd be turning up traces everywhere."

"I have four answers to that," the Archeologist replied. "The first is the most obvious. Time. Geologic ages of it. The second is more subtle. What if we should have been looking in the wrong place? I mean, what if the creatures occupied a very different portion of the Earth than our own? Third, it's possible that atomic energy, out of control, finished the race and destroyed its traces. The present distribution of radioactive compounds throughout the Earth's surface lends some support to this theory.

"Fourth," he went on, "it's my belief that when an intelligent species begins to retrogress, it tends to destroy, or, rather, debase all the things it has laboriously created. Large buildings are torn down to make smaller ones. Machines are broken up and worked into primitive tools and weapons. There is a kind of unraveling or erasing. A cultural Second Law of Thermodynamics begins to operate, whereby the intellect and all its works are gradually degraded to the lowest level of meaning and creativity."

"But why?" The Explorer sounded anguished. "Why should any intelligent species end like that? I grant the possibility of atomic power getting out of hand, though one would have thought they'd have taken the greatest precautions. Still, it could happen. But that fourth answer—it's morbid."

"Cultures and civilizations die," said the Archeologist evenly. "That has happened repeatedly in our own history. Why not species? An individual dies—and is there anything intrinsically more terrible in the death of a species than in the death of an individual?"

He paused. "With respect to the members of this one species, I think that a certain temperamental instability hastened their end. Their appetites and emotions were not sufficiently subordinated to their understanding and to their sense of drama—their enjoyment of the comedy and tragedy of existence. They were impatient and easily incapacitated by frustration. They seem to have been singularly guilty in their pleasures, behaving either like gloomy moralists or gluttons.

"Because of taboos and an overgrown possessiveness," he continued, "each individual tended to limit his affection to a tiny family; in many cases he focused his love on himself alone. They set great store by personal prestige, by the amassing of wealth and the exercise of power. Their notable capacity for thought and manipulative activity was expended on things rather than persons or feelings. Their technology outstripped their psychology. They skimped fatally when it came to hard thinking about the purpose of life and intellectual activity, and the means for preserving them."

Again the slow shadows drifted overhead.

"And finally," the Archeologist said, "they were a strangely haunted species. They seem to have been obsessed by the notion that others, greater than themselves, had prospered before them and then died, leaving them to rebuild a civilization from ruins. It was from those others that they thought they derived the few words and symbols common to all their languages."

"Gods?" mused the Explorer.

The Archeologist shrugged. "Who knows?"

The Explorer turned away. His excitement had visibly evaporated, leaving behind a cold and miserable residue of feeling. "I am not sure I want to hear much more about them," he said. "They sound too much like us. Perhaps it was a mistake, my coming here. Pardon me, old friend, but out there in space even *our* emotions become undisciplined. Everything becomes indescribably poignant. Moods are tempestuous. You shift in an instant from zenith to nadir—and remember, out there you can see both.

"I was very eager to hear about this lost species," he added in a sad voice. "I thought I would feel a kind of fellowship with them across the eons. Instead, I touch only corpses. It reminds me of when, out in space, there looms up before your prow, faint in the starlight, a dead sun. They were a young race. They thought they were getting somewhere. They promised themselves an eternity of effort. And all the while there was wriggling toward them out of that future for which they yearned . . . oh, it's so completely futile and unfair."

"I disagree," the Archeologist said spiritedly. "Really, your absence from Earth has unsettled you even more than I first surmised. Look at the matter squarely. Death comes to everything in the end. Our past is strewn with our dead. That species died, it's true. But what they achieved, they achieved. What happiness they had, they had. What they did in their short span is as significant as what they might have done had they lived a billion years. The present is always more important than the future. And no creature can have all the future—it must be shared, left to others."

"Maybe so," the Explorer said slowly. "Yes, I guess you're right. But I still feel a horrible wistfulness about them, and I hug to myself the hope that a few of them escaped and set up a colony on some planet we haven't yet visited." There was a long silence. Then the Explorer turned back. "You old devil," he said in a manner that showed his gayer and more boisterous mood had returned, though diminished, "you still haven't told me anything definite about them."

"So I haven't," replied the Archeologist with guileful innocence. "Well, they were vertebrates."

"Ah?"

"Yes. What's more, they were mammals."

"Mammals? I was expecting something different."

"I thought you were."

The Explorer shifted. "All this matter of evolutionary categories is pretty cut-and-dried. Even a knowledge of how they looked doesn't mean much. I'd like to approach them in a more intimate way. How did they think of themselves? What did they call themselves? I know the word won't mean anything to me, but it will give me a feeling—of recognition."

"I can't say the word," the Archeologist told him, "because I haven't the proper vocal equipment. But I know enough of their script to be able to write it for you as they would have written it.

293

Incidentally, it is one of those words common to all their languages, that they attributed to an earlier race of beings."

The Archeologist extended one of his eight tentacles toward the blackboard. The suckers at its tip firmly grasped a bit of orange crayon. Another of his tentacles took up the spectacles and adjusted them over his three-inch protruding pupils.

The eel-like glittering pet drifted back into the room and nosed curiously about the crayon as it traced:

RAT

The Life Hater

Fred Saberhagen

Carr swallowed a pain pill, and tried to find a less uncomfortable position in the combat chair. He keyed his radio transmitter and spoke to the rogue ship that hung before him in space.

"I come in peace. I have no weapons. I come to talk to you."

He waited. The cabin of his little one-man ship was silent. His radar screen showed the berserker machine still many light-seconds ahead of him. There was no reaction from it, but he knew that it had heard him.

Behind Carr was the Sol-type star he called sun, and his home planet, colonized from Earth a century before. It was a lonely settlement, out near the rim of the galaxy. Until now the war waged on life by the berserker machines had been a remote horror in the news stories. The colony's only real fighting ship had been sent to join Karlsen's fleet in the defense of Earth, when the berserkers were said to be massing there. But now the enemy was here, and the people of Carr's planet were readying two more ships in feverish haste—they were a small colony, and not wealthy in resources.

Even when the two ships were ready, they would hardly be a match for a berserker.

When Carr had taken his plan to the leaders of the colony, they had thought him mad.

Go out and talk to it of peace and love? *Argue* with it? There might be some hope of converting the most depraved human to the cause of goodness and mercy, but what appeal could alter the built-in purpose of a machine?

"Why *not* talk to it of peace?" Carr had demanded. "Have you a better plan? I'm willing to go, I've nothing to lose."

They had looked at him, across the gulf that separates healthy planners from those who know they are dying. They thought almost any scheme would be better than his. But they could imagine nothing else to do until the warships were ready, which would be at least ten days. The little one-man ship was expendable, being unarmed. Armed, it would be no more a provocation to a berserker. In the end, they let Carr take it, hoping there was a chance his arguments might delay the inevitable attack.

For Carr himself, of course, they wasted no thought. For Carr was dying. Was as good as dead.

When Carr came within a million miles of the berserker, it stopped its own unhurried motion and seemed to wait for him, hanging in space in the orbital track of an airless planetoid, at a point from which the planetoid was still several days away.

"I am unarmed," he radioed again. "I come to talk with you, not to damage you. If those who built you were here, I would try to talk to them of peace and love. Do you understand?"

He felt sure it would understand his language. All the berserker machines had learned the universal space-travelers' tongue, from human prisoners or from each other. And he was serious about talking love to the unknown Builders. Grudges and vengeance seemed tiny things to a dying man. But the Builder would not be aboard; the berserkers had been constructed, probably, when Earthmen hunted the mammoth with spears. The Builders were lost in spacetime, along with their enemies of long ago.

Suddenly it answered him: "Little ship, maintain your present speed and course toward me. Be ready to stop when ordered."

"I—I will." In spite of being ready for it, Carr found himself stuttering and shaken at the sound of its voice, the uneven mechanical reproduction of the words of human prisoners, recorded aboard or borrowed from another machine. Now the weapons which could sterilize a planet would be trained on him alone. And there was worse than destruction to be feared, if one tenth of the stories about berserkers' prisoners were true. Carr did not let himself think about that—although the pain that racked him in a momentary flood of agony made death seem almost welcome.

When he was within ten thousand miles, it ordered: "Stop. Wait where you are, relative to me."

Carr obeyed instantly. Soon he saw that it had launched toward him something about the size of his own ship—a little moving dot on his video screen, coming out of the vast black fortress that floated against the stars.

Even at this range he could see how scarred and battered that fortress was. He had heard that all of these ancient machines were damaged, from their long senseless fighting across the galaxy; but surely such apparent ruin as this must be exceptional.

The berserker's launch slowed and drew up beside his ship. Soon there came a clanging at the airlock.

"Open!" demanded the radio voice. "I must search you."

"Then you will listen to me?"

"Then I will listen."

He opened the lock, and stood aside for the half-dozen machines that entered. They were not unlike robot valets and workers, except that these were old and limping and worn, like their great master. Here and there a new part gleamed. But often the machines' movements were unsteady as they searched Carr, searched his cabin, probed everywhere on the little ship. One of them had to be half-carried out by its fellows, when the search was completed.

Another one of the machines, a thing with arms and hands like a man's, stayed behind. As soon as the lock had closed behind the others, it settled itself in the combat chair and began to drive the ship toward the berserker.

"Wait!" Carr protested. "I didn't surrender!" The ridiculous words hung in the air, seeming to deserve no reply. Sudden panic made Carr move without thinking; he stepped forward and grabbed at the mechanical pilot, trying to pull it from the chair. It put one metal hand against his chest and shoved him across the cabin so that he staggered and fell in the artificial gravity, thumping his head painfully against a bulkhead. "In a matter of minutes, we will talk about love and peace," said the radio voice.

Looking out a port as his ship neared the immense berserker, Carr saw the scars of battle become plainer and plainer, even to his unpracticed eye. There were holes in the hull, square miles of bendings and swellings and pits where the metal had once flowed molten.

Rubbing his bumped head, Carr felt a faint thrill of pride. *We've done that to it,* he thought, *we soft little living things.* His own martial feeling annoyed him, in a way. He had always been something of a pacifist. Of course it could hardly be thought immoral to use violence against a dangerous but inanimate machine. After some delay, a hatch opened in the berserker's side, and Carr's ship followed the berserker's launch into darkness.

Now there was nothing to be seen through the port. Soon there came a gentle bump, as of docking. The mechanical pilot shut off the drive, turned toward Carr, and started to rise from the chair.

Something in it failed. Instead of rising smoothly, the pilot reared up, flailed for a moment with arms that sought a grip or balance, and then fell heavily to the deck. For half a minute it moved one arm, and made a grinding noise. Then it was still.

In the half-minute of silence which followed, Carr realized that he was again master of his cabin; chance had given him that. If there was something he could do—

"Leave your ship," said the calm voice. "There is an airfilled tube fitted to your airlock. It will lead you to a place where we can talk of peace and love."

Carr's eyes, with a sort of reluctant horror, had dragged themselves to focus on the engine switch, and beyond that, to the C-plus activator.

The C-plus jump was not usable as a drive anywhere near the huge mass of a sun. In such proximity as this to a mass even the size of the surrounding berserker, the effect became only a weapon—a weapon of tremendous potential power.

Carr did not—or thought he did not—any longer fear sudden death; he was too near to the slow, sure kind. But now he found that with all his heart and soul he feared what might be prepared for him outside the airlock. All the horror stories came back. The thought of going out through that airlock now was unendurable. It was less terrifying for him to step carefully around the fallen pilot, to reach the controls and turn the engine back on.

"I can talk to you from here," he said, his voice quavering in spite of an effort to keep it steady.

After about ten seconds, the berserker said: "Your C-plus drive has safety devices. You will not be able to kamikaze me."

"You may be right," said Carr after a moment's thought. "But if a safety device does function, it might hurl my ship away from your center of mass, right through your hull. And your hull is in bad shape now. You don't want any more damage."

"You would die."

"I'll have to die sometime. But I didn't come out here to die, or to fight. I came to talk with you, to try to reach some agreement."

"What kind of agreement?"

At last Carr took a deep breath, and marshaled the arguments he had so often rehearsed. He kept his fingers resting gently on the C-plus activator, and his eyes alert on the instruments that normally monitored the hull for micrometeorite damage.

"I've had the feeling," he began, "that your attacks upon humanity may be only some ghastly mistake. Certainly we were not your original enemy."

"Life is my enemy. Life is evil." Pause. "Do you want to become goodlife?"

Carr closed his eyes for a moment; some of the horror stories were coming to life. But then he went firmly on with his argument. "From our point of view, it is you who are bad. We would like you to become a good machine, one that helps men instead of killing. Is not building a higher purpose than destroying?"

There was a longer pause. "What evidence can you offer that I should change my purpose?"

"For one thing, helping us will be a purpose easier of achievement. No one will damage you and oppose you."

"What is it to me, if I am damaged and opposed?"

Carr tried again. "Life is basically superior to non-life; and man is the highest form of life."

"What evidence do you offer?"

"Man has a spirit."

"I have learned that men claim that. But do you not define this spirit as something beyond the perception of any machine? And are there not men who deny that this spirit exists?"

"Spirit is so defined. And there are such men."

"Then I do not accept the argument of spirit."

Carr dug out a pain pill and swallowed it. "Still, you have no evidence that spirit does not exist. You must consider it as a possibility."

"That is correct."

"But leaving spirit out of the argument for now, consider the physical and chemical organization of life. Do you know anything of the delicacy and intricacy or organization in even a single living cell? And surely you must admit we humans carry wonderful computers inside our few cubic inches of skull."

"I have never had an intelligent captive to dissect," the mechanical voice informed him blandly, "though I have received some relevant data from other machines. But you admit that your form is the determined result of the operation of physical and chemical laws?"

"Have *you* ever thought that those laws may have been designed to do just that—produce brains capable of intelligent action?"

There was a pause that stretched on and on. Carr's throat felt dry and rough, as if he had been speaking for hours.

"I have never tried to use that hypothesis," it answered suddenly. "But if the construction of intelligent life is indeed so intricate, so dependent upon the laws of physics being as they are and not otherwise—then to serve life may be the highest purpose of a machine."

"You may be sure, our physical construction is intricate." He wasn't sure he could follow the machine's line of reasoning, but that hardly mattered if he could somehow win the game of Life. He kept his fingers on the C-plus activator.

The berserker said: "If I am able to study some living cells—"

Like a hot iron on a nerve, the meteorite-damage indicator moved; something was at the hull. "Stop that!" he screamed, without thought. "The first thing you try, I'll kill you!"

Its voice was unevenly calm, as always. "There may have been some accidental contact with your hull. I am damaged and many of my commensal machines are unreliable. I mean to land on this approaching planetoid to mine for metal and repair myself as far as possible." The indicator was quiet again.

The berserker resumed its argument. "If I am able to study some living cells from an intelligent life-unit for a few hours, I expect I will find strong evidence for, or against, your argument. Will you provide me with cells?"

"You must have had prisoners, sometime." He said it as a suspicion; he really knew no reason why it must have had human captives. It could have learned the language from another berserker.

"No; I have never taken a prisoner."

It waited. The question it had asked still hung in the air.

"The only human cells on this ship are my own. Possibly I could give you a few of them."

"Half a cubic centimeter should be enough; not a dangerous loss for you, I believe. I will not demand part of your brain. Also I understand that you wish to avoid the sensation called pain. I am willing to help you avoid it, if possible."

Did it want to drug him? That seemed too simple. Always unpredictability, the stories said, and sometimes a subtlety out of hell.

He went on with the game. "I have all that is necessary. Be warned that my attention will hardly waver from the control panel. Soon I will place a tissue sample in the airlock for you."

He got the medical kit, took two pain-killers, and set very carefully to work with a sterile scalpel. He had had some biological training.

When the small wound was bandaged, he cleansed the tissue sample of blood and lymph and with unsteady fingers sealed it into a little tube. Without letting down his guard for an instant, he dragged the fallen pilot to the airlock and left it there with the tissue sample. Utterly weary, he got back to the combat chair. When he switched the outer door open, he heard something come into the lock, and leave again.

He took a pep pill. It would stimulate some pain, but he'd be alert.

Two hours passed. Carr forced himself to eat some emergency rations, watched the panel, and waited.

He gave a startled jump when the berserker spoke again; nearly six hours had gone by.

"You are free to leave," it was saying. "Tell the leading life-units of your planet that when I have refitted, I will be their ally. The study of your cells has convinced me that the human body is the highest creation of the universe, and that I should make helping you my purpose. Do you understand?"

Carr felt numb. "Yes. Yes, I have convinced you. After you have refitted, you will fight on our side."

Something shoved hugely and gently at his hull. Through a port he saw stars, and realized that the great hatch through which his ship had entered was swinging open.

This far within the system, Carr necessarily kept his ship in normal space to travel. It meant he could see the berserker as he fled from it, and he kept it in sight as long as possible. His last sight of the berserker showed it moving as if indeed about to let down upon the airless planetoid. Certainly it was not following him.

A couple of hours after being freed, he roused himself from contemplation of the radar screen, and went to spend a full minute considering the inner airlock door. At last he shook his head, dialed air into the lock, and entered it. The pilot was gone, with the tissue sample. There was nothing strange to be seen. Carr took a deep breath, as if relieved, closed up the lock again, and went to a port to spend some time watching the stars.

After a day he began to decelerate, so that when hours had added into another day, he was still a good distance from home. He ate, and slept, and watched his face in a mirror. He weighed himself, and he watched the stars some more, with great interest, like a man examining something long forgotten.

In two more days, gravity bent his course into a hairpin ellipse around his home planet. With his whole world bulking between him and the berserker's rock, Carr began to use his radio.

"Ho, on the ground! Good news."

The answer came almost instantly. "We've been tracking you, Carr. What's going on? What happened?"

He told them of his encounter with the berserker. "So that's the story up to now," he finished. "I expect the thing really needs to refit. It is seriously damaged. Two warships attacking it now should easily win."

"Yes." There was excited talk in the background. Then the voice was back, sounding uneasy. "Carr—you haven't started a landing approach yet, so maybe you understand. We've got to be careful. The thing was probably lying to you."

"Oh, I know. Even that pilot's collapse might have been staged. I guess the berserker was too badly shot up to want to risk a battle, so it tried another way. Must have sneaked the stuff into my cabin air, just before it let me go—or maybe left it in my airlock."

"What stuff?"

Carr said, "The stuff you're worrying about. The poison it thinks will kill us all. I'd guess it's some freshly mutated virus, designed for specific virulence against the tissue I gave it. It expected I'd hurry home and land before getting sick, and spread a new plague. It must have thought it was inventing biological warfare, using life against life, as we use machines against machines. But it needed that tissue sample to blood its pet viruses. It didn't know our chemistry. It must have been telling the truth about never having a human prisoner."

"Some virus, you think? What's it doing to you, Carr? Are you in pain—I mean, more than before?"

"No." Carr swirled his chair to look at the little chart he had begun. It showed that in the last two days his weight loss had started to reverse itself. He looked down at his body, at the bandaged place near the center of a discolored, inhuman-looking area. That area was smaller than it had been, and he saw a hint of new and healthy skin.

"What *is* the stuff doing to you?"

Carr allowed himself to smile, and to speak aloud his growing hope.

"I think it's killing off my cancer."

Linkage

Barry N. Malzberg

My name is Donald Alan Freem. I am eight years old. I can do anything with the power of my mind. I can make people say what I want them to say; make them perform actions which I have predetermined. I have always had this gift.

Because of my power, people fear me. They know that I can control them and take away their free will, and this terrifies them because they wish to hold onto their pitiful illusions of freedom. Resultantly, I have been institutionalized since the age of five with the full consent of my parents and at the expense of the society which traps me.

I am not concerned. This institution cannot control the power I have. My mind sweeps and soars, moves far beyond their pitiable effort to entrap me. I can do anything I want. It will always be this way.

"You must face reality, Donald," Dr. Nevins says to me at our weekly session. "If you do not face reality you will live this way all your life, and I do not want it to be this way. You are very young, you are highly intelligent, you are malleable. We believe in your ability to break this. But you must help us."

I recline on the chair, look at the round, disturbed face of Dr. Nevins, then out the window to the grounds where some of my peer-group are playing mindlessly with a ball. "I made you say that," I point out. "You said that because I ordered you to say it."

"Donald, you can no longer function this way. We must make progress—"

"I knew that you would say that. I sent through an order from my mind telling your mind to say 'We must make progress.' Everything that you do is because I make you do it."

Dr. Nevins slams down a palm on his desk, stands awkwardly.

This is the way in which our interviews usually terminate. "I don't want to lose patience," he says, "but you're not cooperating. You're not even trying—"

"I knew you would say that. I knew it before you did, and I made you hit your hand on the desk. You are afraid of me," I say, "but there's no need to be frightened. I would never do anything bad to you. I would never make people hurt themselves."

Dr. Nevins exhales, puffs his cheeks, shakes his head. "We'll discuss this again next time, Donald," he says. "You're going to have to think about these things—"

"I wanted you to say that," I point out, and as Dr. Nevins stands, I send orders from my mind for him to open the door for me and send me out with a small flush of rage sending red sprinkles through his clear cheek. He does so. I leave. At the end of the corridor I disperse a message for him to slam the door, which he does with a metallic clang.

I did not develop the powers of my mind. They came to me full-blown. I cannot remember a time, even when I was very young, when I could not make people do what I wanted. When I was six years old I was visited by an alien with whom I had a long discussion. The alien told me that I was the first of a super-race, the first human being with my abilities, and that he had been sent back from the future to investigate and to guard my health. He promised me that my powers would breed true and that when I was an adult I would be able to reproduce with a female who would bear children like me. Tens of thousands of years in the future, my descendants would be the dominant race of the planet and would have, with their great powers, long since conquered the stars and invented time machines. One of these machines was being employed as a means for one of their scientists to come back and check on me, measure my progress and assure me that in the long run, all of my difficulties would work out. "You will be kept in the institution for a long time," the alien said, "but eventually, during adolescence, you will finally learn to lie and conceal your powers from them. You will say that you realize you control nothing and no one, and they will release you as 'cured.' Quietly then you will sow your seed and so on."

"I don't want to lie to them," I told the alien. "I'm proud of my powers and I know that it infuriates them when I brag but I see no reason why I have to treat these inferiors with any courtesy." Perhaps I did not put it quite that way. I was only six. In the last two years I have learned to read well and have been able to express myself in a far more sophisticated fashion. Probably, I merely told the alien that I would do exactly what I wanted and he and no one else could stop me. At six I was very grandiose, but I have calmed down somewhat since then. I say and feel the same things but have learned to take a little of the edge off them.

"I will be back occasionally to check on your progress," the alien told me, "but essentially you have to live your own life." I have lived my own life. The alien has returned only once so far for a very brief discussion. I accept the fact that I am on my own.

Dr. Nevins loses his temper and says something about giving me more "injections" and "needles" and "drugs" if I do not cooperate with him, and for the first time he truly angers me. I tell him about the alien and the pact he made with me about my future. It takes me a long time, and when I am finished, Dr. Nevins shakes his head with a pleased expression and says finally, "I'm very pleased, Donald. At last you're opening up to me."

"I made you say that."

"I'm beginning to see the fantasies which are at the root of your condition. Now we can begin to work. You've enabled us to make a start. I'm grateful."

"I *ordered* you to say *grateful.* Anything I tell you to say you will say."

"Yes," Dr. Nevins says, patting me, and leading me to the door, "this is very helpful, Donald," and he ends our interview so rapidly that I realize I have not had a chance to make it finish the way I ordered. This is the first time it has ever happened, and I am somewhat disconcerted. I remind myself that even Dr. Nevins has a kind of cunning and must be watched.

The alien comes to see me that night and tells me that he is extremely disturbed. I can sense his agitation. "You shouldn't have told them about me," he says. "That was not very smart, Donald. You could upset all of our calculations, the whole projected future.

Now they will concentrate on exactly those elements which are most central."

"I don't care," I say. "Besides, I made you say that."

"No, Donald; this is very serious business. This was supposed to be our secret. I am very upset."

"I wanted you to be upset. I did something to your mind to make you upset."

"They will focus on specifics, Donald, and may even convince you that this is a fantasy. You may upset the whole track of time."

"I want to upset the track of time," I say, "the track of time is anything I want; I think that I'll get rid of you," and I do something to him with my consciousness and with a roar the alien vanishes; was never there in the first place, as a matter of fact; I never knew of any aliens, and quite weakly it occurs to me that all these years Dr. Nevins has only been trying to help me and I owe him nothing less than my assistance: the two of us, perhaps, can work this out together, and I am beginning to find it very boring to have things turn out exactly the way I make them. The other way would be more exciting. I will let them do what they want for a while.

Listen, Love

George Zebrowski and Jack Dann

Uheh sat next to the rodasz bush. Its glow cast thin rods of yellow onto her features; the rods changed color one after another, shifting from yellow to red to orange and back again. She stared at the small glowing branches; she felt the numbness of sleep stealing over her. Soon the sun would set and the quiet-time would begin, the time of darkness and rest. The colors swept her away into a whirlpool of sensation, and she fought back. It seemed too soon yet, she must wait; sleep-time was far, far away. She came up close to the bush and brushed her face gently against the delicate branches. She drew back; the plant was trying to lull her to sleep.

Uheh listened. Her large, finely shaped ears gathered in the small sounds of her world, and she was expert at interpreting them. There were few loud sounds in her experience, and she had been taught to fear them: she knew how to cover her ears with the large palms of her hands and then bring her elbows together until they touched. As she listened now, she heard only the sounds of small living things getting ready for the dark-time. The sun was low over the trees in the distance. The world was at peace, yet she felt fearful.

She closed her eyes and turned her face to the sun, and felt its evening warmth, its quiet embrace which seemed to touch and not touch at the same time. The soft pink skin of her naked form said a silent goodbye to the departing star that was the sun of her world.

Suddenly there was a blast of light, so strong that she sensed it even through her delicate eyelids. A rumble came across the distance toward her, but it was only a deep bass sound and couldn't hurt her. She listened to the low pitched sound; it was almost comforting. She sat down on the grass and closed her eyes again. Her entire body tingled to the sound, until it died away and she was almost asleep.

Uheh sat up suddenly, awake again and full of fear. For a brief instant the sound had become shrill and painful, and even the grass around her, the caghfr green on which she had played since she had been a little girl among the little ones of the kuu, seemed frightened. She looked at the rodasz bush; its color now was a drab green, its glow gone. Did it wake her? Had it been calling her, to warn her? The momentary shrill sound had been so loud. She shuddered and crawled into the vegetation around the rodasz bush, thinking that it would be a good place to hide; and perhaps she could spend the dark quiet-time here. That would certainly prove to the old ones of the kuu that she had come of age, and was unafraid of the dark quiet-time: the mark of a woman who could begin to bear young. A moment of pride went through her, but it was cut short by what she saw coming across the caghfr grass toward her.

The small flyer settled on the alien grass. Uheh felt the ground tremble slightly under her feet. She peered out from the vegetation; her hand held a branch on the rodasz bush.

The sun was very low when she saw the two figures get out of the silver flyer. This could not be any kind of calling, she thought. It was too harsh. Dimly she understood that the low sound from before had something to do with the silver flyer now before her. She wondered if the old ones from the kuu were watching this new thing. They would know what it was, and protect her.

The pain-sound came from the new thing and throbbed in her temples for a moment, and was gone.

The two space-suited figures walked on the caghfr grass while Uheh watched. She pushed her head through the branches of the rodasz bush to get a better view, and a leaf touched her cheek, lovingly.

She stood up and made herself visible. One of the figures waved his arm and came toward her. What could she fear from them? They were like her, and yet not like her. She wanted to run toward the flyer, the new thing that had come from the sky; but the voice of her upbringing was strong: be cautious. She looked at the figure who came up to her now, and she wondered why he wore the clear thing over his head. She could see that he was smiling at her, and she could see his teeth; there was a lot of hair on his dark face. Surely he did not wear the clear thing to keep warm? He should take it off, she thought, and smiled back at him.

The other one came up behind him, and as if in answer to her thought they took off their helmets. She stared at the strange texture of their skin. The first one was handsome enough to make any in the kuu jealous; yet different. He motioned to her with his suited and gloved hand. Could this be dangerous? He looked so pleasing. Surely he was like her, but from somewhere far off; perhaps from the other side of the blue hills, or the far side of the world? She sat down on the grass and motioned for them to do the same. They hesitated, then followed her example; they put their helmets down on the grass in front of them.

The first one gestured at her strangely and pointed at the sky, and she nodded and smiled her understanding. Then she tried to make the sign of the kuu for them—the sign of her home; but it was difficult without the sandy lakeshore where the elder had first taught it to her. The first stranger smiled at her efforts and looked at his companion.

He was good. She would try to keep him. The elder would be happy when she brought him home to the kuu. She touched his hand. It was very warm without the glove and she drew back. Then she stood up and gestured him to follow her. She waved the other one away, but he didn't go. Didn't he understand? She was puzzled. All elders made the same rules. Had she done something wrong?

"I think she wants you, and she wants me to clear out," the second one said. She heard the pain-sound coming from his mouth, and she put her hands up to her head in pain. The sound was so high, so harsh! So unlike the quiet world that cared for her, nourished her. The pain-sound cut through her entire body and she shuddered uncontrollably. It ran along her nerves and seemed to burst in her head.

"Just like a woman," the first one—(her favorite!)—said.

Run! the world cried to her. The pain-sound became worse; it squeezed her. Could such a sound have meaning? The sun was almost down now, and the dark quiet-time was coming swiftly now. In the sky the stars winked into existence, and would soon march in their promenade from horizon to horizon. The two men were gesturing at her. She saw their lips move and again the pain-sound reached her ears. She turned and began to run toward the kuu, away from the sunset three hills away by the lakeside.

"Hey, beautiful, don't go!"—the pain-sound followed her. "Come on back!"—it shrieked and screamed across the darkening sky after her.

At the top of the first hill she fell and turned over to look at the starry sky, and felt for the last time the caghfr grass against her back. Her body shuddered again from the pain-sound and was still.

Mail Supremacy

Hayford Peirce

It all seems so inevitable, now that mankind is spreading out through the galaxy. The only question is: Why wasn't it done sooner? Why did the road to the stars have to wait until 1984, when an Anglo-Chinese merchant fell to musing over his correspondence? But perhaps all of mankind's greatest advances, from fire through the wheel, from penicillin through hydrogen fusion, seem inevitable only in retrospect.

Who remembers the faceless thousands who unlocked the secret of nuclear energy, the man who dropped the first atomic bomb? Mankind remembers Einstein.

Who remembers the faceless thousands who built the first moonship, the man who first stepped upon an alien world? Mankind remembers Verne and Ley and Campbell.

As mankind remembers Chap Foey Rider.

Chap Foey Rider's main offices were in New York, not far from Grand Central Station. From them he directed an import-export firm that blanketed the globe. On November 8, 1984, a Friday, his secretary brought him the day's mail. It was 11:34 in the morning.

Chap Foey Rider frowned. Nearly noon, and only now was the mail delivered. How many years had it been since there had been two deliveries a day, morning and afternoon? At least twenty-five. Where was the much-vaunted progress of the age of technology?

He remembered his childhood in London, long before the war, when there had been *three* daily deliveries. When his father would post a letter in the morning, asking an associate to tea, and receive a written reply before tea-time. It was enough to make a bloke shake his head.

Chap Foey Rider shook his head and picked up his mail.

There was a bill of lading from his warehouse in Brooklyn, seven miles away. Mailed eight days ago.

There was a portfolio print-out from his investment counselor in Boston, 188 miles away. Mailed seven days ago.

There was an inquiry from his customs broker in Los Angeles, 2,451 miles away. Mailed four days ago.

There was a price list from a pearl merchant in Papeete, Tahiti, 6,447 miles away. Mailed three days ago.

Chap Foey Rider reached for his slide rule.

He then called his branch manager in Honolulu. He told him to mail a letter to the branch manager in Capetown, 11,535 miles away.

The Capetown manager called Chap Foey Rider two days later to advise him that the letter from Honolulu had arrived. Although still Sunday in New York, it was early Monday morning in Capetown.

Chap Foey Rider pondered. The length of the equator was 24,901.55 miles. No spot on Earth could be farther than 12,450.78 miles from any other.

He reached for the World Almanac.

Bangkok was 12,244 miles from Lima. He smiled. He had offices in each city.

A letter from Bangkok reached Lima in a single day.

Chap Foey Rider returned to his slide rule.

The extrapolation was staggering.

One further test was required to prove his theory. He pursed his lips, then carefully addressed an envelope: *Occupant, 614 Starshine Boulevard, Alpha Centauri IV.* He looked at his watch: good, the post office was open for another hour. He personally pushed the envelope through the Out-of-Town slot and strolled home.

Returning to his office the next morning, he found in his stack of mail the envelope addressed to Alpha Centauri. Frowning, he picked it up. Stamped across the front in purple ink were the words: *Addressee Unknown, Returned to Sender.*

Chap Foey Rider lighted his first cigarette of the day and to conceal his discontent puffed perfect rings toward the ceiling. Was the test actually conclusive? True, the envelope had been returned. But with suspicious speed. He reviewed his chain of logic, then studied the envelope with a magnifying glass. There was, after all, nothing to indicate *which* post office had stamped it.

He ground the cigarette out and reached for a piece of paper. He wrote firmly, without hesitation:

The Rgt. Hon. Chairman
of the Supreme Galactic Council
Sagittarius
Sir: I feel I must draw to your attention certain shortcomings
in your General Post Office system. Only yesterday I mailed a
letter . . .

Chap Foey Rider awaited the morning's delivery. Eventually it arrived.

There was an envelope-sized piece of thick creamy parchment, folded neatly and held together by a complex red seal. His name appeared on one side, apparently engraved in golden ink.

Expressionless, he broke the seal, unfolded the parchment, and read the contents. It was from the Executive Secretary, Office of the Mandator of the Galactic Confederation:

> *Dear Sir: In reply to yours of the 14th inst. the Mandator begs me to inform you that as per your speculation the Galactic Confederation does indeed exist as primarily a Postal Union, its purpose being to promote Trade and Commerce between its 27,000 members. Any civilization is invited to join our Confederation, the sole qualification of membership being the independent discovery of our faster-than-light Postal Union. His Excellency is pleased to note that you, on behalf of your fellow Terrans, have at long last fulfilled the necessary conditions, and in consequence, an Ambassador-Plenipotentiary from the Galactic Confederation will be arriving on Terra within the next two days. Please accept, Mr. Rider, on behalf of the Mandator, the expression of his most distinguished sentiments.*

". . . to promote Trade and Commerce . . ."

Chap Foey Rider restrained himself from rubbing his hands together in glee. Instead he pushed a buzzer to summon his four sons to conference. The stars were coming to mankind. Rider Factoring, Ltd. would be ready for them; he called the mailroom to tell them to be on the alert for a large package from Sagittarius.

Man of Destiny

John Christopher

They clock the spaceships in from the main control tower seventeen miles southeast of Tycho. The magnesium flares blossom out against the stars and the searching telescopes find them and name them. The *Elistra* back from Procyon, the *Alte Wien* from Lumen III, the *Winston* from Sirius. Ships laden with passengers and freight from halfway across the visible universe, controlled corks bobbing up through the maelstrom of time and space to that same narrow arc of the lunar sky. They come in on time—solar time. There's no danger to life or goods or schedule.

It wasn't always so. When the slip process was first being developed, there were both danger and uncertainty for those isolated men, strapped in their bubbles of metal and plastic, who voyaged out across an alien dimension to the far reaches of the sky. Their job was to take routine star pictures and then come back on the reverse. But the reverse did not always work. They were stranded then, hundreds or thousands of light-years from the planet they had known as home.

From the moment the reverse failed, Theodore Pike concentrated on the lucky side of his situation. He might have been lost in the remotenesses of interstellar space, condemned to suffocation when his meager oxygen supply gave out—a week of waiting for death unless he had the courage to seek it out first.

As it was, he was slap in the middle of a solar system, a matter of three hundred million miles from a blue giant. The system, as he had planned it for the report that would not now be made, was not of any notable size. There were only three planets. One was very large and impossibly distant from the sun. But there was some hope in the other two. In size they were reasonable enough. He arrowed down toward the first of them three days later; and at once set the coracle climbing up again, through a methane atmosphere, from a barren and unrewarding surface.

That left one planet. Only one.

When he released the hood and the planet's air came in, it was like the first time he had tasted wine, in the late spring at Heidelberg, under the gaudy cherry blossoms. He lifted his body clear and slid down the still warm metal of the spheroid to the mossy ground. The moss was dark green, and deep and springy. His feet went down two or three inches, but there was resilience even beneath that.

He looked up at the sky. It had a strange and strangely warm green tinge; the sun was hidden behind tufted blue-green clouds. He looked toward where it should be with contemptuous, good-humored acknowledgment. It had done its job; he was all right now. Then he stood easily erect beside the spheroid, watching the natives hesitantly approaching from the village fifty yards away.

They were humanoid bipeds, with a natural green-tinged fur, but wearing artificial decorations and the beginnings of clothing. He stood quite still as they approached. Ten yards away, with a slow and somehow graceful ceremony, they all knelt. They rested their heads on the green moss. When he spoke, they looked up. He beckoned and they came closer. Their leader knelt again at his feet. Quite casually Theo put one foot on the prostrate head.

It was accomplished. The natives had found their god.

The first few months passed very quickly. He had set himself one task—to learn the language. After that, the life of Reilly. Things were already very pleasant. The bed made of something like swansdown, the spiced and delicate foods, the sweet yellow wine which, by a dispensation of Providence, had a far less intoxicating effect on him than on the natives. They got drunk on it; a cheerful, happy drunk every seventh or eighth day. He was able to preside over their revels benignly enough, mellowed and happy enough himself in—as he reflected sardonically—his divine way.

He had been figuring on a week of seven days and only later discovered that the natives had a ten month year. The four months thus far had been rather less than one of them, but at the end of that time he could communicate well enough.

He called the chief, Pernar, into the hut that he had once owned and gave the preliminary directions for the building of his palace. The natives already had fire, but had not applied it to the working of metals. He gave them that, and the spoked wheel. They were enough to be going on with, in addition to the supreme, never-ending boon of his own personal godhead. He had found an outcrop of good granite, tinged with rosy green in the prevailing light of the planet, less than three miles from the village.

The palace went up fast. He took it over with due ceremony. The natives were puzzled but respectful.

That was where the settling down began. At one time, at the beginning, he had held vague hopes of being rescued through the slip. He had even planned great beacon towers spaced across the planet. But more sober reflection proved them futile. Even with every imaginable success, the Mendola process could not be studding the universe with ships enough to make the possibility of this planet's discovery more than fantastically remote. This was a life sentence.

He had something bigger to do now. He would leave something for the exploring slip-ships to find: a civilization founded on a manifest divinity. At its heart a shrine, and in its shrine the memory of what Theodore Pike had made of his exile.

In the eighth month of the planet's year, he provided the steam engine.

The natives stood around with their usual impeccable gravity; Pernar surrounded by his men, and even the bolder of the women and children. The tiny model hissed; the small piston began to work the wheel.

"In this, my people, is your future," Theo told them. "With this your labor will be lightened, your fields made fruitful. Your ships and wagons will cross the wide spaces of the world. All this your lord brings to his people."

They nodded solemnly and bowed. The sun was at its zenith, where its light concentrated into an astonishing blueness. Every day at this time the green became blue for an hour; by now, an ordinary miracle. He looked over their heads toward the dazzling sapphire of his palace. At its threshold stood the two gigantic replicas of his own image. The small white jet of steam climbed unwaveringly. Eventually there would have to be a larger palace, he reflected. But still here, in this spot, still enshrining the spheroid and the spot where it had landed.

Who would be in it? he wondered to himself. He had thought of it before; it was his most sustaining fantasy. The great slip-ship settling down into this blue-green world, being taken (as the tradition would demand) to the shrine of the great palace-temple, looking with astonishment—and respect? pride?—on the first interstellar coracle, the tomb of Theodore Pike. What would the visitors be like? They would be respectful, anyway. They would be proud of the memory of the first of their line. His name would leap through the vast gulfs that now cut him off from all his youth might have enjoyed. That made up for everything.

But everything was quite a lot.

Following Theo's demonstration, the natives seemed in no hurry to adopt the steam engine. Every now and then the elders would come to watch the little model puffing away. Theo explained it to them several times, and they nodded their heads in respectful approval. But all their working time now was being devoted to the harvest. The whole tribe—men, women, children—toiled in the fields through the long hot days.

Even in his natural indolence he was aware of a sense of urgency about their labor; they worked on their holiday now, only getting drunk when the green twilight had darkened into night. He had the shrewd sense not to interfere. A natural rhythm of the tribe, he guessed, best modified by the fundamental change in environment which his technology would inevitably create.

He went out into the fields one day to watch them. Pernar, the chief, was sweating with the rest. Theo lay back in the springy moss and watched them. He noticed idly that the wagons carrying produce—mounted now on his wheels, the old crude wooden skids having been discarded—did not go back to the village, but away up the slope, in the opposite direction. He asked Pernar why.

Pernar explained, "Against the Time, Lord."

"The time?"

Pernar paused for a moment, fumbling. At last he used a word Theo had not heard before.

"What's that?"

Pernar said awkwardly, "The wild air . . . the water."

A rainy season! Theo understood. It was reasonable enough that the harvest had to be in before the rains came. But that didn't explain the wagons trekking away uphill. He asked Pernar again.

"At the Time, we retreat. It is necessary."

"Necessary" was a common and useful word in the vocabulary of the natives; it stood for anything they were in the habit of doing. Eventually he would do something about it himself. But now it was pleasant enough to lie back in the green moss and watch his people going about their business. Let this coming rainy season pass in the usual way; next year he would really get down to pouring them into his mold—into the necessary mold for the empire that he would build and leave as his record to those ships a thousand years in the future.

The sky thickened into cloud over a period of several days; from thin twists and strands low on the horizon to ropes and bunched masses, and, finally, a universal, paralyzing gray. Two days after this unbroken canopy had settled over them, Pernar came to him in the palace.

"Lord, it is the Time."

Theo said, "How long will your people be gone?"

Pernar was startled. "You are not coming with us, Lord?"

"For you in your huts, the retreat may be necessary; these granite walls are protection enough against the wild air. In other years, you, too, will have refuges like this. Go in peace now."

Pernar nodded reluctantly. "Your other servants, Lord . . ."

He was referring to the personal servants who attended the god-king in his palace.

"They will be safe here," Theo said.

"They will not stay, Lord. They dare not stay."

The best argument, Theo realized, was acquiescence. When they returned to find the palace still standing beside the storm-blasted huts of the village, that would be the real conviction. He said simply, "Let food and drink be made ready. For how long?"

"Two weeks."

"Two weeks, then."

He was aware of loneliness when the last of them had gone, up the rising ground to whatever ritual refuge they used against the storms. Now once more he was conscious of his isolation, cut off from his own people by uncountable galactic miles, by the long sweep of time itself. Only the realization of destiny made the future seem worthwhile. He was pleased, in a way, when the rising wind began to howl about the village. The savageness of the elements gave him something to measure himself against.

But he was not prepared for the fury that developed. The storm rose from climax to climax; rain belted down torrentially from the raging skies. On the third day it rose to hurricane force.

From an embrasure slit, he watched the pitiful native huts torn from their moorings and flung like tattered leaves about the swirling sky. It seemed impossible that there could be more violence, but more came. The air shrieked in protest, a high-pitched wail under the constant lash. Theo watched it in amazement.

He was more amazed still when Pernar came to him, drenched and battered from his voyage through the storm.

"You must come, Lord."

"Into that?" He pointed out into the storm. "You'd better stay here yourself now."

"The water . . . the water that rises."

"Floods? This place is high enough. We're all right here."

"You must come, Lord."

The argument between them went on as the late afternoon passed into night. And with nightfall, astonishingly, the rain stopped and the gale dropped. Theo said to Pernar triumphantly, "You see?"

For answer Pernar insisted on dragging him outside into the open. The ground was soggy underfoot; the mashed remains of the huts lay before them. Pernar pointed. On the far horizon a glow became increasingly brilliant against the thinning clouds. The cloud strands twisted and broke, and, in the interval of clear sky, he saw it.

A moon. A giant, gibbous moon poised above the skyline like a grinning skull.

But how? He knew this planet had no satellite.

When he considered things, it was obvious enough. One of the other two planets in the system, almost certainly the nearer one, with the methane atmosphere, was eccentrically orbited. It was this the natives measured their year by—the regular approach and the attendant perturbations. All their life, inevitably, must be regulated by it.

Pernar said, "The rising water, Lord . . ."

He understood that, too. With one last glance at his sand-castle palace, he said, "Let's go."

The refuge was under the rocky knob of the hill's carapace, a natural cave hollowed out and improved by the work of generations. They arrived there with less than an hour to spare. Theo watched, with Pernar and the others, the brilliant globe that put out the light of the usual stars in a sky now clear and unclouded again. And he watched the tidal wave surge like a moving mountain of water to within twenty feet of where they crouched.

Watching it lap the land, almost at their feet, he considered the kind of courage that could have made Pernar go down into that doomed valley to rescue him. Nor was it any easily dismissed compulsion of religion. He had been fooling himself about that. You did not rescue a god from the consequences of his folly.

They were a peaceable and docile people. They had accepted his commands and they had given him service; if he wanted to be a god, they were willing to let him. But they weren't his subjects or his disciples. More important than those things, they were his friends.

There was still much he could give them, but more, he suspected, that they would give him.

Finding himself not a god was a relief, somehow. It was less of a strain to be human and fallible.

The floods receded, and the tribe moved again into the valley. As the great blue sun burned the water out of the steaming soil, they set to work to plant the seeds again and to rebuild the vanished huts.

Theo worked with them. He found an unexpected satisfaction in these labors, and an increasingly deeper realization of the nobility of these creatures who seemed to be without even the slightest trace of mutual hostility or anger. They accepted his working with them in the fields as casually as they had previously accepted his over-lordship; the difference was that now he was one of them and wanted no more than the awareness of that oneness.

Sometimes, especially when he passed the broken and scattered stone of what had been his palace, he remembered the world he had come from, and that great ship that—in a hundred years, a thousand, a hundred thousand—might drop through the green glow of the sky.

But the memory and the thought were tinged with *fear*. Fear of anything that might come to disrupt the beauty and peace of this undemanding life.

When the planting was over, there was the season of recreation. They danced, supple, graceful, unhurried dances, to the music of flutelike instruments; and chanted poems whose tenderness he understood more clearly as his mind grew more at home in their liquid but sinewy tongue.

Day after day, week after week. Work and rest and laughter and song. Where he had once asked for worship, he found himself almost reverent.

He had not guessed there could be such joy in humility.

When he died, twenty of the planet's years later, he had been their loved and respected chief for nearly fifteen years. Only you couldn't call it chief, nor had he done so.

They buried him in his former palace, which had gradually become a mausoleum. His last request was to have the steam engine buried with him.

The Man Who Came Back

Brian M. Stableford

There was a pool of light above him, and he was staring straight into it. His eyes refused to focus, and the pool seemed to eddy and swirl gently. The light seemed to emanate from a brighter but still indistinct patch, which he thought was a light bulb. There was something wrong with his eyes, as though he couldn't use them properly.

A round object appeared at the side of the pool. He couldn't make it out but he knew it was a human face, looking down on him. A second dark blob eclipsed another section of the light.

Oh God! They're here again . . .

"Can you hear me?"

Don't answer. Perhaps they'll go away.

"Hello, Jason, can you hear me?"

"Yes. Away." The words were slurred, as though pronounced through a mouth full of saliva.

"Now, Jason, listen carefully. You know me, I'm Doctor Yorke. This is Doctor Angeli. You remember, don't you?"

"Yes." *You were here yesterday with your bloody questions. And I'm not answering them today either.*

"You must try to remember, Jason." Yorke pronounced the words slowly and deliberately. "Remember exactly what happened. We'll try to help you all we can. You were on a ship—the *Stella*. Remember?"

"Yes." *Of course I remember. I remember everything. But I'm not telling. You go on thinking I can't remember.* Pleased, he nodded his head.

"What is he doing?" asked a new voice—Doctor Angeli.

"I think he's nodding his head," replied Yorke in a low voice. *You think. Can't you see? You know what a head looks like, don't you? Well, I'm nodding mine.* "At least," amended Yorke, "he's trying to."

"Ready, Jason." Slow and clear again. "The *Stella*. All right? Now you were going to Vesta. Vesta is an asteroid." *I know what Vesta is. I haven't lost my mind. Stop talking to me as though I were a bloody child.* "While you were going to Vesta the alarms rang, didn't they?"

Nod.

"Those alarms meant that a slug ship was on the screens. Did you know that?"

Nod. *Of course I know that. I'm an officer in the navy. I told you. You think I'm mad?*

"Now after the ship was attacked, you escaped in a spaceraft. The raft was picked up by the slugs after they blasted the *Stella* apart. Is that all right so far?"

Nothing. *No, it isn't right, imbecile. And here's where I stop answering, and your logic goes off the rails.*

Yorke started talking in his low voice again, to Angeli. "He always stops there. I don't know what happened then or afterward. He closes up entirely, and I can't worm even another nod out of him. Only thing he says is 'Away.'"

"Try again," requested Angeli.

"Jason, I'm talking again. Understand?"

"Yes." Nod.

"You were captured by slugs. What does a slug look like, Jason?"

Nothing. *A slug looks like a colossal coenocytic mass with thousands of nuclear blobs, modifications to serve for eyes and ears, and a mouth with no lips. It can repeat most things we say, but it can't make all the sounds we can. Vocal apparatus different. God what an understatement! All its apparatus is different. Alien. But I won't tell you.*

"Could it be just that he can't speak?"

"Oh, he can speak all right. After a fashion anyway. He can't say everything we can, but with improvisation he can manage enough to get along. He did quite a lot of talking in the beginning. About his family, mostly. Had to, to convince us he was William Jason."

"Then why won't he tell us?"

"I don't know. We can only keep trying." Louder again. "Jason, what did the slugs do to you?"

Nothing.

"Jason, you must tell us. We are at war with the slugs. You are the only man, as far as we know, who might have seen one. We need every last little bit of information you can give us. Now what did they do to you to make you look like this?"

Look like what? I'm Bill Jason. I've always been Bill Jason. I look like Bill Jason.

"Jason, this body you have. Is it a slug's?"

Slug's? What the hell? I'm Bill Jason, human. Go away.

Angeli chipped in again. "How can we be sure that it is Jason anyhow, wearing a body like that. Couldn't the slugs have picked Jason's mind, sent a spy with his memories?"

"Where would be the point?" said Yorke tiredly. "What good would a spy be to them, locked up in this place? And he isn't ever going to get out, Jason or not."

"Then why won't he talk?"

"I don't know. If he can talk, and he can, I can only see one conceivable reason, and that's that he doesn't want to talk. But that doesn't fit either. Why should he withhold information after they did *this* to him?"

Did what to me? I'm Bill Jason, and I'm not talking. Do what you like, you'll get nothing out of me.

"Jason!" began Yorke again. "Can you remember when you were picked up? You were in a slug spaceraft. Now, can you remember getting on that liferaft? Where was it? What happened? Were you released, or did you escape?"

Nothing. *I'm not telling you. Get nothing from me.*

"Jason! Where did they take you?"

Nothing.

"Look, Jason, you've got to tell us. For the sake of your family, for your own sake. Now, you escaped from the *Stella* in a spaceraft. Is that correct or not?"

"No!"

"But you must have. The *Stella* was completely wrecked. You could only have survived in a spaceraft."

A pause. Then Angeli said, "He's not telling. I think he honestly believes we're the enemy. After all, he is in a slug body. Or what we think is a slug body. He may even be a slug."

One of the round black blobs moved from side to side.

"You must tell us," protested Yorke desperately. "What did the slugs do to you? Why won't you tell us?"

Oh hell! If I tell them why, maybe they'll leave me alone. I doubt it though. They don't seem to think my way. I wish they'd stop plaguing me.

Slowly, his lipless mouth formed the syllables. He managed to slobber out the barely intelligible words:

"They killed me . . ."

The Martians and the Leadfoot

William F. Nolan

Maybe some of you remember "Big Ed" Timberland. He was a pretty hot sports car pilot who did all right for himself in local events not so long ago. Now he's out of the game. And the reason he gives for quitting is real gone.

First of all, Ed never believed in Bug Eyed Monsters or Fireballs from Outer Space or any stuff like that. So when he saw this Flying Saucer land smack next to him on the front straight at Riverside he figured it was some kind of gag—maybe a publicity stunt or a TV quiz show routine. Anyway, he was all alone on the circuit on this particular afternoon, taking a few hot laps in his Chevy-Special, when this big silver thing comes buzzing down, a panel slides back, and three little green guys step out with notebooks.

In a way, they look like Ed. I mean, they have goggles and crash helmets on; but they're all pint-size. Ed figures them for a trio of midgets.

"Your name?" asks Number One. His voice is like sandpaper.

"Big Ed, pal, what's yours?" Ed is playing it cool, riding the gag.

"*Our* names are unimportant," says Number Two.

Number Three doesn't say anything. He just takes notes like mad with a weird looking stick.

"You are testing this machine?" asks Number One, indicating the Special.

"You bet, Mac. An' she's a goin' bomb."

"Ummm," says Number Three. "A warhead."

"Just what, Mr. Biged, is your method of operation?" This from Number One.

"You mean how does she go?"

"Precisely."

"Like stink, Mac. I mean, she moves out. You just stand on the loud pedal, tach way up, pop the clutch and drive up a storm."

"Ummm," says Number Two. "A complex procedure."

"And just what is your pattern of atmospheric acceleration?" asks Number One.

"She goes like a scalded kitty. Zero to sixty in about five."

The three of them stare at Ed for a long moment. Then Number One asks another question. "What of actual performance under power?"

"Man, she handles like I carried my own set of rails. Bat her down the chute, drift the dogleg, whomp her through the chicane, climb on the binders, snap a downshift and crank her round the hairpin with your tootsie in the carbs."

"Please excuse us for a moment, Mr. Biged," says Number One. And all three of them go into a huddle. Finally, after a lot of mumbling, they break it up.

"Could you elaborate on the portion having to do with a 'tootsie in the carbs?' " asks Number Three.

"Sure," Ed nods. "You know, Mac—you leadfoot it through the esses. You stomp it, but good. You bury your boot in the firewall."

"Ummm." Number Three pauses, then tries another question. "And what, may I ask, is the direct result of this procedure?"

"Man, you drop the fast boys in your back pocket. You lap the field. You carry home the happy hardware."

"I am afraid we are losing contact, Mr. Biged," says Number One. "Could you possibly simplify your explanations?"

"I'm givin' you the straight jazz, Mac."

By now Ed is having a ball. He figures himself way ahead of the gag, that he has turned the table on these nutty little guys, whoever they are.

"What, in effect, do you plan to do with this machine?" asks Number One.

"Bomb the competition," says Ed. "Man, I'm gonna go like Jack the Bear in this rig soon as I get all the bugs out. Ten to one she outhauls the spaghetti wagons with no sweat. Hell, I can tach up to seven now without floating. She's solid."

The three green guys immediately go into another huddle.

"Obviously," states Number Three after a couple of minutes, "you have progressed alarmingly far beyond our present scientific horizons. We find it impossible to relate what you have just told us of this machine to any known technical data of our own. Therefore, you leave us no choice—" The others nod slowly. "—We must take your machine back with us."

Ed bristles at this. "Fun's fun, pal, but nobody is makin' off with my heap. But nobody. Like—take three drop dead pills. Get lost."

But at this point, Ed says, he suddenly knew the whole bit was for real. Number Two greenboy puts away his writing stick and flips out a metal gadget. He aims it at Ed and presses something and Ed feels like he's just been dropped headfirst into a vat of glue. He can't twitch a muscle.

Then, out of the sky, swoops this mammoth cigar-shaped whatchamacallit with maybe ten dozen windows but no wings, and a big panel slides open along the bottom. Out comes a huge claw and scoops up Ed's Chevy-Special as neat as you please.

By the time Ed can move again the three green characters have hopped back into their Flying Saucer and taken off after the big cigar.

And that, according to Big Ed, is why he's out of the racing game.

Now I, personally, figure this. Either Ed is the biggest liar this side of Detroit—or some pretty hot laps are going to be turned up on Mars.

Because, like Ed says, one thing is for sure: That Chevy-Special of his goes like *stink!*

A Matter of Taste

Esther M. Friesner

I should do what?" The butler's eyes goggled worse than those of the stuffed carp he had carved only last night.

"You heard me, Rawlins." The housemaid fixed a steely gaze upon the priceless antique dinner plate in the butler's hands. He held it tentatively just above the place of honor at the elegantly laid table, but not for long, if Mrs. Connor had her way. "Break it."

The idea set Rawlins's underlip atremble. "Part of the Trafalgar service, Mrs. Connor? On purpose? Me?"

"Yes, you." Mrs. Connor pursed her lips. "I'd do it quick enough myself, if I hadn't Mother to support. Smash it in a minute, sooner than let that one eat from it."

She cast a meaningful gaze at the closed living room doors, beyond whose mute oaken barrier a select contingent of the Georgetown *haut ton*—and one other—were presently enjoying Mrs. Ruth Longworthy's hospitality. "They'll just be finishing their drinks now—and I shudder to think what that one's drinking—coming in here next, that one a-slithering over the very floors poor Ina spent half her life holystoning. Yes, poor Ina, lying on her bed this very minute without even the comfort of her faith to see her through these awful times!"

Ina was a low blow—a younger Rawlins once had shared a carefully banked passion with said lady—but it had a galvanic effect on the butler. Purposefully he strode towards the Carrara marble fireplace, the guilty plate held high. Mrs. Connor smiled a silent *alea jacta est*. No crockery could survive a tumble to that adamantine hearth.

Rawlins paused. "This will mean my job, you know."

"A-slithering!" Ruthless, that reiteration.

And effective. Rawlins let drop the irreplaceable plate just as the great doors rolled back on their brass casters and the first guests entered the dining room.

"Ah!" the Ambassador exclaimed, and swiftly flicked out his second-lower-left tentacle to snatch the falling plate from doom. He caught it a foot above the hearthstone. "How lucky for you that I am omnidextrous." He passed it back to the butler with an approximated smile.

Rawlins took the plate, being scrupulous to avoid all contact with the Ambassador's rippling cyan flesh. Without a word of acknowledgment or thanks, without even the ghost of a bow, he set the platter in its place and retired to his carving station, ignoring Mrs. Longworthy's glare and the extended and pointed clearing of her sapphired throat.

"I do apologize for Rawlins," she said, a bit testily.

"You cannot blame him, dear lady," the Ambassador replied. "The populace of this city—this country—I will go so far as to say this world in its entirety!—has hardened its heart against me and mine. Yet the crime was so ancient. Had we not had the bad luck to mention it ourselves—"

"Do have some of the duck, Your Excellency," Mrs. Longworthy exclaimed, a bit too brightly, a tad too sharply. At mention of the now-famous abomination, polite dinner chat ceased. All eyes turned to the Ambassador; unfriendly eyes.

"No, thank you," he returned. "We no longer indulge." He gave his full attention to the salad.

"Why not?" It was the son of the Moravian attaché—or perhaps the Brazilian sub-chargé d'affaires—a most disagreeable lad, in any case. "Not as tasty as what you'd really like, is it? After all, duck's only a dumb beast. Why not nibble on our hostess's ear, for old times' sake?"

"Sebastian!"

"Oh, come off it, Ruth!" Sebastian retorted. "You only invited him for the notoriety of it, and we're only at the same table with this—thing—because we're all dog-leg level on our ministerial to-tem poles. I've put up with this charade through cocktails and hors d'oeuvres—and did you see the wistful way he stared at those Swedish meatballs?—but nothing says I have to swallow dinner at the same table with—with—that one!" He indicated the Ambassador with the same disgust he reserved for his pedigreed but unhousebreakable Afghan hound. The Ambassador's nictitating membranes lowered in shame. He poked his arugula listlessly.

"We're risking our necks being seen with him!" a flighty specimen of local journalistic fauna shrilled.

"I fail to see the risk involved." Mrs. Longworthy's generous mouth was sullen. This scenario had not occurred to her while laying out the place-cards.

"You know what risk," the columnist cheeped. "Revenge, damn it! And not just the nut-groups. Ordinary people. Decent people who aren't about to forgive or forget what he and his kind did to us!"

"Not to you." The Ambassador's voice was barely audible. "We have already tendered our regrets—"

"Don't you dare tender another thing while you're under my roof, Your Excellency!" Mrs. Longworthy was not about to let the

Lower Orders win without a tussle. "You aren't responsible for the actions of your ancestors."

"But if further apology is called for—"

"I forbid it. Have you no pride?"

The Ambassador pondered this. "No," he said at last. "That is, I don't think I have. A strange concept. . . ."

"Not so strange as your concept of a family barbecue!" Sebastian sniped.

The alien sagged further in his chair. "How could we suspect? Had we but known what you would become—the evolutionary potential—!" He waved his tentacles vaguely, helpless to recapture the past. "We were not so wise, then."

" 'That was then, this is now'?" The British Third Assistant Under-Minister for Culture curled his lip. "God, I hate a sanctimonious vegetarian!" A proud member of the C. of E., he still smarted under the horrendous changes it had undergone in the wake of the revenants' shocking confession. When he thought of the new Primate of England, he shuddered.

The closed dining-room doors flew back into their wall-sleeves with a resounding crash. The dinner guests dropped their hostilities to stare. A small, elderly woman tottered in, clad only in a white flannel nightgown. Gray hair streamed down her back in a tousled mane and framed her wrinkled face in a wispy halo.

"Gubba!" she shrieked.

"Ina . . ." The pain in Rawlins's face was immeasurable.

"Ina Harvey," Mrs. Longworthy whispered to the Ambassador. "My housekeeper. She's—not well."

As if to confirm Mrs. Longworthy's understated diagnosis, Ina Harvey lurched forward still gibbering, "Gubba! Gubba!" Rawlins attempted to intervene, leaving the half-carved duck abandoned on the sideboard. His former inamorata staggered towards him. She seemed about to tumble into his arms, but at the last moment she nimbly sidestepped, lunged for the duck, seized the unattended carving knife, and with a cry of, "Sweet Saint Gubba, guide my hand!" plunged the knife blade into the Ambassador's back.

The wound would not have killed an Earther, but alien physiology being the random thing it is, she connected with the main heart, three of the kidneys, and the durb.

*　*　*

The outcry in diplomatic circles was loud, though not all of it was outraged. The Ambassador was dead, and public opinion was evenly split between Serves them right and What will they do to us now?

Terror seized the planet. Survivalists took to the woods in hordes, sure of civilization-levelling retaliation on the part of the extraterrestrial nostalgiaphiles. The faithful jammed the newly founded First Church of Darwin, laying their petitions for salvation before Saint Simian and Saint Scopes. Saint Gubba the Australopithecine had her adherents, too, for the Right Reverend Doctor Billie-Joe Chase had been vouchsafed a divine revelation on prime-time TV proving that the families of both Saint Elizabeth and Saint Anne had descended in direct genetic line from this sole protohominid ancestress. Followers of Saint Lucy of Olduvai begged to differ.

"Suddenly it's illegal *not* to teach evolution in Tennessee." Brian Greeley of the recently formed Exogaian Liaison Authority folded his newspaper and passed it on to his subordinate, a skittish young thing with a B.A. in English from Harvard and a government job as a last resort.

"How can you read the paper so calmly?" the underling squealed, letting the daily flutter to the floor unread. "They're going to blast us off the face of the earth!"

"Oh, I don't think so."

"Why shouldn't they? They've got the technology, and we've given them the motive. They came in peace, and what did we do? We killed their Ambassador! We treated them like lepers! We—"

"My dear Hollis, they are reasonable beings. The very fact of their peaceable return proves it. What could they have expected from us, once the secret was out? What sort of reception would Colonel Sanders get if he walked into a coop full of suddenly sentient chickens?"

Hollis moaned. "I'll never see another Yale game!"

The interoffice line beeped once, discreetly. Greeley picked up the receiver, listened, then said, "Show him in."

The Ambassador was dead, but his successor had not been dilatory in assuming diplomatic duties. Greeley's secretary stood well away as she held the door open to admit him. She made no attempt to hide her distaste.

Hollis took one look at their caller and wove his fingers into a Turk's-head knot. "Don't eat me!" he cried.

The new Ambassador furrowed his brow and several other areas of exposed skin in perplexity.

"Ignore Hollis," Greeley said, providing a chair wide enough to accommodate the Ambassador's hummocky body. "He's a twit. Aren't you, Hollis? Now, if you've come to discuss reparations for the death of your colleague—"

Fully three tentacles were raised in a staying motion. "By no means. That sad incident has but emphasized our urgent need to learn what really underlies your animosity."

"Well, there is the semantic difference we have when it comes to the phrase, 'have lunch together'. . . ."

"No, no, it is more; it must be. We continue to assure you by our most holy vows that we no longer eat meat—not merely yours, but that of more succulent species. Surely there is some other reason—?"

Greeley scratched his head. "Oh, hell, you've been honest with us. Why not tell you the truth? It's pride."

"Pardon, that concept has no equivalent in our lexicon."

"Lucky you. I'll say this for our species, sir: We can take being eaten a lot easier than we can take being force-fed humble pie. Creationists said humanity was put on this earth, Evolutionists said it developed here. Suddenly out of the clear blue sky—literally— you folks come to say, yes, humanity was put here: put here by your colonists as beef cattle! Whole herds of hominids, with no greater role in the Universal Scheme than to serve as the Sunday roast."

The Ambassador's membranes lowered halfway. "Stew," he murmured. "Too tough for a roast; though you do—did—travel well."

"—and when the colony failed, many of the herds escaped. Evolution took it from there. Like our wild mustangs descending from domesticated horses the Spaniards brought to the New World. Now back you come—our former masters and consumers—to establish friendly relations. How friendly did you think we'd be, once we learned the truth? We're no longer a little below the angels, we're one step from the Quarter Pounder! You've knocked every earthly religion on its sainted ear, you've gutted our language of every food-based idiom, and it's become high treason for someone to tell the old 'I met a bum who hadn't had a bite in days so I bit him' joke."

The Ambassador's frown-lines were trenches now. "I don't understand. Pride. . . ."

"Self-love, if you will," Greeley suggested. "Esteem, self-image. The value we set on ourselves, the worth—"

"Is that it, then?" The alien's skin smoothed somewhat. "Because our ancestors ate yours, you believe we do not value you highly? Love you with sufficient sincerity?"

"Something like that."

The Ambassador brightened. "But that is most easily rectified!" He rose slowly from his seat. "Tell me, will your television crews be present at our comrade's funeral?"

"We'd need the Marines to keep them away."

"Excellent. Then directly after the rites, I can promise to show your people proof of the high regard, the esteem, the abiding love we cherish for your breed."

"Uhhh, this proof . . . Could you specify—?"

"Permit me the indulgence of surprise." The alien ignored the look of misgiving on Greeley's face as he started for the door. "Gentlemen?"

The funeral was held at the Washington Monument reflecting pool. The alien delegation performed the simple yet elegant rites as the late Ambassador's body was reduced to its component elements and dispersed in the atmosphere. The new Ambassador took it upon himself to explain the whole procedure for the cameras, and for the benefit of the few jittery Terrans present in person at the obsequies.

"Such complete disposal of the corporeal form is an old, old way of ours. This is why you never suspected our previous presence on your world. We did not leave behind even our bones."

"And artifacts?" Greeley asked.

"We were—how would you say it?—minimalists. Also tidy." He shrugged off his ceremonial robes and faced the cameras. "Cherished watchers, now attend and witness. In the interests of the harmony between our peoples, let the sending that here follows end all your doubts: to love and value you is truly our second nature; to consume, ingest, or even think of nutritionally assimilating you, anathema."

An oblong section of air behind the Ambassador turned hazy and resolved itself into a holographic projection that was eagerly picked up by the cameras. It was, the alien explained, a transmission directly from the homeworld—only the first of many, if their Terran friends would forgive, forget, and allow. He had arranged it as easily as a college student might phone in a pizza order, no anchovies. The eyes of every Earther with access to a boob-tube were transfixed by the panorama of a civilization from beyond the stars.

The initial epic sweep of that miraculous transmission narrowed to a single-family dwelling. A small alien bobbled across the equivalent of a front lawn, pursuing a multicolored floating star. While earthbound toy tsars barked orders at their R&D departments to develop a knockoff in time for Christmas, the youngling lost its plaything in a tangle of nasty-looking scrub. Tentative probings with its tentacles yielded painful results. The youngster put the wounded extremities to its mouth like any thorn-stung Terran child. For a moment, that one gesture evoked a twinge of sympathy from the human audience.

But only for a moment. The child turned back toward the dwelling, raised two opposing pairs of tentacles overhead, and snapped them like whips. The transmission of sound was as sharp as the picture. No one on Earth could fault it, or later deny what they saw.

The dwelling irised open and a man emerged. He was somewhat hairier and smaller than the norm, with slack posture and no hope of making the Best Dressed list—unless one counted the shiny bangles on his wrists and ankles. But for all his sartorial primitivism, he was bright-eyed, healthy, and eager to please. He fairly scampered across the lawn, listened attentively to the little alien's bubbly syllables, then bounded into the scrub with a happy cry.

When he fetched out the wayward toy, his owner gave him a lump of something green and scratched his back in the one spot no human can reach on his own. It was evident that Mrs. Ruth Longworthy would serve *chat au vin* at her table sooner than that small alien would consent to eat its adored pet.

Hollis needed a winch to get his jaw off the ground.

"Well, hel-lo, Grampa," Greeley said *sotto voce.* "What big brow-ridges you have."

After a lengthy conference in the office of Exogaian Liaison, the new Ambassador was brought to see the error he had made, albeit with the best of intentions.

"Yet if we make amends, why can you not forgive?" he asked plaintively. "Have I not sent instructions to the homeworld, directing the immediate institution of programs to speed the evolution of your ancestral beings? We have the bioforming technology to do this—a simple affair, the stimulation of certain nexi of the brain. No longer shall they be pets to us, though I weep for my daughter's sake; she was very attached to hers."

"I'm sorry, Your Excellency," Greeley replied, "but that changes nothing. Your broadcast riled folks up worse than before. Now we need time to decide which hurts worse: being your lunches or your Lassies."

"Lassies?"

"You wouldn't understand."

"That appears to be the durb of the problem." The alien's whole massive body seemed to droop. "I agree, Mr. Greeley. It is hopeless to strive for diplomatic relations so long as your people will not understand our position. We shall leave you for a time. Only the mutually guilty can share the pain of inadvertent crime. But you will learn."

"Of course." Greeley really didn't follow the alien, but as a career diplomat he was paid to be agreeable.

The aliens' departure was received with sorrow only within the scientific community. "Did you see what they did with their ship's mascot in just the short time they were here?" one lab tech groaned to another.

"Well, I don't usually stay up for the *Tonight* show, but I made an exception," his partner replied. "A thousand years of evolution leaped in one week. I hear that Johnny's going to let Rover be guest-host for April. What we might have learned!"

On the other hand, the majority of Just Plain Folks said much the same as Mr. Fred Nicely, family man, solid U.S. citizen, Iowan, and pig-farmer, viz.: "Good riddance!" He rattled the newspaper for emphasis.

His hired man, Randy Morse, tried to read the article about the alien exodus over his boss's shoulder. It shared front-page space with the new Supreme Court judgment making it a felony to sing "Love Me Tender" in a public eatery. The two men leaned their elbows on the top bar of the breeding sty as they shared the news of the day. "Says here they'll come back when we call 'em," Randy pointed out.

"Ha!" Mr. Nicely's short, harsh laugh was rank with the after-traces of a hearty bacon-and-eggs breakfast. "They think we'd ever tell 'em to come back? In a pig's eye!"

"Watch your language, Nicely!"

The paper was snatched from the good farmer's hands. Automatically he cursed Randy's rudeness; unjustly, for Randy was incapable of such discourtesy to his employer. At the moment, Randy was incapable of anything. Petrified, paralyzed, only his lips flapping like longjohns on the line, Randy gawked at the real culprit, a prize Spotted Poland China boar who was exercising his newly acquired opposable trotters to turn the newsprint pages.

The boar ignored the hired man's frozen stare and the farmer's guttural scream. He only had eyes for the page-one story on the aliens. He sighed deeply over the photos of his benefactors' leavetaking. He'd miss them, though their mutual acquaintance had been brief and confined to the cover of darkness. Their initial encounter was shrouded in the mists of pre-sentience, but what came after was crystal clear in newfound porcine memory. What they'd done to him and the others hadn't hurt a bit that he could recall. Even if it had, it was a trifling price to pay for facing a tomorrow that now held more than scrapple.

He thumbed to the farm news and remarked, "Says here that pork futures are up."

So they were.

The Mission

Arthur Tofte

The two figures descended warily from the tiny scout ship. They knew their descent through the atmosphere had created a meteor-like streak of brilliant light. They hoped that the valley where they had landed was well enough hidden to conceal them and their craft.

The two looked at each other grimly. They were unhappy with their mission, and with the orders that brought them to this strange, gloomy planet.

"I know what our duty is," the older and taller of the two said in the sibilant language of his race, "even though I can't agree with what we are expected to do."

The other nodded agreement with the thought.

The leader handed his companion a small bundle he had brought out of the ship with him. "Here, you carry it for a while. I'll lead the way."

He looked up into the night sky as though trying to catch a glimpse of the great mother ship that had brought them to this troubled, savage place. Mother ship indeed!

He peered anxiously at the dark knuckles of hills surrounding them. He pointed. "According to the instructions the Watchers gave us, the settlement is that way."

The two plodded slowly up the long slope of the hill. Suddenly the leader held out his arm for the other to stop.

"Strange beasts ahead!" he said. Using a shielded lightbeam, he flashed it at a group of white, rather round animals that stood silently in their way.

For only a moment the creatures stared at the light and then scurried off with little bounds.

"They don't appear to be dangerous," the younger stranger said as he moved his burden from one arm to the other.

The ground, they found, was hard and dry under their feet. Vegetation was thin and brittle. Overhead the stars sparkled with the sharp intensity that comes on a cold, cloudless night.

As they approached the sleeping village, they proceeded with increased caution. Occasionally small animals ran out to sniff and bark softly at them.

After they had passed several stone huts and a cave entrance or two, the leader murmured, "As the Watchers said, these people are indeed very primitive. They live in caves and stone hovels. I doubt if they know how to work metals. Almost certainly they have no written language. A truly sub-civilization—possibly like our own two or three thousand generations ago."

A single torch light gleamed ahead of them. Making their way through the stone rubble next to the path, they came to a wooden shed, half open to the night sky. Carefully and in secret they watched from the side.

A male and a female were in the shed. The woman, quite young and obviously in the final stages of exhaustion, held out a naked baby for the man to hold while she wrapped cloths around it.

This was what they had been told by the Watchers they would find—a native child being born.

From their vantage point, the two strangers saw the young mother sink with a sigh to the floor. The man carefully placed the child next to her. Then, he too lowered himself to the dirt floor. In a matter of moments both were asleep.

Quietly the tall visitor went over to look down at the newborn child. Its mouth was moving soundlessly and its tiny fingers groped futilely at the empty air.

He reached for the bundle his companion had brought so carefully from the ship and opened it. He lifted out the naked baby it contained. It too was a newborn.

In the time of half a dozen heartbeats, he had exchanged the two infants, even switching their covering cloths.

As the two turned to leave, the strangers looked back for a last look at the sleeping man and his wife. And they peered for the last time at the child they had brought with them and were now leaving in this primitive place.

Hurriedly, their mission completed, they headed back toward their ship. The leader carried the infant they had stolen.

"Our Watchers were right," he said once they were away from the village. "The people on this planet are extremely primitive. And yet they appear to be more like us in appearance than those of any other planet we have ever studied."

"Yes," the other replied, "our scientists should be pleased with getting this fine, healthy specimen."

"What makes me feel badly is that we had to leave one of our own in its place."

"Of course you know it has always been our policy never to let the natives of any planet know we have visited them. That's why we had to wait for one of our women on the mother ship to give birth so we would have a newborn to put in place of the one we took."

"But that child of ours back there, won't he be different from the natives when he grows up? After all, he has thousands of generations of our advanced civilization behind him."

"Yes, I suppose he will be different. It would be interesting to come back when he is grown to see how he has developed in this primitive life."

As they reached their ship and started to climb up, the leader turned to his companion. "What was the name of that village? It was listed by our Watchers."

The other replied. "It is called Bethlehem."

Mister Magister

Thomas F. Monteleone

Mister Magister was not his real name.

He was tall, and his skeleton thinness was enhanced by the dark clothing he wore. He fancied a sweeping black cape that hung upon him like a scarecrow's rag, fastened by a single silver clasp in the shape of a bird's taloned claw. His face was pale, gaunt, accented by sunken cheeks, a pointed nose, thin bloodless lips, and dark eyes that seemed to glow faintly like the coals of a dying fire. His hair was black and thick and greased against his skull, although it was mostly concealed by his broad-brimmed, drooped-down black hat.

Mister Magister had come from a far-flung star system to perform his appointed tasks—to seek out intelligence on likely worlds, then test it for certain qualities. To accomplish this, he was forced to pretend to be something he was not: on Earth, a traveling road-showman.

And so he was Mister Magister, the proprietor of a most unusual wagon, a portable carnival shooting gallery. It was a magnificent affair: gingerbread paneling, filigreed ironwork, polished brass, and shining paint with pinstripe. The folks of a small midwestern town were righteously impressed with the rig when he appeared on Main Street one early autumn evening, upon the heels of a dusty carnival of loud barkers and gypsy workers. They assumed he was but a straggler from the main troupe, and they patronized his wagon with no great suspicion.

There were others among us at that time, all of them conducting their own specialized tests upon our species, but we are concerned only with Mister Magister's test.

It went something like this:

At one end of the carnival wagon was a section of boards that hinged down to form a countertop where several BB guns were anchored with generous lengths of chain. Past the counter was an open space, an *emptiness,* that suggested a gulf far greater than the mere length of the wagon, beyond which there was a dimly lit stage where targets seemed to float effortlessly.

The targets were the important things.

On the first evening, when the townspeople lined up at the counter and squinted down the thin barrels of the rifles, the target they saw was the half-grinning face of one of the town's Negroes—a young man who ran deliveries for the grocer. Although the people thought this odd, it did not stop them from taking careful aim at the familiar black face.

But they were stunned the next morning when news spread through the streets that the young Negro had been found shot to death in the alley behind the grocery store. The sheriff was prevailed upon to investigate the death, but there was a strange feeling in the town. It was as though everyone understood what had happened, but chose not to talk about it.

The next evening, a different face appeared under the shrouded light of the gallery. Mister Magister quietly took their coins as they all took their turns squeezing off rounds at the melancholy face of the town shoemaker—an old Jewish man who spoke with a funny accent.

And it was really no surprise when they found the Jew slumped over his cobbler's bench shortly after sunrise. But still they pretended not to know. And still they would not talk. Much less would they look oddly toward the southern end of town where Mister Magister had set up his wrinkled canvas tent alongside his magnificent wagon.

The next evening brought a steady stream of people to his counter, where the shifting target now became the familiar features of a big immigrant auto mechanic—a well-intentioned Swede who spoke so little English so poorly that most people laughed at him. Coins were dropped. The guns were fired.

And in the morning the Swede was dead.

In the evenings that followed, the business was brisk at Mister Magister's wagon. The townspeople each secretly wondered who would be next at the wrong end of the gallery.

Most of their wonderings eventually came to pass: an Indian who pumped gas at the Texaco; another Negro, who was the janitor at the boiler factory; the addled, cross-eyed boy who did gardening in the summer and snow shoveling in winter to earn his meager keep at a boardinghouse in the north end; an Italian immigrant who washed dishes in the hotel café.

All targets; all now dead.

And the strangest part of this story was that the remaining townspeople went about their business as if nothing were amiss. Perhaps they knew—of course they knew!—that Mister Magister and his wagon were to blame, but no one said a word against him.

No one, until a young girl of thirteen named Stella. She was wiry-lean, with reddish-blond hair that fell down her back in a thick braid. She had green-gray eyes, full pouting lips, a turned-up nose. She came to the wagon after dinner, watching the dark road-showman set up for the evening's entertainment.

"I know who you are," she said, looking into those cold dark eyes.

"You *do?*" he said in his low, solemn voice.

Stella nodded as she continued to stare at the tall thin man. "Yes. You're *Death,* aren't you?"

"Death?" Mister Magister smiled and shook his head.

"Yes, you know . . . the one that takes us. The Reaper."

"I know of whom you speak, little girl," said Mister Magister. "But I must confess that I am not . . . that person."

"Then who *are* you? Why're you killing us like this?"

"It is not I who is killing you. You are killing yourselves."

Stella stared at him for a moment. A wind touched her neck coolly and there was the sound of scuttling leaves. The sunlight was almost a memory now. "But we wouldn't be doing it . . . if you and your shooting gallery wasn't here. Don't you see what I mean?"

"Oh, I see what you mean. But you are wrong, child. . . ." Magister paused, turning over that last word—"child"—in his mind. She *was* a child, but she spoke with the directness, the power, and the maturity of someone far older, far stronger. "It seems to me," he continued once again, "that your people were killing them long before I came along. Only much more slowly."

Stella considered the dark one's words. She understood what he said. She was not so young that she had not already noticed the hate in the world, the mindless dislike for things that people did not understand, for things that were *different.*

But another question occurred to her. "There's something else, though. . . ."

"And what is that?" he said, as he began carefully to lay out the shooting gallery rifles, make small adjustments to the wagon's trappings.

"How long are you going to let this go on?"

"It could go on for a very long time. I really don't know." Mister Magister shook his head slowly, then turned his back on the little girl.

She knew that he was finished with her, and so she wandered off, seeking a deeper meaning to his words.

Later that evening, the customers came to play at Magister's game. The faces seemed to change in the swirling half-light of the gallery stage. But they did not seem to care.

The new deaths were no longer the feared, the foreign, and the hated. News spread each morning of violent passings: neighbors, cousins, councilmen, and brothers. The little girl, wise Stella, having spoken so openly to Mister Magister, stood apart from the rest of the town and its trancelike attraction to the strange and terrible gallery. She thought she knew now what was really happening, and she went again to see the master of the black wagon.

It was late and he was lowering the flaps, hinging the boards that would lock away the rifles and the counters for the night. "So," he said upon seeing her in the light of an almost full moon, "you have come back."

"You're not going to *ever* stop, are you?" she said, trying to hate this strange man, but failing.

Magister smiled. *Yes, this child knows,* he thought. "That's correct," he said. "It is not my decision to stop this thing. I am only a tool, a means to an end, not the agent."

"We *are* the agents," said Stella. "And we must stop it."

Mister Magister nodded slowly; the fire behind his dark eyes seemed momentarily to flare.

Stella tried to smile. There was something about this man that made her feel, almost *know,* that he was not of her familiar world. There was a coldness about him, a detached aspect, that, while it was not good, was not evil either.

"We would all keep coming," she said. "All of us who were left . . . until there was no one left at all."

Mister Magister could only nod his head, and she thought she caught a hint of sadness in this gesture.

"It's always been our way, I think," said Stella, the words now rushing out of her. "As long as it's somebody else, it doesn't seem to matter. But I want to stop it. I want to stop it right now!"

The dark, thin man looked down at her and she shuddered. He threw hard the bolt that locked up the wagon and said, "You already have, little one. You already have. I will leave you now. My business here is done."

"You're leaving?" Stella was shocked indeed to hear such words.

"Yes, I have discovered what I came here to know."

"And what is that?" she asked.

"That there is hope for this race of beings, for this tiny world of selfish creatures." He paused and walked to the front of the wagon.

"Know this, child, and never wonder why I came here: I have come for *you*."

As Stella heard these words, the moon slipped behind a passing cloud and darkness settled upon them. The wind grew suddenly chillier, and the thought of being swept away in the shadowy wagon passed icily through her.

But Mister Magister turned away from her and climbed upon the wagon. He rattled the black reins and slowly rolled away from that place. As the distance grew between himself and the town, Mister Magister found himself alone with waving fields of wheat. It shimmered like a ghostly sea in the moonlight. Looking up into the starry sky, Magister smiled. Somewhere, out among the stars, there would be another race of beings, another town, another role for him to play.

He wondered if the next world would be so lucky as to have a Stella in their midst. If they did not, he felt truly sorry for them.

Mr. Iper of Hamilton

Carl Jacobi

"Come, follow me into the tunnel of oblivion and I will disenchant you."

—Rices'
Palimpsest and Fragments

Actually the strange one in this story is Mr. Paxton Iper—he pronounced it Eeper—though everyone regarded Herman Watt as the oddity. Herman was odd all right but in a different way.

Mr. Iper arrived in Hamilton Corners in a work-cruiser on a sultry Monday morning in October and, after talking with the sheriff a half-hour, drifted around to the shady side of Sam's gas station where some of us sit and smoke and pass the day. Right away he puzzled us.

He introduced himself as territorial representative for the Third

Estate Environmental Council and said he had come to make a test of the town's water supply. "Understand you've had several cases of Magnetic Fever," he said.

"If you mean summer complaint, we get that every year 'bout this time."

He nodded. "You get your water from the river, I understand."

"That's right, and we've got one of the finest filtration plants in the state."

He was a small man with hair so black it looked as if it had been stamped out of a piece of blotting paper. His eyes, cat-green, had a trick of slowly closing, then blinking rapidly. He wore a copper medallion with the embossed design of a clarinet, apparently the emblem of some music society.

Presently his gaze turned across the road to the fenced-in corner of Watt's meadow.

"What's that?" he demanded.

We all smiled. You couldn't help but smile when a stranger first set eyes on Herman Watt's "machine." Though we always sobered up quickly when we thought of the tragedy behind it.

Paxton Iper was looking at a heavy platform about four feet square upon which were mounted three triangular metal boxes. Projecting from one of these boxes was a wheel-gear connected with a chain to a rusty burned-out five-horse motor. At each corner of the wooden platform a steel rod was fixed upright and these rods supported a sort of helix of twisted copper wire. Half a dozen white porcelain insulators, positioned aimlessly, gleamed in the sunlight. A panel, covered with defunct dials and gauges, stood to one side.

This was Herman Watt's "machine," put together during his convalescence from the accident at the Fission Mill.

Even before his accident Herman had been no mental genius. But after he came into contact with that conduit stopping his heart for a matter of minutes before respiration could be applied the resultant brain damage left him a cross between a vegetable and a man. Parabonic hypnotherapy had done wonders for him but it couldn't completely restore his blood-starved think-box.

The fact that the machine did nothing seemed not to concern him. Referring to it as his "device," he always spoke of it as "nearing completion" and accepted gravely "parts" for it that were proffered him from time to time by sympathetic town citizens.

"What's that?" Mr. Iper asked again, looking toward the machine.

Somebody told him the story. While he listened he idly took from his pocket a pair of folding-scissors and picked up a newspaper one of us had discarded. He folded the paper an odd way and began to cut a chain of paper dolls joined together by their outstretched arms.

Just then, the subject of our conversation, Herman Watt, joined our group.

"Hi, Herman," we said.

"It's a nice day," Herman said, looking up at the sky.

We agreed that the weather was tolerable.

In the silence that followed Mr. Iper sat staring at Herman Watt with unblinking eyes. His fingers moved to his medallion and began to caress it as he said softly:

"Sele mobas ante lium."

For a week the stranger continued his investigation of Hamilton Corners, if you could call it an investigation. Aside from taking samples every morning from the taps at the water tower and the filtration plant and filling a big test tube every afternoon with water from the river, he didn't seem to do much but ask questions. He did open an office above Garson's drug store and slept there too. What seemed particularly to interest him was the Selfridge Addition at the north end of town. The Selfridge Addition was composed of ultra plastic homes in the seventy-five thousand dollar class, surrounding the Mason Selfridge mansion. They and their residents were a unit apart. Except to pay taxes, they had no contact with the rest of the town. They had their own wells, their own sewage disposal, even their own power system. In the language of the sheriff they were "a bunch of snobs." "And, the worst snob of them all," he said "is Mason Selfridge, president of the Fission Mill."

Thereafter Mr. Iper drove his work-cruiser to the various homes in the Addition, remained inside each a half hour or so, then came out, red-faced and tense with anger. Not until October 15th, however, did he make public his report. It went something like this:

The Fission Mill, a dozen miles out of town, used "heavy" water, and other elopsi-chemicals in its operations and dumped the residue in the river. In spite of the Hamilton filtration plant the water remained contaminated when it poured from the faucets of the town's houses. The only reason there weren't more cases of Magnetic Fever was because a lot of the people who drank the water had developed a tolerance for it. But that tolerance would disappear as the contamination grew.

The home of Mason Selfridge and the other houses of the Addition got their water from deep electro-hydron wells and this water was pure. But neither Selfridge nor the other Addition residents would consent to share their water with the rest of the townsfolk.

In frustration Mr. Iper interviewed Mason Selfridge at his Mill office, queried him on the possibility of underwriting a bond issue to finance a series of wells for the town proper.

Selfridge shook his head. "Certainly not," he said. "I may live within the confines of the town, but I have no connection with it at all."

"But it's your mill that's contaminating the water supply."

"That's a matter of question," Selfridge said. "Besides the town has a filtration plant."

Next day there were three more cases of Magnetic Fever—old Doc Bentle had finally come around to Mr. Iper's diagnosis—and by late afternoon the widow Edwina Woods had succumbed. But Mr. Iper didn't quarantine the town nor stop the use of the water. "I have no authority to do that," he said in his room over the drug store where several of us had gone to ask him to contribute to the flower-fund for the Edwina Woods' funeral. He put aside the clarinet he had been playing and stopped the metronome on the table with an air of shy embarrassment. "No," he repeated, "I have no authority to condemn the water supply or anything else. I'm just a—survey man."

Two days after the posting of the Iper report the town council held an emergency general meeting. The mayor was there, the sheriff, Doc Bentle, Druggist Garson, as well as Paxton Iper who, seated at the speakers' table, amused himself by cutting endless rows of dancing dolls, some out of paper, some out of foil. There was something odd about the foil dolls. Although he worked the scissors around a single pattern, the folded figures always came out half with skirts, half with trousers; that is to say, half boy-dolls, half girl-dolls. Herman Watt was there too, long legs thrust out before him.

The meeting was hot and heavy. The water contamination was discussed pro and con but it all ended with no decisions. As we were starting to leave Mr. Iper motioned Herman to his side. "I've got something for you," he said.

He reached under the table and brought up his finish-scratched metronome. He fastened a string to the top end of the measure-beating arm, the other end of the string to one of his chains of foil dolls and then with a flip of his finger started the metronome. The dolls came to sudden life. With each swing of the timing-arm the silver images appeared to kick up their heels in a gay rigadoon.

Herman Watt broke out in a grin of pleasure. "For me?" he said.

Mr. Iper nodded. "For your machine."

Next morning Mason Selfridge phoned the sheriff. The voice of the fission mill president shook with anger.

"Do you know what some of your fine citizens did?" he demanded. "They threw a barrelfull of junk down my well. Just because I refused to turn it into a public watering place. I want to know what you're going to do about it."

"Junk?" repeated the sheriff. "In your well?"

"In the ornamental one with the pagoda roof in the front grounds."

"I see," the sheriff said vaguely. He hesitated. "Well . . . I'll put a man on it right away."

It was true all right. Somebody had thrown a lot of metal and wood down the Selfridge well. Much of it had lodged half way down, wedged against the side walls. But the sheriff did a double take when he saw the nature of that material. It was Herman Watt's machine!

"Now," said the sheriff, "who'd do a thing like that?"

He leaned farther out over the well and saw something he hadn't seen the first time.

The machine was wedged half way down all right but it hadn't been dropped or thrown there. It must have been lowered by a rope fastened to a hook which had been swung free when the machine had stopped its descent. This was made apparent when the sheriff probed the darkness with a powerful flashlight. He could even see the string of foil dolls and the metronome which Herman had added to the machine.

The sheriff was a reasoning man. He had gone to Aldebaron Tech and he had his own ideas of science and philosophy and metaphysics. Although in his studies—much more complete and offbeat than a man in his occupation normally would have—he had seen many problems dissipated by logic, this time it seemed he was up against a brick wall. Why would anyone throw a mentally incompetent's "machine" down a well? Simply as a reprisal for Mason Selfridge's refusal of the use of his water? That didn't make sense. There were things nearer, lighter and far less cumbersome than the machine. But perhaps the perpetrator had an entirely different reason, had progressed along a different line of thought. Perhaps he wanted to surround the machine with permanent darkness. Wasn't it true that some metaphysical activity required the absence of light to function? But this would presuppose Herman Watt's machine embraced a psychic motivation, a supposition which the sheriff knew simply did not exist.

The sheriff got a rope and a grappling hook from his car, let it down the shaft and attempted to draw the machine to the surface. It wouldn't budge. Nor would it move when the tow truck windlass ordered from Sunderson's Garage tried to pull it out.

These proceedings were watched by Mr. Iper who stood some distance off smoking a cigar.

"What're you doing here?" the sheriff asked. He was annoyed by the presence of the environmental man who seemed to be wherever any activity took place but never seemed to accomplish anything on his own.

"Three more cases of Magnetic Fever," Mr. Iper replied quietly. "I came to ask Mr. Selfridge and the rest of the Addition if they don't reconsider opening their wells to the town."

"Mr. Selfridge won't reconsider anything. He's a stubborn snob."

Iper stroked his jaw slowly. *"Paklo narum colaris,"* he said.

The sheriff frowned. "What's that mean?"

"It means 'judge not until you have heard the final answer.' "

Mr. Iper walked up the gravel drive and disappeared in the direction of the side entrance.

That was Friday. Tuesday was Hallowe'en and we in the town were thankful we expected no vandalism or trouble from our juveniles beyond perhaps a few soaped windows. As for the kids of the Addition, not even soaped windows were on the docket. Those little darlings were to be entertained at a party at the Selfridge house. No messy Jack-o'-Lanterns there, no painted witches' faces. Each of the

Addition juveniles was to be furnished with a satin domino mask. All were very correct; all very proper.

Nevertheless a sense of unease settled over the town.

You could feel it underlying the unseasonal warmth of the patchwork sunshine that angled into the streets with a melancholy brilliance. You could sense it in the raucous screams of the jays that soared in the autumn sky.

It rained a little during the afternoon and toward evening a lozenge-shaped cloud-bank began to build up in the southwest. Protected by the wide eave of Sam's station, we sat and talked.

The storm held off. A white moon rose in the east and the October countryside became a woodcut of light and darker shadow. Someone suggested we walk down to Church Lake and see how high the muskrats were building their houses this year. We set off through the town and down the lake road.

Church Lake was a disc of burnished silver in the moonlight. Out from shore were a dozen or more muskrat houses.

"They're bigger all right," said Sam Kellogg. "It's going to be a cold winter."

We listened for a while to the water lapping the piles of the old dock and then we turned and headed back for town.

Abreast of the Selfridge house again we suddenly stopped. Silhouetted against the moonlight the figure of a man stood motionless in the center of the lawn. His head was thrown back, his arms were partially extended and he held in his hands something that looked like a clarinet.

"Say," said Sam Kellogg, "isn't that Mr. Iper?"

His question was never answered. At that moment peals of muffled laughter rang out from the pagoda well. Up from the shaft, like smoke in the moonlight, rose a line of dancing images. The light was deceptive and we were some distance away, but we could see they were cut-out dolls of foil, endowed, it seemed, with magic motion. As they danced over the lawn they grew to life-size, mingled with vagrant wisps of autumn miasma.

Suddenly the door of the Selfridge mansion burst open and a group of domino-masked children rushed into the moonlight. Their legs were swinging, they leaned first to one side and then to the other. When they reached a point directly before the pagoda well their laughing and shouting ceased and one by one they grasped the foil dolls and blended with them. Dolls and children became a unit.

Like a fencing master before his pupils Mr. Iper took a stand before them and then led them in a zig zag procession across the lawn. Into the road, white as a bone in the moonlight, the children followed like a troupe of ballet performers, swinging with mindless delight. To the end of the lane we watched them go; there they turned and, still following their leader, retraced their steps to the pagoda well. Sweet music poured from Mr. Iper's instrument. Around the well they danced, gesturing in high glee. And then Mr. Iper paused. All in one motion, he climbed up and over the side of the well, raised his hand as in farewell and disappeared in its depths. The dancing children followed. One by one, in blind mimicry they leaped into the well . . . and vanished.

The uproar was nation wide. For two weeks Hamilton Corners overflowed with police, sheriff and deputies, state and NSC—National Secret Constabulary—strangers, reporters and wire press men, to say nothing of TV and radio field-operatives. Mason Selfridge screamed for action, demanded that the children and Mr. Iper be found. But they were not found. And no fingerprints or identity dossier of a Paxton Iper was in existence. There was no such organization as the Third Estate Environmental Council which he claimed to represent. In a search of his room over the drug store a paper was found, written in a language no one had ever seen. Somehow this paper got into the hands of Herman Watt who, of all people, insisted he was able to translate it.

Herman said the printed words at the top meant: *On-location Inter-world Report.* He said the writing went something like this: *Thorough investigation convinces me that these people are deplorably undeveloped. They don't even know the application of the Basic Galactic Law. Action: Removal of offspring for elemented instruction.*

Herman said he wasn't sure but he thought the Basic Galactic Law was the same as the golden rule.

Open, Sesame!

Stephen Grendon

In the morning he went thoughtfully out into the woods to seek the source of the explosion he had heard in the night. He walked leisurely; at sixty-seven, he was more than ever inclined to take his time. The morning was bright with October, but the leaves were still predominantly green.

The explosion had taken place after midnight. He could not truthfully say that it had been an explosion—a low, rumbling roar had briefly awakened him. It had come from the direction of the woods behind his house, and very probably whatever it was had occurred in the vicinity of the ancient oak which brooded among the cedars. Cedar and oak, he thought, the ancient haven for gods and sprites. He had made a study of superstitions and strange religious beliefs for a seminar he had once taught at Indiana. The vagaries of faith were strange and wonderful.

Just beyond the oak he came upon a curious sight. There was manifest evidence that this was the place of the explosion—but strangely ominous evidence; it was not that the cedars were twisted and torn, as one might expect—no, they were simply not there. For a distance of over a hundred feet beyond the oak tree, the cedar trees had simply vanished. The earth was oddly wounded; it lay as if it had boiled and churned and bubbled, and then dried; and over it in the rough shape of a gigantic lozenge lay a film of grey that was neither liquid nor dust, but something grained and metallic, like a sand made of millions of grains of metal.

He estimated that more than forty trees of various heights had simply vanished; there was not even a fragment of stump left to show where they had stood. He stood looking at the scene with puzzled eyes. Being a methodical man, he groped for some basis from which to explore what he saw. He found none. Presently he took an envelope out of his pocket and scooped up some of the metallic grains, together with the earth beneath.

He took this carefully back to the house and returned to the spot with a shovel.

He dug.

No roots.

No stones.

The soil was peculiarly pulverized.

He went down three feet and found nothing before he abandoned digging.

Coming around the oak tree he saw on the ground quite close to it, on the side away from the place of the explosion, a metallic object. Something roughly octagonal, about six inches or less in diameter. It looked like platinum. He picked it up.

Someone said, "Good morning, Professor Septimus Quince."

Somewhat startled, he looked around.

There was no one within range of his vision.

"Possibly it may seem strange to you that a tree should address you so familiarly," pursued the voice. "If so, I shall be glad to address myself to you from some other point of vantage."

Amazed as he was, he was yet unaware that the octagonal piece of metal he had picked up had grown unbearably hot in his hand. He slipped it into a coat pocket, and, still looking around him, he waited for the voice to resume.

Nothing happened except a small sound of irritation that might have been wind in the oak tree.

Professor Quince made his way back to his home in unseemly haste.

"I assure you, Royde, it might have been an unnerving experience if it were not that I am fully aware of the tricks the human mind is capable of playing on one," he said that afternoon to his colleague, Professor Darrel Royde, who was in nuclear physics and extremely practical.

"Yes, of course," said Royde casually. "But the metal piece interests me. I can't tell you what it is. It resembles platinum, but it isn't that. I'd better take a sample of that dust along."

"Do, by all means."

"And if I can manage the time, I'll have a look at that place in your woods."

There was something Professor Quince was trying in vain to remember. He could not seem to bring his thoughts into focus. He sat there for a puzzled moment before he managed to ask, "What is the most recent theory about the possibility of interplanetary travel, Royde?"

"Newspaper supplement stuff," said Royde tersely.

"It does not occur to anyone that the possibility of such travel exists?" persisted Quince.

Royde shrugged. "Only the impractical and imaginative."

"I see. They are conceiving of all else as akin to us, and not considering an alteration in basic elements."

"What do you mean?"

"I mean a being not constructed like us."

"Ghosts? My dear fellow—I warned you about interesting yourself in all that rigmarole about primitive superstitions and religions."

"What is a ghost?"

Royde leaned forward and gazed intently at his companion. "Quince!" he said sharply.

"Oh, yes!" said Quince, blinking his eyes rapidly.

"You just now asked me in all seriousness what a ghost was," said Royce dryly.

"How extraordinary!"

And indeed, it was extraordinary, reflected Quince. On reflection, however, quite a number of things about this day were extraordinary. There was that troubled moment when the mirror's image had startled him; what was it he had expected to see but the image of an amiable professor of anthropology? Quite clearly he had expected to see someone else; he had never expected to see his own image there and to think for one intense moment that it was an alien who looked back at him from the glass.

"This thing appears to have the peculiar property of growing warm in the hand," said Royde.

"Yes, I noticed it. Just put it down."

"Not an alloy, I feel certain."

"No." There was a moment of silence before Quince said, with no alteration in the tone of his voice, "But, on the other hand, you did mention something about the unpredictability of static on your radio. Have you ever thought of interplanetary communication?"

Royde's jaw dropped. "My dear Quince—you *have* been unnerved!"

"Oh, yes, I have—profoundly," agreed Quince amiably.

What in the world had got into him? he asked himself after Royde had gone. He had no more interest in such fantastic subjects as interplanetary travel and communication than he had in the atonality of Schönberg. He was vaguely troubled, but he could not quite decide whether he was troubled because of his lack of interest in these subjects or because of some more obscure reason.

Approaching the mantel on his way to return the octagonal metal to that stone ledge, he was once again sharply aware of seeing himself in the mirror there as someone incredibly alien and far away. He winked his eyes shut. The mild-mannered gentleman in the glass was actually repellent to him; his appearance was so foreign that he could hardly bear to look at it. This lasted but a moment.

He put down the metal octagon and stood examining it anew. It resembled, absurdly, a very large compact, save that there appeared to be no opening in it. It was twice as thick in the middle as along its rim, though its rim was not tapered off, being as blunt as a compact's.

He put one hand on the metal, to wait for it to warm under his touch, as it always did. At the same time he raised his eyes to the mirror. A kind of shimmering was there, like heat waves rising, like a transparent flame separating object from reflection. It faded, and the face he knew came to the fore from behind it. He was aware of a beading of perspiration on his forehead.

"I am Professor Septimus Quince," he said to the glass, "ex-instructor in anthropology at Princeton. B.S. from Purdue, M.A. from Chicago, D.S. from Princeton. Single, white, aged sixty-seven. Resident at Princeton, New Jersey, United States of America, Earth. Author: *Ancient Man in the Southwestern United States, The Mayan Culture.* Member: International Anthropologists' Society. . . ."

In his daybook late that night he wrote:

"The feeling which I have experienced ever since returning from the wood today has been one of profound *dislocation.* The illusion of being spoken to by the oak tree, the extraordinary solution of the explosion of last night—which may indeed have been another illusion, the incredible conversation with Royde, the metal object which is in any case real enough, the experiences at the mirror—these are all patently a part of the affliction. Doubtless a symptom of some mental lapse which will bear inquiry. Peculiarly, I feel dislocated not only from my customary daily routine, but also from something else which as yet does not come at all clear, though there are moments of terrifying vision when I appear to see an utterly alien landscape suggestive of Egypt of the Lower Nile, though abounding in vegetation with which I am completely unfamiliar. As were it a struggle of two personalities, each striving for mastery. (Inquire of Dr. Mason relative to this symptom.) Presumably the feeling of dislocation commenced with the problem of what happened to the cedar trees, which would seem to have been reduced to powder or ashes in the same way that the soil was affected. The subjects of interplanetary travel and communication apparently do not present a problem. It would seem quite clear that the inhabitants of Earth do not look upon either as practicable, and it may be that for them interplanetary travel would afford insurmountable difficulties. The Earthling in the focus is a creature of routine habits; someone younger would have been preferable, but it was he who completed the contact which automatically released the controls. From such observations as have been practical, it would seem inescapable that the planet has none but the most elementary defenses, atomic research having only begun, though the Earthling in the focus is convinced that the present elementary status of atomic weapons foreshadows the doom of his civilization. Earthlings would appear to be possessed of few faculties warranting their survival . . ."

He stood up and went over to the mirror.

The face looking out at him was detestably alien. It was not the face to which he was accustomed. It was the face of the Earthling, Professor Septimus Quince, which was henceforth to be his own.

He put his hand on the metal octagon and waited for it to warm beneath his fingers.

In the house of Professor Darrel Royde half a mile down the road, the radio began to chatter with static. For a few moments Royde paid no attention to it. He had just received an extraordinary laboratory report on the peculiar metal grains Quince had given him. "Metal unknown. Not an alloy. Further examination will be made. Material radio-active."

The static impinged.

Before he turned the knob he reflected absently that the incessant static came in a pattern, like speech, like atonal sounds which might have meaning if one had a way of interpreting them.

On Alpha Orionis a sentient being like a shimmering flame methodically read the static:

"Geth to the Members of the Supreme Council: Mission accomplished.

"Geth to the Interplanetary Legion: Contact made. Focus open."

The Opening

Bruce Boston

Raging . . . he yanked the liquor bottle from the cabinet. He strode across the kitchen tiles, the utility room with its built-in washer and dryer. Out the back door, slamming it behind.

"Howard," she yelled, "come back here!"

Beyond her voice he could still hear the drone of the television. Damn her, he thought, damn her to hell anyway. He kept moving. Through the yard, knocking the gate open with the heel of his palm so it banged against the fence post and the length of the structure rattled. Feeling the sting upon his palm, the jarring to his elbow as a kind of satisfaction, he started up the hill which rose behind the house.

A clear night for the Valley, for anywhere in the Los Angeles Basin. Despite the city lights for miles in every direction, a smattering of stars prevailed. The climb was mostly dirt, some bushes and weeds, a few scraggly trees Howard had never been able to identify.

By the time he was halfway up he was breathing heavily. He was no longer young and each day there were reminders.

Slowing his pace he uncorked the bottle, took a pull and coughed in surprise. The mouthful erupted back onto the earth. He had meant to grab the scotch and had somehow come up with the creme de cacao. Cursing his wife once more, Howard continued to climb.

What the hell, he thought, he didn't really want to get drunk. He'd been on top of the booze for months and wasn't about to go back to it now. Of course every time he even sniffed a cork Beverly was after him about it. She was always starting something, he thought. He'd already forgotten what had set her off tonight. Sure enough it had ended with the same stupid and vicious game: each of them dredging up the past, hurling back and forth resentments stockpiled over the years of their marriage.

Howard took another drink. His face scrunched up at the unpleasant taste. He swallowed anyway.

As he neared the crest of the hill he began to wander back and forth, searching the invisible ground more by touch than sight. He found the depression, a natural seat in the hard dirt, and collapsed into it. Wedging the bottle next to his leg, he sighed deeply. This was not the first time he had found himself here after one of their battles. Not the first and he knew it wouldn't be the last. Sometimes he would kick the dirt and tear at the scratchy weeds as if he were a frustrated child. Only he had children of his own. Grandchildren.

"Bitch," he whispered to the night air.

It was quiet except for the background hum of the freeway on the far side of the hill, a noise to which Howard was so accustomed he hardly noticed it anymore. He fished a cigaret from his shirt pocket and lit up. All across the valley, singly and in irregular clumpings, the anonymous lights shone. And higher, in the sky, the faint outlines of constellations he had once studied but could no longer name. He exhaled a cloud of smoke and the slight breeze streaming up the hill caused it to rise about his head. He breathed the night. Clean, with not even an aftertaste of the smog which seemed to cling to the palate on even the clearest days. Instead, something else, a faint sweetness, like sage or honeysuckle. Maybe that's what the trees were? Honeysuckle. Only he'd never seen any blossoms.

"Bitch," he repeated to the mute trees, and took another drink.

Maybe the smell was only the creme de cacao, wafting from the open bottle.

Howard remembered how it once was. They had fled the East for California in the first year of their marriage. California, land of sunshine and opportunity. He had found his opportunities and made what he could of them . . . and they had not done badly. Each year their tans were good, their cars were new. Except for an occasional consultation he was retired, and still they were not doing badly. Yet he had discovered with the passing years that one's opportunities narrowed. There was never any turning back, he had learned that too. At times he felt trapped, when it seemed as if he could spy a way out he must bolt. As he looked across the valley at the sea of lights, he consoled himself once again with the assurance that they were **all** trapped, locked into worlds of their own making yet locked drum tight nonetheless. If freedom was what counted, then freedom was a full plate, a space of one's own.

A crushing of leaves in the bushes to his right, a heavy breathing. All at once the dog was upon him. Howard rolled back laughing as a slippery tongue fluttered against his cheek, a cold snout explored his ear. A low whistle from the same direction and the animal was bounding away. As Howard came up from the grass the sweet smell was overwhelming. He had spilled some of the liquor on himself.

"Sorry. I should have kept him on a leash." The man had come along the crest of the hill. "I didn't really expect to find anyone up here."

"That's okay," Howard laughed. "Surprised me for a second, but he's friendly enough." He could hear the dog crashing through the bushes behind him.

"Yes," the man answered, "it's in his nature."

He was slight and wore coveralls. The moon was not yet up and it was too dark to make out his features. Howard normally avoided his neighbors, expecting the same courtesy. Yet he realized that at this moment he welcomed the intrusion. Anything to take his mind off Beverly.

"Have a seat," he told the man. "It's a beautiful night."

"Yes, the stars are very bright."

The fellow sat down a few feet away, forearms resting on his knees and the dog's leash hanging between them. Despite the fact that Howard was sitting in a depression, their heads came to the same height.

"You live around here?"

"Over there." The man gestured, but Howard couldn't be sure in which direction.

"Have a drink?" Howard offered the bottle.

"No, thank you."

"Sorry, I should have brought a glass. I didn't expect to find anyone up here either. Just had a run-in with the wife and I had to get away for a while."

The man laughed. "We all have to get away sometimes."

Howard realized he must be half drunk already if he was confessing his domestic squabbles to a complete stranger. What the hell, he thought. He upended the bottle once more. "It's a beautiful night," he repeated.

"Yes, the valley is lovely."

"Not like it used to be though." Howard gestured with one arm to take in the scene before them. "I remember when half this land was orange groves, lemon trees, avocados. During the harvest you could smell them every evening. No damn pollution! And there didn't used to be a freeway over there either. It's sure not what it used to be."

"Everything changes."

That was some consolation, Howard thought. Digging in his pocket for another cigaret, he looked back at the sky. "Not everything," he said.

"Hmn?"

"The stars." Howard lit up, cupping his palms for the flame. "They're just like when I was a kid. I used to be able to name quite a few. Now I have trouble even spotting the Dipper."

"There's Polaris," the stranger pointed to the northern sky, "that's part of your Little Dipper." His hand swung to the west. "And that's the Big Dipper."

Howard could see his face more clearly now. He was young, hardly more than a kid. Yet he was completely bald. Unless he shaved his head.

"There's Procyon. Castor and Pollux, the twins. And that red one, that's Betelgeuse, in the constellation Orion."

With each pronouncement the man's forefinger seemed to jab at the heavens. There was something in his manner which Howard distrusted. He was too sure of himself. Like he was a saint or something. It all made sense, Howard thought. The shaved head. Those funny coveralls, incongruous on such a small man. There were some pretty strange religions knocking about Southern California these days.

"What are you, an astronomer or something?" Howard asked.

"Not really," the man laughed again, knowingly, "let's just say I'm interested in the stars. I've studied them. And you're wrong, you know. The stars change just like everything else. And the worlds with them. Just think, a million upon a million worlds up there, all changing."

Howard noticed that in profile the man's head was not only shaven but oddly shaped, elongated, almost like a bullet. Not far behind them the dog had found something and was pawing at the dirt. And I'm drunk, he thought, and so what? Running his finger around the grooved glass of the bottle's neck, he took another sip, allowing the liquor to pool on his tongue before swallowing.

"A million upon a million worlds." The man seemed strangely intent upon the subject of the stars. "Just think what it would be like to visit them."

"If there are even any worlds up there." Howard burped noiselessly. "We don't know for sure, do we?"

"They're up there all right. Believe me."

The knowingness again, the superiority. "Well," Howard countered, "it's not likely we'll find out in our lifetimes."

"Don't be too sure. Have you ever thought about this?" The man paused for emphasis. "People disappear all the time, sometimes without a trace. No final messages. Their bodies never turn up. Have you ever thought that maybe they've gone to the stars?"

Howard laughed. "What are you trying to tell me? That you think little green men in flying saucers are kidnapping people from Earth and taking them to other planets?"

"Let's not say kidnapping," the man answered. "Let's say 'by invitation.' And let's **not** call them little green men."

This chance conversation on a hillside was surely taking a peculiar turn, Howard thought. Then the dog was by his side once more, nuzzling his shoulder. The sweet smell was back and it was stronger than ever. It was the dog, he realized, not the creme de cacao.

Though it was not unpleasant. He ran his hand over the animal's head, tousling its fur, along its side, down the leathery spines running the length of its back.

The leathery spines running the length of its back!

Howard sat frozen in drunkenness and sudden fear while the stranger continued to speak.

"A million upon a million worlds up there. Just about any kind of world a person could want to live on. Why you could take your pick. Tell me, suppose you had the chance. Would you go?"

And then the man touched his arm and the stars in the sky, the lights of the valley, seemed to lose their moorings and come spinning toward him in a sickening rush.

He was sitting on a hillside in the San Fernando Valley. He could feel the sharpness of a rock wedged against his thigh. On one side of him was a . . . dog? . . . who smelled like honeysuckle, and he was touching its fur. On the other side, a man with a bullet-shaped head was touching his arm. There were chills, not so much running up and down his back, but lodged solidly in his shoulder blades. His vision was somewhere else. And wherever that somewhere was, the worlds were there, just as the man had promised. Changing landscapes rose up before him and fell back behind.

Rain forests with trees the size of mountains, mountains the size of moons. A green sunset on a geometric plain littered with ancient statuary, broken columns, toppled giants. Worlds still volcanic and in flux with huge slabs of rock wrenched perpendicular to the earth. Ice worlds sealed in the stillness of perpetual winter. Cities of perpetual light where thousands of strangely human configurations thronged the arching streets and colored waters flowed. Beneath a naphtha sky grey-blue tentacles reaching . . .

Howard bolted. He wrenched his arm free, staggered to his feet and began to run. Not in the direction of his house—god forbid the man should discover where he lived!—but down the opposite side of the hill, toward the freeway. He fell once on the uneven ground, but tottered to his feet once more. He kept moving.

Where the bushes grew thickest, ignoring the branches scratching his bare arms and face, he dived among them. Hugging the ground in this temporary shelter, Howard felt nausea clawing its way up his belly, the beating of his heart. Somehow he had held on to the bottle through it all and now he swallowed more of the liquor to keep down what was already there. He heard the familiar noise of the freeway, louder now, and he fastened upon it. The coming and going of ordinary people, ordinary commerce. He prayed that the animal could not track by smell like its earthly counterpart.

When Howard came to on the rough ground he thought he was having a nightmare. His head was splitting and his joints were stiff. For several moments he wasn't sure where he was. The noise of a semi passing on the freeway brought him back. He uncurled and sat up. Then he remembered the fight with his wife. The heel of his palm was sore where he had banged it against the back gate. He remembered meeting someone on the hill. Further recollection seemed to descend into a haze of drunkenness.

The moon was now up and it was easier for him to make his way. He stumbled over the crest and back down the hillside to his house. He found the television still running and he turned it off.

"Beverly," he called. "Bev!"

Off to her goddamn sister's again, he thought before falling fully clothed across the bed. Not until the next morning did he discover both cars still in the garage.

The Other Tiger

Arthur C. Clarke

It's an interesting theory," said Arnold, "but I don't see how you can ever prove it." They had come to the steepest part of the hill and for a moment Webb was too breathless to reply.

"I'm not trying to," he said when he had gained his second wind. "I'm only exploring its consequences."

"Such as?"

"Well, let's be perfectly logical and see where it gets us. Our only assumption, remember, is that the universe is infinite."

"Right. Personally I don't see what else it *can* be."

"Very well. That means there must be an infinite number of stars and planets. Therefore, by the laws of chance, every possible event must occur not merely once but an infinite number of times. Correct?"

"I suppose so."

"Then there must be an infinite number of worlds *exactly like Earth,* each with an Arnold and Webb on it, walking up this hill just as we are doing now, saying these same words."

"That's pretty hard to swallow."

"I know it's a staggering thought—but so is infinity. The thing that interests me, though, is the idea of all those other Earths that aren't exactly the same as this one. The Earths where Hitler won the War and the Swastika flies over Buckingham Palace—the Earths where Columbus never discovered America—the Earths where the Roman Empire has lasted to this day. In fact the Earths where all the great *if's* of history had different answers."

"Going right back to the beginning, I suppose, to the one in which the apeman who would have been the daddy of us all, broke his neck before he could have any children?"

"That's the idea. But let's stick to the worlds we know—the worlds containing *us* climbing this hill on this spring afternoon. Think of all our reflections on those millions of other planets. Some of them are exactly the same but every possible variation that doesn't violate the laws of logic must also exist.

"We could—we *must*—be wearing every conceivable sort of clothes—and no clothes at all. The Sun's shining here but on countless billions of those other Earths it's not. On many it's winter or summer there instead of spring. But let's consider more fundamental changes too.

"We intend to walk up this hill and down the other side. Yet think of all the things that might possibly happen to us in the next few minutes. However improbable they may be, as long as they are *possible,* then somewhere they've got to happen."

"I see," said Arnold slowly, absorbing the idea with obvious reluctance. An expression of mild discomfort crossed his features. "Then somewhere, I suppose, you will fall dead with heart failure when you've taken your next step."

"Not in *this* world." Webb laughed. "I've already refused it. Perhaps *you're* going to be the unlucky one."

"Or perhaps," said Arnold, "I'll get fed up with the whole conversation, pull out a gun and shoot you."

"Quite possibly," admitted Webb, "except that I'm pretty sure you, on this Earth, haven't got one. Don't forget, though, that in millions of those alternative worlds I'll beat you on the draw."

The path was now winding up a wooded slope, the trees thick on either side. The air was fresh and sweet. It was very quiet as though all Nature's energies were concentrated, with silent intentness, on rebuilding the world after the ruin of winter.

"I wonder," continued Webb, "how improbable a thing can get before it becomes impossible. We've mentioned some unlikely events but they're not completely fantastic. Here we are in an English country lane, walking along a path we know perfectly well.

"Yet in some universe those—what shall I call them?—*twins* of ours will walk around that corner and meet anything, absolutely anything that imagination can conceive. For as I said at the beginning, if the cosmos is infinite, then all possibilities must arise."

"So it's possible," said Arnold, with a laugh that was not quite as light as he had intended, "that we may walk into a tiger or something equally unpleasant."

"Of course," replied Webb cheerfully, warming to his subject. "If it's possible, then it's got to happen to someone, somewhere in the universe. So why not to us?"

Arnold gave a snort of disgust. "This is getting quite futile," he protested. "Let's talk about something sensible. If we don't meet a tiger round this corner I'll regard your theory as refuted and change the subject."

"Don't be silly," said Webb gleefully. "That won't refute anything. There's no way you can—"

They were the last words he ever spoke. On an infinite number of Earths an infinite number of Webbs and Arnolds met tigers friendly, hostile or indifferent. But this was not one of those Earths—it lay far closer to the point where improbability urged on the impossible.

Yet of course it was not totally inconceivable that during the night the rain-sodden hillside had caved inward to reveal an ominous cleft leading down into the subterranean world. As for *what* had laboriously climbed up that cleft, drawn towards the unknown light of day—well, it was really no more unlikely than the giant squid, the boa-constrictor or the feral lizards of the Jurassic jungle. It had strained the laws of zoological probability but not to the breaking-point.

Webb had spoken the truth. In an infinite cosmos everything must happen somewhere—including their singularly bad luck. For *it* was hungry—very hungry—and a tiger or a man would have been a small yet acceptable morsel to any one of its half dozen gaping mouths.

The Pair

Joe L. Hensley

They tell the story differently in the history stereos and maybe they are right. But for me the way the great peace came about, the thing that started us on our way to understanding, was a small thing—a human thing—and also a Knau thing.

In the late days of the hundred-year war that engulfed two galaxies we took a planet that lay on the fringe of the Knau empire. In the many years of the war this particular planet had passed into our hands twice before, had been colonized, and the colonies wiped out when the Knau empire retook the spot—as we, in turn, wiped out the colonies they had planted there—for it was a war of horror with no quarter asked, expected, or given. The last attempt to negotiate a peace had been made ten years after the war began and for the past forty years neither side had even bothered to take prisoners, except a few for the purposes of information. We were too far apart, too ideologically different, and yet we each wanted the same things, and we were each growing and spreading through the galaxies in the pattern of empire.

The name of this particular planet was Pasman and, as usual, disabled veterans had first choice of the land there. One of the men who was granted a patent to a large tract of land was Michael Dargan.

Dargan stood on a slight rise and looked with some small pride at the curved furrow lines in the dark earth. All of his tillable land had been plowed and made ready for the planting. The feeling of pride was something he had not experienced for a long time and he savored it until it soured within him. Even then he continued to stare out over his land for a long time, for when he was standing motionless he could almost forget.

The mechanical legs worked very well. At first they had been tiring to use, but in the four years since his ship had been hit he had learned to use them adequately. The scars on his body had been cut away by the plastic surgeons and his face looked almost human now, if he could trust his mirror. But any disablement leaves deeper scars than the physical ones.

He sighed and began to move toward the house in his awkward yet powerful way. Martha would have lunch ready.

The house was in sight when it happened. Some sixth sense, acquired in battle, warned him that someone was following and he turned as quickly as possible and surveyed the land behind him. He caught the glint of sunlight on metal. He let himself fall to the earth as the air flamed red around him and for a long time he lay still. His clothes smoldered in a few spots and he beat the flames out with cautious hands.

Twice more, nearby, the ground flamed red and he lay crowded into the furrow which hid him.

Martha must have heard or seen what was happening from the house for she began shooting his heavy projectile "varmint" gun from one of the windows and, by raising his head, Dargan could see the projectiles picking at the top of a small rise a hundred yards or so from him. He hoped then that she would not kill the thing that had attacked, for if it was what he thought, he wanted the pleasure for himself.

There was silence for a little while and then Martha began to shoot again from the window. He raised his head again and caught a glimpse of his attacker as it scuttled up a hill. *It was a Knau.* He felt the blood begin to race in him, the wild hate.

"Martha!" he yelled. "Stop shooting."

He got his mechanical legs underneath him and went on down to the house. She was standing in the doorway, crying.

"I thought it had gotten you."

He smiled at her, feeling a small exhilaration. "I'm all right," he said. "Give me the pro gun." He took it from her and went to

366

the small window, but it was too late. The Knau had vanished over the hill.

"Fix me some food," he said to her. "I'm going after it."

"It was a Knau, wasn't it?" She closed her eyes and shuddered, not waiting for his answer. "I've never seen one before—only the pictures. It was horrible. I think I hit it."

Dargan stared at her. "Fix me some food, I said. I'm going after it."

She opened her eyes. "Not by yourself. I'll call the village. They'll send some men up."

"By that time it will be long gone." He watched her silently for a moment, knowing she was trying to read something in him. He kept his face impassive. "Fix me some food or I will go without it," he said softly.

"You want to kill it for yourself, don't you? You don't want anyone to help you. That's why you yelled at me to stop shooting."

"Yes," he admitted. "I want to kill it myself. I don't want you to call the village after I am gone." He made his voice heavy with emphasis. "If you call the village I won't come back to you, Martha." He closed his eyes and stood swaying softly as the tension built within him. "Those things killed my parents and they have killed me. This is the first chance I've ever had to get close to one." He smiled without humor and looked down at his ruined legs. "It will be a long time dying."

The trail was easy to follow at first. She had wounded it, but he doubted if the wound were serious after he had trailed awhile. Occasionally on the bushes it had crashed through were droplets of bright, orange-red blood.

Away from the cleared area of the farm the land was heavily rolling, timbered with great trees that shut away the light of the distant, double blue suns. There was growth under the trees, plants that struggled for breathing room. The earth was soft and took tracks well.

Dargan followed slowly, with time for thought.

He remembered when his ship had been hit. He had been standing in a passageway and the space battle had flamed all around him. A young officer in his first engagement. It was a small battle— known only by the coordinates where it had happened and worth only a line or two in the official reports of the day. But it would always be etched in Dargan's brain. His ship had taken the first hit.

If he had been a little further out in the passageway he would surely have died. As it was he only half died.

He remembered catching at the bulkhead with his hands and falling sideways. There was a feeling of horrible burning and then there was nothing for a long time.

But now there was something.

He felt anticipation take hold of his mind and he breathed strongly of the warm air.

He came to a tree where it had rested, holding on with its arms. A few drops of bright blood had begun to dry on the tree and he estimated from their height on the tree that the Knau had been wounded in the shoulder. The ground underneath the tree was wrong somehow. There should be four deep indentations where its legs had dug in, but there were only three, and one of the three was shaped wrong and shallower than the others.

Though he had followed for the better part of half the day, Dargan estimated that he was not far from his farm. The Knau seemed to be following some great curving path that bordered Dargan's land.

It was beginning to grow dark enough to make the trail difficult to read. He would have to make cold camp, for to start a fire might draw the Knau back on him.

He ate the sandwiches that Martha had fixed for him and washed them down with warm, brackish water from his canteen. For a long time he was unable to go to sleep because of the excitement that still gripped him. But finally sleep came and with it—dreams. . . .

He was back on the ship again and he relived the time of fire and terror. He heard the screams around him. His father and mother were there too and the flames burned them while he watched. Then a pair of cruel, mechanical legs chased him through metal corridors, always only a step behind. He tore the mechanical legs to bits finally and threw them at Knau ships. The Knau ships fired back and there was flame again, burning, burning. . . .

Then he was in the hospital and they were bringing the others in. And he cried unashamedly when they brought in another man whose legs were gone. And he felt a pity for the man, and a pity for himself. . . .

He awoke and it was early morning. A light, misty rain had begun to fall and his face was damp and he was cold. He got up and began to move sluggishly down the trail that the Knau had left, fearing that the mist would wash it out. But it was still readable. After a while he came to a stream and drank there and refilled his canteen.

For a time he lost the trail and had to search frantically until he found it again.

By mid-suns he had located the Knau's cave hideaway and he lay below it, hidden in a clump of tall vegetation. The hideaway lay on the hill above him, a small black opening which was shielded at all angles except directly in front. The cave in the hillside was less than a mile from Dargan's home.

Several times he thought he could detect movement in the blackness that marked the cave opening. He knew that the Knau must be lying up there watching to see if it had been followed and he intended to give it ample time to think that it had gotten away without pursuit or had thrown that pursuit off.

The heat of the day passed after a long, bitter time filled with itches that could not be scratched and nonexistent insects that crawled all over Dargan's motionless body. He consoled himself with thoughts of what he would do when he had the upper hand. He hoped, with all hope, that the Knau would not resist and that he could take it unawares. That would make it even better.

He saw it for certain at the moment when dusk became night. It came out of the cave, partially hidden by the outcropping of rock that formed the shelf of the cave. Dargan lay, his body unmoving, his half-seeing eyes fascinated, while the Knau inspected the surrounding terrain for what seemed a very long time.

They're not so ugly, he told himself. *They told us in training that they were the ugliest things alive—but they have a kind of grace to them. I wonder what makes them move so stiffly?*

He watched the Knau move about the ledge of the cave. A crude bandage bound its shoulder and two of the four arms hung limply.

Now. You think you're safe.

He waited for a good hour after it had gone back inside the cave. Then he checked his projectile weapon and began the crawl up the hillside. He went slowly. Time had lost its meaning. *After this is done you have lost the best thing.*

He could see the light when he got around the first bend of the cave. It flickered on the rock walls of the cave. Dargan edged forward very carefully, clearing the way of tiny rocks so that his progress would be noiseless. The mechanical legs dragged soundlessly behind him, muffled in the trousers that covered them.

There was a fire and the Knau lay next to it. Dargan could see its chest move up and down as it gulped for air, its face tightened with pain. Another Knau, a female, was tending the wound, and Dargan felt exultation.

Two!

He swung the gun on target and it made a small noise against the cave floor. Both of the Knau turned to face him and there was a moment of no movement as they stared at him and he stared back. His hands were wet with perspiration. He knew, in that instant, that they were not going to try to do anything—to fight. They were only waiting for him to pull the trigger.

The fire flickered and his eyes became more used to the light. For the first time he saw the male Knau's legs and knew the reason for the strangeness of the tracks. The legs were twisted, and two of the four were missing. A steel aid was belted around the Knau's body, to give it balance, making a tripod for walking. The two legs that were left were cross-hatched with the scars of imperfect plastic surgery.

Dargan pulled himself to his feet, still not taking the gun off the two by the fire. He saw the male glance at the metallic limbs revealed beneath his pants cuff. And he saw the same look come into the Knau's eyes that he knew was in his own.

Then carefully Dargan let the safety down on the pro gun and went to help the female in treating the male.

It should have ended there of course. For what does one single act, a single forgiveness by two, mean in a war of a hundred years? And it would have ended if the Knau empire had not taken that particular small planet back again and if the particular Knau that Dargan had tracked and spared had not been one of the mighty ones—who make decisions, or at least influence them.

But that Knau was.

But before the Knau empire retook Pasman it meant something too. It meant a small offering of flowers on Dargan's doorstep the morning following the tracking and, in the year before they came again, a friendship. It meant waking without hate in the mornings and it meant the light that came into Martha's eyes.

And Dargan's peace became our peace.

/S/ Samuel Cardings,
Gen. (Ret.) TA
Ambassador to Knau Empire

Paths

Edward Bryant

The reefs and domes of City South gleamed beneath the stars. It was late night; little traffic disturbed the waterways. On the top level of the *Harbinger-Communicator's* dome, a single office was occupied. Soft ultraviolet spilled out through the wall apertures.

"Just who the hell are you, really?" Morisel sank back in the warm fluid. His visitor stood and lumbered to the edge of the newsman's meditation pool.

"Think of me as a distant relative." The words grated across the edges of his serrated beak. "A good many generations removed."

"Look," said Morisel. "I don't want to seem cynical. You may be my ten-times-removed egg-father or something, but right now it's awfully hard not to believe you're just a run-of-the-mill aberrant. I mean, here you crawl into my office close to midnight, spread yourself down, and then calmly announce you're a traveler from the future. That takes either incredible gall, or. . . ."

"I spoke truth," said Morisel's visitor. He towered over the reclining newsman. The writhing cilia around his beak settled in no specific emotion; sincerity flashed briefly, before collapsing back to chaos.

"Don't try to intimidate me," Morisel snapped. The self-proclaimed time traveler moved back. The newsman tried to assume conciliatory signals. There might be a feature-story here, he speculated. *What the hell, the silly season may as well start early.*

"Some sort of alien being from another planet, I might accept," said Morisel. "If he had suitable proof. It's unlikely, but scientifically possible. Now time travel? No. That's out."

"Your skepticism is laudable," replied the man. He settled himself on his lower coil of tentacles. "I suppose logic is one of the attributes that has made you so successful in your profession. But don't let it trap you in blind dogmatism."

"All right," said Morisel. "Well, I'm doing my best to be understanding." He played abstractedly with a stylus. "Then supposing you *are* from the future, what are you doing back here?"

The visitor's voice reverberated hollowly. "I have returned many millennia to warn you. I realize that sounds rather melodramatic, but it is essentially the substance of my mission."

"Oh?" Morisel glanced at his chronometer and suppressed an expression of annoyance. "Warn me of what?" He roughly sketched a cartilaginous skull on the gell pad beside his electric scriptor.

The traveler folded a row of extensipods, the limbs angling stiffly. "I did not come back to warn specifically you. Rather I am, or at least I have been, trying to alert your entire world."

"What do you mean, 'have been trying'?" Morisel asked. "You tried to contact others?"

"Thus far, only one." The man's cilia settled grimly. "A fellow in the communications field, one of your acquaintances, I believe. His name is Connot."

"Des Connot?" Morisel, startled, looked up. "The office said he left the *Sentinel* for extended recreation. I wondered. . . ."

"Connot is confined."

"Des?"

"His price for believing my story."

Slightly shaken, the newsman erased the skull on his gell pad and drew a pattern of interlocking circles. "All right, just because Connot turned aberrant doesn't mean anything. I can't believe a good reporter like Des would come apart just because of a ghost story or something." He paused, expecting his words to draw the man across the pool into a response. The bait failed; the man only stared silently back at Morisel.

372

"Go ahead and tell it," Morisel said finally. "Whatever you've got."

"You still do not believe me," said the traveler. "Not yet, anyway, but you will." He uncrossed his extensipods and slid closer to the pool.

"Suppose, Brother Morisel," he began. "Suppose that time is analogous to a current. I imagine you are at least vaguely familiar with the concept?"

"More or less. Sunday supplement stuff."

"Indeed. But the image of time as a river is essentially accurate. It is a flow which contains certain points that are crucial to the past and future. These dates are like forks in a current; they are points when history may have alternative destinies. Sometimes these circumstances can be manipulated."

Morisel listened attentively. He drew another skull on the gell pad.

"It is because of a critical fork approaching in your time-stream that I was chosen by my colleagues to travel here," the man continued. His voice rasped harshly. "This, you see, is an experiment—a trial born of desperation. The approaching split in the time-stream is critical. My mission is to influence its direction, to utilize any means so that your people follow one certain branch of the divergence."

"It sounds ambitious," said Morisel.

"Perhaps it is impossible. My colleagues and I have never before tried such an experiment. Interference, with the attendant paradoxes, could prove dangerous for all the alternate futures."

"So why this one now?" asked Morisel. His notepad displayed the silhouette of a sandclock superimposed on the skull.

"Desperation. This approaching point of divergence is utterly crucial to mankind's future. It is imperative that my efforts ensure the choice of a certain path—and deny existence to the other possibility. This is my mission—to make sure that your people take the better of two possible courses."

Morisel realized he was beginning to lose a measure of his skepticism. The stranger's voice, for all its stilted syntax, struck a premonitory chord. The newsman's tentacles began to widen the lines of the skull.

"Let me describe a possible future awaiting you, Brother

Morisel. One of the problems receiving much popular attention in this time is the pollution of our natural environment; correct?"

Morisel registered agreement. "Ecology."

"That desperately vital balance between sentient being and this planet is about to break down. You have hesitated too long. The rape of your world should have been interrupted long before."

Morisel started to speak, but his visitor waved an extensipod. "Please hear me out. Air and water, all are irreparably poisoned. Unnamed terrors are about to ride the planet. The tiny diatoms will die first. Then the smaller beings, the plants, finally yourselves. There will be oases of a fashion, for a while. Then the scramble for life will pit bands of survivors against each other. Thermonuclear weapons, poisons, bacteriological bombs will be used. It will be madness.

"There will be nearly no life left on a virtually sterile world. If ever a similar civilization rises, it will not be for hundreds of millions of years. That is how far ahead our probability scanners can operate. The world will remain a bleak cinder."

Morisel was shaken by the conviction in his visitor's voice. The portrait of civilization's self-destruction had been suitably graphic. "Consider," he said, "if you're from the future, then you must be from the other branch of our time-stream where life evidently wasn't wiped out. Is that our other choice—your own future? Is that our chance to avoid the world's destruction?"

The man opened his beak, then paused. A silver glow began to surround his body and the amorphous lines of his form wavered.

"I am sorry, Brother Morisel." The words seemed to come from a great distance. "I fear my power resources are more greatly depleted than I realized; I can no longer maintain the mask." The nimbus intensified and deepened to a mirror-bright haze obscuring the stranger from Morisel's fascinated gaze.

Then the luminous mist vanished and Morisel looked upon his visitor's actual face.

"Do you really want to know what the other path is?" asked the being. "The tale I have already told you is the one that I am working with all dedication to bring into reality; your final, total suicide is the optimistic view. Are you sure you want to hear the other alternative, the pessimistic choice?"

Morisel stared at the matted hair, the clumsy anthropoid form reared erect on its hind limbs. He didn't answer. He began to scream.

Punch

Frederick Pohl

The fellow was over seven feet tall and when he stepped on Buffie's flagstone walk one of the stones split with a dust of crushed rock. "Too bad," he said sadly. "I apologize very much. Wait."

Buffie was glad to wait, because Buffie recognized his visitor at once. The fellow flickered, disappeared and in a moment was there again, now about five feet two. He blinked with pink eyes. "I materialize so badly," he apologized. "But I will make amends. May I? Let me see. Would you like the secret of transmutation? A cure for simple virus diseases? A list of twelve growth stocks with spectacular growth certainties inherent in our development program for your planet, that is, the Earth?"

Buffie said he would take the list of growth stocks, hugging himself and fighting terribly to keep a straight face. "My name is Charlton Buffie," he said, extending a hand gladly. The alien took it curiously, and shook it, and it was like shaking hands with a shadow.

"You will call me 'Punch,' please," he said. "It is not my name but it will do, because after all this projection of my real self is only a sort of puppet. Have you a pencil?" And he rattled off the names of twelve issues Buffie had never heard of.

That did not matter in the least. Buffie knew that when the aliens gave you something it was money in the bank. Look what they had given the human race. Faster-than-light space ships, power sources from hitherto non-radioactive elements like silicon, weapons of great force and metalworking processes of great suppleness. His wife's aunt's brother-in-law, the colonel, was even now off in space somewhere in a highly armed space ship built according to their plans.

Buffie thought of ducking into the house for a quick phone call to his broker, but instead he invited Punch to look around his apple orchard. Make the most of every moment, he said to himself, every moment with one of these guys is worth ten thousand dollars. "I would enjoy your apples awfully," said Punch, but he seemed disappointed. "Do I have it wrong? Don't you and certain friends plan a sporting day, as Senator Wenzel advised me?"

"Oh, sure! Certainly. Good old Walt told you about it, did he? Yes." That was the thing about the aliens, they liked to poke around in human affairs. They said when they came to Earth that they wanted to help us, and all they asked of us in return was that they be permitted to study our ways. It was nice of them to be so interested, and it was nice of Walt Wenzel, Buffie thought, to send the alien along to him. "We're going after mallard, down to Little Egg, some of the boys and me. There's Chuck—he's the mayor here, and Jer—Second National Bank, you know, and Padre—"

"That is it!" cried Punch. "To see you shoot the mallard." He pulled out an Esso road map, overtraced with golden raised lines, and asked Buffie to point out where Little Egg was. "I cannot focus well enough to stay in a moving vehicle," he said, blinking in a regretful way. "Still, I can meet you there. If, that is, you wish—"

"I do! I do! I do!" Buffie was painfully exact in pointing out the place. Punch's lips moved silently, translating the golden lines into polar space-time coordinates, and he vanished just as the station wagon with the rest of the boys came roaring into the carriage drive with a hydromatic spatter of gravel.

The boys were extremely impressed. Padre had seen one of the aliens once, at a distance, drawing pictures of the skaters in Rockefeller Center, but that was the closest any of them had come. "God! What luck." "Did you get a super-hairpin from him, Buffie?" "Or a recipe for a nyew, smyooth Martini with dust on it?" "Not Buffie, fellows! He probably held out for something *real* good, like six new ways to—oh, excuse me, Padre." "But seriously, Buffie, these people are unpredictably generous. Look how they built that dam in Egypt! Has this Punch given you anything?"

Buffie grinned wisely as they drove along, their shotguns firmly held between their knees. "Damn it," he said mildly, "I forgot to bring cigarettes. Let's stop at the Blue Jay Diner for a minute." The cigarette machine at the Blue Jay was out of sight of the parking lot, and so was the phone booth.

It was too bad, he reflected, to have to share everything with the boys, but on the other hand he already had his growth stocks. Anyway there was plenty for everyone. Every nation on Earth had its silicon-drive space ships now, fleets of them milling about on maneuvers all over the Solar System. With help from the star-people, an American expedition had staked out enormous radium beds on Callisto, the Venezuelans had a diamond mountain on Mercury, the Soviets owned a swamp of purest penicillin near the South Pole of Venus. And individuals had done very well too. A ticket-taker at Steeplechase Park explained to them the reason why the air jets blew up ladies' skirts, and they tipped him with a design for a springless safety pin that was earning him a million dollars a month in royalties. An usherette at La Scala became the cosmetic queen of Europe for showing three of them to their seats. They gave her a simple painless eye dye, and now 99% of Milan's women had bright blue eyes from her salon.

All they wanted to do was help. They said they came from a planet very far away and they were lonely and they wanted to help us make the jump into space. It would be fun, they promised, and would help to end poverty and war between nations, and they would have company in the void between the stars. Politely and deferentially they gave away secrets worth trillions, and humanity burst with a shower of gold into the age of plenty.

Punch was there before them, inspecting the case of bourbon hidden in their blind. "I am delighted to meet you, Chuck, Jer, Bud, Padre and of course Buffie," he said. "It is kind of you to take a stranger along on your fun. I regret I have only some eleven minutes to stay."

Eleven minutes! The boys scowled apprehensively at Buffie. Punch said, in his wistful voice, "If you will allow me to give you a memento, perhaps you would like to know that three grams of common table salt in a quart of Crisco, exposed for nine minutes to the radiations from one of our silicon reactors, will infallibly remove warts." They all scribbled, silently planning a partnership corporation, and Punch pointed out to the bay where some tiny dots rose and fell with the waves. "Are those not the mallards you wish to shoot?"

"That's right," said Buffie glumly. "Say, you know what I was thinking? I was thinking—that transmutation you mentioned before—I wonder—"

"And are these the weapons with which you kill the birds?" He examined Padre's ancient over-and-under with the silver chasing. "Extremely lovely," he said. "Will you shoot?"

"Oh, not *now*," said Buffie, scandalized. "We can't do that. That transmutation—"

"It is extremely fascinating," said the star-man, looking at them with his mild pink eyes and returning the gun. "Well. I may tell you, I think, what we have not announced. A surprise. We are soon to be present in the flesh, or near at any rate."

"Near?" Buffie looked at the boys and the boys looked at him; there had been no suggestion of this in the papers and it almost took their minds off the fact that Punch was leaving. He nodded violently, like the flickering of a bad fluorescent lamp.

"Near indeed, in a relative way," he said. "Perhaps some hundreds of millions of miles. My true body, of which this is only a projection, is at present in one of our own interstellar ships now approaching the orbit of Pluto. The American fleet, together with those of Chile, New Zealand and Costa Rica, is there practicing with its silicon-ray weapons and we will shortly make contact with them for the first time in a physical way." He beamed. "But only six minutes remain," he said sadly.

"That transmutation secret you mentioned—" Buffie began, recovering his voice.

"Please," said Punch, "may I not watch you hunt? It is a link between us."

"Oh, do you shoot?" asked Padre.

The star-man said modestly, "We have but little game. But we love it. Won't you show me your ways?"

Buffie scowled. He could not help thinking that twelve growth stocks and a wart-cure were small pickings from the star-men, who had given wealth, weapons and the secret of interstellar travel. "We can't," he growled, his voice harsher than he intended. "We don't shoot sitting birds."

378

Punch gasped with delight. "Another bond between us! But now I must go to our fleet for the—hum. For the surprise." He began to shimmer like a candle. "Neither do we," he said, and went out.

The Rebel Slug

Basil Wells

U ncharted asteroid dead ahead," sang out the watch in the control blister of the *Gallun.*

The ten passengers, and the four remaining members of the *Gallun's* crew, boiled forward to inspect the tiny speck of matter that came swimming toward them. Perhaps they could make contact with this lifeless lump of chill metal and rocks and find enough frozen oxygen to replenish their dwindling supply.

Here at least would be a place to repair the sheared-off rocket jets, and their outer sheathings—used to encase the heat-resistant troxodite of the jets—might be replaced with metal from the asteroid's deposits.

As they drifted, powerless, nearer the unknown body the Skipper cried out in amazement. In a sunken rift there lay a meteor-riddled space ship of archaic design. Here would be material in plenty for the swift repair of the *Gallun.*

"Twenty-second century ship," he rumbled.

Closer they moved. They could make out the name of the quaint old vessel at last.

"The *Arnheim*," mused an excessively blondined female passenger. "Idealistic writer, Old Germany. Three centuries or longer."

Mutual gravity gripped the orphan blobs of matter. They drifted more rapidly together. There was a dull thud of airless impact telegraphed back along the *Gallun's* metal framework, and then the damaged ship came to rest on a near-even keel.

Space suits were broken out for the crew and for three passengers who volunteered, and work was started on two of the ruined jets. The *Arnheim*'s battered hulk was nearby and the Skipper went over toward it to learn what could be salvaged there.

Inside the asteroid opened a great, hollowed-out cavity. There was no horizon—the walls curved upward and overhead. Everywhere up there 2ARE could see the identical little huddles of his race's dwelling places.

Dua Ree, as he liked to call himself, was a formless, ugly blob of yellowish-gray. He owned two arms, two legs, and a lump that served as his head. His whole body and face was formless and featureless. It was as though his flesh had been overflowed by a spongy layer of rubber or opaque, impure plastic.

Now he walked over toward the ancient gateway to the outer emptiness from which his people had escaped in ages past. He spent much time at the lock peering out through its transparent ports at the endless reaches of space. He dreamed of the exotic huge worlds rolling majestically along their appointed course about fiery Sol.

Dua Ree was a dreamer, an uncertain thinker of antisocial thoughts. He had read many of the forbidden books smuggled from the space ship by some ancient rebel, that he had come across, while his fellows slept. To them, of course, he was only one more of their colorless, antlike community. Only the legend, 2ARE, stamped in dull purple ink across his front, belonged to him.

But within that shapeless bulk lived Dua Ree, the dauntless space explorer—the brave explorer of a dozen new savage planets.

Some of the books from the abandoned spacer were magazines smuggled aboard by the crew members and left behind, as worthless trash by the single-minded pioneers. Dua Ree read the stories of ancient writers dealing with fictional heroes of the spaceways and he ached to emulate them. He saw illustrations of men and women from his home world, and he wondered if he too resembled them beneath this ugly covering that he had always worn.

For the sluglike appearance of the asteroid's inhabitants was artificial. From the moment of birth a flexible spongy suit of hideous pseudo-rubber was worn continuously. Even in death it was not removed.

This helped them to achieve such uniformity of appearance and character that only their numbers marked them apart.

The men from crowded green Earth who had founded this lost

perfectionist colony were not content that all things, good or bad, be shared in common. They had determined that any superior strength, beauty, or other physical characteristic must be buried for the good of the whole community. And after three centuries of practice their theory seemed to be correct—all the human slugs looked, acted, and even thought alike.

Save for a few half-hearted rebels like Dua Ree they were no more human than a swarm of bees or a flock of sheep.

So now Dua Ree was looking forlornly out through the port.

A whimper of terror was in his throat as a black shape was suddenly blocking his vision. He backed away. His heart was thudding madly.

But there was something familiar about the alien shape. Yes! The illustrations in the thinner books! Space suits as the artists pictured them in the future. Not exactly the same. This was no bulky, knobbed collection of hardware and plastics. This was a thin, transparent balloon and the warmly clad shape of a man was within it!

Dimly the Skipper saw a humanoid shape within the lock set into the cliff beside the *Arnheim*. That it was a human being he was certain—only the men of Earth had penetrated into this sector of outer space. Perhaps a descendant of the old *Arnheim*'s survivors he surmised, living a precarious existence in some air-filled cavity of the tiny world.

He motioned for the man to open the inner lock and permit him to enter. The man seemed reluctant to obey but eventually the thick, round outer door groaned open. Escaping air frosted the barrier thinly.

"Poor devil," he muttered. "So stunned by the realization that rescue is at hand that he can barely move."

He closed the outer lock. He felt the pressure of air that built up about him. At approximately four pounds the inner lock inched slowly open and a four-limbed slug-creature came obscenely toward him.

The Skipper's boltray leaped into his grip. He backed toward the outer lock. What sort of devilish beast was this?

Then his audiophones picked up the ragged words of the thing. He could understand them! This was perhaps some subhuman creature of the asteroid domesticated and trained by the Earthmen. It was identifying itself.

"Take me to your master, Dua Ree," he said, slipping his head through the unsealed top of his now-deflated suit.

"No masters in Coom," came the slug-thing's ghastly muffled voice. "We all alike. Little, yes, big, yes. But all alike."

"You do not understand, Dua Ree. I mean people like myself."

"I am like you," said Dua Ree. "I too wish to visit the stars. I would like to go Mars, Venus, Mercury. My people from Earth."

"Your people," said the Skipper quickly. "Take me to them."

"Perhaps they not like you," demurred Dua Ree. "You look like monster to them. They not see pictures of Earthmen like me. They fear—maybe kill you. Then I never get to see Earth."

"Go along with you," barked the Skipper impatiently at the small slug-being. "They will be glad to see me."

The shapeless creature shrugged what should have been shoulders and led the way down a rocky slope toward a huddle of rudely constructed stone huts. A crooked path, worn deep into the dusty soil of the asteroid's inner skin, rumbled among irrigated sunken patches of vegetables and cereals toward a squat building of grayish stone blocks and boulders.

"Here we grow our young," he announced.

The Skipper saw a series of once-transparent, time-stained tanks ranged along the inner walls. Inside these cloudy warm cells he saw human infants in all stages of development from the foetus upward. He felt reassured by what he saw. There must be a number of human beings in this hidden inner world.

Dua Ree then led the way toward the village. Up ahead there was a stir of movement and then two larger slug creatures moved up the dusty path toward him. Old they must have been for their blubbery bodies sagged yet more shapelessly than that of Dua Ree. Some strange disease, also, seemed to have eaten away or corroded patches of their yellowish claylike flesh.

They carried crooked metal bars as weapons.

"Proctors!" murmured Dua Ree. "The time of sleep is ended."

"What monster is this you have found, 2ARE?" the proctors grunted, their metal clubs upraised menacingly.

"A man from Earth," Dua Ree told them.

"It does not look like a man," one of the proctors grumbled. "Its covering is misshapen. There are useless appendages upon its head. You are deceived. This is a monster—an animal!"

"It can talk," Dua Ree insisted stubbornly.

"It is not a man." Both proctors said this loudly. "We must capture it. It will supply food for all of us."

"Nothing doing," the Skipper snapped out, his space-darkened hand slipping about the comforting ridged grip of his boltray. "I wish to see your masters at once. Take me to them."

The two creatures gasped. Their ugly blobby heads touched. There was an angry exchange of conversation.

"There are no masters in Coom," one of them announced. "We all the same. All of us be men."

The Skipper thought hard for a moment. These untidy monsters of the asteroid must have destroyed the human beings who domesticated them. Yet, why were there human babies in the incubation vats if that was the case? He scowled. Could it be that mutation, over the long centuries of exposure within the poor shielding of the asteroid's shell, acted to change those perfectly formed babies into these travesties of humankind?

One thing was certain. There was nothing to be gained by antagonizing the slug creatures needlessly.

"I am going back to the ship," he told Dua Ree, briskly, and turned to retrace his steps to the locks.

Abruptly he realized that while they had been talking a swarm of the faceless slug-things had gathered about him. Slowly they were closing in. The stench of foul bodies, many of them marred with loathsome patches of decaying yellowish hide, was strong in his nostrils.

The boltray leaped into his hand. He lifted it.

"Get back," he commanded, "before I blast you!"

Dua Ree cried out in protest. He flung himself before the Skipper.

"Do not hurt them," he whispered. "They never see real Earthman before. Your muscles strong. Spring over their heads. Go back to the ship. I will come to you later."

Like some mindless pack of animals the slug people closed in about the Skipper and Dua Ree. The man reluctantly slipped his weapon back into its holster and closed the retaining flap. He tensed for the leap. Dua Ree was right. No need to ray down the bloblike monsters. Perhaps later they could be tamed again.

The two proctors launched themselves at him. His hard fist crashed twice into their pulpy flesh and they went spinning away a dozen yards or more. The Skipper grinned. Then he sprang into the air toward the airlock, high above their heads.

He had been aching to fight someone since his ignoble defeat by the space pirates had left him undermanned, the ship crippled, and his cargo gone. His knuckles tingled pleasantly.

He went rocketing over the building of the incubator vats and touched ground lightly on the slope below the airlock. His many years of travel in weightlessness had trained his muscles and brain to gauge his speed and attitude correctly.

The Skipper turned to look back at the seething mass of sluggishly moving, bewildered asteroid dwellers. A single pursuer was bounding slowly up after him. He saw the blotchy number and smiled. It was Dua Ree. He had decided to join him now rather than later.

He waited for the small monster to join him.

Dua Ree tightened the last corroded fitting of the ancient space suit that was kept inside the lock. He signaled to the Skipper that he was ready. Slowly the outer lock swung open and the two of them shuffled out upon the airless rockiness of the asteroid's exterior.

He waddled slowly along at the Skipper's elbow. It was an uncomfortable way to travel. The suit was too large and it was leaking slowly, and chilling.

They came to the *Gallun* at last and were admitted quickly. The Skipper told his story and then all of the crew and passengers gathered about Dua Ree. At last he had an opportunity to explain the strange appearance of himself and his people. Then he asked for a knife to slit and tear apart the hateful body covering.

"Now I go see the planets," said Dua Ree in his high boyish voice as the Skipper led him to the privacy of his cabin. "I go with you in ship. I learn to navigate. I find pretty girls on Earth and Mars and kiss. I explore new worlds."

"Sure, sure," agreed the Skipper, grinning at him in a friendly fashion as he handed over a knife. They both started cutting.

As they stripped away the hideous yellow-gray covering Dua Ree discovered how resilient the synthetic plastron shell could be. It was porous yet incredibly tough, but little by little they cleared his legs and arms and started on his torso. White flesh gleamed patchily through the accumulated grime of years.

The Skipper tore away a great section of the artificial covering from Dua Ree's chest—and the breath caught suddenly in his throat. Dua Ree heard the gasping sound. Then the Skipper eased a whistle slowly through his teeth.

Dua Ree slipped the hollow mask that capsuled his head free at last and long reddish hair flooded down upon his white shoulders. He smiled up at the Skipper and wrinkled up his nose.

"That feels better," he announced, sniffing deeply. "I feel almost human at last."

Then his eyes followed those of the startled Skipper and his hands came slowly up to his chest.

"You're a woman—a girl!" cried the Skipper. "All these years—and you didn't know it."

Tears flooded Dua Ree's eyes. Did this mean the end of her dreams of conquering and exploring space? Or was there to be a new dream?

A dream that included the stalwart, pale-haired Skipper perhaps?

The Remorseful

Cyril M. Kornbluth

It does not matter when it happened. This is because he was alone and time had ceased to have any meaning for him. At first he had searched the rubble for other survivors, which kept him busy for a couple of years. Then he wandered across the continent in great, vague quarterings, but the plane one day would not take off and he knew he would never find anybody anyway. He was by then in his forties, and a kind of sexual delirium overcame him. He searched out and pored over pictures of women, preferring leggy, high-breasted types. They haunted his dreams; he brooded incessantly with closed eyes, tears leaking from them and running down his filthy bearded face. One day that phase ended for no reason and he took up his wanderings again, on foot. North in the summer, south in the winter on weed-grown U.S. 1, with the haversack of pork and beans on his shoulders, usually talking as he trudged, sometimes singing.

It does not matter when it happened. This is because the Visitors were eternal; endless time stretched before them and behind, which mentions only two of the infinities of infinities that their "lives" included. Precisely when they arrived at a particular planetary system was to them the most trivial of irrelevancies. Eternity was theirs; eventually they would have arrived at all of them.

They had won eternity in the only practical way: by outnumbering it. Each of the Visitors was a billion lives as you are a billion lives—the billion lives, that is, of your cells. But your cells have made the mistake of specializing. Some of them can only contract and relax. Some can only strain urea from your blood. Some can only load, carry and unload oxygen. Some can only transmit minute electrical pulses and others can only manufacture chemicals in a desperate attempt to keep the impossible Rube Goldberg mechanism that you are from breaking down. They never succeed and you always do. Perhaps before you break down some of your specialized cells unite with somebody else's specialized cells and grow into another impossible, doomed contraption.

The Visitors were more sensibly arranged. Their billion lives were not cells but small, unspecialized, insect-like creatures linked by an electromagnetic field subtler than the coarse grapplings that hold you together. Each of the billion creatures that made up a Visitor could live and carry tiny weights, could manipulate tiny power tools, could carry in its small round black head enough brain cells to feed, mate, breed and work—and a few million more brain cells that were pooled into the field which made up the Visitor's consciousness.

When one of the insects died there were no rites; it was matter-of-factly pulled to pieces and eaten by its neighboring insects while it was still fresh. It mattered no more to the Visitor than the growing of your hair does to you, and the growing of your hair is accomplished only by the deaths of countless cells.

"Maybe on Mars!" he shouted as he trudged. The haversack jolted a shoulder blade and he arranged a strap without breaking his stride. Birds screamed and scattered in the dark pine forests as he roared at them: "Well, why not? There must of been ten thousand up there easy. Progress, God damn it! That's *progress,* man! Never thought it'd come in my time. But you'd think they would of sent a ship back by now so a man wouldn't feel so all alone. You know better than that, man. You know God-damned good and well it happened up there too. We had Northern Semisphere, they had Southern Semisphere so you know God-damned good and well what happened up there. Semisphere? Hemisphere. Hemi-semi-demisphere."

That was a good one, the best one he'd come across in years. He roared it out as he went stumping along.

When he got tired of it he roared: "You should of been in the *Old* Old Army, man. We didn't go in for this Liberty Unlimited crock in the *Old* Old Army. If you wanted to march in step with somebody else you *marched* in step with somebody else, man. None of this crock about you march out of step or twenty lashes from the sergeant for limiting your liberty."

That was a good one too, but it made him a little uneasy. He tried to remember whether he had been in the army or had just heard about it. He realized in time that a storm was blowing up from his depths; unless he headed it off he would soon be sprawled on the broken concrete of U.S. 1, sobbing and beating his head with his fists. He went back hastily to *Sem*-isphere, *Hem*-isphere, *Hem-i-sem-i-dem*-isphere, roaring it at the scared birds as he trudged.

There were four Visitors aboard the ship when it entered the planetary system. One of them was left on a cold outer planet rich in metal outcrops to establish itself in a billion tiny shelters, build a billion tiny forges and eventually—in a thousand years or a million; it made no difference—construct a space ship, fission into two or more Visitors for company, and go Visiting. The ship had been getting crowded; as more and more information was acquired in its voyaging it was necessary for the swarms to increase in size, breeding more insects to store the new facts.

The three remaining Visitors turned the prow of their ship toward an intermediate planet and made a brief, baffling stop there. It was uninhabited except for about ten thousand entities—far fewer than one would expect, and certainly not enough for an efficient first-contact study. The Visitors made for the next planet sunward after only the sketchiest observation. And yet that sketchy observation of the entities left them figuratively shaking their heads. Since the Visitors had no genitals they were in a sense without emotions—but you would have said a vague air of annoyance hung over the ship nevertheless.

They ruminated the odd facts that the entities had levitated, appeared at the distance of observation to be insubstantial, appeared at the distance of observation to be unaware of the Visitors. When you are a hundred-yard rippling black carpet moving across a strange land, when the dwellers in this land soar aimlessly about you and above you, you expect to surprise, perhaps to frighten at first, and at least to provoke curiosity. You do not expect to be ignored.

They reserved judgment pending analysis of the sunward planet's entities—possibly colonizing entities, which would explain the sparseness of the outer planet's population, though not its indifference.

They landed.

He woke and drank water from a roadside ditch. There had been a time when water was *the* problem. You put three drops of iodine in a canteen. Or you boiled it if you weren't too weak from dysentery. Or you scooped it from the tank of a flush toilet in the isolated farmhouse with the farmer and his wife and their kids downstairs grotesquely staring with their empty eye sockets at the television screen for the long-ago-spoken latest word. Disease or dust or shattering supersonics broadcast from the bull horn of a low-skimming drone—what did it matter? Safe water was what mattered.

"But hell," he roared, "it's all good now. Hear that? The rain in the ditches, the standing water in the pools, it's all good now. You should have been Lonely Man back when the going was bad, fella, when the bull horns still came over and the stiffs shook when they did and Lonely Man didn't die but he wished he could . . ."

This time the storm took him unaware and was long in passing. His hands were ragged from flailing the broken concrete and his eyes were so swollen with weeping that he could hardly see to shoulder his sack of cans. He stumbled often that morning. Once he fell and opened an old scar on his forehead, but not even that interrupted his steady, mumbling chant: " 'Tain't no boner, 'tain't no blooper; Corey's Gin brings super stupor. We shall conquer; we will win. Back our boys with Corey's Gin. Wasting time in war is sinful; black out fast with a Corey skinful."

They landed.

Five thousand insects of each "life" heaved on fifteen thousand wires to open the port and let down the landing ramp. While they heaved a few hundred felt the pangs of death on them. They communicated the minute all-they-knew to blank-minded standby youngsters, died and were eaten. Other hundreds stopped heaving briefly, gave birth and resumed heaving.

The three Visitors swarmed down the ramp, three living black carpets. For maximum visibility they arranged themselves in three thin black lines which advanced slowly over the rugged terrain. At the tip of each line a few of the insects occasionally strayed too far from their connecting files and dropped out of the "life" field. These staggered in purposeless circles. Some blundered back into the field; some did not and died, leaving a minute hiatus in the "life's" memory—perhaps the shape of the full-stop symbol in the written language of a planet long ago visited, long ago dust. Normally the thin line was not used for exploring any but the smoothest terrain; the fact that they took a small calculated risk was a measure of the Visitors' slightly irked curiosity.

With three billion faceted eyes the Visitors saw immediately that this was no semideserted world, and that furthermore it was probably the world which had colonized the puzzling outer planet. Entities were everywhere; the air was thick with them in some places. There were numerous artifacts, all in ruins. Here the entities of the planet clustered, but here the bafflement deepened. The artifacts were all decidedly material and ponderous—but the entities were insubstantial. Coarsely-organized observers would not have perceived them consistently. They existed in a field similar to the organization-field of the Visitors. Their bodies were constructs of wave-trains rather than atoms. It was impossible to imagine them manipulating the materials of which the artifacts were composed.

And as before, the Visitors were ignored.

Deliberately they clustered themselves in three huge black balls, with the object of being as obstreperous as possible and also to mobilize their field strength for a brute-force attempt at communication with the annoying creatures. By this time their attitude approximated: "We'll show these bastards!"

They didn't—not after running up and down every spectrum of thought in which they could project. Their attempt at reception was more successful, and completely horrifying. A few weak, attenuated messages did come through to the Visitors. They revealed the entities of the planet to be dull, whimpering cravens, whining evasively, bleating with self-pity. Though there were only two sexes among them, a situation which leads normally to a rather weak sex drive as such things go in the cosmos, these wispy things vibrated with libido which it was quite impossible for them to discharge.

The Visitors, thoroughly repelled, were rippling back toward their ship when one signaled: *notice and hide.*

The three great black carpets abruptly vanished—that is, each insect found itself a cranny to disappear into, a pebble or leaf to be on the other side of. Some hope flared that the visit might be productive of a more pleasant contact than the last with those aimless, chittering cretins.

The thing stumping across the terrain toward them was like and unlike the wave-train cretins. It had their conformation but was material rather than undulatory in nature—a puzzle that could wait. It appeared to have no contact with the wave-train life form. They soared and darted about it as it approached, but it ignored them. It passed once through a group of three who happened to be on the ground in its way.

Tentatively the three Visitors reached out into its mind. The thoughts were comparatively clear and steady.

When the figure had passed the Visitors chorused: *Agreed,* and headed back to their ship. There was nothing there for them. Among other things they had drawn from the figure's mind was the location of a ruined library; a feeble-minded working party of a million was dispatched to it.

Back at the ship they waited, unhappily ruminating the creature's foreground thoughts: "From Corey's Gin you get the charge to tote that bale and lift that barge. That's progress, God damn it. You know better than that, man. Liberty Unlimited for the Lonely Man, but it be nice to see that Mars ship land . . ."

Agreement: *Despite all previous experience it seems that a sentient race is capable of destroying itself.*

When the feeble-minded library detail returned and gratefully reunited itself with its parent "lives" they studied the magnetic tapes it had brought, reading them direct in the cans. They learned the name of the planet and the technical name for the wave-train entities which had inherited it and which would shortly be its sole proprietors. The solid life-forms, it seemed, had not been totally unaware of them, though there was some confusion: Far the vaster section of the library denied that they existed at all. But in the cellular minds of the Visitors there could be no doubt that the creatures described in a neglected few of the library's lesser works were the ones they had encountered. Everything tallied. Their non-material quality; their curious reaction to light. And, above all, their dominant personality trait, of remorse, repentance, furious regret. The technical term that the books gave to them was: ghosts.

The Visitors worked ship, knowing that the taste of this world and its colony would soon be out of what passed for their collective mouths, rinsed clean by new experiences and better-organized entities.

But they had never left a solar system so gratefully or so fast.

Ripples

Ray Russell

An invisible starship stood at rest near a canal. If the eye could have seen it, the sight would have been one of immense beauty, for it was a thing of harmonious circles: an outer rim, hollow and transparent, in which the crew of four lived and worked and looked out upon space and suns and exotic worlds; contained in this circle, another, the core of powerful engines whose surging, flaming energy propelled the ship across galactic distances. And all of this unseen.

Inside, the captain spoke briefly to his specialist, first class. "Your report is finished, then? We can embark?"

"Yes sir."

"That was fast work."

"These rudimentary cultures are all very much alike. The report is simple—planet's inhabitants too primitive to comprehend our presence here; therefore suggest a return in a few millennia when the species may be more advanced and we can set up cultural and scientific exchange, trade, and so on."

The first mate drew near them. "Do you really think they're too primitive? They already have language, laws, religion. . . ."

"But no technology," said the specialist. "They couldn't possibly understand that we come from another planet; the very concept 'planet' is beyond them. . . . No, no, to try to establish contact now would be traumatic for them. If we revealed ourselves—flicked off the invisibility shield—there would be . . . ramifications . . . repercussions . . ."

"Ripples?" said the captain.

"Ripples," replied the specialist with a nod. "An apt word. Like a pebble dropped in a pond, spawning ever larger and larger and more grandiose images of its own smallness, so even an instantaneous glimpse of us and our ship could, with time and retellings, become magnified and elaborated and distorted—into something far beyond anything we could dream."

"Then, let us head for home and a well-earned leave," said the captain.

The first mate added, "And a well-shaped young lady I *hope* has been pining away in solitude!"

"Ah, youth—" began the captain, but broke off as his navigator approached with a worried air. "Trouble?" the captain asked.

"Yes, sir, I'm afraid so," said the navigator.

"Serious?"

"A little. The main engine is inoperable—just as I feared."

The first mate said, "That rough landing damaged more than our pride."

"What about the auxiliary?" asked the captain.

"It will get us home, just barely, but it won't hold up under the strain of lift-off—"

"What?"

"—unless we conserve all other energy. That means switching off lights, chart banks, communications, sensors, air, invisibility shield, everything—but only for those first few vital seconds of lift-off, of course."

"Then, do it."

"Yes sir."

The specialist, alarmed, said, "Captain! Not the invisibility shield! We must not turn that off!"

"You heard the navigator. It's our only chance—and it will just be for a few seconds." He nodded to the navigator, saying, "Lift off." Then he looked out through the transparent hull at the world they would soon depart. "Primitive, you say. Well, you're the expert. But it's too bad we can't contact them now. It might have been interesting. They're so much like us, they're almost *human*."

"Well, hardly that," said the specialist as the starship moved. "They're monofaced, and their feet are different, and they completely lack wings. But I know what you mean. . . ."

Outside, a bearded denizen of the primitive planet blinked, stared, pointed.

"Behold!" he cried to a companion. "A whirlwind! A great cloud! A fire! Men with wings and many faces! A wheel . . . in the middle of a wheel!"

"Where? What?" said his companion, turning a second too late. "I saw nothing, Ezekiel."

But, roiled by that whirlwind, the waters of the Chebar canal were a dancing spiderwork of ripples.

Roadside Rescue

Pat Cadigan

Barely fifteen minutes after he'd called Area Traffic Surveillance, Etan Carrera saw the big limousine transport coming toward him. He watched it with mild interest from his smaller and temporarily disabled vehicle. Some media celebrity or alien—more likely an alien. All aliens seemed enamored with things like limos and private SSTs, even after all these years. In any case, Etan fully expected to see the transport pass without even slowing, the navigator (not driver—limos drove themselves) hardly glancing his way, leaving him alone again in the rolling, green, empty countryside.

But the transport did slow and then stopped, cramming itself into the breakdown lane across the road. The door slid up, and the navigator jumped out, smiling as he came over to Etan. Etan blinked at the dark, full-dress uniform. People who worked for aliens had to do some odd things, he thought, and for some reason put his hand on the window control as though he were going to roll it up.

"Afternoon, sir," said the navigator, bending a little from the waist.

"Hi," Etan said.

"Trouble with your vehicle?"

"Nothing too serious, I hope. I've called Surveillance, and they say they'll be out to pick me up in two hours at most."

"That's a long time to wait." The navigator's smile widened. He was very attractive, holo-star kind of handsome. *People who work for aliens,* Etan thought. "Perhaps you'd care to wait in my employer's transport. For that matter, I can probably repair your vehicle, which will save you time and money. Roadside rescue fees are exorbitant."

"That's very kind," Etan said, "but I *have* called, and I don't want to impose—"

"It was my employer's idea to stop, sir. I agreed, of course. My employer is quite fond of people. In fact, my employer loves people. And I'm sure you would be rewarded in some way."

"Hey, now, I'm not asking for anything—"

"My employer is a most generous entity," said the navigator, looking down briefly. "I'll get my tool kit." He was on his way back across the road before Etan could object.

Ten minutes later, the navigator closed the power plant housing of Etan's vehicle and came around to the window again, still looking formal and unruffled. "Try it now, sir."

Etan inserted his key card into the dash console and shifted the control near the steering module. The vehicle hummed to life. "Well, now," he said. "You fixed it."

That smile again. "Occasionally the connections to the motherboard are improperly fitted. Contaminants get in, throw off the fuel mixing, and the whole plant shuts down."

"Oh," Etan said, feeling stupid, incompetent, and worst of all, obligated.

"You won't be needing rescue now, sir."

"Well. I should call and tell them." Etan reached reluctantly for the console phone.

"You could call from the limo, sir. And if you'd care for a little refreshment—" The navigator opened his door for him.

Etan gave up. "Oh, sure, sure. This is all very nice of you and your, uh, employer." What the hell, he thought, getting out and following the navigator across the road. If it meant that much to the alien, he'd give the alien a thrill.

"We both appreciate this. My employer and I."

Etan smiled, bracing himself as the door to the passenger compartment of the limo slid back. Whatever awkward greeting he might have made died in his throat. There was no one inside, no one and nothing.

"Just go ahead and get in, sir."

"But, uh—"

"My employer is in there. Somewhere." Smile. "You'll find the phone by the refrigerator. Or shall I call Surveillance for you?"

"No, I'll do it. Uh, thanks." Etan climbed in and sat down on the silvery grey cushion. The door slid partially shut, and a moment later Etan heard the navigator moving around up front. Somewhere a blower went on, puffing cool, humid air at his face. He sat back tentatively. Luxury surroundings—refrigerator, bar, video, sound system. God knew what use the alien found for any of it. Hospitality. It probably wouldn't help. He and the alien would no doubt end up staring at each other with nothing to say, feeling freakish.

He was on the verge of getting up and leaving when the navigator slipped through the door. It shut silently as he sat down across from Etan and unbuttoned his uniform tunic.

"Cold drink, sir?"

Etan shook his head.

"Hope you don't mind if I do." There was a different quality to the smile now. He took an amber bottle from the refrigerator and flipped the cap off, aiming it at a disposal in the door. Etan could smell alcohol and heavy spicing. "Possibly the best spiced ale in the world, if not the known universe," the navigator said. "Sure you won't have any?"

"Yes, I—" Etan sat forward a little. "I really think I ought to say thank you and get on. I don't want to hold you up—"

"My employer chooses where he wants to be when he wants to be there." The navigator took another drink from the bottle. "At least, I'm calling it a he. Hard to tell with a lot of these species." He ran his fingers through his dark hair; one long strand fell and brushed his temple. Etan caught a glimpse of a shaved spot. Implant; so the navigator would be mentally attuned to his employer, making speech or translation unnecessary. "With some, gender's irrelevant. Some have more than one gender. Some have more than *two*. Imagine taking *that* trip, if you can." He tilted the bottle up again. "But my present employer, here, asking him what gender he is, it's like asking you what flavor you are."

Etan took a breath. One more minute; then he'd ask this goof to let him out. "Not much you can do, I guess, except to arbitrarily assign them sex and—"

"Didn't say *that*."

"Pardon?"

The navigator killed the bottle. "Didn't say anything about sex."

"Oh." Etan paused, wondering exactly how crazy the navigator might be and how he'd managed to hide it well enough to be hired for an alien. "Sorry. I thought you said that some of them lacked sex—"

"Never said anything about sex. Gender, I said. Nothing about sex."

"But the terms can be interchangeable."

"Certainly *not*." The navigator tossed the bottle into the disposal and took another from the refrigerator. "Maybe on this planet but not out there."

Etan shrugged. "I assumed you'd need gender for sex, so if a species lacked gender, they'd uh . . ." He trailed off, making a firm resolution to shut up until he could escape. Suddenly he was very glad he hadn't canceled his rescue after all.

"Our nature isn't universal law," said the navigator. "Out there—" He broke off, staring at something to Etan's left. "Ah. My employer has decided to come out at last."

The small creature at the end of the seat might have coalesced out of the humid semidark, an off-white mound of what seemed to be fur as close and dense as a seal's. It would have repelled or disconcerted him except that it smelled so *good,* like a cross between fresh-baked bread and wildflowers. The aroma filled Etan with a sudden, intense feeling of well-being. Without thinking, he reached out to touch it, realized, and pulled his hand back.

"Going to pet it, were you? Stroke it?"

"Sorry," Etan said, half to the navigator and half to the creature.

"I forgive you," said the navigator, amused. "He'd forgive you, too, except he doesn't feel you've done anything wrong. It's the smell. Very compelling." He sniffed. "Go ahead. You won't hurt him."

Etan leaned over and gingerly touched the top of the creature. The contact made him jump. It didn't feel solid. It was like touching gelatin with a fur covering.

"Likes to stuff itself into the cushions and feel the vibrations from the ride," said the navigator. "But what it *really* loves is talk. Conversation. Sound waves created by the human voice are especially pleasing to it. And in *person,* not by holo or phone." The navigator gave a short, mirthless laugh and killed the second bottle. "So. Come on. Talk it up. That's what you're here for."

"Sorry," Etan said defensively. "I don't know exactly what to say."

"Express your goddamn *gratitude* for it having me fix your vehicle."

Etan opened his mouth to make an angry response and decided not to. For all he knew, both alien and human were insane and dangerous besides. "Yes. Of course I do appreciate your help. It was so kind of you, and I'm saving a lot of money since I don't need a roadside rescue now—"

"Never called it off, did you?"

"What?"

"The rescue. You never called to tell Surveillance you didn't need help."

Etan swallowed. "Yes. I did."

"Liar."

All right, Etan thought. *Enough is too much.* "I don't know what transport services you work for, but I'll find out. They ought to know about you."

"Yeah? What should they know—that I make free repairs at the bidding of an alien hairball?" The navigator grinned bitterly.

"No." Etan's voice was quiet. "They should know that maybe you've been working too long and too hard for aliens." His eyes swiveled apologetically to the creature. "Not that I mean to offend—"

"Forget it. It doesn't understand a goddamn word."

"Then why did you want me to talk to it?"

"Because *I* understand. We're attuned. On several frequencies, mind you, one for every glorious mood it might have. Not that it's any of your business."

Etan shook his head. "You need help."

"Fuck if I do. Now finish your thanks and start thinking up some more things to say."

The bread-and-flowers aroma intensified until Etan's nerves were standing on end. His heart pounded ferociously, and he wondered if a smell could induce cardiac arrest.

"I think I've finished thanking your employer." He looked directly at the creature. "And that's all I have to say. Under more pleasant circumstances, I might have talked my head off. Sorry." He started to get up.

The navigator moved quickly for someone who was supposed to be drunk. Etan found himself pinned against the back of the seat before he realized that the man wasn't jumping up to open the door. For a moment, he stared into the navigator's flushed face, not quite believing.

"Talk," the navigator said softly, almost gently. "Just talk. That's all you've got to do."

Etan tried heaving himself upward to throw them both off the seat and onto the floor, but the navigator had him too securely. "Help!" he bellowed. "Somebody help me!"

"Okay, yell for help. That's good, too," said the navigator, smiling. They began to slide down on the seat together with Etan on the bottom. "Go ahead. Yell all you want."

"Let me up and I won't report you."

"I'm sure I can believe *that.*" The navigator laughed. "Tell us a whole fairy story now."

"Let me go or I swear to Christ I'll kill you and that furry shit you work for."

"What?" the navigator asked, leaning on him a little harder. "What was that, *sir?*"

"Let me go or I'll *fucking kill you!*"

Something in the air seemed to break, as though a circuit had been completed or some sort of energy discharged. Etan sniffed. The bread-and-flowers aroma had changed, more flowers, less bread, and much weaker, dissipating in the ventilation before he could get more than a whiff.

The navigator pushed himself off Etan and plumped down heavily on the seat across from him again. Etan held still, looking first at the man rubbing his face with both hands and then turning his head so he could see the creature sliding down behind the cushion. *We scared it,* he thought, horrified. *Bad enough to make it hide under the seat.*

"Sir."

Etan jumped. The navigator was holding a fistful of currency out to him. The denominations made him blink.

"It's yours, sir. Take it. You can go now."

Etan pulled himself up. "What the hell do you mean, it's mine?"

"Please, sir." The navigator pressed one hand over his left eye. "If you're going to talk anymore, please step outside."

"Step outs—" Etan slapped the man's hand away and lunged for the door.

"Wait!" called the navigator, and in spite of everything, Etan obeyed. The navigator climbed out of the transport clumsily, still covering his eye, the other hand offering the currency. "Please, sir. You haven't been hurt. You have a repaired vehicle, more than a little pocket money here—you've come out ahead if you think about it."

Etan laughed weakly. "I can't believe this."

"Just take the money, sir. My employer wants you to have it." The navigator winced and massaged his eye some more. "Purely psychosomatic," he said, as though Etan had asked. "The implant is painless and causes no damage, no matter how intense the exchange between species. But please lower your voice, sir. My employer can still feel your sound, and he's quite done with you."

"What is that supposed to mean?"

"The money is yours from my employer," the navigator said patiently. "My employer loves people. We discussed that earlier. *Loves* them. Especially their voices."

"So?" Etan crossed his arms. The navigator leaned over and stuffed the money between Etan's forearms.

"Perhaps you remember what else we were discussing. I really have no wish to remind you, sir."

"So? What's all that stuff about gender—what's that got to do with . . ." Etan's voice died away.

"Human voices," the navigator said. "No speech where they come from. And we're so new and different to them. This one's been here only a few weeks. Its preference happens to be that of a man speaking from fear and anger, something you can't fake."

Etan took a step back from the man, unfolding his arms and letting the money fall to the ground, thinking of the implant, the man feeling whatever the creature felt.

"I don't know if you could call it perversion or not," said the navigator. "Maybe there's no such thing." He looked down at the bills. "Might as well keep it. You earned it. You even did well." He pulled himself erect and made a small, formal bow. "Good day, sir," he said, with no mockery at all and climbed into the transport's front seat. Etan watched the limo roll out of the breakdown lane and lumber away from him.

After a while, he looked down. The money was still there at his feet, so he picked it up.

Just as he was getting back into his own vehicle, the console phone chimed. "We've got an early opening in our patrol pattern," Surveillance told him, "so we can swing by and get you in ten minutes."

"Don't bother," Etan said.

"Repeat?"

"I said, you're too late."

"Repeat again, please."

Etan sighed. "There isn't anything to rescue me from anymore."

There was a brief silence on the other end. "Did you get your vehicle overhauled?"

"Yeah," Etan said. "That, too."

Roog

Philip K. Dick

Roog!" the dog said. He rested his paws on the top of the fence and looked around him.

The Roog came running into the yard.

It was early morning, and the sun had not really come up yet. The air was cold and gray, and the walls of the house were damp with moisture. The dog opened his jaws a little as he watched, his big black paws clutching the wood of the fence.

The Roog stood by the open gate, looking into the yard. He was a small Roog, thin and white, on wobbly legs. The Roog blinked at the dog, and the dog showed his teeth.

"Roog!" he said again. The sound echoed into the silent half darkness. Nothing moved nor stirred. The dog dropped down and walked back across the yard to the porch steps. He sat down on the bottom step and watched the Roog. The Roog glanced at him. Then he stretched his neck up to the window of the house, just above him. He sniffed at the window.

The dog came flashing across the yard. He hit the fence, and the gate shuddered and groaned. The Roog was walking quickly up the path, hurrying with funny little steps, mincing along. The dog lay down against the slats of the gate, breathing heavily, his red tongue hanging. He watched the Roog disappear.

The dog lay silently, his eyes bright and black. The day was beginning to come. The sky turned a little whiter, and from all around the sounds of people echoed through the morning air. Lights popped on behind shades. In the chilly dawn a window was opened.

The dog did not move. He watched the path.

In the kitchen Mrs. Cardossi poured water into the coffee pot. Steam rose from the water, blinding her. She set the pot down on the edge of the stove and went into the pantry. When she came back Alf was standing at the door of the kitchen. He put his glasses on.

"You bring the paper?" he said.

"It's outside."

Alf Cardossi walked across the kitchen. He threw the bolt on the back door and stepped out onto the porch. He looked into the gray, damp morning. At the fence Boris lay, black and furry, his tongue out.

"Put the tongue in," Alf said. The dog looked quickly up. His tail beat against the ground. "The tongue," Alf said. "Put the tongue in."

The dog and the man looked at one another. The dog whined. His eyes were bright and feverish.

"Roog!" he said softly.

"What?" Alf looked around. "Someone coming? The paperboy come?"

The dog stared at him, his mouth open.

"You certainly upset these days," Alf said. "You better take it easy. We both getting too old for excitement."

He went inside the house.

* * *

The sun came up. The street became bright and alive with color. The postman went along the sidewalk with his letters and magazines. Some children hurried by, laughing and talking.

About 11:00, Mrs. Cardossi swept the front porch. She sniffed the air, pausing for a moment.

"It smells good today," she said. "That means it's going to be warm."

In the heat of the noonday sun the black dog lay stretched out full length, under the porch. His chest rose and fell. In the cherry tree the birds were playing, squawking and chattering to each other. Once in a while Boris raised his head and looked at them. Presently he got to his feet and trotted down under the tree.

He was standing under the tree when he saw the two Roogs sitting on the fence, watching him.

"He's big," the first Roog said. "Most Guardians aren't as big as this."

The other Roog nodded, his head wobbling on his neck. Boris watched them without moving, his body stiff and hard. The Roogs were silent, now, looking at the big dog with his shaggy ruff of white around his neck.

"How is the offering urn?" the first Roog said. "Is it almost full?"

"Yes." The other nodded. "Almost ready."

"You, there!" the first Roog said, raising his voice. "Do you hear me? We've decided to accept the offering, this time. So you remember to let us in. No nonsense, now."

"Don't forget," the other added. "It won't be long."

Boris said nothing.

The two Roogs leaped off the fence and went over together just beyond the walk. One of them brought out a map and they studied it.

"This area really is none too good for a first trial," the first Roog said. "Too many Guardians . . . Now, the northside area—"

"*They* decided," the other Roog said. "There are so many factors—"

"Of course." They glanced at Boris and moved back farther from the fence. He could not hear the rest of what they were saying.

Presently the Roogs put their map away and went off down the path.

Boris walked over to the fence and sniffed at the boards. He smelled the sickly, rotten odor of Roogs and the hair stood up on his back.

That night when Alf Cardossi came home the dog was standing at the gate, looking up the walk. Alf opened the gate and went into the yard.

"How are you?" he said, thumping the dog's side. "You stopped worrying? Seems like you been nervous of late. You didn't used to be that way."

Boris whined, looking intently up into the man's face.

"You a good dog, Boris," Alf said. "You pretty big, too, for a dog. You don't remember long ago how you used to be only a little bit of a puppy."

Boris leaned against the man's leg.

"You a good dog," Alf murmured. "I sure wish I knew what is on your mind."

He went inside the house. Mrs. Cardossi was setting the table for dinner. Alf went into the living room and took his coat and hat off. He set his lunch pail down on the sideboard and came back into the kitchen.

"What's the matter?" Mrs. Cardossi said.

"That dog got to stop making all that noise, barking. The neighbors going to complain to the police again."

"I hope we don't have to give him to your brother," Mrs. Cardossi said, folding her arms. "But he sure goes crazy, especially on Friday morning, when the garbage men come."

"Maybe he'll calm down," Alf said. He lit his pipe and smoked solemnly. "He didn't used to be that way. Maybe he'll get better, like he was."

"We'll see," Mrs. Cardossi said.

The sun rose up, cold and ominous. Mist hung over all the trees and in the low places.

It was Friday morning.

The black dog lay under the porch, listening, his eyes wide and staring. His coat was stiff with hoarfrost and the breath from his nostrils made clouds of steam in the thin air. Suddenly he turned his head and leaped up.

404

From far off, a long way away, a faint sound came, a kind of crashing sound.

"Roog!" Boris cried, looking around. He hurried to the gate and stood up, his paws on top of the fence.

In the distance the sound came again, louder now, not as far away as before. It was a crashing, clanging sound, as if something were being rolled back, as if a great door were being opened.

"Roog!" Boris cried. He stared up anxiously at the darkened windows above him. Nothing stirred, nothing.

And along the street the Roogs came. The Roogs and their truck moved along, bouncing against the rough stones, crashing and whirring.

"Roog!" Boris cried, and he leaped, his eyes blazing. Then he became more calm. He settled himself down on the ground and waited, listening.

Out in front the Roogs stopped their truck. He could hear them opening the doors, stepping down onto the sidewalk. Boris ran around in a little circle. He whined, and his muzzle turned once again toward the house.

Inside the warm, dark bedroom, Mr. Cardossi sat up a little in bed and squinted at the clock.

"That damn dog," he muttered. "That damn dog." He turned his face toward the pillow and closed his eyes.

The Roogs were coming down the path, now. The first Roog pushed against the gate and the gate opened. The Roogs came into the yard. The dog backed away from them.

"Roog! Roog!" he cried. The horrid, bitter smell of Roogs came to his nose, and he turned away.

"The offering urn," the first Roog said. "It is full, I think." He smiled at the rigid, angry dog. "How very good of you," he said.

The Roogs came toward the metal can, and one of them took the lid from it.

"Roog! Roog!" Boris cried, huddled against the bottom of the porch steps. His body shook with horror. The Roogs were lifting up the big metal can, turning it on its side. The contents poured out onto the ground, and the Roogs scooped the sacks of bulging, splitting paper together, catching at the orange peels and fragments, the bits of toast and egg shells.

One of the Roogs popped an egg shell into his mouth. His teeth crunched the egg shell.

"Roog!" Boris cried hopelessly, almost to himself. The Roogs were almost finished with their work of gathering up the offering. They stopped for a moment, looking at Boris.

Then, slowly, silently, the Roogs looked up, up the side of the house, along the stucco, to the window, with its brown shade pulled tightly down.

"ROOG!" Boris screamed, and he came toward them, dancing with fury and dismay. Reluctantly, the Roogs turned away from the window. They went out through the gate, closing it behind them.

"Look at him," the last Roog said with contempt, pulling his corner of the blanket up on his shoulder. Boris strained against the fence, his mouth open, snapping wildly. The biggest Roog began to wave his arms furiously and Boris retreated. He settled down at the bottom of the porch steps, his mouth still open, and from the depths of him an unhappy, terrible moan issued forth, a wail of misery and despair.

"Come on," the other Roog said to the lingering Roog at the fence.

They walked up the path.

"Well, except for these little places around the Guardians, this area is well cleared," the biggest Roog said. "I'll be glad when this particular Guardian is done. He certainly causes us a lot of trouble."

"Don't be impatient," one of the Roogs said. He grinned. "Our truck is full enough as it is. Let's leave something for next week."

All the Roogs laughed.

They went on up the path, carrying the offering in the dirty, sagging blanket.

Sequence

Carl Jacobi

By noon Carston had made his daily inspection circuit of the drome. He had surveyed the commissary, loitered past the new structure that was to house the courts and exchanged a few pleasantries with the sergeant of the constabulary. He had checked the oxygen and humidity gauges on the big board outside the power building. And he had climbed to the drome's Central Observation Platform within the quartz bubble, where he stood now, gazing out at the incredible landscape of Nida 255.

A jigsaw pattern of tumbled monolithic rocks in a myriad of pastel colors stretched before him as far as he could see. Off to the left where the rock formations descended into a low bluish plain, a mass of girders and steel ribs crouched like some huge spider—all that was left of the *Centauria*. As Carston looked at the dismantled space ship now, a wave of repugnance swept over him.

Ten years! Ten years he had spent in that ugly hulk while it had bored through space, crossing the incalculable distances from Earth to this planet. He had lived perhaps an eighth of his life imprisoned with two thousand others in a man-constructed projectile that was such a leviathan not even he nor his officers had completely explored its galleries, its courts, its corridors, its great hydroponic growing chambers.

But success, such as it was, could partially be claimed theirs. They had reached this new System and they had landed on Nida 255, not because conditions were ideal—they were far from that—but because the planet was on the outer fringe of the unknown. Beyond lay mystery. Here they could establish a base for deeper exploration, and here they would perhaps be sighted by the next vessel from Earth, if one ever came.

Carston prided himself that his company of two thousand had accomplished a lot since their landing five months ago. First and foremost, they had erected this huge drome over the settlement, protecting themselves against the outside rarified atmosphere and the fierce herds of two legged goat-like creatures that seemed to migrate constantly from one pole to the other. Second they had maintained their social structure without a hitch. Five marriages, one divorce, three petty crimes—all had been settled, including an election of minor officials, in as smooth a procedure as if they had been still back on Earth. Within the drome, houses had been built, streets laid out, shrubbery planted. But at a cost!

Material for the drome had been obtained by ologizing a form of igneous rock that was abundant on the planet and spinning it into a film-like composition that slowly hardened when exposed to light. The superstructure that was required to support this huge envelope, however, had to be taken from their ship, the *Centauria*. It had meant dismantling the vessel, and it had meant burning their last bridge behind them. They were marooned on Nida 255 now, for better or for worse.

A buzzer sounded abruptly and a light glowed on a small panel at Carston's side. He pushed a stud and watched the view panel illuminate with the likeness of young Stewart who was on duty at East Tower. Stewart had been a lad of eleven playing hand ball in the upper galleries when the *Centauria* had started its voyage. Now he was a fine strapping young man of twenty-one. It didn't seem possible . . .

"Yes?" Carston spoke into the disc.

"Hello, Davis, you old walrus. How's tricks? Hourly report. Stewart speaking."

Carston smiled. "Davis isn't here," he said. "I gave him temporary relief. This is Captain Carston." He switched on his own reflector screen.

There was a pause and Stewart's face grimaced in embarrassment at his blunder. "Oh, beg pardon, sir. I didn't . . ."

"All right, Stewart," Carston smiled again. "Go on with your report. I'll take it."

"Yes, sir. East Tower 12:15. Visibility . . . five. Sectors one, two, three, and four . . . okay. Probascope reading: zero-zero."

"All right, Stewart," acknowledged Carston. "I'll record it. Yes, what's wrong?"

On the panel, the young watch-officer's face showed some anxiety. "If you please, sir, I'd like to have someone take my place for a few hours. My eyes have been bothering me a bit, sir."

"Scanner strain?"

"I don't think so. I seem to see streamers of white light, little pin points, that is. It's probably only a temporary condition."

Carston personally gave the order for Stewart's relief, and then sat there a moment, frowning. At twelve thirty West Tower reported in, and Carston recorded it as he had Stewart's. When the watch-officer had finished, Carston asked:

"How're your eyes, McIver?"

There was a moment's hesitation. Then: "Now that you mention it, sir, they've been giving me a little trouble. Little streaks of light. I expect it will pass shortly."

By now Carston's worst fears were realized, and he went into action at once. He pulled over the mike of the P.A. system, and an instant later heard his voice go resounding over the entire drome-settlement.

"Attention! It is quite possible we are being observed by enemy craft. I want each one of you to remain calm but be ready for any emergency. The settlement is now under martial law and will remain so until further orders from Central Tower."

Twice he repeated this statement, then clicked off the mike and glanced at the general view screen. It gave him a feeling of satisfaction to see that his orders had produced no hysteria. Like a well-oiled machine the settlement dropped its civil routine and geared itself for the unexpected.

Carston remained in Central Tower three hours more, watching the wan daylight cast by Nida's distant sun slowly fade. With the coming of darkness he went down the lift to the street level, and walked the short distance to his quarters. He had left word to be called at the first sign of any trouble, but what sort of trouble did he expect? He had said 'enemy craft' but he had used that expression for mundane rationalization only. They were on the brink of the unknown. Who could tell what cosmic horrors lay out there? Or had he suddenly become over-cautious?

At eleven fifty-two a call from Central Tower brought him to that watch post on the double. He arrived to find Williamson, the night watchofficer in a state of tense excitement.

"We spotted them, sir, but so far there's only one ship. That is, I guess you could call it a ship. It's an odd looking disc with a cylinder-like midsection and at intervals it gives off a powerful light."

Carston looked through the probascope, and for a moment saw nothing but black sky and the myriads of stars that paraded through it. Then a lighter shadow focused itself in his vision, advancing toward him slowly it seemed, but at a rate which he could not even estimate.

"Where do you suppose they're from?" Williamson asked nervously.

Carston said nothing. He was thinking, curiously, of his home back on Earth and the sunlit mornings he had tramped down a dusty road with the call of a meadowlark sounding in his ears. He was thinking of green fields and red-roofed houses and the fragrant honey locust trees in blossom. Williamson's voice cut into his reverie.

"They're heading directly toward us, sir."

"Light the landing platter," Carston ordered. "Full power. Light all tower beacons."

One look at the powerful ship had convinced him that the settlement's defenses—two comparatively small ato-guns taken from the dismantled *Centauria,* one weakened warp-impinger—were inadequate and a bold move of welcoming the stranger the only alternative.

But somehow as he waited for the ship to acknowledge his signal, his mind kept reverting to the past. Ten years ago he had not had to face any emergencies such as this. He was a military man, yes, but a military man retired from active service at the age of thirty-two because of a bad left arm, caused ironically, by a fall down a flight of stairs. Then had come the *Centauria* and a recommendation for him to command by his old friend, Senator Stanley. His jaw tightened suddenly. He didn't intend to lose everything now that the project was on the verge of accomplishment. He would use trickery, cunning, diplomacy, everything at his command, if the approaching craft were hostile, and somehow he would . . . he must . . . win out.

And now the strange ship had checked its forward impetus and was hovering just above them. Gently as a falling leaf, it descended to the landing platter and came to a standstill. A drum-shaped object protruded from a trap on the side and slowly revolved while a diffused red light gleamed above it.

"Testing us for something," mused the Captain. "Perhaps they'll attack without coming out."

Presently, however, the hatch opened, a ladder was slung over the side and two figures climbed down. They were heavily encased in queer-shaped space suits with rectangular helmets. Carston, staring in the glare of the white lights, could not be sure whether or not the two figures were human, though they seemed man-size with four appendages. Three more figures climbed out, and then the five began to move slowly, cautiously across the platter to the drome entrance chamber.

Not until then did Carston leave his post. He rode down the lift quickly and hurried across to the drome-side door. Before entering, he touched a lever on a panel, saw a dull-surfaced metal wall roll across from one side to the other effectively dividing the room into two parts. That wall was constructed of the new aluminum alloy that would permit him to see and hear everything on the opposite side of that wall and yet remain invisible to the strangers, as well as safe from any weapon discharge. He took his place in the chair behind the metal desk and waited.

A moment later the five strangers entered the chamber on the other side of the wall. They remained standing, one slightly in advance of the others. Their helmets presented a solid metal surface completely hiding their features. Carston reached out, pulled over the thought transcriber on its bracket and began to direct his thoughts into it.

"You are on an inhabited planet. As commanding officer of this settlement, I bid you welcome. Will you please state your mission and where you are from."

He was following the *Spaceways Manual* to the letter, following the paragraph which read: *In contacting any form of alien life suspected of not previously being in contact with Earthians, reveal as little about yourself as possible but attempt to elicit at once such information as will enable you to appraise those aliens with a view to a common 'esprit de corps.'*

But the leader of the strangers was likewise noncommittal. The transcriber recorded his reply,

"We have lost our way and are not sure of our present position. What planet is this and to what race do you belong?"

"Do you come from far?" Carston parried.

"From far and near. Our origin is far out in space. Will you reveal yourself, sir?"

"Where?" Carston persisted.

The strangers bent their heads together, held a consultation. At last the helmeted leader looked up. Slowly the transcriber recorded his answer.

"We come from a planet called Earth."

Earth! A pulse began to throb in Carston's temple. He stared at the transcriber, half rose in his chair while beads of perspiration broke out on his forehead. So the cycle was complete. Not *one* but *two* ships had crossed the trackless void. The expedition could now be considered a success from all angles. Carston reached toward the panel at his side. Move back that damned wall and greet your fellow men with the warmth and hospitality they deserved. Shake their hands! Clap their backs! . . . But wait. . . !

Earthmen wore no such outlandish space suits, did not build queer disc-shaped ships like that one out on the platter. Another paragraph in the *Manual* came back to him. *In contacting aliens always establish positive identity and beware of false claims of origin. Cases have been known where outlanders learning of conditions on Earth, have attempted to pose as inhabitants of our System.* All at once Carston's brain became crystal clear, and he weighed the facts and sought the truth. The *Centauria* had landed here but five months ago. At the time of their departure from Earth no other ship capable of making such a voyage had been in process of construction. On the other hand the strangers had all the attributes of Earthmen in spite of their shapeless suits.

Far back in Carston's mind an impossible thought began to whisper for recognition. He turned to the transcriber again.

"Your place of departure on the planet, Earth, of which you speak . . . It has a name?"

"Carstonville."

Cold sweat bathed the Captain from head to foot.

"Your date of departure?" he demanded.

"July sixth, just forty-nine days ago. Our ship is equipped with the new Ganlor Drive, of course, or this speed would not have been possible."

Behind the metal desk Carston was staring with glazed eyes. A mirthless laugh sounded in his throat.

"Ten years . . ." he muttered hoarsely. "Ten years . . ."

The Sky's an Oyster; the Stars Are Pearls

David Bischoff

Thank you, ladies and gentlemen; thank you very much for your kind applause. I certainly hope you enjoyed your dinner. I enjoyed mine quite a bit and would like to thank NASA for instructing the nutritionists present in the proper way of preparing my foods. Not that I'm particular, mind you. Just a necessity. My metabolism is not quite the same as yours, you know.—Can you hear me in the back there? No? Herb, do you think you might put this mike up on something a little taller so it can reach my head? Yes, I know: my height is a real pain. Sorry but that comes from growing up on the moon.—Yes, that's just fine, thank you. Now I can properly begin this speech.

"Uh hum. Mr. President, Mrs. President, heads of state of so many countries I've quite forgotten the exact names and for fear of leaving someone out I won't attempt to name them; may I take this opportunity to express my appreciation for this grand banquet you have put on here at the White House in my honor. As you know, I have been out of quarantine now for only a week and this is the first enjoyable time I've really had since the successful completion of my journey.

"May I also make it plain that I will not be offended if you do not look directly at me during the course of this address. I realize that my countenance is quite horrifying to the average human. NASA apologizes to both you and me but my lack of beauty is a simple by-product of the genetic manipulation effected upon me from the time of my laboratory conception in order to make the trip of the type I have just undertaken possible. But then, that shall be the text of this little talk, which (I hope you don't mind) will be as informal as I can make it.

"Since the time that mankind got it into their heads that space travel is possible, there have been many failures and many successes. It is my honor to be the key factor in what has proved to be the greatest victory of all: man's first exploration of a star system other than the one we inhabit. For years, even after the successful conquest of our solar system, most scientists thought it impossible to send a man out to the stars. The distances were simply too great. Decades would be required to traverse to other suns. But then the exciting discovery of a different dimension where distances in time & space are much shorter than those we know in this universe, was effected by the scientists at NASA. If a spaceship could penetrate this so called 'subspace,' it could easily negotiate distances thought impossible in regular space & time. And of course it was discovered that this was entirely possible, indeed (cough, cough) ridiculously (cough, excuse me) easy.

"Pardon me (cough) but I need a little of my special air from my respirator. Frank, would you hand it here? Thanks.

"There. That's better. I can take normal Earth air for much longer when I'm not speaking.

"Yes. Where was I? Subspace you say? Right. Anyway, there was a very difficult dilemma. Regular, normal, everyday human beings were incapable of inhabiting subspace for various physiological as well as psychological reasons. Even in the closed environment of a spaceship. These reasons were analyzed carefully and scientists determined the necessary sort of organism that would be capable of traveling through subspace. Which is me. And of course my brothers and sisters currently being raised in the proper environment on the moon bases. Because I, their first experiment, was so completely successful.

"I set out somewhat less than a year ago, much of my traveling time taken up by the act of getting past the orbit of Pluto where the gravity of the sun is effectively nil. Entrance into subspace is a bit difficult with any sort of gravitational field near. I and my ship, the *Explorer 5,* were designed for one another, and many mechanisms in it can only be controlled by my specially created mind and body. But let's not get too scientifically detailed. I suppose you may read the scientific reports concerning the structure of the *Explorer* and myself, if you are so inclined.

"Our course was plotted toward the Tau Ceti system, for years the source of radio transmissions picked up by our radio-telescopes that seemed to indicate intelligent life. We could have headed for Proxima Centauri, our closest neighbor sun, but with the nature of subspace what it is, it was just as easy to go to Tau Ceti.

"A moment. Another whiff from the respirator before I get to coughing again. Thanks, Herb. There.

"Doubtless my past few words have been merely a repetition of what you already have read in your Faxsheets or have seen on the holocube. I hope you will forgive my repeating them but I merely wanted to be sure that all present, all you world leaders, have sufficient background to understand what I am going to say.

"Those of you who have studied the information provided you will recall that it states that although the journey was a success in most senses, no intelligent life was discovered in the Tau Ceti system.

"Gentlemen, may I take this time to say that that is not the truth; there is indeed intelligent life in that system and I made contact with it.

"Please! Please! My ears are not accustomed to such an uproar. I suggest you shut up so that I may complete what I am saying. It is of the utmost importance that I do so. No questions now. Let me finish. Sit down, Dr. Haskell. And the rest of my associates in science; be still. I have not let any of you know this, so none of you were kept out of a secret that others of you knew. I alone was its keeper. Along with the Makpzions, of course. The intelligent rulers of Makpzio. They intercepted me as soon as I shifted out of subspace. They too have interstellar travel, you see. In fact, they have had it for centuries and have used it to acquire quite an empire, colonizing other planets. Because they all travel in subspace, they are like me in many ways. Communication was no difficulty. They were delighted to hear of Earth's existence. We are in such a far away corner of the galaxy they never bothered to check out the Sol system.

"Wait a minute! Yes! Look outside that window over to the Mall just by the Washington Monument. That's one of their ships coming down. Exactly on time. I led them here, you know. Several hundred more starships are no doubt orbiting Earth with their incredibly advanced weapons sighted on various strategic targets. And gentlemen, that is why I chose tonight for this banquet. So that all of you can be here together to listen to the terms of conquest the Makpzions will deliver. Oh, I might as well tell you this now: I get to be dictator.

"My goodness, aren't you outraged! Please, no violence upon my person. My conquering friends would not take that at all well. They might get nasty and destroy a few million of you.

"Benedict Arnold, you scream, Mr. President? A traitor to my own race?

"But then, I'm not really human, am I now? Your scientists saw to that.

"Pass that respirator here, Herb. There's a good boy."

Slow

Ramsey Campbell

Gradually he became aware of the cottage around him, as he emerged from himself again. This time he'd gone back as far as his childhood. A landscape of hills, green beyond green beyond green: he hadn't thought of that for years, he'd decided the memory was more frustrating than useful. He was grateful for it now. It was somewhere to go.

He stretched, taking his time. The clock showed 8:37. He was hungry. No wonder, he thought as he glanced at his wrist: he'd stayed within himself for over two hours, he should have eaten an hour ago. Well, it didn't matter. He'd achieved self-discipline, he needn't overrate routine.

He picked his way between his games to the kitchen, and reached through the trap in the wall for the plate of food. Meat and vegetables—or at least, that was what it looked disgustingly like. For a long time he hadn't been able to touch the food. At last, starving, he'd discovered that it tasted synthetic enough; he could even manage to eat it with his eyes open.

He knelt down and peered through the trap. In twelve hours a larger plate of meat and vegetables would click into place; twelve hours after that, a smaller one again. He could see the plates lined up in their cool colourless store, just beyond his reach. A vague irrational hope—why hope?—made him count them again. But he knew (they) had left him enough food to last almost a year. (They) had gone away.

There was no use denying his feelings. He had been hoping they hadn't really gone; incredibly, he found himself already missing (them).

He shook his head wryly. He would never have believed how much he could adjust to. Returning to the living-room he poked the wall with a finger, and felt the surface yield a little, like rubber. He wouldn't have believed he could grow to bear that, yet now he didn't mind it, so long as he avoided thinking how the appearance of the cottage should have felt. And how soon he'd grown used to the view from the cottage windows, the steely blue shine of the folds of rock, the icy glow they retained for an hour after the white sunsets. Even (they) weren't unpleasant to look at, though sometimes he wondered whether they disguised themselves for him.

Staring out at the empty landscape, he began to wish (they) would appear. Perhaps they hadn't gone far, perhaps they would come back occasionally to look at him. Surely they wouldn't leave him for a whole year without a glimpse of life, with nothing but the bare metallic rock.

Not entirely bare, he realized with a disagreeable shock. There was something outside the window—the thing (they) had once chased away.

It was almost the colour of the rock. It might have been a shadow, except that there was nothing to cast it. Its head resembled a swollen egg, precariously perched on a long thin neck that bulged toward the midriff. Beneath the belly, if that was what it was, the body tapered; the thing seemed to float on the point of its tail. It was more than a foot taller than he.

It hung in the mouth of a passage through a low table of rock, a metre away. There was no way to tell whether the blank egg was watching. When the thing had first appeared (they) had rushed at it, whirling and blazing; they'd waited until it had retreated into the rock passage. Let it watch, if it were watching. It couldn't reach him.

After a while he tried to assemble the cube, the most difficult of the games (they) had provided. One of these days he'd solve it. But whenever he glanced up, his gaze was drawn from the wide retreating levels of rock to the nearby rock table, to the thing hanging balanced on its tail. An hour later he could see that it was coming toward the window.

Let it come. Whatever the windows were made of, they were unbreakable. He'd tried violently enough to break them when first he'd found himself here. He only wished (they) had supplied curtains, so that he could close out the sight of the thing. No, he didn't really need curtains, he wouldn't let it worry him.

The cube defeated him again. It was made of hundreds of slotted metal planes; whenever he fitted them together there were always five or six left over. He'd find the secret. He had plenty of time.

He accepted his defeat. The memory of the green day had calmed him. Somehow the memory seemed to reach back further than itself; it touched something at the centre of him. Tomorrow he might find out what that was, or the next day.

When he'd eaten his evening meal he returned to the livingroom, and frowned. The thing had almost reached the window. How slowly it moved, to have advanced hardly a metre since he'd caught sight of it. Surely it must be vegetarian, surely there couldn't be living prey that was slower than it was. He had no idea what lay beyond the rockscape: there must be vegetation.

He wasn't frowning because of the thing's sluggishness, however. Now the sun had set, the folds of rock were shining like a steely afterimage. Something in this light must be playing a trick with the window, for an image of the blank egg on its scrawny neck clung to the glass. Although he moved about the room, changing his angle of vision, the image overlapped its source, blurring the blank head. It was unpleasant to watch, his eyes smarted. Besides, although he knew the thing couldn't reach him, he found its encroaching presence disturbing. It reminded him he was—Perhaps in the morning it would have gone away, baulked.

Around him the cottage began to glow. The furniture, the low beams, the clock-face set at 8:37, glimmered grey; the dim light trembled like almost-stagnant water. Perhaps (they) had meant it to imitate electric light, but it was the one thing he found impossible to bear. At least he'd trained himself to sleep once it began. He climbed the luminous stairs. Lying on the bed, eyes closed, he hoped the thing outside was turning away.

When he came downstairs the next morning, it was entering the cottage.

What he'd taken for an image on the glass was nothing of the kind. It looked more solid now than its source outside the window. Nor was it confined to the glass; there was a shadow of the rest of the body, outlined more darkly in the wall beneath the window. In the room, an arm's length in front of the shadow, a faint transparent darkness was forming. It already had the shape of the faceless thing.

Before he could hold on to his control, it broke. He grabbed a handful of planes from the slotted cube and hurled them at the intruder. They passed through the darkness, disturbing it not at all. He threw another handful, then he began to curse (them) for bringing him here. Them. His owners.

For the first time in years all his paranoia flooded over him, all the nightmares and suspicions he'd thought he had disciplined out of himself. Had (they) really rescued him? Or had they snatched him out of space, for a pet?

All the memories he'd dismissed as useless filled him. He had been ferrying supplies between the outer orbits. Suddenly the ferry was whirling helplessly, spinning out beyond the outermost orbit. He'd never known what had happened. Had that been (them) snatching him?

He'd blanked out. Regaining consciousness, he'd recognized he was drifting somewhere beyond the star maps, beyond rescue. His distress beacon was only interorbital. He was going to die. Eventually the knowledge helped him toward peace; there was no point in panicking. He'd used the techniques he had learned to help himself sleep when he'd first gone into space, as a member of a crew: he'd become his breathing, he'd drifted deep into his memories. He had thought of Old Earth, which he'd never seen. Then, as he'd eaten the last of his food and gazed out at space—abruptly: nothing. He had awakened in the cottage.

It was the cottage in the pictures in his book, the book of Old Earth, he always kept sealed into his pocket. He'd bought the book in a bazaar; it was centuries old, each page coated with preservative. He'd paid its price, for he had always wanted a glimpse of Old Earth. Now it was as though he'd fallen into the book. It had taken him weeks to soothe his nerves, to regain some sense of inhabitating reality.

And longer to be sure of what he saw through the window: the three glittering veils—crimson, indigo, luminous green, the colours swarming over one another in two-metre curtains of light—that stood fluttering outside the cottage for hours. Eventually he saw them surrounding the food-store; when he looked through the trap, the store had been replenished.

He'd tried to communicate with them, shouting in the close silence of the cottage, gesturing. But the only response he ever got was another, more complicated puzzle or game; the cottage was full of them. (They) never entered the cottage while he was awake, however hard he fought sleep. They simply weren't interested in what he had to say. They'd tried to provide what they thought was a familiar environment; they gave him food that looked like the food in his book, they pumped something like the ferry's air through a valve in the wall above the staircase; often they watched him for hours. But they didn't think he was so important, they went away somewhere, leaving him at the mercy of the planet's wild life. The faceless egg stood on the stalk of its neck.

All right. He didn't need them to protect him, he thought furiously. He could easily outdistance the thing. It was too slow to trap him, he would outmanoeuvre it all over the cottage, until it became frustrated and went away. He was sure it must be stupid as well as slow; no doubt it wouldn't think to use the empty doorways, it would retard itself further by seeping through the walls.

But it was unnerving. Though he knew he wasn't in danger he found himself unable to look away from the thing. The fascination infuriated him, he felt helplessly resentful; as long as it was in the cottage the thing would distract him from the peace he'd achieved.

He watched the thing enter the cottage. Gradually the outline, hardly more than a misty silhouette, began to round, to fill out.

Beyond the window the original shape was suddenly empty air. Now the shape that stained the glass and the wall was fading. The thing in the room swelled darker, opaque now. When the outline in the wall drained completely, he knew the thing was full. It stood next to a low flowered couch. It was in the room with him, little more than a metre away.

For a moment there was nothing between him and terror. The thing stood glistening, dull blue; its bald featureless head almost touched the beams. Close up the thing looked slick and oily. He felt a nervous horror of touching it, of feeling the swollen glistening skin.

Never mind. It couldn't touch him. It was wasting its time, he reassured himself as he saw—with a snigger as much of unease as of mirth—that while entering, it had begun to poise itself to catch him: the head was stooping forward on the neck, and at the top of the egg an orifice was puckering. Within the orifice he could make out rows of fangs, pointing inward. They didn't look like the teeth of a vegetarian.

They wouldn't touch him. He could soon be calm. All he need do was measure the thing's speed. Then he'd be able to ignore its impotent menace. He watched the thing creep forward toward him. To reach the window it had moved at a rate of about ten centimetres to the hour. There was no reason to suppose it would move faster now. No reason to suppose so—but it had doubled its speed.

He glared at his chronometer. It never lied, but neither did his eyes in judging distances. The thing had advanced ten centimetres toward him in half an hour. Perhaps the nearness of its prey gave it the impetus. The head had stooped a fraction more, the mouth had opened further, imperceptibly.

He could still stay out of its reach without trying. It couldn't double its speed indefinitely. It couldn't. In half an hour he knew he was right; it had moved only ten centimetres. He snarled at it, at its fatuous empty face, its trailing tail. It didn't frighten him. It just annoyed him. He wished he could block it off so that he needn't look at it.

Block it off. Yes. He might not be able to hide the thing away, but at least he could slow it down further; perhaps then, happily triumphant, he could ignore it. He carried one of the games down from the second bedroom. It was a cubical maze, as high as his waist. He thumped it down in the thing's path. It wouldn't get through that in a hurry.

He forced himself to leave the thing for a while. He gazed out of his bedroom window. The white sunlight bared the landscape, the gleaming metallic corrugations of rock. At the horizon the sky was bright silver. Were there more of the things out there? Oddly, he found himself almost welcoming the notion. At least it made the landscape feel less barren, now the sparkling coloured veils were gone.

He made himself wait for an hour, then went downstairs. The thing had reached the block; a shadow of its tail was seeping into the far face of the cube. Three hours later, when he returned again, two pale silhouettes confronted each other patiently across the cube. Before he went to bed the thing hung half-embedded in the cube, looking exactly like a retarded Jack-in-the-box. He couldn't control his laughter. He wondered whether he might grow fond of the thing. It was beginning to amuse him, in its ugly stupid way.

He lay on the glowing bed. He must be sure to lure the thing into one of the downstairs rooms each evening—never to allow it to reach the hall late in the day, where it could begin coming upstairs while he slept. As the room dimmed slowly, he visualized the layout of the cottage. No, he would never be trapped. He could always keep at least one wall between him and the thing, if he felt he needed to.

He let his breathing carry him down into himself. He remembered the green day, the hills multiplying green to the horizon. For a while, when he'd found himself in the cottage's parody of Old Earth, that memory had seemed flat, false as the cottage's clock—he was sure the clock was empty inside, or solid. The green of his remembered hills had been metallic, not like Old Earth's at all.

But now the green of the metal hills seemed to lead him back further. Perhaps it was inherited memory, perhaps it was only the book: but for a moment the green was the swaying of grass, which he'd never seen. The swaying was peaceful, was sleep.

He awoke refreshed, feeling as if he'd slept for days. The room was dazzling with light. Too dazzling. He twisted round; the white sun stood at the centre of the window. He had overslept.

At once he remembered the thing. He glanced warily toward the doorway, glad (they) had omitted the doors. The landing was empty. He rose hastily, hardly glancing at his clothes beside the bed—he never wore them now, the cottage was too hot. He hurried across the landing. His gasp of shock was the only sound in the cottage.

The thing was waiting for him on the staircase, on the third stair up. The egg had stooped further; if it reached him, it would be on a level with his head—the mouth would, and the mouth had gaped wider now, a fanged ridged hole as wide as his fist.

Did it move faster at night? Had he slept for days? The questions tumbled about in his mind, but his panic was ahead of them. He musn't be trapped upstairs, there was a nightmare in that somewhere. He musn't be cut off from food. He climbed over the banisters, hung by his fingertips from the edge of the landing, let himself fall.

Too fast! He hadn't time to bend his knees, the fall jarred his ankles painfully. Panic must be blocking his responses somehow. Well, it was only a four-metre drop, it hadn't killed him. The thing was already backing downstairs toward him. Its averted head wobbled on the thin neck, as if about to turn.

It was moving faster. It was going to overtake him. But he forced himself to time it. The chronometer insisted the thing was still restricted to twenty centimetres an hour. It must be his fear that had lent it the seeming of speed.

He hurried into the kitchen. He felt as if he were trying to run through the marsh of a nightmare. Each step seemed slower than the last. He'd grown unused to panic. He must reach deep into himself for calm, otherwise the situation would overcome him. But first, food. He reached into the trap and took the plate.

Though he knew he should carry the plate across the hall, to manoeuvre further out of reach of the thing, his panic seemed to have exhausted him; he had to make an effort even to cross to the kitchen table. The surface of the table gave like elastic beneath his elbows.

He must time the thing tonight. If it moved faster at night, he could block its path effectively. But if it could somehow make him oversleep—He ate sluggishly, irritably, staring nervously at the blank wall of the kitchen for the thing's outline. He ate, he ate. How much time it took.

He was still eating when the thing glided into the kitchen doorway and stood waiting, head lowered, mouth almost as wide as his head.

His panic burst, flooding him. Then almost at once he felt very calm. So the thing could move faster, but only did so when he wasn't watching. And it must have learned that it could move more quickly through space than through walls. It wasn't as stupid as he'd thought.

But he was still faster. If it could have moved as fast as he, it would have been able to catch him by now. He'd always outdistance it. Except that it wasn't pursuing him now; it seemed content to block the doorway.

He laughed out loud. It had trapped him with the food, trapped him in the one place he couldn't have afforded to be blocked from. He could live in here if he had to. There were games and chairs in the kitchen, they'd slow the thing down while he slept. Did it expect him to walk over and stuff his head into its mouth? What could it gain by standing there?

Well, let it stand. He felt calm, unnaturally so. He ate slowly—no hurry, the thing was two metres distant. Chew, chew. His jaws were racing the sun, which had nearly reached the horizon.

When he realized what that meant he felt himself become slowly, slowly cold. He hardly needed to consult his chronometer. Even to raise his wrist toward his face, and turn it to be read, took minutes. At once—though even the thought seemed to drift very slowly into focus—he knew that the thing wouldn't move from the doorway until he was slower than it was.

So that was how it caught its prey. Well, it wouldn't catch him, he'd block it. But in the time it took him to rise from his chair the sun sank beneath the horizon. There was no use pretending, he was caught. Time surrounded him thickly, like amber.

Night gathered, and the room began to glow. Beneath his hands the table yielded treacherously, glowing. The walls glimmered grey; the glow shone faintly on the figure waiting in the doorway. The mouth was ready for his head now. The faceless egg was hardly more than a thin stretched frame for the dim fanged tunnel.

He began to writhe frantically within himself, within his stopped body. All he managed was a scream, and even that seemed weak; he tried to make it louder, more raw, but it sank into the silence. Darkness was seeping into the dim glow now. He heard the oppressive silence of the cottage, of the dead clock. He heard his slow harsh breathing, each breath slower than the last. The thing waited near him in the dark, mouth ready.

He heard his breathing. And he knew that the thing hadn't quite trapped him. He couldn't move, but he could still escape.

Perhaps the calm he'd felt before had been false, part of the thing's preying. It didn't matter. He could use that too, to take him to his own peace. He made himself relax, to sink into the green day, the green hills.

The day had gone. There was nothing but the mouth, waiting for him in the darkness. He wouldn't know when it was coming closer, not until it reached him. It might be coming now.

He struggled wildly, feebly within himself, within the dark. At last he gave up, exhausted. That wasn't the way. He couldn't reach for the memory, for escape. It was in him already. He must let it come to him. Listen to his breathing. His slow breathing. Become his breathing, slow. Become all of himself. There was green in the dark, in his mind. There were the hills.

He lay calm, cradled in his breathing. His arrested body stood hunched over the table, but it didn't matter. In a moment the green would begin to sway slowly in the wind, the wind of Old Earth. He knew Old Earth was there at his centre, inherited. He must be aware only of his breathing. The darkness didn't matter. His breathing would take him to his centre. His breathing was slow as the swaying of leaves.

The Spy

Theodore L. Thomas

Jehn Dofan was a very human-looking and highly intelligent young man, but sometimes he did not show good sense. Any young man might meet a girl night after night in an apple orchard, but Dofan had to do it in time of war, behind enemy lines, with the daughter of the mayor. On top of that he had to try to pry information out of her.

Even this might have been all right if Dofan had used a little more sense. After four consecutive nights of pressings and squeezings and heavy breathings, one does not maintain a stony silence when a girl like Betty Fuller nestles up closer and says, "We will be so happy together." The situations swiftly deteriorated after that. He wound up under arrest.

Flung into a root cellar, Jehn Dofan underwent a short but intense period of questioning by three burly soldiers, aided by the butt end of their flintlock rifles and directed by a second lieutenant bent on promotion. Dofan told them nothing. But it did not matter. As the soldiers left, the second lieutenant said, drawing himself to attention, "You hang at dawn, scum. We know how to treat spies."

For the first time Dofan saw that he was in trouble.

Betty Fuller rushed in as the soldiers went out. She flung herself on Dofan and covered his bloodied face with kisses and wept into the hollow of his neck. "My darling," she wailed, "what have I done to you?"

With this to work on, Dofan might have extricated himself even then, for Betty Fuller's father was the mayor, and a friendly mayor wields much influence even with the military if he puts his mind to it. But Dofan, although very human-looking and highly intelligent, did not show good sense for the second time in the same night.

He looked at Betty Fuller coldly and said, "You've done enough. Why don't you let me alone?"

Her eyes widened in disbelief and then flashed in hatred. She turned and tapped calmly on the door, and the soldiers let her out.

Dawn was close, and Dofan had no time to lose. He went to a corner of the root cellar and listened to make certain no one was coming. With his right thumb he probed deep up under his right jaw. He found the tiny button imbedded there, and he pushed it and held it.

He said softly, "Jehn Dofan calling Base. Jehn Dofan calling. . . ."

"We have you, Dofan. Talk."

"I'm captured, heavily guarded. They plan to hang me at dawn, less than an hour. Condition appears desperate. I need help."

"Will this rescue constitute a major interference with the natives? And, if so, are you willing to stand court-martial?"

"Yes," said Dofan. "I believe it will require major interference, and I am willing to stand court-martial."

"Stand by for instructions."

Dofan removed his thumb and paced back and forth in the root cellar in the candlelight.

Now that he had committed himself, he was a little sorry. But there seemed no other way out. This would spoil a perfect record here on the planet Earth. Betty Fuller had succeeded in ruining him. He would be drummed out of the Controllers, and she and the other Earth people did not even know such an organization existed. There would come a time when he could. . . .

A series of sharp buzzes echoed inside his head. It startled him; he had not expected his instructions so soon. He went to the corner and pressed the switch under his jaw and said, "Jehn Dofan."

"This is Charn Dofan. How are you, brother?"

Dofan felt his breath catch in his throat, and for a moment he could not speak. A real feeling of relief swept over him. Charn Dofan was here, his older brother, come to him in a time of trouble as always.

He said, "Charn, it is good to hear your voice. Where are you calling from, brother?"

"About a mile away. I command a troop of cavalry stationed in Brooklyn. I heard your call to Base and came out. Are you well?"

"Very well, brother. And you?"

"Very well."

A silence fell. The silence rested uncomfortably and strangely with Jehn Dofan. There had never been any strained silences between him and his brother. Something was wrong. He asked, "Is all well at home?"

There was a perceptible pause before the answer came. "Our parents and our family are all in good health." Again the silence.

Jehn Dofan said, "Tell me what is wrong, Charn. Base will call soon to tell me of the rescue procedure. What is it?"

A pause, then Charn Dofan began to speak. "Our Islands at home are ready to demand full statehood. The Mainlanders are trying to find some way to keep us out. A vote will be taken next week. As things stand now, we can just about muster the necessary strength, but it won't take much to change things. We won't get another chance for a long while. We'll have to keep paying the taxes, letting them bleed us white, controlling our production."

Jehn Dofan nodded in understanding. "Yes, our people have worked toward statehood for a long time. I hope we make it."

Again the silence. Jehn Dofan was puzzled.

He said, "What is wrong? What can we do about it from here?"

This time his brother's words poured out, wrenched from the heart. "Base commander is a Mainlander! He will have to interfere openly with the natives to rescue you, and this will reflect on all the Islanders. No question about it, Jehn. It will tip the vote the wrong way. Your rescue will be an international incident back home."

Jehn Dofan shook his head regretfully and said, "I suppose you are right. But I don't know how we can stop him from here. We are. . . ." And then he understood.

He felt sick to his stomach and he began to perspire. His breath caught in his throat. His heart pounded. He refused to accept the full realization—kept thrusting it out of his mind—but it kept intruding.

His brother continued, "Base will be calling in a few moment. I will be nearby, no matter what happens. Call on me for anything. I will abide by your decision. Good-by." The radio fell silent before Jehn Dofan could speak.

He was alone in the cellar. He slumped to the dirt, too weak to pace.

He was frightened. He had not seriously considered the possibility of dying on this planet. Yet here he was, in a position where his own brother had to point out the desirability of letting himself be executed instead of rescued. The Islands needed a hero now, not a goat. He needed time to think this out.

But there was no time. The buzzer sounded inside his head. He jumped. He went to the corner and pushed the switch and spoke.

"Base commander," was the response, and without further preamble the commander launched into a description of the rescue plans. In spite of the turmoil that raged in his mind, Dofan recognized that the plans were more violent and complex than they needed to be. It was apparent that the commander was seizing the opportunity to make trouble. The recognition steeled his mind.

"There will be no rescue, Commander. I have decided that I do not want to be the cause of such open interference."

The commander started to speak, but then fell silent, recognizing the impropriety of arguing with Dofan about such a matter. But his fury was apparent. Feeling it, Dofan said, "There is no need to talk further, Commander. I sign off now. Do not risk open interference by contacting me again. Good-by, sir."

They came for him shortly. They marched him between two columns of red-coated soldiers to the slow beat of muffled drums. He climbed the gallows steps in the bright morning sunshine and looked out over the Long Island countryside. As they adjusted the noose around his neck, his eyes swept the assembled crowd. There to the left, among the others, stood a tall, black-haired figure in a red coat. The eyes and nose were the same as his eyes and nose, and he looked at his brother and smiled.

A few feet from his brother, all unknowing, stood Betty Fuller, and for a wild moment he considered calling out to her for help. He saw the sneer on her face, and he was immediately ashamed of his momentary weakness. He gritted his teeth and tried to think of a way to die well.

He looked up to the sky, in a westerly direction. He could not see it, for it was light-years away, but he knew it was there. A lovely island on another planet, bathed in warm breezes, the place where his people were.

His executioners asked him, "Do you have anything to say, schoolmaster?"

Then he knew what to do to swing the vote; it came to him all of a sudden. With his face raised toward home, he said, "I only regret that I have but one life to lose for my country."

Starting from Scratch

Robert Sheckley

L ast night I had a very strange dream. I dreamed that a voice said to me, "Excuse me for interrupting your previous dream, but I have an urgent problem and only you can help me with it."

I dreamed that I replied, "No apologies are necessary, it wasn't that good a dream, and if I can help you in any way—"

"*Only* you can help," the voice said. "Otherwise I and all my people are doomed."

"Christ," I said.

His name was Froka and he was a member of a very ancient race. They had lived since time immemorial in a broad valley surrounded by gigantic mountains. They were a peaceable people, and they had, in the course of time, produced some outstanding artists. Their laws were exemplary, and they brought up their children in a loving and permissive manner. Though a few of them tended to indulge in drunkenness, and they had even known an occasional murderer, they considered themselves good and respectable sentient beings, who—

I interrupted. "Look here, can't you get straight to the urgent problem?"

Froka apologized for being long-winded, but explained that on his world the standard form for supplications included a lengthy statement about the moral righteousness of the supplicant.

"Okay," I told him. "Let's get to the problem."

Froka took a deep breath and began. He told me that about one hundred years ago (as they reckon time), an enormous reddish-yellow shaft had descended from the skies, landing close to the statue to the Unknown God in front of the city hall of their third largest city.

The shaft was imperfectly cylindrical, and about two miles in diameter. It ascended upward beyond the reach of their instruments, and in defiance of all natural laws. They tested and found that the shaft was impervious to cold, heat, bacteria, proton bombardment, and, in fact, everything else they could think of. It stood there, motionless and incredible, for precisely five months, nineteen hours, and six minutes.

Then, for no reason at all, the shaft began to move in a north-northwesterly direction. Its mean speed was 78.881 miles per hour (as they reckon speed). It cut a gash 183.223 miles long by 2.011 miles wide, and then disappeared.

A symposium of scientific authorities could reach no conclusion about this event. They finally declared that it was inexplicable, unique, and unlikely ever to be duplicated.

But it did happen again, a month later, and this time in the capital. This time the cylinder moved a total of 820.331 miles, in seemingly erratic patterns. Property damage was incalculable. Several thousand lives were lost.

Two months and a day after that the shaft returned again, affecting all three major cities.

By this time everyone was aware that not only their individual lives, but their entire civilization, their very existence as a race, was threatened by some unknown and perhaps unknowable phenomenon.

This knowledge resulted in a widespread despair among the general population. There was a rapid alternation between hysteria and apathy.

The fourth assault took place in the wastelands to the east of the capital. Real damage was minimal. Nevertheless, this time there was mass panic, which resulted in a frightening number of deaths by suicide.

The situation was desperate. Now the pseudo-sciences were brought into the struggle alongside the sciences. No help was disdained, no theory was discounted, whether it be by biochemist, palmist, or astronomer. Not even the most outlandish conception could be disregarded, especially after the terrible summer night in which the beautiful ancient city of Raz and its two suburbs were completely annihilated.

"Excuse me," I said, "I'm sorry to hear that you've had all this trouble, but I don't see what it has to do with me."

"I was just coming to that," the voice said.

"Then continue," I said. "But I would advise you to hurry up, because I think I'm going to wake up soon."

"My own part in this is rather difficult to explain," Froka continued. "I am by profession a certified public accountant. But as a hobby I dabble in various techniques for expanding mental perception. Recently I have been experimenting with a chemical compound which we call *kola,* and which frequently causes states of deep illumination—"

"We have similar compounds," I told him.

"Then you understand! Well, while voyaging—do you use that term? While under the influence, so to speak, I obtained a knowledge, a completely far-out understanding . . . But it's so difficult to explain."

"Go on," I broke in impatiently. "Get to the heart of it."

"Well," the voice said, "I realized that my world existed upon many levels—atomic, subatomic, vibrationary planes, an infinity of levels of reality, all of which are also parts of other levels of existence."

"I know about that," I said excitedly. "I recently realized the same thing about my world."

"So it was apparent to me," Froka went on, "that one of our levels was being disturbed."

"Could you be a little more specific?" I said.

"My own feeling is that my world is experiencing an intrusion on a molecular level."

"Wild," I told him. "But have you been able to trace down the intrusion?"

"I think that I have," the voice said. "But I have no proof. All of this is pure intuition."

"I believe in intuition myself," I told him. "Tell me what you've found out."

"Well, sir," the voice said hesitantly, "I have come to realize—intuitively—that my world is a microscopic parasite of you."

"Say it straight!"

"All right! I have discovered that in one aspect, on one plane of reality, my world exists between the second and third knuckles of your left hand. It has existed there for millions of our years, which are minutes to you. I cannot prove this, of course, and I am certainly not accusing you—"

"That's okay," I told him. "You say that your world is located between the second and third knuckles of my left hand. All right. What can I do about it?"

"Well, sir, my guess is that recently you have begun scratching in the area of my world."

"Scratching?"

"I think so."

"And you think that the great destructive reddish shaft is one of my fingers?"

"Precisely."

"And you want me to stop scratching."

"Only near that spot," the voice said hastily. "It is an embarrassing request to make, and I make it only in hopes of saving my world from utter destruction. And I apologize—"

"Don't bother apologizing," I said. "Sentient creatures should be ashamed of nothing."

"It's kind of you to say so," the voice said. "We are non-human, you know, and parasites, and we have no claims on you."

"All sentient creatures should stick together," I told him. "You have my word that I will never ever again, so long as I live, scratch between the first and second knuckles of my left hand."

"The second and third knuckles," he reminded me.

"I'll never again scratch between *any* of the knuckles of my left hand! That is a solemn pledge and a promise which I will keep as long as I have breath."

"Sir," the voice said, "you have saved my world. No thanks could be sufficient. But I thank you nevertheless."

"Don't mention it," I said.

Then the voice went away and I woke up.

As soon as I remembered the dream, I put a Band-Aid across the knuckles of my left hand. I have ignored various itches in that area, have not even washed my left hand. I have worn this Band-Aid for a week.

At the end of next week I am going to take off the Band-Aid. I figure that should give them twenty or thirty billion years as they reckon time, which ought to be long enough for any race.

But that isn't my problem. My problem is that lately I have begun to have some unpleasant intuitions about the earthquakes along the San Andreas Fault, and the renewed volcanic activity in central Mexico. I mean it's all coming together, and I'm scared.

So look, excuse me for interrupting your previous dream, but I have this urgent problem that only you can help me with . . .

Steel

Alan Brennert

The glen was quiet this time of night, the last stars dimming over the horizon, the sun's light cresting the near hills. Ken abandoned his star-gazing and poked his way through the underbrush, moving back toward the cabin. The thorns scratched his fingers, but did not, of course, draw blood; his bare feet trod uncut over the sharp pebbles and bits of broken glass. Coke bottles. Ken picked up the pieces, disgusted, balled his hand into a fist and crushed the glass to powder. Then, stuck with the deadly powder, he had to dig a hole in the hard clay and bury it—harmlessly, he hoped—half a foot under.

He returned to the cabin—more a cottage, really, nestled in the rapidly despoiling woods—and, to avoid waking either Laney or the kids, didn't enter by the creaking front door but instead leaped up to the second-story window. Gently he pried it open, climbed in, and padded down the hallway to their bedroom.

Laney was already awake, brushing her graying black hair absently, an old nervous habit. She looked quite as beautiful as when Ken had first seen her, so long ago, when they had both worked on the same paper; she turned and smiled at his entrance.

"Out in the glen again?" she said. He nodded. Her quick eyes misted over a moment, sadly. "Why now? You've let it go by for thirty years. Why worry about it now?"

He went to the window, seeing his own reflection—the strong face, tousled black hair graying prominently—against the lightening sky. "I don't know," he said distantly. "I never used to think it was important. I mean, I just assumed . . . that this was my place, and that it didn't matter where I was born, or why I'm—the way I am."

"And now?"

He turned, half-smiling. "Now I want to know."

"Middle-aged identity crisis?"

He laughed. "Like none the world has ever seen."

She touched his arm. "Let's go to breakfast."

They ate a light meal, bacon, eggs, toast, while the radio droned on about the crisis in the Mideast in the background. Ken sat staring out the verandah window into the distance for some minutes, finally smiling and looking back at Laney. "Raccoons about fifty yards into the brush. Have to tell the landlord about it."

She nodded. She was used to nodding mutely at his sudden pronouncements of things she couldn't see. It might only have been a raccoon in a bush, or a car on a distant road, but it might as well have been half a world away for all that she could see what he saw.

"When should we start back to the city?" she asked. Ken shrugged. "Day after tomorrow," he said. "Unless you want to get back early."

"Me? God, no. I don't relish putting together the August issue." In point of fact, she did not relish putting together *any* issue; editing a women's magazine for an audience she didn't understand and only marginally believed in was a long way from where she had once hoped to be.

He touched her hand, his eyes no longer focused distantly but firm and penetrating. "I know how you feel." And the hell of it was, he did.

The kids whooped in just then, Lucy promptly spilling her grapefruit juice all over her jeans, Tom laughing uproariously at his sister's clumsiness. Looking at them, Ken felt a recurring gladness, a sense of accomplishment. Years ago he would have laughed at the idea of simple paternity counting for anything in this world, but that was years ago. Things had changed a good deal since then.

And thank God they hadn't inherited his—strength. His curse, his glory. He didn't know why, exactly; genetically he should have passed on some of his—abilities—to them; but no, they were normal, and thankfully so.

And, in the end, they might turn out to be his only vindication.

They returned to the city two days later, the kids to school, Laney to the offices of *Fem*, Ken to his editorial desk at *Life*. There was a sheaf of photos waiting for him—several sheaves, in fact: some blurred shots of the fighting in the Middle East, a couple of hot exclusives showing the ultimate dissolution of the League of Nations peacekeeping force, some spectacular color shots of Mars taken by one of the Mariner probes . . .

Ken stared at the Mariner photos a long moment, at the rugged terrain, the wasteland grayness in between the darknesses. Not there, he thought. Not anywhere in the whole damned solar system. *Where? How? Why?* He put aside the space scenes and thumbed the intercom.

"Rose, have Jim come in, will you? I want to dummy up the war pages right away . . ."

By lunchtime, Ken had had quite enough of spectacle and famine; he left Jim in charge of the office and hurried out of the building, pleading a headache. The magazine ran well without him; he had no qualms about leaving.

That afternoon, for the first time in months, he flew.

He stripped in an alley, jogged to its mouth, and leaped up. Within moments he was airborne, arcing halfway across the city before he realized that he had no place to go. No matter. He rarely had anywhere to go these days. The important thing was that he was flying, skirting the tips of skyscrapers, chasing the clouds, high above the smogline. Up here, the city was a gray tundra, soot and mist cloaking the skyline like London fog.

Disgusted, he veered west, toward open country.

(But below, he could see the small blurred figures of men and women, pointing, waving, shouting his name, and he was pleased that they remembered, even now.)

He flew into the night, seeking the darkness and the stars. He sought and named to himself the constellations; he squinted, trying to discern the planets as they popped into view. He picked up speed as he progressed, a blue streak against blackness, until he noticed ocean below him; then, reluctantly, he turned and headed home.

That night, in bed beside him, Laney stroked his face and kissed him lightly on the lips. He drew her closer to him, always careful to be gentle, afraid of the power in his arms, and they made love slowly, and didn't speak of it at all.

Word of the attack came Friday, just after the issue had gone to press. There was no deadline rush, no frantic writing, as in the old days; everyone knew all too well that there might not even *be* a next issue.

The Israelis had tactical nukes; everyone had known that. The Arabs had nuclear reactors; everyone had known that, too. Why in God's name had no one expected what had to come? Ken had, though, even as he anticipated this moment in his career—the moment in which he would, ultimately, have to pit himself against everyone, take no one's side, act from his own morality.

Laney rushed into the office minutes before he left. "Ken, for God's sake," she pleaded, taking him aside, "let them kill themselves. You can't stop it."

He licked his lips and touched her face. "I've been trying for thirty years, love. If I stop now, I . . ." He paused, forcing a thin smile. "I never could break old habits, Laney."

Within minutes he was over the Atlantic, the wind tearing at him savagely. There were limits to his strength, and he was straining those limits, now; he could only go so fast and so far before the force of his own speed battered him into unconsciousness. But he kept at it, and within two hours he was over the Mediterranean.

The fleets were converging, Americans to the south, Russians to the north. The fools who had started it all were nursing their radiation burns and had no time for the end of the world; they would leave that to the major powers. Miles above, the Chinese satellite eyed the tableau with patient silence.

Ken swooped down, the dazzling blue waters of the ocean nearly blinding him; half-sightedly, he dropped toward the U.S. flagship, snapping the aft cannons in two as he fell.

Machine guns turned on him. Volleys of ammunition pounded at him, sending him toppling backward but doing no further damage. At least he was drawing their fire away from the other ships, he thought, and then suddenly a starboard gun began firing from the Russian fleet. Damn it! He leaped up, hands outstretched, and shot toward the second cannon. It exploded, the concussion catching the flying figure off-balance. With a grunt of pain, Ken fell back into the water.

The Russian ships began their counterattack . . . but their missiles were quickly intercepted as a fount of water shot up between the two fleets. The geyser knocked the missiles off-course and they fell harmlessly into the sea.

At the tip of the waterspout, Ken halted his upward flight and the water cascaded down into the ocean again.

He made for the Russian flagship, dodging the cannon fire, snapping their guns in half with a curse. It was getting too damned hard, all this exertion after two hours' flight; he felt drained, he wanted time to rest. Perhaps they would stop now, pause at least to rethink their positions.

When the two American and Russian missiles hit him simultaneously, he knew that they were not going to stop. Not now, not ever.

He fell into the sea, letting the cold biting waters refresh him. The damned fools. They needed him, once, or said they did. As long as he was capturing bank robbers or mending broken dams, they needed him; as long as he flew above the city, lending his power and courage to their lives, they wanted him, or the symbol of what he was.

Not now, though. Not now.

With a sudden, bitter anger, Ken dived to the very bottom of the sea, touching the ocean floor. He stood there, holding his breath, clenching his fists . . . then, with one surge of strength, he vaulted up, up, through the waters, above the waves, surface tension slamming into him like a brick wall, and into the sky.

He peaked at a distance fifty yards above the two fleets . . . and then came down.

He plunged through the Russian carrier, feet first, screaming as the tough steel tore at his limbs—but he plummeted all the way through, four, five, six decks, out the bottom of the hull and into the sea once more.

He zoomed out and into the air again, heading for the American ship, repeating his actions: down through the bowels of the carrier, steel splintering around him, and back into the ocean.

When he flew shakily out of the water, exhausted, the two ships were sinking rapidly and lifeboats were being dispatched from the other carriers. Picking up the sound of radio signals, Ken heard the first halting overtures toward a cease-fire. Perhaps his intervention had slowed the battle long enough for Washington and Moscow to reconsider their options; Ken found that he no longer cared. He hovered a moment in the still air, then shut his eyes and veered to the east, homeward.

He landed in the glen, unseen, he hoped, near dawn. His costume was tattered and he was bleeding slightly, but he would live. Easily. Still as strong as ever, he thought bitterly. But they've gotten stronger. He lay down and breathed heavily.

Behind him, he heard the crackle of dry grass, and he turned around. Laney stood in the clearing, holding her bathrobe tightly around her. She ran to him and they held each other.

After a while, Ken kissed her, and then he lay back once more in the soft grass, his eyes shut to the stars.

"I know where, Laney," he said quietly, unmoving. "I know, now."

She looked at him, so large, so impervious, so deathly afraid of his own strength. All those years, she had had to have enough courage for both of them; had to give him strength enough to touch her. He was a man who never wanted to hurt, but they had forced him to hurt, in their name and their justice; and it had taken her years to convince him he would not, could not, harm her. And he hadn't. Not once in thirty years.

"Where?" she said softly.

He opened his eyes and looked up at the sky. "They made me," he said quietly. "They needed me for a time, or thought they did. The time was right. I was there." He shut his eyes again.

She took him gently by the arm and got him to stand. "Come on," she said. "Let's go to bed."

He looked at her and smiled. "If it weren't for you . . . and the kids . . . what the hell would I have to show for it all?"

"Let's go to bed."

He nodded. Together they poked their way through the thick underbrush, and Laney thought she had never seen him quite so happy.

A Stranger from Atlanta

Hugh B. Cave

Right from the start I felt there was something different about this Duane Rogers. Ever meet someone you like a lot but can't quite figure out? He was one of those.

Harry is my name, and I was forty-three years old when I met him. Just Harry, if you don't mind. And I lived in farm country then. Never mind where; it doesn't matter.

I was driving my pickup to town to buy some groceries that afternoon, and saw this fellow walking along the roadside. He had long hair and a beard and was wearing a kind of robe, like what a priest might wear at times, so I stopped and asked him did he need a lift.

"Thank you, friend," he said, climbing in. "Where does this road lead to?"

I told him, and asked where he was from.

"Atlanta," he said. He was about my age, maybe a year or two younger.

"Anywhere special I can drop you off?" I asked.

He said he was looking for a place to stay.

"Stay? You mean to live?"

He nodded, and I got an idea. I think I know now where the idea came from, but I didn't then. It really surprised me.

"If it's just a room you want, I could put you up for a while," I offered.

"That would be kind of you, friend," said he.

I told him my name, and he told me his. "I been living alone since my wife died, four years ago next month," I said. "You looking for work around here, Duane?"

"Well, yes, I believe I should have a job of some kind."

"What you do?"

"I'm a scientist. But any sort of work will do until I—ah—become acclimated, so to speak."

As it happened, the grower I worked for as bookkeeper was hiring just then, so I was able to tell Duane I was pretty sure I could help him. And on the way home, after buying some extra groceries because he'd be staying with me, I stopped there and waited outside the personnel office while he was interviewed.

He came out smiling. "I start Monday," he said. This was a Saturday. "The man was doubtful about me at first. He asked if I had a car, and when I said no, he asked where I lived and how I would get to work. When I told him I was living with you, everything was all right."

"He knew you'd be riding in with me," I said. "He ask if you had any experience?"

"Only if I were healthy and had a strong back. And oh, yes, he advised me to dress properly for the work. So I am wondering, Harry, if you—"

"Sure," I said. "I got some things I sort of grew out of. They should fit you." And that wasn't my idea, either, I know now. Not any more than telling him he could live with me.

One evening a week or so later, while we were watching *The X Files* on TV, I asked Duane what kind of work he'd done in Atlanta.

"I was in charge of a science sector," he said.

"A what?"

"A government science sector." Then when I didn't answer, he turned his head to look at me. "Didn't I tell you?"

"Well, I guess you mentioned being a scientist. You never told me what kind, though, or anything else about yourself. Where you were born, for instance. Or if you have any family."

He laughed. "Some other time, Harry. But I warn you, you'll be bored to death."

I never asked him again, figuring if he wanted me to know, he'd tell me.

One thing he didn't keep bottled up was his opinions. Before he'd been living with me a month, I was sick and tired of hearing them.

First, the Spranglin Brothers, where we both worked, was using the wrong kind of fertilizer, and too much of it. If they kept it up, they'd eventually poison not only the land they were farming but the water under it.

"How you know that?" I challenged him.

"I told you I worked in a science sector, didn't I?"

"Well, if you're that smart about such stuff, why'd you leave Atlanta?"

He changed the subject.

One evening he was at the kitchen table, reading a book he'd got from the town library. I was bagging garbage for the truck to pick up in the morning, and he'd been telling me garbage would be one of our biggest problems if we just kept dumping it in landfills. Then he looked up at me and made some remark about trees.

"What?" I said.

"Says here they've done it in Haiti."

"Done what?"

"Cut down almost all the trees, letting the wind blow the topsoil away or the rains wash it out to sea, so now there is no way they can grow enough food to feed themselves. But all over the U.S. people are still cutting down trees to build houses. Another thing: trees help clean the air. When enough of them are gone, what we breathe into our lungs will kill us."

I'd been hearing things about him at work, so after taking the garbage out to the road, I sat down to have a talk with him. "Duane," I said, "you been preaching this save-the-earth stuff to other people, haven't you?"

"Of course," he said.

"You know what's gonna happen if you keep it up? You'll get both of us fired. You for sounding off, and me for letting you."

"All right," he said. "But in time you'll wish there'd been more people like me sounding off, as you call it. You mark my words."

He didn't keep his promise to stop, though. Next thing I knew, he was writing letters to newspapers and had joined some organizations that were saying pretty much the same things he was saying.

"Duane," I told him one evening, "you're a nut."

"No, Harry," he said. "I'm a prophet."

"Well, you're going to be a sorry one. You keep this up and you'll be run out of town on a rail."

A week later, sure enough, he got fired.

"What will you do now?" I said. "The way you been carrying on, nobody around here is going to hire you, that's for sure. The growers have you pegged for a trouble-maker."

"I won't need another job right away," he said. "I've saved up enough to pay my share of our expenses. Unless you want me to leave, that is. You don't want me to leave, do you, Harry?"

I thought it over. Living alone I'd been pretty lonely, and at least he was someone to talk to. Besides, some of what he said made sense when you thought about it. And I hadn't been fired along with him, so what the hell.

"No, you can stay," I said. But I couldn't help wondering if he'd been fired from his job in Atlanta, too. The one with the science sector, whatever that was.

Well.

He went on writing letters to the newspapers. And articles, now, for various magazines. With the money he was paid, he bought himself a secondhand car and began giving free lectures around the area. But for every article of his that I saw, there were half a dozen others condemning him.

So when it happened, I wasn't surprised.

Duane Rogers had been living with me for almost two years by then. I don't know how to explain our relationship exactly. I thought he was a little crazy, I suppose. At the same time I have to admit he'd become kind of like a brother to me, doing his share of the housework and cooking. I didn't want to see anything bad happen to him.

They came in the night, like they were the K.K.K. about to lynch some poor fellow they'd taken a dislike to. Duane and I were watching a late-night movie because it was Saturday and we could sleep next day.

My house being at a bend of the road, I saw lights travel across the front window shades as the cars hit the turn. It happened all the time, of course, but this time there were too many cars for it to be natural.

"Must be some kind of meeting going on somewhere," I said, getting up to look.

The first car stopped just past my yard, with a whole string of headlights boring through the dark behind it. "Duane!" I yelled. "Come here!"

We stood there at a window and watched between twenty-five

and thirty cars stop as close to the front of my house as they could get, lining both sides of the road. Then people piled out of them and came marching toward the house like an army. As they came, the ones in front struck matches and held them against sticks that had rags wrapped around the ends of them, and the rags burst into flames.

"Duane!" I said. "They're going to burn the house down!"

"So it would seem," he agreed, taking hold of my arm. "Come, Harry. Come with me."

"Let me talk to them!"

"They won't listen," he said. "Mobs never listen. Come."

Well, I tried to reach the door, but he was a lot stronger than I'd ever suspected. Holding on to my arm, he sort of dragged me to the stairs and up them to the hall at the top, and along that to his room. Even there he didn't trust me to be sensible, but pulled me along with him to the closet where he kept his clothes.

Reaching in, he pulled out the robe he'd been wearing that first day I met him. You remember the robe? I hadn't seen it on him since then, and was surprised he still had it. Now he stuck his hand into one of its two deep pockets and the hand came out holding a black plastic box that looked like a remote control for a TV.

At that very second I heard a crash downstairs that told me the mob had broken my front door open, and I began to shake. But Duane said, "Don't be afraid, Harry. Hold my hand."

I grabbed the hand he held out to me. With his other one he pressed some of the little buttons on the box.

Well, I don't exactly know what happened. I mean I wasn't conscious of being swept off my feet and shot through space or anything. But all at once I wasn't in Harry's bedroom anymore, listening to mob noises on the staircase. I was in a big, long room that looked like a laboratory of some kind, and still clutching Duane's hand for dear life.

The black box was still in his other hand. I looked at it and said, "What *is* that thing? Where are we?"

"A mover," he said. "And we're in Atlanta, where I came from."

"A mover?"

"For travel through time or space. Or both. In this case I had to use both and get us back here in my time because if we'd returned in yours we'd be in trouble. I read about what happened here in one of those books I got from your town library."

I didn't have a clue what he was talking about. "You're crazy," I said.

"No I'm not. And I wasn't crazy back there when I was trying to hammer some sense into people. Come on," he said. "Let me show you."

We walked out into a kind of marble hall and down the hall to a big door that slid open sideways when he spoke to it. The next thing I knew, I was out on the street trying to get used to the idea that Atlanta was nothing like what I'd always thought it was. I'd been to New York once and always figured Atlanta was pretty much the same.

It sure wasn't. The buildings all around us weren't made of anything I recognized, but of some shiny light-gray material I'd never laid eyes on before. At one time they must have been really beautiful.

They looked seedy now, though, as if nobody had used them in years.

"Come," Duane said, and walked me on down the street.

Well, the city was the same all over, seedy and cruddy and looking like nobody lived in it anymore. We did meet a few people, though. They were dressed in rags and stumbling along in a daze, as if they didn't know or care where they were going.

After a while we left the city proper and I saw we were in what must have been a nice residential suburb at one time. But it too was dead or dying. Most of the trees along the roadside were skeletons, and the sidewalks were cracked, and the houses looked abandoned.

"There's no safe water anymore, Harry," Duane said. "And air and soil pollution killed not only the trees but all other growing things. Those people back there who wanted to kill me for warning them—I wish we could have brought them here and shown them this."

By now I was kind of numb. "I never knew this happened to Atlanta," I said. "It was never on TV or the papers."

"Of course," he said, "now that I know what happened here later, it doesn't seem such a tragedy. I mean, the place was doomed anyway, wasn't it? But it's not too late for the rest of the planet, if only people will listen."

We walked up to a house—one of those they call a geodesic dome. Back home it wouldn't have been more than a few years old because they haven't been around much longer than that. But this one looked like it had been standing there neglected for ages. We sat down on the steps to rest awhile and Duane said, "Well, what do you think?"

"What do you mean, what do I think?"

"You want to see more of what I've been talking about? Abandoned farms that won't grow anything anymore, and wells that produce only foul water, and lakes and streams with no fish left in them? Or I can show you some cities a little different from this one, where whole manufacturing sectors have been abandoned because they were causing some of the problems. We can't go the usual way because there's no transportation left, but I can take you on a tour with my mover here. Or shall we go back?"

"For God's sake, Duane, we can't go back," I said. "By now I don't have a house to go back to. Those people were gonna burn it!"

"We could pick another spot. I selected your town at random before."

"With the mover, you mean?"

He took it out of his shirt pocket. "Yes, with this."

"You invented that thing?"

"Of course. I told you I worked in the science sector."

"That's how you got from here to there, huh? How long were you there before I picked you up that day?"

"Only a few minutes, actually. I landed right there at the side of the road. I had a real problem, you understand, when using this to project myself into the future that time. I knew I had to go somewhere because I could see Atlanta was dying. At the same time, I didn't know if there *was* anyplace better. So I just sort of took blind aim and hoped for the best." He shook his head. "It's a good thing I opted for both a time-change and a place-change, isn't it? Because if I'd only moved forward in time but remained here in Atlanta, I'd have ended up at the bottom of the sea."

I was too tired to even try to sort it out. "So if we don't return to my house, where do we go?" I said.

"Where would you like to start over?"

"Well," I said, "I have a brother Wilbur who owns a nice farm in

Vermont. Since my wife died, he's asked me half a dozen times to come live with him and share the work. I guess if I went there I could be useful. You'd be welcome too, at least to rest awhile before you start preaching again."

"Where in Vermont?" Duane said. "I know the big cities from the books I read, but you'll have to pinpoint me."

"Could you aim us at Burlington?"

"No problem."

"We can make it the rest of the way easy. There's just one thing."

Duane was on his feet by now, with the black box in one hand and reaching for me with the other. "What's that?" he said.

"Wilbur is going to ask me how come I turned up without even phoning him, and I'm gonna have to tell him. I mean the whole story. So I have to know the real name of this place we're in right now. You understand?"

"I've told you," Duane said with a frown. "It's Atlanta. I don't know why you—" He stopped talking when a big bug with long wings and legs zoomed in out of nowhere and landed on the front of my shirt. Then he stepped forward and snatched it off me and flung it away.

"We don't want to take any Atlanta wildlife to your brother's place," he said. "There's no telling what kind of trouble an alien insect might cause. That was a praying manta," he added, watching it fly away.

I'd seen what it was. "Mantis," I corrected. "You mean a praying mantis."

He reached for my hand again. "That's what I said, didn't I?" he replied, just before he used his little black box and moved us to Vermont.

Strangers to Straba

Carl Jacobi

hey sat in Cap Barlow's house on the lonely planet, Straba. It was early evening and Straba's twin moons were slowly rising from behind the magenta hills. Outside the window lay Cap's golf course, a study in toadstool cubism, while opposite the flag of the eighteenth hole squatted the kid's ship.

The kid had landed there an hour ago. He had introduced himself as Clarence Raine, field man for Tri-Planet Pharmaceutical, and had announced urbanely he had come to make a botanical survey. All of which mildly amused Cap Barlow.

The kid was amused too. From the *Pilot Book* he had learned that Cap was the sole inhabitant of Straba, and he regarded him—and rightly so—as just another hermit nut who preferred the spacial frontiers to the regular walks of civilization.

The old man packed and lit a meerschaum pipe.

"Yes, sir," he said, "efficiency . . . regulation . . . order . . . that's what's spoiling all life these days. Those addle-headed scientists aren't satisfied unless they can dovetail everything."

Raine smiled and in the pause that followed cast his eyes about the room. It was circular and no attempt had been made to conceal its origin: the bridge-house of some discarded space-going tug. Along the continuous wall ran a triple tier of bookshelves, but it seemed that most of the books lay scattered on the table, chairs, and floor.

Above the shelves the wall was decorated with several three-dimensional water colors, pin-up girls in various stages of undress and mounted trophies of the rather hideous game Straba provided.

"About this survey," the kid began.

"Only last month," Cap Barlow continued, unmindful of the interruption, "a salesman stopped off here and wanted to sell me a gadget for my golf course. Said it would increase the gravitation over the fairways and prevent the ball from traveling any farther than it does on Earth."

He spat disgustedly. "You'd think any fool would realize it's an ideal course that can offer a Par three on a thousand yard hole."

But Raine hadn't come this far to listen to the dissertations of an old man. He was tired from long hours of sitting at the console of his ship. He stood up wearily.

"If you'll show me where I can stow my gear," he said, "I think I'll turn in and get some sleep. I've got a lot to do tomorrow."

For a week the kid didn't bother Cap at all. Each morning he went out with a reference book, a haversack and a canteen, and he didn't show up again until dark. Cap didn't mention that Straba had been officially surveyed ten years before or that results of this survey had been practically negative as far as adding to the *Interplanetary Pharmacopoeia* went. If Tri-Planet wanted to train its green personnel by sending them on a wild goose chase, that was all right with Cap.

But the old man had one thing that interested young Raine: his telescope mounted in a domed observatory on the top floor. Every night, Raine spent hours staring through that scope, sighting stars, marking them on the charts. Cap tried to tell him that those charts were as perfect as human intellect could make them. Raine had an answer for that too.

"Those charts are three years old," he said. "In three years a whole universe could be created or destroyed. Take a look at this star on Graph 5. I've been watching it, and the way it's acting convinces me there's another star, probably a Wanderer, approaching it from here." He indicated a spot on the chart.

He was efficient and persistent. He watched his star, checked and rechecked his calculations, and in the end, to Cap's amazement sighted the Wanderer almost exactly where he said it would be.

That discovery only excited him more and after that he spent an even greater amount of time in the observatory. Then late one night he came to the top of the stairs and called for Cap.

Cap went up to the scope, and at first he didn't see anything. Then he did see it: a darker shadow against the interrupted starlight.

"It's a ship," the old man said.

Raine nodded. "My guess too. But what's it doing out of regular space lanes?"

"You forget you landed here yourself. Straba does occasionally attract a visitor. Her crew may need water or food."

Raine shook his head. "I hedge-hopped in from asteroid Torela. This fellow seems to be coming from deep space."

They continued to watch that approaching shadow, taking turns at looking through the scope. It seemed to take a long time coming; but finally there was a roar and a rush of air and a black shape hurtled out of the eastern sky. The two men ran outside where Cap began to curse volubly. The ship's anti-gravs were only partially on. It had hit hard, digging up three hundred yards of the sixteenth fairway and completely ruined two greens.

Then the dust cleared and the two men stared. The ship was a derelict, a piece of space flotsam. There was no question about that. It was also a Cyblla-style coach, one of the first Earth-made passenger freighters to utilize a power-pile drive, designed when streamlining was thought to mean following the shape of a cigar. On her bow was a name but meteorite shrapnel had partially obliterated the letters.

"Jingoes," said Raine, "I never saw a ship like this before. She must be old—really old!"

The hatches were badly fused and oxidized, and it was evident that without a blaster it would be impossible to get in. Cap shrugged.

"Let her stay there," he said. "I can make a dog-leg out of the fifteenth, and keep the course fairly playable. And if I get tired of seeing that big hulk out of my dining room window I can always plant some python vines around the nearside of her."

Raine shook his head quickly. "There's no telling what we may find inside. We've got to find an opening."

He went over the ship like a squirrel looking for a nut. Back under her stern quarter, just abaft her implosion plates, he found a small refuse scuttle which seemed movable. He took drills and went to work on it.

Three hours later the two men were inside. There was nothing unusual about the crew quarters or the adjoining storage space. But when they reached the control cabin they stood and gaped.

It was like entering a museum. The bulkheads were covered with queer glass dials, and several panels of manual operating switches. The power pile conduits were shielded with lead—lead mind you— and the lighting was apparently done with some kind of fluorescent tubes bracketed to the ceiling. It brought Cap back to the time he was a kid and his grandfather told him stories and legends of the past.

Just above the pilot's old fashioned cosmoscope was a fancy metal plate with the ship's name stamped on it. *Perseus!*

"Do you know what ship this is?" demanded Cap, excitedly.

"I can read," said Raine.

"But do you know its history and the story behind it?"

Raine shook his head without interest.

Cap Barlow was still staring at the nameplate. *"Perseus!"* he repeated slowly, "it goes back to the First Triad Empire when the planets of Earth, Venus and Mars were grouped into an Oligarchy, when Venus was still a frontier. Life there was pretty much a gamble in those days, and the Oligarchs enforced strict laws of eugenics. They set up Marriage Boards and all young men and women had to undergo physical and mental examinations. Couples were paired off only after scientific scrutiny. In other words it was a cold-blooded system which had no regard for what we call love."

The old man paused. "Did you ever hear of Mason Stewart?" he asked suddenly.

Raine shook his head.

"As an individual he's pretty well forgotten today," Cap said. "I suppose you might call him a promoter. At any rate he figured a way to make himself a few thousand extra credits. He got hold of two condemned passenger freighters and with a flair for classical mythology named them *Perseus* and *Andromeda*."

Raine, listening, lit a cigarette and blew a shaft of smoke ceilingward.

"The *Perseus* was moored in North Venus," continued Cap. "The *Andromeda,* in the South. Stewart managed to spread the word that these two ships would be heading for Alpha Centauri to start a new colony. He also let it be known that the passenger lists would be composed of couples who were in love with each other without scientific screening or examination."

"Well, what happened?" demanded Raine with an air of acute boredom.

Cap bit off a piece of plug tobacco. "The rumor spread, and berths on the two ships sold for fabulous prices. Of course, the Constabulary investigated, but that's where Stewart was clever. The couples were to be split up: all females in one ship, all men in the other. The Constabulary warned them that it would take years to cross such an immense distance—those were the days before the Wellington overdrive, of course.

"But the couples wouldn't listen, and the two ships took off. People of three worlds made a big fuss over them. The theme invaded the teletheater and the popular tape novels of the day. Newscasters went wild in their extravagant reports.

"And then the truth came out. Stewart got drunk and let slip the fact that the boosters on the two ships were absolutely worthless and capable of operating for only a short time. By then the ships were several hundred thousand miles beyond the System and out of radio range. Rescue ships were sent out but found nothing though they went as far as they dared. Stewart was jailed and executed. That's the story of the *Perseus*."

Raine nodded and ground his cigarette stub against a bulkhead. "Let's get on with the examination," he said.

They continued down the dark corridors, Raine leading the way with a magno search lamp. Some of the cabins were in a perfect state of preservation. Others were mere cubicles of rust and oxidation. Once Cap touched a chair which apparently had been made of wood or some similar product; it dissolved into dust on the instant.

This was the *Perseus,* the ship which had carried the male passengers of that strange and ancient argosy, but as yet they had come upon no skeletons or human remains. What then had happened to them?

Five minutes later they entered the captain's cabin and found the answer. On the metal desk, preserved in litnite, lay the rough log. Cap picked it up, opened it carefully and began to read:

January 21—All hands and passengers in good health, but God help us, booster reading: Zero-Zero. By radio we have learned that our sister ship, the Andromeda, is also without auxiliary power and adrift. Such a dual catastrophe would certainly argue for something other than coincidence.

Our charts show an asteroid of sizeable proportions to lie approximately midway between the two ships. Under ordinary circumstances I would order the lifeboats run out at once and attempt to reach this planetoid, hoping that by some miracle it will be capable of supporting life. But the circumstances are far from ordinary.

We sighted them at 4:30 P.M., Earth-time, a few moments after the booster went dead and the ship lost steerageway. Absorbers! They hover out there in space, clearly visible through the ports, waiting for us to open the air-lock. There are two of them, but even as I write, one has turned and with unfailing accuracy has headed in the direction of the *Andromeda*.

Absorbers! What a world of myth and legend surrounds them! Are they organic or inorganic? I do not know. I only know they have been mortally feared by sailors since the first rocket blasted through Earth's orbit. They are what their name implies: devourers of life, with the peculiar, apparently meaningless power of transforming themselves into a physical facsimile of their victims.

One of them is out there now, swirling lazily like a miasmic cloud of saffron dust . . .

Cap handed the book to Raine who read it and handed it back without comment. And at that moment Cap saw the kid in his true light: a cold-blooded extrovert who was interested in the ship only for what he could get out of her.

Next day, without asking permission, Raine began the task of dismantling the *Perseus*. He knew he had a potential fortune at his fingertips, for every portable object he could transport back to Earth or Venus would bring a high price from curio-hungry antique hunters.

For a week he worked almost unceasingly at the salvage operations. He unscrewed the ship's nameplate and made a little plush box for it. He took down the dials of the cosmoscope, the astrolog and other smaller instruments and made them ready for shipment. He stripped out the entire intercom mechanism, the old fashioned lighting fixtures, to say nothing of the furniture and personal effects which hadn't spoiled by time.

It was on a Sunday evening that matters came to a head. In the early dusk Straba's twin moons were well above the horizon, shining with a pale light. Cap was in the kitchen brewing himself a cup of coffee when through the window he saw Raine emerge from the *Perseus* and carry an armful of equipment across to the little lean-to shed where he stored the salvage. He came out of the shed and something prompted him to look upward. An instant later he ran to the house and took the steps three at a time to the observatory.

He was up there a quarter of an hour before he came down again, a queer look on his face.

"Mr. Barlow," he said, "what's that thing that looks like a gun emplacement on the flat on the other side of the house?"

"That's exactly what it is," Cap told him. "A Dofield atomic defender. I've had that gun here a long time. When I first set up housekeeping on Straba, this part of the System was pretty wild. Pirates weren't unusual."

"What's its range?"

"Well, I don't know exactly. But it has a double trajectory that makes it a pretty potent weapon."

Raine looked at the old man for a long moment. "You probably don't believe in coincidences," he said. "But come upstairs. I want to show you something."

Cap followed him up to the observatory and looked through the scope. At first he couldn't believe his eyes. If he had been alone he would have said he was dreaming.

But there it was, a miniature satellite caught helplessly in the planet's polar attraction, midway between Straba's twin moons. He was looking at another antiquated space vessel; a ship that almost detail for detail was a replica of the *Perseus*. The truth dawned on him gradually.

It was the Andromeda—*the sister ship of the* Perseus!

The kid didn't hurry himself, bringing in the *Andromeda*. For two nights he did nothing but watch the sister ship through the scope. Then he carefully removed the preservative covering from the Dofield defender, cleaned and oiled the barrel and made the gun ready for a charge.

"If I can put a shot abaft her midsection," he said, "it might spin her out of polar draw long enough to fall into Straba's linear attraction . . ."

"Why don't you take your ship up and tow her in?" Cap said.

Raine shook his head. "Too dangerous. I'd have to come to a dead stop to fasten my grappler and at that range I'd likely become a satellite myself."

Meantime the *Perseus* lay neglected save for the tour of inspection Cap took through her on Friday morning. Cap hadn't been in the ship since Raine had started his salvage operations, and the old man was curious to see how work had progressed.

He entered through the refuse scuttle and proceeded to the control room. The bulkheads were bare expanses with only a few nests of torn wires and broken conduits to show where the dials and gauges had been ripped from their mounting places. The place looked desecrated and defiled.

Cap left the control room and mounted to the pilot's cuddy. Here, too, Raine's work was in evidence. The old man stood there, looking at the dismantled chart screens and thinking about the ship's strange and tragic past.

Her life boats were gone and the inner door of the airlock was still open. Her passengers and crew must have attempted escape in the end. Had they managed to slip by the Absorber and reached the asteroid, the name or chart number of which the captain had neglected to mention in the log? And were there such things as Absorbers or had the captain under stress of the situation given in to his emotions and flights of fancy?

Cap had heard the usual sailors' stories, of course. How a freighter had come upon one of them off Saturn's rim and sent out a gig to investigate. How the gig and all men in it had simply dissolved and become a part of the writhing cloud of mist. And how that cloud had then slowly coalesced into the shape of the six men and the gig.

As he stood there, Cap abruptly became aware of a vague pulsation, a rhythmic thudding from far off. He put his ear to the wall. The sound lost some of its vagueness but was still undeterminable as to source.

He went down the port ladder to the tween deck. Here the sound faded into nothingness, only to return as he descended the catwalk to the engine room. But in that cavern-like chamber he became conscious of something else.

He had a feeling he was surrounded by life as if he stood within the body of a living intelligence whose material form included the ship itself.

Clearly audible now was that distant thud . . . thud . . . thud . . . like the beating of a great heart.

Saturday Raine announced he was ready to "shoot down" the *Andromeda.* Unfortunately Cap figured he wouldn't be there to see the show. He had had a signal from one of his weather-robots on the dark side of the planet that morning, reporting that a cold front was moving down and the migration of the Artoks was about to begin. The Artoks could be mighty troublesome when they came en masse. If Cap didn't want his golf course eaten to the roots he'd have to stop them before they started. The generators which powered the barrier wires across the Pass would have to be turned on and the relay stations set in order.

It was late before he made his return. Dusk had set in and the Straba's twin moons were riding high when he reached the hill over-looking the house. On the flat below him he could see the moonlight glint on the barrel of the Dofield defender, and he could see Clarence Raine standing by the gun as he made preparations to fire.

For a moment Cap stood there, drinking in the scene; his golf course spread out in the blue light like a big carpet and in the center of it the black cigar-shaped *Perseus*. There was something virile about that antiquated ship, something different from the *Andromeda* he had seen through the scope. It was as if the *Perseus* were all masculine, while the *Andromeda* were its daintier feminine counterpart.

And then Raine touched the trigger. There was an ellipse of yellow flame, a mushroom of white smoke and a dull roar. Cap was flung backward by the shock-wave. The hills fielded the explosion, flung it back, and the thunder went grumbling over the countryside.

In the empty silence that followed, Cap's wrist watch ticked off the passing minutes. The moonlight returned from behind a passing cloud, to reveal Raine by the Dofield defender, binoculars to his eyes. Time snailed by. The night was passing.

And then the roar came again, this time from above. Cap saw a great cylindrical shadow slanting down from the sky. The *Andromeda* struck far out on the flat beyond the house. It struck with a crash of grinding metal and crumbling girders.

For an instant after that a hush fell over everything. And then from the *Perseus* in the golf course came a sound, low at first, growing louder and louder. To Cap it sounded like a moan of anguish, of hatred and despair that seemed to issue from a hundred throats.

The *Perseus* trembled, began to move.

Cap stared. The ship moved on its belly across the fairway. Like a timeless juggernaut it entered the flat and slid out across the table-land toward the crumpled wreckage of its sister vessel.

Raine twisted about as he heard the thunder of that advancing hulk. Fear and disbelief contorted his face. He uttered a cry, leaped from the mount of the Dofield and began to run wildly across the flat. For an instant Cap thought he was going to reach the first low hillock that led to higher ground and safety. But Cap had reckoned without the terrific drive of that vessel.

Was it the Absorber—that strange creature of outer space—which had transposed its own inexplicable life into the shell of the dismantled *Perseus* and now *was* that ship *alive* with all the ship's hates, joys, and sorrows? Organic into inorganic—a transmutation of a supernormal life into a materialistic structure of metal . . . cosmic metempsychosis too tremendous for the finite mind to grasp.

The *Perseus* came on, bowling across the flat like a monster of metal gone mad, grinding over rock outcrop and gravel, throwing up a thick cloud of dust. It came on with a terrible fixation of purpose, with a relentless compulsion that knew no halting. It met and engulfed the helpless figure of Clarence Raine and a cry of mingled hate and triumph seemed to rise up from its metal body.

The *Perseus* continued along the moonlit plateau, heading straight for the wreckage of the *Andromeda*. Not until it had reached that formless mass did it stop. Then it shuddered to a standstill and ever so gently touched its prow to the prow of the sister ship.

For a long moment Cap stood there motionless. Then, head down, he slowly made his way down the hill toward his house.

A Tale of the Lonely Larva

Del Stone, Jr.

Renfro stood naked in the center of Merriwether Street, wondering which house would be a good place to die.

Renfro wanted to die. He could no longer abide life on this planet, and he could not go home. He wanted to die.

He crossed the street and made his way up the asphalt driveway of the house to his left. So many of his brethren had died after the catacoombia had crashed in the wheat field in Alberta. He had seen the aftermath on television, a miles-long scar on the landscape that had culminated in a splash of wreckage that covered an entire farm.

And later, Renfro remembered as he rang the doorbell, the tales of horror emerging from a tiny Canadian town near the crash site. Stories about people being killed and eaten, and man-sized larvae pupating into likenesses of the victims, which staggered onto the streets in search of more victims.

The crash and subsequent escape of aliens had caused worldwide panic. People were terrified—especially when they discovered the aliens reproduced by injecting larvae into people's mouths. The larvae consumed the person, then each other, until only a single larva remained. After a short metamorphosis, what emerged was an exact likeness of the host. The alien even retained some of that person's memories, and that's what scared people—the idea that their families might not be who they appeared to be. And that a kiss could bring horrible death.

Renfro rang the doorbell again. A woman answered. She did not seem surprised by his nakedness.

"I'm selling magazine subscriptions," Renfro said. "Would you care to purchase one?"

The lady smiled radiantly. "Why, yes," she beamed. "Wait just a moment." She closed the door.

Renfro felt a satisfied glow spread through his body. She would return with a gun, and she would kill him, and he would be done with this awful, alien place.

After the crash, the world had gone berserk. Aliens were killed on the streets. Towns set up crematoriums for disposal of the bodies. Nobody asked many questions.

The first two or three generations of aliens were easy to spot, because they did not know enough about people to hide themselves well. It was not unusual to see them walking the streets naked, trying to pass themselves off as salesmen or fund-raisers. But as the aliens reproduced, they gained more and more knowledge about human behavior and were better able to disguise themselves. People lived in constant fear, because a 14th-generation alien could pass for human in every way.

But Renfro no longer wanted to pass for human. This world was a lonely, inhospitable place for him. Days and nights of nothing but television, and solitary meals, and a purposeless life that offered nothing in the way of challenges or rewards.

A Containment Division car pulled to the curb and stopped. Two men stepped out. One stood at the side of the car, his hands on his hips, and shook his head. He seemed to smile a little.

So the lady had called the CD, Renfro said to himself. That's just as well. They would haul him off to one of the public crematoriums and burn him.

The lady opened the door. The men strolled up, and indeed, the one man was smiling. Renfro said, "I am raising funds for the American Cancer Society. Would you care to make a donation?"

The CD cop sighed. "Did you stop taking your pills, Mr. Renfro? This is the second time in a week we've been called out here because of you."

Renfro felt a flash of anger. "I am NOT a man. I'm an ALIEN. You need to kill me before I bite somebody."

The cop slid a mirror from his shirt pocket and held it before Renfro. "Open and say 'ahhhh,'" he chided.

Yes, Renfro thought. That will show them. The one feature an alien cannot hide is his teeth. An alien's mouth is filled with hundreds of fangs through which larvae are injected into the host.

Renfro opened his mouth and stared. Teeth. People teeth. Molars, with fillings. Incisors. Canines.

Just teeth.

"Sorry, Mr. Renfro," the woman said lightly. "If you need a ride to the pharmacy to refill your prescription, let me know."

And as the cops led him to their car to take him back to his empty house, he spotted another pair of cops down the street, their guns aimed at the head of a man who was kneeling in the street. They shot him—a single, concussive pop—and maggot-like larvae erupted from his shattered skull.

And God how Renfro envied him—the drama of his tragedy and the almost glandular thrill of his brief existence.

Because now, and until the next time he forgot the damnable pills, Renfro was just a man. A lonely man.

That Strain Again

Charles Sheffield

Dear Werner,

I see what you meant about Vega IV. After the places I've been posted for the past three years, it's Paradise. An atmosphere you can breathe, and people who seem like humans (only, dare I say it, nicer). What more could you ask for?

Did you know that their name for themselves translates as "The Ethical People"? It seems to apply a lot better than "The Wise People"—*homo sapiens*—ever fitted us. Maybe it's the Garden of Eden, *before* the Fall. You know, just a little dull, all the days the same length, and no change in the weather. It takes some getting used to, but I'm adapting.

One other thing. Remember the way that Captain Kirwin described the Vegans' reaction when he first landed here? "They were surprised to see us, and they seemed to be both relieved and rejoicing at our arrival." A lot of people have puzzled over Kirwin's words—and today I found out why he sensed that reaction. The Vegans *were* relieved, and they were surprised, when we appeared.

You see, they'd made an expedition to Earth themselves, just a few years ago.

Sorrel has been translating the diary of that expedition for us, and he gave it to me today. I'm enclosing part of it here. To make it easier to read, I have translated the times and places into terrestrial terms. Otherwise, it's just as they wrote it.

September 12th. All arrived safely. The transmatter worked perfectly and has deposited us in an unpopulated forest area of the northern hemisphere. We will make no attempt to look for a native civilization until we have settled in. Gathor's warning is being well-heeded. We are watching closely for evidence of infection from alien bacteria and microorganisms. So far, no problem and we are all in good health.

September 23rd. All goes well. A beautiful and fertile planet this, but a strange one. Surface gravity is only five-sixths of ours and we all feel as strong as giants. This world is tilted on its axis, so days and nights are not all the same length. This has caused some confusion in our sleeping habits, but we are adjusting satisfactorily.

October 8th. Strange things are happening. The trees all around us look less healthy, with a strange blight spreading over their leaves. We thought at first that it was a trick of illumination when the sun is lower in the sky, but now we are sure it is real.

October 20th. We must return to Vega IV. Gathor was right, in an unexpected and terrible way. Alien microorganisms have not harmed us—but we have infected Earth. All around us the great blight spreads. Everywhere we look the Earth is dying. We are contagion and bear guilt for the murder of this world. Tomorrow we must transmit home.

—and they came home, Werner, back to Vega IV. Do you see what I mean about "The Ethical People"? I've looked up the climate records, and I find that fall in Vermont was exceptionally beautiful that year, all glorious reds and browns and yellows. It made me think. Somewhere out there we are going to run into a planet with as big a shock in store for us as our seasons were to the Vegans. Want to speculate? I just hope we can come out of it as well as they did . . .

Jory

They Live Forever

Lloyd Biggle, Jr.

Before he stepped out of his hut into the clear morning air, Mathews repeated his calculations of the night before. The result was the same. In Earth-time, this was the Day. And if it were not, if an error had crept into his records down through the years, this particular day was close enough. It would do.

He stood looking at the village below him, at the laboriously-cultivated fields on the lower slope, at the peacefully grazing *zawyi*, some of which were still being milked. From the village street the little chief saw him, and raised both hands. Mathews returned the greeting, and took the down path.

The chief approached him humbly. "Is your Day of Days satisfactory?"

Mathews looked down at the breath-taking panorama this strange planet served him each morning with his breakfast. The haze of ground mist was shot through with riotous colors that drifted and spread and changed before his unbelieving eyes. Without warning the jungle would suddenly flip into the sky and hang above itself in a dazzling, inverted mirage. In the distance the broad surface of a mighty river mirrored the pink-tinted clouds of early morning. The sight awed and stirred Mathews as it had on thousands of other mornings, and as it would each morning as long as his eyes served him.

"The Day is satisfactory," he told the chief.

The chief gave a little grunt of satisfaction, and shouted a command.

From nearby huts came warriors, eight, ten, a dozen. They carried an odd miscellany of weapons, and Mathews was responsible for many of them—spears, blowpipes, a boomerang, bows and arrows, and odd items that Mathews had invented. They were a resourceful people, these *Rualis*—quick, intelligent and brave. They reacted with rare enthusiasm to a new idea.

Women came forth to approach Mathews with shy respect. They bowed before him with their gifts. He accepted a skin of sweet wine, bread cakes, and pieces of dried meta. A whispered request, and a small boy scurried into a hut and returned with a hoe.

"The Day waits," Mathews said. He took the downward trail, and the *Rualis* marched behind him, singing lustily.

They moved quickly down the cool, sunny mountain slope, and the torrid heat of the jungle rolled up in waves to meet them. The natives moved ahead of him when they reached the jungle path. It was a custom, almost a ritual, that they should precede him into the jungle, to protect him from the nameless terrors that lurked there. Mathews had never seen these terrors, and frankly doubted their existence, but he never protested. His ability to yield graciously on matters that were really unimportant was one reason for his success with these people.

The Tree was their objective. It had been a forest giant when Mathews first saw it—fifty-eight years before, by his calculations. The Tree held some mysterious significance for the natives which he had never fathomed. They conducted ceremonies there, and their dancing kept a broad, circular track cleared. But they never invited his presence, and he never attempted to intrude.

The *Rualis* seated themselves in a circle about the tree. They had removed their clothing, and perspiration glistened on their sun-tanned bodies. Insects swarmed around them. Mathews waved his hand in a friendly salute, and turned off the jungle trail. The path he followed was faint, overgrown, almost obliterated. The *Rualis* never used it, and it had been ten days since his last visit.

He moved a dozen yards into the jungle, slashing at the under-growth with his hoe, and reached a small clearing. He seated himself on the ground, and drank deeply from the wine skin. Insects droned incessantly overhead, colossal insects, but they did not bother him. That was one of the many mysteries of this strange planet. The insects plagued the *Rualis*, but ignored the Earthman.

Back at the Tree, the *Rualis* continued their singing. The song tossed swingingly on the breeze, backed up by intricate thumping on a dried *liayu* fruit. Mathews suspected that they were a highly musical people, though he knew too little about music himself to share their extreme pleasure in it.

He pushed the wine skin aside, and chewed solemnly on a piece of meat, feeling a deep, relaxing peace within himself. It was his Day—his birthday, by Earth-time, as well as he had been able to keep it. It was also, by a coincidence he had often pondered down through the years, the anniversary of the tragedy that had placed him on this planet.

The ship had crashed on his sixteenth birthday. It rested somewhere in front of him, hidden by the impenetrable curtain of green. Long years before the roaring jungle had swallowed it up in its clinging, rusting embrace. It had been years—decades, even—since Mathews had last hacked his way through to visit it. Now he was content to leave it undisturbed. There was nothing entombed there except memories, and the clearing had memories enough to satisfy him.

On the other side of the clearing were the graves—six of them, side by side. At one end Mathews had buried his grandfather. At the other end rested the mortal remains of old Wurr, the immortal man who was not immune to accidents. Between them lay the four-man crew of the *Fountain of Youth*.

"Seven is a lucky number," his grandfather had said. "Come along, and bring us luck." So Mathews had come, and brought luck only for himself. Of the seven, he alone had survived the crash.

At the time the *Fountain of Youth* set forth bravely for the far reaches of the galaxy, he'd had little understanding of his grandfather's quest. The adventure, the excitement was enough. He hadn't particularly cared whether they reached their objective or not.

Now he was an old man, and he understood—too well. It was not an idle whim that led his grandfather to name the new star ship *Fountain of Youth*. Grandfather Mathews quite literally sought the source of eternal life, but his objective was a planet of youth, rather than a fountain. He sought the home of old Wurr.

Wurr, the kindly old immortal! Mathews' memory could still search back over the years and bring him vividly to life. Bushy hair, black, twinkling eyes, low, husky voice, he never seemed anything but ordinary.

And the known facts about him were nothing less than staggering.

Wurr had survived a precipitous arrival on Earth when the space ship on which he was a passenger plunged into the Pacific Ocean. Wurr was found bobbing on the surface in a space suit, the only survivor. He was a mature man then, and from that day until he left Earth on the *Fountain of Youth,* three hundred and seventy-two years had elapsed. That much was documented history.

During those centuries he had not aged perceptibly. Doctors examined him, and x-rayed him, and studied him repeatedly, and their only comment was a rather frustrating shrug of the shoulders. He was an ordinary man, with a single difference.

He lived forever.

Ordinary man and immortal man, man of simple, unaffected habits, man of mystery. He was a sly and candid observer of the human scene. Historians sought him out—an eye-witness of more than three centuries of Earth's history. He submitted willingly to examinations, but he balked at answering questions. He was no different, he said, from anyone else—where he came from.

Grandfather Mathews became acquainted with him, and reached a conclusion on a subject that had been giving rise to much speculation ever since Wurr had completed his first hundred years on Earth. Wurr's home was a planet of immortality, a planet of perpetual youth.

Supposing an alien, a native of Earth, were to visit that Planet. Would he receive the gift of immortality? Grandfather Mathews conferred with Wurr. The immortal man was reluctant. He liked Earth. Eventually Grandfather Mathews convinced him, and the *Fountain of Youth* expedition was born. Earth had lately developed star travel, and Wurr knew with the exactitude of a skilled navigator the stellar location of his home planet in the Constellation Scorpio. Grandfather Mathews was confident.

Mathews understood, now, that the old man had not taken him along as a whim. He had frankly sought immortal life for himself, but he was a practical old fellow. He admitted the possibility that he might already be too old, too near to death, to be redeemed by the powers of that miraculous planet. But his grandson, only a boy in his teens—surely the planet could work the miracle for him!

That was the legacy the old man had sought for Mathews. Not wealth, not prestige, but immortality. Mathews gazed at the six graves with a searing pang of regret. Perhaps the bones had already dissolved in the moist jungle soil, but he carefully tended the graves as a lasting monument to his own loss, to a loss that seemed more tragic with each passing year as his life drew to a close, to the loss of life itself. But for the stupid accident, he might have achieved that which men of Earth had dreamed of for as long as there had been dreams.

And life was good. Even on this savage planet it was good. He had been too young when he arrived to feel deeply the loss of the civilized splendors of Earth. His very youth had given him much in common with the child-like *Rualis*. He had enjoyed love and laughter, the hunt, the occasional, half-coming tribal war. He had helped the *Rualis* to become strong, and they gave him lasting honor.

Life was good, and it was beating its measured way to the inevitable end, to the damp soil of the jungle. And it might have been otherwise.

Mathews got wearily to his feet, and went to work with the clumsy, stone-bladed hoe. He cleared the green shoots from around the headstones he had carved with such care so many years ago. The mounds had to be reshaped after every rainy season. The jungle was perennially encroaching upon the clearing. The open ground had been much larger in his younger days, but as he grew older he allowed the jungle to creep back. Now it seemed a struggle to hold the space remaining.

There were times when he thought he should remove the graves to a high, dry place on the mountain side. But this place seemed to belong to them, and they to it—here, where their quest had ended, hundreds of light-years from Wurr's planet of immortality, wherever it might be.

He could not work long in the savage jungle heat. He gathered up his things, and followed the faint trail back to the Tree. Still singing, the *Rualis* took their places behind him, and he led them out of the jungle.

The climb up the slope seemed harder with each trip. When he reached the village he was quite content to sit down and rest, and watch the children play, before he attempted the steep path to his own hut. He held a special affection for the village children, and they for him. Perhaps, he thought, it was because none of his wives had been able to bear him children, though when he gave them to men of their own race they always proved fertile. It was as though fate were not content with denying him physical immortality, and must also cut him off from the perpetuity that children could have secured for him. In his more bitter moments he believed that the six who died had been dealt with more kindly.

But he had to admit that life was good. The *Rualis* were an attractive, graceful, light-skinned people—small of stature, much smaller than he, but sturdy and strong. The children matured with astonishing rapidity. It was only three Earth years from birth to adolescence, and then, alas, perhaps another seven or eight years from maturity to death. The *Rualis* who reached the age of fifteen, by Earth standards, were rare. Mathews had watched many generations come and go, and he'd had wives from every generation, but no children. He had long since given up the thought of children.

When he had rested, he got to his feet and walked slowly down the village street. A child caught his attention, a girl, and even among the charming *Rualis* children her beauty was exceptional. With a smile, he stopped to admire her.

The mother appeared in the doorway of the hut, and turned aside shyly when he saw him. "You have a beautiful child," Mathews said to her. "She is the image of her great-great grandmother. Or perhaps it was her great-great-great grandmother—I do not recall exactly. But she, too, was a beautiful child."

The mother was pleased, but held herself apart with proper good manners. The child prattled excitedly. "Today is my birth festival," she told Mathews.

He said gravely, "Today is also my birth festival."

The child seemed startled. "What is your age, Earthman?"

Mathews smiled wistfully. How was he to explain seventy-four Earth years to this child? And the *Rualis* had no number large enough to embrace the quantity of the fifty-seven day months they called years that Mathews' life had spanned.

"I do not know," he said. "I cannot remember."

He turned, and sought the path to his hut. . . .

The child watched him until he disappeared. "Mother," she said, "Why does the Earthman not know his age?"

"Hush," the mother said soothingly. "Age does not matter to the Earthman. Like the Tree, his kind lives forever."

They're Playing Our Song

Harry Harrison

Love, love, love-lee love—my love's forgotten me-eee . . . !!"
stomp-stomp-stomp—
STOMP-STOMP-STOMP!! echoed through the cavernous
Paramount as the thousands of teenagers stamped their feet in hys-
terical unison, drowning out the amplified efforts of the quartet on
the stage, writhing and tearing at their guitars unheard but not
unappreciated. Squealings and stampings shattered the air and
more than one flat-chested thin-flanked and orgiastic young thing
leaped in frenzy and collapsed unconscious in the aisle. The bored
ushers—with ear plugs—dragged them onto the waiting stretchers
and carried them out.

The closing number was the Spiders' top-hit-favorite, "Were My
Pitying Heart To Break From Pitying You," and they hurled themselves into it with reckless abandon, black hair falling low over their
foreheads, arms thrashing and hips rotating like epileptic mario-
nettes. They ended with a flourish and their enamored audience had
one last sight of them bowing as the curtains closed, and with love
swelling their hearts hurled after them a final hoarse chorus of cries
of worship. There had never been anything like it in the history of
show business—well, there had been things like it—but The Spiders
were surely the latest and best.

They were ushered down a back stairway and through an un-
marked exit to avoid the press of autograph hounds at the stage
door.

Their yellow Rolls-Royce spun them back to their hotel and the
bowing manager personally showed them into the service elevator
and up to their suite.

"Quickly!" he cozened. "Screams approach—they are coming
down the hall." They pushed in hurriedly and Bingo locked the
door just in time.

"That was close," Wango said, throwing his guitar onto the couch.

Then the door to one of the bedrooms burst open and at once four lank-haired, autograph-book clutching girls rushed out: they had bribed a chambermaid and lain there in concealment the entire day.

"Shall we?" Bingo asked.

"Sure," Lingo said and unbuttoned his coat.

The girls screamed even louder when they saw the many, hairy arms concealed there, and tried to flee. But the black suited figures leapt with strange agility and arrow-sharp egg-laying ovipositors penetrated the quivering flesh.

Their heightened screams were drowned in the other screams from beyond the door:

"The Spiders! The Spiders!! We want THE SPIDERS!!"

Three Fingers in Utopia

Philip Sidney Jennings

I seated myself in a Spaceport booth opposite a large middle-aged man whose hair curled down to his shoulders and from whose open face two eyes peered in that keen look, these days attributed to twentieth-century cowboys, men who had spent too long in the saddle, riding against a dust storm that nagged on and on, eroding a man's nerve until finally he toppled from his horse and became part of the desert—unless . . . unless he were tempered of a finer quality, a more durable belief.

"Good morning," I said, "I'm Tevo, journalist en route for Olympus 11. I'm covering the Space Games, may I join you?"

Spaceports were friendly places in those days. Intergalactic travellers were still quite rare and a good companion was a blessed thing.

The man looked at me quickly and for a moment I had the

strangest feeling that I was shaking hands with his eye-brow. The feeling passed. I waited for him to say something. He said nothing, instead he sipped his coffee and made a noise.

"Something wrong?" I said.

He shook his head and sipped the coffee again.

"I don't believe in the coffee, that's all."

I touched a paper knob and released my tuna fish sandwich from its everypol container.

"Looks like coffee to me," I said, glancing at his cup.

The man beamed:

"For sure it's called coffee but I don't believe it originates from a bean that's come out of the ground. Therefore I don't believe it is what they say it is. You must BELIEVE in a consumer product in order for it to taste . . . right. It's no good going by taste buds any more either, they've learnt how to swindle too. No. You have to approach it with the spirit in order to ascertain the spirit of the brew. This brew has no spirit. It remembers only the ashes of pulverised acorns. It is not coffee."

I nodded as an oceanic memory of tuna fish swept over my tongue. I swallowed:

"I know what you mean. We have space travel through at least three galaxies and a lousy cup of coffee."

I swallowed the rest of my sandwich. The man nodded and went on: "That's well said, but do you believe there is a good cup of coffee anywhere in the universe? Anywhere?"

I gulped and let my mind go blank like a screen—an Indian doctor had taught me the method—I then waited for the truth to emerge in some shape or pattern on the screen. I waited. I waited for a decent cup of coffee. Nothing. Negative . . . wasn't that the reason I drank tea?

"I guess you can probably forget about coffee anywhere."

The man nodded his head so that the spiraling locks of his black and white hair seemed suddenly like staircases and up and down those winding stairs stepped column after column of pouring humanity, rising and falling to an unheard music.

"Not quite right though."

I looked across at him sharply. For a long time there was silence between us. I waited for him to go on.

"There's good coffee in Kareebah. I can tell you that because I was there."

"I don't know the planet."

"Few do. It's a tropical world-lazy unruffled lagoons, children and grown-ups bathing and singing, making love and music. Fruits drop off the trees into your waiting hands. Vegetables are anxious to show their shape above ground. And beans, they perk at the people. The people! Perhaps you would think they had nothing to say or do with a planet like that, you'd be wrong, they never stop wagging their tongues until both suns have gone down and the first guitar is echoing the cry of the small orange-throated dragons, who've waited all day in the shade so that they may sing when it is their time."

The man shook his head:

"The people sing by day and night and the creatures choose their time for their songs."

I had heard stories of such places but had never met anyone who had experienced such a way of life.

"It sounds like a Utopia. A place where all people were free and secure."

The man sipped his brew again and said quite levelly:

"It is a planet without a system."

I marvelled at that and couldn't resist:

"So all men were free?"

"Logically yes."

"Were they in fact?"

"I said there was no system but I should have added there was a ritual . . . a strange ritual. Maybe I shouldn't call the ritual strange—all rituals seem to have that built in their essence, by definition—nevertheless for me, at first, it was strange, incomprehensible . . ."

He stopped talking.

"Tell me about the ritual," I said.

"When I arrived in Kareebah I was a young man, about your age. I didn't know what to do with my life. I was a respectable jack of all trades and really a master of none. I adapted myself and my abilities as I travelled from planet to planet in a small ship my father had left me when he died. Life had thrown me good health and a small spaceship so—I became a star traveller. I left Earth in the sixties, by the early seventies I was looking for a place to rest for a while, you know, to look back along the road I'd been travelling. That's when I alighted on Kareebah. It was the furthest out I'd ever taken that ship and it was the most welcoming planet I'd ever seen. Oh the Karees are a blue coloured people. Their skin is a light blue. Sometimes when they stand up beneath the blue sky with the green-blue water at their backs, they hardly seem to be there at all. I was amber amongst opals. And they welcomed me with their shine. We reflected in each other's light. That was the feeling. A man called Hahah took me by the arm and led me to a grove where the finest suck-fruits grew. By the way he showed me that place I knew it was Haha's secret place and he had at once given me his secret and made me instantly special and loved. Later I loved Hahah all the more when I came to understand that he showed *everyone* his secret place and each person he showed felt loved and special. He pointed at the pink swollen suck-fruit and said with a grin:

"Haha shows you so you know."

I looked at Haha and at the fruit and I offered him thanks, which I probably meant for the first time in my life . . . and for the first time in my life felt they were pointless, irrelevant. Hahah welcomed me to Kareebah.

And there was a woman, Reejah. Since the day I had landed I had felt our eyes locking and holding and galloping away suddenly like insane horses only to return later docile and breathing regularly as though the fit were over. I sat with her, hour after hour, listening to the sound of the Up and Down music, which never dies there but builds for ever on the memory of itself so that it seems as though there has always been music and it grows from the ground like a tree or plant. One day I said to her:

"I like you Reejah."

She said: "You don't know I have such a want on you?"

I was loved. I felt wanted. I was able to shine for the first time in my life. I had landed on a planet of dreams spawned in the purest sleep . . . but real, you understand, real!

Then I stopped holding my breath and began to breathe normally and the days, they passed in peace and contentment. I sailed around the Lagoons in a wooden boat I made and spent hours staring down into the ocean. You could see through the water for about a quarter of a mile and through it there were a myriad worlds of light and movement and shifting shadows.

I climbed trees and toned my muscles and spoke to dragons and handled snakes. And the Karee laughed with me and helped me and caught parrots with their hands and chattered and screeched with them.

I built a house in the crescent that swept along the bay and by and by Reejah moved in with me. I became a happy man, loved, self-sufficient, untroubled . . . except in one respect . . . the ritual. I could do what I liked, go where I liked, sing what I liked, dance how I liked—but the ritual . . . I couldn't grasp it! I didn't understand what was going on and that disturbed me. You know how a boxer goes for his opponent once he has opened a cut on him? That's how my mind went for me. Every time it jabbed at me it said the same thing: the ritual, you don't understand it! Do you? Do you? Do you? And the answer was: No, I didn't understand.

Dawn would break. I would hear the pulse of the music in the ground murmuring like a tremor. Reejah left the bed and went out onto the beach where a small fire was burning and a band was playing the Up and Down music. I followed after her and joined her and the Karees seated around the fire, which was stirred by the early morning breeze, coming in from the sea like a sigh of expectation for the two suns which would shortly emerge from either end of the planet.

I took my seat next to Reejah and was immediately aware that the ritual had already begun. There was no telling when it had started. I suddenly saw Hahah stretch out his hands as though he had caught something. For a moment he struggled with it in his grasp. Then he hurled "it," whatever "it" was, towards the fire. But the fire would not burn "it" because now someone else had "it" and was struggling and gesturing at the fire. And all the time the Up and Down music was playing and pumping. Then I saw a musician get "it" and for a moment his hands fell away from his skins and were throwing, throwing at the fire. As this happened the men on the guitar called and pulled at the drummer with their music as though they needed to feel him behind them. And then he felt their need and was back again on the drums. And then a guitar player . . . his fingers were falling away from his instrument as he gestured at the fire. The drummer called out to the guitarist. His beat was undeniable. The guitarist came back to life, back to his strings . . . The music was very powerful. The musicians were marvellous men.

I never saw a musician run screaming out into the bush. That was the thing about the ritual, you see. It could go on for three minutes or three hours but sooner or later one person, one Karee, would jump to his feet and run screaming and shouting at the top of his voice out into the bush. You wouldn't see that person for a day, perhaps two, but after that he or she would be back at the dawn fire just as though nothing had happened. And there it would be—once more as always, the dawn, the gemini glow in the sky, the snorting little fire, and the blue blue Karees, throwing, struggling, giving the thing to the dancing flames.

"It was the only thing that disturbed me about Kareebah and it disturbed me all the more because I felt reluctant to ask Reejah, Hahah or my friend Tallyo what it all meant. I sensed that was the wrong approach. It didn't feel right. It would be like asking a fish why he didn't swim in the sky or a bird why she didn't lay her eggs at the bottom of the sea. A wrong kind of question. I had to see and feel for myself. It was Tallyo who helped me at that time. He brought me Kareebahan herbs with which strong aromatic teas were made. He advised me to drink them if I wished to understand everything. He said:

"These will fill you up so you know where you are. When you know where you are the tea will taste good. You won't be troubled that often, believe me!"

I followed Tallyo's advice and began each day with a gourd of tea. Then I followed Reejah out to the beach. It was just a week later that I found myself seated with the Karee, seated in the half light while the music rose and fell with an energy that you could believe in—it was the falling of the beat which caused the next to rise and one followed the other like the day follows the dawn.

I saw as usual the ritual had begun, for already, next to me, Reejah was attempting to throw something out of her hands and into the fire. And then I shuddered. For a moment I thought I had seen something, something wriggling and shapeless, something that filled me with fear and repulsion . . . a human liver torn from a body and tossed in the air while wolves waited and broke their teeth in expectation of its taste . . . I saw something and I was more afraid than I have ever been for not only had I felt and instantly seen it but now Reejah was on her feet and screaming from her belly and running like she was on fire out of the circle of blue faces into the bush. Trembling, I stood up and started after her. Hahah touched my arm—I thought for a moment restraining me—but no—Tallyo said:

"Let the man go and let him see."

See What?

I ran after Reejah. I ran beneath the huge bread-fruit trees. I ran through the suck-fruit groves. I ran uphill into the places where the vegetation was thicker and darker and the small dragons blew out their orange throats. Then directly ahead of me I heard a sound. A panting squirming sound as though an animal had caught itself in the bush. I went on. Then I saw Reejah. She was like I had never seen before. Her naked body was covered in a fungoid slime, her mouth and hair were tangled with leaves and earth. She was scratching clawing herself into the ground as though to bury or clean herself. She rolled over in the earth and bush and I saw the pupils of her eyes had disappeared so all that I saw was her blue round face and a white space where her eyes should shine.

"Reejah!" I shouted and her eyes came back and to my horror I saw they were full of poison, full of a wriggling ugliness. There it was in her eyes: the thing the fire had rejected. She had it and it was ugly. Now it seemed her mouth was dripping snakes and her hair was full of nits and lice. I felt her ugliness in every part of my body. I felt snakes dropping out of my own mouth and roaches running between my fingers stuffing their cases of young beneath my finger-tips. Was I the man who shared the want with this woman and was she the same woman? I took her by the wrist and pulled the leaves out of her mouth. I wiped at her body with them. And she fought and screamed and sobbed and we rolled over and over in the decaying debris of undergrowth until at last, mercifully, we were both exhausted and lay together in a panting heap, all our energies burnt and the thing from the ritual—gone.

In the evening we went down to the sea and bathed and listened to Tallyo telling the story about the Karee who rode a shadow beneath the sea. The Up and Down music was pumping life! life! life!

into the night and then it felt that what had happened between Reejah and myself earlier that day had not really happened at all. It was only a memory.

That night Reejah said:

"You know that one day you will run out into the bush and be ugly until a time or two is gone and you come back again to the Karees on the sea-shore."

I nodded. I had already begun to see the thing, the ugliness, that the music could not dissolve and the fire burn.

But I still didn't understand how. I asked: "What is it? Where does it come from?"

Reejah shook her head and I watched her as she nibbled at the rind of a suck-fruit.

"It has always been here. It has always been like that. Tallyo says it is a memory which is buried deep in our planet. It goes back to the earliest and cruellest times. Something happened on Kareebah. Something ugly. We do not know what it was, nor does it matter, since it weakens from generation to generation and we are a happy people. But it is here. It comes out of the ground and we bury it again and each day it dies a little more and we grow stronger in our lives. Why examine an ugliness? Perhaps it is different for each Karee?"

I poured coffee which was brought down from the Blue hills. I had no answers to Reejah's questions. The coffee was good. The only good cup of coffee I have ever drunk."

I stared across the everypol table at the man who was finishing his cup of spaceport coffee and I suddenly jumped in my seat for now I saw that the hand which was holding the cup—three fingers were sky blue in colour, almost translucent.

"Your hand!"

A door opened in the man's eyes. I looked in and for a moment I saw the fire on the sea-shore and a thousand laughing blue faces moving around it. And then the door was closed and I was nibbling on the lip asking myself why this man had left Kareebah, a utopian planet flawed with only an ugly memory. He began speaking again as though to answer my question:

"The Karee were right. One day I caught the memory in my hands and sobbing I ran away with it, up into the hills where I had left my spaceship. Somehow I put myself behind my controls and moved up into the atmosphere. For three days I travelled through a desert of space, not knowing where I was going, not caring, for every moment of those three days I saw in front of my eyes the Kareebahan memory and handful after handful I threw out of the ship, into the winking depths of cold space until it was all gone and I was alone and clear . . ."

"What did you see? What was the memory?"

"Reejah was right, for every person it is different. It is different for the Karee than it is for me and for each one of them it is different again. But you are a journalist, you want to know what the memory looked like . . . for me it was like a baby in a translucent sack, it was a thousand tiny planets in a capsule, it was a man in a spaceship sealed in behind his controls, safe from space and free to travel . . . and there was the feeling that it was all a mistake and really the coffee was not coffee at all, only the memory of pulverised acorns . . . it was ugly and it wriggled and then it was gone. That is how it was, a paradox in that utopia."

The man shook his spiralling locks:

"Now I am going back to Kareebah. It is a Utopia, make no mistake! You asked if men were free there and I said there was no system, only a ritual. The ritual grows like a planet or music out of the ground. It frees the spirit to travel in time, back to the past, into the future and all the time it hovers in the space of the present. The spirit is a time traveller in a human body . . . for too many years I made my human body a star traveller in a rocket ship, confusing the two, seeking the space where the two would coincide, seeing only a rush of stars and worlds like ashtrays strategically placed . . ."

The man was silent for a few moments, then he went on: "But now I know all these things and I am going back to Kareebah, a real Utopia. You noticed my hand earlier on, I saw you, the knowledge I have gained has made me part-Karee, three of my fingers are a translucent blue . . ."

At that moment a voice came over the intercom:—"We have clearance for star traveller 998K. Please stand by Hatch X17."

The man rose to his feet and stretched his hand across to me. I grasped the sky-blue of his fingers and I heard myself saying: "Three fingers in Utopia . . . and the rest to follow."

The man nodded. Doors opened in his eyes. Then he was gone. Like a memory.

To Serve Man

Damon Knight

The Kanamit were not very pretty, it's true. They looked something like pigs and something like people, and that is not an attractive combination. Seeing them for the first time shocked you; that was their handicap. When a thing with the countenance of a fiend comes from the stars and offers a gift, you are disinclined to accept.

I don't know what we expected interstellar visitors to look like— those who thought about it at all, that is. Angels, perhaps, or something too alien to be really awful. Maybe that's why we were all so horrified and repelled when they landed in their great ships and we saw what they really were like.

The Kanamit were short and very hairy—thick, bristly, brown-gray hair all over their abominably plump bodies. Their noses were snoutlike and their eyes small, and they had thick hands of three fingers each. They wore green leather harness and green shorts, but I think the shorts were a concession to our notions of public decency. The garments were quite modishly cut, with slash pockets and half-belts in the back. The Kanamit had a sense of humor, anyhow.

There were three of them at this session of the U.N., and, lord, I can't tell you how queer it looked to see them there in the middle of a solemn plenary session—three fat piglike creatures in green harness and shorts, sitting at the long table below the podium, surrounded by the packed arcs of delegates from every nation. They sat correctly upright, politely watching each speaker. Their flat ears drooped over the earphones. Later on, I believe, they learned every human language, but at this time they knew only French and English.

They seemed perfectly at ease—and that, along with their humor, was a thing that tended to make me like them. I was in the minority; I didn't think they were trying to put anything over.

The delegate from Argentina got up and said that his government was interested in the demonstration of a new cheap power source, which the Kanamit had made at the previous session, but that the Argentine government could not commit itself as to its future policy without a much more thorough examination.

It was what all the delegates were saying, but I had to pay particular attention to Señor Valdes, because he tended to sputter and his diction was bad. I got through the translation all right, with only one or two momentary hesitations, and then switched to the Polish-English line to hear how Grigori was doing with Janciewicz. Janciewicz was the cross Grigori had to bear, just as Valdes was mine.

Janciewicz repeated the previous remarks with a few ideological variations, and then the secretary-general recognized the delegate from France, who introduced Dr. Denis Lévêque, the criminologist, and a great deal of complicated equipment was wheeled in.

Dr. Lévêque remarked that the question in many people's minds had been aptly expressed by the delegate from the U.S.S.R. at the preceding session, when he demanded, "What is the motive of the Kanamit? What is their purpose in offering us these unprecedented gifts, while asking nothing in return?"

The doctor then said, "At the request of several delegates and with the full consent of our guests, the Kanamit, my associates and I have made a series of tests upon the Kanamit with the equipment which you see before you. These tests will now be repeated."

A murmur ran through the chamber. There was a fusillade of flashbulbs, and one of the TV cameras moved up to focus on the instrument board of the doctor's equipment. At the same time, the huge television screen behind the podium lighted up, and we saw the blank faces of two dials, each with its pointer resting at zero, and a strip of paper tape with a stylus point resting against it.

The doctor's assistants were fastening wires to the temples of one of the Kanamit, wrapping a canvas-covered rubber tube around his forearm, and taping something to the palm of his right hand.

In the screen, we saw the paper tape begin to move while the stylus traced a slow zigzag pattern along it. One of the needles began to jump rhythmically; the other flipped halfway over and stayed there, wavering slightly.

"These are the standard instruments for testing the truth of a statement," said Dr. Lévêque. "Our first object, since the physiology of the Kanamit is unknown to us, was to determine whether or not they react to these tests as human beings do. We will now repeat one of the many experiments which were made in the endeavor to discover this."

He pointed to the first dial. "This instrument registers the subject's heartbeat. This shows the electrical conductivity of the skin in the palm of his hand, a measure of perspiration, which increases under stress. And this"—pointing to the tape-and-stylus device—"shows the pattern and intensity of the electrical waves emanating from his brain. It has been shown, with human subjects, that all these readings vary markedly depending upon whether the subject is speaking the truth."

He picked up two large pieces of cardboard, one red and one black. The red one was a square about three feet on a side; the black was a rectangle three and a half feet long. He addressed himself to the Kanama.

"Which of these is longer than the other?"

"The red," said the Kanama.

Both needles leaped wildly, and so did the line of the unrolling tape.

"I shall repeat the question," said the doctor. "Which of these is longer than the other?"

"The black," said the creature.

This time the instruments continued in their normal rhythm.

"How did you come to this planet?" asked the doctor.

"Walked," replied the Kanama.

Again the instruments responded, and there was a subdued ripple of laughter in the chamber.

"Once more," said the doctor. "How did you come to this planet?"

"In a spaceship," said the Kanama, and the instruments did not jump.

The doctor again faced the delegates. "Many such experiments were made," he said, "and my colleagues and myself are satisfied that the mechanisms are effective. Now"—he turned to the Kanama—"I shall ask our distinguished guest to reply to the question put at the last session by the delegate of the U.S.S.R.—namely, what is the motive of the Kanamit people in offering these great gifts to the people of Earth?"

The Kanama rose. Speaking this time in English, he said, "On my planet there is a saying, 'There are more riddles in a stone than in a philosopher's head.' The motives of intelligent beings, though they may at times appear obscure, are simple things compared to the complex workings of the natural universe. Therefore I hope that the people of Earth will understand, and believe, when I tell you that our mission upon your planet is simply this—to bring to you the peace and plenty which we ourselves enjoy, and which we have in the past brought to other races throughout the galaxy. When your world has no more hunger, no more war, no more needless suffering, that will be our reward."

And the needles had not jumped once.

The delegate from the Ukraine jumped to his feet, asking to be recognized, but the time was up and the secretary-general closed the session.

I met Grigori as we were leaving the chamber. His face was red with excitement. "Who promoted that circus?" he demanded.

"The tests looked genuine to me," I told him.

"A circus!" he said vehemently. "A second-rate farce! If they were genuine, Peter, why was debate stifled?"

"There'll be time for debate tomorrow, surely."

"Tomorrow the doctor and his instruments will be back in Paris. Plenty of things can happen before tomorrow. In the name of sanity, man, how can anybody trust a thing that looks as if it ate the baby?"

I was a little annoyed. I said, "Are you sure you're not more worried about their politics than their appearance?"

He said, "Bah," and went away.

The next day reports began to come in from government laboratories all over the world where the Kanamit's power source was being tested. They were wildly enthusiastic. I don't understand such things myself, but it seemed that those little metal boxes would give more electrical power than an atomic pile, for next to nothing and nearly forever. And it was said that they were so cheap to manufacture that everybody in the world could have one of his own. In the early afternoon there were reports that seventeen countries had already begun to set up factories to turn them out.

The next day the Kanamit turned up with plans and specimens of a gadget that would increase the fertility of any arable land by 60 to 100 percent. It speeded the formation of nitrates in the soil, or something. There was nothing in the newscasts any more but stories about the Kanamit. The day after that, they dropped their bombshell.

"You now have potentially unlimited power and increased food supply," said one of them. He pointed with his three-fingered hand to an instrument that stood on the table before him. It was a box on a tripod, with a parabolic reflector on the front of it. "We offer you today a third gift which is at least as important as the first two."

He beckoned to the TV men to roll their cameras into closeup position. Then he picked up a large sheet of cardboard covered with drawings and English lettering. We saw it on the large screen above the podium; it was all clearly legible.

"We are informed that this broadcast is being relayed throughout your world," said the Kanama. "I wish that everyone who has equipment for taking photographs from television screens would use it now."

The secretary-general leaned forward and asked a question sharply, but the Kanama ignored him.

"This device," he said, "generates a field in which no explosive, of whatever nature, can detonate."

There was an uncomprehending silence.

The Kanama said, "It cannot now be suppressed. If one nation has it, all must have it." When nobody seemed to understand, he explained bluntly, "There will be no more war."

That was the biggest news of the millennium, and it was perfectly true. It turned out that the explosions the Kanama was talking about included gasoline and diesel explosions. They had simply made it impossible for anybody to mount or equip a modern army.

We could have gone back to bows and arrows, of course, but that wouldn't have satisfied the military. Besides, there wouldn't be any reason to make war. Every nation would soon have everything.

Nobody ever gave another thought to those lie-detector experiments, or asked the Kanamit what their politics were. Grigori was put out; he had nothing to prove his suspicions.

I quit my job with the U.N. a few months later, because I foresaw that it was going to die under me anyhow. U.N. business was booming at the time, but after a year or so there was going to be nothing for it to do. Every nation on Earth was well on the way to being completely self-supporting; they weren't going to need much arbitration.

I accepted a position as translator with the Kanamit Embassy, and it was there that I ran into Grigori again. I was glad to see him, but I couldn't imagine what he was doing there.

"I thought you were on the opposition," I said. "Don't tell me you're convinced the Kanamit are all right."

He looked rather shamefaced. "They're not what they look, anyhow," he said.

It was as much of a concession as he could decently make, and I invited him down to the embassy lounge for a drink. It was an intimate kind of place, and he grew confidential over the second daiquiri.

"They fascinate me," he said. "I hate them instinctively still—that hasn't changed—but I can evaluate it. You were right, obviously; they mean us nothing but good. But do you know"—he leaned across the table—"the question of the Soviet delegate was never answered."

I am afraid I snorted.

"No, really," he said. "They told us what they wanted to do—'to bring to you peace and plenty which we ourselves enjoy.' But they didn't say *why*."

"Why do missionaries—"

"Missionaries be damned!" he said angrily. "Missionaries have a religious motive. If these creatures have a religion, they haven't once mentioned it. What's more, they didn't send a missionary group; they sent a diplomatic delegation—a group representing the will and policy of their whole people. Now just what have the Kanamit, as a people or a nation, got to gain from our welfare?"

I said, "Cultural—"

"Cultural cabbage soup! No, it's something less obvious than that, something obscure that belongs to their psychology and not to ours. But trust me, Peter, there is no such thing as a completely disinterested altruism. In one way or another, they have something to gain."

"And that's why you're here," I said. "To try to find out what it is."

"Correct. I wanted to get on one of the ten-year exchange groups to their home planet, but I couldn't; the quota was filled a week after they made the announcement. This is the next best thing. I'm studying their language, and you know that language reflects the basic assumptions of the people who use it. I've got a fair command of the spoken lingo already. It's not hard, really, and there are hints in it. Some of the idioms are quite similar to English. I'm sure I'll get the answer eventually."

"More power," I said, and we went back to work.

I saw Grigori frequently from then on, and he kept me posted about his progress. He was highly excited about a month after that first meeting; said he'd got hold of a book of the Kanamits' and was trying to puzzle it out. They wrote in ideographs, worse than Chinese, but he was determined to fathom it if it took him years. He wanted my help.

Well, I was interested in spite of myself, for I knew it would be a long job. We spent some evenings together, working with material from Kanamit bulletin boards and so forth, and with the extremely limited English-Kanamit dictionary they issued to the staff. My conscience bothered me about the stolen book, but gradually I became absorbed by the problem. Languages are my field, after all. I couldn't help being fascinated.

We got the title worked out in a few weeks. It was *How to Serve Man*, evidently a handbook they were giving out to new Kanamit members of the embassy staff. They had new ones in, all the time now, a shipload about once a month; they were opening all kinds of research laboratories, clinics, and so on. If there was anybody on Earth besides Grigori who still distrusted those people, he must have been somewhere in the middle of Tibet.

It was astonishing to see the changes that had been wrought in less than a year. There were no more standing armies, no more shortages, no unemployment. When you picked up a newspaper you didn't see H-BOMB or SATELLITE leaping out at you; the news was always good. It was a hard thing to get used to. The Kanamit were working on human biochemistry, and it was known around the embassy that they were nearly ready to announce methods of making our race taller and stronger and healthier—practically a race of supermen—and they had a potential cure for heart disease and cancer.

I didn't see Grigori for a fortnight after we finished working out the title of the book; I was on a long-overdue vacation in Canada. When I got back, I was shocked by the change in his appearance.

"What on earth is wrong, Grigori?" I asked. "You look like the very devil."

"Come on down to the lounge."

I went with him, and he gulped a stiff scotch as if he needed it.

"Come on, man, what's the matter?" I urged.

"The Kanamit have put me on the passenger list for the next exchange ship," he said. "You, too, otherwise I wouldn't be talking to you."

"Well," I said, "but—"

"They're not altruists."

I tried to reason with him. I pointed out they'd made Earth a paradise compared to what it was before. He only shook his head.

Then I said, "Well, what about those lie-detector tests?"

"A farce," he replied, without heat. "I said so at the time, you fool. They told the truth, though, as far as it went."

"And the book?" I demanded, annoyed. "What about that—*How to Serve Man*? That wasn't put there for you to read. They do *mean* it. How do you explain that?"

"I've read the first paragraph of that book," he said. "Why do you suppose I haven't slept for a week?"

I said, "Well?" and he smiled a curious, twisted smile.

"It's a cookbook," he said.

Too Many Eggs

Kris Neville

Coxe, an unusually phlegmatic citizen, came to buy the new refrigerator in the usual fashion. He was looking for a bargain. It was the latest model, fresh from the new production line in Los Angeles, and was marked down considerably below standard. The freezing compartment held 245 lbs. of meat.

"How come so cheap?" Coxe wanted to know.

"Frankly," the salesman said, "I asked myself that. Usually there's a dent in them or something, when they have that factory tag on them. But I checked it over and I can't find anything wrong with it. However, she goes as is."

"At that price," Coxe said, "I'll take it."

It arrived, refinished in a copper color to his specifications, the following Tuesday. It was plugged in and operated perfectly. He checked it out by freezing ice cubes.

Wednesday evening, when he opened the door to chill some beer, there was a package in the freezing compartment. He took out the package.

It was some sort of plastic and appeared to contain fish eggs.

Coxe had not seen fresh fish eggs, considered by some a delicacy, for a number of years.

He chilled the beer and fried the eggs.

Both tasted about right.

The following Friday, his girlfriend came over to fix dinner for him, and when she looked in the freezing compartment, she said, "What's this?"

"Fish eggs," Coxe said. "How many of them?"

"Two packages."

"We'll fry them up for breakfast," he said.

Saturday morning, there were three packages of eggs in the refrigerator.

"Where do they come from?" his girlfriend wanted to know.

"They just appear. I ate some and they're very good."

She was reluctant, but he talked her into preparing a package. She agreed they were very good.

"What are you going to do about it?" she asked.

"I don't think there's anything to do about it," he said. "I like fish eggs."

On Sunday, the package they had eaten Saturday had been replaced. They were coming at a steady rate of one a day. Coxe cooked a package for breakfast and took the other two to his parents.

By Tuesday, he was getting tired of the eggs, and by the end of the week, he had four more packages. He succeeded in giving two packages to the neighbors.

At the end of another week, he had eight packages.

He explained to his girlfriend. She suggested they visit all their friends, leaving a package with each of them.

At the end of another two weeks, this method for disposing of the eggs had worn thin. They finally managed to give the last two packages to the landlady.

At the end of still another week, there were seven more packages. Otherwise, the refrigerator was a good buy.

Coxe calculated that, at the present rate, had he left the packages in the compartment, it would have been filled by the end of the month. He felt that once that point was reached, the eggs would stop coming. Should this prove to be incorrect, he was prepared to arrange for some method of commercial distribution for the product.

On schedule, the eggs stopped coming.

He waited two days. No more came. It was over.

He ate the last package.

The refrigerator worked perfectly, and he began to stock it with things freezers are conventionally stocked with.

It was almost two weeks after the last package had appeared, early one Sunday morning, when the doorbell rang.

At the door was a small, nondescript man with a vaguely—and really indefinably—unpleasant aspect. His head was bandaged.

"Mr. Coxe?" he asked.

"That's me."

"May I come in?"

"Come on."

The man seated himself. "Something terrible has happened," he said. "A horrible mistake has been made."

"I'm sorry to hear that. You look as if you were in an accident."

"I was. I've been in the . . . hospital . . . for nearly two months. But to come to the point, Mr. Coxe. I've come about the refrigerator you recently purchased. It was a special refrigerator that was erroneously shipped out of the plant as a second. When I didn't come in, it got shipped out and sold."

"Good refrigerator," Coxe said.

"Perhaps you've noticed . . . ah . . . something unusual about it?"

"It runs okay. For a while there were a bunch of packages of fish eggs in it."

"Fish eggs!" the little man cried in horror. After he had recovered sufficiently, he asked, "You do, of course you do, I'm sure you still have all the . . . little packages?"

"Oh, no," said Coxe.

"NO? Oh, my God. What did you do with them, Mr. Coxe?"

"Ate them."

"You . . . ate . . . them? Ate—? No. You didn't. Not all of them. You couldn't have done that, Mr. Coxe. Please tell me that you could not have done that."

"I had to give a lot of them away, and everybody said they were delicious. And really . . . Uh, Mr.—? Mr., uh. . . ."

The little man got unsteadily to his feet. His face was ashen. "This is horrible, horrible." He stumbled to the door. "You are a fiend. All our work . . . all our plans . . . and you, you . . ." He turned to Coxe. "I hate you. Oh, I hate you."

"Now, see here."

". . . Mr. Coxe, you'll never realize the enormity of your crime.

You've eaten all of us!" With that, he slammed the door and was gone.

Coxe went back to the other room.

"Who was it, honey?"

"Ah, some nut. Seems he had first claim on the refrigerator."

"I'll bet it was about the fish eggs."

"Yeah, he wanted them."

"Oh, dear. Do you think he can do anything to us?"

"I don't think so, not now. It's too late," Coxe concluded. "We ate them all."

Top Secret

Donald A. Wollheim

I cannot say whether I am the victim of a very ingenious jest on the part of some of my shackier friends or whether I am just someone accidentally "in" on some top-secret business. But it happened, and it happened to me personally, while visiting Washington recently, just rubbernecking, you know, looking at the Capitol and the rest of the big, white buildings.

It was summer, fairly hot, Congress was not in session, nothing much was doing, most people vacationing. I was that day aiming to pay a visit to the State Department, not knowing that I couldn't for there was nothing public to see there unless it's the imposing and rather martial lobby (it used to be the War Department building, I'm told). This I did not find out until I had blithely walked up the marble steps to the entrance, past the big bronze doors, and wandered about in the huge lobby, wherein a small number of people, doubtless on important business, were passing in and out.

A guard sitting near the elevators made as if to start in my direction to find out who and what the deuce I wanted, when one of the elevators came down and a group of men hustled out. There were two men, evidently State Department escorts, neatly clad in gray, double-breasted suits, with three other men walking with them. The three men struck me as a little odd; they wore long, black cloaks, big slouch hats with wide brims pulled down over their faces and carried portfolios. They looked for all the world like cartoon representations of cloak-and-dagger spies. I supposed that they were some sort of foreign diplomats and, as they were coming directly toward me, stood my ground, determined to see who they were.

The floor was marble and highly polished. One of the men nearing me suddenly seemed to lose his balance. He slipped; his feet shot out from under and he fell. His portfolio slid directly at my feet.

Being closest to him, I scooped up the folio and was the first to help raise him to his feet. Grasping his arm, I hoisted him from the floor—he seemed to be astonishingly weak in the legs; I felt almost that he was about to topple again. His companions stood about rather flustered, helplessly, their faces curiously impassive. And though the man I helped must have received a severe jolt, his face never altered expression.

Just then the two State Department men recovered their own poise, rushed about and, getting between me and the man I had rescued, rudely brushed me aside and rushed their party to the door.

Now what bothers me is not the impression I got that the arm beneath that man's sleeve was curiously wooly, as if he had a fur coat underneath the cloak (and this in a Washington summer!), and it's not the impression that he was wearing a mask (the elastic band of which I distinctly remember seeing amidst the kinky, red, close-cropped hair of his head). No, it's not that at all, which might be merely momentary misconstructions on my part. It's the coin that I picked up off the floor where he'd dropped his portfolio.

I've searched through every stamp and coin catalogue I can find to borrow, and I've made inquiries of a dozen language teachers and professors, and nobody can identify that coin or the lettering around its circumference.

It's about the size of a quarter, silvery, very light in weight, but also very hard. Besides the lettering on it, which even the Bible Society, which knows a thousand languages and dialects, cannot decipher, there is a picture on one side and a symbol on the other.

The picture is the face of a man, but of a man with very curiously wolfish features: sharp, canine teeth parted in what could be a smile; a flattened, broad, and somewhat protruding nose, more like a pug dog's muzzle; sharp, widely spaced, vulpine eyes; and definitely hairy and pointed ears.

The symbol on the other side is a circle with latitude and longitude lines on it. Flanking the circle, one on each side, are two crescent-shaped moons.

I wish I knew just how far those New Mexico rocket experiments have actually gone.

Tu Quoque

John DeChancie

Lunchtime.

Food smells, cafeteria food, the unmistakable effluvium of rancid meat and reheated gravy mixing in the hallways with bathroom disinfectant and the faintest whiff of old vomit dusted up by the janitor long ago. Recess time: from the playground come shouts, taunts, imprecations in singsong rising on the fall air.

Book mold, old wood. School is an insular sensorium, a self-contained universe of smells, sights, sounds: the feel of fresh, slick textbook paper, the smell of its ink; the waxy odor of crayons and the musty one of pencil shavings . . . the slant of afternoon light through rows of classroom windows, birdsong outside—

He walks along the hallway, not very afraid of meeting an adult, because he has a hall pass. Forged, but he is a good forger. He should be out on the playground. Who would suspect him of playing hooky from recess? They might ask to look at the slim book he's carrying, but maybe not. Probably not.

The piano practice room is locked; but he is prepared. A credit card—his credit card, fully functional, with a five-thousand-dollar line of credit—applied to the crack between door and jamb, and he's in. The room is dark.

He flips on the light, goes to the piano, a battered console upright with gouges taken out of its faded walnut finish. The keyboard is not locked, and he is glad for that. He sits on the bench and puts the music score up on the rack.

CONCERTO IN A MINOR

FOR PIANO AND ORCHESTRA

EDVARD GRIEG

Flipping pages, he runs his eyes over the tiers of staves, the various parts: *Fagotti . . . Violino . . . Corni . . .* Bassoons, strings, horns. He knows Italian and several other languages. The piano solo part is three-quarters of the way down the page. The concerto begins with a tympani crescendo, the piano coming in immediately in a descending series of minor chords.

He puts his fingers to the keys, his long delicate fingers. He can play intervals of a tenth easily. He heard this piece once and fell instantly in love with it.

He plays the first four measures. It sounds like the CD he heard. The arpeggio looks daunting until he plays it. He reads music instantly, easily. He probably could have played this piece by ear—he has perfect pitch—but he wanted to study the score.

There are many parts. He plays the string parts, then the woodwinds, then the brass. Abstracting, he plays them all together, reducing the octave-spanning harmony to accommodate human hands.

He is enjoying himself. He loves music, though most of what he hears coming out of the radio is banal, juvenile, silly, boring. This is different. He likes other sorts of music besides classical, but classical pieces seem to have more going on inside them—structural things: towers of harmony, dancing counterpoint, long, thoughtful meditations on themes—more. "Serious" music is interesting and a lot of it is actually fun.

He is well into the second movement *(Adagio)* when the door opens.

It is the math teacher, Mrs. Schaeffer.

"I thought someone was playing the radio in here."

He looks up at her. He decides to play innocent. He should have brought a portable radio, though. Should have thought of that. Best to hedge his bets—

But she knows. "That was you, wasn't it, Ramon?"

Ramon is silent, regarding her impassively. She is tall with long brown hair. Attractive, for an adult female. Her eyes are steel gray.

She closes the door and leans against it. "Did you ever take lessons, Ramon?"

He nods. "Sure."

"Who gave the lessons to you? When?"

"Oh, when I was . . . younger. A teacher taught me. A piano teacher."

She nods, but she isn't buying it. "You've never had a lesson in your life, have you, Ramon?"

No use denying it. "No. I just picked it up."

She comes to the piano, takes the score, flips through it. "This is hardly the kind of thing you just 'pick up,' Ramon." She smiles a sly, knowing smile. "Grieg. A Romantic. You like Grieg especially?"

Ramon shrugs. "No. I just heard it on the radio."

"You got this score from the public library? Yes. And not only can you play the solo part like an accomplished pianist, you can play the orchestra part, too. You can read music as if you were trained in the best conservatories."

Ramon lifts his shoulders again. "I just picked it up."

"You're a musical genius, a child prodigy, possibly on the order of Mozart or Saint-Saëns—you've heard of them?"

"Sure. I like Mozart."

"But you are possibly greater, at least in theory, because you are self-taught."

Ramon looks away.

She sits on the piano bench next to him, and he feels her thigh against his hip.

"You're in my class, Ramon, and I know you. I've had my eye on you. To all appearances you're a bright student in math, you get good grades . . . but not the best grades. Otherwise, you seem to be an average twelve-year-old boy."

Ramon plunks out a random chord on the piano, then lets his hand drop.

"You hide your abilities," she goes on. "Sometimes the extent of your abilities scares you a little. You know people would think you strange, so you hold back. You learned long ago to hide your light under a bushel basket. Safer that way."

Ramon says nothing. He stares at the concerto score.

"You wonder sometimes," she continues. "You wonder how the human race has managed to accomplish anything at all, because the people around you, the vast majority of them, are so doltish, so inept, so far beneath you that you suspect . . . it's just a sneaking suspicion, something that gnaws at you late at night, when you're about to doze off—just a notion, a stray thought—you suspect that you are not human at all."

Slowly, he turns his head toward her. "How do you know what I think at night?"

"Because I have thought it, too. Do you want to know the answer, Ramon?"

"What answer?"

"The answer to the question. The answer is no, you're not human, not quite. And neither am I."

Ramon bangs out a loud chord. He sneers. "You're crazy."

She smiles again, this time indulgently, condescendingly. "You've read history. Is human history the story of a great and noble race? Or is it the sorry record of a species of pathetic creatures who regularly miss disaster by the skin of their rotting teeth?"

"There are some good things."

"Of course. But most of human accomplishment rests upon the work of a handful of geniuses, men and women at the farthest points along the great bell curve of intelligence, insight, and creativity. You know what a bell curve is, don't you, Ramon?—though we haven't covered it in class."

"Sure."

"Of course you do. Ramon, listen to what I'm saying. We . . . you and me, and others like us around the world, aren't even on that curve. We're off the graph paper."

Ramon laughs. He slams the keyboard cover down. "Listen. Why don't you get to what you're driving at, Mrs. Schaeffer?"

She chuckles. "So you're dropping the kid act? I know only too well that you're an adult—far above a human adult—trapped in a child's body. I know the tragedy of it. The ache, the loneliness. But you don't have to be lonely anymore. *Tu quoque,* Ramon. You know Latin, don't you?"

"A little."

"You're probably capable of reading Juvenal's satires in the original. Juvenal knew the depths of human folly. But you know what the phrase means."

"Yeah. It means 'you, too.' "

"Or 'you're another.' I'm *tu quoque*-ing you, Ramon Sanchez. It's the ancient, customary greeting of our kind, usually spoken in hushed tones. It's the recognition of one superhuman by another."

Ramon gets up from the piano bench and goes to the window. It is a brisk winter day, a bright sun low in the southern sky. He watches his schoolmates mill about the playground like so many ants from a disturbed anthill.

"I say you're crazy."

"Let me tell you a story," she says. "It's about a race of beings, an alien race—noble, powerful, intelligent beyond human imagining—who once ruled a galaxy. Not this one, but another, millions of light-years away. They were called the Kweii. Can you say that?"

"Cut the crap," he says.

She smiles thinly, then spells it for him. "Say it."

"Kway-ee."

"That's right. They ruled with an iron hand, showing no weakness, doing what was necessary to preserve order. They ruled for tens of thousands of years. But a rebellion among the lesser races, one that had brewed for a long time, finally came to a boil. The Kweii were overthrown, dethroned. They were hunted down almost to the last individual, and killed. But a few Kweii managed to escape. And they have been hiding ever since. Hiding here, on this planet."

Ramon interrupts. "Pardon me for sounding like a kid again, but that's dumb. Sounds like comic-book stuff."

"Perhaps, but it's true," Mrs. Schaeffer says. "When the Kweii arrived here, some fifty thousand years ago, they found an almost uninhabited world. Most of the advanced species were doomed to eventual extinction, including the so-called 'dominant' species of bipedal mammals. I don't have to ask you if you know any paleontology."

"Fifty thousand years ago?" Ramon thinks about it. "Neanderthals—but what about the Cro-Magnon?"

"An improved version, our creation. The aboriginal subspecies was simply too primitive. The Cro-Mags and their descendants proved useful. Their improved DNA was complex enough to accommodate and conceal the Kweii genome. Again, I will assume that you know at the least the rudiments of biochemistry and molecular biology."

"You can assume that, yes," Ramon says.

"Then I don't have to spell it out for you. The Kweii genetic material is interwoven with the human double helix. The alien Kweii genome is programmed to produce Kweii individuals now and then, quite at random, regardless of the genetic makeup of the human parents. Not too many racial specimens, not too few. Just enough to maintain a level of racial consciousness across the span of fifty thousand years."

Ramon steps toward her. "Why?"

"Why?"

"Why is the genome hidden?"

"To deceive our enemies, to conceal our presence here. Our life spans are long, but we are not immortal. Many new generations would have to be born in exile. For appearance's sake, we have had to suffer the humiliation of a short life span. There was no other way. Long-lived individuals would surely attract attention. No, the first Kweii generation here had to die knowing only that their progeny would live on, down through the ages. Until the Rebirth."

Ramon nods noncommittally. "I see. How long do we have to stay in this form?"

She answers, "Until the heat is off, to use movie gangster lingo. Until they give up looking. Then we will regroup and return to the home galaxy. And take it back."

Ramon sits on a chair beside the sooty iron radiator. "Won't we be discovered eventually?"

"No. When our enemies observe this planet, as they no doubt have already, they see a race of bumbling bipeds who can't think of anything better to do with nuclear energy than to make big firecrackers with it, or to heat water. So far they haven't been able to summon the wherewithal to design a simple fusion reactor. Laughable. No, our enemies will observe, dismiss Earth entirely, and go on, not even suspecting that we Kweii are here, biding our time, and will one day return to wreak vengeance."

Ramon rises again and begins to pace slowly, the peeling, cracked linoleum gritty under his feet.

"You don't know whether to believe me," she says. "I can understand. But if you think about it, if you think back on history, on the human record, it all makes sense."

He turns to regard her, his dark eyes hotly suspicious. "Perhaps."

"It does," she says. "You'll see that in time. And you'll be ready to join us. We have regular meetings, you know."

"You don't say."

"Yes. And the worldwide front organization is one you might even have heard of. Completely innocuous, but one not easily infiltrated. Baseline humans—that's what we call the host race—are a dead giveaway, for obvious reasons."

Ramon returns to his seat. Restless, he crosses his growing young legs. "All very interesting. Extremely interesting."

Mrs. Schaeffer raises her thin eyebrows. "Not convinced? You will be, in time. You'll be contacted when we want you to attend a meeting."

"My parents?"

"You'll have a good cover story. Leave that to us. You'll be able to attend the meeting, alone."

"You have everything worked out, don't you?"

She nods. "Of course. Formerly, we could have taken our time with you. But now, time is of the essence."

"Why so?" he asks.

"Recent work in decoding the human-Kweii megagenome is getting dangerously close to the truth. Some baselines may already begin to suspect that something anomalous is going on."

"Perhaps the baselines aren't as stupid as we think?"

She dismisses the notion with a derisive laugh. "It's taken them millennia to even begin to glimpse the truth. I suppose there's something to be said for dogged determination, but the notion that they're anything but backward and obtuse is a joke." She shakes her head, and her long hair sways. "I will grant that they've been up to surprising things lately. We've speculated—perhaps the baseline part of the genome has been mutating. But we can't be sure."

"What will happen at the Rebirth?"

"We'll leave," she tells him, her eyes cool and gray and serene.

"And the baselines?"

She shrugs it off. "We might not be able to return to the home galaxy immediately. All evidence of our stay here must be destroyed."

"I see."

"Simple, really. A rapidly mutating and absolutely deadly virus, ninety-nine percent mortality. And the remainder can be dealt with easily. No one will suspect, no one will ever know, including our enemies."

"DNA residue," he suggests.

"No one will think of conducting a racial postmortem. Why?"

He has no answer.

"Come here," she commands.

He remains seated for a moment, then gets up and approaches her.

She says, "You will mate with me, when you finish maturing."

"I will?"

"Of course. We will live to see the Rebirth. Our new bodies—our *old* ones. Glorious, transfigured! They are to these flabby lumps as champagne is to ditchwater, as baselines are to their old gods."

He says nothing as she rises and embraces him. He is almost as tall as she. Her warm wet mouth finds his, and her tongue probes deeply. Moments pass.

Suddenly she withdraws. Her gaze is analytical.

"There is . . . something about you."

He meets her gaze levelly.

They stare at each other for a time.

"No," she says finally. "No. It couldn't be . . ."

Her hand goes tentatively to his cheek. "You and I . . . we will be good together. You will see, Ramon Sanchez."

She turns toward the piano. "Finish your playing. You're young, you still enjoy games. Music is just a game, really. A frivolous pastime." She picks up the score and pages through it. "This is mawkish, saccharine. You'll evolve beyond this. And then you'll evolve beyond baseline amusements such as making rhythmic noise."

When she leaves, he reseats himself at the piano, lifts the cover, and plays a bit more. But his thoughts are on the future, and on what he has just learned.

He has had an eye on Mrs. Schaeffer. He suspected her, and she took the bait. Soon he will know more about how the Kweii were organized here. He will infiltrate. That is part of his mission, and the first major step toward his ultimate mission objective.

Yes, she almost intuited it, guessed that he is a plant, a deep-cover agent, a mole. An agent of the Kweii's "enemies"—in reality their victims, races who had suffered under the Kweii yoke, who for countless eons had endured their enormities, their humiliations, their unspeakable oppression.

This is his objective: to destroy the Kweii once and for all, to rid the universe of this curse forever. If all goes according to plan, the plague will come before the Kweii can build their ships and leave the planet, not after. All the Kweii humans will die. And with them all the host humans, every last one of them, but that can't be helped. They all carry the deadly Kweii genome within their genetic structure.

He takes his hands from the keyboard and closes the score.

Music, rhythmic noise. It has much to recommend it. Yes, he has decided. He will recommend that some of these worthy cultural artifacts be preserved. He will also recommend that an attempt be made to resurrect the aboriginal subspecies. Their art might never attain the heights of that of the altered species, but one never knows about these subjective matters. Perhaps the hosts, the base-lines, have tapped into something primal, something they had lost.

He cannot absolutely guarantee that he can save anything, or resurrect anyone, but he will try. He will surely try. After all, he and those of his culture are not Kweii. They are not ruthless, cruel, inhumane . . .

The Twerlik

Jack Sharkey

I t lay like a blanket over the cool gray sands, its fibrous substance extended to ultimate length in all directions, like a multi-spoked umbrella shorn of its fabric.

From each of its radiated arms—or legs; the Twerlik could employ them as it chose—innumerable wire-like filaments stretched outward at right angles to these limbs, flat upon the gray sands. And from them in turn jutted hair-like cilia, so that the entire body—had it been suitably stained and raised against a contrasting backdrop—resembled nothing so much as an enormous multi-plumed fan, opened to a full circle and laid over an area of ten square miles. Yet weighed upon Earth-scales, its entire mass would have been found to tilt the needle barely beyond the one-pound mark. And its arms and filaments and cilia clung so tightly to the sand, and were so pallid of hue, that even were a man to lie face down upon it and stare with all his might, he would not be certain he saw anything but sand beneath him.

It could not break apart, of course. In its substance lay strengths beyond its own comprehension. For the planet upon which it had been born was too distant from its star to have developed cellular life; the Twerlik was a single, indestructible molecule, formed of an uncountable number of interlinked atoms. But—like the radar-grid it resembled—it could see, by the process of subtraction. Mild waves of light from the cold, distant star bathed it eternally. And so, objects that thrust in between the Twerlik and its source of life were recorded as negations upon its sensitive cilia, and the composite blotting-out of the light was sorted and filed and classified in its elongated brain in a fractional instant, so that it knew what went on in its vicinity.

It could see. And it could think. And it could do.

What it did, over endless ages, was convert some of the energy

500

absorbed from the distant star into power. It used the power to work upon the atoms of the gray sand upon which it lay, and at a peripheral rate of about half an inch per Earth year, it turned the sand into its own substance and thus grew. The larger it became, after all, the more its surface could catch the faint light from the star. And the more light it could catch, on its planet whose rotation was equal to its period of revolution, the more sand it could transmute; and the more sand it transmuted the larger it became.

That was its entire cycle of life. The Twerlik was content with it. Absorb, transmute, grow. Absorb, transmute, grow. So long as it could do these things, the Twerlik would be happy.

Then, partway through its hundred billionth trip around the dim, distant star, the men of Earth came.

Its first awareness of their arrival was a sort of bloating sensation, not unlike a mild twinge of nausea, as the cilia far beneath the gleaming fires of the rocket-thrust began hungrily to over-absorb.

The Twerlik did not know what was occurring, exactly, but it soon got itself under control, and would not let those cilia nearest the descending fires partake overly of the unexpected banquet. It made them take a share proportionate to their relationship in size to the rest of the enormous body, and it urged the rest of itself to partake similarly. By the time the slim metal rocket had come down, midway between the outermost fringes of the Twerlik and its splayed-out central brain, the creature had been able to feed more than in the previous three periods of the planetary revolution.

"This thing which has come," it told itself, "is therefore a *good* thing."

It was pleased at this new concept. Until the ship had come, the Twerlik had simply assumed that life was being lived to its peak. Now it knew there were better things. And this necessity to parcel out absorbable energy to its limbs was new, also. It gave the Twerlik a greater awareness of its own brain, as the key motivator of this farflung empire which was itself. "I am a *me,*" it realized, "and the rest of my extensions are but my parts!" It almost glowed with delight—not to mention an overload of absorbed energy—at the thought of all it had learned in a few moments. And then it realized what "moments" were, too; until the arrival of the ship, everything had been the same, and so the vast eons it had been there registered as no longer than an eyeblink would to a man, because it had had no shorter events for comparison of time. "So quickly!" the Twerlik mused. "I know what goodness and betterment are; I know that I am a *me;* I know the difference between a moment and an eon."

The Twerlik was abruptly aware, then, of yet another new sensation; gratitude. "This tall thing," it said, and at the same time filed away its first knowledge of differentiation in heights for later reference, "has done the *me* a service, in a moment, and the *me* is *bettered,* and *grateful!*"

And then it knew its first pain, as this rush of new concepts attempted to file themselves in sub-atomic synaptic structures incapable of coping with such a swift influx.

The Twerlik's brain throbbed with this cramming. To ease the pain, it used a fraction of the energy it had absorbed from the fires of the rocket, and enlarged the surface of the thinking-section. Wisely—for it was growing wiser by the moment—it over-enlarged it, that it might not again know pain should more concepts try and engrave themselves upon its consciousness. And just in time, too. For it suddenly needed room for concepts of foresight, prudence, headache, remedy, and alertness.

Being lost in its own introspections, it turned its mind once more to the New Thing on the planet as it felt another increase in the absorption of its cilia. It did some rapid subtraction from the shifts in light from its star, and then it "saw" that there were things like unto itself emerging from the tall thing.

Its brain instantly added the concept of pity to the collection.

For these like-creatures were stunted travesties of the Twerlik. Only four limbs, and a limb-stub on top. And these four fairly developed limbs had but five filaments to each, and no apparent cilia, save upon the useless limb-stub. And the five filaments upon each of the two limbs nearest the *me* were bound up in layers of something that was not part of the creatures at all.

"These magnificent creatures," mourned the Twerlik, "having so little of their own, have yet shared their largesse with me!" For the creatures were bearing bulky objects out of the tall thing, and setting them upon the gray sand and upon the Twerlik itself. And from these objects there flared a great deal of brightness and warmth, and the creatures were standing amid this brightness and warmth, and doing incomprehensible things with four-limbed objects that had no life at all . . . and the cilia of the Twerlik were absorbing all they could of this unexpected feast.

"I can grow now!" it told itself. "I can grow in a short period as I have never in my life grown before. I can spread out until I cover the entire—planet." The Twerlik puzzled over the latest addition to its increasing concepts. From where had this strange idea come, this idea of a gigantic ball of solid material swinging about a star? And it suddenly knew that those other four-limbed non-living creatures were called "chairs" and "tables," and that the poorly developed things were named "men."

The Twerlik tried to solve this puzzle. How were these concepts reaching it? It checked its subtractions, but there was nothing new blocking the starlight. It checked its absorptions, but its rate of drainage upon the spilled-over warmth and light from the "electric heaters" and the "lamps"—and it realized, again enlarging its brain to store these concepts—was just as it had been. Yet these new ideas were reaching it somehow. The ideas came from the "men," but in what manner the Twerlik could not determine.

Then it checked into yet another one of its newfound concepts, "pressure," and found that there was something incomprehensible occurring.

Its first awareness of this concept had been when the "space-ship" ("Larger, brain, larger!") had pressed down upon the limbs and filaments and cilia of the *me.* Then secondary awareness that told the Twerlik of differentiations in "pressure" came when the "men" had trodden upon it, and again when the "chairs" and "ta-bles" and "electric heaters" and "lamps" had been "set up." ("More room, brain, more room!") But there was a new kind of "pressure" upon the *me.* It came and went. And it was sometimes very heavy, sometimes very faint, and it struck only near the "men" at its fullest, being felt elsewhere along the cilia in a "circle" ("Grow!") about them, but less powerfully, and in a larger "circle" about that one, but much less powerfully.

What was it, this thing that came and went, and rammed and fondled and stabbed and caressed, so swiftly, so differently—and all the time kept filling its increasing brain with new concepts?

The Twerlik narrowed its field of concentration, starting at the outermost "circle," moving inward to the next, and drawing closer and closer to the "men," seeking the source of this strange alternating pressure. And then it found it.

It came from the "mouths" of the men. They were "talking." The Twerlik was received "sound."

Its brain began to hurt terribly, and once again it made use of its newly absorbed energies and grew more brainpart for the *me*. Then it "listened" ("More! More!") to the "talking," and began to "learn."

These men were only the first. There would be others, now that they knew that the "air" and "gravitation" and "climate" were "okay." There would be "houses" and "streets" and "children" and "colonization" and "expansion." And—the Twerlik almost shuddered with joy—*light!*

These men-things needed light constantly. They could not "see" without light. There would be more heaters, more lamps, campfires, chandeliers, matches, flares, movies, candles, sparklers, flashlights—("Grow! *Grow!* GROW!")

Right here! On this spot they would begin! And all that spilled over from their wanton use of energy would belong to the *me!*

"Gratitude" was a poor word to express the intensity of the Twerlik's emotions toward these men-things now. It had to help them, had to repay them, had to show them how much their coming meant.

But how? The greatest thing in creation, so far as the Twerlik was concerned, was energy. And they had energy to spare, energy aplenty. It could not give them that as a gift. It had to find out what *they* valued most, and then somehow give this valued thing to them, if it could.

Desperately, it "listened," drawing in concept upon concept, seeking and prying and gleaning and wondering. . . .

It took all that they said, and filed it, cross-indexed it, sorted it, seeking the thing which meant more than anything to these men-things. And slowly, by winnowing away the oddments that cluttered the main stream of the men-things' ambitions and hopes, the Twerlik learned the answer.

And it was within its power to grant!

But it involved motion, and the Twerlik was not certain it knew how motion might be accomplished. In all the eons of adding to its feathery perimeter, it had never had occasion to shift any of its limbs from where they lay upon the sand. It was not quite certain it could do such a thing. Still, it told the *me,* if there were a way, then it was obligated to use this way, no matter what the difficulties thus entailed. Repayment of the men-things was a legitimate debt of honor. It had to be done no matter what the cost.

So it attempted various methods of locomotion.

It tried, first, to flex and wriggle its filaments as the men-things did, but nothing happened. Bewildered, it checked through its file of new concepts and discovered "leverage." On this principle did the men-things move. They had "muscle" which "contracted" and caused a "tendon" to shift the angle of a "bone." The Twerlik had none of these necessary things.

So it tried "propulsion," the force which had moved the space-ship, and discovered that it lacked "combustible fuel" and hollow channels for the energy called "firing tubes" and some built-in condition of these tubes called the "Venturi principle."

It pondered for a long time then, not even bothering with things the men knew as "pistons" and "cylinders" and "wheels"—since the use of these involved a freemoving segment and the Twerlik could not operate save as a whole.

Finally, after thousands of those intervals which it had come to think of as "moments," it came upon the concept of "magnetism." The forces involved came well within its scope.

By subtle control of the electron flow along the underside of one of its five-mile limbs, and the creation of an electronic "differential" flow along the top, it found that the consequent repulsion-attempts of its upper and lower surfaces resulted in the tip of the limb describing a "curl." Once this basic motion had been achieved, the rest was simple, for the Twerlik learned swiftly. In a few short moments, it had evolved a thing called "coordination" and found to its delight that it could raise, lower or otherwise manipulate limbs, filaments and cilia with ease, in a pleasant, rippling whip-motion.

This new power being tested swiftly and found quite enough for its purposes, it set to work repaying the men for their great kindness to it.

The men, it noted as it worked, were undergoing a strange somnolence called "sleep," inside the spaceship. The Twerlik realized with joy that it could indulge in what men-things called a "surprise" if it worked with sufficient rapidity.

Draining its energies with uncaring profligacy, it coiled and swirled and contracted itself until its cilia and filaments and limbs lay all about the spaceship and everywhere within it save upon the men-things. The Twerlik found that it was greatly weakened by this unwonted output, but it was a dedicated Twerlik now, and did not stop its continuation to the task at hand. It worked, and molded, and rearranged. It grew dizzy with the effort, until a stray groping strand of cilum found the energy-crammed metal housed in the tank near the firing-tubes of the spaceship. Into this metal the cilium burrowed, and then began drawing upon the energies therein like an electronic siphon, feeding out the particles of raw powder to the rest of the Twerlik, that the entirety of the creature might perform this labor of love.

It took many thousands of moments for its task to be done, but it was a contented—if desperately weary—Twerlik which finally uncoiled its incredible barely-greater-than-a-pound enormous size from the spaceship.

Once again it retreated in all directions, to lie weakly in the dim light of the distant star and await the awakening of the men-things.

It noted, disinterestedly, that the shape of the spaceship was slightly altered. It was widening slowly near the base, and bulging about the middle, and losing height. The Twerlik did not care. It had shown its gratitude, and that was all that mattered.

Abruptly, men-things were leaping from the doorway of the ship, shouting empty sounds which the Twerlik could only interpret as signs of "fear," though no "words" were used. They were—ah, that was the term—"screaming."

It could make no sense of it. Were the men-things mad? Had it not given them what they desired most? Had it not even worked upon the "food" and "water" for them, so that every item they possessed would be vastly improved?

The Twerlik could not understand why the men were acting so strangely. It waited peacefully for them to use the now-improved heaters and lamps, that it might restore some of its deeply sapped strength. But they made no move to do so. They were using words, now, having gotten over their "screaming." Words like "trapped" and "impossible" and "doomed."

506

They were, sensed the Twerlik, terribly unhappy, but it could not comprehend why.

It seemed to have to do with its gesture of repayment. But along this line of reasoning the Twerlik could not proceed without bafflement. It thought momentarily of removing the gift, and restoring things to what they had been, but then realized that it no longer possessed the necessary energies.

So it sat and pondered the ways of men, who seemed to desire nothing so much in life as the acquisition of an element called "gold," and yet acted so oddly when they were given a spaceship made of it.

The Twerlik sadly filed "screwy" in close juxtaposition to the men-concept in its brain, and when at last the men-things had laid upon the gray sand and moved no more, it transmuted their elements into that substance they loved so well with its last burst of waning strength.

Then it lay there upon the cool gray sand, sucking life from the dim, distant star of its planet, and thought and thought about men-things, and wondered if it would ever be satisfied to be nothing but a Twerlik forever, with no more creatures to be good to.

It knew one thing, however. It must not give men gold again.

The next spaceship to land upon its planet, after two revolutions about the sun, was filled with men-things, too.

But these men-things had had an accident to a thing called their "reclamation tanks." They were all thick-tongued and weak, and a quick analysis of their conversation showed the Twerlik that these men were different from the others. They desired nothing so much as a comparatively simple molecule known to them as water.

The Twerlik was only too eager to help.

And, when the transmutation of this second spaceship had been completed, right over the thirsty gray sands, the Twerlik proudly added "permeability" to its vocabulary.

Upstart

Steven Utley

You must obey the edict of the Sreen," the Intermediaries have told us repeatedly, "there is no appeal," but the captain won't hear of it, not for a moment. He draws himself up to his full height of two meters and looms threateningly over the four or five Intermediaries, who are, after all, small and not particularly substantial-looking beings, mere wisps of translucent flesh through which their bluish skeletal structures and pulsing organs can be seen.

"You take us in to talk to the Sreen," the captain tells them, "you take us in right *now,* do you hear me?" His voice is like a sword coming out of its scabbard, an angry, menacing, deadly metal-on-metal rasp. "You take us to these God-damned Sreen of yours and let us talk to them."

The Intermediaries shrink before him, fluttering their pallid appendages in obvious dismay, and bleat in unison, "No, no, what you request is impossible. The decision of the Sreen is final, and, anyway, they're very busy right now, they can't be bothered."

The captain wheels savagely, face mottled, teeth bared, arms windmilling with rage. I have never seen him this furious before, and it frightens me. Not that I cannot appreciate and even share his anger toward the Sreen, of course. The Sreen have been very arbitrary and high-handed from the start, snatching our vessel out of normal space, scooping it up and stuffing it into the maw of their own craft, establishing communication with us through their Intermediaries, then issuing their incredible edict. They do not appear to care that they have interfered with Humankind's grandest endeavor. Our vessel is Terra's first bona fide starship, in which the captain and I were to have accelerated through normal space to light-velocity, activated the tardyon-tachyon conversion system and

508

popped back into normal space in the neighborhood of Alpha Centauri. I can understand how the captain feels.

At the same time, I'm afraid that his rage will get us into extremely serious trouble. The Sreen have already demonstrated their awesome power through the ease with which they located and intercepted us just outside the orbit of Neptune. Their vessel is incomprehensible, a drupelet-cluster of a construct which seems to move in casual defiance of every law of physics, half in normal space, half in elsewherespace. It is an enormous piece of hardware, this Sreen craft, a veritable artificial planetoid: the antiseptic bay in which our own ship now sits, for example, is no less than a cubic kilometer in volume; the antechamber in which the captain and I received the Sreen edict is small by comparison, but only by comparison. Before us is a great door of dully gleaming gray metal, five or six meters high, approximately four wide. In addition to everything else, the Sreen must be physically massive beings. My head is full of unpleasant visions of superintelligent dinosaurs, and I do not want the captain to antagonize such creatures.

"Sir," I say, "there's nothing we can do here. We're just going to have to return home and let Earth figure a way out of this thing. Let them handle it." Absurd, absurd, I know how absurd the suggestion is even as I voice it, no one on Earth is going to be able to defy the edict. "We haven't any choice, sir, they want us to go now, and I think we'd better do it."

The captain glares at me and balls his meaty hands into fists. I tense in expectation of blows which do not fall. Instead, he shakes his head emphatically and turns to the Intermediaries. "This is ridiculous. Thoroughly ridiculous."

"Captain—"

He silences me with an imperious gesture. "Who do these Sreen think they *are*?"

"The true and indisputable masters of the universe," the Intermediaries pipe in one high but full-toned voice, "the lords of Creation."

"I want to see them," the captain insists.

"You must return to your ship," they insist, "and obey the will of the Sreen."

"Like hell! Like bloody Goddamned hell! Where are they? What makes them think they have the right, the *right*, to claim the whole damned *universe* for themselves?" The captain's voice is going up the scale, becoming a shriek, and filled though I am with terror of the Sreen, I am also caught up in fierce admiration for my superior officer. He may be a suicidal fool to refuse to accept the situation, but there is passion in his foolishness, and it is an infectious passion. "How *dare* they treat us this way? What do they *mean,* ordering us to go home and stay there because *they* own the universe?"

He takes a step toward the door. The Intermediaries move to block his path. With an inarticulate screech, he ploughs through them, swatting them aside with the backs of his hands, kicking them out of his way with his heavy-booted feet. The Intermediaries break easily, and it occurs to me then that they are probably as disposable a commodity among the Sreen as tissue paper is among human beings. One Intermediary is left limping along after the captain. Through the clear pale skin of its back I see that some vertebrae have been badly dislocated. The thing nevertheless succeeds in overtaking the captain and wrapping its appendages around his calf, bleating all the while, "No, no, you must abide by the edict, even as every other inferior species has, you must abide . . ." The captain is having trouble disentangling himself, and so I go to him. Together, we tear the Intermediary loose. The captain flings it aside, and it bounces off the great portal, spins across the polished floor, lies crushed and unmoving.

Side by side, we pause directly before the door. My teeth, I suddenly realize, are chattering with fear. "Captain," I say as my resolve begins to disintegrate, "why are we doing this?"

"The nature of the beast," he mutters, almost sadly, and smacks the palm of his gloved hand against the portal. "Sreen!" he yells. "Come out, Sreen!"

And we wait.

"If we don't make it home from this," I say at length, "if they never hear from us back on Earth, never know what became of their starship—"

"They'll just keep tossing men and women at the stars until someone does come back, Sreen or no Sreen." The captain strikes the door again, with the edge of his fist this time. "Sreen!" A bellow which, curiously, does not echo in the vast antechamber. *"Sreen!* SREEN!"

The door starts to swing back on noiseless hinges, and a breath of cold, unbelievably cold air touches our faces. The door swings open. The door swings open. The door swings open forever before we finally see into the next chamber.

"Oh my God," I whisper to the captain, "oh, oh my God."

They are titans, they are the true and indisputable masters of the universe, the lords of Creation, and they are unhappy with us. They speak, and theirs is a voice that shatters mountains. "WHO. ARE. YOU?"

The captain's lips draw back over his teeth in a mirthless grin as he plants his fists on his hips, throws back his head, thrusts out his jaw. "Who wants to know?"

Varieties of Technological Experience

Barry N. Malzberg

So for his various crimes against the Federation, none of which had to be explained to him (since he knew his guilt; since his entire life, he thought, was a stain of implication), they exiled Fritz to the fourth division of the Doom World which in real life was the climate-controlled sixth satellite of Neptune and there for his various crimes against the Federation explained that in order to buy his release Fritz would have to invent a universal solvent. In return for a sample they would grant him full remission and allow him to return to his old life, although of course under Federation surveillance. Fair was fair.

Fritz explained to them that the basic problem with a universal solvent was that it would dissolve any container and therefore could not be segregated. They responded that this was his problem. He asked if a formula would be sufficient with the various technicians of the Doom Planet actually preparing a batch for use. They said that this was impossible, that they already had many formulas. What they needed was proof of utility. They were very kind. Everyone on the Doom Planet was reasonable. They were not there to be punitive; it was assumed that banishment was sufficiently traumatic. What they were seeking, they explained in the most pleasant way, was results. They offered him full laboratory facilities and assistants if he desired.

Fritz, embittered, discussed the situation with his three roommates in the Dark Quarter, all of whom had been confined much longer than he. He found that he was unable to elicit much sympathy. One of them had been working on a perpetual motion device for some years, another had failed with antigravitation despite some new observations into metallurgics, and the third who thought he had had a workable disintegrator some years ago had blown out half of his laboratory facilities but in demonstration before the administrator had been unable to produce any results other than a slightly charred hand, which he claimed still gave him trouble in delicate work. "What you have to understand," the perpetual motion man said, "is that we have been handed ancient scientific paradoxes, impossibilities by definition. We have been given a life sentence, in other words, but on the other hand if we were able to defy physical laws it would be to the advantage of the Federation and they would certainly release us in gratitude. They have no shortage of potential prisoners, you know."

Fritz had become very cynical about the Federation since his detention and exile—he was beginning to suspect that it was an autocratic government interested only in self-perpetuation and any popular resistance would be defined as a "crime"—but the influence of his early technological training still sat heavy upon him and he found himself unable to accept what the perpetual motion man was saying. "They would never assign an impossible task," Fritz said. "Ultimately the Federation is a rational agency, founded upon rational principles. If there were not a way, they would not have assigned this to us. Actually, it is a test."

"It is a test, all right," the antigravity man said, "a test of our gullibility."

"A universal solvent would eat out its container," the disintegrator man said, "it could not be conveyed."

"I pointed that out to them."

"He pointed that out to them," the perpetual motion man said and poked antigravity in the ribs. "And they of course agreed and assigned you something else."

"Oh no," Fritz said, "they said that it was my problem."

"That it is," the perpetual motion man said. "And that is what they told me. I have, incidentally, been here for more than half my lifetime and until you joined us here I was the newcomer of this group. Of course there are those like you coming in all the time so I have accumulated a fair amount of seniority, haven't I, lads?"

The call to serving quarters interrupted the harsh laughter of the others and Fritz found that he had no desire to continue the discussion later. It was true what he had heard of the Doom Planet: despite the fact that the felons lived together and were exposed, almost mercilessly, to one another's personalities they tended to lead very solitary lives without much connection. Part of that came from the consuming and obsessive nature of the tasks they were assigned, of course, and another part came from the personality-set of a person foolish enough to try to overthrow the Federation. Stubborn, self-willed, monomaniacal types, Fritz had decided, never *actually* attempted overthrow. Like him, they had merely paused to consider in the interstices whether the Federation might be as benign as it pretended and that pause, it would seem, had been enough to attract the interest of the Surveyors.

In any case, it was too late for that kind of concern now. He had had a different kind of life on Mars and many associations which, if he had thought about them, he would have keenly missed, but his perspective narrowed, as perspectives on the Doom Planet tended to do, to his situation and he had decided that he would accept the conditions of his internment. He would create a universal solvent and find a container of some sort and he would present it to the Board and would be released. Once released he might carry the news of conditions far and wide to all the towns of Mars, but then again he might not. It was impossible to project that far ahead. One thing he resolved was that he would have nothing to do with his roommates or with any of his fellow felons. He considered himself to be several levels above them intellectually and he found their cynicism corrosive.

How Fritz was able to fulfill at last the conditions of his assignment and how he invented not only the universal solvent but a varying propane ring which enabled the solvent to possess other strange powers of alteration must fall without the proper scope of this history. As the various Acts & Regulations have established, the release of technological information is not only dangerous should it fall into the hands of enemies of the Federation, it is extremely boring to the majority of the populace who have no interest in the devices that manage their lives as long as these devices are workable. (Nor should they!) Sufficient to say that over a period of some time Fritz, relying heavily upon laboratory facilities and ignoring the jeers of his fellows, was able to accomplish his task and under procedure applied for an appointment with the Board to whom he presented himself in due course. When his roommates heard through the usual network of inference that Fritz had actually scheduled an appearance before the Board their contempt and amusement was virtually unbounded, but Fritz did not allow it to affect him. "You are a fool," the perpetual motion man, the harshest and most persistently abusive of his roommates, said, "you are making a mockery of their very concept of punishment. The problems are insoluble by nature."

"Not with a universal solvent," Fritz said, permitting himself the most careful of private smiles.

"You will never be welcome in these walls again."

"That is of no concern," Fritz said. "After all, I will have obtained my release."

"A fool," the perpetual motion man said, "a fool," and stalked to the doorway, attempting a dramatic exit but forgetting in his choler that exitways were barred during this period and succeeding only in causing slight but painful damage to his nose. At this the antigravitation and disintegrator men roused themselves from their quarters to laugh almost as harshly as he, but Fritz, all in all a kind and thoughtful man, had already detached himself from the conversation, preferring to think of his confrontation with the Board on the morrow.

It had long since occurred to him through his period of internment and researches that the Federation was indeed a cruel and frozen regime engaging in repression at all levels of administration solely for the purpose of decadent self-perpetuation and that the Doom Planet was a fiendish means of not only interning dissidents but exploiting their very creativity, but these insights were virtually incidental to the overall element of his growth which was that he had managed to solve one of the oldest of all scientific paradoxes. Beside this accomplishment the corruption of the Federation fell away, it was of no significance whatsoever. Of course the Federation was corrupt but then again, Fritz, not a particularly introspective man, had decided that almost all of history was a matter of corruption and that ultimately only individual ends, not collective destinies, suited. He therefore presented himself to the Board in a sanguine and optimistic manner and without questioning described what he had been able to accomplish.

"That is remarkable," they said to him and indeed their expressions showed much approbation and astonishment, "but where is the solvent itself?"

"I am carrying it with me."

"You are?" the Board said. There was a slight pause. "That is even more interesting. Where is the container?"

"Ah," Fritz said, "*I* am the container."

"Pardon?"

"*I* am the container," he pointed out, "and the solvent reposes within me."

"But that is impossible."

"Certainly not."

"Of course it is," the Board said with more emotion than was its wont. "By definition you would have been dissolved. You could not be here, the solvent is a deadly poison—"

It occurred to Fritz that under pressure the Board lost its dignity, which he could have anticipated anyway if he had given the matter some thought. There was his own loss of dignity to consider; the Board was, in its lovable way, no less human than he. There was a message there, the ultimate prevailing of humanity that was to say, but he did not want to pursue the matter at this time. "But of course," he said gently, instead, "that is the point, I am in the process of being dissolved right now. There was a calculated Lag Effect."

Gently he extracted from his pockets schematics and diagrams to place before them in verification, gently he laid them in front of the gibbering old men, and then as the solvent finally reached its critical point he consequently, and with the most lingering of sighs, began to break down.

Ah, the breakdown! First the walls of molecules, then the outer edges of cells, the viscera themselves coming with relief askew the wall of self, the persona, and he became those mindless constituent atoms which under the influence of the amalgam . . .

. . . moved out.

Moved out to dissolve the floor, the walls, the Board itself to say nothing of the planet, consuming all of it utterly as the famous prophet had pointed out concerning another matter so that all that was left of the oppressive Federation in this difficult sector was a planet-sized glob of universal solvent, hanging there in space quite unapproachable (as one might suspect) by stabilizing forces and therefore a beacon to all who would in their own way seek to assert their individuality. A planet-sized signal of Revolution to absolutely clarify, a symbol of individual human will.

But, of this glimmer of triumph from the very jaws of defeat, of the fall of the Federation, and of the heroic, brave, and finally successful efforts of the Opposition (many of whom survived in the most cunning of ways) little enough need be said at this time, the tale being part of our great and arching folklore, so we will merely pass now to our next exhibit which will depict in diorama to please all of you the history of the first and final Squaring of the Circle.

Very Much Like a Game

Adam Niswander

Fifteen-year-old Billy answered the doorbell and found himself confronted by a very strange and obviously nervous individual.

"Uh . . . pardon me for intruding, sir," said the stranger, "but my name is Grax and I represent a trading concern that would like very much to develop a new market . . . uh . . . here in your matrix."

Billy couldn't help himself. He began to laugh out loud. The stranger, no taller than he was, wore a crimson skintight suit with brilliant green cape, a skullcap of black, and soft black slippers with curled toes.

The stranger looked down at his clothing. "My staff assured me that this style of dress would be appropriate for this period—obviously a mistake. If you'll pardon me . . ."

With that, he turned and walked out of sight around the corner of the house.

In what seemed to be only a moment, the stranger returned, dressed impeccably in a gray business suit. This time, he even managed to get a foot in the door.

"Good day, sir. I am prepared to offer you the finest of products in the universe in exchange for elements you find common and valueless."

Jeeze, thought Billy. *An alien traveling salesman!* He smirked and said, "No thanks."

The little alien seemed to crumble in self-pity. "Oh, dear," he mumbled to himself, green coloring his face. "What shall I do? This is my first day on the job and the supervisor will be furious."

"What exactly are you selling?"

Grax brightened. With the oily smile, he produced a colorful brochure. "Perhaps something here will interest you, sir," said the visitor a little smugly.

Billy took the brochure and opened it. He read.

UNIVERSAL EXCHANGE, LTD.

There followed page after page of products—none of them even comprehensible.

Billy shook his head. All the pages were essentially the same. "What kind of junk is this?"

"Junk, sir?" exclaimed the stranger. "Why these are the most sought after items in the universe."

"Not in this neighborhood," commented Billy dryly.

Grax took a deep breath, then sighed. He folded the brochure and spoke in a quiet voice. "I must apologize, sir. It is apparent to me that my staff has failed dismally at providing the market research needed for this matrix. I feel badly about wasting your time, sir," he said. "For your trouble, you may select any item in my inventory. What do you say?"

"Free?" asked Billy.

"Of course," replied the little man, stepping through the open doorway. At that moment, he saw Billy's computer in the living-room.

"Is that yours, sir?" Grax asked pushing past the boy and examining the machine.

"Yes," said Billy.

A look of pure joy came over Grax's face. He pulled a small package from his pocket and handed it to Billy. "Here. Look at this, sir. I'll guarantee you'll find it a challenge." He smiled. "This is manufactured by the reality fanatics on Hestor IV and, with a few small adjustments, can be made compatible with the machine you possess."

Billy looked at the listing. It read:

REALITYGAMES
The ultimate in games and challenges.
Are you the gambling sort?
Try **Nova**—
Challenge your race.
How will they react when your primary goes?

"Is this really a good game?" Billy asked doubtfully.

Grax seemed to hesitate a moment, and his face took on a look of genuine concern. "This is very much like a game," he said. "I believe that every being has the right to determine its own destiny, but it would be unfair of me to mislead you by failing to caution you about the. . . ."

Whatever he had been about to say was lost when Billy interrupted, finally out of patience. "Look, I'll take this one. Is it okay or not?"

Grax looked angry for a moment, then shrugged and smiled a very alien smile.

"That will be fine, sir," he replied. "Activate the program by typing the word NOVA." With that, he gave a formal bow and exited.

Sighing, Billy closed the door and went to his machine. *What a stupid waste of time.* He took the disk and put it in his computer.

When the prompt came up, Billy typed "NOVA."

The computer responded with "OK."

As Billy waited for graphics to begin, it got suddenly brighter outside.

The Voice from the Curious Cube

Nelson Bond

All Xuthil seethed with excitement. The broad highways, the swirling ramps that led to the public forum were thronged with the jostling bodies of a hundred thousand inhabitants, while in the living quarters of the capital city millions unable to witness the spectacle first-hand waited anxiously by their *menavisors* for news.

The curious cube had opened. The gigantic slab of marble, its sheer, glistening walls towering hundreds of feet above the head of the tallest Xuthilian, its great square base more than a hundred home-widths on each side, but a few hours ago had opened—one smoothly oiled block sliding backward to reveal a yawning pit of blackness in its depths.

Already a band of daring explorers, heavily armed, had penetrated the depths of the curious cube. Soon they would return to make a public report, and it was this which all Xuthil breathlessly awaited.

None living knew the purpose—or dared guess the fearful age—of the curious cube. The earliest archives in Xuthilian libraries noted its existence, presupposing divine origin or construction. For certainly even the accomplished hands of earth's dominant race could not have built so gigantic a structure. It was the work of Titans, or a god.

So, with *menavisors* dialed to the forum for the first mental images to be broadcast therefrom by members of the exploration party, Xuthil hummed with nervous activity.

Abruptly a pale green luminiscence flooded the reflector screens of the *menavisors,* and a thrill coursed through the viewers. The exploration party had returned. Tul, chief of all Xuthilian scientists, was stepping upon the circular dais, his broad, intelligent forehead furrowed with thought. His band of followers trailed after him. They too walked leadenly.

Tul stepped before the image-projecting unit. As he did so, a wavering scene began to impress itself into the minds of his watchers—a picture that grew more clear and distinct as the mental contact strengthened.

Each Xuthilian saw himself walking behind the glare of a strong torch down a long straight marble passageway, through a high vaulted corridor of seamless stone. Cobwebs and the dust of centuries stirred softly beneath his feet, and the air was musty with the scent of long-dead years. A torch swung toward the roof of the passageway, and its beam was lost in the vast reaches of the chamber above.

Then the passage widened into a great amphitheatre—a tremendous room that dwarfed to insignificance the wide Xuthilian forum. Telepathically each viewer saw himself—as Tul had done—press forward on eager feet, then stop and swing his flaring torch around the strangest sight a living eye had ever seen. Rows upon rows of recessed drawers, bronze-plated and embossed with hieroglyphs—these were the contents of the curious cube. These and nothing more.

The picture wavered, faded. The thoughts of Tul replaced it, communicating directly with each watcher.

"Undeniably there is some great mystery yet to be dissolved concerning the curious cube. What these drawers contain we do not know. Archives, perhaps, of some long-vanished race. But it will take long years of arduous labor with the finest of modern equipment to open even *one* of the mighty shelves. Their gigantic size and intricate construction defies us. If living creatures built the curious cube—and we may suppose they did—their bodily structure was on a scale so vastly greater than our own that we are utterly unable to comprehend the purpose of their instruments. Only one thing found in the cube was in any way comparable to machinery we know and employ."

Tul turned and nodded to two of his assistants. They moved forward, staggering under the weight of a huge stone slab, circular in form, set into a greater square of some strange fibroid material. Attached to this giant dais was a huge resilient hawser, larger in width by half than those who bore it.

"The cable attached to this slab," continued Tul, "is very long. It reaches all the way into the heart of the curious cube. Obviously it has some bearing on the secret, but what that bearing is, we do not know. Our engineers will have to dismember the slab to solve its meaning. As you see, it is solid—"

Tul stepped upon the stone. . . .

And as Tul stepped upon the push-button, quiescent current flowed from reservoirs dormant for ages, and from the dark depths of the curious cube an electrically controlled recorder spoke.

"Men—" said a human voice—"men of the fiftieth century—we, your brothers of the twenty-fifth, need you. For humanity's sake, we call on you for help.

"As I speak, our solar system is plunging into a great chlorine cloud from which it will not emerge for hundreds of years. All mankind is doomed to destruction. In this specially constructed vault we have laid to rest ten thousand of the greatest minds of Earth, hermetically sealed to sleep in an induced catalepsy until the fiftieth century. By that time the danger will be ended.

"The door to our vault at last has opened. If there be men alive, and if the air be pure, pull down the lever beside the portal of our tomb and we will waken.

"If no man hear this plea—if no man still be alive—then farewell, world. The sleeping remnants of the race of man sleeps on forever."

"Solid," repeated Tul. "Yet, as you see, it seems to yield slightly." He continued dubiously, "Citizens of Xuthil, we are as baffled by this mystery as you are. But you may rest assured that your council of scientists will make every effort to solve it."

The green glare of the *menavisors* faded. Xuthil, perplexed and marveling, returned to its daily labors. On street corners and in halls, in homes and offices, Xuthilians briefly paused to touch antennae, discussing the strange wonder.

For the voice from the curious cube had not been heard by any living creature. Sole rulers of the fiftieth century were ants—and ants cannot hear.

A Walk in the Wet

Dennis Etchison

The letters burned warm in the night:

cold
BEER
o
n
t
a
p

Spane's labored *thump-slide, thump-slide* rhythm carried him closer to the alley that stretched out behind the sign. He stopped only long enough to rub his gnarled hand once over the half-inch growth of beard on his face and to wipe the sweat out of his eyes. A man on crutches must learn to make a hundred such moves every day of his life, but for Spane it came to be a battle by this time of night, complicated by the amount of wine he had consumed and the fact that he had only one crutch with which to maneuver, and one hand. But he moved ahead. He clenched his teeth, echoing his determination with a rheumy clatter from within the hollowed and sunken cavern of his chest, and moved ahead.

He had his job to do and, by God, he would do it.

As he passed under the sign, the letters reflected a liquid sanguineness over his glistening features and the glistening surface of the pavement and its oily, rainbow-streaked puddles. He looked grimly down at his clenched hand and saw in its perspiring ridges a blurred reflection the color of watery, gritty blood, and in the greasy clockwork springs of the white hairs curling on his corded arm a glow as if from the inner heat of a moving piston.

"Hey, old guy!"

The lights of passing cars at the end of the alley streaked the street, casting long, deep shadows toward him along the rows of garbage cans that lined the backs of the buildings.

And then suddenly a shadow moved.

Spane felt his shoulder lurch reflexly as he moved to put his other hand to his forehead, but the hand was not there. *Damn,* he muttered silently somewhere behind the sweetsour breath and the churning waters of his consciousness. But his body would never forget, and he knew it. He would die reaching for something that was not there with an arm that no longer existed.

Except in the black spaces of his memory.

"Hey, you!"

He squeezed his eyes shut, the perspiration dripping down from the creases like dirty tears. *Concentrate.* He had come this far— almost three miles across the city on foot—and now he had to know.

The shadow sprang out from the wall between two garbage cans; the old man slitted his eyes for an instant to see the batlike figure waving its arms in silhouette.

He clenched his eyes shut. He had to be sure! The glimmer had been faint all across the city and now, if he was right, if he had found him at last, he would feel a spark in the special place beyond the backbrain where he always felt it when he was right, and then he would *know.*

"HEY!"

A hand grabbed him.

He shuddered, attempting to shake it off. I must not lose this thought! His trembling cheeks protested before his lips could form the words. *I must—not lose—it now!*

"Awrr, old man."

A sliding shuffle scraped to a stop at his back, and the clammy, meaty hand gripped his neck.

Spane's fist raged up from its hold on the crutch and shook at the night in front of his brow, and he bellowed a guttural animal roar deep in his throat.

The old woman lumbered around into full view as he staggered for the crutch grip again, her hand never leaving his neck, steadying him.

There was a shivering of flesh as his face rescinded, the painful ungluing of eyes to what now filled his vision, and the sound of automobile horns in the city streets beyond the alley. His breath labored into resignation.

"You made me *lose* it!" he growled.

"Come on."

The woman's hulking body turned and the meaty hand and the neck it held turned with it, blocking from his eyes the shadow in the alley.

He was aware that he was being led up the cracked stone steps of a back entrance to the bar, and now the woman's pungent odor enveloped him, overpowering even his own rotgut breath. But he knew the sickening sweet smells of the bar as well as if they were his own, and he did not think of the creaking floorboards of the hallway down which she navigated him, nor of her intentions, for he knew them full well, and these were things that were of no importance to him. He thought, with an overwhelming and brutal melancholy, only of his prey, what had been left behind to escape in the alley.

She prodded him to the left, then right along the corridor that stank faintly of urine, and left again and pushed him down into the wooden chair.

"No-ow." She rolled into her sagging chair across the table from him, the rickety door slamming closed seemingly from the current of air she stirred as she moved to settle. "Tell me about them rockets . . . and people."

Spane felt the joints of his back crack as he straightened to protest, and to leave, but then he let his body subside and decided to go along with her, at least for a while. He saw her pawing inside her distended sweater for the bottle. He heard the giggle of female voices from the rooms nearby, and the rhythmic din of techno-rock from the floor below, and he sighed into his filthy arm and the stained wooden table on which it rested. She was too big for him to fight. He closed his eyes and felt his mind reeling backwards in space end over end as the wine resurged through his body. But he caught himself in time. When he looked up, Zenna was filling the plastic tumblers in front of her. He knew, however, that he must not take any more to drink tonight; not until he had done what he had come all this way to do. He would wait, pretending to drink with her, until she dropped off to sleep as she always did, and then he would make his way back down the stairs . . .

"Well?"

She sloshed a glass of cheap bourbon into his hand. Catching the sudden smell in his nostrils like a whiff of fermenting candy, he started to push himself up from the table. At the same time his eyes were caught, as his head turned, by a view of the night sky from the second-story window. And there were the stars. He had an instant recollection of the way the stars had looked from the *Deneb,* and he blinked, feeling himself relax to the notion of telling her, of telling anyone, what it had been like. Saturn: standing on Minas, her rings cutting the sky. Or what it was like on Deimos. Or Phobos.

But he knew that she did not want to hear of these things, nor did she want to hear about the rockets, not really. . . . And people, she had said. That was what she always said. No matter how many times he spoke to her of the wreck she never grew tired of hearing it over and over: the collision cutting the two ships almost in half, and the survivors wriggling free in space and spinning out to drift like cosmic cartwheels in all directions while their oxygen was used up slowly and they were swept toward some unthinkable alien sun. The ones with space suits, that is. What she liked most to hear, he knew, was the way the other less fortunate ones fared in that horrible instant when the protective fabric of the ships was rent apart and the night rushed in too soon to meet them. . . . That was what she wanted to hear, all right, and he felt a new wave of nausea warp through his body.

He sat down, his eyes searching the street below as a single thought returned to take the place of this room, this travesty of a woman.

He had not forgotten.

He gazed at her tiredly. Already she was pouring another glassful for herself.

"Here, drink yer hap'ness." When he did not move, she tossed her medusa head in the direction of his empty shoulder, which was nearer to the glass than his right arm. "Ya really oughta get that fixed, ya know."

His bloodshot eyes narrowed. From beneath the floorboards drifted the pulse of the dance music, and Zenna's foot began to throb against the floor in an insistent counter-rhythm of its own.

Yeah, he thought bitterly, mockingly, I oughta get it fixed—but why? His lips curled back over his ragged teeth. "Why-can't-you-just-let-me-alone!" he said, as much to her as to the old aching that he felt now where his arm should be. He winced in pain, remembering for a mercifully brief but vivid flash just what it had been like, swinging free of the *Deneb,* his lifeline drifting out and away with the torn shard of his arm still gripped to it as his suit sealed itself off and his eyes bulged behind his faceplate in unimaginable horror; and all the while he was sinking into unconsciousness, the seconds impaling him for eternities on the rays of the glaring twin suns, hearing across the soundlessness of space the soul-deaths of the 130 others, screaming silently the agony of the dying, screaming inside his own mutant skull. (They had not known when they took him on, the US Space Force, of his mother's passing through the Hallendorf Barrier on the way to Venus Base in her seventh month, nor of the finger-like projection that had been thus stimulated into development at the back of his brain. Later, when random children were discovered in their wild talent, the mutated telepower lobe would be named, the Barrier declared off-limits "pending further study," and the doctors would begin their futile attempt to trace the tens of thousands born on the Base; now, with a second generation imminent, their memories would be weak. But not Spane's; he knew the curse and he would not forget.) His shoulder nerves spasmed as he thought for the billionth time in twenty years, Get it fixed—I got no right to get it fixed! I can't let myself forget, not even for a minute—

And just then he felt a spark struck somewhere behind his back-brain, and he knew he would never be able to forget. Not even if he wanted to.

"Awrr, old one, you're a vet'ran . . . ya know the gov'ment'll pay to restore that ol' arm o' yours. Why dontcha . . ."

Spane jammed his eyes shut.

It hit him.

Now he was no longer trying to concentrate, but to bear the screeching signal as it pierced the back of his head.

He had found it, all right. The other's presence was so intense—

". . . git yourself . . ."

His chin pressed against his chest as the mental probe pressed deeper, an ultra-frequency only he could hear, then subsided. But the other's involuntary signal had been received. His head and mind reeled back up to the surface. He was aware once again of the rocking beat below his feet.

". . . fixed back up good as new."

The words the woman was saying, which would have angered him a moment ago, now buzzed meaninglessly in his ears.

He gripped the corner of the table between his thumb and forefinger and pushed his chair back, flailing for his crutch.

"Naw, you, you'd rather go on feelin' sorry fer yourself."

She swooned drunkenly over the table, her eyes rolling, her thick fingers slipping listlessly up and down her glass.

He dug his crutch into the boards and moved toward the door.

"No-ow, jus' wait a minute here, you ain't finished yet."

He fumbled the door open.

"You ain't even begun. . . . You haveta tell me 'bout them *people.*" Her face contorted in misshapen folds of flesh. "Yeah! That's what I wanna hear. I wanna hear 'bout all them pret-ty people swimmin' 'round in the dark like fish. . . ." Her glass tipped over.

He was halfway out the door. She rolled to her feet and lunged, groping unsteadily. Her overstuffed arms struggled to fit between the edge of the door and the wall, and as she lurched forward for the last time it was only her oversized head that emerged into the hall.

Bracing himself against the wall, he growled and swung his crutch, pointing it at her. His jaws parted and he snarled his warning:

"ZENNA!"

She huffed at him. Her attention floundered then as did her body, crouching close to the floor.

"Yeah. Who needs ya. Yer an ol' bum, anyway. You was prob'ly never no rocket jockey anyhow. Yeah."

He turned as she spat at him and hunched his way down the stairs.

"Yeah." Her rasp withdrew into the room. "The hell with ya!" And as the door slammed she threw up one last oath:

"Some spacer . . . Hell!"

He lowered his head, breathing heavily, and made for the back door.

There were two young servicemen who passed him, led from the bar by two girls who wanted them to climb the stairs.

Spane did not glance up but continued to scowl down at his own progress until he was bumped into deliberately.

"Well look who came back for more," sang one of the girls above the blare of the synthetic music. She stuck out her hip and propped her hand on it, then shifted insolently, folding her arms over her breasts. "It's Spame the lame!"

"C'mon, Rena," said the other girl, pulling at her young man.

Spane noted the USSF insignia on the uniforms and felt an echo of kinship, melancholy and finally pity stir within him.

"Aw, how 'bout some lovin', Spame the lame? I'll bet you taught Zanna a thing or two with that crutch of yours . . ."

The girl threw herself at him, mouthing vulgar sounds, pretending to offer her arms and the cheap fragrances that exuded from her gaudy professional's dress.

He felt revulsion, and a bitter thankfulness that he had conditioned himself to block off her thoughts and Zenna's and the thoughts of all the others, of the masses of non-telepaths around him. It had taken years, but his brain had had to grow a kind of callus to protect itself after that horror of consciousness, floating with the wreckage in the Mars-Jupiter asteroid belt and receiving each wrenching pain, each death as though it were his own. But never again.

He shrugged her off with his strong right arm and shouldered his way outside.

The girls' laughter and the cacophony of dance rhythms faded, as he heard again the swishing of automobiles along the wet streets. A wind hit him as he felt mist settle in his eyebrows. He swayed.

And there.

There in the dark he saw a movement.

He took a step.

Thump-slide.

Suddenly there was the sound of a trash can overturning.

Spane focused his mind.

Something jumped out in the alley, silhouetted in the headlights of a passing car.

aaahhhhh

Spane's mind constricted. This, the signal of a mind like his own, he could not shut out.

aaayahhh

He pulled himself forward a step at a time. He strained his eyes against the dark, and then—

Swish.

—another car passed in the street and there for an instant, reflecting pinpoints of light, were the wide and terrified eyes of—

Thump-slide.

God, thought Spane, the eyes, they're so small this time.

The figure froze like a startled cat as their eyes locked, then bolted.

Wait.

He said it with his mind.

Thump-slide.

Thump-slide.

It was only a boy, not more than eight or nine. See, Spane thought. He saw the stealthy movements like those of a frightened cat, a supersensitive creature with senses so acute that he has learned to avoid people, cruel people with their vicious, stabbing thoughts.

The boy gazed up at him, confused. The fur collar on his jacket was turned up over his ears and in one mittened hand he clutched the rubber ball he had been playing with. His mouth opened but he made no sound, clearly uncertain about what to do as he faced another like himself for the first time in his young life.

Do not be afraid.

See, thought Spane, already he has found that he must avoid the streets, the crowds, his own house and the thoughtless thinking people in it. But does he know yet what it will be like? Every day that there is a fire, a crash on a nearby highway, the agony of a drunken lovers' quarrel that ends in a knifing or worse, every time a man is beaten and dumped bleeding in just such an alley as this . . . or a baby dies screaming in a scalding tub, or is born . . . every time, every time he will be that person. He will know what it feels like for a man to suffer so much that he begs to be killed so there can be an end to it. And he will not be able to stop it. He might one day teach himself to shut his mind, but that would take years and years and years. And by then he may have gone mad.

The boy looked up at him, a flicker of a smile playing over his chill lips.

Hey mister, he thought, *you wanna play with me?*

Spane stood thinking, He does not know what he is. If he did he would kill himself.

Then, feeling an almost unbearable weariness in his bones, he moved his hulking body close to the boy.

He held a breath for a long, very long minute.

Then.

He raised his crutch in the night, and brought it down as hard as he could, as many times as he could.

And presently the boy's thoughts—were over.

Spane turned his face to the night sky. He felt his teeth chattering, grinding together. And this one, he thought, this one, too.

And then, the swishing of the traffic sounding so far away to him that it was like the tides going out on some unseen shore, and leaving the light from the distant and inconceivably indifferent stars to reflect through the drizzle onto the wet pavement and the unmoving shape he left lying there, Spane went home.

What's He Doing in There?

Fritz Leiber

The Professor was congratulating Earth's first visitor from another planet on his wisdom in getting in touch with a cultural anthropologist before contacting any other scientists (or governments, God forbid!), and in learning English from radio and TV before landing from his orbit-parked rocket, when the Martian stood up and said hesitantly, "Excuse me, please, but where is it?"

That baffled the Professor and the Martian seemed to grow anxious—at least his long mouth curved upward, and he had earlier explained that its curling downward was his smile—and he repeated, "Please, where is it?"

He was surprisingly humanoid in most respects, but his complexion was textured so like the rich dark armchair he'd just been occupying that the Professor's pin-striped gray suit, which he had eagerly consented to wear, seemed an arbitrary interruption between him and the chair—a sort of Mother Hubbard dress on a phantom conjured from its shagreen leather.

The Professor's Wife, always a perceptive hostess, came to her husband's rescue by saying with equal rapidity, "Top of the stairs, end of the hall, last door."

The Martian's mouth curled happily downward and he said, "Thank you very much," and was off.

Comprehension burst on the Professor. He caught up with his guest at the foot of the stairs.

"Here, I'll show you the way," he said.

"No, I can find it myself, thank you," the Martian assured him.

Something rather final in the Martian's tone made the Professor desist, and after watching his visitor sway up the stairs with an almost hypnotic softly jogging movement, he rejoined his wife in the study, saying wonderingly, "Who'd have thought it, by George! Function taboos as strict as our own!"

"I'm glad some of your professional visitors maintain 'em," his wife said darkly.

"But this one's from Mars, darling, and to find out he's—well, similar in an aspect of his life is as thrilling as the discovery that water is burned hydrogen. When I think of the day not far distant when I'll put his entries in the cross-cultural index . . ."

He was still rhapsodizing when the Professor's Little Son raced in.

"Pop, the Martian's gone to the bathroom!"

"Hush, dear. Manners."

"Now it's perfectly natural, darling, that the boy should notice and be excited. Yes, Son, the Martian's not so very different from us."

"Oh, certainly," the Professor's Wife said with a trace of bitterness. "I don't imagine his turquoise complexion will cause any comment at all when you bring him to a faculty reception. They'll just figure he's had a hard night—and that he got that baby-elephant nose sniffing around for assistant professorships."

"Really, darling! He probably thinks of our noses as disagreeably amputated and paralyzed."

"Well, anyway, Pop, he's in the bathroom. I followed him when he squiggled upstairs."

"Now, Son, you shouldn't have done that. He's on a strange planet and it might make him nervous if he thought he was being spied on. We must show him every courtesy. By George, I can't wait to discuss these things with Ackerly-Ramsbottom! When I think of how much more this encounter has to give the anthropologist than even the physicist or astronomer . . ."

He was still going strong on his second rhapsody when he was interrupted by another high-speed entrance. It was the Professor's Coltish Daughter.

"Mom, Pop, the Martian's—"

"Hush, dear. We know."

The Professor's Coltish Daughter regained her adolescent poise, which was considerable. "Well, he's still in there," she said. "I just tried the door and it was locked."

"I'm glad it was!" the Professor said while his wife added, "Yes, you can't be sure what—" and caught herself. "Really, dear, that was very bad manners."

"I thought he'd come downstairs long ago," her daughter explained. "He's been in there an awfully long time. It must have been a half hour ago that I saw him gyre and gimbal upstairs in that real gone way he has, with Nosy here following him." The Professor's Coltish Daughter was currently soaking up both jive and *Alice.*

When the Professor checked his wristwatch, his expression grew troubled. "By George, he is taking his time! Though, of course, we don't know how much time Martians . . . I wonder."

"I listened for a while, Pop," his son volunteered. "He was running the water a lot."

"Running the water, eh? We know Mars is a water-starved planet. I suppose that in the presence of unlimited water, he might be seized by a kind of madness and . . . but he seemed so well adjusted."

Then his wife spoke, voicing all their thoughts. Her outlook on life gave her a naturally sepulchral voice.

"What's he doing in there?"

Twenty minutes and at least as many fantastic suggestions later, the Professor glanced again at his watch and served himself for action. Motioning his family aside, he mounted the stairs and tip-toed down the hall.

He paused only once to shake his head and mutter under his breath, "By George, I wish I had Fenchurch or von Gottschalk here. They're a shade better than I am on intercultural contracts, especially taboo-breakings and affronts . . ."

His family followed him at a short distance.

The Professor stopped in front of the bathroom door. Everything was quiet as death.

He listened for a minute and then rapped measuredly, steadying his hand by clutching its wrist with the other. There was a faint splashing, but no other sound.

Another minute passed. The Professor rapped again. Now there was no response at all. He very gingerly tried the knob. The door was still locked.

When they had retreated to the stairs, it was the Professor's Wife who once more voiced their thoughts. This time her voice carried overtones of supernatural horror.

"What's he doing in there?"

"He may be dead or dying," the Professor's Coltish Daughter suggested briskly. "Maybe we ought to call the Fire Department, like they did for old Mrs. Frisbee."

The Professor winced. "I'm afraid you haven't visualized the complications, dear," he said gently. "No one but ourselves knows that the Martian is on Earth, or has even the slightest inkling that interplanetary travel has been achieved. Whatever we do, it will have to be on our own. But to break in on a creature engaged in—well, we don't know what primal private activity—is against all anthropological practice. Still—"

"Dying's a primal activity," his daughter said crisply.

"So's ritual bathing before mass murder," his wife added.

"Please! Still, as I was about to say, we do have the moral duty to succor him if, as you all too reasonably suggest, he has been incapacitated by a germ or virus or, more likely, by some simple environmental factor such as Earth's greater gravity."

"Tell you what, Pop—I can look in the bathroom window and see what he's doing. All I have to do is crawl out my bedroom window and along the gutter a little ways. It's safe as houses."

* * *

The Professor's question beginning with, "Son, how do you know—" died unuttered and he refused to notice the words his daughter was voicing silently at her brother. He glanced at his wife's sardonically composed face, thought once more of the Fire Department and of other and larger and even more jealous—or would it be skeptical?—government agencies, and clutched at the straw offered him.

Ten minutes later, he was quite unnecessarily assisting his son back through the bedroom window.

"Gee, Pop, I couldn't see a sign of him. That's why I took so long. Hey, Pop, don't look so scared. He's in there, sure enough. It's just that the bathtub's under the window and you have to get real close up to see into it."

"The Martian's taking a bath?"

"Yep. Got it full up and just the end of his little old schnozzle sticking out. Your suit, Pop, was hanging on the door."

The one word the Professor's Wife spoke was like a death knell. *"Drowned!"*

"No, Ma, I don't think so. His schnozzle was opening and closing regular like."

"Maybe he's a shape-changer," the Professor's Coltish Daughter said in a burst of evil fantasy. "Maybe he softens in water and thins out after a while until he's like an eel and then he'll go exploring through the sewer pipes. Wouldn't it be funny if he went under the street and knocked on the stopper from underneath and crawled into the bathtub with President Rexford, or Mrs. President Rexford, or maybe right into the middle of one of Janey Rexford's Oh-I'm-so-sexy bubble baths?"

"Please!" The Professor put his hand to his eyebrows and kept it there, cuddling the elbow in his other hand.

"Well, have you thought of something?" the Professor's Wife asked him after a bit. "What are you going to do?"

The Professor dropped his hand and blinked his eyes hard and took a deep breath.

"Telegraph Fenchurch and Ackerly-Ramsbottom and then break in," he said in a resigned voice, into which, nevertheless, a note of hope seemed also to have come. "First, however, I'm going to wait until morning."

534

And he sat down cross-legged in the hall a few yards from the bathroom door and folded his arms.

So the long vigil commenced. The Professor's family shared it and he offered no objection. Other and sterner men, he told himself, might claim to be able successfully to order their children to go to bed when there was a Martian locked in the bathroom, but he would like to see them faced with the situation.

Finally dawn began to seep from the bedrooms. When the bulb in the hall had grown quite dim, the Professor unfolded his arms.

Just then, there was a loud splashing in the bathroom. The Professor's family looked toward the door. The splashing stopped and they heard the Martian moving around. Then the door opened and the Martian appeared in the Professor's gray pin-stripe suit. His mouth curled sharply downward in a broad alien smile as he saw the Professor.

"Good morning!" the Martian said happily. "I never slept better in my life, even in my own little wet bed back on Mars."

He looked around more closely and his mouth straightened. "But where did you all sleep?" he asked. "Don't tell me you stayed dry all night! You *didn't* give up your only bed to me?"

His mouth curled upward in misery. "Oh, dear," he said, "I'm afraid I've made a mistake somehow. Yet I don't understand how. Before I studied you, I didn't know what your sleeping habits would be, but that question was answered for me—in fact, it looked so reassuringly homelike—when I saw those brief TV scenes of your females ready for sleep in their little tubs. Of course, on Mars, only the fortunate can always be sure of sleeping wet, but here, with your abundance of water, I thought there would be wet beds for all."

He paused. "It's true I had some doubts last night, wondering if I'd used the right words and all, but then when you rapped 'Good night' to me, I splashed the sentiment back at you and went to sleep in a wink. But I'm afraid that somewhere I've blundered and—"

"No, no, dear chap," the Professor managed to say. He had been waving his hand in a gentle circle for some time in token that he wanted to interrupt. "Everything is quite all right. It's true we stayed up all night, but please consider that as a watch—an honor guard, by George!—which we kept to indicate our esteem."

Zoo

Edward D. Hoch

The children were always good during the month of August, especially when it began to get near the twenty-third. It was on this day that the great silver spaceship carrying Professor Hugo's Interplanetary Zoo settled down for its annual six-hour visit to the Chicago area.

Before daybreak the crowds would form, long lines of children and adults both, each one clutching his or her dollar, and waiting with wonderment to see what race of strange creatures the Professor had brought this year.

In the past they had sometimes been treated to three-legged creatures from Venus, or tall, thin men from Mars, or even snake-like horrors from somewhere more distant. This year, as the great round ship settled slowly to earth in the huge tri-city parking area just outside of Chicago, they watched with awe as the sides slowly slid up to reveal the familiar barred cages. In them were some wild breed of nightmare—small, horse-like animals that moved with quick, jerking motions and constantly chattered in a high-pitched tongue. The citizens of Earth clustered around as Professor Hugo's crew quickly collected the waiting dollars, and soon the good Professor himself made an appearance, wearing his many-colored rainbow cape and top hat. "Peoples of Earth," he called into his microphone.

The crowd's noise died down and he continued. "Peoples of Earth, this year you see a real treat for your single dollar—the little-known horse-spider people of Kaan—brought to you across a million miles of space at great expense. Gather around, see them, study them, listen to them, tell your friends about them. But hurry! My ship can remain here only six hours!"

And the crowds slowly filed by, at once horrified and fascinated by these strange creatures that looked like horses but ran up the walls of their cages like spiders. "This is certainly worth a dollar," one man remarked, hurrying away. "I'm going home to get the wife."

All day long it went like that, until ten thousand people had filed by the barred cages set into the side of the spaceship. Then, as the six-hour limit ran out, Professor Hugo once more took microphone in hand. "We must go now, but we will return next year on this date. And if you enjoyed our zoo this year, phone your friends in other cities about it. We will land in New York tomorrow, and next week on to London, Paris, Rome, Hong Kong, and Tokyo. Then on to other worlds!"

He waved farewell to them, and as the ship rose from the ground the Earth peoples agreed that this had been the very best Zoo yet. . . .

Some two months and three planets later, the silver ship of Professor Hugo settled at last onto the familiar jagged rocks of Kaan, and the queer horse-spider creatures filed quickly out of their cages. Professor Hugo was there to say a few parting words, and then they scurried away in a hundred different directions, seeking their homes among the rocks.

In one, the she-creature was happy to see the return of her mate and offspring. She babbled a greeting in the strange tongue and hurried to embrace them. "It was a long time you were gone. Was it good?"

And the he-creature nodded. "The little one enjoyed it especially. We visited eight worlds and saw many things."

The little one ran up the wall of the cave. "On the place called Earth it was the best. The creatures there wear garments over their skins, and they walk on two legs."

"But isn't it dangerous?" asked the she-creature.

"No," her mate answered. "There are bars to protect us from them. We remain right in the ship. Next time you must come with us. It is well worth the nineteen commocs it costs."

And the little one nodded. "It was the very best Zoo ever. . . ."

Acknowledgments

Grateful acknowledgment is made to the following for permission to reprint their copyrighted material:

"All Cats Are Gray" by Andre Norton, copyright © 1971 by Ben Bova. First published in *Fantastic Universe*, August–September, 1953. Reprinted by permission of the author.

"And So On, and So On" by James Tiptree, Jr., copyright © 1971 by James Tiptree, Jr. First appeared in *Phantasmicon* under the title "And Shooby Dooby Dooby." Reprinted by permission of the author's Estate and the Estate's agent, Virginia Kidd.

"A Bad Day for Vermin" by Keith Laumer, copyright © 1964 by Galaxy Publication Corporation. Reprinted by permission of Baen Books.

"The Beautiful Doll Caper" by William F. Nolan, copyright © 1956 by Nugget Magazine, Inc. Copyright renewed 1984 by William F. Nolan. Reprinted by permission of the author.

"Beyond Lies the Wub" by Philip K. Dick, copyright © 1952 by Philip K. Dick. First published in *Planet Stories*, July 1952. Reprinted by permission of the agent for the author's Estate, Scovil-Chichak-Galen Literary Agency, Inc.

"The Big Trek" by Fritz Leiber, copyright © 1957 by Mercury Press, Inc. First published in *The Magazine of Fantasy & Science Fiction,* October 1957. Reprinted by permission of the agent for the author's Estate, Richard Curtis Associates, Inc.

"Blood Lands" by Alfred Coppel, copyright © 1952 by Alfred Coppel. First published in *Dynamic Science Fiction,* December 1952. Reprinted by permission of the author.

"Brave New Hamburger" by Philip Sidney Jennings, copyright © 1989 by Philip Sidney Jennings. Reprinted by permission of the author.

"Capsule" by Rosalind Greenberg, copyright © 1982 by Mercury Press, Inc. First published in *The Magazine of Fantasy & Science Fiction.* Reprinted by permission of the author.

"The Client from Hell" by Richard Curtis, copyright © 1995 by Richard Curtis. Reprinted by permission of the author.

"Collector's Fever" by Roger Zelazny, copyright © 1964 by the Galaxy Publishing Corporation. First appeared in *Galaxy,* 1964. Reprinted by permission of the author's agent, Kirby McCauley.

"The Crawling Chaos" by Elizabeth Neville Berkeley and H. P. Lovecraft, copyright © 1921 by H. P. Lovecraft and Elizabeth Berkeley. Reprinted by permission of the authors